Tempting My Mafia Boss

AURA ROSE

Copyright © 2022 Aura Rose

All rights reserved. This book or any portion thereof may not be reproduced or used in any manner without the express written permission of the author except for the use of brief quotations in a book review.

This is a work of fiction. Names, characters, places, events and incidents are products of the authors imagination. There may be some references to real places but any resemblance to actual persons, living or dead, and actual events is purely coincidental.

ISBN: **9798833687017**

For S.B who always believes in me.

For Aurawrites mob (my crazy ladies) and my spicy girls for supporting my dreams and being the best cheerleaders a girl could ever ask for.

Letter to my Readers

Dear Reader,

Thank you so much for purchasing this book- I hope you enjoy it as much as I enjoyed writing it.

I think I have felt more emotionally invested in the characters from Tempting My Mafia Boss than my previous books I've created. Perhaps it is because I wanted to use many of my own personality traits in the female lead, Olivia or perhaps because I strongly connected with the characters imperfections and struggles.

This story is a steamy romance with twists and turns and family drama, but it also touches on a number of sensitive material and is suggested for those over 18. There is explicit language and sexual scenes throughout.

I love to interact with my readers so please come and join me on social media for extra content, mood boards on each character and upcoming projects. If you enjoy this book, please follow me on amazon and leave a review. It would mean the world to me as a new author!

Lots of love,

Aura Rose x

@aurawrites31

Facebook.com/AuthorAurawritesReadersPage

Prologue

Skipping down the stairs two at a time, I swung around the bannister and into the kitchen, grabbing a piece of buttered toast off my mum's plate.

"Oi you little menace! Get your own!" She chuckled, hitting my hand away, but it was too late. Shoving the toast in my mouth, I gave her a toothy grin.

I was going to be late to meet Nate and I didn't have time for chitchat. I also didn't want to hang around for *him* to wake up. Giving my mum a hasty kiss on her cheek, I turned abruptly to grab my school bag from the table.

His imposing glare stopped me in my tracks as he slowly looked up and down my body with disgust. "You are not actually going to let her go to school like that?" He snarled, his cold blue eyes lingering on my bare legs in my school skirt.

My mum turned and looked between us both anxiously. "There is nothing wrong with what I am wearing. It's a school uniform," I quipped back, rolling my eyes. The atmosphere thickened with tension as he continued to stand in the door frame, blocking my way to the front door.

"It's too short. You look like a slut," he spat. I blinked twice and turned to my mum but, of course, she had lowered her eyes and pretended she hadn't heard. This was how it was. He could say and do what he liked with hardly any repercussions. Taking a deep breath, I pushed past him down the hallway. I could feel him following me. His eyes scanned my body as if he owned it. Well, he didn't own it. No one fucking owned it and if I wanted to wear a short ass skirt, I bloody well would.

Opening the front door, I raged down the overgrown garden path. I could feel him hot on my heels, so I sped up. Not quick enough, apparently. His tight grip on my arm spun me around and he pulled me into him. His eyes were blazing with anger and his face was so close to mine, I could feel his hot breath on my skin. I tried to pull away from him, but it was no use. He was older, stronger and way more muscular than me.

"You like being a little slut, don't you, Livvy? You want all the boys to stare. It makes you feel like you exist when actually you are nothing. No one loves you; no one cares about you. You are a worthless piece of shit," he growled at me and I gritted my teeth together.

"Get off me!" I hissed back but he grabbed my jaw in his hand, pushing my lips into a pout. His vindictive eyes flickered down to my mouth, and he licked his own as the longing and desire in them made me feel sick.

"You let anyone touch you today, especially that little boyfriend of yours, and you are dead. Do you hear me?"

I narrowed my eyes and shrugged out of his grip just as he looked over my shoulder and released me quickly.

"Everything alright Liv?" I heard Nate's soothing voice behind me, and I walked towards him quickly. He was staring at Henry with malice, and I pulled his arm frantically to get him away. I knew deep down that Henry wouldn't physically harm me; it was all mind games, but with Nate I wasn't so sure. Henry's temper gets the better of him and, to be honest, I have seen him beat guys to a pulp for a lot less.

"Come on, we are going to be late," I tried to distract him. Reluctantly, Nate turned away and started to walk down the road with me. I could feel Henry's eyes burning into the back of our heads and when Nate tried to reach for my hand, I quickly moved it away.

"Not yet. Just wait until we get around the corner," I whispered, which caused his handsome face to twist in irritation.

Once we were out of sight, I exhaled deeply and reached for his hand.

"What is going on with your brother Liv? Why does he act like that towards you?" He asked softly, but I could hear the concern and rage masked in his tone.

"Stepbrother," I corrected him. "And I don't know."

He pulled at my hand and forced me to look up into his light brown eyes. He lifted his hand and smoothed my cheek with a brush of his fingers. "You know you can talk to me. If he is… hurting you, you can tell me."

I shook my head. "It's just words and… he just likes to think he can control my life. Don't worry about it, Nate. Come on, we really are going to be late, and I don't want another detention from Mr Dace."

"But will you tell me if things get worse, Liv? Or speak to someone? Does your Mum know?"

I swallowed my emotions and continued to walk as he ran to catch up with me. "She knows some of it. She's scared of him. And of his dad. She doesn't like to get involved. But I promise Nate, I will tell you if it gets worse, okay?"

His kind eyes studied my side profile and I saw him nod out of the corner of my eye. He dropped the subject, and I linked my arm with his before smiling up at him. "So tonight?"

He smiled down at me, kissing my nose. "Tonight."

∗∗∗

Sitting in maths as Mr Dace droned on and on about algebra, I couldn't help but stare out of the window and let my mind wander to thoughts of how things might go this evening. It was the end-of-year party at Chelsea's house, and she had pretty much invited the entire school. It was going to be the party of the year and the night that I finally lost my virginity to Nate.

We had talked about it for weeks and I knew I was ready. I didn't want to go to university as a virgin and I liked Nate. Maybe I even loved him. What was there not to love? He was sweet, clever, caring and hot. I couldn't believe it when he started showing an interest in me a few months ago. Most boys in school knew Henry's reputation and 'overprotectiveness' around me and decided I wasn't worth the hassle. I scoffed and rolled my eyes. Overprotective my ass. He was a psychopath.

He hadn't always been like this. When my mum first met my stepdad, Neil, and they moved into our house, he was nice. He was friendly. Sometimes a little flirty, but I just put that down to his nature. He was the most popular kid at school. Head of year and Captain of the football team. He had girls falling at his feet and a group of friends that were forever going to parties and on road trips. And then something changed. On his sixth form graduation, he got so drunk and stumbled into my bedroom when he got home. He tried to kiss me. He tried to force himself on me and I punched him in the nose. I will never forget the anger and rejection in his eyes. It still sends a shiver down my spine. That was two years ago and ever since, he has made my life a living hell. I hoped he would move away. Go to college or Uni but he decided to stay put and get a job at the local building site down the road. I swear he did it just so he could torment me.

Now it was my sixth form graduation. I was eighteen and ready to get the hell away from this place and him. I was going to go to Plymouth University and study education. I want to be a primary teacher and it was the furthest university I could get into from my little hometown on the outskirts of London.

"Olivia Bennett! Earth to Olivia!"

I whipped my head around in a daze as the whole class sniggered. Mr Dace was standing right in front of my desk, holding my latest test in his hands. Shit.

"Sorry Sir," I muttered as I took it from him timidly.

"I was just saying that the class could learn a thing or two from you about perseverance and hard work but perhaps I was wrong," he narrowed his eyes, before turning swiftly to the next student. I looked down at the paper. A+. Perfect. I smiled to myself as I thought about how I was going to celebrate tonight. I just needed to make sure I got out of the house before Henry got home from work.

The school bell rang and I quickly scooped my belongings into my bag. Racing down the school corridor to catch my best friend Millie before the next class took some skill through the mass of teenagers messing around.

"Mills!" She turned sharply, books in hand, and smiled at me.

"Hey hun! What class do you have next?" She asked as I fell in with her steps.

"English Lit. Can I get ready at your house tonight? I am just going to run home and grab my stuff and I can be at yours at 4?" My eyes pleaded with her and she could hear the desperation in my voice.

"Of course, Liv! You know you are always welcome! I don't know why you don't just move in with me. My family loves you! And it would get you away from that asshole."

"I can't leave my mum and you know it," I sighed. God, I wish I could move in with Mills. Her family was the perfect 2.4 loving family with all the trimmings. Her mum was sweet and kind and oh so motherly. Her dad was cheeky and funny with his giant moustache and quirky dress sense. Her brother was the same age as Henry but a bit of an introvert and geek. A lovely person. They all were.

"Well, you can sleep over mine tonight after the party. That's if you aren't going to sleep at Nates?" she gave me a cheeky wink. I had already told her our plans to go all the way tonight and she was just as excited as me.

"Thanks, but Chelsea has actually let us have one of her spare rooms for the night. Nate's parents are having their own little dinner party so we can't sleep there."

She looked surprised. "Well, that is nice of Barbie! Perhaps she does have feelings after all!"

I chuckled, "Chelsea isn't that bad once you get to know her. Yea, she is obsessed with looks and materialistic shit, but she was brought up like that. What do you expect?" Millie rolled her eyes, not convinced.

The rest of the day went by painfully slowly. Why was it when you always had something exciting to look forward to, it was as if the universe prolonged every minute just to torture you? Racing home after school, I ran up to my bedroom and started to grab everything I would need in my bag; my dress that I had saved up for weeks for, sexy matching lace underwear, my make-up, heels, toothbrush, straighteners. What else was I missing? Ah. I pulled open my bedside drawer and threw the unopened packet in my bag. Condoms.

Throwing the bag over my shoulder, I opened my door and listened. Quiet. He wasn't home yet; the coast was clear. I thundered down the stairs as fast as my little legs could take me and grabbed my phone and keys from the side table just as my mum walked out the living room. I could tell from her puffy eyes that she had been crying. Another argument with Neil, no doubt. I don't know why she didn't just leave him. We would be so much better off without Neil and Henry in our lives. Guilt riddled me as I hesitated by the door. I couldn't leave her like this, but I really needed to go before Henry got back.

"Are you okay mum?" I asked carefully.

"Oh yeah. Everything's fine," she lied with a wave of her hand. Her tired eyes and haggard skin told the truth. She used to be so full of life. So vibrant. Now she was a shell of her former self. "You sure? Because I can stay if you like?"

"No. No. You go to your party. Have fun darling," she smiled at me and I gave her a weak smile back.

"I am staying at Millie's tonight," I lied. She didn't need to know what I was really up to.

"Okay my love. I'll see you in the morning," she turned and walked back into the kitchen. I sighed. I didn't have time to dwell on this. I had to go.

The party was in full swing and I was having more fun than I had ever had before. Chelsea's house was a mansion. She had a huge swimming pool in the back garden, so many rooms that it felt like you were walking through a maze of different vibes throughout the whole party. There was something for everyone. A beer pong room, a techno dance room with a DJ, a making out room, a chilling room, a room where everyone seemed to be hot boxing and smoking weed. And then the main room and open-plan kitchen where people were dancing and drinking, having the time of their lives. The atmosphere was electric. Everyone was buzzing that we had finally finished sixth form and would all be moving onto bigger and better things. This was what I had waited for. One last wild blow out with my friends and boyfriend before we went out into the big wide world.

"Have I told you how incredible you look?" Nate whispered in my ear as his hand snaked around my waist from behind.

"Only a thousand times," I giggled before taking a sip of beer from my plastic, red cup.

"Well, it's true. This dress. It does things to me," he nibbled at my ear lobe, and I felt my stomach flutter. Turning in his arms, I stared into his beautiful eyes and ran my hand through his floppy brown hair. His eyes were full of admiration and want, not like when Henry looked at me.

"Well, how about we take my little dress upstairs?" I cocked my head to one side and smiled seductively. The alcohol was definitely giving me some Dutch courage and I was determined to make this an experience I would remember forever.

He leaned down, holding my face in his hands and kissed me passionately. Our tongues danced together as the intense need to have his hands explore my body and to feel what it was like to satisfy that ache between my legs grew.

Without saying a word, he took my hand in his and led me up the clear staircase to the top floor. Chelsea had already shown us our room when we arrived, so it didn't take us too long to push past the couples who were eating each other's faces on the landing and the girls who were tripping over their feet, giggling as they made their way back downstairs.

Once Nate closed the door behind us, only the dull vibrations of the blaring music downstairs could be heard and the pounding of my heart in my ears. I stepped towards him and started to unbutton his shirt, my eyes flicking up at his every now and again. He watched me intensely and once they were all undone, I pushed it away from his shoulders as it fell to the floor. Tracing my hands across his athletic chest, his breathing hitched and he leaned down, capturing my lips once more.

He slowly walked me backwards until my legs hit the end of the bed and we both fell back on it, giggling. He turned on his side and ran his fingers over the swell of my breasts that were rising and falling under my silver dress.

"You are so beautiful Liv," he smiled down at me and I fluttered my eyelashes. He was so sweet, but I wanted to get on with it. I wanted to feel the passion. The 'I need you now' feeling that I read about in books. I grabbed the nape of his neck and pulled him down to my lips, placing his hand on one of my boobs. He squeezed it gingerly, and I moaned into the kiss, trying to encourage him to do more. Luckily, it worked and his hand found its way down my body and between my legs. He started to rub me over my underwear and I gripped his shoulders tighter. We had tried everything else and I was eager to get to the main event. The anticipation was killing me and the alcohol was making me needy as hell.

"Get a condom. They are in my bag," I panted against his lips. He moved off me quickly and I removed my dress, leaving me only in my new lacy underwear set I bought especially for this occasion. He removed his trousers and boxers, kneeling on the bed between my legs. He was already standing to attention and slid the condom on easily. Thank God for sex-ed classes and bananas! I pulled down my underwear and kicked them onto the floor as he leaned over my body, resting his weight on one arm as he positioned himself at my entrance.

Suddenly, the nerves built. This was it. After this, I will no longer be a virgin. I will be changed. He hesitated as he looked into my eyes, and I saw the doubt in his own. This was his first time too. I lifted my head to meet his lips and kissed him softly, showing him I was ready. He inched himself into me and the feeling felt so overwhelming. I felt so full, and it hurt. Hurt like hell! I winced into our kiss, and he pulled back to look at me with concern.

"It's okay! I'm okay, just go slowly to start with," I rushed, and he nodded. His face scrunched up in pleasure as he pushed himself a little further in and held himself there, letting me get used to the sensation. I wasn't sure if he was fully in yet but I felt like I was going to snap in half if he went any further. But he did. And then he was completely inside me. I cried out at the pain, but as he slowly pulled out and pushed back in, it started to subside. Instead, it started to feel good. Sore but good.

"Oh my god Liv," he breathed through his slow thrusts, and my chest swelled with pride. I wasn't even doing anything, but the pleasure on his face was amazing. He started to quicken his pace a little and I gripped his shoulders and moaned as the feel of him moving in and out of me, started to really make my body tense in the most delicious way. I closed my eyes and got lost in the feelings as I moaned and cried out like I'd seen them do in porn films. Suddenly, he stopped.

My eyes snapped open and my heart raced as I looked into his wide eyes that were laced with fear. His face was slowly turning red as if he couldn't breathe and that's when my world froze. I glanced over his shoulder at the figure who loomed over us, his face almost unrecognisable as it twisted with evil intent. *Henry.*

I watched in horror as he pulled the knife out from Nate's back, only to ruthlessly stab him again. My eyes widened and I wanted to scream, but I couldn't. I had lost all ability to do anything. All I could do was stare into Nate's haunted eyes as he was stabbed repeatedly by my stepbrother. Nate's body fell on top of mine as he passed out and the blood started running down his back onto the bed. I looked up at the sweaty face of his killer and he locked eyes with me.

"Look what you made me do, Livvy," he snarled, before turning and fleeing the room, the bloody knife in hand.

And that's when reality hit me. And I screamed.

Olivia Bennett I Mean Jones
Five years later

Checking the address on the small piece of paper again, my face scrunched up in confusion as I peered through the grand, iron gates. This cannot be right. Giulia must be playing a prank on me. There is no way I am in the right place.

Pulling out the old school Nokia phone and clicking on one of the three numbers I had saved on it; I called my new Italian roommate to give her an earful for wasting my time.

"Ciao Liv, are you done already?"

"No, I haven't even been in! Are you joking with this address? I can't even see the house; the drive is so fricking long! It's like royalty are living here or something!" I stood up on my toes to glance over the gate to get a better look. Only luscious lawns and trees were in sight. It looked like some kind of health spa hotel from back home.

"Well, the Buccini family are very wealthy, so I expect you are in the right place. I mean, what unemployed woman needs a full-time nanny if she isn't filthy rich?" Giulia chirped down the phone, and I frowned.

"I'm not sure about this anymore. I am not dressed for an interview with the rich and famous!" I glanced down at my informal outfit choice of a lemon and navy-blue summer dress that had huge sunflowers all over it and a white-washed denim jacket. I thought I was just coming to a modest, little Italian family's house for an informal interview as their nanny.

"Liv! You need this job! I love you but I cannot sit back and watch you eat those hideous microwave things any longer. You are in Italy, my love! You need to live it to experience its true beauty! And to do that you need money! And this job pays really well!"

I sighed as I pushed one strand of my dark hair behind my ear that had fallen out of the messy bird's nest of a bun on top of my head. She was right. I really did need the money and on paper this job sounded too good to be true.

Two children. Six and four years old. A boy and a girl, needing homeschooling and wrap-around care. And the bonus, they wanted English-speaking applicants. Well, I had that covered. I was born and raised in England.

"Okay. Okay. I'll see you later. Wish me luck!"

"Good luck, Livvy! Ciao!" I heard her loud smacking lips sending me air kisses through the phone before she hung up, but hearing that nickname still sent a shiver down my spine. I hated being called that. It reminded me of *him*.

I had only known Giulia for a few weeks, but we had quickly hit it off and become good friends. Something I desperately needed when I stepped off the plane into a foreign country where I didn't know a soul. She was positive, intimidatingly confident and a little bitchy, which I liked. She reminded me so much of Millie and my heart ached. Gigi had quickly taken me under her wing and showed me the authentic side of Verona and managed to secure me with this interview. Her brother's girlfriend works as their cleaner and had mentioned to her that they were rehiring a nanny. Everyone seemed to know everyone in this town, and I loved the support they all had for each other. Most of the Italians I had met so far were nothing but warm and welcoming and I knew I had picked the right place to hide from my dark past.

I nervously pressed the modern intercom button on the stone wall next to the gate and was surprised to see my reflection staring back at me on a built -in TV screen. I quickly checked my newly dyed chocolate brown hair, trying to tame any of those pesky wisps that were sticking out by my ears before moving onto my teeth. I had just eaten, and I really did not want the embarrassment of showing them what I might have had for lunch.

"Si?" A loud male voice boomed through the speaker, causing me to jump back and my face to flame, knowing he probably caught me on camera.

"Oh…er…Ciao…er…I…E sono qui in orario per il colloquio," I cringed at my terrible attempt to tell him that I was here for the interview from my handy little translation book.

"Come si Chiama?" The voice replied and I scrambled through the pocket-sized lifeline for a translation. "Ciao?" His tone was impatient, and I slammed the book shut in a fluster as I felt sweat starting to build on my brows.

"Er. Yes. I am still here. I'm sorry I don't speak Italian. My name is Olivia Benn- I mean Jones and I am here for the nanny position."

There was a long pause and I glanced down the isolated road as the nerves started to build. This was a disaster already. I could still make a run for it. I am wearing my converse high tops so I am sure I could get away before the gate opens and…

BUZZ!

The automatic gate started to pull open slowly and I jumped back. Shit. Looks like I am going through with this after all. Stepping over the threshold, I was met with a long, winding road framed with towering greenery all the way up. A black car suddenly appeared, speeding towards me and I leapt onto the neatly mowed lawn to get out of its way. My mouth hung open when I realised it was a Bentley and had pulled to a stop next to me. A smartly dressed man climbed out and opened the back door for me.

"Ciao Ms Jones. I will escort you to the house," he greeted me formally with a thick Italian accent. My eyes widened slightly as I looked up the never-ending driveway and back at the car. I forced a small smile on my face and nodded at the man before scrambling onto the luxurious cream seats. He started up the engine and did a quick U-turn at the gate before zooming back up the driveway at an insane speed. I peered out the window as tennis courts, an Olympic-sized swimming pool and horse stables as well as an enormous garage made of glass that housed nearly every luxury car on display inside, blurred past me. This was not just filthy rich. This was something else.

I gulped as the house came into view. No, not house. Palace. It was breath-taking. From the outside, it had all the traditional elements of a stylish Italian villa with a large fountain in the driveway, black iron balconies off every room that was decorated with beautiful vines of greenery and flowers snaking around the bars. But it was the sheer size of the place that really left me speechless. It must have been at least three stories high and the size of a small shopping mall. I couldn't even fathom why anyone would need this much living space. I was going to go crazy at Giulia and her brother's girlfriend, Natalia. I was so not prepared for this!

"Please. Follow me," An older man wearing an expensive suit addressed me rather coldly at the top of the stone steps by the grand entrance to the mansion. I trailed behind him, and my mouth fell open as I entered the lobby. It was a drastic change from the traditional exterior of the building. Inside, everything was pristine and elegant. Marble floors that looked as though they must be polished numerous times a day and a spiralling staircase going up both sides of the room that led to the top floor with a cream carpet. God, this place must be a nightmare to keep clean. I suddenly felt sorry for Natalia.

Leading me through the lobby, turning left down a wide corridor and stopping at the door of one room, he nodded to another man who was standing guarding the entrance. This man was dressed entirely in black. Black shirt, black trousers and black sunglasses. I almost laughed at his serious face. Why the hell was he wearing sunglasses inside? But his intimidating aura forced me to bite my lip and swallow my amusement.

"Please. Take a seat and fill out the forms. You will be called in for your interview shortly," the older man replied, and I nodded, taking a clipboard from him with a pen attached. Walking into the room, I nearly stumbled over my feet. It was beautiful. Creams and whites everywhere gave it an almost tranquil vibe if it wasn't for the three or four butch men standing around the room in menacing stances. What were they doing? They looked like bodyguards or something. Taking a seat on a clear, glass chair which I instantly recognised as a famous designer but couldn't for the life of me remember the name, I gazed down at the form in my hand. Oh fuck.

I grimaced in alarm as I realised the entire form was written in Italian.

"Oh… excuse me?" I called, but the man had already left. Glancing at the statues of men who were ignoring me completely, I didn't feel like I was meant to speak to them. They were clearly doing something extremely important. I scoffed at the thought. That's when I noticed another woman on the far side of the room. She was sitting elegantly on the cream sofa, flicking through a magazine. She was very beautiful in that supermodel, high cheekbones and stern expression kind of way. She was wearing a tight pencil skirt and silk blouse, open a little too low to be appropriate for an interview, but I am guessing that is what she was here for. I couldn't exactly talk. What the hell was I wearing? I wore this over-the-top sunflower dress because I thought it looked sweet and fun and the kids would like it. Now, I just feel ridiculous.

"Excuse me? I don't suppose you could tell me what the first question on the form says please?"

She turned her flawlessly made-up face to me and looked me up and down like I was so far beneath her she could squash me with her stupid killer heels. She flicked her immaculate blonde ponytail over her shoulder and narrowed her eyes. "Can't you read?"

I immediately wanted to wipe that smug smirk off her face, but instead I plastered on a fake smile. "Not Italian, no."

She tutted and dismissed me rudely, flicking back through her magazine. *Bitch.*

Just then, another woman arrived and took a seat next to me. She was also dressed more formally than me, but in a tight bodycon dress that I swear would be more appropriate for a night out, not an interview to work with children. Perhaps this was the norm in Italy? I couldn't deny that she was just as stunning as the ice queen over there. I gave her a smile which she returned before looking down at the clipboard and starting to fill out her form. Well, that was promising. At least she smiled.

"Ciao! Hi, could you help me please? I can't read Italian. What does this say?" I asked her. She peered up and regarded me thoughtfully.

"It says, what are your three worst traits," she replied with a smile and I frowned. That seemed like a weird question to ask first, but I shrugged and wrote my answers down in English. My frown deepened as I tried to recognise any of the Italian words in the second question. I couldn't keep asking the poor girl next to me, she was trying to focus on her own form. I am going to have to rely on my handy little translator. He was quickly becoming my dependent and best friend.

Lifting my rucksack onto my lap, I started rummaging around frantically for the pocket-sized book. God, I had so much crap in here, it was like a lucky dip. Suddenly, the bag slipped off my lap from my manic search and all its embarrassing contents flew out across the marble floor and my dignity with it.

"Shit!" I cursed under my breath as I dropped to my knees and started to clamber around the floor grabbing lipstick, tampons, the half-eaten baguette I had for lunch and… I paused as my hand reached for the black lacy thong that I just so happened to have with me as a spare. I don't even know what it was doing in my bag. But it's not the thong that has me frozen, it's the shiny black shoes that have approached them. Please don't be the old man who can't crack a smile. I slowly lifted my head to take in the man that was standing between me and my underwear and, oh, it was so much worse.

My eyes travelled up the smart black suit trousers that hugged thick thighs with an expensive-looking belt to the muscular torso and broad shoulders in a tight-fitting black shirt. The sleeves were rolled up slightly, showcasing strong forearms, one covered with tattoos. I gulped as I continued up to his face. Oh my…God. Seriously, this man was so damn hot it should be illegal.

He was unfairly gorgeous. Possibly the most gorgeous man I have ever laid eyes on. His handsome face was perfectly symmetrical, his strong jaw line decorated with neatly groomed stubble, an annoyingly straight nose and high cheekbones. His jet-black hair was slicked back and swept over to one side, but it was his eyes that had me forget my own name. They were burning into mine with intrigue and I felt my body temperature rising. They were so dark, the deepest shade of brown I had ever seen. He was the definition of perfection and I swear my mouth was watering at the sight of him. Although, there was one thing about him that did not sit right with me. The one thing that I could never be okay with…danger.

His face remained expressionless and stern as he slowly lowered himself down to my level on the floor and picked up my thong in his fingers. He tore his intense gaze away from mine and studied them as my cheeks flamed with mortification.

"Good try. I agree, these would look better on my bedroom floor," his deep voice laced with an Italian accent made my stomach flutter until I registered what he said. He winked at me and tossed them towards me before standing up and walking away without looking back. What an arrogant ass! I groaned as I threw them in my bag quickly and sat back on my chair. It was only then that I noticed how the other two women were practically foaming at their mouths at the sight of him and then turned their deadly glares towards me.

"That was pathetic," the blonde one hissed at me, giving me the bitchiest look she could muster.

"I – I wasn't trying to…" I didn't even know what I was trying to say. Did they really believe I did that on purpose for his attention? I don't even know who he is! And why for the life of me would I do something so stupid?

I decided not to bite back in this situation. They already thought what they did about me so what was the point in trying to change their minds? One thing was for sure. I hate arrogant assholes even if they are sex on legs.

They could have him. And from the way they reacted to his presence, I am pretty sure that's what they were here for, not the job.

I just hoped I would never have to see him again. I'll just get this interview with Mrs Buccini done and dusted and go home with my tail between my legs. I mean the chances of getting this job are non-existent anyway.

"Olivia Jones," The older man had returned and called my new name, gesturing to the door which that man had just walked through. I inhaled deeply, before standing up and brushing my dress down nervously. Ok. Here goes nothing.

Interview from hell

Walking through the door into the elegant office, I couldn't help but feel intimidated. Behind the grand desk was a beautiful woman in her early fifties, although from the way she was dressed and her immaculate make-up she could have passed for forty easily. She was wearing a colourful satin dress that screamed designer brand and was drumming her acrylic nails on the expensive oak desk in front of her.

I gulped as she turned her head in my direction and looked me up and down. Her face slowly turned from serious to amused as a smile played on her lips. I gave her my most charming smile before my eyes flickered over to the intimidating man who was burning a hole in my head with the intensity of his stare. Fuck not him again. His giant frame was leaning back on a white leather sofa, one leg resting casually over his other knee and his arms stretched out along the back. He regarded me as if I was on auction as his dark eyes slowly raked over my body. It felt like he was undressing me with his deep brown eyes and I shifted uncomfortably on my feet.

"Please, Miss Jones, take a seat," The woman who I assumed was Mrs Buccini held out her hand in the direction of the glass chair a few metres in front of them. "My name is Cecilia Buccini and this is my son, Giovanni Buccini."

I smiled politely at her but as my eyes met his, I felt the heat spreading across my skin again. *Fuck sake Liv. Get a grip. Stop reacting to him.* Dragging my gaze back to the blonde woman in front of me, I decided I would solely focus on her and ignore him completely. "It's a pleasure to meet you both," I smiled, lying through my teeth.

She leaned back in her chair and studied me with mischief in her eyes. There was something odd about this woman, but I couldn't put my finger on it. She was almost youthful in her nature, but she also had an underlying sadness behind her eyes. Something that warned me that she was not perhaps all as perfectly together as she seemed.

The room pulsed with tension as the seconds ticked by and no one spoke. Were they waiting for me to speak? I thought they were supposed to ask the questions.

After studying me for what felt like eternity, Cecilia leaned forward on her desk and placed a pair of cat-eye glasses on the bridge of her nose before opening a file on her desk.

"Olivia Jones. 23 years young and from London." She nodded her head in approval before she continued. "It says here that you studied at Plymouth University to become a primary school teacher but you never graduated. Why not?"

I swallowed my nerves at her directness and lifted my chin a little higher. "Family circumstances. I hope to finish my degree soon, but I thought I would take some time out to try something new. A new life experience."

"That being?" she prodded, looking over the rim of her glasses.

"To live in another country. Learn a new language and culture," I said confidently. I had rehearsed these answers numerous times, but I still felt sick talking about it. I knew they would have questions about why there was a two-year gap from when I left school until I attended university and then why I left university in my third year, so close to the end. But I didn't need them to know the real reason why.

She narrowed her eyes at me as she assessed my answer. "So why should I employ you to take care of my children if you have no real experience or qualifications?"

I shuffled on my seat awkwardly and did my best not to look in the direction of the piercing gaze of Giovanni Buccini. "Because I love children. I may not have a degree in teaching yet, but I am practically at the end of my course and was the highest in my classes. I am trained in education, first aid and safeguarding. I was an A* student in high school and at the end of the day, I care. I believe children should work hard to get what they want in life, but also to have fun. To have a real childhood full of happy memories and great experiences. I know I could provide that, and I saw that you wanted them to learn English. Well, it's the only language I can speak…fluently."

Her face slowly lit up into a broad grin and she threw her pen down on the desk, causing me to jump. "I like her!" She shouted, glancing over at her son.

"Mamma," Giovanni's deep voice had a warning in it and my eyes darted over to him. Sitting there in all black, cloaked in shadows, he looked every inch the kind of arrogant bad boy I despised. I was surprised to see that his face was tense, his jaw clenched as he looked me over before meeting her gaze. He said something quickly in Italian to her and I squeezed my thighs together after hearing his natural Italian voice so dominating and sexy as hell. I cursed myself internally. All men who can speak Italian fluently were sexy. There was nothing special about this one, I tried to convince myself.

She dismissed whatever he said with a wave of her hand. "Tell me Olivia. Do you want to sleep with my son?"

My mouth dropped open, and my eyes widened at her shocking question. What kind of interview was this? Giovanni looked just as outraged as he sat up and glared at his mother, shouting something at her again in Italian. She ignored him and kept her gaze on me.

Was this a trick? What was I supposed to say? Obviously, the right answer was no. But something about the way she was looking at me, made me want to be completely frank with her.

"I'm sorry but I am not sure what this has got to do with the job?" I asked carefully. A little glimmer of amusement flashed across her eyes, and I felt her son's gaze return to me. He seemed surprised by my forwardness.

"It has everything to do with the job. Could you please answer the question? Honestly," she encouraged with a smile. His eyes moved to mine and his expression softened. In fact, he now looked intrigued and a little smug as he waited for my answer.

Honestly, my body wanted him. Yes. He was dark, mysterious and drop dead gorgeous, but he was also everything I hated in a man. I could tell he was controlling, cocky and dangerous. A combination that triggered me to the core. And no one should be this good-looking. It was annoying.

"Honestly, there is no doubt that your son is attractive, but no, I do not want to sleep with him. Definitely not." I replied with conviction. The man snorted and shook his head, his black-olive eyes challenging mine. I squinted my eyes with a deep scowl. He thinks I am lying. He is that up himself. I am sure he is used to every woman falling to his feet and doing whatever he wants. Well not me. He has met his match.

His mother looked between us with interest, before sitting up in her chair and pulling my attention back. "OK, one more thing, Olivia. You say here your best traits are stubbornness, forgetfulness and overthinking."

My eyes bulged in panic. Fuck that traitor! She told me the wrong question! I stumbled over my words as I tried to explain, "I'm sorry. My Italian is not great, and I must have interpreted the question wrong. I thought it said 'what are your worst traits?'"

She chuckled and shook her head, removing her glasses as she did. "Well, I have to say Ms Jones. I enjoyed this interview far more than I normally do. My children would love your dress as well. We have some more candidates to see, so we will be in touch."

I nodded and stood up, thankful that this was over, and I could get the hell out of this place. "Thank you for your time."

I turned to leave the room, but as I reached the door, I suddenly felt a surge of courage power through me. No matter how much money these people had or how good looking they were, they couldn't treat me like shit. Turning on my heels, I glared straight into Giovanni's dark eyes.

"Just so you know. My underwear will never look good on your floor, so you can keep on dreaming." Shock possessed his devilish features before he frowned deeply at his mother's raucous laughter. I opened the door and walked out with my head held high. There would be plenty of other jobs. I definitely didn't need this one.

The Underboss

Giovanni

"And why do you think you should get the job?" Mamma asked the third woman we had seen in a bored tone. It was clear from the moment she strutted into the room and pretended to drop her pen right in front of me, bending over and giving me a full view of her rounded ass in that tight pencil skirt that it wasn't so much the job that interested her but me. Mamma didn't try to hide her irritation as she rolled her eyes at the gesture and gave me a pointed glare.

Normally, I would revel in such obvious flirtation and attention. It wasn't rare that beautiful girls threw themselves at me at any chance they had. But since that little firecracker stepped into my mother's office an hour ago, she was all I could think about. And it was bothering me. No, it was infuriating to me. I scowled at the blonde woman who clearly didn't give two shits about my siblings and just wanted a way to get my attention and ultimately get into my bed.

"Well, I am flexible... and eager to learn new things. I will always give you my best," she batted her eyelashes at me with a sultry smile. I fixed my sinister eyes on her, trying to warn her to cut the crap. I wasn't in the mood for this. She clearly had no shame, flirting outrageously with me in front of my mother. Her face paled slightly, and she cleared her throat as my deathly glare had the desired effect and forced her to submit. That's more like it. So why didn't that girl, Olivia, act the same way? Who did she think she was talking to me the way she did?

"And how will those...skills help you to care for and teach my children?" Mamma's sharp voice made the woman gulp and her blue eyes widen. I decided to zone out of the rest of the interrogation. It would only be more of the same. Mamma would be drilling the girl to the point she made her cry. It was strange. She has many personalities, and you never know exactly which one you will get. The strong, intimidating, and shrewd Mafia wife or the sweet, vulnerable and comical woman. It was surprising to see she acted in the latter with Olivia. She also had a dark side too. One that she had battled with since the death of my papi. Hence, why we needed a full-time nanny. We never knew day to day if it would be one of her good days or not.

Thoughts of that defiant girl swarmed my mind. There was something about her. She was... different from other girls. It was amusing to see her so flustered out in the waiting room, scrambling around on the floor for her bizarre bag contents. Exactly where I liked my women. On their knees. I'd had a semi from the moment I caught a glimpse of her soft, bouncy cleavage in that cute little dress. But the moment she lifted her flushed pretty face and I looked into those eyes; I knew I had to have her. Maybe it was purely the fact that she seemed so unaffected by me and didn't cower in my presence like others did. She had a backbone. A fighting spirit, but at the same time, she seemed so innocent. Naïve to what she had just walked into. From the way she dressed in that flirty little summer dress, to her messy, unkempt hair piled on top of her head, she was oblivious to how gorgeous she was. Images of fisting her messy bun in my hand while I dominated her from behind, that dress up around her waist had my dick stirring.

She had no idea who I was. If she did, she would fear me. She would never have spoken to me the way she did. And it only made me want to corrupt her more. The devil in me couldn't help but be enraptured by her ethereal beauty. She was so naturally stunning. Her eyes. Fuck. Those exquisite green irises that were haloed with an outer ring of blue as well as speckles of gold. But when she opened her mouth and insulted me at every opportunity, the desire and filthy thoughts that entered my mind of what I could teach that smart little mouth to do shocked me to the core. I was floored. Sucker punched. Name the cliche. I had never felt such an immediate intense longing for a woman before. Women to me were beautiful but just a pass time. They never plagued my mind for longer than a few minutes. A way to relieve stress and meet a need. I gave them what they wanted and in return I got what I needed. But this was different… This was dangerous. She was dangerous.

I am Giovanni Buccini. The underboss of one of the largest and most violent and powerful families in Italy, otherwise known as the Mala del Brenta. I am next in line to take over from my zio (uncle), The Boss. And the last thing I needed right now was a distraction. Albeit a beautiful, enchanting distraction. No. She wasn't even qualified for the job. It's fine. I won't have to see her again. Life can continue exactly how it was. Making money, fucking and killing. That was who I was. And her innocence had no place in my world.

"We will be in touch," My mother concluded the interview, and I glanced up to see the woman close to tears. She looked my way but I didn't give her even an inkling of hope that her plan had worked. She had not interested me in any shape or form and her feeble attempt to seduce me was unsuccessful. She stood up abruptly and left the room without saying goodbye.

Lifting my hand to my face, I rubbed my forehead and closed my eyes. This was becoming exhausting. We had been interviewing for a nanny for weeks now and mamma insisted I sit in on them all, but no one was good enough for mamma.

"So shall I call her?" She leaned back in her white leather swivel chair with a mischievous glint in her eyes. I frowned.

"Who?" I already knew the answer, but I didn't want to believe it.

"The first one. Olivia Jones. She is perfect," Mamma said excitedly. The sternness and authority had dissolved and she was in one of her playful moods again. I couldn't keep up.

"No. She was not perfect," I groaned, but my forbidding heart fluttered at the lie. She was perfect. The perfect little package. She was curved in all the right places and soft and inviting. Everything about the way she looked screamed effortless femininity, yet when she opened her mouth, she was a lioness. If I was just some normal man who spotted her on the street, I wouldn't hesitate to make her mine. But she didn't deserve to be thrown into this world. I couldn't offer her the kind of thing she would want or need from a man. "She had no qualifications and there was something off about her."

"Why? Because she is not interested in you?" She teased and my frown deepened.

"I couldn't care less if she was interested in me or not. She is not even my type. You saw her. She was scatty, unprofessional and stubborn." I tried to argue with some conviction but failed miserably as my mamma's smile grew.

"Exactly. She was perfect. She is exactly who I had in mind," her thoughts seemed to travel somewhere else for a few moments and my dark eyebrows pulled together in confusion. She was up to something. "Think about it, Gio. She does not speak a word of Italian. She cannot understand it. She won't be aware of what goes on within these walls and therefore, the children will be happy and unaffected. She will treat them like any other children and not the most feared underboss's siblings. You know I am right. And it helps that she is a strong character. She is not going to take any shit from anyone, and I like that."

I rolled my eyes and leaned my head back on the sofa. I would never win this argument. When my mother set her sights on something, she would make my life a living hell until I gave in. "That is a problem, mamma. She cannot walk around here causing havoc. She will get herself killed."

Her painted lips turned up into a knowing smirk as she spun around on her chair. "That is why she will be under your protection. You know no one can touch her if you forbid it."

I exhaled deeply. It wasn't everyone else she needed protecting from. It was me.

"Fine. Give her the job on a two-week probation. Let's see how she handles Soraya and Santino first," I smirked. My siblings were rascals. They were super hard work and I gave her two days with them before she cracks and hands in her notice like the last one.

"You can do it yourself," she held her file out to me and I glared at her. Fuck sake. This is the last thing I needed. Taking the folder from her hands,

I kissed her on the top of her head and made my way to the door. "Oh and Gio…" I turned and she gave me one of her icy scowls. "Don't sleep with her. I like this one."

I scoffed and left the room. I was in for absolute hell.

***

Pouring myself a whiskey on ice, I strolled over to my large mahogany desk. It was the only room in the house that wasn't white and cream. My office was dark. Grey walls, dark furniture and black décor. It reflected my mood when I was at work. It helped me to do what was needed and reminded me of who I had to be when I entered it. With my mamma and siblings, I was Gio. They were the only ones who saw the real me. The very small part of me that was still buried deep within. But most of the time, I was Giovanni Buccini. The ruthless, unforgiving and arrogant underboss. I could never show weakness. I could never let my guard down. After my papi's brutal murder, I was forced to grow up quickly and take on the responsibility of all the capos under our regime. And I was set on avenging my father's death. One day soon. I was just waiting for the right time to strike.

I opened the folder and saw the picture of the girl that had been tormenting my mind all morning. How did this happen? How is she the girl my mamma wants? Staring into her unique eyes that held so much depth, I allowed myself to get lost in them. There was something lurking behind her pretty face and stunning eyes. Pain. I would recognise it anywhere because I had it too. Every time I stared into my own reflection; all I saw was emptiness. A void that can never be filled. A wound that will never heal. She had it too. Scanning her file, I read through her CV for anything that stood out.

She lived in a small village called Stratford-upon-Avon outside of London. Went to Niall Tawn High School. Attended university and did a BEd degree in primary education, majoring in English Literature. She was clearly a clever woman from her impressive school grades and essay results, but something didn't add up. There is a two-year gap between when she finished her A levels and started university. No job or travel, just a blank space. And then there is the mystery as to why she dropped out of university this year and came to Italy. Family circumstances, she had said. That could mean anything. There was nothing alarming about her file and normally I would let something like this go. She wasn't a threat to our family, but I wanted to know more. I wanted to know everything about this woman. I told myself it was because I was trusting her with the care of the two little people I loved most in this world, but really, I knew it was more than that.

Dialling Antonio's number, I leaned back on my leather chair. Antonio is my zio, Salvatore's, trusted consigliere. He advised my uncle and me on all matters. He was not family by blood, but he may as well be. He has served our family faithfully for over twenty years and a lot of our success has come from his expert ideas at drawing up the best business deals.

"Ciao Giovanni,"

"Ciao Toni. I need a thorough background check on Olivia Jones. We are hiring her as the kids' new nanny and I want to make sure we have all the information. I will send you over her CV," I said firmly, speaking in my mother tongue over the earpiece.

"No problem. Give me a couple of days. A new deal is coming through with the Columbian channels and it is going to take up a lot of my time with Boss. He wants you in on this deal, so meet us tomorrow at 9am."

I sighed, rubbing my forehead again. "See you tomorrow." This was a deal we had been working on securing for months. The fact that we were close to closing, should make me elated. This kind of deal would bring in millions, but it was dirty money.

Picking up my whiskey and downing the contents in one go, I started to dial the phone number provided for Olivia Jones. The rings resounded through the phone and each second that ticked by made me more impatient. Why was I so eager to hear her voice again?

"Hello?"

I sat up straight in my chair as her soft voice entered my ear.

"Hello, Olivia Jones?" I said, clearing my voice quickly when it came out hoarser than normal. What was wrong with me?

"Yeah. Who is this?"

I smirked at her fiery tone. She was a feisty woman. I like my women wild; it makes it that much more fun to tame them. *No! She is off limits now.* "Giovanni Buccini. We met earlier today at the interview."

She paused for a moment, "I remember."

Her curt response surprised me and I took a moment to regain my composure. No woman has ever had the balls to address me like this. It was refreshing although annoying as hell too. But as much as I wanted to put her in her place, *over my knee*, I couldn't scare her away. I scoffed at the inappropriate thoughts my mind took me to. "We would like to offer you the job starting tomorrow."

There was a silence at the end of the phone, and I waited impatiently for her response. My foot started tapping on the floor.

"Why?" Her surprised voice made me want to laugh. Of course, she didn't think she would be hired. She shouldn't after the way she spoke to me, but that was my mother's doing.

"My mother liked you. She thinks you will do well with my brother and sister. You will need to arrive here by half seven-tomorrow morning to go through some security procedures before you start. This would be on a two-week probation to see how you get on." I could hear her panting through the earpiece, and it sounded like she was out of breath. "Is everything alright?" I asked. The image of her panting on top of me as she rides my di...*snap out of it Gio!*

"Yeah…um sorry I was just out for a run. Thank you for the offer but I am afraid I am going to have to turn it down."

I blinked rapidly as I digested her words. What? Turn it down? Is she insane? This time it is my turn to be shocked, "Why?"

"I just don't think I am the right fit for what you are looking for. I'm not what you need," her words travelled straight through my body, causing a flurry of alien emotions to emerge. *She is everything I am looking for. She is what I need.* I shook my head quickly. What the fuck is wrong with me?

"I would have to disagree, Olivia. My mother thinks you are perfect for this job, and she is very adamant that you take it," I relished the way her name rolled off my tongue.

"Well, I am sorry to disappoint her. But I don't think this is going to work for me," her voice had a sharper edge to it now, as if she was getting annoyed. I should be the one getting annoyed! No one says no to me.

I sighed and rested my head on my hand on the desk and ran my fingers through my dark hair. This was not playing out how I expected and this woman was giving me a headache already. And for some strange reason, panic was setting in. I should just accept her refusal and move on. But I couldn't. It was just another sign of her defiance and I needed to break her.

"What would you say if we doubled the salary?" I spoke quickly. There was another long silence at her end and I waited with bated breath for her response.

"I would say you are insane. Why would you pay a nanny 100,000 euros a year?"

I chuckled through the phone and my dick stirred against my trousers. I was starting to enjoy this girl's spunkiness.

"Because I can. So?" I pressed, my patience wearing thin.

"Okay," her voice was small, unsure, and I smiled. Good. Mamma would be pleased.

"Don't be late and bring your passport as ID." I hung up the phone before she could change her mind and leaned back in my chair as I raised my hands behind my head. Without even realising, my mood had been lifted and I felt a flutter of excitement. As soon as I realised how widely I was smiling, my face fell. No fucking way. I was going to have to keep my distance from this woman. There were no two ways about it. I had to stay away from her.

A Tempting Offer

Olivia

I stared at the battered, second-hand phone in my hand, breathing rapidly, partly because of the exertion of running, but also because I had just been offered 100k euros for a job! What the hell! These people have far too much money to know what to do with! As much as I never wanted to set foot in that place again, I couldn't refuse that kind of money. I was down to my last 100 euros of savings, and I was desperate.

I suppose I was just going to have to try to avoid Giovanni Buccini as much as possible. I couldn't deny that hearing his deep, husky voice through the phone had sent my body into overdrive. I hated how much my body reacted to him. But luckily my mind was stronger. I will be able to ignore these feelings eventually. This attraction I felt towards him. It was only because he was so good-looking. It was like if you walked down the road and ran straight into Tom Hardy's chest. Your body will react! How could it not? I just had to train myself to ignore it.

Putting my phone back in my leggings pouch, I started to pick up the pace again and head back to the flat. Running has become my own form of therapy. It always helped me clear my mind and shake the unwelcome feelings or flashbacks that threatened me. I have had a lot of therapy since that night. Community therapists tried to help me come to terms with what had happened. Sex therapists tried to help me overcome my fear of going all the way with someone again and not suffering the panic attacks it evoked. I wanted to move on with my life. I wanted to get a boyfriend and enjoy sex like everyone else my age, but the memory of him was always lurking in the shadows.

It has been five years since Henry killed Nate while he was still inside me. The guilt I would have to live with for the rest of my life sometimes becomes so great that it cripples me. There would be days where I was just a mess. Crying for no apparent reason over the smallest things. Retreating into myself and pulling away from the world. It has been tough, but I keep reminding myself that it is nothing compared to the grief Nate's family were feeling every day. They lost their son in a brutal attack. He had done nothing wrong except get involved with me. I was the reason he was dead. The therapists tried to convince me that it wasn't my fault. What Henry did that night was nothing to do with me. He had an illness. A disease. That's what the courts decided. He pleaded guilty by reason of insanity or mental illness and was granted a sentence in a mental health institution instead of jail. It wasn't justice. Henry knew what he was doing that night. He knew the difference between right and wrong and still picked up the knife. He should be in jail but he was clever. Manipulative. So was his father who helped him get the most ruthless lawyer to sway the case and plead insanity. I don't deny that he was insane, but he was also evil. Through and through.

After the worst two years of my life, I managed to find the strength to get myself together. To go to university as planned and train to be a teacher. Nate would not have wanted me to fall apart like I had and it was his spirit that gave me strength. I had to live for him. I wasn't going to give Henry the satisfaction of ruining two lives.

I was slowly getting on with things. I was reserved and kept myself to myself through university, barely going to any parties and just studying hard. People thought of me as a bit of an outcast. I was a few years older than the other freshers because of my two-year breakdown. Millie was my rock. Without her, I wouldn't have survived. This last year, I was finally starting to feel myself again. Starting to enjoy my life, making new friends and trying new things. And then I got the call that changed everything. He had escaped from the mental institution. Strangled a warden with a telephone cable in the middle of the night. He was out there somewhere, and I knew he was coming for me. The police offered me surveillance protection for a few weeks until they could find him, but I knew I couldn't live like that. I was already the most talked about girl in my hometown and I didn't want to be a prisoner in my own dorm either. So, Millie and I made the difficult decision to make me disappear. I changed my last name, dyed my ashen hair dark brown, deleted all my social media and left the country with only a rucksack of belongings and a handful of cash from Millie and my savings. I got a burner phone, hence the shitty Nokia, and the only numbers I had saved were Millie, Giulia and my lawyer. I hadn't called Millie since I left. I didn't want to risk putting her in danger. It was better if I was no longer in her life or my mum's. No one knows where I am or what I am doing. Until he was found, that was the way it had to be.

As I reached the idyllic little side street my apartment was on that I shared with Giulia, I slowed my pace. Sweat trickled down my chest and face from the heat of the afternoon sun and I pushed open the little green door that was barely hanging on for life to enter the building. It was old and falling apart but had a rustic charm to it. I loved it here. The first night I arrived in Italy, I slept in a hostel in Venice and that's where I met a girl who went to school with Giulia. She said she was looking for a roommate and lived in Verona. I jumped at the chance and felt so lucky that this opportunity fell into my lap. Climbing the steep steps to our little two-bed apartment, I bumped straight into Luca on the stairwell. He was one of Giulia's friends.

"Ciao Liv! I was just asking Gigi where you were!" he smiled kindly at me, but I still noticed his eyes flickering down to my breasts in my little sports top. Men.

"Hi! Just been for a run. It's such a lovely day for it," I smiled back politely as I leaned against the wooden bannister.

He wrinkled his nose up. "It is too hot for a run today! You a crazy lady!" He chuckled and I couldn't help but feel charmed by his thick Italian accent as he spoke in broken English. I really felt bad that I didn't know their language. I was in their motherland and yet they had to try and communicate with me. "A few of us going to the bars tonight. Will you come?"

Normally, I would come up with an excuse as I had no money to spend in bars, but after today's events, I could really do with a few drinks. "Yea sure. I'll come with Giulia."

His handsome face broke into a cheesy grin and he looked cute. "Fantastico! I will see you later."

He turned and skipped down the steps as I opened the door to our apartment. Loud music blared around the room and I saw Gigi's light brown hair bouncing up and down as she danced around the kitchen, unaware of my presence. I threw my keys and phone down on the table and pulled my trainers off.

"You are back! You just missed Luca…he was asking about you," she winked at me suggestively and I rolled my eyes.

"I know, I bumped into him on the stairs. He said about us all going out tonight?" I perched on one of the mismatched bar stools and leaned on the small wooden kitchen island.

"Si. You coming?" her eyes widened in excitement as I nodded. "Yes! You can finally meet the whole group. And Luca will be pleased. You know he has the…how do you say it… 'Hots for you' right?" I groaned as I picked up an apple from the fruit bowl and took a bite out of it. "What is wrong with Luca?"

"There is nothing wrong with Luca. He is great but I am not getting involved with anyone romantically right now," I tried to make my voice as stern as possible so she would drop the subject, but I knew that was wishful thinking. She didn't know about my past, just that I had a violent stepbrother who I left home to get away from. I didn't go into the horrific details of what actually happened. I didn't want to scare her away. She was the only friend I had in this place.

"Who said anything about romance? Just good sesso is all you need! You must try the Italian men out. They are spectacular in bed!" she laughed and I rolled my eyes at her. If only she knew. I was a sexual person. I wanted to have sex. Badly. But every time I attempted to go all the way with a man, it would end in a panic attack. Which is pretty much a mood killer and fair to say, they never want to see me again.

And now there was the danger of Henry looming over me. I would not risk getting close to anyone until he was safely behind bars. I wasn't about to put another man's life in danger.

"Oh, guess what?" I tried to change the subject and she faced me with a curious expression. "I got the job. The nanny one. And they doubled the salary."

Her mouth hung open before she raised her hands dramatically in the air and started to shout in Italian. I was pretty sure she was cursing from her shocked expression.

"Double?! Why? What did you do?"

I shrugged my shoulders. "I told him I didn't want the job. But it turns out they really wanted me to take it."

"And by him you mean Giovanni Buccini himself?" she said in disbelief.

"Yes."

She grabbed her iPad off the side and I tensed my eyebrows, trying to sneak a peek at what she was doing.

"You are going to get to see this insanely hot man every day and get paid a ridiculous amount for it? Are you sure you are just expected to look after the kids?" she teased as she pushed the iPad towards me, and I glanced down at a picture of Giovanni standing in front of a huge hotel. It was an article about him opening the largest hotel in Northern Italy. I skimmed the text and wasn't shocked to read that this was just one of ten hotels he owned, as well as two nightclubs and three restaurants.

"Yep, that's him and I don't know what you are insinuating, but I shall definitely only be looking after those kids," I said flatly as I stared at his perfectly symmetrical face that was set in a deep, brooding scowl as he stared into the camera. Fuck why did he have to be so damn fine?

"Well girl, you have landed on your feet there. I'm jealous! You are one lucky lady!"

I slid off the stool and made my way to the bathroom. Lucky isn't the first word that comes to mind…

***

Sitting outside at a table in a pretty courtyard bar, I felt relaxed. Happy. The balmy evening atmosphere mingled with the soothing sounds of chatter and soulful music filled the air. I leaned back and took in the group of people I was with as I sipped my Aperol Spritz. They were trying to speak in English throughout the night to keep me involved, but as the drinks flowed their mother tongue was creeping back in. I didn't mind one bit, as I loved listening to the beauty of their language even if I couldn't understand a word. I locked eyes with Luca across the table, who gave me a smile before grabbing his chair and moving around to sit next to me.

"Hi."

"Ciao!" I smiled at him. Pretty much the extent of my Italian. I really needed to start taking classes or something.

"Are you enjoying it?" he gestured to the group and the bar and I smiled, nodding my head.

"Yes. It's so nice to just be out and doing something so normal," I replied, taking my straw between my teeth. His face creased with confusion or intrigue at my comment.

"Normal? This is not normal for you?"

"Not really. I don't tend to go out much back home. But that doesn't mean I don't enjoy it," I added.

"So would you like to go out again sometime?" he leaned on one arm of his chair, so he was a little closer to me and I eyed him suspiciously. Was he asking me out or just asking an innocent question?

"I guess. You mean as a group?"

He smirked and shook his head. "No. I mean with me. Me and you. For drinks. So, I know you better," he explained, and I looked down at my glass. I really didn't want to upset him. He seemed like a really nice guy and someone I could be friends with. But I also didn't want to lead him on.

"I would like that, but just as friends. I am not really looking for a relationship right now," I said honestly, but his features maintained the cheeky smile and twinkling eyes.

"Friends is good for me. For now," he winked, and I couldn't help but chuckle. The Italians never gave up, that's for sure.

When it reached midnight and the bars were calling last orders, I excused myself as I had a very early morning and a new job to start. Many of Giulia's friends seemed shocked to hear where I was going to be working, some even seemed a little concerned. On the way home, I let curiosity get the better of me and asked Giulia why they reacted that way.

She sighed, linking her arm with mine. "The Buccini family is a pretty intimidating name in our region. They own many businesses but there are also rumours that they are involved in some dodgy dealings. Drugs and stuff. But they are very private people. No one really knows what they are like and most of it is just hearsay, so try not to let it bother you."

I nodded and looked ahead as we walked over the Ponte Pietra Bridge and the serenity of the backdrop of this city gave me a warm, fuzzy feeling. This city was everything I had imagined it to be. Romantic, idyllic and beautiful.

"Anyway, you are just going to be with the kids and at the house all day, so I don't expect you will even see him much," she added, trying to ease my anxiety.

"That's what I am counting on," I mumbled. But something was telling me, I was about to be seeing a lot more of Giovanni Buccini and I knew I wasn't the least bit prepared for it.

Playing With Fire

Olivia

"Miss Jones. Nice to see you again," Cecilia greeted me warmly as I entered her plush office. I was relieved to see that her son was not lounging on the sofa like yesterday.

"Please call me Olivia or Liv," I smiled at her and she cocked her head to the side as she studied me intensely like she had previously. Her expression remained friendly but there was something going on behind it. A secret that seemed to amuse her somewhat.

"I like Olivia. I shall call you that," she nodded to the chair for me to sit. "So, I hear you didn't want to work for me?"

A blush crept up my cheeks as I looked down at my hands. Shit. He told her. Of course, he did. "Yes. Sorry. I was just surprised to hear you chose me over the other candidates. I didn't feel like I made a very good first impression," I said honestly.

She regarded me carefully before leaning forward on her desk.

"Oh, you made quite an impression," she chuckled, but moved on before I could question her. "I have four children. Gio is my eldest, Elenora, who is at university, and then my two youngest, Santino, who is six, and Soraya, who has just turned four. Sani and Raya for short. They are my world. So, I am trusting you to take exceptional care of them, Olivia."

I nodded carefully. "You will notice the guards placed around the house. They are for the family's protection. Don't be alarmed if you see them carrying weapons. They will not bother you unless necessary, so just try to ignore them as much as possible. Marco is the children's and your personal bodyguard and will escort you and the children if you choose to leave the premises."

I frowned and decided now, if any, was the best time to interrupt her. "Sorry, but why do I need a bodyguard?"

She leaned back in her chair and clasped her hands together. Her face was neutral as she explained. "We are a very wealthy family, Olivia. There are many people who would like to harm us to get our assets. The children could be taken for ransom etc. so it is vital you do not take them anywhere without first checking with myself or Gio. I am a pretty laid-back person, Olivia, but this is one thing I will not be lenient about."

I nodded and swallowed my fear. A cold, hard mask had slipped down her face as she spoke and suddenly her aura changed. She was terrifying. A woman I did not want to get on the wrong side of. "I understand."

She held my gaze for a few moments before the mask was removed once again and she seemed like a different woman. "Good. So here are your things." She lifted a box and pushed it towards me across the table. What things? I shuffled forward, intrigued by what could possibly be in this box. Lifting the lid, my eyes widened in shock as I saw a brand-new Apple mac laptop, the latest iPhone, a set of keys with so many different colour coded handles and a Mulberry purse. Lifting the purse out first and opening it, I was speechless to see a number of credit cards and some cash in there.

"These aren't my things?" I glanced up at her. She must have made a mistake.

"They are now. How do you expect to teach my children without a laptop? The phone is for work use only. My number, Gio and Marco's are saved, as well as the children's personal doctors, dentist, tailor and stylists."

I was momentarily frozen. Did I just hear her correctly? The four-year-old has a personal stylist?

"Let me explain the keys. The red is for access into the children's living quarters. The blue is for your office. The yellow is for the garden and tennis courts. The pink is the gym and spa. The swimming pool is opened daily after 7am by our housekeeper and you are free to use it anytime. And black is for my living quarters. That is only to be used in emergencies. I like my privacy."

I definitely was not going to remember all of that. I picked up the huge collection of keys in my hand and studied each one. This was insane. Suddenly my head snapped up. "What about the front door? And the main gate?"

She giggled as if I had asked a ridiculous question, "The main gate will always be locked, and you will always have to be granted access through. The front door is heavily guarded so there is no need for a key."

"Okay." I said slowly.

"Okay," she repeated, standing up. "Let's go meet my little angels. Just to warn you, they may take a little time to warm to you. They are like that. But they are sweethearts really. Just be sure to set firm boundaries," she smiled as if it was no problem at all, but I could tell from her tone that she was slightly anxious. Great. This wasn't the most hopeful of beginnings.

We made our way through the 40-room mansion as she pointed out the different areas of the house to me. It was overwhelming. They had a bowling alley, cinema and their own mini club/bar on the bottom floor, as well as three living areas, Cecilia's office, the kitchen and the dining room. On the second floor were the children's living quarters to the left and their mother's to the right. They each had their own wing of the house. And the entire top floor was reserved for Giovanni. We paused at the bottom of the cream stairs that led up to his floor and I couldn't stop my heart from racing a little at the thought of him up there.

"He is not here. He is taking care of business. He is a very busy man, and you will find that he is rarely around the house." Her tone seemed off, so I didn't respond but instead followed her into the children's wing. There were many doors turning off the long corridor. A games room, a playroom, an education room and they each have a bedroom with an adjoining bathroom connecting the two. We headed towards the games room where an enormously built man in a black suit was standing rigid at the door.

"Olivia, this is Marco," she introduced the bodyguard to me, and I couldn't help but feel intimidated as he nodded his head once in my direction, his face passive. Cecilia knocked on the door of the games room and pushed it open slowly.

"Sani! Raya! I have someone here to meet you," she announced. I stepped inside and saw the back of a young boy with a mop of black curls sitting forward in a huge racing chair, eyes glued to the 46-inch flat screen on the wall as he tapped violently at the remote in his hand. A little girl with white, blonde curls was sitting in the window seat on an iPad watching some kids' YouTube videos. Neither of them looked up from what they were doing. "Right, I will leave you to get acquainted," Cecilia said with a clap of her hands as she backed out of the room. Oh. Right. Straight in at the deep end. Okay.

I strolled towards the little girl first and glanced over her shoulder to see what had her so engrossed. "Oh, I love Barbie. Is this your favourite show?" I attempted to interact with her, but she kept her brown eyes cast down and shook her head. I bent down to her level and watched the screen for a little while, pretending to be interested. "My name is Olivia. What's yours?"

Silence.

"Non le piacciono gli estranei," the little boy spoke without taking his eyes off the screen. I stood up and walked over to the chair.

"Can you speak English, Sani?" I asked softly.

"Si."

"Do you mind telling me what you said? My Italian is a little rusty. I was hoping you could teach me and in return I could teach you both some English."

"I said she doesn't like strangers. And I do not need your help. I can speak English good," he replied coldly. Okay, this was going to be harder than I anticipated, but I was always up for a challenge.

"Wow. Your English is very good. I am from England. Have you ever been?"

He shrugged his shoulders and carried on shooting at the zombies on the screen. I don't know much about video games, but I am pretty sure this was very inappropriate for a child of his age. I picked up the case, *Zombie Apocalypse*. 18+. Ah brilliant.

"OK well, I think ten more minutes on the game and iPad and then we will go outside for some fresh air," I tried to keep my voice friendly but with an air of authority.

"Why?" Sani quizzed as he shot a grotesque zombie between the eyes.

"Because it is a beautiful day and I think we can have some fun in the sunshine. What do you say?"

"No. We do not go outside."

I frowned and placed my hand on my hip. "OK. What do you do then?"

"We do this," he said, refusing to look up from the screen. He hasn't even looked my way once to see who he was talking to. I can't believe that to be true. He must be exaggerating.

"Well, your English is very good, so you must have had some lessons. Can Soraya speak English too?" I glanced over at the little girl, who was sucking at her finger as she concentrated on the screen on her lap.

"I am a genius. I just know it," he replied nonchalantly. I couldn't help the smile that tugged at the corners of my lips. He seemed a lot like his older brother. Arrogant as hell. "And Raya won't talk. Not to you."

I sighed, feeling exhausted already. Today was going to be a long day.

***

Giovanni

"Dimitri wants another favour," my zio, and boss of our empire, said calmly as he walked over to the floor-length window that overlooked his estate in Verona.

I rolled my eyes behind his back as I flicked open my Zippo before closing it again. The sound of the metal clicking each time was keeping my mind from swaying to unwanted thoughts of that girl in my house right now. I could not allow myself to be distracted when in the presence of Salvatore Buccini. He would not hesitate to punish such recklessness.

"What does our amico want this time?" I asked carefully. Dimitri was a respected and influential political figure in our country by the Italian citizens, but we knew him better as a greedy, corrupt and unforgiving man. He swore a vow of silence, what we call an omerta, which is punishable by death if not upheld to become a friend to our family. He gives us important political information on the stock markets and government enquiries and, in return, we give him what he requires to keep his squeaky-clean appearance sparkling brightly. He was the kind of man I would never respect.

Toni opened a file and slid a picture of a middle-aged man across the table to me. I picked it up lazily to study it.

"Massimo Novalli. Businessman, husband and father of two. Gambled away a hefty amount against Dimitri in an underground poker night. 750k euros to be exact. Hasn't paid a cent," Salvatore, my zio, turned and walked towards the table, picking up a cigar and lighting it.

"So, he wants us to shake him up? Make him pay?" I threw the picture of the man back down on the table.

Salvatore shook his head while he blew out clouds of smoke, momentarily masking him from my view. "He wants our little friend to walk the bridge."

My dark eyebrows tensed and I clenched my jaw. That seemed extreme. To murder a man without at least threatening him into paying first. He had a fucking family for fucksake.

"Why don't we give him a wake-up call first? Break a few bones? Hospitalise him? I am sure he will quickly right his wrongs," I folded my arms across my chest. My uncle glared at me with his notorious death stare. It was the only look that could make a full-grown man piss himself in public. Even though it did have some effect on me. I knew it was an empty threat. He may punish me in certain ways, but he would never kill me. I was far too valuable to him.

"You sound just like your papi, Giovanni. The weak, sensitive Vincenzo Buccini. Always trying to do what was best. Where is he now?" His voice was calm but hard. It was his eyes that warned me. Anger bubbled under the surface of my skin at his insult towards my father and I held his stern gaze. I would not look away even if he called his henchmen in to fight me.

His face slowly opened up into a sadistic grin as he realised I was not going to submit to him. "Good. Not as like your papi as I thought," he smirked, turning his back to me again. "But what Dimitri wants, Dimitri gets. As much as I would love to cut his tongue from his vulgar mouth, we need him. So, I don't care who you get to do it, but do it well."

His tone was sharp and authoritative, leaving no room for retaliation. I was already on thin ice, so I stood abruptly and merely gave him a blunt nod before leaving the room.

I felt drained as I left his estate, climbed into the back of my Rolls Royce Phantom and nodded at Lori, my driver. I unbuttoned my cuffs and rolled my sleeves as well as a few more buttons down my chest. Leaning my head back against the leather headrest, I closed my eyes and exhaled deeply. The meeting went well, all things considered, and clearly, business is good in all areas right now, legal and illegal, but I wasn't happy with the contract killing. Dimitri was an important political figure in our country, and we needed him on our side, so as much as I did not enjoy killing a man for no good reason, if he needed someone dead…it was my job to fulfil the order. It's the way our hierarchy worked. My uncle (or zio in my native language) was the boss. The Don if you will. He dealt with the main threats to our empire and his word was final in all matters. Toni was his consigliere. His advisor in all things financial and political. It was his job to keep our heads above water and our accounts clean. And then there was me. The underboss. Next in line to take over the empire. I oversee all the Capo's who work beneath me in different regimes, keeping the legal and illegal businesses running smoothly, while also delegating deals to the Capos. Under them were the soldiers or bodyguards. The lowest ranking in the hierarchy devoted their lives to protecting the elite and did most of our dirty work for us. We mainly dabbled in drugs, gun running, contract killing, protection and loan sharking. Our hotels, clubs and restaurants were what we call racketeers. Laundered businesses where we could tie all our money and assets into as a cover up for all the dodgy shit we deal with behind the scenes. We also paid many influential people for their silence and to keep us out of the spotlight. Police, government officials, business owners. They were all corrupt, which kept us untouchable to a certain extent. It was only rival families who posed a threat. The Leone family, to be precise. They were our biggest competitors and the people also responsible for my father's death. We had no real proof that would stand up to the commission, but we knew it to be true. And one day they will pay at my hand.

As the car pulled up to the gates of my home, I ran my fingers through my thick, black hair. I sat up a little straighter as we approached the house and I knew what was putting me on edge. *Olivia Jones.* I wonder if she is still here. Or if, in fact, she had already called it quits. A strange prickly feeling quickly passed through my chest as I thought I might not see her. This was fucking stupid. I didn't even know the woman. She was nothing to me. She was my sibling's nanny and someone I needed to stay the hell away from for her own sake.

Perhaps though, if she quits, then there would be no reason not to sleep with her. I could get it out of my system. Because that's what it was. A need to have something that was off limits. It was the only way to explain why this woman was affecting me so much. I wasn't used to not getting what I wanted, and I didn't like the feeling.

Stepping out of the car and marching up the gravel driveway, I nodded to the two soldiers who opened the front door for me. I stopped at the bottom of the staircase and weighed up my options. Go check on mamma. Go see if Olivia was still there with the kids or the sensible thing, go to my floor until I knew for sure she had gone home. Checking my Rolex, I tapped it when I saw it was 7.30pm. She is probably putting them to bed. I should just go to my office. Climbing the stairs two at a time with large strides, I stopped on the first floor. I could hear screaming coming from the bathroom. That is Raya alright. Curiosity and protectiveness got the better of me as I headed towards the shrill hysterics of my little sister. Pushing open the bathroom door, Soraya was standing naked in the bath, screaming at the top of her lungs as Sani ran circles around a stressed and dishevelled looking Olivia, wrapping her in toilet roll. My lips thinned into a straight line to try to stop myself from laughing at the chaotic scene before me.

"Gio!" Sani dropped the toilet roll and ran towards me, barrelling into my legs. Raya immediately stopped screaming and looked up at me through tear-stained eyes, reaching her arms out for me.

"What is going on here?" I raised one eyebrow as I ruffled Sani's hair and walked towards Raya, taking the towel from a stunned Olivia's hands. Wrapping it around her little body and lifting her into my arms, she nestled her head on my shoulder.

"Raya didn't want to get out of the bath, and I was turning Olivia into a zombie walking dead enemy that I could shoot with my nerf gun," Sani spoke quickly in Italian, and I stifled a chuckle. I made him repeat it in English for Olivia to hear. She stood up, tearing the toilet roll off her and glared at me.

"He plays too many inappropriate video games," she said so seriously that I was now really struggling to suppress my laughter. I looked at Sani, who gave me an innocent shrug and we both burst out laughing. Her cheeks turned red and her nostrils flared as she looked between us both before an embarrassed giggle escaped her as well. My chest tightened at how beautiful and carefree she looked when she laughed.

"Right. Bedtime you two! And no more tears," I pulled Raya back to give her a pointed glance and she nodded slowly.

Sani ran out of the bathroom towards his own room as I handed Raya over to Olivia. Our hands innocently brushed as we exchanged her, and my eyes flickered to her lips instinctively. They were so full and plump. So kissable. She lowered her head, stroking Raya's hair out of her face as she walked past me into the corridor. She quickly turned and I locked eyes with those magnificent green irises with specks of gold.

"Thank you, Giovanni," she muttered quietly before turning and walking briskly into Soraya's room. Something fluttered inside me at her submissiveness and hearing my name for the first time leave her lips. I felt my dick harden. I stood rooted to the spot. Fuck sake. I should have gone to my office.

***

Olivia

Once Soraya was tucked into bed and I had checked in on Sani, who was already passed out on top of his racing car duvet covers, I closed their doors and rested my forehead against the cold wall.

"Was it really that bad?" A low, husky voice echoed down the corridor, and I turned to see Giovanni leaning against the bannister with a cold beer in his hand. I slowly tiptoed towards him as I put my finger to my lips. I don't think I could take it if they woke up and demanded an ounce more of my energy again. Even though he shook his head, there was laughter in his eyes as he gestured to the bottom step of the staircase that led up to his floor. We both sat down, only a fraction apart from each other, and my nerves grew. He seemed so arrogant, cold and intimidating yesterday, but after seeing him with his siblings tonight, I realised I might have read him wrong. I could smell his masculine cologne mixed with whiskey and cigars and I fought the urge to breathe in deeply.

"I thought you might need a drink after your day?" he held the beer out to me and I took it gratefully, taking a swig of the icy liquid that felt oh so good as it slid easily down my throat. I suddenly froze. Shit. Was this a trick? I was still technically working.

"Sorry," I said quickly, handing it back to him and his handsome features creased with confusion. "I'm still working so I shouldn't be drinking on the job."

His face lit up and amusement flickered across his smouldering eyes. "I am your boss and I offered. And your shift has finished now. They are asleep."

We sat in silence as I took the beer from him again and gulped down a few more mouthfuls, wiping my mouth after. I could feel his dark gaze focused on me like a laser as I stared straight ahead and tried to ignore the fluttering of butterflies in my stomach.

"You are not scared of me, are you?" His voice was laced with some kind of emotion. Pride or intrigue? I couldn't quite tell.

I turned and stared into his enticing eyes that seemed so mysterious and haunting. "Should I be?"

His eyes narrowed and flickered down to my lips and when they returned to my gaze, I felt my body fail me again. That unwanted warmth rose through me as his gaze was filled with so much desire and heat that I thought I might burst into flames at any moment.

"Most people are," he answered, his voice deeper than before, and I swallowed. He screamed danger. Warning alarms and red flags were going off in my head. But I couldn't tear my eyes away from him. It's like he had me hypnotised. Those eyes of his were lethal. "But you are not like other people, are you?"

I didn't know how to answer that question. So instead, I tore my gaze away and took another swig from the beer bottle. A drop of liquid missed my mouth and ran down my chin and before I could wipe it away, he did something that had my whole body frozen in shock. His masculine, rough hand reached up and he ran his thumb down my chin, wiping it away before turning my face towards him with his firm grip on my jaw. My breathing hitched and my heart started racing as he brushed my bottom lip with his thumb roughly and I saw his eyes darkened with lust at the action.

"You sure about what you said yesterday, bambola? Because I really think your underwear would look ravishing on my bedroom floor."

My eyes widened at his words and my anger overtook my unwanted desire to have this man. For a moment, I really thought I saw a different side to him. With his siblings and coming to my aid. But he was still this arrogant playboy and I saw red.

I pushed his hand off my face aggressively and watched his expression turn to one of shock and then anger. "You will not take me to bed. Ever."

I stood up and went to walk away, but his hand grasped my wrist. He yanked me back as he stood up and I slammed straight into his muscular chest. My eyes couldn't help where they travelled down to as the buttons of his shirt were undone, giving me a mouth-watering sight of his defined pecs. The smell of him up close alone made my knees weak.

"You are playing with fire, Olivia. I am a man who gets what he wants," he growled, his eyes burning with desire and rage. A dangerous combination. But he didn't scare me. I have witnessed worse. I had been at the end of worse.

"Then maybe it's about time somebody told you no!" I snarled and ripped my arm out of his grip. He let go and stayed rooted to the spot as I stomped down the stairs, grabbing my belongings by the door and running out into the night.

Me, Tease Him?

Olivia

I was furious at myself. Why did I let this man affect me so much? I have barely exchanged a few sentences with him and yet he seems to have the ability to get right under my skin.

You are playing with fire Olivia. I am a man who gets what he wants.

He can't know how those words would trigger me. How they would cause rage to burn through my veins. I hated men like him. Men who thought they could control women. Take what they want without any regard for the other person. No matter how much my body reacted to his touch, his eyes, his voice, I wouldn't allow myself to go there. He was no good for me, I knew that much.

I slammed the flat door behind me and fell with a huff on the sofa. Giulia raised her eyebrows at me but said nothing as I quickly sat up and poured myself a glass of red wine from the already opened bottle on the coffee table.

"Rough day?" she teased as I downed an entire glass in one go before refilling it.

"I can't do it. I don't care how much they are paying me. The kids are a nightmare and don't listen to a word I say. The little girl won't even speak to me and the boy, well, he finds it hilarious to keep speaking to me in Italian knowing full well I can't understand him. They refused to leave the games room the entire day and then…" I paused mid rant to take a sip of wine. "I had an unpleasant run in with the boss."

"Mrs Buccini?"

"No, the other one," I quipped, and she sat up. Suddenly, I had all her attention.

"Unpleasant how?"

I leaned back on the sofa and closed my eyes. "He propositioned me AGAIN! Assuming I am one of those girls that will fall at his feet and do anything he says with a few seductive words and heated glances."

"You mean he tried to come on to you? I knew he offered you more money for a reason!" she shouted, and my eyes bulged.

"Is that what you think he did? He doubled my salary, thinking I would sleep with him?" I could feel my anger coming into full force again, burning me from the inside out.

Giulia nodded her head, and I clenched my fists. "Then first thing in the morning, I will go and give him a piece of my mind. He can take back his offer and I will hand my notice in."

"Liv! No way! You can't do that! You need this job, remember? And so what if you have a hot boss who wants you and two little brats to tame? You can handle it. I know you can! Give him a piece of your mind and refuse the double salary by all means, but don't quit!"

I took another sip of my wine as I thought about what she said. She was right. I wasn't a quitter. I wasn't going to give up on a decent job so easily. I just needed to change my tactics with the kids. And as for Giovanni, he could go fuck himself or some other woman, but not me.

Feeling better about the whole situation and with a newfound determination to make this work, I settled down for a night with my friend. Giovanni had just messed with the wrong woman.

***

I arrived at the Buccini mansion earlier than I needed to get my plan in motion. Pulling out the black tape, I covered the games room doorway, blocking their entrance and locked the door. They would not be going there until they had both had some genuine fun that didn't involve a screen. These kids may have had all the latest trends and technology, but they were deprived of a childhood. Silly games, running around the lawn chasing the sprinklers, that kind of stuff. Today was going to be all about that. FUN.

Happy with my masterpiece, I stood back with my hands on my hips as I noticed a huge, bulky figure heading towards me. He took one look at the door and gave me a confused glance. Today was a new day and I was even going to attempt to get on the good side of this man.

"Good morning Marco, how are you today?" I smiled genuinely up at him, and his eyes widened slightly in surprise.

"Good signorina. Although I think you are a little crazy to be restricting the games room from those two," he looked over the black tape zigzagging across the door and then back at me.

"I think I have to be a little crazy to be doing this job altogether, don't you think?" I asked and I saw a little ghost of a smile play on his lips. "Could you let me know when the little darlings wake up Marco? I am just going to have a word with Mr Buccini."

He nodded his head as I walked away and made my way up the carpeted stairs to the top floor. I wasn't even sure which room was his office or if he would even be awake yet. I saw an older woman come running frantically up the stairs towards me, her face crippled with irritation and fear.

"Signorina Jones. You are not authorised to be up here. Please come down immediately," she ordered, but I shook my head.

"No, I need to speak to Mr Buccini. It's very important. Could you please go and inform him that I am waiting?" I said confidently as her face paled with shock.

"No need," said that husky voice that created an unwanted, pleasurable bubble to form in my stomach. I turned quickly and my heart started thundering in my chest. Holy fuck. The man before me was wearing nothing but grey joggers, his raven hair that was normally styled back so smartly, looked soft and messy on top of his head. And his body… I had never seen a more deliciously formed male torso in my life. His eight pack was ripped and carved by the gods and his pec muscles were so large, causing his chest to look broad and intimidating. His biceps were nearly the size of my head, and one arm adorned an impressive sleeve of tattoos. I gulped as my eyes drank him in and when they settled on his sleepy face, I saw him failing to hide the smug grin at catching me ogling.

"Like what you see?"

I lifted my chin higher and narrowed my eyes at him. A moment of weakness. That was all that was. It took me by surprise. That's all. I had composed myself and I was still determined as hell to give him a piece of my mind.

"Oh, mi dispiace signore…" the housekeeper mumbled in a timid voice, clearly terrified she was going to be blamed for my actions, but Giovanni held up his hand and she stopped talking instantly.

"It's okay. I will see Olivia in my office now," he nodded, and she curtsied before turning to walk back down the stairs, but not before shooting daggers at me.

Giovanni strode confidently towards me and opened the door right in front, gesturing for me to enter first. I kept my face blank as I walked past him into the room. I was momentarily stunned by the drastic change of décor. Everything was so dark and depressing. A huge contrast from the cream, white and gold theme that ran through the house.

I stood still in the middle of the room and refused to take a seat when he pointed to an armchair in front of his desk. Seeing my refusal, he perched on the front of his desk and folded his arms across his chest, causing his biceps to bulge.

"Are you not going to put a top on?" I didn't try to hide my distaste. He smirked.

"Is the sight of me half naked really so tempting that you cannot control yourself?"

I rolled my eyes and folded my own arms across my chest, mimicking his stance.

"Fine. This won't take long anyway," I started as I glared directly into his dark eyes. "I would like to retract my acceptance of the double salary." A deep frown set on his face. "I know why you did it and I will not be guilt-tripped into whoring myself out to you for money. I don't know who you think you are but I am not the kind of woman who- "

Before I could finish my sentence, his hand was wrapped around my throat, and he had slammed me up against the drinks cabinet, his body caging mine. His grip was firm but not painful, yet my eyes widened in fear all the same. He glared down at me and, for the first time, I saw what everyone else seemed to know. He was someone to be feared. His inky eyes danced with pure rage as his chest rose and fell in shallow breaths. I hated to admit it but even in his anger, he was hot as hell.

"You think that is why I doubled your salary? To sleep with you? I am Giovanni Buccini and I can fuck whoever I like whenever I like. I don't have to pay for it, sweetheart."

My lips parted and his angry glare turned into one of intense desire when he looked down at my lips hungrily. My breathing was coming out in quick, sharp gasps as I stared into his eyes, his musky scent causing my head to sway. He loosened his grip on my throat, instead, he slowly traced his fingers down to my collarbone, brushing my wavy dark hair away from one shoulder. I stood motionless. The fear had evaporated and was now replaced by an intense burning need to feel his hands everywhere on me. His fingertips grazed along the swell of my breast in my tight strappy top and then he travelled them back up towards my neck. Every feathery touch left a trail of tingles in its wake and a need ached between my legs.

"Don't play these games with me, Olivia. I will always win," he husked and I bit my lip without realising. His thumb pulled it out from between my teeth and he leaned in slowly, brushing his lips against mine so lightly. I was surprised by how soft they felt as my eyes fluttered closed. I could smell his minty breath as I sucked my breath in. "If you bite your lip one more time, I won't hesitate to bite it for you," he whispered against them.

My eyes snapped open and my brain suddenly caught up with the precarious situation I was in. What was I doing?

I needed to get some distance from this man. I shoved at his chest hard, and he took a step back from me. I finally felt like I could breathe again.

"I could sue you for sexual harassment in the workplace," I breathed, but to my horror, my voice was laced with just as much need and lust as his. I wanted to curse myself. His face creased with amusement as a low, soft chuckle left his lips. The sound was so alluring, my core tightened in response.

"I'd like to see you try, bambola. You can deny it all you want, but your body is so receptive to me. You want me and I want you. Why torture ourselves?" His eyes held mine in challenge and I felt the anger starting to rise again. This was always just about sex for him. His mind was always in the gutter, and I would be damned if I gave into him.

"Your ass must be pretty jealous of your mouth right now with the amount of shit that comes out of it," I snarled, glaring at him.

Mirth flashed across his features which for some reason pissed me off more. I wanted to make him angry but instead he just seemed entertained by my insult.

"You've got quite a mouth on you, don't you? Maybe I should teach you how to put it to better use," he flirted outrageously, and I sent him a disgusted look before turning to leave the room. "You should get better at staying away from me, Olivia Jones. I am not someone you want to keep teasing," he called out as I opened the door. I slammed it shut behind me with force and marched down the stairs.

Me, tease him? He is insane. I am doing nothing of the sort! I am trying to stay away from him. Well, except for this morning. Now he has asked for it. I will pretend he doesn't even exist.

You're Wet

Giovanni

This was getting ridiculous. Why couldn't I get her out of my fucking head? I promised myself and mamma that I would stay away from the girl, but at every opportunity, there I was making shit worse. Why couldn't I just leave it alone? What was this spell she had me under?

Last night was a problem. I hadn't intended on coming onto her so strongly. But I couldn't help it. I wanted her so fucking bad. As soon as I brushed that soft bottom lip of hers with my thumb and got lost in her enchanting eyes, I didn't give a fuck about my promises. Calling her bambola just slipped out too. It was at that moment that she reminded me of a beautiful, precious doll that my crazy nonna was so obsessed with in her old age. She used to make me sit with her and brush the doll's long brown hair as a small boy, which I hated but did out of love. Olivia was just like that doll. Beguiling but with a cold exterior. And then, after that compromising situation this morning, I was ready to throw all sense out the window and take her up against that cabinet. Yet, she was playing hard to get. Something I had never experienced before. I had never had to work this hard to get a woman's attention and it was fucking with my head.

Maybe I just needed to get laid. It had been a few days. Actually, the morning of her interview was the last time I found any release. Maybe that was all this was. A build up of sexual frustration. I do not feel shit for women. I do not feel shit for anyone but my family. Family first. Always. This girl had a strange effect on me and I didn't like it one little bit. I needed it to stop.

Picking up my phone from my desk, I typed out a text to Mia's number. She was the most likely to come at the drop of a hat, no questions asked. We had an agreement. You could call us fuck buddies. There were no emotions involved on either side, I made sure of that. She knew what this was and was more than okay with it. Within five minutes, she had texted me back that she would be over in half an hour. I headed out of my office towards my bedroom but froze on the landing when I heard Sani's whining voice.

"What!? You can't! It's not fair!" I watched him stamp his feet as I leaned over the railing and peered down below at Sani, Raya and Olivia in the corridor of their wing.

"This is a lesson in compromise. Today, we will spend the day outside playing, learning and having fun. I have an amazing day planned for both of you and I know you will love it. At 3pm, when you come back inside for your afternoon snacks, you can tear down the games room barricade and spend as much time in there as you like. That is called a compromise."

Sani folded his arms across his little chest and scowled at her, but she just ruffled his hair and took Raya's hand in hers as she stood up. "Let's go party, people! Your day of fun starts now!"

I watched as she dragged them reluctantly down the stairs and out of sight. I couldn't help but be impressed by her courage and perseverance. I wouldn't dare block off that room from Sani. He was terrifying when he went into full melt-down mode. She had some iron balls. Perhaps mamma was right after all, she was perfect for them.

I pushed the thoughts of her deep down into the depths of my mind and focused on showering before Mia arrived. The intercom in my room buzzed and it was Mattio, my head of security, asking for permission to send Mia up. After a few minutes and a faint knock on the door, I pulled Mia into the room by the belt on her dress and slammed her lips against mine. I didn't want to have to talk. I just needed the release. Her hands gripped up into my hair as I lifted the cotton dress over her body and head.

"Someone is in a rush today?" she smiled seductively, and I just pulled her back to my lips as her answer. I wasn't in a rush, yet I felt like I wanted to get this over with. This wasn't for enjoyment for me. I realised that her kiss, tongue and hands did nothing to set my world alight. Just caressing Olivia's neck this morning caused more passion and desire to erupt through me than this. I squeezed my eyes shut tighter as I tried to black out any thoughts of her and focus on the woman in front of me.

Lifting Mia by the waist, I threw her onto the bed aggressively before pulling the fluffy towel around my waist off and discarding it on the floor. Her hooded eyes scanned my body appreciatively as I grabbed her ankles and yanked her down the bed towards me. She squealed in delight, but it had no effect. Flipping her over onto her front so I didn't have to kiss her, I spat on my hand and rubbed between her legs. I don't go down on women I am not really into. It's too intimate. Luckily, I didn't need to as she was more than ready for me. Lifting her backside into the air, in one swift thrust I slammed into her, causing her to cry out. I squeezed my eyes shut as she continued to moan and say my name as I pounded relentlessly. It was irritating the fuck out of me. I didn't want to hear her. Leaning forward, I grabbed a fist full of her black hair and put my hand over her mouth to muffle her moans. But it was still no use. I could feel myself losing my erection. The tension was still in my body but I couldn't find my release. I closed my eyes again and allowed the images of Olivia to come to the forefront of my mind. Her lips were so full and inviting. The feel of them brushing against mine this morning. Her delicate neck and lightly tanned skin. Those eyes that seemed to always be set in a menacing glare towards me. The feel of her body moulded against mine, trapped between the cabinet and my strong frame, completely at my mercy. That did the trick as I groaned out my orgasm and shuddered to a halt.

I opened my eyes as I pulled out of Mia swiftly and disposed of the condom. Sitting down on the bed, panting heavily, I ran my fingers through my hair. What the fuck was that? That had never happened to me before.

I felt Mia's hand rest on my shoulder as she climbed down the bed to sit next to me. "That was amazing as always," she purred in Italian. I gave her a small smile.

"I have a meeting. Can you see yourself out?" I stood up and walked towards the bathroom.

"Sure. See you next time," she winked as she picked up her clothes from the floor and started to dress. I ignored her comment and turned the shower on for the second time that morning to wash away any trace of her on me. I had a feeling that there wouldn't be a next time for Mia. She had not helped to relieve this ache and need deep inside me. And I wasn't sure anyone could. Anyone that wasn't Olivia. I was screwed.

***

"Giovanni, who do you want to delegate the killing contract for Massimo Novalli to?" My capo of Trieste and closest cousin, Maximus, asked.

I rubbed my hand down my face as I thought about who to give that burden to. This was an important client and the job needed to be done seamlessly, but I also knew whoever I gave the order to would have to live with the guilt for the rest of their lives. Just like I do. I may not be the one pulling the trigger, but I am the one giving the order, so I am just as much a killer as them. This target had a family, a wife and two young children. He owed Dimitri hundreds of thousands of euros through a gambling debt and he had stopped paying. Apparently, that was enough to warrant his death.

"Tommas. He proved himself to be a skilled soldier and deadly assassin in the last contract. Ask him. He will receive 20% of the fee beforehand and the other 30% once the job is complete," I commanded, and Maximus nodded his head.

"What of the Leone family? Any inside information from our spies?" I asked my Capos. These were my most trusted men. Most of them were family, distant cousins who were each in charge of their own area of Northern Italy. We were the largest of the Northern families and controlled Venice, Verona, Trieste and Vicenza. The Leone family also had a presence in Venice, which meant they were our biggest threat.

"No Boss. Everything seems pretty low key right now," Leo, my Capo of Venice answered. That wasn't good. That meant something was brewing. The Leones are never low key. They like to rave and flaunt their successes, no matter how small, in our faces.

I stepped towards the window of my meeting room that overlooked the back lawn of the grounds. My eyes fell upon three figures running around the lawn, weaving in and out of the sprinklers, squealing with delight. I smiled at the faces of my siblings who had pure joy written all over them. Their hair was wet and their clothes were soaked through but they were having the time of their lives. And then I saw her. The same look of happiness on her face as the kids. Her chocolate-coloured hair looked almost black as the water dampened it and her tight white strappy top started to go see through, slick against her skin, as she ran through the fountains of spray, chasing after the kids. She looked so different when she wasn't scowling and full of rage. She was mesmerising. I couldn't take my eyes off her.

"Boss? Giovanni!"

The sudden raised voice of Maximus pulled my attention back into the room and I turned around to see all three of my Capo's and Toni staring at me with concern.

"What were you saying?" I took a seat at the top of the table and forced myself to get my head in the game.

"Francesco Aiani would like an invitation to visit. The Boss has agreed that you will host him and his men here as well as open the in-house club and bar for the night."

I gritted my jaw at this information. That was all I needed. Francesco Aiani was the boss of the Aiani family who were important allies of ours. We needed to keep them on our side as they had great connections with the best clients for gun running and armouries. Their equal hatred for the Leone Family made us natural allies. They were the third largest Mafia family in Northern Italy after us and the Leones. But I hated hosting in my home. I liked to keep my family life and my work separate. Very rarely did I ever do work here. Only the weekly Capo meetings taking place right now are scheduled at my home. And that is because I trusted these men with my life and my family's. But I didn't trust outsiders. I did not trust Aiani, even if he was an ally. But if my zio had already agreed to it, there was not much I could do.

"When?" I growled, not hiding my obvious annoyance.

"In two days' time."

Rubbing my hands up and down my face, only one thought crossed my mind. Olivia was going to have to stay with the kids for the night. Mamma would for sure have to make an appearance and I would need someone I trusted to keep them in their rooms with so many people on the premises. Realising what I had just admitted, I frowned. Did I trust her? I hardly knew her but for some reason I knew that I could. Though it would be risky for her to be here when she doesn't know the truth about who I really am.

I ended the meeting and glanced down at my watch. 3pm. They would be getting their afternoon snack according to what Olivia said this morning. Do

I dare? Why can't I stay away from her?

It's so much harder being in the house knowing she is in arms' reach. And after her little confrontation this morning and my very unsatisfying encounter with Mia, I wanted her more than ever. I had never allowed anyone to speak to me the way she did. Normally, such disrespect and defiance would send me into a violent rage, but with her, it just turns me on. Our little moment this morning just confirmed what I wanted to know. That as much as she was fighting it, she wanted me too. Or at least her body did. She was so receptive to my touch. She didn't even realise that her breathing had shallowed, goose pimples adorned her soft skin when I caressed her neck and her perfect tits pushed up against my chest when I brushed my lips against hers.

Fuck I was getting hard just thinking about it again. But I had a rule. One that I was failing miserably at. Never fuck employees. It always ends badly. They catch feelings and it gets messy. They think they can change me. No one can change me. Not even her. Continuing with whatever this was between us was a terrible idea. I knew I would break her eventually if I persisted, but for the first time in my life, I was actually thinking of someone else's needs before my own. I don't have relationships. I don't feel things the way a normal person should. I was taught from a very young age that feelings and emotions were a sure as hell way to get yourself killed in the world I lived in. I would never give anyone that kind of power over me. I couldn't. I had to be seen as cold, hard and ruthless. That was the hand I had been dealt.

My father wasn't like me. Yes, he was feared and respected, but he was also soft. He loved my mother more than life and, in the end, it resulted in his death. He died protecting her. Proving everything my zio and boss, Salvatore, had always told me since I was a young boy. Love is weakness. And I had a feeling that this was the kind of thing that a woman like Olivia would need. She wouldn't just sleep with me, no matter how much her body craved it. She had too much self-worth. Too much self-respect. No, she wanted the whole package. The doting, the romance, the…relationship. It was obvious she was that type. And I could never provide her with that. So, knowing all of this…why am I even contemplating trying to 'bump into her' around the house? *STAY AWAY*. It is so simple.

But I'm hungry. And where is food kept… In the kitchen. She is probably not even there anymore. Before I could think any more about what I was doing, I made my way down the stairs to the ground floor.

"Boss," the soldiers, who were stationed in the main lobby, bowed their heads to me as I stormed past them. I reached the doorway of the kitchen and stopped dead at the sight before me. Olivia was on her tiptoes, failing to reach up to the top cupboard for a tub of aioli. The way she was leaning over the worktops slightly was forcing her rounded and perked ass in her tight jeans to stick out even more. Her dark hair was still damp but was starting to curl naturally as it cascaded down her back, nearly touching her tail bone. Her white camisole is soaked through and clinging to her olive skin. My eyes roamed her from head to toe hungrily and before I could stop myself, I was standing right behind her. I pressed my body against her back, her ass brushing against my semi-hard cock as I reached up over her shoulder and grabbed the spread. She jumped and looked over her shoulder with a shocked expression. Placing the aioli on the counter without taking my eyes off hers, I gripped the countertop either side of her body, keeping her trapped. Her stunning irises that held so many mysteries, blazed in irritation.

She quickly grabbed the tub and turned slightly, lifting her hands in surrender and avoiding my face.

"Excuse me," her tone was stern but held none of the normal sassiness she gives me. For a second, I was surprised. I had at least expected a little bit more of a reaction. Even a scolding. Reluctantly, I lifted my hands off the kitchen surface, allowing her to escape, and she marched around the huge kitchen island to get as far away from me as possible. She opened the tub and started to spread the butter over some bread, her eyes cast down, ignoring me completely.

I frowned. I didn't like that. At least before, she gave me something to work with, even if it was disgust.

My eyes flickered down to her chest and I fought a groan that was itching to rumble from my throat when I saw her pebbled nipples through the thin, wet fabric of her top. Fucking hell. I could see the details of a white lace bra and both that and her drenched top were leaving nothing to the imagination.

"You're wet," I smirked, and her eyes darted up at me in shock at first and a cute blush formed on her cheeks. Ha, she has a dirty mind too. She relaxed when she realised what I meant.

"So I am," she responded in a flat tone. Annoyed at her brush off again, I felt that instant darkness crawling to the surface. Why is she being so…normal? Why is she not reacting to me?

I stepped towards her and leaned against the island, taking a piece of salami off the plate and lifting it to my mouth. She momentarily froze, knife in hand as she watched me suck my finger clean. There it was…ever so brief but a flair of attraction in her eyes before they turned hard and she returned to making the sandwiches.

"Can I help you, Mr Buccini?" She asked professionally as she cut the sandwich into finger strips like my mother used to do for me as a child.

I frowned at the formality. I liked it better when she called me Giovanni last night. "Depends. What are you offering?" I gave her a smouldering gaze, but she didn't even look up to allow its full effect. This woman was aggravating.

"Well, right now, sandwich soldiers or salt and vinegar crisps."

My jaw ticked. This was ridiculous. Why won't she look at me? This morning she was seconds away from kissing me and now she is acting like I am nothing to her. She glanced up at me when I didn't respond. The moment those stunning eyes locked with mine, I lost control. I grabbed her roughly by her soft upper arms and slammed her back into the fridge behind, trapping her with my body. Her eyes widened and a gasp escaped her lips from the shock of my sudden movement.

"What game are you trying to play here, Olivia?" I gritted through my teeth.

Her eyes filled with relentless rage but she kept her tone low and cold. "I am not playing any games, Mr Buccini. I am just trying to do my job. The job you are paying me to do and *not* anything else." She curled her eyebrow up with sass and my immediate frustration turned to amusement. How did she do that? How could she control my emotions so effortlessly?

My eyes rested on her tempting, plump lips as she talked and it took everything in me to fight the overwhelming urge to kiss her. To taste them. To tug at that bottom lip with my teeth until it bled.

"I don't like it when you call me that."

"Then what should I call you…*sir*," My dark eyes snapped up to hers and we both knew she did that on purpose. The way 'sir' slid off her tongue so seductively with challenge. She fucking knew what she was doing to me and she was enjoying it.

Just at that moment, Mamma came striding into the room and looked from me to Olivia with a blank expression. Olivia immediately pushed past me and grabbed the sandwiches and crisps from the island as I straightened up.

"Olivia," my mother greeted her as she raced past, head down and avoiding mamma's curious eyes. As soon as she left the room, I turned around and poured myself a glass of iced water from the fridge. I could feel my mother's deadly glare on me as she watched my every move.

"I warned you Giovanni," she said coldly, which I ignored as I gulped down the drink. She only ever calls me by my full name when she is pissed.

"Non stressarti mamma," I replied coolly, but inside I was cursing myself. The last thing I needed right now was her on my back about Olivia. I was already finding it hard enough to figure out what the fuck was going on with me. I didn't need her input either. I kissed her cheek as she shot me a look that would have most men quaking in their boots before leaving the room. My stomach grumbled fiercely, and I rolled my eyes. Fuck sake. I'll have to ask Lucinda to make me a sandwich now. There is no way I am going back there.

A Mother's Mission
Cecilia

As I watched my beloved son stalk away from me at the speed of light, I dropped my 'outraged and judgmental' mother act and my lips curled up into a twisted smile. This was all going swimmingly. Even better than I had hoped. From the eavesdropping I had just done, it was clear to see that Gio was interested in her and she was…putting up a fight, shall we say? I knew from the moment Gio entered my office with a little twinkle in his eyes and a secret smile that morning, that the girl I had been looking for was in that waiting room.

The girl that would save my son's life.

My son is not a complicated creature, just like many other men, but he is misunderstood. Not only by those around him, but also by himself. He believes he needs to be a certain type of person. A certain man to gain power and respect. To have success. I saw it happening before my eyes. From a young age, my brother-in-law and his uncle, Salvatore, had taken an extra interest in Gio. At any opportunity, I would find him speaking of horrific murders to my infant child like they were trophy stories to be achieved. He would buy Gio the most inappropriate gifts for no reason. After spending any amount of time with Salvatore, Gio would mimic his attitude or the way he spoke. Wanting to be just like him or trying to impress him. Ultimately, his zio was grooming him. But what for, I wasn't so sure. If Salvatore had any children of his own, the empire would be passed down to them, but he hasn't. I often spoke of my concerns to my Vinny, but he dismissed it as that's just the way Salvatore was. That we should be appreciative that he is taking the time to mentor our son who could one day be in charge of our empire if Salvatore never had children of his own. But I hated it. I tried my best to never leave Gio alone with his uncle. Luckily, he had a wonderful, loving papi who balanced him as he grew up. But it never changed the fact that Gio always looked up to Salvatore and wanted to learn from him. But that is not who he is. He is good. He is kind and loving. He is just like his papi. The love of my life.

After the night that turned my world upside down, my boy no longer had that balance in his life. That calm presence who could keep him in check when life turned dark. And it always would in the world we live in. That was inevitable. *It's how you handle the darkness that is your secret power.* That's what my Vinny used to say.

I didn't want this life. The life of a Mafia wife. But I fell in love. And love does not discriminate or judge. I did my best to understand it. I turned a blind eye when I needed to. I learnt how to grow a thick skin and a backbone so not to be walked all over by the powerful men of the family. I earned their respect slowly and became a useful and vital member of our family. With my law degree, I helped on certain contracts ensuring we were given the best possible deals, which was rare for the Mala Del Brenta. Most women were silent and obedient. Their place was in the home and in their man's bed. But my Vinny demanded I be given respect. Like I said, he was different.

His death has affected me more than I could ever describe. He was the other half of me. The shore to my sea. Without him, I was drowning. The only man I will ever love. Apart from my children, of course. Which brings me back to why I am doing this. Since his papi's death, Gio has given himself fully to the pledge of the Buccini regime. He stepped up into Vinny's role as underboss immediately. He never cried or grieved for the loss of his papi. Salvatore made sure there was no time for it. He had a responsibility. An honour bestowed upon him and he must not let his dead papi or supportive zio down. That was how it was sold to him. I have helplessly watched from the side-lines as my son loses himself to the darkness a little more each day. The last two years have made him colder, harder and more ruthless. I know he is still in there from the small moments of affection and pure love he shows me and his siblings, but as Sal works him harder and keeps him out of the house for longer, it is becoming less frequent. He is forgetting how to find any joy in his life, and I fear that he will turn into the clone of his zio. Someone who I despise more than Satan himself.

So, I am desperate. I have watched as Gio fucks numerous women on a weekly basis. They parade in and out of the house in their skimpy outfits and flicks of their sleek hair extensions believing they will be the woman that makes the formidable Giovanni Buccini fall in love. But they never are. They fall at his feet, kissing the ground he walks on. He snaps his fingers and they come flocking. That is satisfying for a man like Gio, but not thrilling. It does not bring him joy. No, he needs chaos. He needs someone strong. Someone who will not bow down to his every need and put him in his place when he is being an ass. He needs someone to make him see that there is so much more to life than deals, money and fighting. He needs a girl to challenge his ego and make him FEEL. Even if it is just pure rage or desire or lust. But I hope eventually he will feel love. That was the girl I was for Vinny and that is the girl I believe Olivia could be for him. I just hope I am not wrong.

Taking careful steps up the first flight of stairs towards the children's wing, I was surprised to hear nothing but the dull sound of the hoover on Gio's floor. Marco was not in the corridor and I wrinkled my nose up in confusion. Walking briskly towards the games room, I was proven right when I saw black tape across it like a crime scene and the door locked. Where are they?

Hearing movement behind me, I turned and saw Lucinda, our very diligent and loyal housekeeper, coming down the second flight of steps.

"Ah Lucinda, do you know where the children are?" I asked as she gave me a respectful nod. The woman is about the same age as me, but we have a completely different vibe. I like to try to keep things light and airy but she is always about formality. Perhaps I should demand she get drunk with me one evening to loosen her up a bit.

"Yes Signora Buccini. They are out in the garden, I believe."

How strange. They hate the outdoors. Making my way out into the extravagant gardens, my heart fluttered and warmed at the sound of innocent laughter and happiness. I followed the noise until I reached the rose gardens and spotted my two darlings kneeling on the grass with Olivia next to them, all shouting and laughing with urgency at something on the floor. Not wanting to disturb them, I watched from behind as Sani suddenly jumped up from the floor, punching the air with his fists. Olivia and Soraya sighed as they lost out on whatever weird game this was, but I smiled when Olivia pinched Raya's nose playfully to make her smile again.

"What are we celebrating?" I asked, causing them all to turn to me. Soraya immediately got up and came bounding into my arms.

"Mamma!" she yelled, squeezing her chubby arms around my neck. I hated that I couldn't spend all my time with them like a normal mother should. But the medication I was on made me very drowsy and sometimes my mood swings were unpredictable.

"We were playing bug races and I won! I had the grasshopper, Raya had the il grillo and Liv had the la formica!" I smiled as he bounced from English to Italian with excitement. I hadn't seen him this lively for ages.

"Ah! Can you remember the English names?" Liv held up her finger to him and he stilled, sucking his lip and thinking hard.

"Cricket and… ants!" he beamed, and she clapped her hands.

"And what do we call this group of bugs?"

"Insects!" Soraya shouted from my arms and my eyes nearly popped out of my head. She barely spoke to anyone apart from her family and never in English.

"Or inv-ir-tbites!" Sani tried to pronounce, and Olivia smiled patiently.

"Yes, insects or invertebrates," she repeated, and I was speechless. She had spent only two days with my children and they were already outside, learning and having fun, not addicted to a TV screen. How did she do it? I don't care. Whatever we are paying her, it isn't enough.

"Mamma, did you know that in-verte-brates don't have a backbone?" Sani asked, his curious eyes alight with interest. I smiled and ruffled his hair.

"No, I did not. What an interesting fact," I looked up at Olivia as she stood up from the floor and brushed down her jeans awkwardly. Placing Soraya back on her feet, I asked them both to go and see if they could catch a butterfly while I had a little chat with their nanny. Olivia immediately looked terrified, so I plastered on my most genuine smile.

Once the little bambinis were out of earshot, Olivia immediately started babbling.

"Mrs Buccini, I want to apologise for what you saw in the kitchen. I don't —" I held my hand up to stop her.

"That is none of my business. I just came here to invite you to stay for dinner this evening. My daughter is coming home for the night from university, and I would like her to meet you. You are about the same age actually."

Her mouth dropped open slightly and she began to fidget on her feet. She didn't want to come. That much was obvious. I kept my face neutral to avoid giving away any amusement and waited for her response.

"Thank you. That is very kind but I- "

"Do you have somewhere you need to be this evening?" I interrupted and from the panic in her eyes I knew she didn't.

"No. But won't I be putting the children to bed?" she asked.

"We will be having an early dinner so the children can see their sister. They can also stay up a little later than normal tonight. I just wanted you to also eat with us as well," I explained, and she nodded nervously. "Good. Dinner will be ready at 6.30pm and served in the dining hall."

I turned on my heels before glancing over my shoulder at her stunned face. "Olivia. You are exceeding my expectations in every way. Keep it up!" I smirked as I walked away.

A Dinner Affair

Olivia

How on Earth did I get myself into this mess? Dinner with the Buccini family. I couldn't think of anything worse than having to sit at a table with Giovanni and refrain from punching him in the face every time he opens that filthy mouth of his. I am not even sure how I agreed to this. Cecilia Buccini was a master manipulator! Hats off to her.

"Why do I have to wear this? It's so itchy!" Sani complained as I did up the shirt buttons. It did seem a little extravagant to be putting the children in their finest designer clothes to eat dinner as a family in their own home, but these were the clothes laid out for them, so help me God if I didn't force them into it.

"You want to look nice to see your sister, don't you? Look at Raya. She looks like a princess," I tilted my head towards the sweet little girl that was holding her tulle lilac dress in her hands and spinning in circles. "Every princess needs her prince."

"Ewww! I can't be her prince. I'm her fratello," he wrinkled his nose up in disgust and I laughed. His face turned curious as he studied my face while I fastened the last few buttons.

"Who is your prince Liv?"

I paused for a moment and felt an unexpected lump form in my throat. The way his big brown eyes were staring into mine so innocently reminded me of Nate's. I shook my head with a small smile.

"I don't have a prince, Sani."

"Then I be your prince?" His sweet voice had tears threatening my eyes as I smiled widely and nodded my head.

"I would love that," I managed to choke out before I quickly stood up and busied myself with tidying their toys. I don't know why his words affected me so much. It was just a sweet, innocent question yet it felt like it had plucked at a hole in my heart and suddenly all the thread previously holding it together was unravelling. I had felt alone for so long. Nate could have been my prince, but he was stolen from me. A moment that was supposed to be so special was stolen from me. And once again, I am living in fear. No prince charming was going to come and rescue me on his white stallion because this was real life. And real life is fucked up.

"Did you make all this effort for me?" A warm voice came from the doorway of Sani's bedroom, and I turned to see a stunning girl the same age as me. Her face held so much warmth as she looked from her brother to her sister before they ran into her open arms. I smiled as she smothered their faces with kisses. One thing for sure about this family was that they really did love each other. It was sweet. "And this must be the famous Olivia Jones I have been hearing so much about."

I felt a prickling heat rise in my chest as my heart fluttered at her words. My first thought had those butterflies appearing in my stomach again. He told her about me? What did he say?

"My mamma has not stopped raving about you these last two days. Olivia this, Olivia that," she smiled, her dark brown lipstick making her lips look larger than they were. Disappointment settled in my chest. Of course, he hadn't spoken about me. Why would he? And more importantly, why do I care?! I can't stand him.

"Hi, you can call me Liv. It's so nice to meet you. I have heard a lot about you too," I smiled, walking towards her and extending my hand. Her hazel eyes looked down at it like it was a snake about to strike and instead, she pulled me into her arms and squeezed me tightly.

"I am not like the rest of my cold, heartless family, Liv. I do hugs," she chuckled, and I nodded, still a little taken aback by her warm and alluring nature. She was so different from Giovanni. Yet I could definitely tell she probably got some of her playfulness from her mother. Though I could never imagine Cecilia pulling me in for a hug. "You best go get ready! I can watch these two monsters now."

My eyebrows furrowed as I looked down at my flimsy white cami and jeans. I didn't bring any spare clothes with me. This was all I had.

"Please tell me you weren't going to wear that to dinner?" Her eyes widened and her mouth dropped open. I nodded slowly, wrapping my arms protectively around myself. "Well, that just will not do! Come on everyone, to my room! We have an angel to dress!"

"She is a princess," Sani corrected and I smiled, ruffling his hair.

Half an hour later and I was standing in front of the floor-length mirror in Elenora's exquisite room, wearing a deep red dress that was far too low cut for a family dinner. I tried to protest but Elle was not having any of it. "You look phenomenal Liv! You should really dress up more often. You have a body to die for!"

I rolled my eyes as I looked back at myself in the mirror and ran my hand over the expensive fabric. I must admit, I did look good but find me somebody who wouldn't in this Dolce Gabbana dress. It hugged all my curves in all the right places and hid the little flaws that always niggled away in my mind. I dreaded knowing how much this was worth. Pulling my long, unruly hair up into a high ponytail, I gasped as Elle grabbed my arms and forced them back down. "What are you doing? Hair down! Always!"

I chuckled at her seriousness. It was as though I had committed a serious offence, not just trying to tie my hair up. "But it got wet today. It's a mess."

"No, it looks beautiful. Your natural curls look lovely over one shoulder like this," she said as she bunched up my hair and placed it over my right shoulder. One ringlet fell forward over the opposite side of my face, and I had to admit, she was right. "Okay! Now make up!"

I held my hands up quickly. "No. No, I draw the line at make-up Elle. Thank you for this but we are going to be late."

She dropped one hip, her hand resting on it dramatically and sighed. "Fine, but at least put on a little red lipstick to match the dress. Here."

Deciding to meet her halfway, I took the designer lipstick and applied it quickly.

"Why do girls take so long to get ready?" Sani moaned from Elle's bed.

"Do it once but do it properly!" Elenora smirked as she picked him off the bed. He gave her a confused look but then shrugged and walked out the room. Elenora and Soraya followed behind him and I inhaled a shaky breath. Please, please…let Giovanni be called away for business. I really did not want to see him tonight. *Liar.*

***

Giovanni

Cecilia Buccini was up to something. I could feel it. Her eyes kept glancing over at the door, waiting for God knows what, and she had that playful twinkle in her eye she only ever had when she was up to no good.

"Che cos'è, mamma?" I asked, but she just shrugged her shoulders and sipped her wine, averting her attention back to the double doors. We were sitting waiting for Elenora to come down with Sani and Raya as well as Maximus to arrive. He was the closest member to all my family and was often invited to our little family occasions. I was looking forward to seeing Elle. It had been a few weeks and she was my sorellina. We had always been close growing up, but in the last two years, as my workload and responsibilities increased and she had her own ambitions to do fine art at university, our relationship had become strained.

"Ah! La mia bella ragazza!" Mamma shouted as she jumped up from her chair and ran towards Elle, pulling her into her arms and kissing both her cheeks.

"Mamma," Elle greeted her just as warmly. Sani and Raya came strolling in behind as I slowly stood up from my chair to make my way over to greet my sister. But a beauty in red had me frozen to the spot. I gripped the marble table so tightly my knuckles were turning white as my eyes took in Olivia's incredible body in that revealing red dress. Her eyes met mine as she stood next to Elle and my heart increased to an unhealthy rate. She looked good enough to eat. And how I would fucking devour her if there was no one else in this room right now. Her gaze quickly darted away from mine as she smiled weakly at mamma who was already gushing over her and telling her how beautiful she looked. So, this was what mamma was up to. Inviting Olivia to the family dinner. But why? Was this a test after what she saw in the kitchen this afternoon? She wanted to try and work out what was really going on between us.

Having no choice but to shove my intense desire down into the pit of my soul, I stood broadly and approached them.

"Elle," I smiled, giving her a kiss on each cheek.

"Jeez! Lay off the weights for a bit fratello! You look like Schwarzenegger more and more every day!"

I rolled my eyes and pulled her in for a hug anyway. My gaze found Olivia's once more over Elle's shoulder but she looked away quickly. Looks like we were both hiding our true desires tonight.

"Liv! Sit next to me!" Sani shouted from the chair he had already scooted himself onto. I groaned when I realised that would mean she would be sitting right next to me too. Taking my place at the head of the table, she stilled when she saw where he meant.

"It's okay Sani. I am going to sit down at this end," she replied with defiance, giving me a cold glare.

"But I am your prince, remember! The princesses always sit next to their prince!" He sulked, looking genuinely hurt. The whole room fell silent as we all took in the exchange between Sani and Olivia. Sani never shows any affection towards anyone but us and what is he going on about...prince? I watched as her resolve faltered and she gave into his puppy dog eyes.

"Of course. I forgot," she muttered, giving him a smile and taking the seat on my left next to Sani. Mamma sat to the right of me as always and Elle sat next to her with Raya on the other side. The staff came and poured our wine as Elle started to chat a million miles an hour in Italian to mamma about her most recent art lecture. Olivia picked up her wine glass timidly and avoided looking in my direction at all. Leaning back in my chair to try and provide some much-needed distance between us, I couldn't help but glance down at her tempting cleavage in that dress. Every rise and fall of her chest as she breathed restricted her tits a little, causing them to strain against the fabric before falling back down. It was mesmerising and caused my dick to twinge in my trousers.

"Don't you think we should talk in English while we have a guest for dinner?" I commanded, forcing my attention on my mother and sister.

"Oh yes! I'm so sorry Liv! I forgot you can't understand Italian," Elle apologised sweetly.

"It's okay really! I don't mind. I love listening to your language. It's so... charming," she smiled and my heart fluttered even though the smile was not directed at me. She liked hearing Italian... Maybe I should try that next time I am trying to get in her knickers. I smirked at my inappropriate thoughts. I really needed an electric shock device to punish myself every time I allowed this woman to enter my dirty fantasies.

"So Olivia," Mamma started as I picked up my wine glass and brought it to my lips carefully. I never knew what was about to leave her mouth and it always had me on edge. "Why Italy?"

My shoulders relaxed slightly as the tension left them. At least she wasn't grilling her about me...yet. Hang on, why did I care how mamma was making this woman feel? I never have before.

"Well, honestly, it was more a question of why not. I had never been, fancied a change of scenery and I had always heard such wonderful things from people who had travelled here," Olivia replied confidently and I couldn't help but hang off her every word.

"What did you do back home?" My sister asked innocently, but I noticed the sudden tension in Olivia's posture. I could sense that the question had put her on edge, but why? What was she hiding?

"Not much really. I am from a small village outside London where there wasn't really much going on, so I was happy to get out of there and head to university to learn to be a teacher," her voice remained calm but there was definitely hesitancy to it. I have undertaken enough interrogations in my time to spot the signs when somebody isn't being 100% truthful.

"But there was a long gap between your A levels and starting university, wasn't there? Two years?" I questioned. I couldn't help it. I needed to find out more about this woman. I wanted to know who she was.

She visibly swallowed and glanced my way, but her expression was nothing but ice cold. She loathed me. I could see the icicles of hatred glimmering behind her eyes.

"Gio! That is none of your business! Don't answer him if you don't want to!" Elle jumped to her defense but I didn't take my eyes off hers in challenge.

"No it's okay," she replied, holding my gaze. "Something happened in my life that I do not like to talk about. It set me back and made me doubt my worth and ability to move forward with my life. I worked on myself for those two years to try and remember the person I was and who I wanted to be. I would like to say it only took two years but, in truth, I am still dealing with it now."

My heart was pounding in my chest as she spoke every word with so much honesty and pain. I could see the anguish of whatever she had been through behind the cold mask that she was wearing. And it did something to me. I felt something. A need. Not a need to kiss her or fuck her or claim her like I had been having. A need to... protect. The room fell silent at her confession but she never took her eyes off mine. I watched as the gold speckles danced against the vibrancy of her bottle green irises and the room faded away to nothing but her eyes. It was only mamma's clearing of her throat that broke our challenging stare and we both looked away awkwardly.

"I am so sorry sweet girl. That you have been through something difficult. Life can be very unforgiving sometimes. As a family we also went through something difficult a few years ago," she started, and my warning glare snapped at her.

"Mamma," I growled, but she just met my gaze with a dismissive glance.

"We lost my beloved Vinny and the children's father in a brutal attack."

I slammed my fist down on the table, making everyone jump. There was one thing I could not talk about right now. Not in front of my younger siblings or Olivia and that was my papi.

"Non qui. Non adesso," I commanded her to not talk about this. She lowered her head and sank back in her chair. I instantly felt like an asshole. Looking around at the awkward and sad faces of each family member made my rage triple. This is who I had to be. This heartless prick. The one that had to carry the weight of responsibility. The weight of our papi's death so they could live the lives they wanted to.

I closed my eyes and focused on my breathing as I tried to calm the storm raging inside my head.

"Don't tell me I have already missed all the drama?" Maximus' deep Italian voice echoed into the room as he strolled in casually. I leaned back in my chair, glad for the distraction, until I saw his leering eyes fall upon Olivia. He looked her up and down hungrily and licked his lips, not even attempting to hide his interest. I clenched my fists on the table, one around the stem of my wine glass. "And who do we have here? A guest?"

"This is Liv. Sani and Raya's new nanny and teacher," Elle introduced them as he took her hand in his and raised it to his mouth like the slimy bastard he is. I squeezed the glass tighter as his lips drew seconds away from touching her skin. I was about to smash the glass over his head but Olivia quickly pulled her hand away.

"Nice to meet you," she said politely. His eyes glistened with intrigue and he smiled back at her.

"I'm Maximus. Cousin of this rowdy lot!" he smirked, pulling his chair out next to Sani. I sighed in relief that he was away from her. I really did not want to have to kill him. He was my favourite cousin and best Capo.

The food came out shortly after and the rest of the meal went by without too much drama. Olivia held her own amongst my opinionated family and I sat back and watched all her interactions with interest. I noticed that when she genuinely smiled, she had an adorable, small dimple in her right cheek. When she felt uncomfortable, she always looked down at her hands and picked at her thumb nail. I also noticed that instead of jewellery she wore nothing but an elastic hair tie around her wrist. I wondered if that was out of choice or whether she just didn't own any jewellery.

"So what do you think, Gio?" Elle's voice invaded my thoughts and I reluctantly turned my attention to her. She was giving me that hopeful look that could only mean one thing. She wanted something she couldn't have.

"About what?" I lifted my wine glass to my lips and took a sip of the sweet white wine from our vineyard in Tuscany. Her face scrunched up in irritation.

"About the trip to France? The art exhibition with the Uni?"

Mamma sat back in her chair and let me take the wheel on this as usual. She never liked being the bad guy. I sighed and rubbed my face. "You know the rules, Elle."

"But it's a Uni trip! It's part of my education! It's only for a few days!" Her voice rose higher with each sentence and I scratched my chin, giving my hands something to do. I hate it when people argue with me. My family knew that better than anyone.

"Elenora. My word is final. You can go if you have five of my men with you at all times or you don't go at all."

"You are so insufferable! What other twenty-three-year-old girl has to have five bodyguards follow her around a museum while she looks at a few paintings? Can't you see you are ruining my life? I am suffocated!" She shouted, losing her temper. Us Buccinis were all known for our fiery dispositions.

I closed my eyes briefly to keep control of my own rising anger. She was suffocated? If only she could walk a mile in my shoes. At least she gets to follow her passions. She gets to go to university (which might I add is a fucking ball ache of organisation and safety procedures on my part) and pursue her dreams. She gets to have dreams full stop. When I opened them, she had chucked her napkin onto the table and stormed out the room, cursing at me in Italian.

"Perhaps, I should take the children up to bed now?" Olivia's small voice came from the side of me as she looked across at mamma. Mamma merely nodded and kissed Raya and Sani goodnight as I watched Olivia walk out with them both. My jaw ticked as I realised I wasn't the only one watching her go.

"Max. She is an employee and off limits," I snarled through gritted teeth and his head whipped round to me with amusement.

"She doesn't work for me," he teased, and I gave him a deadly glare. He may be family but he knew when not to push me and this was one of those times. He nodded once and lifted his glass to his lips as I felt my mamma's blazing glare on the side of my face.

"You seem to have a soft spot for the girl Gio," she taunted, and I sighed heavily. I was really hanging on by a fucking thread tonight.

"You told me she was under my protection while she worked for us. That is all I am doing," I ran my hand through my black hair as my body felt tight with tension. I only released it this morning and now I am wound up like a fucking knot again.

"Are you sure?" mamma probed and I stood up from my chair abruptly. I can't deal with this shit any longer.

"Yes, I am sure, mamma. I do not know what game you are playing to entertain your pass time but I promise you that I will not be a part of it. Unlike some of us, I have a business and a family to run and I do not have the luxury to plot schemes and play games. So, whatever it is you are doing, leave me out of it," I thundered down the dining room and out the door, but I heard my mamma call after me.

"You cannot RUN a family, Gio! That is not how this works!"

I growled in rage as I stormed up to my office to pour myself something stronger than wine.

Who Is the Real Giovanni?

Olivia

"Is Gio mad at us?" Sani asked quietly as I placed his duvet under his arms and tucked him. His handsome little face showed so much worry and it made me even angrier with Giovanni than I already was.

"No. You did nothing wrong. Sometimes...sometimes adults get stressed and take their problems out on those they truly love," I tried to explain. He nodded slowly and rolled over onto his side.

"Will you come back tomorrow?"

Smiling down at him, I replied, "Of course!"

"You are the only one who plays with us, Liv. I wish Gio or mamma would," sadness pulled at his features and I stroked his ebony curls away from his face.

"I am sure they want to play with you just as much as you want them to." I wasn't sure what else to say. I didn't know this family well enough to make any judgments, but from what I had seen in the last few days, they were busy people. But it broke my heart that they rarely seemed to spend any time playing with Sani and Raya and if tonight's dinner was anything to go by, most family time was tense and not much fun for those kids.

He shook his head slowly, "No they don't. They are always busy. Especially Gio."

I chewed at my bottom lip as I looked down at this lonely little boy. I would make it my mission to ensure that every minute I spent with these kids was fun and engaging. I know nothing will take away from the longing to spend time with their family, but at least I could try to take their minds off it.

"I'll see you tomorrow, Sani. Sleep tight," I leaned over and turned off his table side lamp.

"Can we get gelato?" He shouted as I reached the door. Chuckling, I nodded and left the room.

Remembering I was still in Elenora's dress, I padded down the silent landing towards her room. My toes were enjoying the soft luxury of the cream carpets below them. My clothes were still displayed on her bed and I pulled the zipper at the back of the dress down and shimmied out of it as carefully as I could. Laying it neatly on the bed, I smiled at myself. I would never own such beautiful clothes as this but it was nice to feel a million dollars for one night. Suddenly, I felt as though I was being watched as I turned to the door that I now realised I had left slightly ajar. I stilled and narrowed my eyes, only stood in my knickers and bra, my heart started thundering in my chest. There was no one there. I must be going crazy. Picking up my ripped jeans and white cami, I got dressed as quickly as I could so I could get out of this place.

After grabbing my bag and jacket from the lobby, I poked my head around the door of the dining room to thank Cecilia for the dinner, but I was surprised to see there was no one in there anymore. The table had been cleared and immaculately polished as if the evening had never happened. I was not about to go on a hunt to look for her in this maze and risk bumping into Giovanni, so I settled to thank her tomorrow.

The bodyguards at the front door nodded to me politely as I left and the humid, Mediterranean breeze hit my skin, causing relief to flood through me. I was starting to get used to all these bulky men around the house. It felt...safe even though they looked anything but. As I descended the stone steps onto the gravel driveway, I noticed a woman's figure sitting on the stone wall by the huge Roman statue of a naked woman. It was the orange glow from the end of a cigarette that had caught my attention, otherwise I would have walked straight past her, completely unaware.

As I approached her and she removed the cigarette from her mouth, I was relieved to see it was Elenora. She smiled at me sadly, swinging one leg and kicking the gravel with her foot.

"I wish I could tell you that family meals are normally a lot jollier than that, but I am a terrible liar," she said after releasing a cloud of smoke which evaporated into the dark night sky. I smiled at her joke and looked down the long winding driveway. It normally takes around ten minutes to get to the bottom by foot and I was eager to get home, but I felt bad leaving this girl like this. She seemed so...sad.

"You smoke?" she held out the packet towards me but I shook my head.

"No. Thank you though," I replied. She nodded once, dropping her hand in her lap and bringing the cigarette back to her lips. "Are you okay?"

She scoffed and sent a few more stones flying across the driveway.

"I just...I need to rant!"

I chuckled and made my way over to the wall to join her. "Rant away."

"He is just so infuriating!" I agreed completely although I tried not to show it. I couldn't forget my place and at the end of the day he was my boss, so I needed to stay respectful. "I get it. I do. I mean...he is only trying to protect me and after what happened to our papi, he is more protective than ever, but I just wish...for one day that I could be normal. Be from a normal family and live a normal life."

I kept my eyes cast down, allowing her to express her inner torment, but I couldn't help thinking that she didn't realise how lucky she was. She had someone looking out for her. Protecting her. And I mean look at the life she lives. Filthy rich, designer clothes, no worries about how to pay the bills or afford her university debts. I am sure Giovanni had probably paid them outright.

"I know what you are thinking. That I sound like a spoiled brat! You wouldn't be wrong. I know I shouldn't complain when I have all this..." she raised her arms out around her before dropping them back. "But money really doesn't buy you everything. Definitely not freedom or, in my brother's case...happiness."

I glanced up at the light that flickered on in the middle of the top floor. The warm glow illuminated the driveway below and we were no longer sitting in darkness. My chest tightened when I realised it was his office. Was that true? Was Giovanni just as unhappy as the rest of us?

"No it doesn't," I replied. "But it definitely helps."

I tore my gaze away from the window and when I turned my head to the side to address Elle, I was surprised to see her already studying me carefully.

"What is it?" I asked as she continued to stare intently.

"I love my brother. But you need to stay away from him, Liv. You'd have to be blind not to notice the heated looks and the subtle touches across the table."

I swallowed as her hazel eyes bore into mine. "I – I don't know what you mean. I didn't – I don't..." I struggled to form a coherent sentence as panic and humiliation threatened to swallow me whole. Was my attraction to him really that obvious? I thought I was doing a better job at hiding it.

"I don't mean you. I can tell you hate his guts. I am talking about Gio. He has set his sights on you and he never backs down from a challenge. Like I said, I love my brother but he is a dick to girls and falling for him will only cause you heartache. I am only telling you this because you seem like a nice girl and I think we could be friends," she smiled at me sweetly and I looked back up at Giovanni's window as a broad figure approached it. My heart started pounding and I stood up from the wall, turning my back on his silhouette and smiled back at Elle.

"Thank you for your warning, but I have no intentions of falling for your brother. He is everything I despise in a man. No offence." She chuckled, shaking her head.

"None taken but let me just say this... Giovanni is playing a part. Right now, you are safe because you might hate this version of him but be careful. He is not what he seems and if he ever allows you to see the real him...you will be in trouble," she stabbed the cigarette out on the surface of the wall and threw it into the bush behind before standing up. I was still trying to process her words when she pulled me in for a hug and kissed both my cheeks. "I will be back next week! I look forward to catching up with you then! Ciao Liv!"

I turned slightly to watch her walk back into the house and my eyes flickered up to his office window once more. My stomach flipped at the sight of his muscular build standing in the window. He was staring down at me and even though I couldn't see his eyes clearly, I could feel the heat they possessed. My breathing quickened as he lifted a tumbler to his mouth and took a sip of the dark liquid, never taking his eyes off me. Spinning abruptly on my heels, I marched down the dark driveway without looking back, Elle's words playing like a record on repeat in my mind.

I already knew I should stay away. I already knew he was wrong for me. But what did she mean that he was playing a part? And why would seeing the real him get me in trouble? As I continued to storm away from the mansion and the man who was starting to embed himself into my mind, body and soul in the most infuriating way, I couldn't help but feel intrigue and anticipation brewing inside me.

With only one question on my mind, I reached the gate as the men on guard opened it, setting me free from his kingdom but not from my thoughts.

Who was the real Giovanni Buccini?

Alone

Giovanni

It was three am before I finally decided to call it a night and drag myself to my room. Pulling today's signature black shirt over my head and throwing it into the laundry basket, I staggered a little on my feet. I had had more than my usual nightly tipple. It was needed though, after a night of relentless, painful mental torture. I kicked off my shoes, hopping around clumsily before falling backwards onto my Versace silk sheets. I chuckled at myself. I hated these sheets. They were demons in disguise. They always felt nice at first. The cool, smooth fabric on my skin when I first make contact every night but within minutes, I am a sweaty mess and end up kicking them off and sleeping nude. I wouldn't mind so much if I had Olivia in bed next to me. We could be a sweaty mess together. I smirked as my mind flooded with indecent images of what I would do to her if she were in my bed right now. Then I groaned and threw my arm over my head as the image of her undressing in Elle's room came to mind. Fuck me sideways, she was a goddess. Of course she was, I didn't expect anything less. Watching her wriggle her delicious ass out of the dress and seeing her standing there in a white lace thong and bra took every ounce of my control not to go into that room and take her up against the door.

I wasn't leering on purpose. I am not a fucking pervert. I scoffed again. Okay, maybe I am. But I overheard Sani and her conversation when she was putting him to bed and it had me frozen on the landing as hurt and rage coursed through my veins. Rage at myself. Sani was right. I never make time for my family anymore. I rarely see them and when I do it always ends with me upsetting someone which then pisses me off even more. It was too late to make it up to my floor before I heard her coming out of his room and I didn't want her to know I had been eavesdropping, so I did the only thing anyone could do in that situation. I hid in the bathroom like a naughty kid. I watched as she crept past the room I was concealing myself in and into Elle's room.

Checking she wasn't up to anything suspicious, I peered through the fraction of the door that was still open and saw her undoing the zipper of that tempting dress. But what was underneath was a far greater temptation. I couldn't walk away. I couldn't tear my eyes from her heavenly body. Every inch and curve of her was calling to me like a beacon of desire. She was a siren and it took everything in me to leave and climb those stairs to my floor. I actually locked myself in my bathroom until I was convinced she had left the house. I didn't trust myself to be around her at that moment.

And just to torment myself some more, I watched her outside talking to Elle. I would have loved to know what they were discussing but I had a feeling I wouldn't have liked it. When she peered up at my window and stared straight at me, I half expected her to look away, embarrassed at being caught. But she didn't. Just like always, she surprised me. I hate surprises. Normally, when I am taken off guard by someone, they bleed. But not her. I would never hurt her.

She stood her ground and continued to stare, the light from the room illuminating her stunning face. Her eyes held a challenge. And then she was gone. Watching her hips swaying as she strolled down the dark driveway until she was out of sight, I downed my whiskey in one. And that is how my night continued. Neat whiskey. Vodka on the rocks. Even my father's brandy made the cut.

The room started to spin as I closed my eyes, so I forced myself upright. Sleep was overrated anyway. It isn't that I don't enjoy sleeping. Nothing beats that feeling of a solid night's sleep but, it's been a long time since I had one of them. I hated falling asleep. I resisted the transition of falling to sleep until as late as possible, procrastinating the inevitable until my exhaustion took over and forced the heaviness of my eyelids to close and freed me of even heavier thoughts. But then the night terrors came. The flashbacks. The regret. The pain. Nearly every fucking night.

Stumbling to the bathroom, I splashed my face with cold water from the tap and leaned my hands on either side of the sink. Maybe I should go down to the gym. Doing a workout always helps release this frustration and tension. But I am not exactly in the right state to be lifting weights. This insomnia was nothing new but it has definitely become worse since a certain vixen came barrelling into my life. The only relief I get from my dark terrors are thoughts of her. She is like an addiction. Images of her swarm my mind every second of every day and it is even more insufferable at night when I'm alone with them in bed. The need to have her just keeps growing. I really believed it would fade away. That this...desire would dissolve as I got to know her or see more of her. That's how it always worked with other women. I got bored of them. The excitement wore off. The instant attraction fizzled to a flicker. But this was something else entirely.

Dragging myself back to my bed, I perched on the side, swaying slightly as I ran my hand up and down my face. The real reason I hated the night so much was chipping away at me like the devil on my shoulder, forcing me to think about it. Forcing me to acknowledge it. *I hated being alone.* But being alone was better than the alternative. Being vulnerable.

Standing up from my bed, I stumbled into my walk-in wardrobe and changed into a pair of grey shorts before making my way down to the first floor. If my men were surprised to see me like this, they didn't show it, as they fixed their gaze forward and focused on their job to protect my sleeping family. Making my way towards Sani's room, I opened the door as silently as I could. The glaring light from the landing flooded his room, putting a spotlight on his sleeping form in his racing car bed. I closed the door just as quietly and tiptoed over to him through the darkness.

Something sharp suddenly sliced through my foot, causing me to curse loudly in Italian before I stepped back on what I can only guess was a collection of marbles which had me losing my balance and falling face first onto the carpet.

"Gio!" Sani's frightened little voice rang out around the room as he reached over and turned his bedside light on. I sat up on the floor, stretching my neck to the side.

"Hey kid. Sorry I didn't mean to wake you," I said softly in Italian.

"What happened? What's wrong?" He asked as his sleepy eyes looked over my crumbled body on the floor.

"I fell. Don't worry little man, I am okay. Go back to sleep," I said, kneeling up and rearranging his duvet.

"Why are you awake?" He asked, yawning.

I smiled down at him. "Couldn't sleep. Just came to check on you."

"Do you have bad dreams Gio?" His big brown eyes searched my soul and I froze before nodding slowly. I couldn't lie to him. His innocence was so endearing that he squeezed the truth out of me no matter how much I wanted to deny it. I needed to be the strong big brother he deserved, but right now, I didn't have it in me. "I used to too. But then mamma got me this magic bed and I don't have them anymore."

I chuckled as I leaned my forearms on the side of his bed and rested my chin on them. "It is a cool bed, Sani. I am jealous."

"You can sleep with me if you like? It might make your nightmares go away too," I stared at him as the warm orange glow of his lamp highlighted his sweet face. At that moment, I realised. He didn't need his big brother looking out for him right now. His big brother needed him. I crawled up onto his bed and settled behind him. He reached out to turn off his bedside light and I closed my heavy eyes.

"Notte, Gio," his tired voice hummed out into the darkness and I draped my arm over his little body.

"Sogni d'oro Sani," I mumbled as I fell into a dreamless slumber.

Think About Ice Cream

Olivia

"Ciao Marco! Come stai oggi?" I smiled as I tried out some of my newly learnt Italian. He nodded in approval as he stood like a giant guarding Raya's door.

"Very well, thank you Signora Jones," he replied politely. It was strange. He had such a warm voice even though he was one of the most intimidating men. After Giovanni that is.

I raised my hands out to my sides as he replied in English. "Italian please! I am trying my best to learn here! And please, call me Liv."

His lips tugged at the corners before he said, "Scusate Liv." I grinned. One day, I would get a big fat smile out of this man if it's the last thing I do.

"Are they still asleep?" He nodded again. "Okay. I will just go and wake Sani first."

Walking to the end of the hallway, I reached the last door and cracked it open slowly. What I was met with this early in the morning, I was not prepared for. There in Sani's bed was Giovanni, fast asleep. His insanely ripped torso was exposed and he was only wearing a pair of grey shorts that stopped just above his knees. He was on his back with one huge arm above his head on the pillow and his black hair was tousled in all directions. His jet-black eyelashes fanned his cheeks and his lips were parted slightly as he breathed deeply. He looked...different. Cute if that was even possible. Ridiculous, because his enormous body barely fit on the bed and his feet hung off the end. I smiled as I stared at this gorgeous man who looked almost angelic while he slept. Unlike when he was awake and took the form of Lucifer himself.

The flush sounded in the adjoining bathroom, which caused me to gasp and Giovanni to be startled awake. Our eyes met and his were filled with complete confusion for a few seconds as he found his bearings. Sani came parading out of the bathroom with a big smile.

"Liv! Gio slept in my bed last night because he was having a nightmare," Sani squealed happily and my eyes filled with amusement as they found Giovanni's wide ones. I couldn't help the smile that formed on my lips as I folded my arms across my chest.

"That is not exactly what happened Sani!" he growled as he pulled himself to a sitting position. My eyes involuntarily roamed his chest and delectable ab muscles as they flexed with his movement. I forced my view back up to his face but the wicked grin that was already there made me realise I was too late. He noticed.

"What a great brother you are, Sani. I am sure Giovanni just used that as an excuse to sleep in your racing car because it is the coolest thing in the world," I smiled down at Sani's beaming face.

"Oh, so we are back to calling me Giovanni now?" His deep, husky voice sent a wave of pleasure to my core as he climbed off the bed with a cheeky grin. Oh hell. He was in a playful mood. I hadn't witnessed this side of him before and I didn't like it. It caused a reaction in me that was extremely unwelcome.

I narrowed my eyes at him as he stalked towards me like a predator. His dark irises twinkled with mischief. "Shame. I liked the way you called me sir," he winked as he stopped a foot away from me. I refrained from admiring his mouth-watering physique and kept my eyes locked on his.

I opened my mouth to give him a snarky remark but Sani interrupted us.

"Liv! Are we going to get gelato today? You said last night. Remember? You promised!" His voice turned to a whine, and I sucked my bottom lip with my teeth. I couldn't help but notice Giovanni's eyes darken as they fixed on my lips and I quickly released them.

"Well, I need to speak with your mamma first, Sani. Check if it is okay for us to leave the premises."

"Or you can ask Gio. Gio please! You can come with us!"

My eyes widened as I watched Sani tug on Giovanni's tattooed arm and something flickered across his features.

"I am sure your brother has lots to do today, Sani," I quickly added, giving Giovanni an easy way out of this, but to my surprise and horror, he looked from Sani to me with a devilish grin.

"Actually, I would love to come. I have to move a few things around and it can only be for a few hours, but it is meant to be a scorching day today and I would really love a delicious...creamy...gelato right now. Cool us down, right Olivia?"

I opened my mouth but no words came out. What the fuck is he doing? No. No, I can't spend a day with him. I won't. Sani was already leaping about the room like a gazelle and Giovanni strolled past me before stopping to whisper in my ear.

"How can I say no to spending the day with you when you are looking like that? A gelato is not all I would like to eat."

My cheeks flamed crimson as I felt a wetness pool between my thighs, drenching my knickers under my green summer dress. Oh my god. I cannot believe he just said that to me. I heard him chuckle before he left the room and I had to try to focus on steadying my pounding heart. I thought last night was unbearable...today is on a whole new level.

***

"Here, put some sunscreen on Sani," I commanded as I squeezed a little into his hand before I smothered Raya's face and arms in the white cream.

"I don't need it," he scrunched his face up into a look of disgust as he stared at his hand. I have figured this little man out now. Everything must be on his terms. If he doesn't understand why or how something works, he won't do it. Even down to simply putting on a little sunscreen. Sighing, I glanced over at him.

"Do you know why you wear seatbelts in the car?"

His little head nodded back at me. "Because it is dangerous if we crash."

"Exactly. Seatbelts protect you from getting hurt. Sunscreen does the same thing but for your skin. It protects you from the ultraviolet rays of the sun."

"But how?"

"You know how Ironman puts on his armour so he is protected?" He nodded again as I finished up Raya's arms. "Sun cream is just like that. It's like armour on your body to protect you from the heat of the sun."

"You really have a way with words."

That deep voice that infuriates yet excites me made me jump and I turned around to see Giovanni striding towards us wearing jeans and a black V-neck T-shirt that hugged his large biceps. He looked so much younger in such casual clothes and I hated to admit it, but hot as hell.

"Are you going to wear it too, Gio?" Sani looked up at him hopefully.

Giovanni pretended to look shocked by his question before answering, "Of course! That's if Olivia wants to share?"

I smirked as I held the bottle out to him, but the mischievous glint sparkled in his eyes again.

"Raya, was Olivia good at putting sunscreen on you?" I glanced down at the sweet little girl in her blue summer dress as she nodded with a big grin on her face. "Well, I think I would like Olivia to put some on me. She can show you how to do it yourself, Sani." His lips pulled into a sideways smirk as my eyes widened and I started shaking my head.

"You have hands! You are more than capable," I shot back, but he wasn't going to back down and I knew it. Taking a step closer to me, my breathing hitched as his masculine cologne invaded my space and he maintained his challenging gaze.

"Ok! I will put it on but Gio has to have it on too, Liv!" Sani shouted up from next to us and I threw my head back in defeat. We were never going to get out of this house if I didn't give in.

"You are such a man-child!" I mumbled under my breath, but I knew he heard me as I squirted some sunscreen in my hand and rubbed it together. When I glanced up, he was smiling so widely, I forgot how to breathe for a moment. It was the first time I had ever seen his true smile. Not a smirk or snigger, but a genuine smile. It was beautiful.

"Maybe start with the face...It's my best feature," he teased. He was enjoying this far too much. I rolled my eyes and reached up to place my hands on either side of his face as I carefully rubbed the cream into his tanned skin. As soon as our skin came into contact, my stomach fluttered and I felt heat rise through me, causing a slight blush to creep up to my cheeks. His smile had vanished and he was staring at my face with a serious expression. Letting my eyes follow the trail of my hands to keep me from buckling under his heated gaze, I suddenly realised how intimate this was. My lips parted in reflex as I ran my fingers softly over his stubbled chin and strong jaw. As my hands came down his thick neck, he noticeably swallowed and my eyes flickered up to his. That was a mistake. The look in them was full of intense want and... danger. My hands stilled as I reached his shoulders and his T-shirt restricted me from going any further. We continued to stare deep into each other's souls and for a moment I had no thoughts. Nothing but him. How perfect his skin felt under my hands. How every contour of his face was so distinguished. I wondered what it might feel like to let my hands wander under that shirt. To feel every rock-hard muscle ripple under my touch...

"There! I did it! Can we go now?" Sani moaned and I leapt away from him and quickly looked away. The spell was broken and I felt my cheeks flame and my heart pound in my chest. *What the fuck was that Liv? He is your boss!*

"Yes. Come on, let's go," I said quickly after clearing my throat and grabbing Raya's hand in mine. I didn't dare look back at Giovanni as we strolled down the stone steps where two Range Rover Vogues were waiting for us. Marco nodded at the man who was causing so much stress in my life behind me and threw him a set of keys. I was surprised when Giovanni pressed the fob key and the blacked-out SUV unlocked. Striding passed me, he opened the back door for the kids to jump in and I stood rooted to the spot.

"You are driving?" I was glad to see my voice had returned to normal after our little moment.

"Yes. Something wrong with that?" He raised one eyebrow in amusement and I shook my head. Opening the passenger door for me, I climbed in carefully, holding my dress under my ass to avoid an embarrassing show as I could feel his hot gaze watching my every move. He closed the door and I fumbled with my seatbelt as he strolled around the front of the car and spoke to a few of his bodyguards. I wonder if they are coming with us? I glanced back and checked that the children had put their own seatbelts on just as he climbed into the driver's seat. As I whipped back around, my eyes bulged when he pulled a gun out from under his top at the back of his jeans and placed it in the middle compartment between us. What the fuck? That is a real bloody gun!

He didn't even seem to notice my reaction as he started up the engine and smiled at the kids in the rear-view mirror. I leaned sideways towards him and whisper-yelled in panic, "What the hell? Why do you have a gun?"

His face turned to mine and I realised how close we were. Our noses were practically touching, so I moved back to my seat quickly.

"Just in case," he said with a wink and turned his focus back onto the road as we started to make our way down the gravel driveway to the gates.

"Just in case of what? They don't sell chocolate chip ice cream?" I was trying so hard to keep my voice low so the children wouldn't worry, but I was close to having a full-blown panic attack. I had never seen a real gun just sitting there in front of me before. I knew the bodyguards around the house had them, which had made me uncomfortable at first, but I soon forgot about it. But why did Giovanni need one? That's what he was paying those men for, surely?

"Well, that would be a crime," he chuckled. He didn't answer me but kept his eyes fixed on the gate that was pulling away slowly to let us out. Nodding to his men who stood guard, we drove through and I looked behind to see another black SUV coming out of the premises behind us. "Who is in that car?"

"Marco and my men," he replied coolly.

"Are they coming with us?"

"Si."

"Then why do you need a gun? If they are going to be with us to protect you, why are you carrying that thing around? And in front of kids?" I couldn't keep the judgement out of my voice. It was one thing, having trained men who knew what they were doing welding guns around, but a completely different matter when it came to Giovanni.

"Full of questions today, aren't we bella?" he smirked and I glowered at him. I wasn't going to get anything of substance out of him when he was in this mood. He was too...happy. Everything I seemed to say or do today was just adding to his annoying amusement. Deciding this was dangerous territory after what had already happened between us this morning, I leaned back in the leather chair, folded my arms and stared out of the window.

Sani spent most of the journey talking about which flavour of ice cream he was going to have and which he thought we should all have too. I entertained him and giggled at his excitement but ignored Giovanni the entire time. I could feel his gaze on me every now and again, but I refused to look. Seeing him in his natural environment, so relaxed, was not helping my situation. I needed distance from this man. I needed resistance. But when I allowed myself to sneak a peek at his toned forearms to his huge, masculine hands that tapped away at the steering wheel to the music on the radio, I felt that warmth spread through my body and settle at my core. As my eyes travelled down to his thighs, which were so thick and muscular, an ache between my legs caused me to squeeze my own thighs together. He turned his striking face towards me and his dark eyes bore into mine. God, why did this man have to be so freaking gorgeous? *But he knows it, Liv. Don't give him the satisfaction of letting him know you know it too!* I quickly turned my attention back to the window.

"Are you excited, Liv? To have ice cream?" Raya asked quietly from the back. I gave her a small smile.

"Yes. I am so excited!"

Ice cream Liv. Think about ice cream.

Love is Tragedy

Olivia

Every time I walk the charming streets of Verona, I fall even more in love with this city. There is always more to see. More to take notice of. From the intrinsic details of Roman architecture to the array of beautiful flowers that hang from walls and pretty piazzas filled with bustling cafes, restaurants and shops. I soaked up the relaxed and happy atmosphere as I took in the many faces of residents, tourists and locals. It always feels as if everyone is on their very own little holiday.

We strolled down the cobbled streets of Centro Storico and weaved our way through the crowds. Giovanni was leading the way with Soraya's little hand in his and I was behind with Sani. Marco and two other terrifying men were marching behind us, constantly scanning the throngs of people for any immediate danger. It seemed like the unlikeliest place on Earth to feel unsafe, but what did I know?

I couldn't help but notice how much attention Giovanni was getting. Mainly from beautiful women who gave him flirtatious glances as he walked past, but also from men who stared at him in disbelief. It honestly felt like I was in the company of an A-list celebrity the way the locals were acting in his presence. Some people even had their phones out and were taking pictures. I lowered my head, allowing my hair to cover most of my face to hide myself from appearing in the background of their photos. Not only because I didn't want to be on their phones, but I had no idea where their pictures would end up. Social media? Magazines? I couldn't risk Henry ever stumbling across something like that. I just couldn't.

We stopped outside a quaint gelato shop and ordered our ice cream. The server seemed extremely nervous but also in awe of Giovanni. I couldn't understand it. Yes okay, he is extremely good looking and filthy rich. Yes, he owns half of Verona, but what was with all the wide eyes and shaky hands? Even the second server, who was most likely his daughter, was frozen like a statue, ice cream scoop in hand, until her father nudged her into making our order. But as I looked up at Giovanni's side profile, I was surprised to see no reaction from all this attention. It was as if he was blind to it all or just amazingly skilled at hiding how much it affected him. I would hate it, but then I am not this man next to me. I bet he loves every minute of it.

"You okay?" Giovanni suddenly turned to me and I blinked back at him in surprise. "I know it can be overwhelming. Don't worry, they will all calm down soon."

So, he is aware...yet he doesn't seem to be entertaining it. Interesting. He handed me my salted caramel gelato and I thanked him, which made his lips pull up into a little smirk.

"You're welcome, although I can think of so many more fun ways you could thank me."

I groaned and turned my back on him, walking away to a bench in the middle of the piazza with Sani. Why did he feel the need to always make everything dirty?

Once we all sat down, Giovanni towered over us from behind the bench and Marco and the others stood around us protectively. I felt ridiculous. This all seemed so unnecessary in the middle of this gorgeous little slice of Italian paradise. My eyes fell upon a huddle of people at one end of the piazza where there seemed to be some commotion going on.

"What's happening over there?" I asked, looking up at Giovanni. It was only then that I realised how closely he was standing to me and his tattooed hand was gripping the bench right next to my shoulder.

His face scrunched up in distaste.

"Casa de Giulietta," his Italian words rolled off his tongue like a seductive melody and I swallowed my instant arousal. "Otherwise known as the house of Juliet. The most overrated tourist attraction this city has to offer."

My eyes flew back over to the crowd and I squealed. I couldn't help it. I was a literature buff. And I had been begging Gigi to take me to see Juliet's balcony since I arrived here but she was always busy working during the day and then I started this job, so I haven't had a chance.

"Did you just squeal?" Giovanni raised one dark, well-groomed eyebrow at me and I spun round on the bench to look up at him.

"Can we go and see it? Please?" His face creased with amusement at my excitement, but I didn't care what he thought about me.

"I don't want to! It's so boring," Sani grumbled with a mouthful of chocolate chip ice cream.

"It is romantic Sani! It is poetic and full of magic! Have you heard of Shakespeare?" I asked, practically bouncing on my seat.

"No. Is he a racing driver?" Sani quizzed innocently. Giovanni scoffed from behind me, but I ignored him.

"No. He is one of the greatest poets and playwrights who ever lived!"

"He sounds boring," he said before taking an enormous lick of his ice cream. I rolled my eyes and looked back up at Giovanni's face. He was trying to suppress his laughter but failing terribly.

"Well, I am going. Can you watch the kids for five minutes please?" I didn't wait for him to respond and started to make my way towards the entrance of the attraction. I knew it wasn't really Juliet's house or had any real historical connection to Shakespeare's most famous play, but it was still an experience that I would love.

"Olivia. Wait," That unmistakable alluring voice called behind and I stopped to see Giovanni strolling towards me. I looked over his shoulder and saw the three men all watching over Soraya and Sani who were still happily sitting eating their ice creams. "You can't walk off alone."

My eyebrows furrowed and I burst out laughing.

"I walk off alone all the time, remember? I am not part of your family and under your protection."

Something flashed across his eyes but just as quickly it was gone and replaced with playfulness.

"I didn't take you as another one of those hopeless romantic types that fly halfway around the world to stare at a balcony that has no real significance to anything," he brushed passed me and joined the back of the queue of people who were filing through an arched passageway.

Scowling at him, I replied, "I am not a hopeless romantic! I just like literature and Shakespeare happens to be one of my favourites. Forgive me for wanting a little culture."

Leaning against the brick wall, he smirked.

"Culture is seeing the opera at Arena Di Verona or learning about Mastiff I of the Scala family in Piazza dei Signori. Not this. If you want to experience the real beauty and romance of Verona, I would be more than happy to...assist you. You will be thoroughly satisfied, I promise."

I huffed and folded my arms across my chest. He just can't help himself, can he?

"You have your whole life to be an arrogant, sex-crazed playboy. Why don't you take a day off?" It was out of my mouth before I could stop myself. I slammed my hand over my lips that seemed to have a mind of their own and stared at him wide-eyed. I can't believe I just spoke to my boss like that. I was so fired!

But to my complete shock, I watched in confusion as his face turned from surprise to utter glee. The sound of his laugh moved through me like the first hypnotic note of a live jazz song, leading to even richer and sweeter notes. I couldn't help but join in with a small giggle at his reaction, but I was still mortified.

Suddenly, he reached out and grabbed my wrist in his large hand. In one swift motion, he slammed me straight into his chest and wrapped his arms around me tightly so I couldn't escape. My hands rested on his rock-hard pecs over his black top and I felt like I couldn't breathe. His laughter had come to a natural end and his deep brown eyes bore into mine with so much intrigue.

"Who are you?" he whispered gruffly, but I just opened my mouth and closed it again like an idiot. I couldn't think straight with him this close to me. With his arms around my body and the feel of his muscular frame up against mine. "I never let anyone talk to me the way you do. You really...really want to be punished by me, don't you bambola?"

"I – I –" I couldn't form my words. I didn't know what to say. I wanted to scream at him for his bold seduction, but there was also a devious part of me that knew they were true. Yes. I wanted to be punished by Giovanni Buccini.

Suddenly, the crowd moved and he released me from his embrace, allowing me to regain my senses. As I stumbled forwards through the arched alleyway towards the mediaeval courtyard, my eyes widened at all the names of lovers written on the stone walls. My mouth dropped open as I took in every little detail. Names were carved and a faded crest of the Cappello household was visible on the building, as well as the beautiful balcony that was the main attraction. Tourists were craning their necks to stare up at it but something else had caught my attention. A teenage girl, maybe no older than seventeen, was tucking a piece of paper in the crevice of a stone wall just below the balcony. It was only then that I realised hers was one of hundreds of little notes that carpeted the walls.

"What is she doing?" I asked quietly as I continued to stare. I could sense Giovanni standing right behind me. My body knew when he was near. All the small hairs on my neck stood up in anticipation and my heart was beating a little faster than normal. I felt his hot breath on my skin as he spoke.

"There is a myth that if you write the names of you and your lover on the wall you will be together forever. But really tourists have just vandalised a beautiful building, so now, people write love notes. Letters asking for Juliet's advice on their love lives and stuff them into the cracks. It's ridiculous," I could hear the cynical tone of his voice and I rolled my eyes.

"I don't think it's ridiculous. I get it. Writing out our own thoughts is a kind of therapy for some people. Telling someone you don't know or who won't judge you can be easier than sharing with the people you love," I said thoughtfully as I watched the young girl weaving her way through the tourists to leave.

"But they are not even real people. Romeo and Juliet. And this isn't even an accurate portrayal of Shakespeare's play. He likely had never even been to Verona and this used to be a house that belonged to a local noble family before they turned it into a tourist attraction."

I remained looking forwards, up at the balcony as he had his little rant. "Romeo and Juliet are alive in the imaginations of millions of Shakespeare fans."

He scoffed loudly behind me. "And let me guess, you are one of them. So, *you* believe that love conquers all? If anything, Shakespeare teaches you that love always ends in your demise. In tragedy."

I turned sharply to look up into the dark eyes that held so much emptiness and saw my own. We were the same but different. Although I understood his view, I would never share it. Because I still had hope.

"You may be right. Juliet risked everything for love. She went against her family, faked her own death and woke up to find her true love gone. It was a tragedy. But what it taught me was that she felt more alive and felt more happiness in the short time she had with Romeo than she had ever felt in her life. So, it was all worth it. What is the point of living if you aren't really living at all?"

His face studied me intensely and I think, for the first time since we had met, I had left him speechless. Not wanting to ruin this little win, I pushed through the crowd back out into the bustling piazza, leaving him to contemplate my words. I could feel him trailing behind and I smiled brightly as I reached the children. Settling myself down on the bench between them, I looked up to see Giovanni staring back at me with a pensive expression. Marco approached him, turning his back to us and muttered something in Giovanni's ear. The look of pure rage that etched on his face, transformed his entire appearance. His eyes had darkened to almost black and his handsome features were fastened into a menacing scowl. His aura radiated violence. He said something sharply in Italian to Marco who nodded to the other two men. They turned abruptly and marched off through the crowd with determination, leaving myself, the kids, Marco and Giovanni.

He stormed towards us and lifted Soraya up into his arms. "We have to go. Now." His voice was so demanding and tense that it made my heart start thundering. Something was really wrong.

"What's happened?" I asked in panic as I grabbed Sani's hand in mine and started to follow him down the cobbled streets to where we parked the car. He didn't answer me. I had to jog a little, pulling Sani along to keep up with his urgent pace as Marco brought up the rear.

"Get in," he growled as he opened the back door. The look on his face warned me not to argue and I swallowed my fear as I slid in next to Sani and Raya. Marco climbed into the driver's seat and, to my horror, Giovanni slammed the door of the passenger's side as he pulled out his gun and pulled back the barrel before holding it in his lap. His eyes were glued on the wing mirror, looking for something.

"When we get home, can we do something fun, Liv?" Sani asked, oblivious to the situation we were in. I smiled and nodded at him, but I couldn't take my eyes off the silver gun poised in Giovanni's hand, as if he was preparing to use it. I tried to remain calm as we sped down the roads of Verona's city out into the suburbs. I gripped the seat below my legs as Marco drove us like we were part of the Formula One races and Sani and Raya giggled and screamed at every insanely sharp bend. I honestly thought I was going to throw up or die. Either one.

When the gates to the Buccini mansion finally came into view, I breathed a sigh of relief. They immediately opened and before the engine had even turned off, Giovanni was out of the car. He marched straight up the stone steps and through the front door, leaving me completely baffled. *What the hell is going on? Will somebody talk to me?*

I climbed out of the car and lifted the children down, who ran off inside with no idea of what had just gone down. *What had just gone down?* "Marco!" I ran up alongside him as he followed the children in. "What the hell was that? What just happened?"

He turned, his face void of any emotion and stated calmly, "Nothing you need to concern yourself with Signorina Jones. You should go see the children."

I narrowed my eyes at him but his face remained completely blank. I would get nothing out of this robot. Stamping my feet a little more aggressively than I needed to, I followed the children up to their wing. There was never a dull moment in this job.

The Darkness Within

Giovanni

"T'hai preso? (Have you got him?)" I demanded on the phone to one of my men that had accompanied us to the city today. I may have sounded unnervingly calm, but inside I was raging. A vortex of anger thrummed through my veins and I needed to find a release.

"Si. Lui è in cantina (he is in the cellar)." I hung up the phone immediately and downed my glass of whiskey, hissing as it burned my throat. Time to let off some pent-up frustration and rage. This is what I do best. No fucker messes with my family and gets away unscathed.

Storming down the stairs, I paused when I heard the laughter of my brother and sister in the education room. Normally, the sound would put a smile on my face, but right now it just fueled my darkness. I would never let anyone hurt them and it's time everyone knew Giovanni Buccini was not to be fucked with.

When I reached the cellar that was located under the garage of my estate, the smell of fresh blood invaded my nostrils. Looks like my men were already having some fun. These cellars were designed especially with this in mind. Soundproof, discreet and with limited access, it was the perfect torture chamber for my enemies. As I strolled into the room, one of my men stepped back from the man who was tied up on a metal chair. His head hung low to his chest and rolled back as he tried to look at me through his half-closed eyes. His nose was broken and blood was pouring from his mouth. My men had been enjoying themselves.

"Boss," Luigi greeted me. "He is yet to talk."

Good. I hated it when they caved immediately. Stepping up to his battered face, I grabbed a handful of his hair and forced his rolling head still so he could look me in the eyes. The eyes that would haunt him forever.

"Name," I commanded, my voice icy cold. He coughed and sputtered and I tightened my grip on his hair. "I don't ask twice."

"Fran-Frankie," he choked out, and I dropped his head aggressively.

"Why were you following me and my family Frankie?" I stood up straight, towering over his pathetic body as I removed my Rolex from my wrist and passed it to Luigi.

He dropped his head to his chest once again and remained silent. I nodded to Luigi as I stepped back. Picking up a packet of toothpicks, he handed them to me and I smirked. This will have him talking in no time. I squatted down on the balls of my feet as I spread his fingers apart that were resting on his leg, restricted by the rope.

"Toothpicks..." I held one up in front of his face with an evil grin and saw his brows crease in confusion. "Great for getting dirt out from beneath your nails. Ever tried it?"

I lined the sharp spike up under his index fingernail and, at a languishing slow pace, eased the toothpick under his nail, causing him to scream out at the intense pain it caused as blood started to run down his finger. Leaving the little wooden stick lodged in his finger, I grabbed his hair again and forced him to look at me. Changing my tone to one of pure malice, I snarled, "Would you like another one? This is just a taster of what is to come if you do not cooperate. Who do you work for?"

"The Leone's," he mumbled through his sharp gasps. I stood up and gritted my jaw. I thought as much but also hoped they wouldn't be so stupid as to send a spy to follow me and my family so openly. This meant I couldn't fucking kill him and he knew it. I would be breaking the code of conduct set by the commission and waging a war against our rival family that would end in complete destruction and blood shed on both sides. Also, Salvatore would never allow it. As frustration grew in me, I clenched my fist and sent it flying into his face, hearing his cheek bone crack under the impact.

"We found this in his possession," Luigi handed me the camera and I scrolled through the first couple of photos. Most were of the four of us, Olivia, Sani, Raya and me, but when I flicked through and saw that he had soon fixed his lenses solely on my brother and sister, I saw red. Following me around and reporting back my business was one thing but taking photos of my brother and sister was something I would not let him get away with. But it was the next photo that had my blood boiling. I gripped the camera so hard it felt like it would break in half under my force. He had zoomed right in on Olivia's beautiful face. She was smiling widely and looked so free and happy. And then the next was of her as well, but of her entire body from a distance. She was looking over her shoulder at me and her little green dress was blowing in the breeze giving a flash of her ass cheeks which this fucker had managed to capture at that moment. I opened the camera and took out the sim card, pocketing it. My hands were trembling with fury. I can't remember the last time I have been this livid.

"What the fuck does Riccardo Leone want to know, huh?" My voice remained oddly calm but I knew my eyes burned with the depths of hell.

When he refused to comply, I lifted my leg without warning and kicked him solidly in the chest, causing him and the chair to fall backwards with a powerful thump. He hit his head on the cement floor, his eyes rolling back into his head as I leaned over him and grabbed him by the collar of his shirt. He was barely conscious now and I already knew we weren't going to get anything out of him. He was a loyal soldier to his family.

"You tell Leone, if he ever comes near my family again, I will come for his precious son, and deliver his severed head to him in a box. And I do not. Fucking. Bluff."

Releasing him with a shove, he groaned as he rolled onto his side, taking the chair with him.

"And as for you Frankie. I think taking your eye will be enough of a reminder not to spy on my family again."

He started to beg and plead, coughing up blood as I opened my hand out to the side and Luigi passed me the toxic alkaline that would blind him instantly. Unscrewing the cap, Luigi pulled the chair up to stand and gripped my enemy's head in his hands to hold him still. As the man whimpered and pleaded in front of me, I felt that flicker of humanity spark and for a second, I hesitated. But only for a second.

Pushing the glimmer of mercy down beneath the darkness that I had grown so accustomed to, I stepped forward and held the man's left eye open with one hand. This was business. This was a message that needed to be delivered. If anyone thought they could come for my family or...for her. They would be met by this man. To my family, I was Gio. But here...I was a whole different entity. I was what I was raised to be. A ruthless, heartless monster.

Pouring the corrosive liquid form into the man's eye as he screamed and writhed against the rope and Luigi's grip, I felt nothing. Numb. I had become skilled at turning off my emotions and doing what needed to be done. No matter how much I hated it. As the formula worked its sick magic against his eyeball, damaging it beyond repair, I released him and stepped back. My jaw clenched as the man's head dropped back to his chest and he spluttered and sobbed shamelessly. After a few minutes, he released the loudest ear-splitting scream as his eyeball burst under the pressure and the jelly-like substance slid down his face.

"Drop him back at Leone's territory. And don't forget to relay my message to Riccardo himself. Or I will come for your other eye too," I growled before turning on my heels and striding out of the room.

Clenching and unclenching my fists, I realised I was shaking violently. A mix of adrenaline but also disgust at what I had just done. This always happens. I never let anyone see me this way. I wasn't meant to feel the guilt I did. I wasn't meant to feel sick to my stomach every time I tortured or killed someone but I did. And I hated it. I despised this softness that was always scratching at the surface, trying to change me. My papi; he had too. And it killed him. I would not be so weak. My world was dark and so I had to be too. It was the only way to survive.

***

Olivia

I felt completely shattered after today and I couldn't wait to get back to the flat, put on some comfies and binge Netflix with Gigi. Rolling my neck as I walked through the main lobby to grab my coat and bag from the security room, I heard a loud, repetitive thumping sound coming from down the hall. There didn't seem to be anyone there apart from the odd men standing guard around the house and they didn't seem the least bit concerned by the noise, so I guess I shouldn't be either. Shrugging on my denim jacket, I placed my shabby rucksack over one shoulder and headed back out to the grand ground floor corridor. The kids were tucked up safely in bed and I hadn't seen Giovanni or Cecilia for the rest of the day. The *whump, whump, whump* sound grew louder and was now mixed with animalistic grunts and growls. What the hell was that?

My mum always used to scold me for being too curious for my own good. Why stop now? Padding along the marble floor in my Havana flip flops, I stopped outside an oak door at the end of the corridor. The noise was deafening from here and I looked over my shoulder to check if the bodyguards were going to do anything about this almost violent sound or if they were, in fact, going to leave me to fend for myself. Looks like the latter. Pushing the door open silently, I squeezed through the crack and found myself in a very modern and sleek-looking gym. My eyes roamed the enormous room and all its expensive torture devices (I am not a fan of working out) until my eyes fell on the sexiest scene I had ever been forced to watch.

There, in the corner of the room, was a shirtless, sweaty Giovanni hitting a punching bag, bare-knuckled over and over. He was wearing those famous grey shorts he seemed so fond of and nothing else. Broad shoulders hunched up and large biceps extending and retracting with every violent assault. He was quilted heavily in muscles that should make him slow-moving, but instead, lent him the grace and the poise of a wild cat. Watching him jab and dance around it so effortlessly, as if this was second nature to him, had my body temperature rising and an ache pulling at my core. I was hypnotised. Every muscle in his upper body and back rippled as he moved. Beads of sweat coated his tanned skin and fell onto his shoulders from his hair. But it was the concentration and focus on his gorgeous face that had my attention. It was obvious that he was pissed about something and was taking it out on that poor piece of gym equipment.

He suddenly stopped, hugging the bag to his shoulder and rested his forehead against it. His toned chest was heaving frantically and he flexed his hand open and closed. Shit. I shouldn't be here. I shouldn't have come in.

Slowly, I backed towards the door, not taking my eyes off him, hoping that by some miracle, I would escape this room without him ever knowing I was here.

Noticing a movement, his head whipped to the side and our eyes locked. My feet remained glued to the floor and my heart was in my throat. His eyes. Oh, how darkly they burned. I have never seen a look like the one he was wearing except on one other person. *Henry.* A look so full of darkness and controlled rage. It was terrifying. I sucked in a sharp breath and took an involuntary step back.

Before I had a second to allow my brain to connect with my body and for my fight or flight instinct to kick in, he had closed the gap between us and slammed me up against the mirrored wall. My bag fell from my shoulder to the floor with a thud. His callous hands were gripping either side of my face as he pressed his muscular frame up against mine, caging me in. I stared up at him, wide-eyed and panting with fear. I didn't know this man. This man was not the same man who bantered with me over Shakespeare a few hours ago. His nostrils flared and a muscle in his jaw flexed as his unblinking intense gaze held me rooted to the spot. I squeezed my eyes shut as the menacing look on his face overwhelmed me and I could feel the panic rising in my body. *No. No. No.* He isn't Henry. He isn't here. This isn't happening. My heart was palpitating so violently that he must be able to feel it. I felt him rest his soaking forehead against mine and felt his hot breath coming out in sharp pants on my face. He was so close. Too close.

"Please," I whimpered. I didn't even recognise my own voice. It was laced with so much terror.

"Open your eyes, Olivia. Look at me," he commanded, and I could feel the tears threatening to spill. I shook my head quickly. "Look at me."

Opening my eyes, I gasped with relief when I saw that his face had relaxed. That the darkness had subsided and only those molten brown irises gazed down at me with a flurry of emotions. His eyes darted between mine, his rough hands still holding my face.

"What are you doing to me, Olivia Jones?" His husky baritone voice was strangely calming and I slowly felt all the fear and panic melt away and desire replace them. "I am no good for you."

I didn't know what to say. I didn't know what was happening. I wanted to run. To get as far away from this man as I could, but his eyes felt like a powerful trap. He was trying to see me. Really see me. But I couldn't let him. He was right. He was no good for me and if I let him in, he would ruin me. I knew that much.

"Then let me go," I whispered, even though every part of my body was arguing with my mind. I craved him. I wanted to give in to this intense need.

"I'm trying. I am fucking trying," came his hard reply and he closed his eyes, inhaling deeply. Seeing my opportunity to get away, I pulled his arms from my face and glared at him with determination.

"Then try harder," I snarled before picking up my bag abruptly and storming out of the room.

Filthy Fantasies

Olivia

Stepping into my flat, I threw my bag aggressively onto the small futon sofa and kicked off my flip flops. I had cycled home from the Buccini mansion, which had given me a little bit of time to get my shit together and calm down after that run in with Giovanni, but I was still shaken. I knew it wasn't his fault. He didn't know about my past or the reaction my brain would have to seeing him so… I couldn't even describe it. He just reminded me so much of Henry at that moment. The rage. The evil. It was in his eyes. The same look that haunts my nightmares.

It was only after I poured myself a large glass of water and sat down on the kitchen bar stool that I heard them. The heavy panting and pleasurable moans were growing louder and more intense by the minute. I scoffed into my glass. At least someone was giving into their urges. There really wasn't anywhere to go to get away from it in this tiny flat. We were living on top of each other as it is and when Gigi has a 'guest' over its best I leave or succumb to listening to the live porn show happening behind her door. She wasn't a shy woman, let's put it that way. I think she even liked the audience.

She screamed something in Italian while the lucky man groaned loudly and then it all fell silent. Good for them. Flicking through a magazine absentmindedly to give myself something to do, I kept my eyes cast down as I heard her door open. She never let them stay for long. Once they had fulfilled their purpose, they were pecked on the cheek and sent on their way. I envied her ability to do that.

"Liv! You are home," her voice was laced with fake shock. I lifted my head and took in her messy hair and flushed face before my eyes scanned the very handsome, muscular Viking that was standing next to her, doing up his shirt buttons. He gave me a wink and I rolled my eyes.

"Yes, I am home," I smiled sweetly.

"Why did you not join us? Instead of sitting out here all alone angel?" The thick Australian twang of his voice and his shameless words made me raise my eyebrows. Where did she find these men?

"Leave her alone! You couldn't handle us both," Gigi smirked and he slapped her ass that was nearly sticking out from her flimsy dressing gown, making her yelp.

"You sure about that tiger?" He grabbed the back of her neck with an enormous hand and pulled her to his lips aggressively. They started snogging each other's faces with so much urgency, I had to look away as my cheeks flamed. Shit. I wanted that so badly. Just to be kissed like that. My mind flittered with thoughts of Giovanni's lips and the way his hands felt on my face earlier. I was pretty sure he would kiss me like that if I gave him half the chance.

I coughed loudly and they broke apart, looking heatedly at each other. "Laters, baby," the long-haired muscle man growled before he walked out the front door, throwing a wink my way. Gigi swivelled on her bare feet, fanning her face and exhaling dramatically.

"Now he was good! And you know you could have joined us if you wanted?" She gave me a devilish grin as she poured herself a glass of water.

"Hard pass," I muttered. "I like my men a little more...reserved than that." *Did I?*

She chuckled, leaning onto the counter towards me. "So, I like dangerous alpha males with big dick energy. Sue me!"

"Oh well, maybe I should give you Giovanni's number then!" I added a little too bitterly. My eyes snapped up to her amused face as I realised what I had said. For some reason my chest tightened at the thought of her wanting his number. Of the thought of her doing what she was just doing with Mr Viking with Giovanni.

She shook her head with a secret smile. "No no. He is all yours."

"He is not mine," I gritted through clenched teeth.

"So, nothing happened between you two today? It is written all over your face, Livvy!"

My smile fell into a deep scowl when I heard that name once again. "Please don't call me that, Gigi. It's Liv or Olivia. And as for Giovanni, he is not even my type." Standing up from the stool, I walked over to the small sofa and fell onto it with a huff.

"Girl. That man is every woman's type. Don't lie to me and tell me you don't get fanny flutters every time he is near," she stalked towards me with a cheeky grin and I groaned.

"You are on another level!" I couldn't help the giggle that escaped my lips as she pretended to smooch herself. "But I will admit that he is becoming harder to ignore every day. It's his eyes...and his hands... and that body...and the hair and..." I stopped rambling when I saw her shoulders shaking up and down with laughter. "OK fine! I admit, he is hot as fuck and I would love to climb that tree but it is not going to happen! He is exactly the kind of man I need to steer clear of. I hate everything he stands for!"

She gave me a sympathetic look as she took a seat next to me. "You know what you need?"

"One of those rampant rabbit dildos?" I asked hopefully, even though I am pretty sure she had a different answer in mind.

"Not a bad idea, but no. I was going to say a date."

I dropped my head back on the sofa with a snort. "Not this again!"

"Liv! I can't bear to see you like this anymore. It hurts me! You need a good shag!"

I raised my head and laughed out loud at her pouty face.

"It hurts you?! And, I don't know if you have noticed, but I don't have a string of men waiting to take me on dates or have the ability to meet sexy Vikings in my line of work…"

Giulia was a PR for a big Italian events company, and she was constantly going to fancy soirees and meeting interesting characters from all over the globe.

"That is not true! Luca is dying to take you out!" I moaned and lifted my hand over my eyes. "Come on! He is gorgeous, charming, a gentleman and funny." She tried to big up her friend but she didn't have to. I already knew all of this. Luca was the kind of man I should be dating. He was all those things and more.

"I can't believe I am saying this but…fine. One date."

She leapt off the sofa with excitement as she squealed and ran to grab her phone. "He is going to be so happy, Liv! Here is his number. Text him now!" She shoved her phone in my face and I reluctantly took it and copied his number into my own shitty Nokia.

"Really? Now?" I hesitated.

"Yes! You already know he will say yes, so there is no reason to be nervous!"

I wasn't nervous. I was…unsure. I didn't want to lead Luca on and make him believe I was in this for anything more than it was. I needed to get my mind off Giovanni Buccini and potentially have some fun in this city while I am still here.

"I can't have anything serious though, Gigi. What if he- "

"I am stopping you right there! Luca likes you. He thinks you are hot. That's all. You are not going to marry the guy. Just go and have fun and if you don't feel it, just stay friends."

"You make it sound so simple."

"Because it is simple, Liv!"

Sighing, I started to type out a message to Luca. She was right. I was overthinking everything again. New rule: live life and go with the flow!

***

I felt the side of my bed dip. The smell of alcohol and cigarettes invaded my senses and roused me from my sleep. Someone's in my room. Lifting my head off my pillow, I squinted my eyes in the dark and could just make out a broad figure sitting on my bed. A hand was travelling up my legs over my duvet and I kicked it off.

"Henry? Is that you?"

"Sorry did I wake you?" his slurred voice came through the darkness and I pulled

myself up to a sitting position, wrapping my duvet tightly around my chest. I was only wearing a little silk cami and shorts set and I felt bare in front of my new stepbrother. I rubbed my eyes as I took in his dishevelled appearance. He had definitely been drinking. His sandy blonde hair was messy and his shirt was open halfway down his chest even though he still had his suit jacket on. His tie was around his head in a knot like boys always do for attention, thinking they look cool and hilarious. He clumsily pulled it off when he saw me staring at it and chuckled.

"Forgot that was there," He turned and looked at me. Even through the dark, I felt his expression change. He was looking at me like…like I had seen him look at Sophie, his girlfriend. But this was more. More intense.

Swallowing down my awkwardness, I asked, "What are you doing here Henry? I thought you were staying at Sophie's after the graduation ball?"

His lips pulled up into a little smirk and I sat perfectly still. He was making me feel so…uncomfortable, but I didn't know why.

"I was meant to but…"

"But?" I whispered. I wanted him to leave. To go to his own room or Sophie's. I didn't want him on my bed or looking at me the way he was.

"But I would rather be right here. With you." My heart was drumming in my ears. What was he talking about? He rested his hand on my leg again over the duvet and I froze. Leaning forward, he brushed my hair off my shoulder. "You are so beautiful, Livvy. I think about you all the time. From the moment I saw you I knew we belonged together, but I wanted to wait until you were a bit older. A bit more…mature."

He climbed up the bed, inching closer to me, and the potent smell of alcohol made me feel sick. I was sitting open-mouthed with shock. What was he talking about? I couldn't find my voice as he played with a strand of my hair between his fingers. His eyes pierced mine.

"I can show you things, Livvy. I have waited so long to show you all the things I can do for you. Have you ever been touched? Down there?"

Suddenly, my senses came forth as his fingers travelled down my chest over my breast and towards my…

"Stop! Henry! What are you doing?" I hit his hand away, my eyes wide in shock and disgust. "You are my brother!"

He sat back and the anger was evident as his eyes narrowed and jaw clenched. "Stepbrother. That means nothing Livvy. I want you and you want me. I know it. You belong to me. You are mine."

He lunged at me. His lips were harsh and demanding against mine, knocking me back against the headboard. His hands were everywhere, in my hair, my neck, squeezing my breasts. His tongue darted into my mouth forcefully and I pushed against his chest with as much might as I could, turning my head away. He moved his lips to my neck as he pinned me down with his body weight and I started to really panic. My survival instincts kicked in and I sent my arms and legs flailing around as much as possible and shouted, "Henry! Stop! Get off me!"

His hand came over my mouth to muffle my screams and my eyes widened. "Livvy.

Don't fight this. This is meant to be. You will see. I will make you so happy."

He replaced his hands with his lips again and I bit down as hard as I could on his bottom lip.

"Argh!" He jumped up, touching his bleeding mouth, and I scrambled away from him out of bed. Running to the door, I felt his hand on my wrist pull me back and courage kicked in. I sent my fist flying into the middle of his face as he spun me with force. I heard a crack. And then his scream. Blood poured onto my fluffy sheepskin rug and he clutched his broken nose. I froze. The look in his eyes was crippling. Pure darkness, rage and…evil.

"You fucking bitch. You will regret this. I will never leave you alone. You are mine and if I can't have you. No one will."

With that, he stormed past me and out of my room, slamming the door behind him.

My eyes flew open as the tightness in my chest intensified and I gasped for air. There wasn't enough. I couldn't breathe. Sweat trickled down my forehead and my body was drenched, soaking the mattress. I was going to die. If I didn't get any air in a few seconds, I was going to die. Time slowed down to a grinding halt. No. I knew this all too familiar feeling. I am having a panic attack. The dream. That was the trigger. Sitting up and clutching my chest, I closed my eyes and focused on taking a deep breath and counting to five like my counsellors taught me. Exhaling out slowly and repeating. It was only a dream. It wasn't real. He isn't here. He doesn't know where I am. I am safe. I pulled at the elastic hairband on my wrist, reminding me that it wasn't happening. This is real.

As my breathing gradually started to even out and I felt the panic simmer down, I lay back against the headboard of my little single bed. It had been at least a week since I had dreamt of him. But I knew all too well what had triggered it.

That flashback was how it all began. How my world became smaller and terrifying after that very night. Sometimes, I actually wonder what would have happened if I had given in to him that night. If I had let him do what he wanted to me. Would he have left me alone? Would his infatuation dissolve to nothing after he had me? Would Nate still be alive? I shook my head. No. He wouldn't have stopped. He would never have let me go. According to the psychiatrist who assessed his mental health after he was arrested, he was obsessed with me to the point that he believed that I belonged to him. That I was his property and no one was allowed to touch me without his permission. He believed what he did to Nate was his purpose. I know he would have been very convincing. But I knew him better. Yes, he was obsessed with me, but it was so much more than that. It was his ego. His pride. I turned him down. I didn't want him. He belittled me, insulted me and tormented me daily for two years because I said no to him. That is more than just an obsession. That is revenge. He knew what he was doing and he knew it was wrong. He just didn't care.

Rubbing my face, I flung the covers off me and swung my legs out of bed. There was no way I was going back to sleep after that. Stumbling out of my bedroom and into the kitchen to grab a drink, I noticed Gigi's iPad on charge. Unhooking it, I made myself comfortable on the sofa with a blanket and opened up her Instagram. I smiled as the screen filled with fun, lovely and bright images of her profile. I have to say I thought I would miss it. Social media. It has been at least two months since I deleted it all. Every trace of me off the internet that I could find from the last few months. But I don't miss it one bit. I hate not seeing what my friends and mum are doing, but apart from that, it has felt more therapeutic than anything. A part of my mind has been set free. I no longer worry about what other people are up to. Are they having more fun than me? Are they happier? Have better clothes? Making more money? The fear of always thinking you could be doing more with your life by holding it up against the lives of so many that don't even care if I existed or not. No. I didn't miss it. But there was one thing it was good for. Getting information about someone you are about to go on a date with.

Typing Luca's name into the search bar, he came up instantly. His main photo was a group shot of him with a few friends. They were all dressed in casual clothes and stood on a wall overlooking the city of Verona. Luca was grinning widely in the picture, maybe even laughing- that's how bright his smile was. His arm around one of his buddies and looking carefree and happy. Scrolling down his page, there was more of the same. His profile said everything about him. Sociable, happy, popular and full of life. He reminded me a lot of Nate. My heart tugged at the thought. Would this be what Nate's profile would look like if he ever had the chance to live?

Dropping the iPad onto my chest, I raised my hands to my head and fought back the tears. Crying does nothing, Liv. Crying won't bring him back. Grief and guilt threatened to overwhelm me as I took a few deep breaths to calm myself. I needed a distraction. Anything.

The first thing that entered my mind was his handsome face. Giovanni. Lifting the iPad again, I hovered my finger over the search bar before giving in. I typed his name and my heart fluttered when his profile appeared. Clicking on it, I wasn't surprised to see that his profile was private. A striking difference between his and Luca's. Clicking on the only photo I had access to, I stared at his striking features that were giving the camera a smouldering look. His arms were folded across his chest and he was leaning on the hood of one of his blood orange Ferrari's. I zoomed in on it. My stomach tingled. Just seeing his face right now was sending my body into overdrive and all thoughts of my past were gone.

Turning off the iPad, I closed my eyes and gave into my body's needs. Allowing my mind to drift freely to thoughts of the infuriating man who is starting to make me feel things I have never felt before. The moments from this morning that felt like a lifetime ago now flood my mind. His body posed in Sani's bed. His sexy smirk when he caught me staring. The filthy words he whispered in my ear that my body reacted to so effortlessly. The feel of his skin as I rubbed the sun cream on his face. The cheeky, playful flirting between us as we stood under Juliet's balcony. To my surprise, my vagina was pulsing. Dying to be touched. My whole body was. I needed to burn away the memories from that dream with something new. I glided my hand down my body, caressing my nipples until I reached my aching clit. Slowly starting to rub in circular motion, I gasped as the more intense moments I had shared with Giovanni came to mind. The scene in his office, when he brushed his minty lips against mine. The feel of his strong hand wrapped around my throat. My back arched off the sofa as my pleasure intensified. The sight of his sweating, ripped body beating the crap out of that bag. His body pressed up against mine and the smell of his musky scent and sweaty skin.

"I'm trying. I'm fucking trying." That voice. That deep, husky Italian accent.

I started to pant as my orgasm built and just as I was allowing my imagination to run wild with ideas of what might have happened if I hadn't pushed him away tonight, I exploded. My body quivered and tensed as I slammed my hand over my mouth to muffle my cries. Fuck.

I have never done that before. Got off by thinking of a man alone. I've always needed one of my smutty books, porn or a toy. But that. That was one of the most intense orgasms I have ever given myself. I need a pat on the back; Gigi would be so proud. I sniggered as I felt all the tension leave my body and sighed in heavenly bliss. Maybe Gigi was right. I really did need to allow myself some pleasure. But Giovanni would not be the one giving it to me, unless he was in my filthy fantasies. Only there was I safe from him.

Meddling Mamma

Cecilia

Opening my bathroom cabinet, I snatched the different prescribed bottles off the shelf and swallowed my happy pills. That's what I call them in front of Sani and Raya. Pills that make mamma feel better when all they really do is make me numb. Numb to the intensity of my emotions that suffocate me on a daily basis. If I even miss one round, I am plunged into a world of stifling multi-tones and walls that close in around me. Rooms feel smaller, life feels heavier and my thoughts are unbearable. A mix of bipolar, depression and PTSD is what the doctor diagnosed. I have been bipolar all my life apparently, but I was just handling it well. Masking it until my mind and body were hit with the trauma of that night. The night I lost my Vinny. After that, I stopped trying. I let whatever I felt, whenever I felt it, consume me. Those six months after his death, I know I was unrecognisable to my children. And Gio carried the burden of it. He tried his best to keep it from the others. The self-inflicting pain and demise of their mother. I have always blamed Salvatore for not allowing him to grieve for the death of Vinny by forcing him into his responsibilities so quickly, but I am just as much to blame. I was absent for those six months. A hollow vessel filled with only grief, self-loathing and intense depression. He didn't have time to grieve when he had me to deal with. To watch over me like a hawk. And he is still doing it now.

The day he found me trying to take my own life in the bath was the day it all came crashing down. Seeing my eldest son's helpless and haunted face as he pulled me up out of the water is a horrific memory I can never erase. He knew I was trying to end it and I no longer had the energy to deny it. I cried and fell apart in his arms as he cradled me to his chest and rocked me like a mother should their child. Not the other way around. That was the turning point. He booked me into the best rehab facility in Italy and I agreed to start trying again. Raya was only two. Sani was four. Elle had just started university. I couldn't leave them no matter how much I wanted to. So every day, I get up. I take my happy pills. And I plaster on a smile. For them.

Closing the mirrored cabinet door, I stared at my reflection. I no longer connected with this woman. I felt like an imposter in her body. Someone who was solely here for the purpose of others. Every day was a battle and today was going to be one full of bloodshed. Because tonight, I will have to play the part. The Mafia Widow who holds her own. We were hosting a rival family, the Aianis. They were not technically our rivals as we have established a good relationship through business, but in this line of work, everyone is your enemy. That is just the mentality we must have. Never trust anyone unless they are family. Family first. That is the Buccini motto.

Brushing down my Stella McCartney dress, I braced myself for the day ahead. I liked these events as much as I liked Salvatore Buccini. Not at all. But it was still my duty. To be present. To sit with the wives and chat pleasantly. As Salvatore, the sleaze, has never married, the role still falls to me. Oh, how I wish that man would just find some pretty little thing off the streets to warm his bed and give him an heir. This was not the life I wanted for my son. Yet, Salvatore seemed set on making it his business.

Strutting out of my wing towards the children, I forced an air of fake confidence and contentment to waft from me like the grace of a butterfly in flight. I had perfected it by now and not many knew that I was screaming inside. Knocking once on the education room door, I opened it to see Olivia and my youngest children sitting on the floor doing a jigsaw and ordering the alphabet. I smiled as they all looked up. The difference in my children since Olivia had started teaching them was phenomenal. They were happy. Genuinely happy. And they were enjoying whatever it was she was doing with them so much that I had barely seen them set foot in that games room during the day.

"Good morning my darlings," I cooed as I strolled towards them. "Olivia, could you meet me in my office in ten minutes please? Marco can watch the children. We won't be long."

She nodded at me briefly with a small smile that didn't reach her eyes. She found me intimidating. That much was obvious. Kissing my children goodbye, I made my way down to my little haven of an office. I loved it here and often redesigned it on a monthly basis to suit my mood. I currently have a new mood board up on a large stand in the corner of the room. I am thinking of a tropical theme next. Large plants, greens, creams and beiges. Calming.

A gentle knock came and Olivia's pretty face poked around the door. I smiled widely and flapped my hand for her to enter and take a seat on my white leather sofa by the bookcase. Smoothing my silk dress behind my legs, I perched on the seat next to her. She glanced around the room nervously before her bright, unique eyes fell on my face. She really did have such beautiful eyes. They reminded me of a cat. Piercing and hypnotic with earthy tones. Cats were my favourite animals.

"Thank you for coming. I have a favour to ask of you my dear." Her face remained blank but she gave me a small nod. "Giovanni will be hosting an evening event tonight for some business associates here at the house. In the onsite club. I am obliged to attend as well, so I was wondering if you would be able to stay over for the night with the children?"

Her beautifully shaped eyebrows pulled into the bridge of her nose and her lips pouted. "Why would I need to stay?"

I loved her boldness. It was the first thing that made me realise she was perfect for Giovanni. No matter how much a situation intimidated her, she would always speak her mind and stand her ground. I smiled as I replied, "Sani and Raya are not used to lots of people in our home. They might be quite unsettled and if they wake up in the night, I would like to know that they have someone they trust there to comfort them."

She nodded her head slowly, understanding my point, but she still looked conflicted. "I understand Mrs Buccini, but I am really sorry. I already have plans this evening."

My smile fell and I sighed. "Please. Call me Cecilia. Oh, that is difficult. Are they plans you cannot get out of?" I prodded. I was also a woman who stood her ground.

She hesitated and shuffled uncomfortably on her bum. Her reaction piqued my interest.

"Well. Actually, it's a date," she mumbled, playing with the elastic hair band on her wrist. My eyebrows raised in surprise. A date? Well, that would not do!

Pretending to be extremely delighted and supportive, I gave her a cheeky look. "Oh, a date! You have a boyfriend? I hadn't realised."

"No. No I don't. It's just a first date…with a friend. I am not even sure about it. My roommate kind of set it up and I… sorry I am rambling. Um. I can probably rearrange it. If it is really important to you that I be here."

Thank God. A first date. This could work in my favour. Nothing will kick Giovanni up the arse like him knowing someone else is interested in his little temptation.

"Well, it is very important for the children's sake, Olivia, but I also don't want to make you change your plans if you are really looking forward to your date. That is important too," I soothed, placing my hand on her arm.

"No. It's okay. I will just see if he can do it another night. It's not a problem," she smiled back at me and I nodded.

"Well, thank you. That is very kind and, of course, we will pay you overtime for staying the night. I will get Lucinda to set up another bed in Raya's room for you. I really appreciate it, Olivia. Truly." She stood up with a polite smile.

"It's fine. I will just go and text my date now and get back to the children." She walked out of my office and I crossed my arms over my chest. This changed things. Now I was going to have to start meddling in my son's love life because he is clearly messing it up!

Climbing the stairs to the top floor of our elegant mansion, I didn't bother knocking as I walked straight into his office. He was signing some papers and had one of his Capo's on the loudspeaker. It sounded like Leo, our Capo of Venice. He was saying something about the hit being ready to go and everything in place. Gio glanced up at me with an irritated expression at my sudden intrusion but pointed to a chair for me to sit all the same. Instead, I walked around the room and glanced at the bare shelves that only held a few crime novels, the history of Mala Del Brenta and one photograph of our whole family. Vinny stood in the centre of it proudly. It was taken a year before his death. Raya was just a baby in my arms. My chest tightened as I swallowed down my emotions. Placing the frame back down, I turned and took in the doom and gloom of this room. Just being in here felt like it was sucking all the life out of me. Why Gio chose this decor I will never understand. It was gothic chic apparently. Very on trend according to my interior designer, but I just couldn't get onboard.

Gio finished up the phone call and hung up, leaning back in his black leather office chair. Underneath the smart, designer suit and neatly styled hair, he wasn't fooling me. He looked like shit. He hadn't slept and I could tell he was already in an unpleasant mood. Well, this might just push him over the edge.

"Mamma, you need something?" he asked as he went back to signing whatever papers had been thrust into his lap by Salvatore. That was the job of the underboss. To do whatever the boss didn't want to do.

"No, I am good," I gave him my most persuasive smile so he didn't worry and noticed his shoulders relaxed a little. "I just spoke to Olivia about tonight." I studied his face and body for any reaction but he kept his eyes fixed on the paperwork and continued to scribble at the bottom of the page.

"Hmmhm," he hummed and I rolled my eyes.

"She said she couldn't stay tonight," I said nonchalantly as I ran my finger down the spine of one of his display books.

His head snapped up to me and his pen paused on the paper.

"Why not?" His voice was calm and even, but his eyes gave away his intrigue. His eyes always gave him away. They were just like his fathers. Windows into his soul.

I shrugged my shoulders, "She has a date or something." I allowed my eyes to flicker over to him to judge his reaction. His face stayed expressionless but his hand gripped so tightly around his pen that I could see the whitened knuckles under his skin.

"A date with who? A man?"

I couldn't contain the giggle that escaped my lips. "It is none of our business who she dates Gio! Man or woman! But if you must know, it is a man because she said she needed to text him to rearrange."

"I don't mean that it was a woman- "he started, leaning back in his chair and running his enormous hand that was decorated with silver rings through his hair. He was stressed. This affected him just like I thought it would. Excellent. "Hang on. What do you mean rearrange?"

"She is going to change her date to another night so she can look after the bambini. Why is that a problem? I could just not attend this evening and stay with them and then she can still go on her date if you think that is best-"

"No." He interrupted sharply and took a steady breath before speaking again. Wow. This girl had really gotten under his skin. More than I even expected. He was smitten. My lips pulled at the sides as I fought the urge not to smile too widely. "You need to attend. Zio will want you there, so she has to stay."

I nodded once and made my way to the door. Looking back at my son who was staring out the window, deep in thought, I smiled. I was doing this for him. The sooner he comes to terms with his feelings for this girl, the better. But my son was as stubborn as a mule. It was going to take more than just the idea of a date to kick him into action. Let's just hope Olivia can handle him when he finally does.

Colourful Background

Giovanni

The sun, a fiery orange glow, was dipping low over the horizon as I took in all its glory from the back of my Bentley. Its beauty brought me no joy or solace that the day was finally over because it meant that the night was about to begin. And all this sunset did was remind me of a certain set of eyes. The colours that danced in them when she was angry were like this sunset. A memorising display of enigmatic wonder. Holy shit am I in fucking trouble. A fucking sunset? Really?

I groaned as I leaned my head back against the leather seats and let the steady movement of the car calm the storm inside me. Out of all the shit I have had to deal with today; a HR problem at one of my restaurants, a livid thug who wanted a drug debt paid by some lowlife who refused to pay it and wanted my family's help in making him, and then the organisation of Tommas' murder of Massimo Novalli that was planned for tonight, none of them affected me like hearing she was meant to be going on a date tonight. A date! Who the fuck was she dating?

I had never even considered that she might have been seeing someone or that there was even another 'man' in the picture wanting to take her on dates. I am a fucking fool. Of course there was! Look at her. The infuriating, indecent images that swarmed my mind all day at the thought of someone else touching her soft skin, kissing those delectable lips or fucking her the way I had been fantasising about for over a week now had put me in a state of fury that I could not get out of no matter how hard I tried.

I had just set my head straight about what happened between us in the gym last night and now this has spun me back into a frenzy of jealousy and desire to have her for myself. Last night, after seeing the pure terror in her eyes, I realised this would never work. She could never find out who I really was because she would run. And she should. She had to run as far away from me as she could. She still hated me even though my feelings were... I don't even know what my feelings were. I used to think she hated me because of my arrogance and her refusal to give into my playboy charms but last night, I saw it. There was more to it than that. But what? Why did she hate me so much? Now I was starting to think I might hate her. For making me feel something. For turning me into this person. Someone who couldn't think straight about anything. I wondered where she was, what she was doing and who she was with every minute of the day. I had even been spending more time working from home just so I was near her. It was ridiculous. I can't sustain this. I had resolved to cut off all communication with her after last night. She wanted me to try harder to stay away and that is what I was going to do. My mamma could deal with her. I didn't need to have any involvement. But then those words left my mother's lips and I forgot all about my vow to never think of her again.

As the car pulled up the winding driveway, I sighed deeply and prepared myself for a gruelling evening. Noticing a few cars had already parked, I groaned inwardly. Antonio and Maximus were already here and I am sure all the preparations in the on-site night club were underway. Exclusive invites went out to associates and women who worked in my clubs to come as entertainment. There will be at least one hundred people here tonight and the thought made me want to grind my teeth. My zio never hosts at his estate. If he wants business done, it's always on my turf. That is the role of an underboss.

Striding into the lobby, I saw Max and Toni bantering back and forth as Max grabbed Toni's shoulder and threw his head back and laughed with fake friendliness. I knew Toni was someone Max barely tolerated. They both turned to me when they felt my presence.

"Boss," Max greeted me with a grin. I nodded once and stretched my hand out to Toni. There was always a formality to be upheld when it came to Toni. I liked the man but he worked for my zio and was his right-hand man. He knew the ins and outs of the notorious Salvatore's mind and how this family was run. You could describe him as the neck of this family, turning my uncle's head whichever way he felt was best. I respected him hugely, but I was also wary of him. One day, he may be my consigliere when I become boss and I need to always show my respect.

"Giovanni," his low voice rumbled from his chest. Noticing a folder in his hand, I nodded and directed the men to follow me up to my office. As we started to ascend the staircase, I glanced up and momentarily froze when my eyes locked with hers. She was on her way down and directly in my pathway. She froze too. Neither one of us made a move and just continued to stare.

"Olivia! Nice to see you again," Max chirped behind me and I felt Toni's gaze taking her in. She quickly looked away from me and I continued up the stairs, making my way to the opposite side so I could get as far away from her as possible. She didn't move but I could feel her gaze on me as I ignored her with the last remaining bit of strength I had from today.

"Even prettier in real life," Toni stated as he dropped the thick file on my desk. My face scrunched up in confusion and also annoyance at his remark. "She is an interesting girl for sure. Colourful background."

I opened the blue file to the first page of Olivia's CV and then the realisation hit me. This was her in-depth background check I had asked Toni to do for me the day I met her. It had completely slipped my mind. What did he mean by colourful background? Intrigue simmered beneath my skin but I couldn't let either of these men know that this was so interesting to me. She was just an employee. Shutting the file, I opened my desk drawer and slid it in. I will read it later. In private. I'm not sure I can handle anymore right now.

"I'll read it later. Thanks Toni," I replied in a bored tone.

Max set about pouring us all a whiskey and I waited for the scolding to start.

"Boss is not pleased."

I was prepared for this.

"Is he ever?" I quipped back, sarcasm in my tone. Toni raised one eyebrow. "What would he have had me do? Give him a slap on his wrist and send him on his way?"

"No. But you know you should have informed him before you touched a hair on his head. He is still running this family, Giovanni, and you showed disrespect."

I couldn't help the smirk that played at the corners of my lips. So, the mighty Salvatore Buccini was feeling threatened. That is what Toni had really just revealed. I know I am supposed to have his permission before I do anything to our rival family's men but I was in the moment.

"He was taking pictures of Sani and Raya, Toni. I saw red. I am sure boss will understand. Family first."

"Family first," Max and Toni repeated in unison and we raised our tumblers in the air before taking a sip. Toni leaned back in his chair, drumming his thick fingers on the arm in a repetitive notion. It was a delay tactic. One that was supposed to make me anxious, waiting to hear what my punishment would be. But I couldn't care less right now. I was already in hell, so why not just add to the torture?

"You cannot be so hot-headed, Giovanni. Especially when it comes to family. That is when mistakes are made. Salvatore agrees with your methods this time, but don't let it happen again. He has final say. Remember that," his cold blue eyes held mine and I gave him a lopsided grin and raised my glass in agreement. One day, I would be boss and I would not have to answer to these old men. They would answer to me. I was counting down the days.

"What time are they arriving?" Max asked as he rested one leg lazily on the other and enjoyed my fine whiskey. His eye caught mine and he gave me a cheeky smirk.

"Our guests or the girls?" I joked and his smirk grew wider. I knew my cousin inside out. His mamma was my papi and Salvatore's sister. He was her first born and so given the next highest rank in the family after me. We were only a few years apart, him at the age of twenty – five and me at twenty -nine, and we had been inseparable growing up.

"Both?" he winked.

"Boss and the Aianis will arrive just before 8pm," Toni said sternly. He wasn't a joker at the best of times.

"And the girls?" Max poked him again with his stick of mischief.

"Any minute," I looked down at my watch. The club needed to be flowing before the main guests arrived. There is nothing worse than walking into an empty bar.

"Fantastico! I might be able to get a quickie in before the real business begins," Max clapped his hands together and I swear I saw Toni roll his eyes.

"That is not a bad plan," I smirked back and Toni's eyes pierced into mine. It was only a joke but I enjoyed winding him up.

"There is someone Salvatore wants you to meet tonight, so you must be on your best behaviour. Especially around women," he warned.

"Who? Is that why you are here now? To prep me," I chuckled into my glass as the ice knocked against it. His gaze was hard and unrelenting. I was tired of this shit. I just wanted to be left alone for five minutes before I had to be the ruthless Giovanni tonight.

"You will find out shortly. Just try not to kill or fuck anyone tonight and all will be well," he demanded as he stood up from his chair. Max gave me a knowing look and I shook my head.

"Not a problem," I smiled back before Toni left the room.

"You sure that is not going to be a problem? Just seeing that sexy little thing on the stairs had my dick hard. How do you walk around her all day without bending her over every piece of furniture you can?"

My jaw ticked and my nostrils flared, but I swallowed my instant rage. This was just how we talked about girls. This was nothing new. If I reacted... he would know. But I can't have him talk about her like that. She was not one of those girls. She is Olivia.

"Like I said, it won't be a problem. On the other hand, not killing someone might prove more difficult," I gave him a pointed look and he laughed loudly.

A Proposal

Giovanni

The barely dressed shot girls came over to our secluded section on a raised platform above the dance floor and lowered their trays full of an array of fluorescent liquor. Max and I immediately leaned forward, grabbing one each and raising the tiny glasses in the air to one another before sinking them and grabbing two more. The music was loud. The room pulsed with electric energy as the techno dance beat vibrated off the walls. Luckily, the booth we were in was sheltered by noise-cancelling glass windows and only the red velvet curtain allowed any of the blaring music in.

My uncle leaned back lazily on the booth sofa with Toni whispering business into his ears. His black eyes were fixed on me as he took slow, deliberate sips of his scotch, but I didn't care to find out why.

Two attractive women who worked for one of my clubs in the city strolled in and gave us all seductive glances before turning to each other and throwing their arms around each other's necks, swaying their hips provocatively to the muffled beats. Max's eyes lit up like it was Christmas morning as he licked his lips and smirked, watching their every move. Women were his weakness. He would give up his whole life for an incredible fuck with a beautiful woman. With his dashing good looks, shoulder-length hair that he always wore up in a man bun, tattooed body and green eyes, he never had a problem getting his dick wet. And on top of that, he had an effortless charm. He was one of those people that could flash a cheeky sideways grin and get away with just about anything.

"Why didn't you make me capo of Verona again? The girls here are fire!" He shouted over to me, never taking his eyes off the two blondes in front of us in tiny hot pants and even smaller tops.

"That is exactly why I didn't. You would never get anything done!" I smirked back and he chuckled.

"Oh, I would get plenty done," he winked, before reaching forward and pulling one of the girls' wrists so she fell back onto his lap with a squeal. His face was immediately submerged in her neck and she smiled with pleasure, although I was never sure if these girls were enjoying themselves or just doing what was expected. The stranded blonde, who no longer had her dance buddy, turned to me with a 'I'm all yours' expression and I waved my hand at her dismissively.

Salvatore shot me a look of approval as she stalked towards one of my other men to try her luck instead. I rolled my eyes and leaned back in my chair as I raised another shot to my lips. It wasn't that I was uninterested because Toni had warned me to keep my head straight tonight. That wasn't the reason, although I will let him think so.

The curtain was pulled to the side and the volume of the booth erupted with music as mamma strolled in looking every bit the elegant and hardcore mafia woman. My body immediately tensed as I saw over her shoulder the short, stumpy man with beady black eyes and a bulbous nose. Francesco Aiani. In his company were about six of his burly men as he approached us and we all stood up to greet him with respect.

"Aiani!" Salvatore walked towards him dramatically with his arms open wide as the men made an exaggerated display of affection, signifying that there was no animosity here. That everyone will be on their best behaviour tonight.

"My amico. It has been too long," Francesco gripped his shoulders and they both smiled. So fake. They wouldn't think twice about putting a bullet between each other's eyes if the commission agreed to it. Turning his attention to me, Francesco looked me up and down with satisfaction and stepped towards me. "The one and only, Giovanni. You are looking more and more like your papi every day. God rest his soul."

I pushed down my anger at him mentioning my father and gave him a tight smile and nod. He would not be getting the same warm embrace from me as my zio gave him. I didn't trust him. I didn't trust anyone. I noticed my mother's narrowed eyes at our guest but she kept her cool, calm and collected persona like a mask. She was in character and it would take a lot to rattle her when she was like this.

"There is someone I would like you all to meet," his slimy smile immediately caught my attention. His bird-like eyes flickered over to my zio's and I saw a look pass between them that had me on edge. Something was going on here. Aiani's men parted and Francesco reached behind and pulled a woman forward by her arm to stand in front of us all. Her eyes were cast down to the floor and she looked nervous as shit, but I applauded her for her courage as she glanced up and locked eyes with me.

"This is my daughter, Camilla."

Her blue eyes held my gaze but I didn't feel a twinge of excitement I normally would have with such a beautiful woman's attention. She smiled politely before turning her glance around the booth and giving them all the same emotionless expression. She was wearing a gold metallic dress that stopped halfway down her slender thighs and fitted her thin body like a second skin. Her large and quite obviously fake tits were nearly spilling out over the top of it and only her curled sandy blonde hair was covering them slightly. She was pretty and the type of girl who would normally grab my attention in a club, but looking at her now, I didn't feel even slightly attracted to her. Glancing over my shoulder, all my men were practically drooling as they stared open-mouthed, especially Max. He still had that little blonde straddling his lap but all his attention was on Camilla as he looked like he wanted to slam her against the viewing glass and take her from behind without giving a fuck about all of us. So, what was wrong with me?

"Nice to meet you Camilla," My uncle broke the ice and gestured for them all to come and join us in the booth. I slid across and wasn't surprised when I saw Francesco pull his daughter's arm to slide in next to me. Ah. So that is what this was. A match-making meeting. It suddenly all made sense. The reason my uncle had insisted I host, the warning from Toni to stay away from women tonight and to be on my best behaviour. I fought my urge to laugh at how fucking ridiculous this was as I tried to catch Max's eye to let him in on the joke but his green eyes were still glued on the striking blonde next to me. I could feel her fidgeting nervously on her seat, clearly trying to think of something to say as her father and my uncle started to chat about business.

"Would you like a drink?" I asked in a bored tone, putting the poor thing out of her misery and she smiled shyly back at me.

"Yes please. A vodka soda please." Even her voice was too sweet for me. I grabbed the barmaid's attention and gave her an order before looking back at Max, who had now pushed his little sidepiece off his lap and scooted closer to us.

"Camilla. This is my cousin Maximus," I introduced him as he held out his hand and she placed it in his. Without taking his eyes off hers, he lowered his face to the top of her hand and kissed it tenderly. I could feel the sexual tension radiating from them both as she audibly gulped next to me and her eyes widened slightly. Feeling like an enormous third wheel sandwiched between them, I was just about to make an excuse to get up when my uncle shouted across the table to us.

"Beautiful girl is she not?" he challenged, his brown eyes shimmering in the red lighting. I narrowed my gaze but gave nothing away.

"Of course, who would ever argue that?" I challenged back and Francesco's smug face lit up with pride as he looked between his daughter and me.

"Don't say I never spoil you, Giovanni. Most enchanting woman in this club and you have me to thank," he smirked.

I bristled at his tone and felt Camilla tense slightly next to me, clearly embarrassed by her father's boldness but also that she was being spoken about as if she wasn't even there. Just some trophy prize for him to flaunt at men to make good business connections.

"Like I said, Camilla is beautiful but the most enchanting woman in this club is sitting right beside you," I smirked as I winked at my mamma, who hid her amusement by taking a sip from her drink. If they thought I was going to fall to my knees and thank them profusely for throwing a pretty girl my way for the night, they really didn't know me very well. My uncle scowled at me across the table in warning.

"Of course," Francesco's beady eyes fell on my mamma next to him and he gave her a creepy smile which she ignored completely. "But you two will make a fine couple. Salvatore and I were just saying that an Autumn wedding would be pleasant."

Did I just hear him right? Mamma spat her drink out, allowing her calm and impassive mask to slip as she gaped at me and then glared at my uncle who was staring intensely into my eyes. A small smile played on his lips and it took everything in me not to flip the table over and dive at him for his smugness. What was he fucking thinking?

"Wedding?" It was Max next to me who spoke first as his shocked eyes darted from Francesco to Camilla and then me.

"There will be no wedding," I leaned back into my chair, never taking my eyes off my uncle.

"Not until Autumn falls, no," he replied calmly with a hint of amusement. "Don't tell me you have forgotten Giovanni?" My eyebrows furrowed as my heart started pounding in my chest. "When you pledged your loyalty as underboss you agreed to take a wife that would benefit the family one day."

My eyes widened in alarm. Fuck. It was a conversation we had briefly had two fucking years ago! He asked me how I would feel about one day in the future taking a wife who would strengthen our family's position. An alliance or transactional deal to make us untouchable. I shrugged and agreed. I didn't see a problem with the idea at the time. I was never going to fall in love and I would rather have a wife who would benefit my position in the family. But sitting here now, next to the woman who my uncle had deemed as a fit choice, I felt sick. I don't want to get married. Especially not to a complete stranger.

"Salvatore. A word?" My mother's harsh tone at everyone still as she stood up from the table and glared at my uncle. She was the only one who dared call him by his first name in the company of others. He should always be addressed as Boss, but clearly, by the rage that was evident on her face, she didn't give a crap. He slowly nodded to all of us calmly before standing and doing up his button on his suit jacket and following mamma, who had stormed out of the room.

"Did you know about this?" Max whispered at me, still in shock, and I lifted my glass of whiskey to my lips.

"Did I fuck," I growled before downing the entire contents. I could feel Camilla trembling next to me and it was pissing me off. She may be the daughter of a mafia boss but she was a timid and shy thing under that bold dress and fake smile. I could never imagine myself being with someone like her and being happy. It was nothing against the girl, but I liked what I liked and she wasn't it. Olivia's face flashed in my mind and I slammed my empty glass down on the table.

What the fuck was wrong with me? The Giovanni from a few weeks ago would probably have thought this was a brilliant idea. I mean it could be worse. Camilla was gorgeous, would be a quiet and obedient wife and it would make our two families untouchable with such an alliance. I could see why my uncle was pushing it. Yet now I was feeling sick to my stomach.

"Did you know?" I turned to the woman next to me who couldn't hold my gaze as she nodded slowly, looking down at her lap. Fuck me, she was a submissive thing. Probably brought up to do anything daddy wants and never have a thought of her own. "I am sorry Camilla. But I won't marry you."

Her head snapped up and the look of pure terror on it confirmed that this was all her father's idea and she was under his control. Her one purpose on this Earth was probably to do her father proud and marry a future Boss and she had just failed him.

Standing up from the booth, I walked over to the large floor to ceiling windows that looked over the small dance floor and watched the bodies of people I barely knew grinding against each other in my club. In my house. I clenched my jaw and tightened my grip around the metal bar I was leaning on as I thought about how much I wanted everyone out of here right now. But that was childish. That was my inner softness wanting to throw a tantrum at the unfairness of this situation and say to hell with this life. I didn't have that luxury. As much as I hated to admit it, I was trapped in this lavish yet brutal world. Until I was boss, I had to answer to someone else. I had to do things his way. But the only way of ever getting to that position was by pleasing him. And refusing to marry Aiani's daughter was not going to please my uncle one little bit.

"You will do well to keep your head, Giovanni. Do not make any rash decisions right now. Think about it," Toni's deep voice echoed into my left ear as he brushed shoulders with me.

"I am guessing this was your idea?" I hissed.

"I am not Boss Giovanni. You know that," he smirked and I shook my head in disbelief. I didn't believe a word.

"Maybe not, but he listens to you. So, your input counts for something. I would have appreciated a little heads up at least."

"Think of it as your punishment for Leone's spy," he muttered, and I snapped my head up to him in anger. I knew my uncle would never let me off with a fucking warning. "Not such a bad punishment, I have to say. Tight ass and huge tits. So, enlighten me Giovanni, what exactly is your problem with this arrangement?"

I was just about to bark back at him when something caught my eye on the dance floor. No. Someone. There in her tiny cotton camisole and shorts set, fluffy slippers and a flimsy robe over her shoulders was Olivia weaving her way through the crowd. Her chocolate brown hair was piled up on top of her head in a messy bun and her face was thunderous. She was dressed ready for a slumber party, not a club. What the fuck was she doing in here?

Forgetting all about my conversation with Toni, I pushed past him and made my way down to the dance floor as the growing rage that I had been trying so hard to keep in check for the entire day had my head feeling like it was about to explode.

Olivia Jones. You are in so much trouble.

Giving In To Sin

Olivia

Boom. Boom. Boom.

I huffed loudly as I picked up the TV remote and turned the volume up to a ridiculous level so the kids and I could actually hear Woody knocking the last of Buzz's self-confidence out of him before he failed to make the flight from the bannister to the window. Dick move.

"Why can't he fly? He has wings," Raya asked, curled up into my side as we sat on Sani's bed watching the enormous screen together.

"Because he is a toy!" Sani shouted, as if it was the most obvious thing in the world. Raya scrunched her nose up and glared at him. Now she had become more comfortable around me, I was starting to see that she was a fiery little thing under the shy exterior. A girl after my own heart.

"But kites fly and they are toys," she quipped back, and I smiled.

"She has you there," I chuckled when Sani frowned deeply.

"Shhhhh! I can't hear! Why is the music so loud?"

I sighed again. I wanted to say that your brother is a selfish A-hole who thinks it's a good idea to conduct business meetings in his on-site club with two young children in the house, but instead I settled with, "I don't know Sani."

"When will it stop?" Raya looked up at me with a worried expression. She hadn't left my side since the music started and it was clearly the first time something like this had happened to them in the house. I could feel the small vibrations through Sani's bed from the club that was directly below us. I mean who has a club in their house anyhow? I understand having a bar or a small scotch room or something, but a freaking club?

We gave up on the film halfway through and instead we put on our own Disney soundtrack and danced around the room together. It definitely took their minds off what was going on downstairs and I hoped it would wear them out enough that they would fall asleep quickly.

After getting them ready for bed (Sani only agreed if I put my pyjamas on too), I tried reading them a story which just made me have to shout over the music that was filtering up to our floor. Had it got louder? It seemed so. I glanced over at the clock beside us. 9.00pm. These kids should have been asleep over an hour ago, but how on Earth were they meant to sleep through this?

"Hey Sani, why don't we all sleep over in Raya's room tonight?" I suggested so I could keep an eye on them both.

He shook his head decisively. "I have to sleep in my bed. It's magic."

I sighed, looking down at Raya. "Do you want to sleep in Sani's magic bed tonight, Raya?"

She nodded enthusiastically and I smiled. That was not ideal for me. Cecilia had ordered a single bed to be put in Raya's room for me to sleep in, but it looked like I would be sleeping on the floor if we all stayed in Sani's room.

Tucking them both up in Sani's bed, they nestled into each other, and I smiled at their adorableness.

"Will you stay with us until we fall asleep?" Sani asked.

"I am staying all night, Sani. So, close your eyes and try to sleep."

He did as I said but anger rose in me with every vibration on the floor and I could hear the drunken laughter of a few people outside on the lawn smoking. Maybe twenty minutes had passed and I could tell neither of them were asleep yet.

"I can't sleep!" Sani shouted in frustration.

"Me too!" Raya joined in. I huffed loudly and stood up from the floor.

"Right. You two stay here and do not leave this room. Marco is just outside your door if you need him. I will be back as soon as possible, okay?"

"Where are you going?" Raya's small voice asked from the bed.

"To tell your brother to turn the music down. I will be right back."

Opening the door, I was met by a surprised Marco, whose eyes fluttered down my body in my shorts and camisole set. Grabbing a little robe from my bag, I pulled it over my shoulders and wrapped my arms around my body. "Marco, when is this 'meeting' supposed to end?"

"I do not know, Signorina Jones."

"Olivia. Please. OK well, can you stay with the children while I go and find out?"

His eyes widened slightly and it was almost comical the look of worry on such a brute. "I really don't think that is a good idea, Olivia. The boss will be very upset if you leave the children unattended."

"They are not unattended. They are with you," I started to walk away from him and when I glanced back over my shoulder, I could see the turmoil on his face but he stayed rooted to the spot. His job was to protect those kids, so there was not much choice in the matter.

I knew I looked a mess with no make-up, my hair piled high on my head, my fluffy sliders and mismatched cotton pyjamas but I was so annoyed that right now I didn't give a shit. My job was to look after those children and make sure their needs were met. They needed to sleep. And so, I was going to make sure they got it.

A few of the bodyguards placed strategically around the house eyed me suspiciously as I approached the doors of the club on the ground floor. Two bulky men blocked my way in, their broad shoulders connecting and stances firm. They looked above my head as if I wasn't even there.

"Excuse me. But I need to see Mr Buccini. It is a matter of urgency," I made my voice serious and one of them glanced down at me, taking in my outfit and a little smile played at the corners of his lips. Neither of them moved or spoke. "Fine!" I shouted, fighting the urge to stamp my feet. "I shall find another way in."

Storming off down the corridor, I paused when I heard raised voices coming from a room where the door was half open. A woman's voice was shouting in Italian. I had no idea what she was saying but I could feel her fury through her tone.

Then a very deep voice grumbled something back in Italian and I heard a loud slap across skin. I gasped as a loud bang sounded behind the door and then glass shattered. Without thinking and needing to know if the woman was safe, I pushed the door open and my eyes bulged.

There was Cecilia being pinned down on a sideboard and a very intimidating, older man in a pinstriped black suit had his hand around her throat. A glass vase was in pieces on the floor beside them and she had her hands wrapped around his forearm, trying to pry him off.

"Get off her!" I shouted in panic and both their heads turned to me in shock. He released his grip on her throat immediately and stepped back. And that's when I saw his face. He was tall and had the same dark features as Giovanni except his hair was greying all over. But where Giovanni has a smoothness to his appearance, this man did not. He was terrifying.

"Olivia," Cecilia choked out as she climbed off the sideboard table and rubbed her neck.

"Who is this?" the man hissed, looking me up and down with distaste.

"An employee. The children's new nanny," she said calmly, as if the man in front of her hadn't just been trying to choke her to death. His eyes locked with mine and he tsked. He actually made that noise and screwed his nose up as if I was beneath him. I kept my glare fixed on this entitled prick and folded my arms.

"Do all your employees sleep here?" He grumbled.

"No. It is just because of the party. The children needed her."

He nodded once before striding towards me, his huge frame towering over me.

"You better rethink that attitude of yours before it gets you killed, little girl. And know your place," he hissed in my face and pushed past me, causing me to stumble backwards. Wow.

Suddenly, Cecilia grabbed my arm and pulled me into the room, shutting the door behind me. "What are you doing here, Olivia?"

For the first time since I had met this woman who always seemed to have so much poise and grace, she seemed flustered.

"I – I was just coming to ask Giovanni to turn down the music. The children can't sleep."

She paced back and forth a few steps in front of me as she fussed with her blonde hair to make it neat again. "What you saw...just now, you cannot say a word to anyone. Especially Giovanni. Do you understand?"

My eyebrows furrowed and I knew my disbelief was written all over my face. "But he was hurting you! He was trying to kill you!"

"No. It was just an argument. A misunderstanding. If Giovanni knew his uncle laid a hand on me, he would go ballistic and that would not end well for any of us."

My eyes widened at her words. "Uncle? That was his uncle?"

"Yes. Vinny's brother. Look Olivia, this family is complicated. It is best you stay out of these things. As for the music, I am sorry. I agree. It is getting late and we should turn it down."

I nodded and she paused in her pacing. Her fingers played on the surface of her lips as she looked ahead into space, thinking hard, "But I am not feeling well. I need to have a lie down after...that. Will you be okay to go and speak to Giovanni yourself?"

"Well, that was what I was trying to do, but your ogres out there wouldn't let me in!"

Her stunning face twisted into a smile and she chuckled.

"Come on."

I followed her down the hall until we stood outside the club doors again and as soon as the men saw her, they stepped aside to let her enter. She pointed her hand to the door and looked at me. "There you go."

I sighed and went to approach the door, but her grip on my arm stopped me. "Remember. Not a word," her voice was blunt and intimidating, that cold mask over her face once again. I nodded and she released me before turning on her Louboutin heels and strutting away.

As soon as I entered the club, I felt all that rage at Giovanni come flooding back. This was not a bloody meeting! This was a full-on rave! There must have been at least a hundred people in here and everyone seemed to be drunk, horny and having the time of their lives. I glanced around for any sign of him, but only frolicking bodies on the dancefloor were in my eyeline. And then I looked up and spotted him standing on a raised platform overlooking the dancefloor, separated by some glass. He was talking to another older man in a suit. Pushing my way through the bodies on the dance floor was a difficult mission. Every bump, grind and grope I felt against my body just added to my anger.

Then, suddenly, I ran straight into a 6ft wall of muscle. The firm grip on my upper arm made me wince as I glanced up to see who was manhandling me. Olive black eyes full of rage. A menacing scowl across his handsome features. Giovanni. He started to push through the crowd, dragging me by the arm with him, and I fought against his strong grip.

"Get off me! Mr Buccini! Giovanni!" I shouted over the music. He quickly turned and, in one smooth motion, he bent down and threw me over his broad shoulder. Very aware my ass was up in the air in a pair of very short shorts, I screamed at him and punched his muscular back, which made no difference what-so-ever. The doors opened and we were no longer in the club but back in the lobby of the ground floor. As I looked up from my position, I caught the two beefcake bouncers at the door sniggering and pointing.

"FUCK YOU!" I shouted at them and gave them the middle finger, which just seemed to make them even more amused. A loud, playful swat on my ass cheek had me yelp and my skin immediately flamed from where his hand had been.

"Curse again Olivia and your ass will be red raw," his voice was husky and I gulped, momentarily startled and... aroused by what he just did. He climbed the stairs two at a time and I clocked Marco standing outside the kids' door still. And there it was. That huge, beaming smile I had been trying to get out of him for days. Fucker. So that was what it took to make that robot smile. Me over Giovanni's shoulder, humiliated beyond belief. But Giovanni kept going. Up to his floor.

He finally put me back on my feet and stepped back. I turned around and saw that we were in a bedroom. A very grand and elegant bedroom that oozed sophistication. My mouth dropped open as I realised this must be his room. I was in Giovanni Buccini's bedroom and he was...looking at me like he was contemplating whether to murder me or have his way with me. Oh fuck this is not good. Not good at all.

"Why am I here? Is this your bedroom?" I shouted in disbelief and his eyes narrowed.

"Why were you at the club?" He ignored my question and asked his own.

"Trust me, I would have rather been anywhere else! I came to tell you to turn the music down. Your poor siblings are exhausted but cannot sleep through the unbearable techno music blaring from your oh-so important meeting." I gave the word 'meeting' air quotations as my tone was laced with sarcasm and his nostrils flared. He took a menacing step towards me and I cursed myself for moving back instinctively.

"Talk to me like that again bambola and I will gladly slam you against the wall and fuck you senseless," his low, raspy voice sent a shiver down my spine in the most pleasurable way and I squeezed my thighs together tightly. My heart sank as I realised how much I wanted that to happen. It annoyed me that I found him so attractive. No, it was more than that. He was everything I should be running from. Controlling, demanding, sex-obsessed and dangerous. Yet, the way he made me feel so alive with just his words was slowly killing me and my body was dying to know what those hands could do to me. I had to admit it. I wanted him or at least his body.

My face must have given away my provocative thoughts as he groaned loudly and charged at me, pulling my body into his. I couldn't miss the feel of his cock, rock hard, against my lower stomach. My breasts were smashed into his chest in his tight black shirt and I could feel the tingle of my nipples hardening under the thin fabric of my cami. His gaze burned into mine with so much intensity, I soon forgot why I was mad. He licked his lips. For some reason, I found that simple gesture both sexy and menacing. Anticipating what he was going to do next, all I could do was stare.

"I want to kiss you so badly Olivia. From the moment I picked up your little lace thong off the floor, you have consumed my mind. I think about you constantly."

His words had my stomach flip and, as Gigi so eloquently put it, fanny flutter. My eyes travelled down to his lips that were so inviting yet forbidden. Kiss me. Please.

"But I won't kiss you." My eyes flickered up to his, which were blazing with raw desire and control. "Not until you admit that you want me too," a slight curve on his lips reminded me of who I was dealing with.

That irritation that always brews inside me whenever he is near bubbled up to the surface. Of course he had to ruin it. I would have let him kiss me. I would have let him do anything to me but he had to go and ruin it. Well, who is the fool now?

Pushing his chest hard, I growled when he didn't budge but kept his hands firmly on my hips, holding me in place against him.

"I will never admit it! You are the most cocky, egotistical player and you think far too highly of yourself! You have no effect on me!"

His eyes flashed with amusement and he squared one eyebrow up in response. "Is that so? So, your panties are not soaked through with your arousal for me?"

A wicked grin played on my lips as I realised he had walked right into that one. "I'm not wearing any panties."

His eyes darkened a few shades of brown and that danger was back in full force. "Don't test me, Olivia, or I will snap."

I held his gaze with determination. Challenging him to do his worst. My eyes widened when I felt his fingers run down my thigh lightly, before tracing them back up my inner thigh until he reached the frilly seam of my shorts. "So, this doesn't affect you?" He husked out, lowering his head a few inches so it was in my personal space. All of him was in my personal space and I was struggling to breathe.

"No," I said more confidently than I felt. My heart was pounding and my skin was tingling from his touch.

"So, this doesn't affect you..." he lowered his head in the crook of my neck and kissed my throat so tenderly as his fingers continued to run up and down the inside of my thigh.

My eyes fluttered closed as I felt his hot breath and lips on my skin and I fought the urge to release a moan.

"Not one little bit," I barely managed to choke out and felt him smile into my neck.

He brushed his lips up my throat until he reached my ear and whispered, "Let's see, shall we?" I felt his fingers climb up the loose short leg and he slid his fingers inward, sliding them over me. I gasped loudly and grabbed his huge shoulders.

"Liar," he growled as he parted my folds and slipped a finger inside me before removing it quickly. My core ached with need and I wanted to scream for him to touch me again. Just like that.

"Shall I stop?" His husky voice was against my neck again as he placed small kisses down it.

I didn't answer as his fingers brushed against my clit and caused me to shudder against him. "Tell me Olivia. Do you want me to stop?"

His fingers left my core and I whimpered, "No."

I hated him. I hated him for making me want this so badly. For making me want him. Within seconds, he had pushed me against the wall of his bedroom and his fingers were working their way inside me while his thumb circled my clit. My legs began to shake under the sheer pleasure he was causing to erupt through my body and I gripped his shoulders tighter.

"Fuck you are so tight, bambola."

Just hearing those words had me moaning loudly as he increased his pace. He pulled his head back from my neck and the look of intense arousal on his own face had my orgasm building at an insane speed. This would be the quickest I have ever come! His hooded eyes and parted lips stared down at me as he pleasured me with his fingers.

"Come for me Olivia. I want to see you."

I squeezed my eyes shut and let the feeling take hold of me. Crying out and panting heavily as the bubble burst and my body melted against his. I lowered my head against his chest as I tried to get my breathing under control. Oh my fucking god, what did I just do? I just gave in to him.

He pulled his fingers out from me and I looked up as he raised them to his mouth and sucked them clean. My eyes widened at his crude action and I felt my cheeks flame.

"Oh my god! That is gross!" I stepped away from him as laughter danced behind his eyes.

"Not gross, baby. Delicious." My eyes narrowed and I folded my arms across my chest. "I bet you are glad you didn't go on your date now. He would never be able to make you come like I can."

Anger erupted like a volcano inside me at his words and the smug grin plastered on his face.

"You are such a dick! I hate you!" I screamed, turning on my heels and racing for the door, but he beat me to it, slamming it shut again. I glared up at him as his face turned thunderous.

"Why?" He snarled. "Why do you hate me?"

Stepping back from him to give myself some distance, I stared up into those dark eyes.

"Are you controlling?"

His face contorted with confusion and his shoulders tensed at my question, but I knew he would answer honestly.

"Yes."

"Are you possessive?"

"Yes."

"Are you... dangerous?" I hesitated. This was the one I really dreaded the answer to. Over the last week, the alarm bells have been ringing in my head over and over. That he is a bad man. That he has done bad things. But then he pulls me back in with his charm and seduction and I convince myself it is just because of my past that I feel like this. That I am pushing him away because of gut feelings rather than facts.

His chest was rising and falling in shallow breaths as he held my gaze. "Yes."

I felt my heart flip and not in a good way.

"Then that is why I hate you. You remind me of someone who broke me. And I am in too many pieces to be broken again."

Hurt and confusion creased his sinfully beautiful features and I took a deep breath before I said what I needed to.

"I am not some employee you can fuck and have fun with until you get bored. I can't do that. I am not what you are looking for, so stop this now. Just leave me alone."

With that, I left his room and didn't look back.

Free

Giovanni

"Then that is why I hate you." Her green and gold eyes swirled with emotion as she stared up into the depths of my black soul. Something inside me flinched at her words. She really meant them. "You remind me of someone who broke me. And I am in too many pieces to be broken again."

What? What did that mean? Who broke her? My immediate confusion turned to pain that she would think that I would ever want to hurt her. That I would ever purposely try and cause her suffering.

"I am not some employee you can fuck and have fun with until you get bored. I can't do that. I am not what you are looking for, so stop this now. Just leave me alone."

My jaw tensed as she turned and fled my room. And I let her go. Because at the end of the day, she was right. She can't do that and what other reason was I doing this for?

As soon as the door closed behind her, I turned and swung my fist into the plaster board of the bedroom wall. The wall crumbled from the impact, leaving a mess on the cream carpet below. Pacing the room, I ran my hand through my hair. How the hell did that go south so fast? One minute I was in fucking heaven with my fingers in her tight, wet pussy and the next...

Now I've touched her...now I have had a taste, I can't let go. I can't leave her alone. Why did she think it would be so easy? Does she not feel this pull towards me like I do her? What am I doing wrong? Who do I remind her of?

Anger prickled all over my skin as I opened my bedroom door and dashed into my office. Pulling out the file that Toni gave me earlier about her life, I flipped it open and skimmed down her CV. Nothing I didn't already know. Next page. Birth certificate. My eyebrows pulled together.

Olivia Rose Bennett.

Bennett? But her last name is Jones? What the hell? I checked the date and place of birth and it was the same as her CV. The only difference was her name. Flicking to the next page, I stilled. A deed poll. She changed her name just two months ago. Personal choice was ticked on the reasons why.

Flipping the pages over some more, seeing her school records, GCSEs and A levels, it all matched what I already knew about her until I stumbled upon a death certificate. Her father's.

Stuart Bennett. Died in a fatal car accident at the age of 38 in 2003. Olivia would have been 4 years old. The same age as Raya. A strange feeling settled in my gut and I quickly flipped the page again to not dwell too much on it.

What I saw next had my heart hammering in my chest. English newspaper articles. Loads of them. With the headings; Local man stabs teenager to death. Stalker's stabbing in small town. Murder in mansion house party. Pulling out the articles one by one, I skim read them looking for any indication as to how Olivia was involved in this. And then I spotted it. In one article with the heading: Obsessed stepbrother kills boyfriend, there was a picture of a younger, happier Olivia hanging off a teenage boy's arm. They both look so youthful and carefree and he is looking at her with admiration. I felt my hands starting to shake as I scanned the article for her name.

Henry Trendall, 20 years old, has been arrested for the brutal murder of Nathanial Ford, aged 18. On Friday 12th May, Henry, who was thought to be unprovoked in his attack, stabbed the teenager seven times at an end of year sixth form party at a fellow student's house. Sources say that Nathanial was the boyfriend of Olivia Bennett, an 18-year-old student who also happens to be Mr Trendall's stepsister.

Fuck.

Sources close to the family report that Trendall had a very unhealthy relationship with Bennett. He was controlling, possessive and obsessed with her for many years before committing such a heinous crime.

Fuck. Fuck. Fuck.

The sentencing will be on July 24th at Her Majesty's court and Trendall is expected to be tried for murder and given a life sentence.

Frantically, I flicked through the file some more until I found the court scripture. As my eyes landed at the bottom and I saw the verdict, I shook my head. He got away with it. He was thrown a get out of jail free card. The jury and professionals claimed he was not in his right mind and suffering from a mental health disorder. That he needed help and belonged in a mental institution, not prison. Anger rose in me at the thought of him getting off so lightly when he caused Olivia so much heartbreak and took that innocent boy's life. Then I checked myself. What a hypocrite. How many fathers, sons, boyfriends, husbands have I killed in my lifetime? Yes, they may not have been innocent, but nor was I. Now I understand it.

Now I understand her. In her eyes, I was a constant reminder of her stepbrother. Arrogant. Controlling. Possessive. Dangerous. She could sense it in me. That darkness that she was trying to forget. Of course, she would recognise it when it was staring her in the face once again.

Dropping my head in my hands on my desk, I felt my body shaking with rage. She was right. This could never work. She could never be in this world with me. She has suffered at the hands of a psychotic killer. And once she knew the extent of who I was, she would never think anything less. Because let's face it. I deserved to be rotting in a prison cell too. Yet, because of the family I was born into, I had protection. I could be a monster and get away with it.

Not able to look at any more of her files at that moment, I closed them all and locked them in my desk drawer. Standing up and walking over to my liquor cabinet, I poured myself a large whiskey and downed it in one. A knock on my door made my heart skip a beat. Was it her?

When Max's man bun poked around followed by his beefy body, I groaned.

"Nice to see you too!" He mumbled as he stepped into my office and closed the door. "Thanks for leaving me to deal with that lot alone you bastard."

I turned and handed him a drink before sitting back down at my desk and putting my feet up on it. When I didn't respond but stared into space, I felt Max's gaze on me.

"So, are you going to marry her?"

My head snapped up to his and my face creased with confusion as for a moment my head was only full of Olivia. Then I recalled what a fucking shit show tonight was before I had seen her sexy, stubborn ass in that club.

"No."

"Then, can I?" he chuckled into his glass and I closed my eyes. "She is something else. Don't think I have ever seen a more gorgeous woman in my life."

"By all means, go for it! She is all yours. You'd be doing me a fucking favour," I grumbled. I didn't have the energy to talk about this right now. I didn't have the energy for any of it.

"Zio is pissed. And I mean another level of pissed."

I threw my arms over my head, gripping the back of my chair and sighed. No. Really did not have the energy for this.

"When he returned and heard you had told Camilla you wouldn't marry her and then stormed out of the club with the nanny over your shoulder, I thought his head was about to explode."

I opened my eyes and looked at Max properly for the first time. His own amusement was dancing behind his eyes but also concern was evident. No one wanted to get on the wrong side of our uncle.

"Let me guess? Toni told him?"

"What were you thinking, Gio?"

"I wasn't...thinking. That is the problem. I can't think straight when it comes to her."

"Camilla?"

I chuckled, shaking my head. "No Olivia."

"The nanny?" His voice raised and eyes widened before he looked like the cat that got the cream. "I fucking knew it! I knew there was something going on there. I've been trying to pry it out of you for days!"

"There is nothing going on. Not now," I muttered, lifting my glass to my lips and looking at the wall.

"What do you mean?" His face creased in confusion. "You haven't fucked her?"

I clenched my jaw and gave him a warning look. "No, I haven't fucked her. Believe me, I've been trying but... it's complicated."

"Ah. The 'it's complicated' girl. They are the hardest to crack." His lips turned up into a twisted grin and I frowned.

"No, it's not that. It's not even about getting her in bed anymore," I groaned as I felt a piercing headache coming on.

"Then what is it about? Wait...do you love her?" He immediately sat forward, his eyes bulging.

"No. Of course, I don't fucking love her. Don't be a daft prick."

"You sure as hell look like a man in love. You look like shit."

"Ah. Thanks." I grumbled as I moved my legs off my desk. "Is the party over? Everyone gone?" I asked, changing the subject swiftly.

"Yeah. Zio apologised on your behalf to Francesco, said you had a personal crisis to deal with but would make it up to him soon, and then stormed out with Toni, his little lap dog padding along behind. The Aianis left shortly after and I kicked the rest out."

"And mamma?"

"She never came back to the club after she spoke to zio. The men said she went up to bed."

I nodded, feeling suddenly exhausted. "Thanks Max. I owe you."

He stood up, sensing my need to be alone, and gave me a pointed look, "Sort your shit out Gio. You know boss will not go easy on you for this fuck up."

"Don't you worry your pretty little man bun about me," I smirked and he chuckled, shaking his head.

"You're a first-class prick, you know?"

"It runs in the family."

After Max took off, I knew I wouldn't be able to sleep until I went down and checked on Sani and Raya...and Olivia. Strolling down to their wing, I nodded to Marco who was standing outside their door and gently pushed it open. There in his bed were my two siblings, cuddled up and sleeping peacefully and on a makeshift bed of pillows and blankets was Olivia, also fast asleep. I crept towards them and stared at her stunning face. Realising she was sleeping on the floor and not the single bed that was assembled in Raya's room made my chest tighten. If she didn't hate me so much right now, I would have carried her to the bed or even better mine, but I didn't have the energy for another fight.

As I took in her delicate features so dainty and enchanting, I felt guilt tug at my core. I had been acting like such a dick. The way I had been towards her. It was the way I had always been with women. Most of them liked it. I think deep down, she likes it too, but she was still not over her past. She cannot separate my actions from his. And I reminded her of it. The thought made me feel sick. No wonder she hated me.

She shuffled onto her back in her sleep and the blanket fell away from her chest, the top of her full breast swelling over her little pyjama top as she breathed deeply. My dick stirred and my mind raced back to how they felt against my chest earlier. How hard her nipples were through the thin layers of our clothing. I longed to know what colour they were. To have them in my mouth. Sighing deeply, I backed out of the room. I had to let her go. I had to stop this.

The realisation and heaviness of her words weighed down on me as I resolved to cut her out of my life. She wasn't just an employee I could have fun with. She was Olivia and... I cared about her. There, I admit it. I have never cared for anyone other than my family. She was the first. And she would be the last. She needed to be removed from my life as soon as possible because caring would make me weak. She already had too much of an influence over my thoughts and actions. Closing the door quietly, I ignored the twisted knot forming in my stomach and made my way back to my room.

Olivia Jones or whoever she was, was free from me. For her sake and for mine.

A Warm Welcome

Giovanni

"You wanted to see me?" Mamma opened my office door widely and I leaned back on my chair and nodded, giving her a small smile.

I noticed her relax when she saw it and wondered what had her so on edge. Mind you, my mother's brain was like a beautifully designed garden maze that no one could navigate through except her, so I am not even going to attempt to question her.

She strolled around with an air of elegance, but I could see the gloom in her eyes. She was not having a good day. Fuck sake, I had enough on my plate today. I had a pretty good idea of how this might go.

"Olivia's two-week probation will be up soon and it is time to let her go." I kept my voice void of any emotion and watched as my mamma's brown eyes widened in shock.

"What?! You mean fire her? Whatever for?" She was livid. Her caramel skin flushed and her nostrils flared. A little trait I had inherited from her.

Keeping my tone firm and calm, I replied, "Well, if you need a list... She didn't want the job in the first place, she has no boundaries when it comes to her role in this household. She left the children in the care of my men twice, once to look at some tourist attraction and last night to come and give me an earful about the music being too loud in the club. She talked to me with disrespect and told my men to 'Fuck off'. Do I need to continue?"

She smacked her lips together and stood up abruptly, turning her back towards me. She was processing. Hopefully, that list was enough for her to realise that Olivia was not the right fit for such a role in this house, even though we both knew that was a lie. I just hoped she would back down easily. No such luck.

Turning quickly, she glared at me with determination.

"I don't give a fuck about any of that, Giovanni! We pay her to look after Sani and Raya and teach them. That is her job. And she is doing it brilliantly. The kids love her and I have never seen them so happy, content and engaged. So what if she has a backbone and a sharp tongue? I am sure your men deserved it. What is this really about Gio? Is it because of the engagement?"

My jaw ticked at the reminder of what I had to deal with and I felt instantly annoyed.

"No. It has nothing to do with that. Why would it?"

"You are not marrying that girl, Giovanni! I will not allow it," she snarled and I scoffed loudly. As if she held any power to do anything about an alliance between Salvatore and Francesco. I even had my hands tied and she knew it.

"Why not? It is a good business deal," I sighed, rubbing my hands down my face.

"Marriage is not a business deal Giovanni!" She screamed, her arms flailing dramatically in the air. "I do not want that for you! Don't you want to experience true love? What papi and I had?"

I lost my temper. Slamming my hand down on my desk, making her jump, I hissed, "No! That is the opposite of what I want. If Papi had married for business, then he would still be alive!"

Her face paled and her mouth fell open as the tears brimmed at the corners of her eyes. I might as well have slapped her; the words were that hurtful. I immediately regretted them and stood up, my face softening. But it was too late.

"Fine. Be a coward and ruin your life. I have never been so disappointed in you. Your papi will be turning in his grave right now. But the girl stays. I signed her contract, so technically, I am her boss and the only one who has the right to sack her. And she is not going anywhere." Turning on her heels, she stormed out of the room, slamming the door with a loud bang behind her.

"Fuck!" I shouted, throwing a glass against the wall as it shattered into pieces.

***

As the Bentley pulled up outside my zio's grand estate, I shook my arms out in my expensive suit jacket and combed my hair back. I knew this would be one of the worst encounters I have ever had with him and I was preparing myself for his wrath. I would take it because that was my place, but I would not forget it. I am always watching him. Learning from him. How he handles situations and his reactions. Deciding whether that is the type of boss I will be someday.

Climbing out of the car, I was immediately met by two of his men who marched behind me as if I was a fucking rival not family. As I reached his office, another man opened the door for me to enter and I saw my uncle sitting behind his black oak desk with gold detail. Toni was sitting in a chair to his left in the corner of the room, one leg over the other and his foot bouncing. Neither of them stood to greet me as I approached. Salvatore's face was frosty. Void of any emotion except malice. Toni was staring at me with mild curiosity as I stood before them.

"Gun," Zio ordered lowly, and I frowned.

Pulling my gun out of the back of my trousers, I placed it on his desk in front. I was pretty sure he was not going to shoot me with my own gun, but

I wouldn't put it past him to wound me. Suddenly, the two beefy men who marched me up, stomped into the room standing either side of me. I looked over my shoulders at each one, their faces fixed on my uncle. I smirked. Ah. A beating.

"Hands," he ordered, and I knew the score. Holding my hands out in front of me, one of the men fastened them together tightly with cable ties to stop me from defending myself or breaking any of their bones. As soon as it was done, a powerful punch to my stomach had me crippled over, wheezing. I quickly stood back up and locked eyes with my uncle again as I waited for the next blow. Another one came but this time I was prepared. I tensed my stomach and took as many of their punches as I could before I felt a kick to the back of my knees. Falling to the grey carpet, a fist connected with my left cheek and my head whipped round from the brutal force, spitting blood onto the floor.

"Not his face! Don't bleed on my floor!" I heard my uncle snarl and I chuckled.

A hard shoe connected with my lower abdomen and I fell to the plush carpet as they both started to really go at me with their feet. They weren't holding back as they kicked my back. My stomach. My chest.

"Enough," Salvatore commanded and they instantly stopped, pulling me back up to my feet and cutting the cable ties from my hands.

"Thank you gentlemen. You are so kind," I grinned, with a blood-stained mouth, and they smirked back before leaving the room. I had no problem with them. They were only doing their duty.

Sitting down across from my uncle, I rearranged my shirt that had come out of my belt and tucked it back in. His eyes regarded me intensely as I leaned forward and retrieved my gun, pushing it down the back of my belt.

"That was a warm welcome," I smiled and saw Toni shake his head in irritation. If he had it his way, he would have me begging for my boss' forgiveness. I could feel every bruise and ache stinging against my clothes as my body caught up with the attack and I relished the feeling. It had been a while since I had received a good thrashing.

"You will marry the girl."

I scoffed and leaned back in the chair. "I will *think* about marrying the girl."

His dark eyes narrowed but he seemed to accept that answer.

"Who is the nanny to you?"

The question surprised me and I felt my heart speed up as I held his gaze.

"She is no one. An employee who doesn't know her place. She tried to get into the club last night and I had to show her that she was not welcome."

My uncle lifted his heavily ringed hand to his chin and scratched along his stubble as he considered my words.

"I met her. Last night. She has a fire in her, that's for sure."

I forced myself to keep my calm and cool mask to hide my panic and surprise that Olivia had had a run in with my uncle. What surprised me even more was that she was still alive after it. When I didn't respond, he leaned forward on his desk clasping his hands together.

"She reminds me of your mamma. Feisty and opinionated. Cecilia will always have my protection, but this girl will not. It is dangerous for her to be in our world if she cannot hold her tongue and know her place."

I nodded once. "I understand. I am dealing with it. Mamma is very fond of her and the kids love her, but I agree she is a liability."

He leaned back in his chair and a small grin teased at the edges of his mouth.

"Good. We understand. I will allow you some time to get your head around this marriage, but Giovanni, it is an important alliance. Marrying Francesco's daughter solidifies our friendship and gives us endless possibilities for his contacts and deals. They will all fall to us or you more specifically. Imagine the power you will have." I breathed in deeply and nodded once more.

"Leo informed me of the Novalli contract killing. It is done." I said curtly.

He bowed his head a few times in approval and clasped his hands together. "And handled discreetly?"

"Sì. It was made to look like a burglary gone wrong. Poliziotto Evori has already closed the case, although I expect the media will have a field day with this."

"Buona. And his famiglia?"

"Unharmed," I replied. Zio nodded his head. Knowing that was about all the praise I would get, I asked, "Is that all?"

"For now. There is a deal I would like to arrange with the French by the end of the week. I am sending you in my place. It is best you take your mamma so she can look over the legal contracts and ensure it is a deal worth considering. I will send you all the information in a few days."

Nodding again, I stood up and headed for the door. This day was just getting better and better.

Peeping Olivia

Olivia

It's been three days since I have seen Giovanni. I caught sight of him getting into his driver's car the morning after that night, but I haven't seen him since. I don't know how to feel about it. I know I should be elated, but my emotions and thoughts are confusing me. For one, I am surprised that he has actually listened to me and is in fact leaving me alone. But on the other hand, I felt...empty. It's so hard to describe. I don't think I even understand these emotions myself. I wanted him to ignore me. To leave me to get on with my job and my life in peace without his constant tempting seduction, but now it was happening...I couldn't help but feel a strange loss.

My days felt longer, bleaker and I found my eyes constantly searching for him around the house. It's ridiculous, but after giving into his charms, I couldn't get him out of my head. The whole scene was on repeat like a scratched record and I cannot tell you how many times I have romanced myself when I am alone in my bed or showering thinking of his fingers inside me. But my fingers are never as satisfying. The climax is never as good.

I shook my head as I started to pick up the kids' toys and rearrange them on their shelves. I had given them an hour in the games room as a treat for actually sitting down and doing some simple math and letter formation.

"Olivia?" A whispered voice came from behind me and I turned to see Natalia in a maid's outfit and hoover in hand. She smiled and gave me a little wave from the door.

"Natalia! I can't believe this is the first time I have seen you working when I feel like I practically live here!" I smiled, walking towards Gigi's brother's girlfriend.

"I know! I do the evening shifts normally, so I have never seen you."

"Why do they need cleaners in the evening?" I scrunched my nose up. Honestly, these people have too much money.

"To tidy and clean up after dinner and do the laundry," she smiled sweetly. I nodded in understanding. "So how are you finding it? Working for the Buccinis?"

I scoffed and placed my hands on my hips with a sassy attitude. "Well, it's interesting, that's for sure! The kids are great though."

Her eyes widened slightly. "Really? They have had three nannies since I have been working here alone! No one ever sticks around for long."

That surprised me. Surely Raya and Sani weren't the reason for that. More likely Giovanni. But then I think back to my first day and how much they both gave me the run around and I chuckled.

"They are not so bad once you get to know them," I smirked and she smiled.

"Well, you are obviously doing well with them if you are keeping the boss happy. You know who he is right?" Her eyebrows raised a fraction and I frowned.

Suddenly, Lucinda, the old witch of the west, sauntered into the room and clicked her fingers at Natalia, who scampered away with her tail between her legs.

"That was rude," I glared at the prickly older woman. She took her job far too seriously.

Ignoring my remark, she stared daggers at me before holding out a white envelope in her hand. "From Signore Buccini."

I took it hesitantly before she turned on her heels and left me standing there alone. There was nothing written on the envelope. I turned it over multiple times in my hands before ripping it open. Pulling out my extended contract to sign for...one year! And my paper copy of my payment. My eyes bulged at the figure for the last two weeks of work. What the...?

Anger bubbled in my chest as I realised he had obviously ignored my request to not accept the doubled salary. Clenching the paper in my hand, I stormed out of the playroom and past Marco, who was standing guard outside the games room. I ignored his raised eyebrows and amused smirk as I stomped up to the top floor, a woman on a mission.

As I approached his office, I saw the door was slightly open and pushed it wider to see that it was empty. Urgh! I wanted to deal with this now, while my anger would overpower my desire for this man. Suddenly, I heard a muffled noise down the hallway which piqued my interest. Someone was up here. Taking deliberate steps towards the shuffling noise, I reached a door that I had never entered before. It was ajar just enough for me to peer through the crack and my hand slammed against my mouth as I took in the sight before me.

There, on a cream leather sofa, was Giovanni, legs spread apart, fully clothed and hands behind his head. But that wasn't what had my heart drumming in my chest or heat rising through my body. It was the black-haired girl kneeling between his legs, her head bobbing up and down as she sucked his cock enthusiastically. Her hands were holding his thick thighs over his trousers that were open just enough for her to have access to what she needed. Oh my god!

I wanted to look away. To run for my life, but as I glanced up at his face, all I felt was...intrigued. As much as seeing him with another girl made me feel physically sick, I also felt extremely aroused. Not by what she was doing, but by him. By watching him. His eyes fluttered shut and his jaw clenched as the girl's head frantically moved up and down his length. But he didn't look like he was enjoying himself all that much. He looked almost bored.

Suddenly, as if he could feel someone watching him, his dark eyes snapped open and he looked directly at me, peeping through the crack in the door. I froze. It was too late to do anything. He had seen me. I should run. I should get the hell out of here but something in his eyes held me in place. They burned with desire and raw emotion as he possessed my soul, challenging me to look away. I don't think my heart had ever raced so hard and the sudden ache between my legs had my lips part and my breathing came out in short, sharp pants. But I couldn't look away.

He never took his eyes off me as his hands moved from the back of his head and tangled into the girl's glossy black hair. He started to guide her head faster and deeper. His lips parted as he started to groan loudly, still holding my gaze. I was transfixed. This felt so naughty. So filthy. It was. But I couldn't stop watching. I watched as he held the girl's head still in his muscular hands and started to lift his hips, fucking her mouth, hard and fast. My clit tingled and my knickers were drenched. Every fibre of my body felt like it was on fire. The longing I felt to touch myself was too much. Losing all my inhibitions, I moved my hands up under my flowy dress and started to rub myself. His eyes flickered down at the action and the guttural growl that escaped his chest had me moan quietly behind the door. Our eyes locked once more and I could tell he was close. The girl was making loud, gurgling noises of panic as he continued his relentless thrusts, but he ignored her. His sole focus was on me. He was putting on a show for me.

I felt my orgasm building as I watched his jaw tense and taut muscles in his neck ripple. He moaned, keeping his eyes on me the whole time as he held the girl's head to him and exploded in her mouth. Revelling in the way his lips parted, chest heaved and skin flushed, I felt my own breathing hitch as I was so close to falling over the edge of pleasure as well.

"Liv! Raya won't let me have a go with the iPad! She's been on it for ages!" Sani's voice yelled from the floor below, bursting this bubble of sin. It was enough to cause me to jump back from the door. My eyes widened at what I was just doing and what I had just been an audience for as I turned frantically on my feet and ran down the stairs. Pushing past Marco and into the games room, I knew I must look so flustered and crazed right now as I tried to regulate my breathing. The kids were playing tug of war with the iPad and I marched over, taking it out of both their hands.

"If you can't play nicely, you both won't have it."

Sani frowned but then looked up at me with a confused expression.

"Why are you all sweaty and red? Did you go for a run?"

I paused. Opening my mouth and closing it, I felt the flush of embarrassment flare up in my cheeks.

"Just...just share, okay?"

They both nodded as I handed it back to them. They sat down next to each other in the window seat and went back to watching their shows. Storming into the bathroom, I closed the door and slid down to the floor. If there was ever a time I wanted the ground to swallow me whole, it was now. Please... please God... How will I ever be able to face that man again?

***

Giovanni

My mind was racing as I stared at the empty space behind the door of my entertaining lounge where Olivia had just been standing. Or had she? Had I just fantasised about that whole thing?

No. I felt it. That was the fucking sexiest thing a woman has ever done and she wasn't even touching me. She wasn't even naked. It was her eyes. Her eyes stole that orgasm as if it was always hers to take.

Mia sat back, releasing my dick with a frown. Pushing it back into my boxers and doing up my trousers, I avoided her annoyed glare. Yep. I had just used her completely and she knew it. She could have been anyone just now because it wasn't her tongue, mouth or throat I was imagining around my cock. It was Olivia's. I had been at the point of giving up and telling her to go home when I closed my eyes and tried to project the image of Olivia on her knees instead, but it wasn't working. Once again, I was finding no pleasure or gratification in anything Mia was doing. It wasn't her fault. It was me.

And then I felt it. My skin tingled and I felt that heated gaze that I had denied myself for the last three days. I had kept myself busy, stayed out of the house as much as possible and locked myself away when I was here to avoid her at all costs. But when I opened my eyes, there she was. Hot and flustered, emerald eyes wide with shock and desire. She knew she had been caught. I kept my eyes on her, expecting her to turn and run. If she had, I would have gone after her. I wouldn't have been able to stop myself. To my utter shock and pleasure, she didn't move a muscle. Instead, her eyes burned with indescribable arousal and I felt myself grow harder in Mia's mouth.

Just having her watching me and liking it, made me almost explode immediately. When I started to fuck Mia's mouth hard and fast, giving Olivia a glimpse of what it would be like to be fucked by me, I heard her faint soft moan and watched as her fingers ran up her thigh and under her dress. Her cheeks became flushed with an adorable shade of pink as she started to pleasure herself. That was it. That was enough to send me into a powerful climax as I exploded at the back of Mia's throat, holding her there. I was a panting mess with sweat dripping down my forehead as I let go, but kept my eyes fixed on Olivia, needing to see her own climax. But then something startled her and she was gone. I felt cheated. I needed to see her come.

Mia stood up and grabbed her jacket off the sofa next to me. She placed one hand on her hip.

"I don't mind a bit of rough Giovanni, but that was too much. Okay?" Her tone was kind and seeking my permission, which instantly annoyed me. She should be pissed. She should be screaming at me and calling me all the names under the sun but she wouldn't. Because she was intimidated by me. They all were. Apart from Olivia. Even if Olivia did fear me, she never backed down from me. She was strong and feisty and everything I desired. She was perfect. So fucking perfect that I am convinced now more than ever, that I will never be satisfied with another woman ever again.

She has ruined me. Completely.

Disaster Date

Olivia

"Okay. Spill. What the hell is going on with you?" Gigi narrowed her eyes as she studied my face. I could feel my cheeks flaming as the flashback of earlier came to mind.

"What? Nothing," I grumbled, turning my back to her at her vanity table to start my make-up for my date with Luca tonight. Yes, I know. What a hussy I am! Participating in sexual acts with a forbidden man and going on dates with another.

"Come on! You look... radiant. Whatever it is that has got you all hot and bothered, I think you should do more of it," she winked as she stood up behind me and started to brush my hair.

"No. No, I definitely should not."

Her eyes widened, partnered with a beaming smile.

"So you *did* get up to something naughty today?"

I groaned loudly and rolled my eyes. She would continue to pester me about this for days if I didn't at least give her something.

"Fine. I – I found myself in a compromising situation."

"Meaning?" Her tone could not mask her excitement as the brush paused halfway down my hair.

"I caught Giovanni getting a blow job off some girl today. And I... watched."

Her mouth hung open and then she started to laugh in disbelief.

"My girl! Yes! Was it hot? I bet it was so hot!"

I hid my face behind my hands as I started to giggle.

"Yes, it was hot. Even hotter when he saw me."

"What! He saw you? Watching him? What did he do?"

I lifted my head and looked at her exhilarated face through the mirror. "He fucked her mouth while never taking his eyes off me."

She suddenly flapped her hands and jumped about the room like she had just been zapped by an electrical current.

"Cazzo! That is sexy as hell Liv! And what did you do?" She was like an excited kid who couldn't wait to find out what happened next in their favourite movie.

I avoided her eyes as I picked up my crimson lipstick, twisting the end. "Nothing. I just watched like I said." I was not about to tell her how far I really took it. I still can't believe I did that. It's like he brings out this side of me that is so daring and sexual. I didn't have control of my body at that moment. I knew what I needed and I had to give it to myself.

"Well, I am impressed. You go girl! And now you have had a little foreplay before your date tonight! Luca is a lucky man," she smirked and I rolled my eyes. Somehow, I couldn't quite imagine Luca making me feel so...alive with his eyes alone. But it was worth a shot. To try and get this man out of my head.

"How do I look?" I asked, spinning around on the stool. Gigi looked me up and down carefully and then clapped her hands.

"Bellissima!"

Smiling, I stood up and looked in her floor-length mirror. I'd decided to go with a simple yellow tea dress that gave a little flirty view of my cleavage but was modest enough for a first date. It was snug around my waist in a flattering way but fanned out at my hips into a flowy skirt. It was pretty, feminine and elegant. I'd taken Elle's advice and left my hair down in soft waves and just added a touch of mascara, bronzer and lipstick to finish the overall look.

The buzz of the intercom signalled that Luca was downstairs and I gave Gigi a kiss on each cheek before I grabbed my bag from the kitchen counter and made my way down. I decided to opt for flats because there was no way I could walk miles around those cobbled streets in heels without making a fool of myself. I don't know how the Italian women here do it!

"Wow! You look... mozzafiato!" Luca exclaimed when I stepped out of the shabby green door onto the street.

"I hope that means something good?" I giggled and his kind eyes crinkled at the sides as he smiled.

"It means breath-taking."

"Oh. Well, thank you. You look lovely too," I wasn't lying. He really had made an effort. He was wearing dark jeans and a short sleeved loose white shirt with a few buttons undone, revealing his toned chest. His arms were on display and it was clear he liked to work out although they were not in the same league as Giovanni's muscles. *Liv...don't go there.*

"So where are we going?" I asked. I had let him take the lead, which he was more than happy to do as he was a local and knew all the best places to go.

"Well...there is a bar at the top of a mountain in the east of the city that has mozzafiato views," He smirked at me, helping me to remember the new Italian word. He knew I was trying to learn more of his language. It was sweet. "Or, we can go for dinner in the piazza and then walk the river."

"Hmmm I like the sound of the mozzafiato views," I smiled as I linked my arm in with his naturally. It felt so easy to be around him. He was like a breath of fresh air. Charming. Sweet. Kind. There were no games here. He was just Luca. Although I couldn't deny that electric chemistry that I always felt when in Giovanni's company was lacking.

"Then that is where we shall go," he smiled back at me.

It took us over half an hour, a taxi ride and a cable car up to the mountain to get us there, but I loved it. It gave me the chance to see parts of this beautiful city that I hadn't before. We chatted easily about his job in a clothes shop in town and his family. We also shared some jokes about Gigi's antics with tourist men and the conversation just naturally flowed.

When we finally arrived at the bar and ordered our drinks, I turned to take in the view over the edge of the hillside. It was stunning. The entire city of Verona was lit up like a Christmas tree, a warm glow of orange streetlights and windows from below and the river ran through the middle. It made you realise how big the city actually was, as when you were in it, it felt so quaint and intimate.

Walking outside of the bar onto the grass, Luca gestured to two large plastic deck chairs that had the perfect view. There were blankets hung over the back of the seat for customers to use if it got too chilly once the warmth of Italian sunshine dissolved for the day.

"So..." he smiled as he took his cocktail up to his lips.

"So..." I flirted back.

"What is your family like?"

I looked down at my hands. This was why I hated meeting new people. Once I had kept them talking about their lives for as long as possible, the questions would always circle back around to me eventually.

"My mum still lives in London. Alone. I have no siblings, so we are not a very big family," I kept my answer short and to the point.

"And your papi?"

"He died when I was four. Car accident." I could say that without the sadness overpowering me now. When I was younger, I used to cry every time someone asked about my dad. But the truth is, I barely remember him. I was too young. I have photos and my mum used to tell me stories before she met Neil, but that's it.

"I am so sorry. I did not think," he frowned and reached for my hand, giving it a squeeze.

"It's okay! Honestly, I don't really remember him. It was so long ago."

He nodded once and we both looked out over the city again as the awkwardness took hold. This was what I hated. Not the actual revelation of my past, but the pity and sympathy that came with it. And Luca didn't even know half of it. Once people find out what I have been through, they change. They don't know what to say or how to act around me. They see me as broken. A victim. And I hate it.

"So have you always wanted to work in fashion?" I asked quickly, trying to get our easy, light atmosphere back.

He chuckled and shook his head. "No. I want to be a doctor. But...money." He raised his fingers and rubbed them together. I frowned.

"Do you mean it costs too much to train?"

"Yes. We must pay lots for university and my family do not have money. I am saving but it is slow." I loved listening to his slightly broken English. The Buccini's were fluent. You could hardly tell they were Italian apart from their thick accent, but Luca hadn't had the same level of education and had learnt English himself through Giulia. Her mother was English. She was fluent too.

"Ah, I understand. Well, I am sure you will make it happen. You seem like a very focused and ambitious man." His handsome face scrunched up in confusion but a broad smile appeared on his lips all the same.

"Ambitious? Thank you, I think that is a compliment?"

I nodded with a chuckle. "Yes, it is. It means hardworking."

"Ah," he nodded. "Yes, I am. And you? You always wanted to be a nanny?"

I laughed loudly. "No. I just kind of fell into that job. I want to be a teacher."

"And what is it like to work for the Buccini family? Are they as… scary as they say?"

I smirked and shook my head. Why does everyone keep asking me that? "It is okay. It has its… difficulties." I giggled at myself as the few cocktails I had drunk mixed with the memory of what happened today came to mind. "But they are not all scary, no."

He doesn't look convinced as he rocks his head to the side and shrugs. It was well past midnight, and at least seven cocktails down when the bar called last orders. I had found my new favourite drink, The Godfather, and I groaned into the glass, knowing it would be my last.

"We should go. It is a long walk back to the city," Luca slurred and held his hand out for me to take as I stood up from the chair a little unsteadily.

"What do you mean? Aren't we getting in one of those little tram thingys in the sky?" OK, I was drunk. I giggled at my words and Luca smirked.

"No bella, they are shut now. We must walk to the bottom and then get a taxi."

My face scrunched up in annoyance as I stopped walking and pulled my hand out of his. He turned and looked amused by my face.

"My name is not Bella. It's Liv. Have you forgotten?" I hissed at him and he burst out laughing.

"No. I have not forgotten. How could I forget your name? Bella means beautiful in my language."

Oh. Suddenly, a memory of Giovanni calling me that once sprang to mind and those butterflies were back.

"Oh. Well, I will let you off then," I said, stumbling towards him again.

"Okay," he smiled, placing my arm in the crook of his. We staggered awkwardly down the hill which was so steep and uneven as well as pitch black. The only thing that could be heard was the sound of our feet on the ground and the owls or were they bats in the trees?

I glanced up as Luca was telling me about a time he had visited England as a child and I saw a dark, broad figure approaching us up the hill. I narrowed my eyes but I couldn't see his face clearly. He was still too far away. His hands were inside the front pocket of a hoodie and the hood was over his head. I instantly looked down at the ground as I got a bad feeling about this guy. My immediate panic was that it was Henry. Coming to get me. But that was absurd. Luca seemed oblivious as he continued to ramble on about Big Ben.

I glanced back up as the man was only a metre away and he lifted his face to stare at mine. He looked menacing. Cold blue eyes and a scar on his left cheek.

He suddenly stopped in front of us and yelled something aggressively in Italian. Luca froze and his eyes were wide with fear. I looked from him to the man.

"Give him your bag, Liv," Luca whispered, the terror making his voice tremble. I narrowed my eyes and frowned.

"What! No!" I shouted. The man stepped forward and shouted in Luca's face again and Luca started rummaging in his pockets, passing him his wallet and phone.

The man turned and set his intimidating gaze on me. I swallowed.

"Give him your bag Liv, and he will leave us alone."

I clutched my handbag under my arm tighter, which made the man hiss. Suddenly, I remembered that I hadn't taken out all my belongings after work today. The Buccini keys to the mansion were in there, as well as the iPhone with Giovanni and Cecilia's numbers and the Mulberry purse with credit cards. Fuck! I could not handle all that low life scum.

"Liv!" Luca shouted as the man reached for my bag and tried to tug it from my shoulder. I fought against him, resulting in a tug of war and Luca tried to push the man off me. The mugger turned and head-butted Luca on the nose, causing him to fall backwards in agony. I saw red. I knew it was probably the alcohol that was making me believe I could take on a man who could easily crush me with his bare hands, but I clenched my fist and sent it flying into the man's face. He stumbled back but the look of rage that now took over his vile features made me scream. The next thing I knew, a brutal force connected with the side of my face and I fell to the ground. I was vaguely aware of the man grabbing my bag and the sound of his shoes on the dirt track, running away.

"Liv! Liv! Cazzo! Are you alright?" Luca ran over to me and pulled me up to a sitting position as he assessed my face. He had blood trickling out his nose and as I licked my lips, I tasted my own. Ow.

"That asshole hit me!" I growled and lifted my hand to my face, which was stinging like crazy. My lip was bleeding but I don't think too much damage was done, although from the look on Luca's concerned face, I wasn't so sure.

"Why did you not give the bag Liv?" he shouted, annoyed at me.

"Shit! The Bag! He's got it! Oh fuck! Oh no, I am in so much trouble!" I pulled myself up to my feet and looked around frantically.

"It is only a bag. Things can be replaced. You cannot," Luca tried to soothe my obvious anxiety.

"No! You don't understand. It had very important things in it! It had the security keys to the Buccini mansion!"

Luca's face paled slightly and his eyes widened. Yep. Now he understands.

"I have to go there! I have to warn them!"

"Now?" he shouted in disbelief.

I started to storm down the hill. "Where are we? Are we near the Buccini mansion?"

"It's about ten minutes that way," he pointed to the left, and I started to jog. He easily caught up with me and tried to grab my arm.

"Liv. You need to get checked over first. We both do. Tell them tomorrow."

I shook my head. If that man got into their house and did anything to those kids, it would be all my fault. I knew I would probably be fired over this. Oh yes, Cecilia will have my head and God knows what Giovanni will do, but I couldn't worry about that right now.

Sensing he wouldn't be able to change my mind, Luca remained silent, walking behind me as we approached the iron gates of the mansion. I pressed the intercom buzzer and waited. I could see two bulky men in black standing just inside the gates with guns strapped across their chests. It didn't even bother me anymore. I was used to it. Luca, on the other hand, looked like he was about to shit his pants.

"Si? Signorina Jones?" Mattio's confused voice bellowed over the speaker and I shuffled nervously on my feet.

"Hi Mattio. I need to speak to Mrs Buccini as a matter of urgency," I tried to hide the slur in my voice but ended with a hiccup giving away my intoxication.

There was a pause and I looked over my shoulder at Luca, who shrugged.

"Please wait a moment," Mattio replied curtly and the intercom cut out. That was weird. We waited for a couple of minutes but I was growing impatient. My head was spinning and the sting of my face was now a throbbing pain. What was going on? Why was it taking them so long to open the bloody gates? I glared at the two bodyguards who hadn't moved but were watching us both like hawks. Suddenly, over their shoulder, I saw a large, tall figure running down the driveway towards us. My heart started fluttering as I immediately knew who it was.

The gate slid open as he reached it and he squeezed through, his chest heaving slightly from running all the way down. His confused face looked over me carefully and soon turned to one of complete rage as he saw my cut lip and swollen cheek. His dangerous eyes snapped up at Luca and before I could stop him, he had a death grip around his throat, had lifted him off his feet and slammed him against the stone wall.

"Giovanni!"

Dr Jekyll And Mr Hyde

Giovanni

"Giovanni!"

Her small hands gripped my bicep trying to pry me off this little prick, but I had tunnel vision. He dared to lay a hand on her. I had never felt rage like it. I was going to kill him.

"Giovanni! Get off him! He is a friend! He didn't do this!"

My head whipped to the side as I took in her battered face covered in dried blood again and I didn't care who he was. I wanted someone dead and he just so happened to be at my mercy.

I glared back at the man who was turning the colour of a beetroot under my grip as his legs dangled above the floor and that's when I noticed he had blood on his face and a crooked nose. Dropping him without warning, he fell to his ass gasping for air, his hand around his throat. Olivia bent down to his level, her hand on his shoulder in comfort, which just added to my fury. She glanced up at me with her own anger evident in her eyes.

"What is wrong with you!"

"You!" I bent down and grabbed her upper arm, pulling her into me. "You are what is wrong with me."

Her eyes widened for a moment and then she burst out laughing. My eyebrows furrowed in confusion and my nostrils flared.

"Sorry but you just look so... *bossy!*"

I let go of her arm and she found her words hilarious, her dark eyelashes fluttering as she staggered on her feet. Fuck sake. She was drunk.

"What is going on? Who did this to you?" I growled, stepping closer to her in case she lost her balance.

"A low life scumbag! He mugged us on the street," she yelled in anger. My blood boiled at the thought of that happening to her. "But I am here because I have to tell you something. And your mum. You are in danger." Now it was my turn to look amused as she leaned into my chest with a serious expression and pointed her finger into my peck. "I had the mansion keys and iPhone and... Mulberry with all the cards. I tried to stop him but he took the lot."

I glanced up at one of my guards behind the gate and nodded to him to go and inform Mattio so we could put maximum security on the premises until we found this fucker. He had just picked the wrong woman to mess with.

"Who is he?" I snarled over her head and she turned to peer down at the man on the floor. I expect he is attractive when he doesn't have blood all over his face and wasn't shaking like a leaf.

"That's Luca. We were on a date," she said casually, and my whole body tensed. This is the guy she is dating?

He glanced up at me and the fear in his eyes was amusing.

"Why the fuck did you not protect her? Why is she hurt?" I hissed at him. If it wasn't for Olivia leaning so close to my chest right now, I would have had him by the throat again.

"I-I -it all happened fast," he stuttered, and Olivia glared up at me.

"Leave him alone! It wasn't his fault! And I can protect myself. I threw the first punch!"

My eyes widened in surprise as I peered into her green eyes, the gold speckles sparkling in the moonlight. That wasn't the point. She shouldn't have to protect herself! Inhaling and exhaling deeply to calm myself down, I wrapped my arm around her waist and started to drag her through the gate when I saw the car coming down.

"See that he gets home," I shouted over my shoulder to one of my men in Italian, who nodded and helped Luca off the floor.

"What are you doing? Where are we going?" Olivia started to struggle against me as she saw the gate closing behind us. I opened the car door and picked her up, placing her on the seat before scooting in myself. "Am I fired? I know I probably am, but can I at least say bye to the children tomorrow?"

I glanced out the window trying to ignore her drunk rambling and ran my hand over my stubble as I tried to control my emotions. I am so on edge right now. First that someone had hurt her. Second, that she was on a fucking date with some other guy. And third, because she was looking so fucking sexy in that lemon dress.

"Are you ignoring me now? Well, that's mature! Fine. I didn't want to talk to you anyway. I asked to see your mother, so take me to her and I will explain everything."

"How is it possible that you can give me a headache and an erection at the same time?" I snapped and her eyes widened before a smug smile spread across her face. I gazed back out of the window to avoid her temptation.

"It's a talent. I also have many other talents. Did you enjoy your blowy earlier? You looked like you were bored shitless."

Snapping my head to hers, I gave her a warning glare, "I'll kiss you if that's what it takes to shut you up!"

Her eyes widened and then narrowed at me. "No you won't. Because you said you would never kiss me until I told you I wanted you and you will be waiting a long time for that to happen *Sir*!"

My eyes darkened and she swallowed when she realised what she had called me. A mischievous grin crept up my face and she looked away.

"You sure as hell looked like you wanted me earlier...I could see in your eyes how much you wanted me." I smirked and she glared at me, a deep scarlet blush flaming over her cheeks. I couldn't help the chuckle that left my lips as she opened the door before shouting back into the car.

"You are such a pig!"

I climbed out after her, following her clumsy, heavy stomps into the house and up the first flight of stairs. She turned halfway up and raised her finger in my face.

"Has anyone ever told you that arrogance is the ugliest trait someone can possess?" Her words slurred slightly and she looked cute as fuck pointing her little finger at me. I sucked my bottom lip to suppress my laughter and she turned, marching back up the stairs. I followed her behind, keeping a little distance as I half expected her to try and slap me at this rate.

To my surprise, she started up the next set of steps towards my floor. I don't think she even realised where she was heading as she turned again halfway up to give me another earful.

"And just so you know, that little performance earlier was great foreplay for my date tonight, so I should be thanking you."

My jaw tensed at her words and jealousy consumed me as I watched her sexy ass swaying up the rest of the steps in that little dress. She had better not have let him touch her. I will lose my shit and right now, I am using more control than I have ever mastered in my life.

Taking a deep breath and closing my eyes, I paused before climbing the last few steps and following her into my office. She huffed down into an armchair and kicked off her shoes. Now in the bright light of my office, I could really see the state of her face.

"Wait here," I growled before storming into the bathroom and pouring some warm water into a bowl and grabbing a fluffy flannel. My hands trembled with anger as I turned the tap off. I would find whoever did this and I would kill him.

When I returned to my office, Olivia had helped herself to a glass of my whiskey. I took it from her hands and sat it on the desk before kneeling in front of her.

"Hey! I am drinking that! Do you have 'the Godfather'?"

"I think you have had enough!"

"There you go again. Mr control freak. Let me enjoy myself. I have earned it."

"And how exactly have you earned it?" I challenged, taking my frustration out on the flannel as I twisted all the water out of it.

"Well I..." She thought hard and then leaned her head back against the chair, staring up at the ceiling. "How much trouble am I in?"

Despite my inner rage and frustration, I felt a smile form on my lips.

"I'd say a lot."

Her head lifted and she stared straight into my eyes. For a moment, I forgot what I was supposed to be doing as I got lost in the beauty of them.

"Am I fired? Is that man going to break in or take all your money?"

I chuckled and looked down at the flannel, folding it into a square and placing it in my hand ready to clean her up.

"No bambola. But I do want you to tell me what he looked like and where you were," I was surprised by how soft and calm my voice came out. She creased her face, her little upturned nose wrinkling.

"What does bambola mean? You always call me that."

I smiled as I lifted the flannel to her cheek that was red and swollen.

"Doll."

She flinched as the cold flannel pressed against her skin and I kept my hand there holding it in place. My hand was nearly the size of her face, it was adorable.

"Doll? Why doll? You aren't from Texas!"

Chuckling, I shook my head.

"No I am definitely not. I am 100% Italian muscle." I winked at her and she rolled her eyes. My smile fell and my gaze became intense as I stared at her face. "You remind me of a doll my nonna loved. I always used to stare at it for hours as a child. It was so beautiful."

She visibly swallowed and I saw her eyes flood with heat. Removing the flannel from her cheek, I drenched it in the water again but could feel her penetrating gaze on me, watching my every move. Fuck I would love to know what she was thinking. To be able to get inside that pretty head of hers for just five minutes. She was an enigma to me. I never knew what she was going to say or do from one minute to the next. It was thrilling and irritating as hell.

"So what did he look like?" I leaned back up, pushing her knees apart and kneeling between them on the floor. I noticed her breathing change just from the small action and I fought my urge to smirk. Gently, I cleaned the dried blood off her chin and cheek.

"He was wearing a hoodie. Black one. He had blue eyes and was probably in his forties I think," she muttered, keeping her eyes glued on me. I nodded and slowly brushed the flannel against her cut lip.

"Anything else?"

"He had a scar on one side of his face and he was ugly." I smirked and nodded again.

"That's good and where were you?" My eyes flickered from hers to her plump lips under the flannel and back.

"We went to a bar on top of the hillside. I can't remember what it was called. We were walking back down the hill when the bar closed."

I knew exactly where she was talking about. That road was known as a crime spot as there were no streetlights or authorities around. It just made me more pissed at Luca for allowing them to walk down there so late at night.

"Are you going to call the police?" she asked and I gave her a cheeky smile.

"Something like that," I said, pulling my phone out of my pocket. I dialled Angelo's number. He was one of my best soldiers and would find this lowlife before the sun rises. Still perched between Olivia's legs, I held her gaze as I explained what had happened in Italian so she would have no clue that I was ordering him to find the fucker and bring him to me. I watched as desire and longing glimmered in her enchanting eyes as she listened to me speaking fluently in my native tongue. Turns out she wasn't lying when she said she loved the language. Hanging up the phone, she cleared her throat quickly and I placed the flannel back in the bowl. My rage subsided a little, seeing that the cut wasn't so bad and she would mainly have a small bruise on her cheek for a few days.

"Do I need to go down to the station and make a statement?"

I shook my head with a smirk. "No. You don't need to worry about any of it anymore. I have it taken care of."

She frowned, her brown eyebrows creasing into the bridge of her nose. I thought for a moment that she was going to fight me about this and try and get more out of me, but she said a simple thank you instead.

"Did you kiss him?" It was out my mouth before I even realised. Once again, that annoyed glare was back on her face.

"That is none of your business-"

"Did you kiss him?" I kept my voice slow and calm and tried to hide my anger from her, remembering who she thinks I remind her of. I couldn't change overnight though, and I needed to know. She held my gaze for a few seconds.

"No." I kept my face neutral but inside I was relieved and could feel the anger dispersing.

The atmosphere prickled with sexual tension as she leaned back in the chair, hands gripping the sides while I kneeled between her legs. My stomach was so close to her pussy, I could feel the heat radiating from it against my shirt. Fuck, I wanted her so badly. But nothing had changed. She was still her and I was still me.

"I- I think I should go home now," she whispered, but didn't make any attempt to move. I could see it in her eyes. She wanted me to make her stay. I placed my hands on her knees and slowly ran them up her thighs, inching her dress higher until I could see the whites of her panties.

"What are you doing?" her voice choked, thick with arousal.

"Just checking you are not hurt anywhere else," I husked. Her eyes widened as my hands went up under her dress and caressed her soft hips. Suddenly, I gripped them and pulled her closer to me, causing her to slide down the chair with a gasp. Now there was no denying that she was wet for me as I felt her heat rubbing against my stomach.

Her lips parted as she looked up at me through her thick eyelashes. "Do you still hate me bambola?"

My fingers continued to trace along her skin, waiting for her answer as her gaze burned into mine.

"Yes."

I stopped. I pulled down her dress and stood up from my position, walking over to the desk and downing the whiskey she poured herself. My body was on fire. I was so close to not giving a fuck and just taking her then and there, but I couldn't do it. Not until she stopped hating me. Not until she could separate me from him. Not for my sake, but because she would hate herself if she did.

When I turned back around. She was sitting up straight, with a look of pure thunder. She was fuming. Drunk and fuming Olivia. Not a fun combination.

"Come on. I am taking you home." I said sternly as I walked past her and opened the door.

She glared at me before standing up straight and pushing passed me. What did she expect? That I was going to pleasure her like the last time just for her to tell me how much she hated me again. I wanted her more than I have ever wanted anything in my life but I realised, for the first time ever, I wanted her to want me too.

She stomped down the steps to the bottom and I grabbed the keys to my Ferrari.

"This way," I muttered as she paused on the empty driveway. I needed a fast car. Once I had dropped her home, I was going to rev the shit out of it down the open roads to release my frustration. She tried to hide her surprise when I opened my blood orange metallic Ferrari door for her to climb into. Without giving me a second glance, she crawled in.

I sped through the empty streets of my city with only the purring of my engine between us. Olivia kept her gaze fixed on the window and I gripped the steering wheel so tightly, I thought my knuckles might pop out of my skin. The entire drive I fought a silent war in my head.

Going from wanting to turn the car around and make her mine. To give in to my desires and the overwhelming need to protect this woman. To care for her. But then the more cynical voice argued against it all. What would be the point? Where would this lead to? Heartache and misery on both our parts. I can never be the man she wants me to be. The man she deserves. She has already been through hell. How would it be fair to drag her into my world? And more to the point, she doesn't even want to. She can't stand me. I can't change who I am for her.

"It's just down this side street," she mumbled. I turned right and pulled up outside a pretty but shabby looking apartment block. Is this where she lives?

She unbuckled her seatbelt and panic rose in me. I hated this. I needed to say something. Anything. Do something to keep her in the car for just a few more minutes.

"You don't see me in colour," I blurted out and she turned her head, glancing up at me with a confused expression. What the fuck was I even saying? Well, I have started now. I need to keep going or I will look like I've lost the plot. Maybe I have.

"You see what you want to see when you look at me. Black and white. Yes. I am controlling, possessive, an asshole and dangerous to many. But that is only what I let the world see. I don't let many people in Olivia. I don't know how to. But you..." I sighed and ran my hand through my black hair, staring out the window. I couldn't look at her. Call me a coward, but once I look into her eyes, I will forget everything I am trying to say. "I want to let you see the other side of me. Or at least try to. I want you to know that I would never hurt you. I may be dangerous to many, but I will never be dangerous to you."

I glanced over and her sparkling eyes were wide with surprise. She didn't move or speak for a few moments and the silence stretched between us.

"Like Dr Jekyll and Mr Hyde," she mumbled and I furrowed my eyebrows. What is she going on about now? "The man with two personas." I smiled sadly and nodded my head. I guess she was pretty spot on with that assessment. "It didn't end well."

I burst out laughing as she smiled widely at my reaction. Just then, the little green door opened in front of us and that fucking soppy prick stepped out with a bandage on his nose. A girl stood next to him and stared at us both wide-eyed. My jaw flexed as I glared at the man who was trying to steal my girl. *My girl.* What was I even thinking?

"I better go," she said quietly, her hand on the door ready to free herself. She paused and looked over at me. "Thank you, Giovanni. For looking after me tonight."

My cold heart suddenly warmed and fluttered in my chest.

"I will always take care of you bambola."

Her lips parted and it took everything in me not to lean over and kiss her. "Don't make promises you can't keep." She gave me a small smile before stepping out of the car and walking over to her friends. I watched as Luca draped his arm over her shoulder affectionately as she walked through the door and I slammed my hand on the car horn, causing the loud beep to echo down the street. He jumped a mile, removing his arm immediately, and they all looked back round at me as I gave him my most menacing glare. Then my eyes softened as I took in Olivia's face. Was that a hint of a smile teasing at the edges of her lips?

"Goodnight Mr Hyde!" She shouted before closing the door of the building behind her. I couldn't help the enormous smile that was plastered on my face. My mind was made up. I didn't know how I would make it happen or care about how long it would take, but I had made my choice.

Olivia Bennett was going to be mine.

An Unlucky Man

Olivia

"Oh my god, are you alright Liv? I have been freaking the hell out since Luca came back and told me what had happened!" Gigi shouted as the three of us climbed the steps to the apartment.

"I am fine! Will you all just calm down!"

"What did Giovanni say? Was he mad? Did he fire you?" The questions came thick and fast from my roommate as I stumbled into the living room and flopped down on the sofa.

"No, I don't think so." I briefly closed my eyes as I tried to figure out exactly what had happened in the last hour, but all I could think about was his final words. *I will always take care of you, bambola.*

He seemed so...sincere. Like he really believed them. Like he meant them. But that was just crazy talk. Why the hell would he say something so...sweet? That wasn't him. Nice things don't come out of that man's mouth.

I opened my eyes as Gigi handed me a glass of water and I pulled myself up to a sitting position. A dull pounding was starting to ebb away in my temples like waves crashing onto the shore and I knew I needed to sleep it off.

"But was he mad? Luca said he was furious!"

I glanced up at my date who, to be honest, I had forgotten existed once I was in the company of Giovanni and he gave me a concerned look. I scoffed.

"He was mad at Luca, yes!" I gave Luca a wink to try and lighten the mood but his face remained strained. "But no. Surprisingly, he wasn't angry with me at all. He was...nice."

Gigi looked taken aback as she kneeled beside me on the floor. "Well, that is good. I guess," she gave me a supportive smile but I could tell that she wanted to say more. It was Luca that opened his mouth first.

"That man is dangerous, Liv. You saw what he did to me. You should get out of that place and away from him fast."

An immediate spark was ignited inside me. A strange feeling of irritation at his words. I instantly wanted to stand up for Giovanni even though the sensible part of me knew Luca was right. But the fire in me won.

"He only lost his mind because he thought you had hit me. He is not as bad as everyone thinks he is."

Gigi and Luca exchanged a look between them that made me even more annoyed. I hated people pitying me. Thinking I couldn't look after myself or make my own decisions. Standing up abruptly from the sofa, I started to walk towards my bedroom but paused. Remembering that I was technically on a date still, I couldn't be rude.

Luca's eyes widened slightly as I turned and kissed him on the cheek hastily.

"Thank you for tonight, Luca. I know it didn't end well but I did have a nice time. Although, I think for now, we are better off as friends."

He looked a little relieved as he gave me a small smile. "I had a good time too, you are lovely. But yes. I do not want a bullet in my head."

I cocked my head to the side, wondering what the hell he was talking about, until I realised he meant Giovanni. I chuckled and said good night to them both before walking to my room. I get that Giovanni scared the shit out of Luca tonight, but he would never actually shoot someone unless he was protecting his family. Would he?

***

The next morning, I chucked back my paracetamol with a glass of iced water and checked my appearance in the mirror. Yep. I looked rough. My eyes had that glassy, red-rimmed tell-tale sign that I had been up late and had had one too many cocktails coupled with my cut lip and slightly bruised cheek. I had smothered the foundation to hide it the best I could from the kids, but the faint outlines were still there. I traced it carefully with my fingertips, remembering the way Giovanni had cleaned and soothed it with a flannel last night. Now the alcohol had left my system and I had a clear vision, I realised just how surprising last night was. I saw a different side to him. Although his angry, demanding and threatening side was still on display, he was also gentle and kind. I expected him to be furious with me about what had happened but he only seemed concerned. And when he ran his muscular hands up my legs and under my dress, I melted at his touch. At that moment, all I wanted was to kiss him. To wrap myself around him and give in to it all. But he stopped. I hated how much it disappointed me and I felt rejected. Why did he stop? I vaguely remember him asking me something but it was hazy amongst the fog of lust that clouded my mind.

Grabbing my hair and pulling it on top of my head in a messy bun, I pulled a few strands out to frame my face. Smiling as I tried to replay as much of the conversation in his car as I could remember. He seemed so flustered and vulnerable, refusing to look at me when he said he wanted me to see him differently. It was kinda cute. That, although he admits he has a dark side, it is not always who he is. I wanted to believe him. In fact, I know I do believe him. But what that means for us…I still don't know.

All I do know is... he is not Henry. I can see that now. There is light behind his darkness. But is it enough for me to trust him? For me to let my guard down around him? I don't know. This suddenly felt too confusing. He was still my boss. He was still a cocky man. He was still a terrifying man, even though I believed him when he said he would never hurt me. But what exactly was he suggesting? As much as I wanted to find out what it would be like to give in to my desires, I knew I was playing with fire. How did I expect this to end? If I could resign myself to accepting it for what it would be; hot, mind-blowing monkey sex, then I could do it. But I know myself better than that. These complicated feelings would only grow. And no good could come from falling for a man like Giovanni Buccini.

When I arrived at work, I couldn't help the little flutter of excitement I felt at the possibility of seeing him today. I berated myself for feeling this way. I was here to do a job, not flirt with my boss. As I hung my jacket and bag up in the security room, Mattio, the head of the house's security, walked in briskly. He nodded at me once without cracking a smile. He was always so serious.

"Signorina Jones. Signore Buccini is waiting for you in his office. He would like to speak to you before you start work."

I swallowed my instant nerves. Shit. What was this about? What could I have possibly done in the last few hours to make him need to see me? Perhaps he has changed his mind. Perhaps he is going to fire me now that he has time to let it all sink in. Or maybe the police are here and need a statement from me.

Following Mattio up to the top floor, I fiddled with the elastic band on my wrist and started to pull at it. The elastic snapping back onto my sensitive skin, reminding me that I was okay. That this was real and I needed to stay calm. It was a strategy one of my counsellors suggested to help with my panic attacks. Forcing my hands to do something kept my mind focused and the feel of the elastic stinging my skin with each snap always helped me to remember that I was in control.

Mattio opened the heavy oak door for me and I walked in, my eyes scanning the room. First, I saw Giovanni sitting behind his desk. He slowly stood up and gave me a warm smile, but his eyes still ran over my body quickly and then over my face as if he was checking that I was okay. That was new.

As I stepped towards the chair, I realised we weren't alone. Turning my head, I saw another man sitting in one of the armchairs with his eyes cast down, hands in his lap which were visibly shaking. I froze. As the man lifted his head and peered up at me, I felt terror run through my body. Now I no longer had the courage of alcohol, facing those bright blue eyes again made me shiver. But I soon regained my composure when I realised that this man looked just as afraid, if not more, as he stared at me. In the light of day, he was nowhere near as scary as he looked last night. Long, dirty brown hair, blotchy skin and a deep scar running down his face. He just looked like someone who had fallen on life's hard times.

"Olivia. Please take a seat," Giovanni said, his tone softer than usual. I carefully dragged the chair further away from my mugger, not taking my eyes off him as I sat down.

"What is going on? Why is he here?" I managed to squeak and glanced over at Giovanni.

A slow, mischievous but oh so sexy smile crept up his face.

***

Giovanni

The low life street scum was shoved into my office with his hands cuffed and a black bag over his head. He was struggling against my men and cursing in our native language before he was forced down into one of the armchairs opposite my desk.

Angelo had tracked him down easily last night. He was a crackhead living on the streets and there was no loyalty among his people. They wouldn't think twice about ratting each other out for a little cash or a gram of coke. I leaned back in my padded, leather office chair, resting my elbows on its arms and clasped my hands together. I nodded to Angelo, who pulled off the hood in one swift action, causing the man to blink rapidly against the dawn that was seeping through my window. He was a fucking state.

His blue eyes narrowed as he looked around frantically and then widened when they fell on me. They suddenly filled with worry and I smirked.

"Where am I? Who are you?" he stuttered in Italian, but I didn't reply. Allowing the tension in the room to grow, I stared menacingly into this man's eyes. He was a pathetic excuse for a human. So consumed by his addictions, that he probably fucked over every single person who ever cared about him and has lost his way to the point that he goes around attacking women to get a bit of cash.

"I don't know anything! I haven't got anything. Please," he started to beg, and I held one hand up to silence him.

"Do you know Olivia Jones?" I asked calmly.

His face twisted with confusion as he shook his head violently. "No. No, I have never heard that name before. I swear."

"Ok. Let's try another one." I leaned forward, my visible forearms resting on my desk as I twisted my skull ring around my finger. "Do you know Giovanni Buccini?"

His mouth fell open and his blood-shot eyes filled with alarm.

"S- si..."

I smirked with evil intent and watched as the colour drained out of his face. He knew who I was.

"Good. There is no need for introductions then. Olivia Jones is someone who is very important to Giovanni. Very important to me."

Sweat started to bead on his forehead as his eyes darted around the room and back to me.

"I told you. I don't know her. There must be a mistake. What is this? Why am I here?"

"Last night... you attacked a couple on the streets. A man and a woman."

He swallowed slowly and his chest started to rise and fall with panicked breaths.

"Yes. I – I took their stuff. I needed money. I had a debt to pay and I- "

I lifted my hand again, not wanting to hear his lame excuses. "You make a habit of attacking women?" My tone was no longer flat but instead took on a sharp edge. He shook his head wildly.

"No – no... she hit me first. She wouldn't give me the bag! I hardly touched her!" I glared at him as his voice rose with every word, the fear evident. I felt rage and darkness slowly crawling to the surface but kept my control.

"That woman you hardly touched had a fat lip, bruised cheek and blood everywhere." He opened his mouth and closed it again. "That woman was Olivia Jones."

He whimpered when he saw the look of rage on my face.

"I- I'm sorry! I didn't know... I won't ever do it again. I swear... I will... I will do anything." He pleaded as the tears started to brim in his eyes.

I sighed heavily and cracked my knuckles, the vile sound filling the room. "You will apologise to her."

"Yes! Yes! Of course!"

"You will return all of her and the man's belongings."

"Your men already took them, sir. They have everything. I promise!" he whimpered and I nodded once. My phone rang and Mattio informed me that Olivia had arrived.

"Cut the ties," I ordered Angelo, who walked over and pulled a knife out to release the man's wrists from the cable ties. "You will not move or speak to her until I command it or you will not leave this room alive," I snarled, ending our Italian conversation before Olivia arrived and he nodded in understanding.

The door opened and Olivia strolled in looking as beautiful as ever. The cut and bruises were masked by her make-up, but you could still see it faintly and a knot formed in my stomach. I gripped the edge of my desk to hide my fury and tried to give her a reassuring smile. She looked nervous.

Her eyes fell onto the man who had done this to her, and she paled slightly but quickly composed herself. I was surprised once again by her reaction. I half expected her to scream or cry or get upset. That would be an understandable reaction to be faced with someone who had attacked you, but she remained calm and composed. My heart swelled with pride as she pulled the chair further away from him, glaring as she sat down. She was my tough bambola.

"What is going on? Why is he here?"

"He is here because he owes you an apology. Don't you?" I glanced over at the man who was now trembling like a leaf and he nodded his head slowly. "Look her in the eyes when you express your sincere regret."

He lifted his head and stared straight at her.

"Sorry miss. For what I did," he spoke in slow, deliberate words, clearly English was not his strongest language and he was trying to find the words. "I need money. I did not mean hurt on you."

I groaned. That was not an ideal apology, but as she looked up at me, I saw a small smile play on her lips. She didn't speak but I knew she appreciated what I had done.

"He has given back your bag and all its contents as well as Luca's phone and wallet," I explained. I knew that was what she was most worried about. The security of my family and the thought made me warm. She nodded once.

"What is going to happen now?" she asked, looking from him to me.

"That is up to you. Police or let him go," I said calmly. I watched as she bit at her bottom lip and thought hard. She looked so fucking cute.

"You decide," she said quietly and stood up. "I don't care enough about this man to make that decision."

I nodded, "Ok. You can go to work now and I will be joining you all for breakfast in a few minutes."

Those gorgeous eyes showed her surprise, but she just nodded before turning and leaving the room.

I lowered my head as I leaned my hands on my desk and took in a deep breath. The room pulsed with anticipation as the man waited to hear my verdict on whether I would let him walk out of here or throw him in jail.

Standing up, I stretched my neck out either side, prolonging his torture, and then took calculated steps towards him. His pleading eyes gazed up at me.

"You are a very unlucky man my friend." I said, glancing out the window as the sun started to shine brightly over the horizon. "You could have picked anyone else to mug last night and you would have mercy. But you chose her. And no one fucks with her."

He gasped in terror as I swiftly pulled my silent capped Glock 19 out from the back of my trousers and pulled the trigger. Life drained out his eyes as the blood poured from the hole in his head down his face. I felt the darkness that had consumed me since I saw her battered face slowly leave my body and I inhaled deeply. He was never going to leave this room alive.

"Clear this up and be discreet," I ordered Angelo, who nodded as I walked out of my office and made my way downstairs for breakfast.

Unforgettable

Olivia

"So, what does the day have in store at the school of Olivia?" Cecilia asked as she picked apart her croissant. I don't think she had actually put more than a crumb in her mouth since we had all been sitting at the grand dining room table. The children would always start the day by having breakfast with their mamma. There had only been a handful of times when Marco had informed me it was not one of her good days and it was just us. But Giovanni had never come for breakfast before. He was normally out of the house before the kids were dressed and ready.

"Ooo, can we play that game again? The one where you hide, and I count!" Raya chirped excitedly from her booster chair. I smiled at her growing confidence.

"Hide and seek? Of course. Raya is very good at hiding from me," I winked, and Cecilia smiled affectionately at her daughter as she lifted her coffee to her lips. "But first we will do some reading and learn our numbers to 100. Then, later, we will play football!"

Sani's eyes lit up and he punched the air dramatically. I had quickly learnt that Sani was extremely fond of three things: racing cars, football and his brother.

"Sounds like a wonderful day," Cecilia smiled at her children, but I noticed it didn't reach her eyes. She had seemed a little out of sorts the last few days. Since that incident between her and Giovanni's uncle the night of the club. I wanted to ask if she was okay, but I wasn't sure it was my place. She had made it quite clear that I wasn't to speak a word of it to anyone and she was acting like it had never happened, so I guess she didn't want to discuss it.

"And you? Do you have any plans?" I asked politely, but really, I was worried about her. I had no idea what it was she did all day long when she didn't come and spend some time with the children. She chuckled sadly.

"Oh, there is plenty for me to do. I am rushed off my feet. In fact, I was just thinking that perhaps I should book a holiday soon. A little get away," she said quietly as she stared into her coffee mug, she held between two hands.

"Great minds think alike, mamma."

Urgh. That voice. Why does it have such an effect on me? My whole body stood to attention and my heart fluttered before he had even come into my eyeline. Keeping my eyes glued to my croissant like it was the most interesting thing I had ever seen; I could feel his heated gaze on me. He was being too nice today. It was unsettling.

"What do you mean?" Cecilia asked as he took a seat at the head of the table.

"We are going to France. We fly out in two days," he replied coolly. My eyes flickered up to stare at him. I couldn't help it. Something in my stomach dropped. Was he going away? For how long? Hang on. Why did I care? This should be a relief. I would finally get the peace and space I had so desperately wanted.

"We?" Cecilia had put her untouched breakfast down and was looking a little unsure.

"Yes. We. All of us."

I coughed loudly as a piece of buttery pastry got caught in my throat and they all stared at me with concern as I flapped my hand apologetically. Surely, he didn't mean *all* of us. Cecilia must have been thinking the same thing as she repeated her question.

"We as in the whole family?"

"Si Mamma and Olivia."

OK, now I really was choking. I grabbed my glass of water and started taking urgent gulps to try and dislodge my breakfast. Placing the glass back down, I stared at him from across the table in disbelief.

"What?" I managed to choke out.

He leaned back in his chair with an amused smirk.

"What is wrong with everyone this morning? Are you all hard of hearing? Yes. We are all going to France. Mamma and I have some business to attend to, so I thought why not take the opportunity to stay in our ski lodge in the Alps for a long weekend? Raya has never been, and Sani was barely walking, let alone skiing the last time we went."

Cecilia's face radiated with glee as her eyes shone brightly. She leaned over the table, grabbed her son's face in her hands and gave him a massive kiss on the cheek. Giovanni merely chuckled lowly and shook his head as she released him. I was still sitting with my mouth hanging open in shock.

"Are we going on holiday? All together? And Liv?" Sani shouted excitedly and Giovanni nodded, a huge, satisfied smile on his face as he popped a grape into his mouth. His eyes found their way to mine, and he winked. Oh, dear lord. I cannot go on holiday with this man. I can barely be in a room with him for more than a few minutes without wanting to strangle him or kiss him.

"I can't go. It sounds…lovely but I don't think it necessary for me to come on a family holiday," I said quickly, causing his smile to fade.

"Nonsense! I need you there! Like Gio said, we will need to do some business, so someone will need to be around to watch the kids. Have you ever been skiing, Olivia?" Cecilia looked about twenty years younger, the way she beamed at me and her eyes twinkled. Gone was the gloom and sadness they held only ten minutes ago.

"No but – I –" I stumbled over my words, wracking my brain to come up with some brilliant excuse.

"You have another date? With your boyfriend?" Giovanni cocked his head to the side playfully and sat back with mischief in his eyes. He hadn't told his mother about what had happened last night, which I was grateful for or maybe he had, but she had politely ignored the small bruise on my face. Who knows with this family?

I narrowed my eyes at this infuriating man. How can I go from actually thinking he was a decent human being from the way he handled the situation with that mugger this morning to finding him so irritating I wanted to stab him in the eye with my fork?

"Maybe I do."

His dark eyes hardened but he kept that shit-eating grin on his face, calling my bluff. "I very much doubt that bambola."

I felt my heart flutter at hearing him call me that again. After last night and his confession as to why he calls me doll, I have to admit, I liked it. Not that I would ever tell him that.

I scoffed loudly, "What is that supposed to mean?"

"The man has more sense than to take you on another date. Trust me," he smirked, and I folded my arms across my chest.

"Did you find a prince Liv?" Sani startled me with his interruption and brought us both back into the room, reminding us of the fact that we had an audience to our bickering. Giovanni chuckled as he reached for another grape and I peered down at Sani, giving him my best fake smile.

"No one as worthy as you Sani," I ruffled his hair and he grinned. Once again, I felt Giovanni's penetrating gaze on me, but I refused to look his way. Instead, I glanced up to see Cecilia leaning back in her chair, her curious eyes darting between Giovanni and me.

"Well, I don't know what that was all about and nor do I wish to, but it is in your contract, Liv, that you will need to attend holidays or trips that the children go on," she smiled sweetly, but her eyes were stern. She was really saying, I didn't have a choice.

"Well, I understand that Cecilia, but I haven't actually signed the contract yet. I was hoping to speak to you about that today," I said in a hushed tone, hoping the children and Giovanni wouldn't hear. No such luck. I saw Giovanni sit up straighter in his chair from the corner of my eye.

"You haven't signed the contract?" His voice was dominant and serious. All his previous mischief and playfulness had evaporated.

I sighed and turned my head to him. "That is what I just said."

"Why not?"

"I wish to speak to your mother about this matter," I replied curtly and watched his strong jaw muscles flex in annoyance.

"Then let's talk, my dear. Later. I need to go and take my medication first. I will come and find you," she smiled down at me as she stood. "I am very excited about our trip, Giovanni. I must start packing right away. You must invite Elle too and she can attend that museum she wants to go to! I have a feeling that this may be a trip to remember!"

Giovanni locked eyes with me as a slow, sadistic smile played on his lips. "Trust me. I will make it my mission to ensure it is unforgettable."

Fuck.

***

It was lunchtime before I saw Cecilia again. Standing in front of the kitchen sink, I started to wash up everything I had used to make the children's lunch as they sat at the kitchen island, happily munching away. I had a perfect view of the outdoor swimming pool from here, which was one of the reasons I was so keen to do the washing up today. Ok. That was a lie. That was the only reason.

There in the pool was the sexiest specimen of the male form I had ever seen in my life. Gliding through the water with grace and agility and, not to mention, power in each of his strokes, Giovanni was putting on quite a show. Obviously, he had no idea I was watching him, and he was just doing his own laps for fitness, but I wasn't complaining. I am pretty sure I have washed the same plate three times over, as I haven't been able to peel my eyes away from his rippling back muscles or that very firm, tight ass in those swimming shorts. Thank God it was a skiing holiday and not a beach resort this weekend. I don't think my libido could handle seeing him like this every day.

"He could have been in the Olympics, you know? If he had stuck at it," A whimsical voice sounded from over my right shoulder and I jumped, dropping the plate into the bubbly sink of water, causing a splash to soak my face and top. I gasped and a small giggle came from the woman who had sneaked up on me and shamelessly saw me perving on her son.

"Sorry, I didn't mean to startle you," her voice was laced with laughter, and I felt my cheeks flaming with embarrassment. "You know we have people who will do that for you? You do not need to clean up."

"It's okay. I really don't mind." *Well, today I don't mind.* "Did you say the Olympics?"

"Yes. He swam every day until he turned sixteen and his hormones got in the way of his talent. Swimming was no longer cool then. He was more interested in teenage boy things and so he let it go to waste. His coach was extremely pissed, as was I. But what can you do?"

I smiled at her and allowed my eyes a quick glance over to see him effortlessly somersault at the end of the pool to push off the wall and start a new lap. He was good. Of course he was. I bet there is nothing this man can't do. Another reason to add to my list of why he is so annoying.

Yes. That is what it has come to. Having to keep a mental list of all the reasons I should ignore this insane pull towards this desirable man. It was getting harder and harder each day. No, each hour, minute, second.

"So, the contract. You wanted to discuss it?" She leaned against the kitchen unit and regarded me patiently.

"Yes. I am extremely grateful for the position and the...um...generous salary but there are a few conditions I wondered about and whether they could be tweaked?"

She kept her face passive as I spoke, allowing me to continue.

"It said that I had to sign a non-disclosure agreement. That I wouldn't share any information about the family outside of the premises. What does that really mean and why? Is it like a confidentiality agreement because I would never discuss Sani or Raya to anyone outside of work and – "

She placed her hand on my forearm to silence my babbling. "Yes and no. It is like a confidentiality agreement, yes. But it is for the whole family and everything you may hear or see behind these walls."

My eyebrows furrowed. "I don't understand."

"It is just a precaution, my dear. We cannot have important information about our businesses leaked outside of this house. I am sure you have heard rumours around the Buccini name. Well, we like to keep them exactly that. Rumours." She gave me a pointed glare and I gulped. It was a warning. Anything that happens inside this household must stay behind these walls. I wasn't really sure how to respond to that, so I decided to move on to the next question I had.

"The contract says it is for a year. Cecilia, I wasn't intending to stay in Italy for a whole year," I said quietly, so the children didn't hear. She blinked slowly a few times, deep in thought.

"I see. How long were you intending to stay?"

I hesitated. I wasn't sure. I can't exactly say until my murderous stepbrother is found and put in prison and I am safe to return to my previous life.

"I don't know. I don't really have a plan, but to sign up to stay for one whole year is quite a big deal. I hope you are not offended."

She smiled at me sweetly. "Not at all. I understand. It is a big commitment. How about this... You can sign the contract for a year, but I will remove the clause that says it is binding. If you decide to leave, just give us two weeks' notice and that will be sufficient."

I was a little taken aback by her kindness. I expected her to be a little harder to sway on these terms.

"That is very kind. Thank you."

"So, will you sign? And come with us to France?" she looked at me hopefully and I nodded once with a small smile. She clapped her hands excitedly and did a little jig on the spot. I couldn't help the giggle that escaped my lips at seeing her so youthful and happy.

I turned when I felt his presence and my laughter immediately stopped. Oh lord have mercy...

Giovanni was standing in the kitchen wearing only his dripping wet swimming shorts that stuck to his skin and his...uhm... substantial package. So, he was gifted in that department too. Just great! Droplets of water zigzagged down his ripped torso and he had a towel hanging around his neck loosely. His mischievous eyes were fixed on me, and I swear I nearly moaned out loud at the sight of him.

"Giovanni! You are dripping all over my floor!! You are soaking wet!!" Cecilia raced towards him, pushing his gigantic back to guide him out the door.

"I'm not the only one..." he smirked and raised his eyebrows at me before strolling out of the room with an arrogant swagger.

For the first time, I had to admit he wasn't wrong...

Locked Away

Giovanni

I was having a great day!

I had timed everything perfectly. I knew the kids' schedules like the back of my hand now, so putting off my morning swim until lunch would mean Olivia would be in the kitchen with a front seat view of my workout. I could feel her eyes on me as I propelled myself through the water as powerfully and skillfully as I could. Yes. I was showing off. Course I fucking was. But the look on her face when I strolled into the kitchen dripping wet and out of breath was priceless. It told me everything I needed to know... She was just as affected by me as I was by her. Now I can really start to put my plan into action.

Now I knew about her stepbrother and why she had been putting up a cement wall around her, I knew what I was doing wrong. For the first time in my life, relying solely on my good looks and arrogant charms was not going to work. I was going to have to actually work hard for a woman's affections. But Olivia would be worth it.

The idea of France came to me last night on my drive back from dropping Olivia home. It would be the perfect opportunity to show Olivia a different side to me. The side that only my family knew. If I was away from work, away from responsibility, I could let go. Or so that was the plan. I have never actually tried to consciously switch off being a gangster before. It was a part of me. But I knew here, in this environment, it was the most dominant part of me. I had to find a way of letting Olivia see that it wasn't always who I was. That around her, I would be different. And the only way I knew how to do that was to be around my family.

Of course, I was still going to flirt outrageously, torture her with seduction and tease her until she cannot take it anymore, because that is who I am. I enjoy it. I enjoy making her squirm. I love seeing how much she wants me but is fighting so hard against it. It will make it even more satisfying when she finally gives in to her needs.

"Has she signed the contract?" I asked mamma over my shoulder, as she pushed me down the lobby away from the kitchen.

She rolled her eyes. "No, but she will. She has a strong head on those shoulders of hers and she is sensible. She doesn't want to sign for a year."

I paused and turned around. "Why not?"

"She doesn't know how long she is going to be in Italy for. I get the impression it is not permanent, and she doesn't want to make it so."

My mood shifted immediately. For some reason, the thought of her leaving or returning to England caused an alien feeling to bubble in my stomach. But what was I really expecting? That she loved it here so much that she would live here forever? That she would work for us forever? I hadn't really thought about it, but now I was faced with it, I didn't like how it was making me feel.

"What did you say?" Mamma's brown eyes were assessing me carefully. She knew me better than anyone. Maybe even more than I knew myself. I knew I couldn't hide my obsession with Olivia from her for much longer, but I just wasn't sure how she was going to react. She had warned me not to sleep with her, but technically I didn't.

"That I would remove the clause about it being binding and make it a flexible contract. As long as she gives two weeks' notice, she can leave when she wants."

Fucksake. For a persuasive woman, that was a shit agreement!

"Why did you do that? You know you could have persuaded her to sign for a year, mamma!"

She tilted her head to the side as she folded her arms and a slow smile spread across her face. "Yes, I could have. But I want her to want to stay because she chooses to. Not because she is forced to."

Her eyes burned into mine and it felt like she was trying to send me some kind of message through her words.

"And what if she decides to leave? We will be back to square one with childcare."

Mamma shrugged and placed one hand on my damp arm. Looking deeply into my eyes, she whispered, "Then you will just have to give her a good enough reason to want to stay..."

Me? She walked away quickly to her office, leaving me standing in the lobby staring after her. Did she just say I had to make her stay? Was she just giving me permission to sleep with Olivia? I shook my head in disbelief. That woman was as much a mystery to me as Olivia.

Taking steps up to my floor, I had a quick shower and got dressed for the day. On entering my office, I could see my phone flashing red, meaning I had a number of missed calls. Pressing the button, the room filled with the thick, deep Italian voices of my men all wanting my immediate attention. Maximus about a knife fight between two soldiers in his regime that had had a heated argument; Leo reporting that the Leone's were making a new deal with a Southern mafia family that would bring them millions and strengthen their position; and then last, my zio. He was brief and frank as always.

"Giovanni. Call me."

Huffing down into my leather chair, I decided to work my way backwards. Salvatore is not someone you could keep waiting, and he would already be pissed that I wasn't here to answer his call.

He answered on the third ring.

"Si."

"Boss, it's me. You called."

"Why have I just been informed by Toni that you have booked the larger private jet to take you to France this weekend? I was planning on using that to fly in the Knowles for a business meeting."

I sighed, "Sorry Boss. I hadn't realised. I am taking the family with me to France and need to take the larger plane."

There was a pause. "Why?"

I knew he wouldn't let this drop. "Mamma needs it. She has not been so good recently and some time with her children away from this place will help."

Another long silence. There was some truth behind my excuse. I had been noticing the signs that she was struggling again the last few days and I know that spending time together as a family will help remind her how much she has to live for. But from a selfish point of view, it wasn't the only reason I was taking the family.

"I see. You can have the jet. I expect you have heard about Leone's new alliance. When you get back, we are sitting down and discussing the agreement with the Aianis. You have had enough time," his voice was stern and dominant. I ran my hand down my face.

"Agreed."

He hung up and I placed the phone back on the receiver. I had been trying to block that situation out of my mind as much as possible. I knew that this was an extremely important alliance, and my hands were pretty much tied, but I couldn't get Olivia out of my head. I couldn't marry another woman. Not when Olivia was in my life. I just needed to figure out what this was between us and if she could ever feel the same way about me as I do about her. But time was not my friend.

Lifting my phone, I dialled Max's number.

"Fratello!"

"Max, please tell me you have sorted out your own fucking shit?"

"Si. Nessun problema! I just wanted to keep you in the loop, that's all."

I sighed and leaned back on my chair. "Good. You are old enough that I shouldn't need to hold your hand anymore."

"Fuck off asshole. You know I have been secretly running this ship for years," his deep chuckle put a smile on my face. Max was a very clever man. We had an inside joke between us where together we would openly have 'innocent conversations' in front of Toni and play them off like it was banter, but within a week or so, our zio would announce his new business idea or interest. He had no idea that most of them were coming from Max.

"Listen. I am taking the family to France for a few days. I am leaving you in charge of holding the fort until I am back. Can you come and stay at the mansion?"

"Course man. Anything for you, fratello. Is that little minx going with you?" he teased.

"Well, I am not leaving her here with you, so what do you think?"

He laughed loudly. "Good move."

I hung up the phone and opened my drawer to grab the folder on the French business deal to go over some notes. As I lifted it out, I noticed Olivia's file below. I hadn't looked at it again since that night. There was more to read but it felt somehow wrong now. Now I had decided to try and earn her trust and respect. I wanted her to be the one to tell me about her past. About why she was here and what she was really running from. It would be too easy for me to read it all in her file and then use it to my advantage to make her mine. I may be a fucking monster, but I still have morals deep down in the depths of my dark soul.

Closing the drawer, I opened the French file and started to read the business proposal. Olivia's past would remain safely locked away until she was ready to share it with me. When that day comes, it will mean more to me than she will realise.

It will mean she will be mine.

Dreams

Cecilia

I can't remember the last time I felt this excited! The cabin was one of my favourite places in the world. Vinny and I bought it after we took a skiing holiday in Courchevel in the French Alps and fell in love with the place. We wanted to make it a family tradition to take the children every year and teach them how to ski. Gio and Elle grew up with it as a second home, but we haven't been back since Vinny died. It was always him who would suggest we go and without him around, it just never happened.

There is a sadness festering in me that this will be the first time I will be back there without him, but I know I am ready. I am strong enough to handle it now and my excitement at having the family together for a mini vacation outweighs the pain. But something else is making me even happier... Giovanni! He is changing. I can see it already. He had never thought of taking the family away since he had become an underboss. It has always been work, work, work. Yet here we are. This was his idea, and he is just as excited as me, I can tell. Although his excitement, I feel, has much more to do with a little British firecracker than the vacation itself. I cannot help but feel a little smug right now. Mamma always knows best.

Packing the last few items into my suitcase, I stood back, hand on hip and tried to work out if I was missing anything.

"Signora Buccini, the jewellery from the safe you requested," Lucinda placed my expensive rings and necklaces on the bed in their velvet cases. I opened the Cartier box to reveal the most beautiful, platinum emerald cut diamond ring. It had been Vinny's mother's, the crazy lady, and she had left it to Giovanni in her will. I was a little pissed off, I'll be honest. It was the most gorgeous thing she owned, and I'd had my eye on it for years. But the old bat left it for my son along with her creepy China doll. I never understood it and nor did Gio. He gave it to me, knowing how much I loved it, but I have never allowed myself to wear it. It wasn't meant for me. It was meant for her. Olivia.

I smiled as I picked it out of the box carefully and admired its beauty. My mother-in-law and I rarely saw eye to eye, but on this...she did well!

"I will only need this one, Lucinda. The rest can be returned to the safe."

She nodded, picked the other boxes up and left the room. I knew I was jumping the gun here, but I wanted to make sure I had this ring on me so that whenever the time was right to give it back to Gio, I could. If she is the right girl for him. He will know why I have returned it to him.

My phone started vibrating on the bed and I answered it with a beaming smile. My beautiful daughter.

"Elle!"

"Mamma! Am I dreaming? Is this really happening?"

I chuckled at her dramatics. She was always the eccentric one in the family. Artsy, creative, vibrant and full of life. She could never be held down in one place for more than five minutes and I knew this lifestyle grated on her more than the rest of us. She craved her freedom. Normality. It is not her fault. She was born into this lifestyle and although it comes with glitz and glamour, it also comes with danger and the feeling of being trapped.

"So, you are joining us?"

"Of course!! Gio called me last night! And listen to this, he even said I could go to the art exhibition with only two undercover soldiers! Did he have a brain transplant or something?"

Walking over to my bedroom window, I smiled as I looked out over the immaculate lawns. "Let's just say, I think we will be seeing much more of the old Gio from now on."

There was a slight pause at Elle's end.

"Mamma..." her tone was accusing, which made me grin even wider. "What have you done?"

"Nothing. I haven't done anything, my love."

"This doesn't have anything to do with Liv, does it?"

When I didn't respond, I heard her sigh loudly.

"Mamma, are you sure about this? She doesn't even know who we really are! What do you think is going to happen when she finds out? And this is just an infatuation for Gio. He will drop her once she no longer interests him, and I feel bad for the girl. She doesn't deserve that. I really like her."

"My love. Please, I know what I am doing and trust me, Gio is different with her. She is the one with all the power and he doesn't even realise it. She will bring him back to us, Elle. I know it."

I could feel her doubt through the phone. "Mamma, have you taken your meds today?"

My smile fell and I immediately felt aggravated. "Yes," I replied curtly.

"It's just you seem a little...manic," she said carefully, and I rolled my eyes even though she couldn't see.

"Can't I just be happy and hopeful about the future without everyone thinking I am having an episode?" My tone was sharp, and I heard Elle take a breath in.

"Sorry mamma. I just worry about you. But if you say this is good for

Gio, then I trust you. Just try to be gentle with Liv. I know she seems strong but there is more going on with her beneath it all. I would hate to see her get hurt."

"I am looking out for her. Don't you worry."

"Ok. Well, I won't be arriving until Saturday so I will see you then!" Her voice was back to its natural jolly tone, and I smiled again.

"Ciao darling. I love you."

"Love you mamma."

I hung up the phone, as there was a knock on my door and I turned to see Giovanni leaning against the door frame, looking devilishly handsome.

"Are you ready, mamma? I have the cars waiting out front?" His face was blank, but his beautiful brown eyes danced with excitement. I walked towards him, lifting my hands to cup his face and pulled him to my lips, giving him a big kiss. When I released him, he was looking a little confused but smiling. "What was that for?"

"For this trip. You have no idea how much it means to me. To all of us, Gio."

"It will be fun," he smiled down at me. "But if it is too much... being there again. Will you tell me?" His face creased with concern, and I stroked his cheek.

"I will be fine, my love. It is time. But yes, I will tell you."

He nodded once, happy with my response. "Well, let's move then. Do you know what time Olivia is expecting us to get her?"

"Oh, she's not. She said she would meet us at the airport. She didn't want to be a burden."

His gorgeous features scrunched up and his eyebrows furrowed as he stood taller. "I will go and get her and meet you all at the airport."

I kept my face neutral and nodded as he walked away from my bedroom. As soon as he was out of sight, I smiled widely and flipped open the Cartier ring box. Yes. She was the one for sure.

***

Olivia

"Gigi, I can't take all this stuff! I am going for four days!" I stared down at my little suitcase that was full of Gigi's outfits that she insisted I cram in just in case. "I am not going to need bikinis for a start. We are skiing!!"

"Haven't you seen all those women skiing in bikinis in the snow on Instagram?" She sat on top of my suitcase with a grin. My face dropped and I must have looked mortified because she burst out laughing.

"I am only joking! But I bet they will have a hot tub or pool at the resort.

Like I said, it is better to be prepared! Now help me zip it up."

I groaned as I leaned forward and pulled the zip round as Gigi jumped up and down on the lid to make it easier for me. If I am honest, I am not really sure what is in this bag as Gigi ended up shoving half her own wardrobe in there when she saw how little I had to take. I had been meaning to go shopping with my new pay cheque, but I just haven't made the time.

Standing upright, I glanced at myself in the mirror as the nerves started to cause those pesky butterflies to surface once again. I had borrowed a pair of high waisted wide leg trousers that were elegant but comfy from Gigi and matched them with an orange and cream striped crop top. It was a boiling day here and I had no idea what the temperature would be like in France, but I couldn't wear more than this right now. I was starting to sweat even though the little crappy apartment fan was blowing hot air into my face, and I was fussing with the strands of dark hair that were falling down from my high ponytail. "Oh my god, is it just me or is it stifling today?"

Suddenly, the flat door buzzed, and we both looked at each other in confusion. The taxi shouldn't be here for at least another twenty minutes. "Expecting anyone?" I asked and Gigi shook her head. She jumped up from the suitcase and walked out of my bedroom to answer it.

"Ciao, is Olivia here?" I froze when I heard that voice that I would recognise anywhere. The one that sent immediate heat through my body. Now I am really sweating. What the fuck was he doing here? Was the trip cancelled?

"Si. Come in. You must be Mr Buccini. It's...er...nice to meet you. Liv has told me so much about you."

OH. NO. She didn't just say that! I walked out of the bedroom to quickly intervene before she said anything else incriminating.

"Giovanni. Please. And all good things I hope," he winked, and Gigi practically melted into a puddle, her eyes all big and doey.

"What are you doing here?" I asked bluntly, trying to ignore how bloody good he looked in his casual white T-shirt that clung to his muscles and black jeans. His dark eyes met mine and he gave me that sexy lopsided smirk. Gigi glared at me wide-eyed, probably for greeting him with so much hostility.

"I've come to take you." He said seductively and my core tightened, "To take you to the airport," he clarified, amused by my shocked reaction.

"I told Cecilia I could make my own way there. I have a taxi coming," I folded my arms across my chest and Gigi nudged me with a 'what the fuck are you doing' look on her face.

"Cancel it. I am here now," he smiled, and I scoffed. This was it. He was trying to set the tone for the whole trip. He was in control, and I had to go along with everything he said. Well, I wouldn't make it so easy for him.

"It's too late. They will charge me."

"I will pay the charge."

"I don't need you to do that."

"Then you can pay the charge."

"And come with you instead?"

"Yes."

"Thank you, but I am more than capable of getting to the airport myself."

"I am sure you are. But like I said, I am here now. So, you have two choices. Walk down the stairs yourself or I'll carry you. I am pretty sure you are just arguing with me because you want to be over my shoulder again. I know how much you enjoyed it the other night."

I clenched my jaw and felt Gigi's amused and shocked face flicking between Giovanni and I as we bickered back and forth. His alluring eyes danced with humour as he knew he had me. He was not bluffing, and I would kill him if he tried that move on me again.

"Fine. I will go with you. If you are really too eager to carry something, my suitcase is in the bedroom."

He chuckled deeply and bowed his head before walking past me into my bedroom. As soon as he was out of earshot, Gigi grabbed my arm and started her frantic rambling.

"Oh, my fucking god Liv. You two are fire! The sexual tension in the air is making me horny! You have to sleep with him! Just imagine how good it would be. How have you not already? You are a bloody saint!"

I ignored her as I slipped my feet into my shoes, holding onto the edge of the dining table for support.

"Honestly Liv, if you don't sleep with him on this trip, I am going to be so fucking disappointed in you girl! He is so much better looking in real life too! And have you seen the size of him? He could chuck you around that bedroom like a rag doll!"

"Gigi! Shut up," I growled, keeping my eyes on the bedroom door.

"You've been saying you need to get laid. Now is the perfect chance!"

"He is my boss! Will you shut it!"

"I am not telling you to fall in love with the man! Just fuck his brains out!"

"No chance of that happening. I would rather stick a pin in my eye!"

"Then fall in love or sleep with him?"

"Both!" I glared at her and she shook her head.

"Liar!"

Just at that moment, Giovanni came strolling out of the bedroom with my suitcase and handbag in tow. He had that smug grin plastered on his face once more and he nodded to Gigi before turning to me. "Ready?"

"Yes."

"Nice to meet you Giulia. I will take very good care of her. Don't worry."

"Please do!" She grinned and gave me a wink behind his back which made me roll my eyes.

At this point, I am just convinced some people were just put on this Earth to test my patience and sanity!

When we got outside, I was surprised to see one of his Ferrari's and a black SUV parked behind it. They were already getting a lot of attention from the passersby on the street, and I felt embarrassed as they all started whispering when they saw Giovanni and I climb into his Ferrari. I was so busy looking out of the window at them all that I jumped a mile when I felt Giovanni leaning over me. His face was inches from mine and my senses were invaded by his peppery and masculine cologne and minty breath. My eyes widened in alarm and my heart started thundering. Then I heard a click. He smiled and moved back as I realised he had put my seatbelt on for me.

"Safety first," he smirked as he turned the engine on and we started to move through the small, cobbled streets, gaining even more attention from the crowds. I wanted to send a snarky comment back his way, but I needed a minute to compose myself from being so close to him. He smelt so bloody good; it should be a crime.

"Where are your family?" I asked after a few minutes of driving in silence.

"We are meeting them at the airport. Why? Did you hope I was whisking you away to keep you all to myself?" His molten eyes roamed my body suggestively and I narrowed my eyes.

"Of course not."

"Shame. Because that's what I dreamed about doing last night."

My head snapped at his as a playful smile spread across his face. He kept his eyes fixed on the road and for a moment I thought I imagined his words. "What?"

"Nothing." He shrugged and I dragged my gaze away from his bulging biceps in that short-sleeved top. "But just so you know, I really enjoyed the sex we had last night. And you did too."

"Oh my god," I folded my arms over my chest as a low chuckle came from his throat.

"That's exactly what you were screaming. But bambola..." I turned my crimson face towards him as he looked into my eyes, making my whole body suddenly feel alive with electricity. "In reality it will be my name you will be screaming, not gods."

I gulped audibly as my core tightened and I felt my arousal soak my knickers. Damn this body of mine! It never cooperated with me.

"Well, you best enjoy those dreams, Giovanni, because they will never become reality."

He smirked smugly but kept quiet. Even I knew my words were futile. He wasn't going to stop and, as much as it made me curse myself, I was beginning to like it.

Know You Better

Giovanni

I parked up on the private runway at the back of the airport where my jet was waiting for us. Mamma and my siblings were already onboard, as well as five of my best soldiers and Marco. I turned off the engine and glanced at Olivia's beautiful face staring open-mouthed at the plane.

"I thought we were getting an EasyJet flight?"

I burst out laughing. "EasyJet? Please. If you were mine, you would never fly commercial again." I opened the door and climbed out as my men from the SUV behind took our luggage onto the jet. I went to walk around to open the door for Olivia, but she had beaten me to it and climbed out herself. Urgh. She is really making this chivalry shit hard to do.

She was glaring at me after my comment, which only made me smile wider. It was the first time I had ever said something like that. Ever acknowledged that she could be mine. I liked it but clearly, she did not feel the same way.

"Maybe I like travelling commercially!"

"No one likes being sandwiched between strangers with minimal leg room and shit food. And whoever says they do, is lying." I said frankly, putting my hand on the small of her back to guide her towards the steps of the plane. My thumb caressed the soft skin that was exposed between her trousers and that sexy crop top she had on.

"It's extremely small-minded to believe you know how everyone feels, don't you think?"

"Have you ever been on a private jet before?"

She hesitated but raised her chin higher in the air. "Not all us commoners have the luxury of hopping on private jets every day."

I smirked. "It's extremely small-minded to presume you wouldn't like it if you haven't experienced it, don't you think?"

She paused on the carpeted steps up to the plane and gave me a deadly look.

"Are you set on making this trip a living hell for me?" She whisper-yelled as we approached the entrance to the jet.

"Oh no bambola. Quite the opposite," I winked and strolled past her onto the plane.

"Gio!" Sani ran down the champagne-coloured carpeted aisle towards me and I lifted him into my arms.

"Excited?" I asked, as his big eyes were so wide, I wouldn't have been surprised if he'd had three espressos.

"YES! Where's Liv?" He wriggled out of my arms as she stepped onto the plane.

"Charming," I mumbled as he raced into her legs. She smiled down at him before looking around the deceptively big and extravagant interior of the plane. This was the most luxurious jet we owned, and I had chosen it especially. I knew Olivia was not accustomed to such a lavish lifestyle and I wanted to treat her. Make her see the way she could live if she chose to be with me.

"Olivia, looking as beautiful as ever," Mamma said as she approached us, giving her a kiss on both cheeks. Olivia looked a little startled by the gesture but smiled politely.

"Thank you. You always look so elegant," Olivia returned the compliment and I excused myself to speak to our pilot. After giving him the green light to start our journey, I walked back through the red curtains that barricaded my little family into the main living area and my eyes immediately searched for her.

I groaned internally when I saw she had already chosen her seat and Sani had taken the one next to her. Mamma and Raya were sitting on the long sofa to the side, so I took the single armchair. At least it was directly in front of Olivia, so I had a nice view. Honestly, I never thought my little fratello would be such a cock block!

Once we took off, the servers came round to take our drink orders and I was irritated to see that one of them was an airhostess I had let entertain me during a past flight. I don't remember her name but she sure as hell made it obvious she remembered me with her flirtatious glances and batting of her eyelashes. I was on the phone to one of my Capo's when she placed my whiskey down next to me on the table and inappropriately ran her hand over my chest and shoulder as she walked away. Glancing up at Olivia, I noticed her glare before she quickly looked away from me. A cute blush crept up her cheeks when I caught her watching me and I smirked. Did she see that? Was she jealous? I couldn't help but feel a little elated that she might be.

It wasn't long until both Raya and Sani were asleep. Sani had his little head resting on Olivia's lap as she gazed out of the window and I felt ridiculous. I couldn't help but feel jealous of a 6-year-old. Mamma stood up with Raya in her arms and carried her down to the end of the jet where there was a small cabin bedroom. She then came back for Sani.

"I'm just going to take him to bed. He will be more comfortable," Mamma said as she lifted Sani off Olivia. Olivia just smiled in response and as mamma turned, she gave me a look that said a thousand words. She was leaving us alone on purpose. *Don't screw it up.* Was she really giving me the all clear to go for it with Olivia? I couldn't work it out, but as soon as she was gone, I took my chance.

I closed my laptop and placed it on the floor before walking over to the now empty cream chair next to her. She saw me coming out of the corner of her eye but kept her gaze firmly on the white clouds in the sky. She shuffled slightly as I sat down, my broad shoulders brushing against hers. Time to charm the living daylights out of this woman.

***

Olivia

Great. If I hadn't known any better, I swear Cecilia had planned that. The air thickened with sexual tension and electric energy as Giovanni came and sat next to me on the super-soft, luxurious seats. I had never felt comfort like it. Everything on this plane screamed how the other side lived. It was dripping with wealth, and it made me feel a little uncomfortable and intimidated to be honest. I had gotten used to the extravagance of the Buccini mansion, but this was just another reminder of just how influential this family was.

I felt Giovanni lean on the arm of the chair that was the only thing separating us and he brushed his shoulder against mine. I shuffled away from him but there was nowhere for me to go as I squashed myself against the plane window. His delicious scent was making my head spin once again.

"So better than EasyJet?" I could hear the laughter in his tone without even looking at him.

"I suppose." *Short answers Liv. That's good.* He might leave me alone and allow me to breathe normally again if I don't entertain him.

"You are one hard woman to impress," he mumbled, and I scoffed loudly. I couldn't help myself.

"Are you saying you are trying to impress me?" I turned my head towards him, which was my first mistake. He was so close to me. His chocolate eyes burned into mine and he smiled. That smile. It could make even the hardest of women weak at the knees.

"Of course. I am always trying to impress you."

I chuckled in disbelief. "Yeah. Me and every other woman with a pulse."

He didn't laugh and when I turned my head again to look at his handsome face, it held a serious expression. "No. Only you."

I gulped as our eyes locked and I felt that all too familiar excitement zapping through my body. Suddenly, we were interrupted by the red curtain moving to the side and that pretty air hostess that can't keep her hands off Giovanni. I quickly returned to looking out of the window as she strutted towards us in her 6-inch heels. Why does she need to wear such big heels to hand out a few drinks?

"Posso portarti qualcosa, signore?" Her Italian voice slipped sexily from her lips as she fluttered her eyelashes with a seductive smile. I rolled my eyes. I had no idea what she said, but I wouldn't be surprised if it was "Would you like me to suck you off sir?"

"No," came Giovanni's curt response, which made me look up at the girl's face. Just like I thought, her smile dropped, and she looked disappointed. Her blue eyes darted over at me, and she gave me a glare that would turn molten lava to ice. I chuckled under my breath as she walked away.

"Something funny?" Giovanni asked and I shook my head.

My curiosity reared its ugly head once more and I had to ask, "What did she say to you?"

His eyes twinkled with mischief, and I instantly regretted it. "She asked if she could get me anything."

"Ah. And by anything?" I made a crude hand gesture and he burst out laughing. "So, I am not wrong?"

"No, you're not wrong. She would do anything I asked," he smirked, and I shook my head, facing the window again. The image of that girl giving him a blow job the other day came to mind. We hadn't even discussed what had happened that day. I think he mentioned it when I turned up drunk at his house after the mugging, but I can't be sure. My memory is a little foggy.

"Well, don't let me stop you... You never have before," I wasn't trying to sound jealous or bitter because, honestly, I wasn't. Not about that incident, but it still sounded as if I was from my tone.

"What is that supposed to mean?" he asked, leaning to the side to give me his full attention.

"Just that I am sure your girlfriend would have something to say about what you get up to on planes with pretty servers, but luckily, I am not her, so don't let me stop you."

His eyes narrowed and I felt his instant irritation at my words. Which part I wasn't sure. "Girlfriend?"

I rolled my head to the side and gave him a knowing look. "The black-haired beauty that was well acquainted with your..." I nodded down to the direction of his trousers and saw the realisation register on his face.

"Mia? She is not my girlfriend. Just a friend," he said with a shrug, and I scoffed.

"Just like the server is 'just your friend?'"

He glared at me again and I held his gaze in challenge. "No. She is a server. Mia and I have an arrangement. Had an arrangement."

That sparked my interest. "Had?"

"It no longer applies."

"Why?" It was out of my mouth before I could stop myself.

His eyes flickered down to my lips for a second before returning to my eyes and I felt my stomach flip.

"Because of you."

"Me?" My voice came out in a squeak.

His slow, lopsided smile made my heart flutter. "Yes you. After that day, I realised."

"Realised what?" I whispered. This felt dangerous. Like I was walking into a burning fire with no way out, but I couldn't stop my legs from moving.

"That you were the only one who could give me any pleasure. Your eyes alone made me come that day. You were the object of my desires, and I would never be satisfied with anyone else." His voice was low and husky as he spoke, causing me to gulp down my instant arousal. What the... "You can't deny that you didn't feel it either, Olivia? The connection. Or are you going to tell me you have a thing for watching people fuck?"

His crude words made my cheeks blush and I looked away.

"No! Of course not!"

"Just me then?" The amount of pleasure and smugness in his voice made me irritated beyond belief. "It's okay, bambola. No need to be shy. I will put on a show for you anytime, but I would rather you were the one I am with."

I grabbed my bottle of water from the table and gulped at it like I hadn't had a drop for days. I can't believe this man. The ego on him! But was he wrong? Of course, he wasn't. I had never done anything like that before in my life, but what surprised me more was how much it turned me on. How much *he* turned me on. That moment wasn't about that girl, Mia. It was about us. And we both knew it.

"What's wrong bambola? Lost for words?" He taunted. I turned and glared at him. "OK." He raised his hands in the air in surrender. "Do you ever loosen up and just have fun?"

"I'm actually a lot of fun and really nice until you annoy me and, unfortunately for you, you seem hell bent on annoying me every day," I folded my arms across my chest.

"OK, let's test that theory. Question round. We each ask light-hearted questions to get to know each other better and we both have to answer." I looked up into his amused face and realised he was serious.

"Really? Why?"

He groaned and threw his head back against the headrest of his chair. "Because... I want to know you better obviously."

I narrowed my green eyes at him to try and work out if he had an ulterior motive or if he was being genuine. I gave up after a few seconds and shrugged, "Fine. But as soon as you start to annoy me, I'm giving you the silent treatment."

"What is your favourite colour?" he asked and I giggled at the innocence of it. It was not what I was expecting.

"Really?"

"Yes really. Humour me."

"Yellow. It's a happy colour. Let me guess, yours is black?"

He kept his eyes on the ceiling of the plane but smirked. "No, actually it's green."

I could feel a small smile playing at the corners of my lips but I focused on the next question. "Favourite food?"

"Easy. Pizza."

I giggled. "Stupid question to ask an Italian! Mine is sushi."

"Okay. Do you have any tattoos?" he lifted his head and looked into my eyes, and I quickly turned away.

"Yes. One. I already know you have hundreds."

"Where is your tattoo?" his eyes twinkled with mischief.

"None of your business!" I scolded him, which only made him smile wider.

"That means it's in a naughty place. I look forward to finding it," he winked, and I lowered my head in my hand. He just can't help himself. "Favourite author?" he asked.

Now this was a question I could get onboard with but was not expecting to come out of his mouth. I mastered English Literature at University so I could talk about books all day.

"That is very hard. Classical – Jane Austen or Shakespeare. Poetry – Edgar Allen Poe and modern, I would probably go for Kenn Follett. What?"

I caught him staring at me with a look of wonder and it made me feel uncomfortable.

"Nothing. There is just nothing sexier than a woman who knows her books."

I smiled broadly and shook my head. "Well, now I know you are lying! So, surprise me, you read?"

He put his hand to his heart and feigned hurt which made me chuckle. "Of course, I read. Classical – Leo Tolstoy, Poetry – Il Lampo and contemporary – Tolkien, of course."

My mouth must have been hanging open ready to catch flies as he laughed at my reaction. What the hell? He knew literature? "I love Tolkien! Tolstoy?"

"Anna Karenina is arguably one of the best pieces of written work to ever exist. And I am a huge Lord of the Rings fan. Don't tell anyone," he winked, and I honestly think he must have been able to hear my ovaries fangirling over him. This was unexpected.

"But Anna Karenina is so tragic!" I argued and he leaned into me, staring deep into my eyes.

"Just as tragic as your Romeo and Juliet?" I nodded in agreement and leaned back in the chair.

"Next question: did you always want to be an entrepreneur?" Something flashed across his face and he sat back in his chair and sighed.

"No. I wanted to be a fireman. Or a swimmer." I couldn't help the beaming smile on my face. "What?" he asked, amused as he noticed.

"You would make the ideal fireman. I can just imagine you now on all the hot fireman calendars hanging on horny housewives' walls."

He started to laugh. Like really laughing. A laugh I have never heard from him before. It's a deep, rich and sexy sound, so beautifully masculine. I stared in awe as he looked so free and youthful. He stopped laughing abruptly, looking a little taken aback by his unexpected outburst. I guess he wasn't expecting it either.

"Did you just give me a compliment? You think I'm hot?" He teased that playfulness back in full throttle. I sighed loudly.

"Maybe I did. But don't get used to it."

"Next question. Have you ever had a dirty dream about me?" His tone was infuriatingly seductive, and I pressed the button on the side of my seat to lower my chair to an angle I could fall asleep at and closed my eyes. "Oh, come on. I told you I'd had one about you earlier, so it's only fair."

"I am tired. Time for a nap," I fake yawned, keeping my eyes closed even though I could feel his heated gaze warming my body.

"Where is your favourite place to be kissed?" He whispered lowly, cheekiness evident in his voice and I shook my head.

When I didn't respond, but instead pretended to snore, a pleasing, husky chuckle escaped his lips, and it was somehow the sexiest thing I had ever heard.

"Sweet dreams, Bambola," was the last thing I heard before the drone of the plane's engine lulled me to sleep.

Twister

Olivia

Arriving at the resort in Courchevel, set in the vast and stunning French Alps, took my breath away. It was an undisputed jewel of beauty with unparalleled luxury and glamour. I read the leaflet front to back on our way to the lodge to find out about the area and all the things we could do here. It was one of the highest, largest and most prestigious ski resorts in France, which didn't surprise me in the slightest. The Buccinis never did anything in halves. There was an idyllic village with upmarket boutiques, gourmet restaurants and picturesque timber chalets decorating the main hub. When we finally stopped outside what looked to be a medium sized hotel, my jaw dropped open as I realised this was the Buccini's chalet. It was unrivalled against the others built around it in size and style. Everywhere you looked, the scene was dusted with powdery, white snow on the roofs of chalets and the floor. It almost blinded me when I climbed out of the tinted car.

Sani and Raya were screaming already, obsessed with the snow as they picked it up in their hands and threw it in the air. I walked towards the steps of the chalet and ran my hand over the beautifully carved timber bannister.

Glancing to the side of me, I saw Giovanni standing tall, taking a deep inhale of the crisp air with his eyes closed. He looked like he was meditating for a moment, but as he released his breath, he opened his eyes and peered down at me. A sweet smile lit up his face and he started up the steps to the front door. This place obviously meant a lot to him.

The rest of us followed him up as his men took care of our luggage and scouted the area for any threats. I had wondered where they were going to stay during this vacation, but quite clearly, the chalet could house at least twenty people comfortably.

Cecilia showed me to my room, which was the size of Gigi's apartment, and told me to take an hour to shower, freshen up and unpack. As I looked around the magnificent room that had bespoke furniture and subtle alpine textures, I let a little squeal escape my mouth. I kicked my shoes off and jumped onto the king-sized bed before falling into the mountain of pillows that surrounded me. This was amazing. I instantly wanted to take pictures to share on social media or to Facetime Mills and show her where I was, but as soon as the thoughts crossed my mind, it dampened my excitement. Pushing those ideas to the back of my mind, I waltzed into the bathroom and turned the three-headed shower on as the room filled up with steam. I took my time to enjoy the balmy water and use the designer products that were displayed in the shower cove before climbing out and wrapping an extremely soft, fluffy towel around my body and one around my hair on top of my head. How on Earth did they make these towels so soft? I would have to ask Cecilia. I chuckled at the thought. As if she would know!

Walking over to the large balcony doors that overlooked the breath-taking mountain landscape, I pulled them open and stepped outside onto the small balcony of my bedroom. Looking over the edge, I spotted a large hot tub on the decking below and smiled. Gigi was right! Mimicking Giovanni earlier, I closed my eyes and inhaled deeply, the smell of fresh snow and pine flooded my senses.

"Hello neighbour," a deep voice snapped me out of my bliss and I screamed, hugging the towel to my body as I looked over at the balcony right next to mine. There, leaning back on a wooden chair, was a gleeful looking Giovanni. His dark eyes roamed my exposed skin and bare legs as he lifted his cigar to his lips and took a deep drag.

"Oh my god! You scared the shit out of me!" I shouted and he smirked, releasing a cloud of smoke as he did.

"Scusate bambola."

"Wait! What do you mean, 'neighbours'? Is this your room?" My eyes widened as I realised that our bedrooms were literally separated by one wall, and I suddenly felt panic looming. Of all the, however many rooms in this place, I was given the room right next to his. That cannot be a coincidence.

"Si. Is that a problem?" He looked so relaxed. Too relaxed. It was unnerving. This Giovanni that was slowly coming to the surface over the last few days was different. He was softer and kinder. And yet that seemed to make him feel more dangerous to me. Because I was starting to like this man before me.

"Depends. Are you going to behave yourself?" I gripped my towel tighter around my chest as his eyes filled with heat and desire.

"I never behave myself, bambola. You should know that by now." He suddenly stood up from the chair and stubbed his cigar out on the ashtray. "But if you are worried about me climbing over your balcony and letting myself into your room, don't be. I will only enter with an invitation." He winked before walking through his own balcony doors and into his room. I turned abruptly and closed the doors behind me, noticing my heart was beating faster than usual. This was going to be complete torture and he was going to do everything in his power to make it so!

***

When I finally made my way downstairs to the open-plan ground floor that had a large living area centered around an open log fire, a dining area and a separate snug which, to my delight, was packed with a definitive and interesting assortment of books and a large kitchen area, I could hear laughter from the children.

I paused at the bottom step and watched the scene before me with bewilderment and warmth. Cecilia was lounging on the sofa surrounded by furs, a large glass of wine in hand and watching her two youngest running around the living room as their ridiculously bulky brother chased them both, making dinosaur noises.

"Ahhhh!" Raya squealed as Giovanni scooped her up effortlessly, hanging her upside down before throwing her onto the empty sofa.

"Don't you dare leave my cave little girl! I will be back with the other one soon!" he growled, making her scream and hide behind a pillow laughing.

Sani leapt over the sheepskin footstool and raced towards me.

"Liv! Help! A T-Rex is after me!"

I stood my ground as Sani hid behind my legs and Giovanni marched towards us. I had to bite my lip to avoid laughing at seeing such a brute of a grown man, pretending to be a T-rex. He even had the little claws up by his chest in character.

"Go away T-Rex! There are no little boys here!" I shouted, unable to hide the laughter in my voice. He came up so close that he was towering over me as Sani's grip clung harder to my jeans.

Giovanni sniffed the air dramatically and then he lowered his head into the crook of my neck, sniffing my skin. Just the feel of his stubble against my sensitive flesh made my knees go weak, but I fought my desire.

"Are you sure? Because I sure can smell him!"

Sani screamed as Giovanni quickly pulled him out from behind my legs and threw him over his shoulder. I laughed, trying to reach for Sani, but just as rapidly, Giovanni had bent down and lifted me over his other shoulder too. Sani and I both giggled as he marched us over to the sofa Raya was on and Cecilia watched on in delight. He threw us down aggressively and we both bounced on the cushioned seat, laughing.

"Now which of you shall I eat first?"

His eyes scanned the three of us but rested on me and I saw the hunger in them. I immediately became transfixed by his dark eyes as they bore into my soul.

"Liv! Liv! Eat Liv! We are only little!" Sani cried, causing me to snap out of my trance and dive at the little traitor, tickling his stomach.

"You little monkey!" I shouted as he rolled around helplessly.

"Santino! I have raised you better than that!" Cecilia laughed, shaking her head.

I sat up, pulling Sani up too, and Giovanni ruffled his hair.

"Mamma is right, Sani. Always protect your women!"

Those words sparked something inside me. Maybe it was just hearing that caveman instinct in him, but my god, I swear I just melted a little.

"Like papi protected mamma?"

The room fell silent and thick with tension as Giovanni's eyes widened and Cecilia froze. I didn't move a muscle and it felt like ages before anyone spoke. To my surprise, it was Giovanni who did first.

"Yes Sani. Papi protected mamma and we must be thankful every day that he did."

Cecilia stood up quickly and walked away into the kitchen with her back to us as she tried to busy herself looking in the fridge. Giovanni met my eyes and I saw his concern in them. He stood from his kneeling position on the floor and walked over to his mother.

"Right you two! Let's go on the hunt for some family board games! I bet there are some hidden around here somewhere," I said in a cheerful tone, and the children jumped up from the sofa unaware of the sudden sadness that had filled the room. I had no idea how their father had been killed apart from what Cecilia had mentioned at dinner and I would never pry. I know what it is like when people ask you about difficult things and I would not be that person. But clearly, this family was still dealing with the trauma of that event.

After dinner, which came as another surprise because Giovanni cooked it himself, we all settled down in the living area to play some family games. Cecilia had insisted that I join her in sharing a bottle of wine and I had to admit... I was having a lot of fun. I had never really had this growing up. The whole family games and silliness. My father died when I was too young to remember the times we shared and then it was always just mum and I until Neil and Henry came along. And those family times were not joyful, to say the least. It normally consisted of Neil and mum watching TV in silence in the front room and me trying to avoid being alone with Henry at all costs.

After playing Pictionary and Charades, we were now onto Twister. Raya's choice. It was only Raya, Giovanni and I left in the game. Cecilia spun the arrow once more for Raya's go and when it landed on the left-hand green, she was falling on her bottom within seconds. We all cheered as she crawled off the mat, leaving only Giovanni or me to take the crown. And I was not going down without a fight.

"Scared?" he teased as his mother spun the arrow again.

"Why would I be? This is my game. I am extremely flexible," I whispered and watched his eyes dilate with desire.

"Right hand blue," Cecilia shouted, and I took this moment while he was distracted to lean over his torso and put my hand on the blue dot. Our faces were inches apart and his breathing suddenly became shallow as we locked eyes. We were in quite a compromising position with me practically straddling his body, which was sprawled out touching different corners of the mat.

"Oh damn. This spinner is jammed," I heard Cecilia say as my heart started drumming in my chest. Giovanni's eyes left mine and stared longingly at my lips as he licked his own. I could feel the room growing smaller around me. The walls caving in on us as the pressure and tension grew. "Ah, here we go. Gio, right foot yellow."

He didn't move for a moment as though he hadn't heard the instruction. "Right foot yellow," I repeated, my voice coming out in a broken husk.

Suddenly, he spun over the top of me and knocked us down, his body caging mine beneath him as we both fell to the floor. I could feel his heart pounding in his chest as his huge body pressed against mine and I am pretty sure that that wasn't his gun in his trousers. We stared into each other's eyes and I was lost.

"Yay! Liv won!" Raya shouted as Sani suddenly dove on top of Giovanni's back, adding to the crippling weight on top of me. Breaking the spell, Giovanni quickly climbed off me, taking Sani with him.

"Right. Bedtime bambinis! Say good night," Cecilia stood up and said sternly as they both whined in protest. "We have a whole weekend of this so don't give me those bottom lips," she ordered.

I stood up quickly and brushed myself down before getting ready to put the kids to bed.

"It's okay Olivia. I will put them to bed tonight. You enjoy your evening," Cecilia smiled at me as she took her children's hands.

My eyes widened in panic at being left alone with Giovanni. "No really, that's what I am here for. I don't mind."

"Nonsense. I want to. I am tired anyway. You finish that bottle of wine for me, will you?" She didn't give me time to argue as she marched up the stairs with the kids.

I turned slowly and saw Giovanni leaning against the fireplace, staring at me intensely. He held out my glass of unfinished wine and smiled.

Breaking Down Barriers

Giovanni

Now there was no doubt in my mind, my mamma was cheering me on from the sidelines. She would never have offered to put the kids to bed if she hadn't wanted to leave Olivia alone with me. For the first time, I thought I saw a flicker of nerves cross Olivia's normally so composed and confident expression, but she raised her chin higher and strolled towards me, taking her wine glass.

She practically downed the remainder of her drink before picking up the half-drunk bottle of mamma's favourite white wine to pour herself another. If I didn't know any better, I would say she was in a rush to drink and get away from me.

"Let me do that for you," I stepped behind her and took the bottle from her hand, causing her to look a little taken aback by the gesture before she glared.

"I am more than capable of pouring myself a drink, Giovanni." I loved hearing my name leave her lips. It was my favourite sound in the world after her laugh.

"But not capable of accepting chivalry, it seems," I smirked as I poured the wine into her glass.

"Oh, is that what this is? You are a gentleman now?"

"I don't know what you mean. I have always been a gentleman." I placed the bottle back in the ice bucket and sat back on the sofa. She scoffed and took a seat at the other end. I frowned at the distance. She was too far away.

"Pouring me a drink doesn't make you a gentleman any more than standing in a garage makes you a car," she smirked, hiding behind her glass as she took a sip.

"Ouch!" I grabbed my chest and pretended to feel the stab to my heart. "You are right. You see straight through me bambola. I am no gentleman." I gave her a seductive glance and she froze, her cheeks blushing slightly. "But I am trying to be... nicer. Better. So just cut me some slack please."

Her pretty eyes widened as she realised, I was being honest and she looked a little sheepish as she stared down at her glass in her lap.

"Sorry. I know you are trying but..." She spoke so quietly, I struggled to hear her. "Why?"

"Why am I trying to do better? Or why am I being nicer to you?"

"Both," she muttered, her beautiful eyes flicking up from her glass to mine, which made my heart start to beat a little faster. She had complete control over it, it seemed. Nothing ever made my heart race like she could, not even an open-fire gun fight which I had had a few of in my time.

"It's simple. You deserve better." Her eyebrows furrowed as she registered my words. She seemed confused by them. "I owe you an apology, Olivia. When we first met, your first impressions of me were spot on. I was an arrogant, sex-crazed playboy who thought he could get any woman he wanted. I didn't treat you with respect and I'm sorry."

I fought to keep a straight face as her features took on a look of utter shock. She opened and closed her mouth a few times before looking away from me and out the window. Ha, she was speechless. Even though it had the desired effect, and I could see the cogs frantically spinning in her mind, trying to understand who the hell I really was, I meant every word.

"Don't get me wrong. I am still all those things," I smirked, and she glanced back at me. "And I will never stop teasing you because I fucking love watching you react, but I am trying to be more... decent. For you."

It took her a few seconds to regain her composure and she nodded once before saying, "Thank you. I appreciate the effort."

I smiled but it wasn't exactly the response I was hoping for. I wanted her to open up to me. To tell me about why it was those traits in me that bothered her so much. About her past. But I forced myself to maintain some patience. I couldn't push her too hard.

"Shall we continue our game?" I asked, standing up to pour myself another whiskey. I hadn't finished my drink yet, but I just needed an excuse to sit back down closer to her.

"Twister?" The alarm in her voice made me laugh.

"God no! The question game?" I returned to the sofa, this time sitting only a few inches away from her and draped my arm over the back of the chair, so my hand was close to her head. She immediately turned her body to face me, bringing her legs up underneath her. Just that little move made her look so fucking adorable.

"Okay but play nice," she smirked.

I smiled and settled myself down for another round. I had kept everything lighthearted and fun earlier, but I wanted to get to know her on a deeper level this time. But I knew I had to ease her into it. "Birthday?"

"22nd of May," she answered quickly.

I nodded. "That makes you a Gemini," I added, and she cocked her head to the side, studying me. "That makes sense."

"What is that supposed to mean?"

"The feisty nature and split personality thing," My lips twisted up into a cheeky smile as I took a sip of liquor. She playfully pushed my shoulder and giggled.

"I guess. You?"

"5th of November. Scorpio," I winked.

She chuckled loudly. "Well that makes sense too!" Raising my eyebrows at her, I urged her to elaborate. "Determined, ambitious, intense and controlling."

"True, but you also left out, deep, loyal, honest and we are known as the sexiest star sign," I mused, causing her to roll her eyes. She regarded me with a thoughtful look which made me feel a little nervous. It was a strange feeling. I don't think anyone has made me feel nervous before. "What?"

"Scorpios are also the most misunderstood sign." She said carefully, her green eyes held mine as if she was searching every corner of my soul, trying to figure me out. "They come across as intimidating and tough-minded, but most are hiding behind that façade and are deeply emotional and sensitive."

I looked away and took a swig of my drink. "You seem to know a lot about star signs."

"I find them fascinating," she added. I could feel her eyes still burning into the side of my face and I coughed slightly to clear my throat. "I think you are fascinating too."

My head snapped up to hers and she had a small smile playing on her full lips. I instantly wanted to lean forward and kiss them.

"You find me fascinating?" I had managed to compose myself and felt my playfulness come back to the surface. This was where I was most comfortable; easy and cheeky conversation. But I knew if I wanted to gain her trust, I would have to start letting her in. Showing my vulnerability, which was fucking hard to do.

She nodded and took a sip of wine. "Next question." She changed the subject quickly. "Your biggest regret in life so far?"

I puffed out my cheeks and exhaled loudly. Fuck me, what a question. "Do you have all night?" I smirked but really I meant it. I have done so much fucked up shit in my life and have a lot I regret, but I couldn't exactly go into detail about any of that. She would run for her life. I knew I couldn't keep my job a secret forever. I would have to tell her one day, but I needed her to see me for who I was outside of an underboss first. That was the only way I had any hope of her not running for the hills. But there was one regret I could tell her. One that lived deep in the depths of my darkness and was my biggest regret to date. I had never said this out loud. I had never even told a soul.

I turned my head and locked eyes with hers, unsure whether I could even allow the words to leave my mouth. But when those green eyes gazed back at me with expectation and I saw the warmth in them, the words started to come on their own accord.

"My biggest regret is the last thing I said to my papi the night he died."

She held my gaze and I exhaled deeply before I continued. "We had an argument. It was over something so trivial, but it ended up escalating into a full-blown row where we both said things we didn't mean. But the last thing I said to him...the look on his face as I said them..." I ran my hand through my ebony hair and realised it was shaking. "I told him I hated him and never wanted to be like him. That he was weak and pathetic and would never be the kind of man I could look up to. That my zio was more like a father to me." My voice cracked as I said the words and I stood up quickly, choking back the lump in my throat.

Olivia remained silent and still on the sofa, giving me the space and time I needed to get myself under control.

"I am sure he knew you didn't mean it," her small, gentle voice made a sad chuckle leave my lips.

I shook my head. "No, from the look on his face before I left the room, I really think he believed every word." I sat back down on the sofa, leaning forward and resting my elbows on my knees. "Sorry. I have never told anyone about that before."

"Not even your mum?" she asked, and I shook my head. "You've been carrying that around with you for all that time and never told a soul?"

I leaned back on the sofa and closed my eyes. "The guilt eats away at me every day. I could never tell mamma. She is... fragile. I know she doesn't seem it, but she was dealing with a lot. Still is. I never want her to know what I said. It would kill her."

I opened my eyes when I felt a warm, soft hand grasp mine. She squeezed it gently and I turned my head to look into her eyes. I expected to see pity, disgust or even hate in them at my confession, but instead she just looked concerned.

"You have had to deal with a lot too." I swallowed as that lump returned to my throat. "I should know. I am a master of living with guilt. It feels like a part of me now. Who I am."

I sat up a little straighter and entwined my fingers with hers. Her hand looked so tiny in mine, and it made my heart flutter. I loved that. The feel of her hand in mine as if it was always meant to be there.

"What is your biggest regret?" I asked carefully. Was this it? Was she going to open up to me?

She pulled her hand out from mine and sighed. The fragility beneath that feisty demeanour came out slowly with each word.

"For not acting quick enough. For not speaking out sooner or asking for help."

My eyebrows furrowed as she took a large gulp of her wine. Should I press her for more information? I had never felt so torn before. I wanted to find out more, but I also didn't want to upset her. Deciding to wait and see if she elaborated took precedence. Thankfully, it was the right move.

"A while ago, there was a bad person in my life," she spoke quietly and refused to look up. My heart started beating frantically in my chest. "He didn't treat me well." She laughed, shaking her head. "That is an understatement, he made my life a living hell. He tormented me daily. He abused me emotionally and tried to force himself on me. Tried to control every aspect of my life. People knew. They could see what was happening but turned a blind eye. My best friend and boyfriend were the only ones who tried to help me, but I played it down because I didn't want them to worry. I didn't ask for help. I thought I could handle it on my own. I thought... It would be over soon. I would be at university, and he would be out of my life."

She paused as her voice cracked and her bottom lip trembled. Rage was manifesting itself inside me at the thought of what this fucker did to her. What he put her through for years.

"Perhaps if I had spoken out more. If I had reported him. Nate would still be alive." A tear slid down her cheek and my overwhelming need to protect and comfort this woman took over. I lifted her onto my lap and wrapped my arms around her tightly as she lay her head on my chest and cried quietly. After a few moments, she lifted her head and wiped her eyes. "I'm sorry. I haven't talked about this in years."

"Don't apologise. These tears? They are not a weakness, Olivia. They show how strong you are and how strong you have had to be. Never apologise." She nodded her head slowly with a small smile. "Who was he?" I asked, even though I knew exactly who the asshole was.

"My stepbrother. He tried to force himself on me when I was sixteen. I fought him off and broke his nose. After that, he made my life hell. And then... one night at an end of year party, he stabbed my boyfriend, Nate, to death." She sniffed and I felt my body tense under her. I had read all of this in the newspaper articles, but it had seemed so distant and formal. Factual. But seeing her now, like this, made me realise just how much this affected her. It explained everything. The walls she has up around herself. The hate she had for me when she thought I was like him. I gulped down my sudden fear of losing this woman when she found out who I really am. How could she ever be okay with it? I am a killer. Just like him.

"It gets worse," she whispered. And I held onto her tighter. How could it get any worse?

"When Henry, my psycho stepbrother found us, we were..." she shuffled off my lap awkwardly and I turned to give her my full attention. "We were..." I waited impatiently to hear whatever was causing her cheeks to turn crimson and her body to tremble. "...having sex. For the first time. Both of our first times."

I froze. My eyes must have widened, and I felt my jaw clench. "He... killed your boyfriend while you were..." I repeated, still not being able to comprehend it.

She nodded sadly. "He stabbed him seven times in the back while Nate was still inside me."

My breathing was coming out in short, sharp rasps. That was fucked up even by my standards. Fuck!

"Don't look at me like that!" she suddenly shouted and stood up from the sofa, spilling her drink on the cream rug. "Shit," she hissed as she bent down and started to try and mop it up.

"Leave it. It doesn't matter," I pulled her up by her arm and she glared at me. "Why are you angry? How did I look at you?"

"Like I am broken. Like I am damaged goods." She scoffed and turned away from me. "Maybe I should have told you sooner. Then you would have wanted to leave me alone. No one wants to sleep with the girl whose only sexual experience was a murder."

I froze again. Wait.

"Hang on...so you have never had sex again... not since?" I didn't mean for my voice to come out so frantic, but I was in shock. I instantly felt like the biggest dickhead in the world, the way I had been coming onto her so aggressively.

"See! There it is again! That look! Please spare me your pity! I am fine! If you must know, I have had sex with other men, just not successfully. I always freak out. Flashbacks and shit. So, there you go! You are off the hook, Giovanni. Now I have burst your little fantasy of having hot sex with the nanny. I have baggage. Fucking loads of it!" She stormed out of the living room and onto the terrace.

I stood rooted to the spot for a moment, trying to digest her words and anger. What the hell had I done wrong now? My own emotions were clouding my judgement. I felt pure rage at what she had been through. I didn't pity her. I wanted revenge for her. I wanted blood for her. It was in my nature to want someone who had wronged a person I cared about dead. But I also felt jealous. Intense jealousy that she had been with other men, which was just ridiculous. I hated that she had always had such shit experiences. That they had made her feel like she was broken or damaged.

I stormed out onto the terrace after her. She was leaning over the wooden bannister, her hot breath evaporating into the chilly air.

"You are wrong. I don't pity you. I don't think you are damaged goods. Fuck if you are damaged goods, what the fuck am I? I think you are incredible and anyone who has made you feel anything less than fucking perfect deserves a fucking beating," I growled. She turned to me with a confused expression. Her cheeks were flushed from the cold night breeze and the tip of her nose was turning a cute shade of pink. Her eyes were so big and bright in the moonlight, that I felt mesmerised by them. I took slow steps towards her, and she leaned her back against the bannister.

"I don't understand," she muttered as I stood directly in front of her now, our toes touching. "Why would you still want someone like me?"

"Because you, to me, are perfect, bambola."

Her eyes flickered up at mine and she bit her lip in that sexy way she does that makes me instantly hard. We held each other's gaze for what felt like eternity and my control snapped. Overcome with desire, I grabbed the back of her neck and pulled her into me, both my hands in her hair as I brushed my lips against hers tenderly.

"Stop me if you don't want this," I husked against her soft, supple lips and her eyes fluttered closed. I could feel her heart pounding in her chest as she pushed her tits into my body and grabbed handfuls of my top in her fists. Her lips parted and her warm breath on my skin felt so fucking sensual against the bitter coldness of the night. "Olivia...I need to hear you say it."

Her eyes opened and she stared deep into my soul. "I want you."

I smiled slowly and lowered my mouth to hers. The moment our lips connected; it sent a flurry of emotions through my body. My veins felt like they were on fire as the sparks erupted inside me, and I pulled her into me tighter. Her arms were wrapped around my neck as I kissed her with all the passion I felt. Slowly, I ran my tongue along her bottom lip, seeking access, which she immediately gave me. It danced with hers in perfect harmony and I heard the most erotic moan vibrate into my mouth from her pleasure. I groaned and lifted her up, giving us a fairer position to really deepen the kiss as she wrapped her legs around my waist. My hands on her tight ass, I lifted her and ground her against my rock-hard erection, causing her to moan again. I couldn't get enough of that noise. It was like heaven to me. I needed to hear it again and again.

Without breaking our now very intense kiss, I lowered myself down onto the bench on the terrace, her straddling my hips. She instinctively started to rock herself against my cock, trying to get the friction her pussy so desperately needed. I felt like I could explode in my jeans right there and then. She was so fucking sexy. Breaking our kiss, I travelled my lips down her neck as she continued to dry hump my crotch and I pulled her top down to reveal her lace black bra. Cupping her perfect tit in my hand, I leaned down and sucked her hard nipple through the thin fabric, causing her to gasp before I bit it gently with my teeth. Her moves became more frantic as I pulled the lace down and wrapped my mouth around her sweet, pink nipple, swirling my tongue and flicking it. Her skin tasted like coconuts. Fucking delicious.

Her moans were increasing, and I released her breast, before pulling down her other side of her bra and watching her perky tits bouncing as she ground her hips against me hungrily. Staring up at her flushed face, parted lips and tilted head to the sky, she was a goddess. I gripped her ass in my hands and pushed my erection against her harder, causing her to cry out. She was close and we were still fully clothed. I wanted to see her cum like this. She was stunning. Her lips captured mine once more and I continued to rub her clit with my erection, until she was a panting mess through our kissing. Her body started to tremble, and I gripped the nape of her neck, holding her lips to mine as she released her orgasm into my mouth and shook on top of me. To my surprise, I felt myself release inside my boxers just watching her. Fuck. That was intense. I felt like a fucking teenager.

We were both panting heavily as she rested her forehead on mine, and I stroked her hair out of her face and behind her ear.

"Whoops," she whispered, which caused us both to laugh freely.

I was suddenly glad that we hadn't gone all the way. After what she told me tonight, I knew it would need to be dealt with sensitively and I wanted to make sure it was the best experience she ever had. That she would never think of that event while she was with me. She would be consumed by me. There would be no room for thoughts when I am inside her. Nothing but pure pleasure.

Because now, she is mine.

Demon Or Saviour?

Olivia

I woke up the next morning with the biggest smile on my face. And it wasn't just the satisfying night's sleep I had in this feathery bed that was like sleeping on a giant marshmallow, but the memory of last night. Of him.

I couldn't believe it when he stepped out onto the terrace with the same intensity of desire, he had shown me since the day we met. How could he still want me, desire me, after what I told him? But he did. And my god was that kiss something else. It was the best kiss I have ever had in my life. The amount of sexual tension between us and finally giving into our desires and tasting him for the first time made me hornier than I have ever been before. I came from just dry humping, fully clothed! I mean, really?

I fully expected him to suggest we go to one of our rooms after that so we could really enjoy ourselves, but to my surprise, he said that that was enough for tonight. I can't lie and say I wasn't disappointed. My brain had finally caught up with my body and my god, I wanted him. More than I have ever craved any man before. But I was also glad. Last night was a lot. We had both revealed things about ourselves that we had barely told a soul before, and it was emotionally draining. And plus, I wasn't the least bit prepared for him to see me naked! I hadn't shaved, and was wearing old, shitty underwear.

Instead, he had walked me to my room like the gentleman he admitted he was trying so hard to be and gave me a steamy goodnight kiss that ended up stealing the breath right out of my lungs. He was such an amazing kisser. Of course he was. I can't even imagine how good he is going to be in bed. He has already given me two orgasms in the short time I've known him and both times, I have been fully clothed.

I looked over at the clock on the wall and cursed when I saw it was after 8am. The kids must be up already! Dashing into the bathroom, I showered and got dressed in jeans and a cable-knit jumper in record time and raced downstairs. When I was only met by a very professionally dressed Cecilia in the kitchen making her coffee, I frowned. She was wearing a trendy grey trouser suit with killer heels and a silk blouse underneath. She looked gorgeous. She turned when she heard me coming and gave me a beaming smile.

"Ah Olivia. Good morning," she chirped. "Coffee?"

"Please. I can do it myself, it's fine." I walked towards her, but she shushed me away with her hands.

"Don't be silly, I have already made enough for two. Did you sleep well?"

"Er... yeah. Um, where are the children? Are they not awake yet?" I asked, looking over my shoulder to check every inch of the ground floor.

"Oh yes, they have been up for hours. They are with Giovanni. He said something about letting you sleep, and he would spend some time with them before we headed out for our meeting." She perched on one of the kitchen stools and placed my coffee in front of me.

Wow. That was…sweet of him. "Oh. Okay. That is very kind of him," I said awkwardly as I felt her intense gaze sizing me up. She had that ability to stare at a person so deeply that they would crumble and tell all their darkest secrets. I took a sip from my mug to ensure that didn't happen to me.

"So will you be gone for long today?" I asked politely to make conversation. Really, I wondered how long Giovanni would be away for. I couldn't help the bubble of excitement I had at seeing him again.

"Most of the day, I expect. It is hard to say with these meetings. If it goes well, it could be over in a few hours, but if it doesn't, then we may have to go back again tomorrow," she rotated her mug as she spoke.

I wondered what exactly she did in their business. Giovanni seemed to be the one running everything, so what role did she play? Sensing me deep in thought, she smiled. "I used to be a lawyer. So, I come in handy when looking over new contracts and business proposals."

Ah, that makes sense. "So is Giovanni looking to open a new hotel or something in France?" I asked, but her eyes flickered up over my head as she beamed.

"Ah here they are!" Sani and Raya ran into the kitchen and said good morning to me before asking what we were going to do today.

"Well, I thought we could go down to the little village and get some lunch and we could make snow angels and build snowmen outside the front of the house," I explained, and they both celebrated before running off into the living room. I noticed Marco following them and sitting on the sofa. Then I felt him. It was hard to ignore that instant electricity in the air as he entered the kitchen behind me. He brushed past me, and I felt his hand stroke down my back subtly and without suspicion of anyone else in the room before, he was standing in front of me and Cecilia. I swallowed my instant arousal at the sight of him. He was wearing a three-piece, light grey suit which fit every inch of defined muscle on his body like a glove, making him look intimidating yet sexy as hell. His black hair was styled back and swept to the side like the day I had met him, and he smelt amazing. He was pure sin wrapped in a beautiful package.

"Good morning ladies," he smiled at us both, but his eyes lingered on me a little longer. "Sleep well?" he asked with a smirk.

"Yes, thank you, you?" I replied, not able to hold his heated gaze. I think I was about to combust.

"Very."

Cecilia looked between us with curiosity, and I swear I saw a secret smile teasing at the edges of her lips. "Shall we go mamma? Get this over with?" He asked and she hopped off her stool and said goodbye to Sani and Raya. Taking the few seconds we had without prying eyes, Giovanni leaned into me, his lips against my ear and whispered, "I haven't been able to get you or the taste of those sweet lips off my mind all night. Later bambola."

My heart pounded, blood rushed to my ears and my core pulsed in anticipation. Holy shit. He had already walked away with that arrogant swagger as Cecilia waved goodbye to me, which I barely registered, and then they were gone.

"Right munchkins, let's get wrapped up warm and out in the snow!" I shouted over to the kids and they both cheered. Head in the game Liv. Children first. Sex later. My priorities are skewed. I laughed at myself.

***

Giovanni

"Good night last night?" Mamma prodded as the car zoomed down the mountains towards the nearest city.

"Hmmhm," I hummed as I tapped away replies to texts that were coming through thick and fast. We never had any signal up at the lodge and now suddenly the world has woken up and apparently no one can do a fucking thing without me while I am out of the country.

"Did you and Olivia talk?" I vaguely heard her ask as I frowned deeply, reading Niccola's message about seeing Riccardo Leone in Verona at one of our fucking restaurants. That was taking the piss. It is an unwritten law that we stay out of each other's territories unless someone wants to get a bullet in their head. But to have dinner in a restaurant I owned was disrespectful. He was sending me a message. A warning.

"Hmm," I muttered back as I told Niccola to keep surveillance footage of the restaurant and send it to me.

"Did you finally tell her how you feel about her?"

"Hmmhm," I replied, until I registered what she said, and my head shot up. Glancing over at her, her face was plastered with a knowing smile, and I froze. "What?"

"Did you finally tell her how much you like her? Did anything happen between you?" she leaned against the car door so she could stare directly into my eyes.

"What are you talking about mamma?" I glanced back at my phone, but I could no longer focus on the messages. Does she know?

"Oh, don't give me that, Giovanni. I have known from the moment she walked into the interview weeks ago."

I stared wide-eyed at her as a manipulative grin lit up her face. "What are you- "

"Why do you think I wanted to hire a girl with no qualifications and limited experience so badly? You may not have known it then, but I sure as hell did," she chuckled.

I felt my eyebrows pull in and a deep frown set on my face. What the hell was she going on about?

"Mamma, what are you talking about? Know what? You are not making any sense."

She groaned and raised her hand to her head. "You men are all the same! You think with your cocks before you think with your heads. It was only a matter of time before you realised that you wanted more than just to sleep with her."

I scoffed and shook my head. "What makes you so sure that isn't just what I want?"

"Because I have seen it. What is between you two is deeper than just a physical connection. Even if you try to deny it, you are falling for the girl Giovanni."

I burst out laughing. That tickled me. "Mamma, I do not fall for women no matter how beautiful or amazing they are."

"So, what are you doing then?" She fixed a stern gaze on me, and I felt her challenging me to try and lie to her. I sighed.

"I don't know. I like her. I will admit that. She is different from anyone I have ever met and I..."

"And you..." she pressed.

"I care about her."

"Did you sleep with her? Last night?"

I groaned. Oh, why on Earth was I having this conversation with my mother of all people and right now?

"No."

"Well, that speaks volumes, doesn't it?"

"What do you mean?" I was getting irritated with all these riddles she was using.

"Well, I am sure you had the opportunity to? And old Giovanni wouldn't have thought twice about it. So, what made you hold back? Were you thinking about what might be best for her?" she smiled wickedly, and she knew she had me.

"It's complicated, mamma. You wouldn't understand."

"As far as I can see. It is actually very simple. You like her and she likes you. You are good for each other, Giovanni. Don't screw this up."

I chuckled, which caused her to glare at me. "I am not good for her mamma. How can you even say that? She doesn't even know who I am. Who we are and when she finds out she will leave."

"You don't know that. I was in her position once. You just have to be open with her Gio. Show her who you really are on the inside and who she is to you. Then she will see past the rest," she said confidently, and I ran my hand down my face.

"I love your optimism but she has a dark past. One that she is still dealing with," I glanced out of the window as the hotel we were meeting the French in came into view.

"We all have demons, Gio. But it all depends on whether she sees you as another one or as her saviour. Only you can help her make that choice." The car pulled to a stop and mamma climbed out. I sat in the car for a few more seconds to clear my head of Olivia and pull down the mask of Giovanni Buccini, the ruthless underboss of Mala Del Brenta. To her I would always try to be her saviour, but right now, I was the devil in disguise. And we were one of the same.

Don't Be Late

Olivia

The late afternoon sun was starting to dip below the peaks of the jagged mountains in the distance and Sani, Raya and I were putting the final touches to our snowmen with the help of a reluctant Marco.

"Watch this Raya!" I exclaimed as I jumped back into a mountain of powdery snow and started moving my arms and legs back and forth, creating a perfect snow angel. I stood up and pointed as they both came over to see.

"Cool!" Sani said as he dived backwards and made his own. I helped Raya down before I climbed back into mine.

We giggled and stared up at the clear blue sky as we moved our arms and legs.

"Do you think papi is an angel now?" Raya's sweet little voice came from the pile of snow next to me. I couldn't see either of them as the snow was so thick on the floor we had sunk down into it. Her words tugged at my heart strings, and I stared up at the sky.

"Yes. I believe he is, and he is watching over you all the time sweetie," I replied.

"When I am older, I am going to kill the bad men that killed papi. Me and Gio will together," Sani's voice came from my left. I scrunched my face and sat up right, turning to look down at him.

"What do you mean, Sani?"

Just at that moment, a black SUV pulled up and Giovanni and Cecilia climbed out. Their meeting must have gone well as it wasn't even five pm yet. The kids jumped up and ran towards them as I pulled myself a little more awkwardly out of the snow. Sani's comment worried me a great deal. He had obviously been playing too many of those video games and it doesn't help that he sees Giovanni and all these men walking around with guns for protection. I should probably broach the subject with Giovanni or Cecilia.

Suddenly, I felt a bolt of ice hit my coat and fall to crumbs on the floor. I glanced up and saw Giovanni grinning widely with mischief as Sani fell about laughing and pointing at me. I narrowed my eyes.

"Oh no, you didn't!" I shouted as I leaned down and grabbed a handful of snow to make a hard snowball. Giovanni winked at me and pushed the kids' backs, shouting "Run!"

They all did, and I sent the ball flying towards Giovanni but missed his head by a mile.

"Is that all you've got?" He shouted as he and Sani ducked behind a bush. Raya ran towards me and we hid behind a tree.

"Right Raya, we've got this! Roll this snow and make balls like this and try to hit them, okay?" She nodded her little head in her bobble hat with an excited grin. The first snowball aimed at us hit the tree and I chuckled.

"Pathetic!" I shouted over my shoulder with my back against the trunk. We screamed and laughed our way through ten minutes of an intense snowball war, darting in between trees and hiding places. Then it all fell silent.

"Okay Raya. Let's make a run for it to the lodge." I said, eyeing the steps that were about fifty metres away. I think we could make it. "One, two, three," I whispered, and we both ran through the snow. Out of nowhere, a bulky body collided with mine and we fell back into the snow together, his hand under my head, protecting it from the fall. I stared up in shock as I peered into those dark brown eyes and a slow, cheeky smile spread across his face. My body was caged under the weight of his in the snow and instead of feeling the bitter cold from my landing, my body burned with the heat of his.

"Miss me?" he smirked as he looked down at my lips.

"Like a hole in the head," I shot back, making him chuckle.

"There's my girl," he climbed off me and held his hand out to help me up. I glanced around for Raya and Sani, but it looked like they had already gone back inside with Marco. He kept my hand in his and pulled me to the side of the house, out of view, and pushed me up against the timber wall. His hands went straight into my hair and his lips found mine possessively and full of want. I grabbed the lapels of his suit jacket and pulled him into me more, needing to feel every inch of him covering my body. This kiss turned heated quickly as he lifted me with one arm gripping my ass and wedged me between his muscular frame and the lodge, as our tongues danced together. When we finally broke apart, we were both breathing heavily.

"I've been thinking about doing that all day," he husked, causing me to want to kiss him again.

"Me too," I whispered against his lips. He sucked my bottom one into his mouth and tugged at it between his teeth, making me gasp.

"I love your little noises," he smirked, and I could feel myself blushing. "Let me take you out tonight."

I pulled my head back to look at him as he lowered me back to the ground. "I – I can't. The kids. I have to put them to bed and- "

He shook his head. "Mamma will put them to bed. I have already asked her."

I frowned when I realised what that meant. "She knows?"

"That I want to take you on a date? Yes."

My eyes widened and I pushed at his chest to give me some space. He chuckled at my reaction. "And is she okay with it? I am not fired?"

"Of course not. She is thrilled actually. She thinks you are good for me," he smirked, and I shook my head in disbelief. "So? Is that a yes?"

I stared up into his handsome face as he waited for my answer. What was I doing? If I agreed to go on a date with my boss, it would change everything. *Bit late for that Liv.* My conscious reminded me that I've already snogged his face off three times, watched him have a blow job, and let him give me two orgasms. But somehow, this meant more. This was him asking me out properly. Not just fooling around.

"You are killing me here, bambola!"

I giggled when I realised I had left him hanging for long enough.

"OK. Yes, I would like that," I said, feeling suddenly shy around him. His face opened like a flower in bloom and I don't think I have ever seen him look so happy.

"It's a date. I will pick you up at 7," he winked, walking away from me. I burst out laughing at his goofiness.

"We are staying under the same roof, remember?"

"7! Don't be late. I have waited long enough for you!" he yelled back before disappearing out of sight. I leaned back against the timber and smiled. What was it Gigi said? 'Don't fall for him, just fuck his brains out.' Shit.

***

I stood back to contemplate which outfit to go with for our date tonight, and I swear I would have no thumbnails left if I didn't make a decision soon.

Choice one: jeans, over the knee boots and a bodysuit top which was a little low cut, just the right amount for a first date. It was practical, sexy and comfortable.

Choice two: Jeans again but paired with a bralet and cream blazer (courtesy of Gigi). It was casual but sophisticated.

Or choice three: the showstopper. Gigi had sneaked in one of her most revealing dresses and one that she knew I loved. It was a simple black, figure-hugging dress that stopped just above the knees but had a narrow deep V corset style at the bust. It was classy yet seductive. I inhaled and exhaled deeply again as I tapped my foot on the floor. Can I really pull choice three off? Would it be too much? All I know is that we are going out to dinner. And if I wore that one, I would have to wear heels and how on Earth am I supposed to walk in heels in the snow?!

A knock at the door made me jump and Elenora's black hair and smiling face poked around.

"Elle!" I smiled, genuinely happy to see her again. She walked into my room, shutting the door behind her and hugged me tightly!

"Liv! I don't know how you did it but thank you!" She pulled back from my embrace with a beaming smile. My confusion must have been obvious as she explained herself.

"I got to go to the art exhibition today and it was wonderful! That would never have been possible if you hadn't convinced Gio to make this a family trip."

Now I am really confused.

"I didn't. It was nothing to do with me," I replied as she bounced down on the edge of my bed and looked over my outfit choices.

"Yeah okay," she chuckled sarcastically, which left me baffled. "So, you are doing a really good job at taking my advice, I see."

I felt a deep flush creep up my chest but when she glanced up at me with laughter in her eyes and a soft expression, I realised she wasn't angry.

"He can be very... convincing," I said quietly.

She rolled her eyes. "Ha! I did try to warn you. It seems we both underestimated his charms."

I looked down at my hands and started fiddling with my thumbs, a nervous trait I have. For the first time since he had asked me out, I suddenly felt overcome with worry. Was I doing the right thing? If you had asked me a few days ago if I would ever contemplate going on a date with Giovanni Buccini I would have laughed in your face. Yet here I am. Was I being a fool? Had I let him suck me into his trap of seduction?

Suddenly sensing my change in mood, Elle stood up and grabbed my shoulders. "Hey! I am only joking. I know what I said, Liv, but... you might just be the right girl for my fratello. I have never seen him this way with anyone before." I looked up into her kind eyes and frowned.

"Trust me! He is downstairs right now, constantly fiddling with his hair and shaking out his arms every few minutes. He is nervous as shit. No one makes him nervous."

I chuckled at the mental image she had just portrayed in my mind. Surely, that was not true. Her eyes cast down my body and back to my bed where the clothes were laid out. "I am guessing you are nervous too due to the fact you are still not dressed and supposed to be leaving in five minutes."

"I can't decide what to wear."

"No brainer. 100% this one. No doubt about it," she leaned over and picked up the little black dress with a grin.

"Isn't it a bit much? And I would have to wear heels... in the snow," I curled my eyebrow up knowingly and she shook her head with a smirk.

"Ever seen mamma without a pair of heels? If she can manage it, so can you. Now get your sexy ass in that dress now before Gio storms up here and gets you himself. He doesn't like waiting, Liv!" She winked and walked out of my room, leaving me holding the dress in my hands. Show stopper it is...

Best Behaviour

Giovanni

"Did she say anything about me?" I asked Elle as she appeared downstairs after checking in on Olivia.

She waltzed past me with that cocky air of arrogance that seems to run in the family.

"Si. I believe her exact words were 'Quick! Help me escape out this window from your whipped brother?'" she chuckled. I don't know why I bothered asking. Winding me up was her favourite pastime. I gave her the middle finger.

"She's late," I muttered as I glanced down at my Rolex.

"Perfection takes time," Elle teased, giving me a smug grin. I rolled my eyes and lifted my tumbler to my mouth in the hope that the strong liquor would settle my nerves. Yes. That's right. I was a fucking jittery mess. What the hell was wrong with me?

The longer I waited, the more I wondered if she had changed her mind. The pressure I felt for tonight was insane. I wanted it to go well. No, it had to go well. I needed to know that she liked me. The real me. That she didn't think I was anything like that asshole of a stepbrother. That I would never hurt her. I had decided I would tell her who I really was once I was convinced that she had accepted the real me. And no matter how fucking hard it was, I wasn't going to sleep with her until I had. I was going to take this slow. At her pace. After everything she told me about her past sexual experiences, I was more convinced than ever that I needed her trust if I was going to make her see how good it could be. How good it could be with me.

Movement at the top of the staircase caught my eye and I lowered my glass from my lips, frozen in mid-air as my eyes took her in. She was a vision. In a black low-cut dress, which gave a tempting display of her perky tits but in an elegant yet teasing way. The dress moulded every curve on her body and my mouth watered. She was wearing her dark hair down in loose waves and she had even put on more make-up than I had ever seen her wear before. She didn't need it as she is naturally beautiful, but I have to admit it made her green and gold eyes pop even more. My heart was pounding at the sight of her.

Conversations died. Time stood still. Her eyes fluttered around the room anxiously until they landed on me. She held my gaze and my heart did a somersault. I clattered my glass down on the kitchen top clumsily, breaking the silence, and Mamma walked towards her as she reached the bottom step.

"Bellissima! You look amazing, Olivia!"

She smiled politely as she ran her hands nervously over her hips, which drew my eyes from her face back down to that enticing body. Realising I was still standing motionless like a fool, I stalked towards her, trying not to look like a predator about to go in on its kill.

"You really do look stunning, bambola," I agreed, and her exquisite eyes locked with mine. A cute blush made her cheeks rosy as I held my hand out for her to take. She hesitated a moment as she looked around at mamma and Elle, who gave her encouraging smiles. She was still unsure of me. Of us. Tonight it was my mission to change that. Finally, she took it and I smiled widely as we walked out of the lodge. She hesitated at the top of the icy steps of the veranda. I looked down and realised she was wearing very sexy but very fucking high heels. Without warning, I bent down and scooped her up in my arms, causing her to squeal and wrap her arms around my neck.

"I know your game," I smirked as she stared at my face. When I reached the ice-clad road, I didn't put her down but instead continued to walk towards the main hub with her in my arms.

"What game?"

"You wear ridiculous shoes just so I have to carry you everywhere," I grinned, keeping my eyes fixed forward, but I knew she was scowling at me.

"I didn't ask you to pick me up!"

"If you hate it so much, I can just put you down," I turned and looked down at her pretty face as she narrowed her eyes.

"Well, you carried me *this* far, you might as well carry me until there's no more snow," she replied with a shrug of her shoulders and I chuckled. She liked being in my arms just as much as I loved her there.

I had booked dinner at a Michelin star restaurant, Baumanière 1850, and paid to have a private room away from everyone. That way, my men could wait outside and we could have some time alone. Having my loyal soldiers around us wasn't exactly setting the scene for a romantic evening.

I couldn't help but stare at her as we walked into the restaurant and her eyes grew wider as the server showed us upstairs and into a beautifully decorated and candlelit room with an open fire. Her mouth dropped open when she saw the huge bouquet of red roses on her chair.

"Are these for me? Did you do this?" she asked, picking them up and smelling them.

I chuckled. "Do you like them?"

"They are beautiful. Thank you," she smiled genuinely, and I instantly wanted to kiss her. Realising I no longer had to hold back from stopping myself possessing those lips anymore, I did exactly that. I felt her melt against me within seconds as my hand firmly pulled her into me at the nape of her neck. She lowered the flowers from between us to her side so I could press my body up against hers. It was a slow and gentle kiss. Nothing too heated. I had remembered to take things slow and if I got too excited this early in the night, I would be doomed.

Stepping back, I smiled as I looked down at her dazed face and hooded eyes. She wanted more. Good start. I gestured for her to climb into the little booth in a charming and intimate cove first and then sat on the side opposite her. The waiter brought over the best champagne they had and we glanced down at the menu. However, watching Olivia was far more appealing. She chewed at her lower lip as she scanned the French menu, and I fought the urge to scold her for making my dick instantly hard. No. Best behaviour tonight Gio.

"Is something wrong?" I asked instead. Her eyes flickered up to mine and I could see the concern on her face.

"I don't have a clue what half this stuff is! It's so fancy! You know you are somewhere expensive when they don't put the prices on the menu."

I smiled at her down-to-earth nature. It was so refreshing from the women's company I normally keep.

"Don't worry about it. I will order for us. I know what is good," I replied, taking the menu from her hand.

She studied me carefully and I knew she had a question she was dying to ask. I waited for her curiosity to take over like I knew it would.

"Exactly how rich are you? I don't care. Obviously, I am not interested in you for your money, or I would have taken a very different tact in my interview." I burst out laughing and she smiled, realising she had taken me by surprise. "Let me guess I only got the job because the other two women were gold diggers?"

I rotated the silver knife in my hand on the table. "Let's just say I do very well for myself and you are correct about them being gold diggers. Or maybe it was not so much my money but my cock they were after."

She spat her champagne as I said the word cock and coughed loudly. Her eyes narrowed slightly but in a playful way. She wasn't jealous, merely interested, I think.

"Don't worry, bambola. Desperate isn't my type. My mind was a little preoccupied with a gorgeous brunette who insulted me in front of my mamma." She looked smug as she sat back against the silk booth chair.

We fell into a silence again and I watched her look around the restaurant nervously. I needed to loosen her up. I needed the Liv back that I had last night. This version of her was too in her head. What was it she said was one of her worst traits in her interview? An overthinker.

"Are you looking forward to going skiing tomorrow?" I asked before taking a sip of the champagne.

She scoffed loudly. "No. I am pretty sure I am going to break a bone."

"So, you really have never done it before? Not even dry slopes?"

She turned her head and looked into my eyes with that charming innocence they sometimes held.

"I once went to a tobogganing party when I was ten."

Chuckling, I leaned forward on the table and held her gaze.

"Don't worry. I will help you. I am a brilliant teacher."

She rolled her eyes and drank her champagne.

"I am sure you are! But that's what instructors are for."

I frowned at the thought of another man teaching her how to ski. His hands on her hips.

"Bambola, I am the only teacher you will ever need. In all things."

That flicker of attraction and excitement was evident in her eyes before they turned into her favourite glare. "Modest as ever."

I leaned back and smirked. Good, she was insulting me again, which means she wasn't thinking so much. The waiter came over and took our order. I spoke to him in fluent French, which made Olivia's mouth drop open.

"You speak French too?" she whispered across the table as the waiter walked away.

"Oui," I responded with a cheeky grin. "And Spanish, Russian and a little Korean."

She huffed loudly and folded her arms across her chest, looking bewildered. "Is there anything you can't do? No one can be this good at everything. It's annoying!"

I leaned over the table and curled my index finger towards her, beckoning her to me. She sat forward and I whispered, "I can't sing a note."

She raised her eyebrows. "Really?"

"Yep. Tone deaf. Don't ever get me to sing you happy birthday, you will never look at me the same way again."

She laughed and it sounded like a melody.

"And how do I look at you?" she teased.

"Like you want to rip my clothes off and lick every inch of my body," I winked, and her mouth dropped open.

"I do not!"

"Or like you want to wrap those tiny little hands around my throat and squeeze."

"That's more like it," she smirked as the waiter placed our plates of fine cuisine down in front of us. There was always one problem with coming to these places. Each dish was bite size! I am glad we have seven of them to come.

Each course came with a different glass of wine to compliment the dish and even though I had explained they were to sip with the food, Liv was doing a great job of not leaving any to waste.

"It would be a crime!" She had suggested, so I agreed and joined her by downing each one.

The meal continued as such with us bantering back and forth, laughing and flirting outrageously. As the alcohol started to take effect, each of the many walls we had around ourselves were slowly being torn down. It was the first time I had ever enjoyed being in the company of a woman so much. I loved her little quirks. No, not love. Liked. The way that one dimple in her cheek surfaced when she smiled genuinely. The way she talked with her hands. So expressive and dramatic. The way she would twist one strand of hair behind her ear without realising she was doing it. But most of all I lov…liked the way she could hold my gaze with those spell-binding eyes. She looked at me as if she was seeing me. Really seeing me. And she wasn't afraid.

My stomach dropped when I thought of how soon that might all change.

Lose Your Panties

Olivia

When the last of our dishes were taken away, I smiled at Giovanni as I raised my wine glass to my lips. I had lost count of the number of different wines I had tasted tonight and even though each glass was barely a quarter full, I was starting to feel that fuzzy warming feeling of the alcohol working its magic.

Giovanni lifted his own glass off the table before sliding out of his seat and coming over to the same side of the booth as me. My heart fluttered a little as I moved along to give him enough room to sit next to me. Oh holy shit, why did he have to look and smell so good all the time? Tonight, he was wearing black smart trousers that hugged his thick, toned thighs perfectly and white shirt with the sleeves rolled up, showcasing his strong, black-haired forearms. He had the first three or four buttons undone, which gave me a mouth-watering view of his collarbone and top of his chest. He smelt crisp. Masculine. Intoxicating.

I wanted to bury my head in his neck and breathe deeply but I fought the urge. He twisted his muscular frame so he was facing me on the seat and I did the same. The air suddenly felt thicker between us. More electric. His face became intense as he stared at me.

"What?" I smiled into my glass, trying to ignore the need that was aching between my legs under his penetrating gaze.

"I just wanted to thank you for trusting me enough to open up about your past last night," his voice was deep and husky, sending a wave of pleasure through me. I masked my surprise at his words and shrugged.

"It was nice to actually talk to someone about it," I said quietly. It was true. The moment the words left my lips, I felt a weight lift off my shoulders. I had been hiding in Italy for nearly a month now and it was the first time I had confided to anyone about Henry.

"Look bambola. I don't want you to feel any pressure from me. You have no idea how much I want to fuck you until you beg me to stop. To worship your body the way it deserves. But after everything, I am willing to wait. I will take it slow. I want you to trust that I will look after you," his hungry eyes bore into mine and I gulped down my arousal.

My belly clenched in anticipation. I didn't want to take it slow. Slow was not what I had in mind. At that moment, I realised that he had just said the words that I needed to hear. His understanding and patience just made him even more irresistible. But now I had heard them, now I knew that he was thinking about me and not his own needs, I wanted the opposite. I wanted him tonight.

I had escaped Henry to try and live my life. But I was still letting him have a hold on me. No more. Giovanni was not like Henry. Yes, he was dominant, intimidating and possessive, but he was also kind and gentle. At least with me and his family. It was unfair of me to compare them.

Gathering my courage, I leaned forwards and placed my hand on his warm, muscular thigh. It radiated heat and strength. His eyes burned with intense desire as I stared up at him. Continuing my exploration of his thigh, I noticed the muscles in his jaw flex and his grip on the stem of his wine glass grew tighter. As I glanced down at where my hand was inching closer to the top of his leg, I saw his erection harden, bulging against his trousers. My god, it looked huge. My mouth went dry and I licked my lips.

"Olivia," his voice was laced with thick arousal as he warned me.

My eyes met his and I whispered, "What if I don't want to take it slow?"

His gaze held mine with challenge and I could see the turmoil, need and dominance in them.

"You have no idea the dangerous game you are playing bambola," he husked, and my core tightened in response. I smiled seductively as I brushed my hand lightly over his erection and he hissed sharply.

"Then show me," I leaned in and kissed his neck sensually, tasting his skin on my tongue, sending warmth through my body. Oh wow, I was feeling bold. I had never been this woman before. This was the effect he had on me. I was a new me, a me that didn't shy away from what I wanted. I had been fighting my bewildering attraction to this man, this inexplicable connection we had, for too long and I was tired. I was tired of fighting.

His hand grabbed my wrist that was caressing his bulge and I pulled away from his neck. His expression was dark, dangerous and so fucking sexy.

"Do you trust me, Olivia? Do you trust that I would never hurt you?"

As I stared into those smouldering eyes that held so much danger, I realised I did. I wasn't afraid of him. I felt no fear. He wasn't Henry. I nodded slowly and he released my hand, turning to the side to whisper in my ear.

"Lean back," his raspy accent caused butterflies to flutter in my stomach, but I did what he said. I leaned my back against the stone wall so I faced him. My lips parted at the look on his face. He was in complete dominant mode and I knew my knickers were ruined. I was not in control and, for the first time ever...I was OK with that.

"Take your panties off," his voice was commanding and firm. It should have scared me, but it didn't. What it did was shock me. My eyes bulged at his order.

"What? No way," I whisper-yelled. His eyes narrowed at my defiance. Oh my lord, now my knickers are definitely ruined.

"Do you trust me?" he repeated, and my eyes scanned the room we were in. We were alone but any of the waiters could walk back in at any moment. This was insane. What was he going to do? As my eyes landed on him again, I realised I didn't care. If he kept looking at me with that much desire and need, then he could do anything he wanted to me. I nodded.

"Lose your panties."

I awkwardly hooked my fingers up under my dress and pulled down my black lace thong, shimmying it down my thighs and then off my legs. Giovanni watched intensely and then put his hand out for them once they had passed my heels. Hesitantly, I placed them in his hand, embarrassed by how damp they were. He pocketed them in his trousers with a small smirk at the corners of his lips. "They're mine now."

I narrowed my eyes at him but he leaned towards me and looked down at my bare legs in my dress.

"Spread your legs," he ordered, his voice rough with need. My cheeks burned with the fire of the sun as my eyes widened. Is he serious?! From the look on his face, he was deadly serious.

Slowly, I lifted one leg up onto the seat between us, the heel of my shoe digging into the silk upholstery and spread my other thigh wider under the table, which was rewarded by an animalistic groan of pleasure from Giovanni at the sight of me laid bare before him.

"Fuck. Just as I thought. A perfect, pink pussy," he whispered, and I slammed my legs together on hearing his filthy words. His eyes travelled up to my mortified face and he held my gaze. "Ah ah. Don't you dare hide yourself from me. Open your legs bambola."

My heart was pounding in my ears and my body felt like it was burning up. How was he doing this to me? Yet, I found myself following his command. Opening my legs wide once more.

"I need to taste you," he muttered as he leaned down on the seat and sank his head between my thighs.

"Giovan- Oh my god!" I breathed as I felt my aching clit throbbing against his greedy tongue. Of course, he was really good at this. Flicking my clit with ruthless precision over and over and then sucking it into his mouth before returning to his skillful rhythm.

My back arched against the cold stone wall and I gripped his black hair in my hand, eyes fixed on the door because someone could walk in at any moment. I moaned loudly when he increased his pace and I dug my heel into the seat. Oh my god, I was going to come already. I could feel it building like a volcano about to erupt. My breathing was coming out in short, sharp pants and moans and when I felt Giovanni's strong hands grab my hips and pull me into his face more, I fell over the edge of pleasure. I cried out his name as my thighs trembled around his head. After a few more slow licks, he raised his head with a smug expression, but his eyes still held that dominance and hunger.

Just at that moment, the door swung open, and a waiter waltzed in as Giovanni sat up right and I quickly squeezed my thighs together and turned towards the table. If he took one look at my sated face, he would know. He would fucking know what we had just done. Giovanni put his firm hand on one of my knees under the table and rubbed my skin with his thumb, causing a spike of need to ripple through me again.

The waiter said something to Giovanni in French, and I am pretty sure Gio just asked for the bill. Once he was gone, he turned to me and that look was back. The one that told me he wasn't done with me yet.

"You taste fucking divine bambola and we need to leave. Now."

He grabbed my hand and pulled me out of the booth as I stumbled on my heels. My legs felt like jelly.

"Can I have my knickers back first?" I hissed at him and he smirked over his shoulder.

"No."

I rolled my eyes as we left the restaurant and the cold night air hit me in the little clothing I had on. I shivered and he looked down at me instinctively.

"Are you cold?"

I nodded. He suddenly bent down and scooped me up over his shoulder effortlessly and started marching back up the hill towards the lodge.

"Giovanni! What are you doing?"

"Getting us home quickly... for more reasons than one," his voice held promises that made my stomach flip and when a firm smack landed on my ass cheek, I yelped, causing him to chuckle deeply.

The anticipation grew as the familiar cabins came into sight. That meant we were nearly there. I was about to have sex with Giovanni Buccini! My insanely hot boss! Oh my god! The nerves were starting to build and panic was setting in as he took two steps at a time up to the front door. He placed me on my feet and looked down at me heatedly. I had to warn him. That even though I wanted it more than anything, I might not be able to do this.

"Giovanni. I- When I-" I tried to start but my words failed me.

"What is it?" He asked with concern.

"Whenever I've tried to go all the way, I always end up having a panic attack. Flashbacks," I mumbled, looking down at my hands. He lifted my chin with his finger and thumb and stared deep into my eyes.

"It's okay. You will think of nothing but me and how good I am making you feel, Bambola. I am going to look after you tonight," he breathed, and then leaned down to capture my lips. This kiss was gentle and sweet and I felt all my worries melt away.

I've Got You

Olivia

The kiss didn't stay sweet and gentle for long. Soon all my inhibitions were gone and I jumped up into his arms, circling my legs around his hips as he squeezed my ass cheeks through my dress. Our lips were fighting for more of each other, panting heavily through our kisses so we didn't have to stop for breath. I had never felt anything like this before. Such intense passion. And it wasn't just because of the insane build up of sexual tension between us that was about to come to a head, because I am pretty sure I will want this man just as intensely again and again.

I was vaguely aware of Giovanni kicking the front door shut with his foot and moving us along the ground floor towards the stairs. Suddenly, I felt a hard surface against my back, and I broke away from his lips to see he had stopped at the bottom of the staircase as his lips devoured my neck, causing me to moan. He pushed his hips into me, making his rock-hard erection press against my soaking and still naked centre and I gripped his hair in my hand. *Oh my god.* His head was in the crook of my neck, biting at my skin, and his hands were roaming my body, setting me ablaze with every touch, caress and squeeze.

"Fuck Gio! I want you so badly." Was that my sultry voice?

He pulled out of my neck and looked down at me with half-closed eyes and parted lips. "I am yours, bambola."

He moved us away from the wall, gripping my ass once again, and took two steps at a time up to the first floor. Our lips were locked in a fierce kiss as he entered his bedroom and slammed the door shut behind him. He broke away from me and lowered me to the floor carefully.

My chest was rising and falling in shallow breaths, and I instantly craved his touch again when he stepped back. He never took his eyes off mine as he reached for the door lock and turned it. My eyes flickered down to his hand and then back up to his face. I suddenly registered why he wanted me to see him do that. He was reassuring me that no one else could enter. It was just us.

"Take off your dress," His voice was low and my core tightened. "But don't take your eyes off me, bambola."

It felt as though I was under his spell as my hands moved to the back of the dress and I tugged down the zip slowly. There was no need to wear a bra in this dress, so as soon as it fell to my ankles, I was standing completely naked in front of him, only in ridiculous high heels.

His eyes raked down my body hungrily and they blazed with desire. He was taking his time to admire every inch of my form and, instead of making me feel insecure or embarrassed like I had felt with other men, it made me feel empowered. The way he was drinking me in was as if I was the most heavenly thing he had ever seen.

"Sei così fottutamente bella," he growled in Italian, and although I had no idea what he said, I knew beautiful was one of the words. Oh wow. I think I just had a mini orgasm.

"What?" I breathed.

He took a few steps towards me, his eyes never leaving mine.

"I said, you are so fucking beautiful." He lifted my chin with his fingers and forced me to look him in the eyes. "If you need to stop, you tell me." It came out as a command but there was a gentleness to his tone. I nodded again like an idiot. I think my voice had given up on me. "Don't think bambola. Just feel," he husked as he let the tips of his fingers trace down my neck, chest, around my pebbled nipples, down my stomach, towards my...

My eyelids fluttered shut as I did what he said. I savoured the tingling sensation his feathery touch provoked all over my body. How my nipples hardened. How such rough hands could be so delicate? And when he brushed lower, between my legs and lightly grazed my needy clit, I moaned out. His other hand grabbed me behind the neck firmly, tilting my head up to him as he pushed one finger inside me painfully slowly. I whimpered as he groaned.

"You're so wet and ready for me," he breathed against my lips before he tugged my lower lip between his teeth. I cried out as he added another finger and started to move inside me so deliciously. I rocked my hips into his hand as I gripped his broad shoulders. When he crooked his fingers inside me and started to massage and pump at my G-spot, my legs started to shake and I moaned loudly into our kiss. If his fingers could do this, I couldn't even begin to think about what he could do with his dick.

"Come for me Olivia. Let me see you," his voice was demanding and my body seemed to respond as an explosion of pleasure rippled through me and I threw my head back and cried out loudly. As I came down from my climax, I had never felt so relaxed. I had just had two mind-blowing orgasms in the space of half an hour and we hadn't even got to the main event. He removed his fingers from me and I sat back on the edge of the bed.

"I love watching you come bambola, knowing I am the one who makes you feel that way."

He grabbed the collar of his shirt and pulled it over his head in one swift movement, dropping it on the floor. My heart raced at the sight of his incredibly chiselled torso and muscular pecs. Those huge biceps could throw me around so effortlessly. I hoped that might be the case tonight. I bit my lip as he unbuckled his belt and pulled it out from his trousers. My lips parted when he dropped his pants and boxers and I was faced with the most perfect fucking dick I have ever seen. I am not kidding. If there was such a thing as a supermodel penis, this would be it, I swear. Perfect length, perfect width, smooth, and rock hard, curving up towards his navel. Oh lord have mercy. My eyes were fixed on it as he stood naked before me. I immediately wanted to taste it. To know what it feels like to have it in my mouth. To give him as much pleasure as he has given me.

I dropped to my knees in front of him without second guessing my dirty desires and heard his shocked voice. "Olivia, you don't have- oh fuck!"

I flicked my tongue over the tip to lick off his salty pre-cum and then took him as far into my mouth as I could without gagging. He was so hard but velvety smooth and I moaned as he hit the back of my throat. It seemed to have the desired effect as his thighs tensed and he raised one hand to his face, hiding his eyes. Holding the base of his cock, I sucked, licked and deep throated him mercilessly as he groaned and swore in Italian above me.

Abruptly, he pulled back from me and grabbed me by the arms, hoisting me up into his chest. "You are too fucking good baby, I want to come inside you not in that pretty mouth yet."

I wrapped my legs around him once again as he moved us to the bed, but this time I could feel every muscle and the smoothness of our skin against each other without the restriction of our clothes. It felt amazing. His mouth possessed mine as he dropped us down onto the bed, me under his bulky body that was being propped up by his elbows. He looked down at me with so much desire but I froze. Nate's face flashed in mind. This exact position. Him on top. Looking down at me. I squeezed my eyes shut; my whole body tensed.

"Olivia, look at me," That voice. It sounded so distant yet calming. I felt my body being lifted to a sitting position and I opened my eyes to see Giovanni sitting up on the bed. He was resting back on his heels and my legs were still wrapped around his waist, so I sat on his lap. It was only then that I realised I was shaking, my arms locked around his neck tightly.

"My eyes. Look at me." He commanded. His voice was soothing, calming me instantly as I stared into his beautiful eyes. He stroked strands of my hair out of my face as I tried to get my breathing under control. "Don't think. Just feel," he whispered as he ran his fingertips up and down the length of my back. "You are safe. You're with me." He repeated twice until all my panic had dissolved and all I could feel was his hands and the power of his eyes. "I've got you, bambola."

As my senses returned, I felt his erection nestled between us as he licked my lips sensually until they parted and I smashed my mouth into his, the desire back in full force. He did it. He stopped my flashback. He...saved me from my demons. An overwhelming feeling of safety rushed over me and I rocked my hips against his dick, needing him to take me now. To make me feel only him. Our breathing was frantic as he lifted my hips and held me above the tip of his cock. He slid between my wet folds and pushed slightly at my warm entrance that was yearning for him. We stared into each other's eyes as he let go of my hips and held me tightly around my waist. His cock slid into my wetness in one slow, deep stroke and we both gasped into each other's mouths.

The feel of him stretching me wide and filling me so deeply was incredible. He lifted me again. Up. Down. The pace was torturing slow but every single nerve ending in my centre was being massaged just right. I felt like he knew exactly what my body needed when it needed it. One of his hands cupped my breast and started to play with my nipple as I moaned his name.

"Fuck you are so tight bambola," he breathed against my mouth as he started to move his hips up into me a little faster. I could feel my walls clenching around him as he hit that sweet spot again and again. Every inch of me seemed to gather in on itself, like a star in the galaxy about to explode.

"Sì piccola vieni a prendermi," from his dominant and sexy tone, I knew it was a command. When his hand moved between us and pinched my clit, I screamed out my orgasm as my body shuddered on top of him. He held my body tightly to his chest, never stopping his thrusts. He was protecting me; keeping me safe as I let go.

He slowed to a stop but remained inside me to give me a moment to regain my senses. He brushed my hair out of my face and gave me the most gorgeous smile. "You did well, bambola."

And that's when I felt it. The freedom. I no longer felt that doom hanging over me. That panic that surrounds me whenever I think of having sex. It was no longer the only memory I had of going all the way. Now this was. He was. As I looked down into his chocolate eyes, a single tear of relief rolled down my cheek and I smiled. He wiped it away with his thumb. "No crying baby girl. I am not done with you yet."

My eyes must have showed my excitement as he chuckled and spun us so my back was on the mattress and he was on top of me.

"Hold on bambola. It's my turn."

I didn't even have time to think of anything as he pulled his rock-hard dick out of me only to slam back in with power. I screamed out in pleasure as he pounded into me repeatedly with so much fire and passion. His lips were devouring my neck, my breasts, my nipples and back to my mouth as he fucked me hard. There was no better word for it. He wasn't gentle any longer, his need to take me the way he had always wanted to was in control. And I fucking loved every damn second of it.

Her

Giovanni

This was unlike anything I had ever experienced before. And trust me, I have had my fair share of women, but none have ever made me feel like that. None have provoked such a profound need to worship and please them before I would even consider coming. It's not been easy. I could have exploded in her mouth earlier and again when she rode my dick and soaked me in her orgasm. But I also felt things. Emotions I have never felt for a woman. Pride. Awe. Intense passion. And then there's her unbelievable body that feels like it was sculpted just for me. The way her skin, nipples, clit and pussy are so responsive to my touch. The feeling of being inside her is complete heaven.

How was I only just experiencing this now? How had I only just found her? I wasn't holding back anymore. I couldn't. I had been gentle and tender, letting her body get accustomed to me and freeing her mind of her demons. And now, I was possessing her the way I demanded. The way I had been fantasising about since the day she walked into that interview.

My cock slid out of her tight, warm pussy only to be sucked back in by her clenching walls as I fucked her hard and fast. She's a screamer, that's for sure, and I loved it.

"Fuck Gio!" she cried as I rotated my hips slightly before thrusting back in deeper than before. She was calling me Gio and it was turning me on even more. I kneeled up between her legs and lifted them so her sexy as fuck heels were around my neck and hugged her thighs against my chest. She was about to have her mind blown in this position.

As I buried myself inside her, hitting her G-spot and pushing in as deep as I could go, her eyes rolled back in her head and she cried out. I started my relentless thrusts as sweat beaded above my brows and I watched her body writhing and shaking beneath me. She was close again and so was I. Leaning forward, I took her legs with me. She wasn't joking when she said she was flexible. Shit. Sinking into her even further, I captured her mouth with mine as she screamed into our kiss and I felt my body tense with the pressure of my looming climax. She squeezed her slender legs around my neck tightly as her inner walls did the same to my cock and I released a loud groan along with her name. I felt myself explode inside her as she milked me dry.

Pushing her legs off my shoulders, I fell onto her chest, breathing heavily, still inside her. That was the most intense fuck I have ever had. Suddenly, her chest started vibrating below my head and the beautiful sound of her laughter echoed around the room. I lifted my head and looked at her with a confused smile.

"I hope you are not laughing at my performance?" I panted, raising one eyebrow at her suggestively.

She shook her head, covering her mouth with her hand.

"No. No. Sorry. It's just – "

"Just?" I waited impatiently for her answer through her giggles.

"It was even better than I imagined it would be!"

My smile grew wider and I felt my chest inflate with pride.

"Well...thank you, I think."

She giggled again and looked down at me through her dark eyelashes. "You're welcome."

"So, you *did* imagine what it would be like? You have been having dirty dreams about me?"

She rolled her eyes at the ceiling but still told the truth. "A few."

I pulled out of her swiftly, which caused her to gasp and I leaned up onto my elbow to gaze down at her stunning face. Her cheeks were flushed, lips swollen and eyes bright. Her hair was tousled, and she looked sexy as fuck. "Well, I am glad the reality was better than the fantasy."

She giggled, looking up at me with those big eyes and bit her fingers, which made her look so cute that I wanted to dive straight back inside her again. But I suddenly realised something. Fuck.

My face must have fallen as she looked concerned.

"What?" she asked.

"We didn't use protection." I had never done that before. I always use a condom. The last thing I need is some bimbo trying to trap me with a kid. But Liv wasn't like that and we were so in the moment that it hadn't even crossed my mind. I wanted to be in her bare. I wanted to feel her properly.

Her face relaxed and she traced her index finger over my lips, which caused a pleasurable shudder to travel down my spine.

"It's okay. I am on the pill."

I exhaled in relief and she chuckled. Suddenly realising what that probably meant, I frowned.

"I thought you said you hadn't really been having sex." I didn't mean it to sound so accusing, but the natural jealousy and possessiveness over her was ten times more after what we just did.

"I haven't. But I get heavy periods, so the doctors suggested it and I thought it was a good idea to be prepared, just in case..." she shrugged but it didn't do anything to calm the jealousy that was stirring inside me.

"Incase what?" I growled and she looked up at me, lifting herself onto her elbows. We were still both stark naked and I was pleased to see that she wasn't one of those girls that immediately hid her body away after having sex.

"Hang on... are you jealous?" Her face was one of delight and bewilderment as she stared into my eyes that narrowed at her in a deep scowl. "Oh my god, what of? All the imaginary men I have been having sex with?" she chuckled and I rolled on top of her, pinning her hands to either side of her head.

"Yes. Okay. That's who I am. Now I have had you, be prepared bambola, because I am not a man who likes to share."

Her eyes darted between mine with humour. She finds this hilarious. Seeing me like this. Which only irritated me more.

"You are insane," she smirked. I bent down and kissed the dimple on her cheek.

"Insane about you." Her face froze as she stared into my eyes and tried to read me. I smirked, knowing she was freaking out inside that pretty little head of hers.

"What happens now?" She asked seriously and I pulled her up onto the pillows of my bed. Her hair spilled over the pillow, a mess of silky dark tresses that I wanted to play with between my fingers. I lay on the pillow next to her.

"Well, we go to sleep. Maybe wake up and have some more sex and then maybe a shower. More sex..." I said while studying her soft hair in between my fingers. She hit me playfully in the chest and I chuckled.

"You know what I mean," her eyes stared into mine and for a moment I just wanted to stay like this forever. In this room. This bed. With her. Forget about all the chaos that was waiting for me outside of this. Here we were safe. Safe to be who we were without the rest of the world's shit interfering. I rolled onto my back and stared up at the ceiling. I couldn't lie to her, but I also couldn't be 100% honest. I needed to sort my shit out quickly.

"Honestly, I don't know. All I know is that I want you. A lot. And I can't let you go."

When she didn't respond, I turned my head to her face and saw a small smile on her lips and happiness in her eyes. She liked me too. That's what she was saying without words. I pulled her onto me and she rested her head on my chest. "Sleep bambola."

She nestled into me closer and I put my arm around her shoulders as I stared out the window at the incandescent full moon, our only source of light in the dead of night. My life was a bigger mess than it has ever been now. All because of this woman. I had to find my way out of a joke of an engagement without pissing off my Zio and the Aianis, I had to deal with whatever threat the Leone's seemed to be posing and I had to reveal to Olivia who I really was. The last one was the one that worried me the most because it provoked an alien emotion in me that I did not like at all. Fear.

From the moment I looked into those hypnotic eyes for the first time, I knew I was in trouble. I want to spend every night curled up in the mystery that is her mind. What is she thinking? What does she want? Is this enough for her? Am I enough? I am good at reading people. Good at reading between the lines, but she is an enigma to me. And it scares the hell out of me. I am not in control when it comes to her. She makes me vulnerable and I have lost all my power to stop it. But what scares me the most is the fear of losing something that I have only just found. That I have only just realised I need.

Her.

Nightmares and Monsters

Olivia

Dawn was flirting with the ink-stained sky as the first rays of light were seeping over the snow-capped mountains hiding the horizon. As my eyes adjusted to the unfamiliar surroundings, I felt a heavy weight over my waist, pinning me down, and noticed a tattooed hand coming out from under my neck. I froze.

Giovanni. I was in his bed. We had sex. And now he's... spooning me? I blinked rapidly a few times as my heart started to race. I was dying to turn around and get a look at the gorgeous man behind me but I didn't want to wake him. Or maybe I did... Maybe he would do all those things to me again if he woke up... I smiled as I let my mind fill with dirty fantasies about what we could still get up to before the world woke up. But first, I realised I really needed some water.

As carefully as I could, I lifted his heavy arm off my waist and raised my neck off his other forearm. Leaning up on the mattress, I turned slightly to get a sneaky look at him. My heart fluttered and my stomach flipped. His long, dark eyelashes were fanned over his cheeks, lips parted as he breathed deeply and his black hair was soft and messy on the pillow. I let my eyes travel north down his taut pecs and abs to the sexy V that snaked down under the white duvet. I bit my lip as I contemplated moving the duvet away so I could see that perfect dick again. Just to be sure...

No Liv. Water.

I felt like a ninja, climbing out of bed as silently as I could and picking up his white shirt he had been wearing on our date. Throwing it over my head, my core instantly pulsed as my senses were awakened by his strong, masculine cologne and I breathed it in deeply. I opened the bedroom door and crept downstairs to grab a glass of water from the kitchen.

I froze on the stairs when I saw the dark shadows of two huge frames outside on the veranda and instantly panicked. But then I realised they were just bodyguards on night duty. As long as I didn't turn any lights on, they wouldn't see me in this... attire. As I reached the bottom step, I looked to my left at the little snug room in the corner where a small lamp was indeed already providing a warm glow to the room. I jumped, hand straight to my heart, when I saw a figure sitting in an armchair in the corner.

"Olivia? Sorry my dear, I didn't mean to scare you," came Cecilia's smooth voice with that silky Italian accent.

My cheeks immediately flamed as I tugged at Giovanni's shirt to try and cover my bare legs more. I was naked under this and as her brown eyes behind her cat-eyed glasses took in my body, she knew it too. A slow smile spread across her face as she lowered the book she was reading on to her lap.

"I – I was just getting a glass of water," I mumbled, wanting the ground to swallow me whole. This was possibly the most embarrassing moment of my life so far. Quickly, I dashed into the kitchen and filled up a glass of water from the tap. *Calm down Liv. She doesn't know this is Giovanni's shirt. She doesn't know you slept in his bed or had the most mind-blowing sex of your life with her son.*

As I turned and saw that mischief dancing in her eyes, watching my every move, I gulped. She definitely knew.

"Goodnight Cecilia," I muttered, my head down as I made my way towards the stairs.

"Olivia." I paused as her voice called out into the darkness. "Won't you come and sit with me for a moment?"

What? Really? Now? Like this? Knowing that I didn't really have many other options, I turned on my bare feet and padded towards her. She smiled and gestured to the other armchair by the bookcase. I put my glass on the side table and pulled the shirt down to cover as much of my lower half as I could before I took a seat. My eyes darted awkwardly around the room and I pretended to look interested in reading the spines of the books.

"Do you like to read?" she asked.

I nodded as I forced my gaze back at her. She was lounging in the armchair, a long silk robe around her body and she looked relaxed. Unlike me, who was wearing practically nothing and sitting rigidly.

"Gio likes to read too. I know he doesn't look like the type," she chuckled. "But looks can be deceiving."

Her words sounded innocent yet they felt as if they were packed with hidden meaning. I remained quiet and she placed the book she was reading on the table between us. I didn't recognise it. It was in Italian.

"Could you not sleep?" I asked when the silence became too much for me. I wanted to steer the conversation to more appropriate grounds, not Giovanni.

She smiled sadly and shook her head. "I rarely do. Side effects of the medication. I often feel like I have insomnia, hence why I need to rest sometimes during the day."

I nodded my head and looked awkwardly back at the books on the shelves. She was being so open with me and it made me uneasy. I was her employee at the end of the day, yet she seemed to be talking to me as if she had known me for years or considered me a friend.

"You have never asked why I am on medication or why I needed a nanny to help with the kids in the first place," she stated, cocking her head to the side to study me. It wasn't a question, but she made it sound like one.

"It is none of my business," I said quietly, and her smile grew.

"That's what I like about you. You are not a gossip. You are someone who can be trusted, Olivia. That is a good trait to have."

I relaxed a little at her compliment and started to fiddle with the bottom of Gio's shirt on my lap. I was curious about her life and had often wondered what she was dealing with behind closed doors.

"You told me on my first day that you liked your privacy. I am a private person myself, so I respect boundaries," I said back. Immediately, I looked away from her embarrassed. *Yeah, alright Liv. You just slept with your boss... Where were your boundaries then?*

"I am bipolar. Always have been but I also suffer from depression and PTSD since Vinny's death," she said seriously, and my eyes darted up to hers, shocked she had shared that with me.

"I'm sorry. That must be very difficult," I replied. I know all too well what PTSD feels like, but to be dealing with all of that at once must be a lot.

She nodded, "It is. Every day is a struggle. But I have the most wonderful family to keep me going," she smiled, and I beamed back, thinking of Sani and Raya and Elle. And then Giovanni.

"You really have raised amazing children, Cecilia. They are a credit to you," I said genuinely.

Her eyes shone with unshed tears, and she raised her immaculate nails to her lips.

"Thank you my dear. They are my world and all I wish for them to be in this life is happy." I nodded and smiled but her face was serious, her gaze piercing. "Out of all my children, I worry about Giovanni the most."

I held her gaze as she shifted in her chair a little. My heart fluttered at his name and my intrigue got the better of me. He was the oldest and a grown man who had done extremely well for himself. Why would she worry about him the most?

"Why?" I asked carefully.

She smiled, putting me at ease for asking such a blunt question. "Because he has been through the most. He has to deal with the most. You have probably realised by now that he is not what he likes the world to believe him to be." Her eyes narrowed on me suggestively and I swallowed my nerves. But once again, that look was one of determination and drew out the honesty in me. I slowly nodded my head, agreeing with her. "I worry about him because he carries the weight of this family on his shoulders, and he allows it to consume him. He is alone in his grief, choices and darkness. And that is a very lonely place to be."

I listened intently and felt my face tense at her words. What choices? What darkness? I realised then, that there was so much I still didn't know about this man.

"He doesn't seem to be lonely," I stated, leaning back in the chair. But then I remembered what he had told me about his dad's death and the regret he felt. He had never told a soul. Perhaps what she was saying was true.

"It is always the people that hide it the best that are fighting the biggest battles. Trust me, I am one of them," she smiled sadly, and my heart went out to her. She was a woman who I could relate to.

"I think everyone is fighting some kind of inner battle, Cecilia. That is just the way this world works."

She leaned forward onto the arm of her chair and looked directly into my eyes. "Very true, but we do not have to fight them alone. Sharing your demons and inner struggles with the right person will set you free. If trust is there, you can overcome anything together."

We held each other's gaze as my breathing became shallow under her weighted words. Was she implying Giovanni and I could be that for each other? Surely not? She suddenly leaned back and relaxed. A soft giggle escaped her lips, and her playfulness was back. "Ignore me amore. Lack of sleep has gone to my brain."

I smiled awkwardly and picked up the glass from my table, sensing now was a good time to excuse myself.

"Just..." she reached out and touched my arm as I tried to stand. "Keep an open mind, Olivia. He may surprise you."

I nodded and stood up carefully. Little did she know, he had already surprised me in more ways than one tonight. "Good night, Cecilia."

"Good night, Olivia."

***

I made my way back into the bedroom and placed the water on the bedside table. Giovanni was still passed out and I took a moment to watch him sleeping. I couldn't shake the feeling that there was so much more going on with this man... this family... That in her own way, Cecilia was trying to prepare me or warn me. But the overwhelming message I felt from her tonight is that she was okay with this. Okay with me and her son. I scoffed and shook my head. Could I really allow myself to believe that this could be more than just sex? Amazing, passionate sex was what we had both signed up for last night. What if that is all this could be? Giovanni didn't strike me as the kind of man who had girlfriends. Or relationships in general and, technically, I still worked for him. What was it he said he had had with that girl? An arrangement. Is that what we will become too? When I asked him earlier what happened now, I was really asking what this meant. Was it a one-night thing? Were we just going to sleep together occasionally? Or was it more? His answer was cryptic. He said he wanted me. But he didn't say how... I suppose I will just have to wait and see how the rest of this weekend pans out. I wouldn't allow myself to get in too deep. I had to protect my heart from this man. I knew he had the ability to break it if I let him get too close.

Walking over to the balcony doors, I moved the sheer curtain away and gazed out at the beautiful scenery. He hadn't lied. This trip was already unforgettable. Suddenly, I heard a low groan behind me and the shuffling of the duvet. I turned my head to see Giovanni thrashing around on the bed, his face creased with pain. My heart flipped. He was still asleep, but he was not okay. He was dreaming or... having a nightmare.

"No!" he shouted, making me leap back in alarm. "No!" Sweat was beading on his forehead and his hands were clenched into fists by his side. My eyes widened in panic as I wondered what to do. Don't they say to never wake someone up during a nightmare?

"Apri la porta!" His voice was loud and haunting, it made me cower back into the curtain. No, I had to wake him. I couldn't leave him like this. Diving onto the bed, I put my hands on his chest gently to try and settle his erratic movements.

"Giovanni! Gio, wake up!" I whispered loudly, trying to keep my voice soft so as not to startle him more.

"Gio! It's just a nightmare," I raised one hand to his cheek and stroked his skin. His dark eyes flew open in alarm and his hand gripped my upper arm tightly.

"It's okay," I whispered, trying to keep the panic out of my own voice. The amount of adrenaline that was pumping through my body must have only been a fraction of what was going through his. His eyes settled on my face as his laboured breath caused his chest to rise and fall rapidly. Our eyes locked and I saw everything Cecilia had told me. The fear. Grief. Darkness.

Abruptly, he sat up and smashed his lips against mine possessively, his hands moving to my hips and pulling me on top of him, so I was straddling his waist. His tongue dominated my mouth in frantic urgency, and I felt my core tighten in response. My wetness grew between my legs as I felt his dick hardening instantly. He ripped open his shirt in one violent movement, revealing my breasts before capturing my lips once more. Wrapping his arm around my waist, he flipped us, so I was pinned below his body and, without warning, slammed himself inside me with one powerful thrust. I gasped at the pleasure of him filling me completely. Moaning into his mouth as he started to rock and move his hips, pulling in and out and never breaking our kiss felt so intense. His hands were everywhere. Dominating, exploring every inch of my body and I felt like my skin was on fire. I gasped as he grabbed a fistful of my hair and tugged it back, causing my mouth to break away from his, giving him exposure to my neck. He bit and sucked hard at my skin as he pounded into me harder and faster. My nails clawed and dug into his back as I hung onto him for dear life. This was so different to before. It was raw and wild. Animalistic even. He wasn't in control. At that moment, I felt all his emotions. I felt how much he needed this. How much he needed me.

His arms went behind my back and his strong hands gripped my shoulders, pulling me into every thrust deeper and harder than before. Circling my legs around his hips, I cried out as he hit places inside me, I didn't know were possible and the euphoric feeling of bursting within built at a staggering rate. His head was buried in my neck as he became rampant with need. I screamed out my orgasm as I felt him release inside me.

"Olivia!" he growled into my collarbone as his last powerful thrust caused his body to shake and shudder on top of mine. We laid motionless in the same position for what felt like eternity. Neither of us spoke. He didn't lift his head to look at me and all I could feel was his heavy panting on my skin. I swallowed as I stared up at the ceiling. That was intense. I didn't know sex could be like that. So raw.

Eventually, he pulled out of me and rolled away, staring up at the ceiling, jaw clenched. I moved onto my side to look at him but refrained from touching him. He looked... upset. Did I do something wrong?

I didn't dare speak as I felt his anger rolling off him. Once again, I suddenly felt like I didn't know this man. This man that I was lying next to and had just allowed to be inside me. Just as I was about to give up and climb out of bed to head for the shower, he spoke.

"Sorry."

It was just one word, but it stopped me in my tracks. I frowned as I stared at his side profile that was still tense and unwilling to look at me.

"What are you sorry for?" I frowned.

He sighed and ran his hand down his face. "For that. I didn't exactly give you a choice or wait for your consent. I never wanted you to have to see me like that. I'm sorry if I scared you."

My frown deepened. See him like what? Vulnerable? Scared? Because that was all I saw when I looked into his eyes after waking him up. It didn't scare me.

"You didn't scare me and I was more than willing to participate," I said simply, and he turned his face towards me for the first time. His expression softened and he reached out to stroke my hair away from my face. "Does that happen often? The dreams?" I asked softly as I stared into those chocolate brown eyes that were quickly becoming my favourite colour.

"My mind has a shitty ability to be dark and demented, especially at night," he groaned and dropped his hand on the bed between us.

"Are you afraid of your dreams?" His eyes searched mine as he thought about my question.

"Yes." My heart fluttered at how open he was being with me.

"So am I," I whispered.

We held each other's gaze and then he leaned in. He brushed the tip of his nose against mine before placing the softest and most fragile kiss on my lips. It made my whole-body ache in a way that made me want to cry. It was an understanding and a promise.

"Maybe we can protect each other from our dreams," he breathed against my lips and I wrapped my arms around his neck, moulding my body into his. My heart pounded at his words. His were just dreams but mine... mine was a reality. Henry was still out there.

"But can you protect me from a monster?" I whispered as his irresistible lips caressed mine lightly and his fingers tangled in my hair. He pulled back to look into my eyes. I saw something flash across them. Worry and something else that I couldn't quite put my finger on.

"I will always protect you, bambola. Against the world and all its monsters. But you should know... I am a monster to many." His intense gaze held mine in warning, but all I saw was the truth. That he meant every word.

"But you will never be a monster to me?" I asked quietly. A sweet smile tugged at the corners of his lips.

"Never."

He pressed his lips against mine and we got lost in each other once again.

Snow Plough

Olivia

"Thanks again for letting me borrow some of your skiing clothes."

I zipped up the expensive, designer ski jacket over my tight white thermal top as we waited in the ski shop to hire some ski boots for my day on the slopes. My stomach was twisted in all kinds of knots at the thought. Me? Skiing? I was never the most athletic kid at school. I was the kid who used to forge my mum's signature to say I had stomach cramps to get out of hockey practice. I was much more into calming sports like running, yoga and...sunbathing. Yes, I class that as a sport.

"No problem. It fits you perfectly. We are about the same size luckily," Elle replied as she leaned against the wooden countertop in the ski shop. She looked flawless in her Gucci ski suit, hair swept up into a high pony and expensive-looking ski goggles resting on her head. She could easily pass as a model for some swanky ski resort catalogue or something.

"Bonjour, size?" The Frenchman who was working behind the counter smiled at Elle and his heated gaze did not go unnoticed by me.

"Oh, not for me. I have my own. Liv, what size boot do you need?" she asked but didn't take her eyes off the sexy instructor who was now smirking at her. I might as well not have been there.

"Oh ummm 5 please. Is the sizing the same as in the UK?" I asked but was completely ignored.

"You are here on vacation?" The infatuated Frenchman asked as his blue eyes twinkled with delight that Elle was shamelessly twisting a lock of her hair and biting her lower lip.

"Yes. From Italy. I haven't been here for a while. Perhaps you could show me the black runs?" she flirted, and he leaned forward on the counter. I huffed loudly. My feet were starting to feel the bitter cold standing only in my socks.

"I will be on the slopes in one hour. I'll meet you outside," he winked. Turning his attention back to me as if he had just suddenly remembered he had a job to do, he smiled cheekily. "Size?"

"Ah well, I was just asking if..."

A pair of clearly very expensive and the latest brand of ski boots was lifted over my head and put on the counter in front of me with a thud. I looked over my shoulder to see Giovanni staring down at me with a smug grin and shimmering eyes.

"She isn't hiring any. She is having these," he ordered. The instructor nodded and ran them through the till.

The price flashed up and my eyes bulged. That is insane! They'd be the most expensive shoes I have ever owned in my life.

"I can't afford those, Giovanni. I am fine hiring some. It's only for two days!" I argued and he handed the guy his credit card before I could whack his arm away.

"I am paying."

"What?! No! I don't need them! I have never even skied before and I most likely will never ski again after this trip, so please don't waste your money."

From the amused look on his face, I could tell I was going to lose this battle.

"You don't want to break a bone? Well, you are more likely to, in those shitty hired boots, so think of it as a precaution." He leaned into my ear and whispered, "Just ensuring that sexy little body of yours stays in one piece so I can destroy it later."

I fought back a moan and bit my lip as my cheeks turned crimson. Oh my god, does he know how to do bad things to me. I still managed to narrow my eyes and glare at him through my apparent arousal, which only made him chuckle. In the meantime, Elle had managed to allow the instructor to scribble his phone number on her hand.

"Elle. Away." Giovanni's voice was back to being cold and intimidating as he fixed his menacing glare on the poor lad behind the till. The man looked like he was about to shit himself as Elle rolled her eyes and walked away. I stood by Gio's side as he paid for the boots, more for the guy's sake than for my own. He never said a word to the man, but his terrifying glare was enough to cause the man's hand to tremble when he handed him back his card.

"That was a bit over dramatic, don't you think?" I whispered as we sat on a bench to put the clumpy things on my feet. I struggled and fussed with them awkwardly until Giovanni got down on his knee and lifted my foot into the boot easily and fastened them.

"No." He picked my other foot up to do the same.

"Elle is my age, Gio. She has a right to be interested in boys. Ow! Do they have to be so tight!"

"Yes."

"They are pinching my skin! Can't you loosen them a little?"

"No."

"Chatty today, aren't we?" I said sarcastically, raising one eyebrow up at him and he paused. His face softened slightly as he stared into my eyes. "All I am saying is let her have a little fun. Even if it is a harmless flirtation with a ski instructor!"

He gripped my knees with his strong hands and pushed them apart aggressively before kneeling between them. My eyes widened and I immediately scanned the shop frantically to check Raya and Sani weren't around. "What are you doing?"

"Do you know that you are the only person I let talk back to me?" His deep voice was a low purr and I saw the desire swirling in those dangerous eyes.

"And why is that?" I challenged back, getting lost in them and no longer caring who could see us. His large hands ran up my thighs over the padded ski pants and he narrowed his eyes.

"That is what I am trying to figure out," he muttered. I held my breath as his hands gripped my hips and he pulled them into his body so I could feel how turned on he was. I bit my lip on purpose, giving him a smouldering look and he growled at me.

"Liv! Come on! The lesson starts in five minutes!" Sani shouted, running towards us, head to toe in his new ski clothes. I shoved Gio's chest and he fell back on the floor with a chuckle at seeing me freaking out. The kids were the only ones in the family that didn't know that Gio and I were... whatever we were and I was nervous as hell for them to find out. What could we even say? They were far too young for the birds and the bees conversation.

"Coming," I tried to stand up in these uncomfortable boots and race after him which was much harder than I thought.

"You will be," I heard Giovanni's filthy mind take control of his mouth and I glared at him over my shoulder, which only made him chuckle more.

I had signed up to do the beginner classes with Sani and Raya. I was relieved to hear that they had never skied either, so I had a good excuse to start on the green runs, which were pretty much equivalent to a small mound. How much damage could I do to myself there?

The hour lesson was nail biting stuff! I was the only adult in a group of children, but that was where I was most comfortable anyway. The instructor was an attractive Frenchman with a kind smile and award-winning patience and by the end of the lesson I had mastered the snow plough and had maybe allowed myself to go faster than 3mph.

"Come on Liv! You can go faster!" Sani clapped his gloved hands as I reached the bottom of the tiny slope at a snail's pace.

"Thanks for the support, Sani," I giggled. He had advanced into the next group pretty quickly and was looking like a little pro in the making. Of course he was. He had Buccini genes.

"There she is! Ready to hit the big time now?" Elle shouted as she zoomed straight up to me on her skis, spraying Sani, Raya and I with powdery snow. She lifted her goggles from her eyes with a smile.

"Er... definitely not!" I shook my head as I looked up at the enormous mountain that people seemed to be whizzing down with grace and style. How were they doing that?

Then I caught sight of Cecilia and Giovanni coming down together. They were hard to miss with Cecilia head to toe in a stunning white ski suit and fur hat and Giovanni's sexy black ski pants and... oh god he had taken his ski jacket off and was only wearing his tight black lycra under top which showed off every defined muscle in his body. He looked like a real-life action man as he skidded to a halt before us and removed his mirrored goggles.

I swallowed my desire to jump him then and there and looked away when he caught me staring.

"Well, I think I am done for the day. I will stay down here with the kids and Marco now, Olivia, so you can go up on the slopes," Cecilia smiled sweetly, but I could see the mischief in her eyes.

I waved my hands frantically. "No, no. I am quite happy to stay down here."

"Don't be silly! You won't get the true experience on the baby bumps! You need to feel the wind in your hair and the breeze on your face and I promise you, you will be hooked!" Elle winked and glared at her.

"What I need is a guide on how to ski for dummies and about 100 more lessons with Andre."

Cecilia chuckled but I felt Gio's pointed gaze at me. I didn't dare look over at him.

"Giovanni would be more than happy to teach you Liv. He won't let you get hurt, I promise," Cecilia gave me a reassuring look and I refrained from rolling my eyes.

"It's okay mamma. Liv is too scared. Don't push her. Let her stay down here where it's safe," Giovanni's smooth and teasing tone made my nostrils flare. I knew he was baiting me. And he knew it would work.

"Fine. I will try it once, but I am not going down that massive mountain!"

All their faces broke into wide grins, but none wider than Gio's. I rolled my eyes as I stepped out of my skis and picked them up awkwardly. These things were surprisingly heavy. Stepping towards me, Gio took them out of my hand effortlessly and propped them on one shoulder before lifting his onto his other shoulder.

"Follow me," he smirked.

It looked like they had all planned this, as Elle decided to hang back with her mum and siblings. Really? Could they be any more obvious? I chuckled as Chandler's voice from Friends entered my mind. Gio glanced over his shoulder at me as we walked towards the terrifying looking ski lift that I had so far managed to dodge.

"What are you chuckling at?"

"Oh nothing. Just the look on your face when I beat you to the bottom of this hill." Okay, so I knew that was impossible, but a bit of self-confidence can go a long way, right?

"If you beat me to the bottom of this hill, I will do *anything* you like tonight," he gave me a seductive look and my heart melted. OK, now I have something to actually focus on. I was competitive by nature, even though I was terrible at sports. Put me in a game of scrabble and I will whip your ass! But I was still going to give this my best shot.

"Anything?" I raised one eyebrow suggestively as we joined the back of the queue.

"Anything," he husked, bending down and kissing my lips quickly. I froze. He just kissed me in public. In front of all these people. "But it is not going to happen, bambola."

"Don't underestimate my newly learnt skills, Gio. Andre said I have a very technical snow plough," I replied smugly, and his eyes narrowed in that dangerous way that made my core ache with need.

"You mention that man's name again and I will plough you!" He growled and my eyes widened. Oh my god!

"You are an idiot," I giggled as we reached the front of the line. Suddenly, my nerves forced me to focus on the tiny disc seats that were swinging through the air on the wire and pulling people up the steep incline.

"You better win than bambola or that will be your punishment." He smirked as he dropped our skis to the floor and stepped into his. That didn't sound like much of a punishment. I copied him and he looked down at me, staring with fear at the fast-moving seats. They didn't seem to be moving this fast a minute ago.

"All you need to do is grab the pole and put it between your legs." His tone made me glance up at him as the playfulness danced behind his eyes. "It shouldn't be a problem. You liked having me between your legs last night."

I shook my head, hiding my amused smile. "Please give up the sexual innuendos. You are not impressing anyone," I chided back and he grinned.

"Oh I will try. But it's hard. Sooooo hard."

I stared up at him a little flustered as images of his perfectly hard dick entered my mind. Without warning, Gio grabbed the pole that came hurtling towards us and shoved it between my legs. I screamed as I was propelled up the mountain. Gripping the pole tightly, I heard Gio's laughter behind me, but I was too focused on not falling off this thing to glare at him.

After a short while, I got used to the feeling and was actually quite enjoying the ride up the mountain. We had passed a few different flags signalling the runs and I was starting to worry that we were going too high. What goes up, must come down!

"Liv! Hop off at the next flag," I heard Giovanni's booming voice behind me. My eyes bulged in panic. Hop off?

"How? How do I get off?" I shouted back.

"Just pull it out between your legs," I could hear his amusement in his tone and I groaned. The blue flag was fast approaching and I took a deep breath. Lifting one leg slightly, I pulled the pole down and, to my genuine relief, it came out from between my legs. My relief was short-lived when I realised I would now have to let go as it was still dragging me up the mountain.

"Liv let go!"

"I can't!" I panicked, well aware that as soon as I did, I would go sliding backwards down the slope.

"Let go!" His commanding tone made me release the pole and squeal as I instantly felt my body slipping down the slope. "Ahhhhh!"

I squeezed my eyes shut stupidly but felt my body slam into a hard wall of muscle. Squinting them open, I peered up anxiously to see that I was no longer moving and was in fact in the safety of Giovanni's arms. I exhaled as I clung to his biceps and he smirked. Pulling us along sideways to the top of the slope, my heart started pounding in my chest. Why, oh why did I agree to this again?

"You look nervous bambola?" Gio smirked, still holding my body close to him in his arms.

"Not nervous. Just fearing for my life," I whispered as I gulped at how high up we had come. Andre better not have been lying to me! My snow plough had better be fucking incredible to get me down here in one piece.

A low chuckle vibrated from his chest, and I looked up into those hypnotic brown eyes. "You are so cute."

I frowned. I did not like being called cute. Realising I was in fact clinging to him like a damsel in distress, I let go and wobbled unsteadily away.

"This is a long slope. You don't want to go in a straight line because you will pick up too much speed. Try to zig zag to the bottom, bend your knees and relax. I've got you, okay?" He spoke beside me but I couldn't focus on what he was saying. I just wanted to get this over with and get back to the bottom and grab a beer.

Of course he wants me zigzagging to the bottom, so he can win!

"Stop talking and let's do this!" I gritted through my teeth and his eyes crinkled at the sides before he pulled down his goggles, hiding them from view.

"I'll give you a head start, bambola! I am kind like that," he mumbled as he pulled up the neck scarf over his chin. I rolled my eyes before pulling down my own goggles and holding my breath. Pushing off with the sticks, I felt my body glide forwards on the pristine, hard snow. Keeping my feet pointed in a triangle shape, I snow ploughed the fastest I had so far but it felt OK. It felt... good. The wind picked up and my hair whipped out of my face and I did enjoy the feel of that sting of bitter breeze against my cheeks. Focusing hard on not falling over, I didn't see the teenage boy in front who was not moving out of my way.

"Move!!" I shouted as I soared towards him, picking up speed. He didn't hear me.

"Liv, turn!" I heard Giovanni shout behind me. How the fuck do I turn? Lifting one leg slightly off the floor and leaning on the other in the hope that I would turn left was a big mistake. I wobbled, slammed my leg back down and my skis were now vertical. I was zooming down the mountain at a deadly speed. Oh my god, this is how I die!

The boy jumped out my way just in time and I screamed as I realised I couldn't stop myself. I had lost complete control of my legs and there wasn't a chance of forcing them into a snow plough against the friction of the icy floor.

"AHHHHHHHHH!! Help!!" I screamed like my life depended on it. Suddenly, a powerful force slammed into my body from the side and strong arms snagged me around my waist. At the last instant, I was twisted in the air and landed with a thud on top of a hard body. I quickly pulled up my goggles onto my forehead and blinked rapidly down at Giovanni. He groaned loudly and his face scrunched up in pain as I realised he had taken all the impact of our fall.

"You...saved me," I breathed.

His goggles were nowhere to be seen and he lifted his head out of the snow and opened his eyes.

"And you nearly killed me," he grumbled, and I tried to scramble off him quickly in case he was really injured. His huge hands gripped my arms and pulled me back down onto his chest. "Where do you think you are going?"

"Are you hurt? Shall I call for help?" I looked up frantically and realised he had veered us completely off the run and we had landed in a pile of snow at the beginning of a thicket of trees.

"My stomach," he grimaced. "Can you check it?" He screwed his eyes shut and dropped his head back in the snow. Shit. I pulled his tight top out of his trousers and put my hand under it on his chiselled abs. He wasn't bleeding.

"Lower," he groaned, and I moved my hand down over his stomach, his taut abs rippling beneath my hand. Fuck sake Liv, this was not the time to get aroused. Everything felt fine and looked normal.

"Owww, lower!" he growled in pain. I realised if I went any lower, I would be in his trousers. *Ah.*

Freezing my hand as it reached the band of his ski pants, I glanced up at his face. He lifted his head and rewarded me with the cheekiest smirk, and I gasped. He was faking it!

"You...!" I went to playfully hit his chest, but he grabbed my wrist and pulled me up to his lips, smacking them against mine. I instantly melted as our lips parted and his hands went up into my hair, deepening our kiss. The sparks that were igniting through my body were causing me to moan as his tongue slipped over mine, the passion between us still rife. How would I ever get enough of this man? He had been the forbidden fruit dangling in front of me, tempting me and teasing me. I knew I would be ruined if I had just one bite. One taste. But did I listen?

I bit. I tasted. And I fell.

Control

Cecilia

"I hate to admit it, mamma, but you were right," my daughter smirked at me from across the wooden table we were currently having a large glass of wine at.

"Of course I was."

She rolled her eyes and chuckled. "Maybe you could put your matchmaking skills to good use and find me a gorgeous man that Gio will tolerate. I can't even look in a man's direction without him scaring them off."

She rotated her fingertip over the rim of her glass as she gazed out at the people zooming down the slopes. We sat in my favourite Après ski bar where the terrace overlooked the runs and you could watch people to your hearts' content. It was where Vinny and I spent most of our evenings, curled up under a fur blanket next to the open firepit.

"He is only looking out for you, mio amore. Men like him are raised to look out for the women in their life. He does not know any other way to be and, since your papi is not here to do it himself, Gio has taken that role on. He will be the same with Raya, I am sure," I explained, sticking up for my eldest son. It was a trait most of society would frown upon. The overprotectiveness and what was deemed as controlling behaviour, but it came from a good place. It came from a need to protect and care. It took me a while to grow accustomed to it with Vinny and Salvatore to an extent. Once mafioso men care for a woman, they see them as their responsibility. When I first met the Buccini brothers, I was an independent, stubborn and feisty lawyer who didn't need a man to take care of her. I still am that girl at heart but I quickly came to realise that Vinny wasn't trying to control me or cage me. He was showing his love in the only way he knew how. He did learn how to let go a little over the years and gave me space when I needed it and we soon fell into an understanding of each other's needs that worked for us. I see so much of myself and Vinny in Olivia and Gio. I just hope their story has a happier ending, but there is one thing for certain in this life. It is short. And there is no point in wasting valuable time with the what ifs or buts. True love is the most powerful thing in the world and the one thing I wanted all my children to experience.

"I understand that mamma, but I am twenty-three and I have never had a boyfriend! It's embarrassing. As soon as men hear the name Buccini they run a mile or I see the euro symbols in their eyes," she huffed. My sweet girl was all about the fairytale. She wanted the perfect man to save her from what she deemed as a life of confinement. It was more than likely that she would marry within the mafioso. A man that Giovanni trusted and had earned his respect. A man who would protect her and care for her. But I knew that was not what my little bird wanted. She wanted to be set free. To find a normal, uncomplicated man who she could explore life with.

"When you meet the one Elle, you will know and so will Gio. He will back off when it is right," I smiled reassuringly, but she tutted in response.

"Mamma, where is Liv?" Sani asked as he, Marco and Raya saddled up onto the wooden benches of our table.

"Skiing with Gio," I smiled down at him fondly. His little face scrunched up, deep in thought.

"But she is *my* friend," he replied, and Elle widened her eyes at me in amusement.

"Oh yes the Buccini men start young," she chuckled, and I scolded her as Sani looked between us confused.

"Yes, she is your friend, Sani, but she is also Gio's... friend," I said carefully. Elle was trying to hide her laughter behind her wine glass.

"I think Gio loves her," Raya suddenly interrupted, causing all of us to stare down at her in surprise.

"Does he mamma? Liv needs a prince," Sani looked up at me hopefully and I couldn't help the beaming smile and fullness of my heart for my youngest children. Clearly, it wasn't just me who could see the importance Liv had on our family. On Giovanni.

"I hope so. But it is best we let them decide."

"I thought you were Liv's prince Sani?" Elle prodded, enjoying this conversation greatly.

His little head dropped down to his chest as he thought about it before he glanced back up. "I am, but I am too little. Gio is bigger and he can look after her until I am grown up."

Elle stuck her bottom lip out and put her hand over her heart as she looked at me. I giggled and pulled Sani to my side, giving him a kiss on the top of his head.

"Sei un bravo ragazzo Sani."

Changing the subject, Elle placed her wine glass down and pulled Raya onto her lap. "I want to go out tonight. Hit the ski bars with Liv. I think we need some sisterly bonding time if she is going to become a part of this family."

I chuckled and leaned back on the bench. "Fine by me, but it is not me you have to ask."

"Ask what?"

We looked to our right and there was the loved-up pair themselves. I couldn't contain my happiness when I looked down and saw that they were holding hands. Liv noticeably tried to pull her hand out of Gio's grip, but he held on tighter, causing her to scowl up at him and him to smirk. Adorable.

We all scooted along and they sat down next to me, Gio keeping Liv's hand in his on his lap. This was huge. This was him declaring her as his and not caring who knew it. I was delighted.

"If I can come down here tonight for a few drinks with Liv," Elle made praying hands and gave Gio her best innocent look.

"Absolutely not," he said firmly, and I rolled my eyes. Elle's face dropped and rage replaced her hope, but before she could give him an earful, Olivia beat her to it.

"Why not? I would love to go out for a few drinks with Elle. That's if it is okay with Cecilia and I will obviously put the children to bed first." She leaned forward so she looked past Gio and at me.

"It is fine by me," I smiled, enjoying seeing how this was going to play out. Let's find out just how much power she has over my son.

"Because it is not safe," Giovanni gritted through his teeth, staring daggers at Elle.

"What are you talking about? We are on a mountain in France and having a few drinks in a private resort ski bar? What is so dangerous about that?" Liv argued, glaring up at him. His head snapped down to hers.

"Two beautiful women in a bar alone are not safe. Ever."

She scoffed and shook her head in disbelief, pulling her hand roughly from his grip. His frown deepened. Shit, he was ruining this. She was pulling away because he was coming on too strong.

"That is ridiculous. If Elle and I want to come here tonight for a few drinks, then we will. I am not even sure why she has to ask your permission in the first place. She is an adult and so am I," she said, giving Elle a smile as my daughter's face turned to one of concern, looking between Gio and Liv. No one has ever spoken to Gio like this and not received his wrath. I swallowed my own nerves.

"Olivia. We will talk about this later," he hissed.

"There is nothing to talk about. If you are that concerned about Elle's safety, then some of your bodyguards can come too, but they need to give us space to enjoy ourselves," she said calmly. My god, she was a firecracker. I was impressed.

Gio's jaw ticked, and I could feel the fury radiating from him. I squeezed his knee, which caused his head to whip around to mine, and I gave him a warning look. I hoped it communicated the need to back off. That he needed to give her a little space. It seemed to work as he exhaled loudly.

"You can have two hours and then I am coming down here to join you," he grunted, and Elle's mouth dropped open before she clapped loudly, but Liv still looked unhappy.

"Two hours? Really?" she glanced up at him with fire in her eyes.

"Really. And that is me compromising." His voice was hard and she rolled her eyes.

"Two hours is great!" Elle shouted, clearly trying to mediate between them. She was probably feeling guilty about causing a rift in their harmony, but what no one here realised except me was that this was an important lesson. Giovanni needs to know when he is being too much and Liv needs to learn what his boundaries are when it comes to protecting Elle and, more importantly, her. If only she knew who he was, his behaviour would make a lot more sense. He needs to tell her soon.

***

Giovanni

"Eyes on them at all times. If men approach them, you subtly warn them away. No aggression unless necessary," I ordered Angelo and Finch. They both nodded seriously. I hated this. I knew Elle went out all the time at uni but she always had her soldier and protector, Finch, with her, who posed as another student and she had a good group of friends. This was just her going to a bar with…Olivia. My need to control the situation was overwhelming. I wanted to be there. Their safety was my responsibility and yet, here I am being ordered to stay away by all the women in my life. And what was even more surprising is that I was listening.

Mamma pulled me to the side while Liv and Elle were upstairs getting ready and advised me to give Liv some room to breathe. To let her have fun and see that I am not who she thinks I am, an overprotective and jealous man. But that's the problem. I am who she thinks I am. My feelings for her have grown immensely this weekend and I know I am in trouble. This isn't just about sex anymore. The need to protect and care for her is more than I have felt with anyone before. Even my sisters and mamma. Just the thought of her being somewhere I am not and around other men is causing my blood to boil. But mamma is right. I know she is. I have to chill the fuck out or I will scare her away.

"I will be there in two hours," I gave both my men a curt nod and walked back inside the lodge. Liv and Elle were already in the living room with a glass of wine in hand. My eyes roamed Olivia's body appreciatively. She looked gorgeous, which only tormented me more. Wearing a tight-fitting lace body suit and tight jeans that showed off her ass had me walking up behind her and giving it a squeeze. She jumped forward, startled by my action, but smiled seductively up at me.

"You look good enough to eat. Be a good girl tonight and I just might have my fill later," I whispered in her ear, moving her straightened, silky locks away from her shoulder.

She hit my chest playfully, but I could see that desire in her eyes.

"Right, drink up Liv and let's get out of here! The clock is ticking and I know Gio will have set a timer," Elle teased and I smirked at her. She was right.

Liv sat on the sofa and started to put her boots on. I was transfixed as I realised they rolled up her leg, above her knee. Sexy as fuck. I wanted to growl and take her to the bedroom so I could fuck her wearing just those but it would have to wait.

"What?" she questioned as she caught me watching her. "You are staring."

"I am admiring."

A small blush crept up her chest in that cute way it always does when she is flustered. She smiled confidently at me and my heart flipped. I held out my hand to help her stand up but immediately tugged her into my chest and kissed the life out of her. She wouldn't be thinking of any other man after that kiss.

She blinked up at me dazed and I felt Elle's impatient glare from the front door.

"One hour, fifty-five minutes now!"

Olivia snapped out of her daze and giggled, walking away from me.

"I'll see you then!" I shouted and she waved over her shoulder as they both walked out the door, giggling.

Now for the slowest one hour and fifty-five minutes of my life.

Turning Tables

Olivia

"So... you and my brother are looking pretty cozy," Elle smirked across the tall bar table we were sitting at by the open fire. The bar had transformed into a warm, vibrant nightclub with live music, fire pits and heaters to keep us warm against the cold breeze.

"I guess," I took a sip of my drink for something to do. I felt a bit awkward talking about Giovanni to her and I still didn't know what exactly was going on between us.

She frowned. "You do like him, don't you?"

I smiled into my wine glass and nodded. "Yeah. But... It's complicated. He is my boss and well...Giovanni. You warned me off him yourself, if you haven't forgotten!"

"No, he is not Giovanni with you. He is Gio. And I told you that if he ever showed you the real him you would be in trouble and here we are," a 'I told you so' look was plastered all over her face.

I tilted my head to the side, "What's the difference?"

"Oh, there is a difference. The fact that you can speak your mind in front of him without fear shows he is Gio with you."

I frowned. "I am not following."

"Giovanni is ruthless, intimidating and downright scary. Gio is sweet, playful and protective. That's the difference and only a very select few get to meet Gio."

That made sense. When I first met him, he was clearly in Giovanni mode, but he slowly let me see Gio. I guess he really was like Dr Jekyll and Mr Hyde. "But who is the real him?"

She thought carefully before answering. "I guess he is both. One cannot exist without the other. It is who he is and if you love him, you must love the good and the bad."

My eyes widened. "I don't love him. I barely know him." I shook my head, but I didn't like the way my heart sped up or felt my temperature rise at the thought of it.

She scoffed loudly and leaned forward onto the table. "You know him a lot better than most people. Anyway, I didn't drag you away from him to spend our night talking about him. So... let's talk about me," she grinned widely, and I laughed. I really liked Elle. She was good fun.

"Okay."

"Please tell me you know some hot, sweet and sexy men that you can set me up with! If it comes from you, Gio might just allow me to go on a date!"

"Hmm, I only know one actually, but I think you would like him," I said with a wink and her eyes lit up.

"Yes! Show me a picture," she shouted excitedly.

"I can't. I don't have social media."

"What?! Who are you? Why? Who doesn't have social media?" She exclaimed with a look of shock.

"Someone who does not want to be found," I said quietly. This definitely caught her interest as she leaned forward, giving me all her attention, brown eyes fixed on mine.

"By who?"

I sighed deeply. Since opening up about Henry to Gio, I had felt lighter and free, but I still hadn't told him everything. Like the fact that Henry was somewhere out there, most likely looking for me.

"My stepbrother. He is not a good person and is dangerous. I left England and came here to hide from him."

Her eyebrows raised a fraction as she sat back and studied me. "Does Gio know?"

"A bit. He knows about him, yes."

"That's good," Elle said, deep in thought. I wanted to ask her why that was good, but we were suddenly interrupted by two attractive men. I immediately recognised one as the ski instructor Elle had been flirting with in the shop this morning.

"Elle!" he smiled warmly as he kissed her on the cheek. In a flash, two of Gio's men were next to us and the one that was always with Elle had a firm grip on the guy's shoulder.

"Finch, it's okay. I know this man, he is a friend," she smiled sweetly at the young but terrifying, muscular man whose face was set in a deep frown. I looked over my shoulder and saw the other man who worked for Gio, hovering over me protectively. Jheez, what did they think would happen? These men would harm us with their cheesy pick-up lines? The man I now knew as Finch looked between Elle and I and then gave the Frenchmen menacing glares before stepping back.

"Liv, you don't mind if Freddie and his friend join us, do you?" Elle gave me a pleading smile and I shook my head and gestured to the stools next to us. This girl needed to have a little innocent fun and who was I to stand in her way?

"I messaged Freddie that we would be here," Elle whispered to me across the table and I smirked. Of course she did.

"Thiz iz my friend, Louis. Would you beautiful ladiez like another drink?" Freddie asked, his French accent made me giggle and we both smiled as they walked over to the bar.

"You better get all your flirting crammed into the space of one hour," I said, looking over at the clock above the bar. "I don't fancy dealing with Giovanni tonight."

She giggled and put her hand on my arm. "Girl, if anyone can deal with Giovanni, it's you!"

The next hour went by quickly. Freddie and Louis were very funny and easy to get on with. They were a year older than us and always came and worked as instructors during the ski season as they were both from a little village not far from here. Freddie and Elle were snogging each other's faces off in no time, which Finch seemed very unhappy about. He was keeping an extremely watchful eye on the situation, which made me laugh internally. Louis was a sweetheart and turned out to be gay, which was a blessing as I didn't have to fight off any unwanted advances.

"So beautiful girl, what iz you zay to a dance? I 'ave all the moves so watch out!" He winked, holding his hand out to me as he climbed down from the bar stool. I giggled, the wine had gone straight to my head and the atmosphere was so enticing that I wanted nothing more than to get up and dance to the blaring music. Taking his hand, we walked to the middle of the terrace where people had created a makeshift dance floor with a backdrop of the mountains. Louis did indeed have the moves, making me laugh with his energetic and dramatic slut drops, shimmies, grinding and Beyonce moves. My stomach was hurting from laughing so much. His eyes fixed on something over my shoulder and his whole face turned into a look of awe and desire.

"'ot damn! I may 'ave to ditch you girl. My dream man iz 'eading my way," Louis shouted over the music. I turned and saw the muscular frame and fierce face of Giovanni, pushing his way through the crowd towards us. Oh shit.

"Louis, run!" I turned back to him, and he laughed, thinking I was joking. I was being deadly serious.

As Giovanni reached us, I slammed my hand on his chest to force him to stop his rampage towards Louis. His face was hard and he didn't even look at me as he glared at the poor Frenchman who thought he was coming for him in a different kind of way.

"Gio!" I shouted. He gripped my wrist and pulled my arm off his chest, stepping up to Louis menacingly. Louis gulped and took a step back.

"I see your hands on my girl again," he lifted his shirt a fraction, just enough for us both to catch sight of his gun in his trousers. Louis put his hands up in surrender and I grabbed Gio's arm, pulling him back.

"Are you insane?! We were just dancing!" I yelled at him and, for the first time since he had stormed in, he looked down at me. The fury in his eyes was causing them to appear almost black. Pulling him by his arm, I weaved through the crowd until we were round the corner of the bar away from everyone.

"What the fuck was that?" I shouted at him, losing my temper.

"I could ask you the same thing," he snarled back, his hands flexing open and closed repeatedly. I could tell he was trying to get whatever was going on inside of him under control.

I moved away from him and crossed my arms over my chest, stumbling on my feet slightly. I hadn't realised until now that I was a little drunk. Not as drunk as the date with Luca but still...

"Why can't you just be nice to people?!"

His face softened slightly and I watched as the rage inside him wavered and a flicker of amusement crossed his eyes.

"That was me being nice."

"You threatened him with a gun!"

"Well, yeah. But I didn't shoot him." He was smiling now. That sexy, irritating smile that made him look devilishly handsome and I narrowed my eyes.

"So, what... you are going to threaten every man who looks my way? Even the gay ones?" I cocked my head to the side and glared.

Realisation dawned on his face that Louis was gay and his smile grew. He stepped towards me and I backed up against the wall. Wrapping his hand gently around my throat to hold me in place, he brushed his lips against mine. My core tightened and my legs turned to jelly. His minty breath mixed with mine in the crisp air and the anticipation for our lips properly connecting was too much. "Yes. No one touches what is mine."

I froze. My whole body tensed. He sensed it immediately and his face turned to one of concern, but it was too late. I shoved his chest hard and stormed away from him, gripping the wall as I went. My breathing was coming out in short, sharp gasps as I clutched my chest.

"Liv! Olivia!"

There wasn't enough air. Inhaling frantically but feeling no oxygen fill my lungs was causing my panic to intensify as images of all the times Henry had said those exact words to me over those two years filled my head. I tried to grab my hair band around my wrist, but it wasn't there. Elle had made me take it off for the night. No. I can't- I ca-

Falling to my knees, the concrete floor was cold and rubbly but I didn't even feel it through my fear.

"Olivia. Look at me," I heard his voice, strong, calming and deep, but I couldn't focus on anything except trying to breathe. Forcing myself to look up from the floor, I locked eyes with deep brown irises that were determined and safe. He was kneeling in front of me, his masculine hands on my upper arms.

"You are having a panic attack. But I am going to make it better. You are okay. You are safe."

I opened my mouth to speak but I couldn't. Shocking me completely, he grabbed the back of my head and pulled me to his lips. His kiss was firm but gentle. I held my breath and focused on his lips moving against mine. I couldn't kiss him back but I could feel his reassurance. His safety. When he pulled away and gazed down into my hooded eyes, I wanted more. I ached for his touch. His lips again.

"That's it," his voice was but a whisper as he stroked my cheeks and held my surprised gaze. I was breathing again. The panic was dispersing. I was calming down. How?

"How...how did you do that?" I whispered.

A small smile played on his lips as he brushed his thumb against my swollen ones from our kiss.

"I heard once that holding your breath can prevent a panic attack, so when I kissed you...you held your breath."

I stared into his eyes, completely baffled. I had been dealing with these dreadful moments of pure panic for five years and never have I been able to stop one so quickly.

"You are a wizard," I breathed, and a deep, sexy chuckle escaped his lips as he pulled us up to our feet.

"Do you want to talk about it? Or go back to the lodge?" he asked with concern. I shook my head. No. I was done with Henry ruining any more moments of my life. I wanted to have fun. Wrapping my arms around his neck, I balanced on the balls of my feet and kissed him with ferocity and passion. His hands moved around my back, crushing me against him as our tongues explored each other's mouths. He slowly pushed me back against the wall and I lifted one leg to hook it around his waist as he ground his groin into me. He was deliciously hard and my stomach fluttered and my core tingled. I wanted him. Needed him inside me. Making me feel alive and safe.

"Not here," he panted against my lips as I rocked my hips against him.

"Not here," I agreed, but he smashed his mouth into mine again with urgency, our bodies fighting against our words. I gasped when he grabbed the backs of my thighs and lifted me, pinning me between his torso and the wall. His lips ran velvety kisses down my throat and I moaned.

"You. Me. Bed. Now," he mumbled into my skin and I smirked. No way was I letting him off this easily. I was going to torture him a little longer after his controlling and possessive display earlier. I was the one in control now and I had never felt more powerful.

"No. I want to dance," I breathed, my voice a husky rasp.

His head snapped back from my neck, and I bit my bottom lip to stop myself from laughing at his expression. "Dance? Really?"

I nodded, continuing to chew my lip and look up at him through my dark eyelashes. The intense desire in his eyes was amusing. The last thing he wanted to do was dance. I slid down his body and pulled at his hand as I walked back towards the crowded terrace. He didn't move and his hand fell out of my grip.

"I am dancing. Join me or watch. Up to you." I flicked my hair over my shoulder as he groaned in frustration. Thank God for alcohol. I had enough courage to give him a show he would never forget.

Hot Tub

Giovanni

I strolled reluctantly behind her sexy ass that was so fucking tempting in those tight jeans. My dick was rock hard and straining against my trousers, demanding to be freed and buried deep inside her. But she was teasing me. I knew it and so did she. She was getting her revenge for the way I behaved earlier.

I couldn't help it. Just seeing her on the dance floor, laughing and being spun around by that albeit innocent man, had immediate rage coursing through my body, driving me to the brink of insanity. How I didn't shoot the guy right there and then, I will never know. But then I fucked up again. When I am in that headspace, when I allow the darkness to come forth, I don't even realise how I am being or what I am saying. As soon as those words left my lips, I saw fear in her eyes. Watching my strong and feisty bambola crumble to the floor and struggle to breathe nearly broke me. I could feel it too. I could see her pain and I felt it in my soul. The need to make her okay again, to stop it, was so overwhelming and I did the only thing I knew how to at that moment. I kissed her. And thank fuck it worked, which just proved to me that she felt this between us too. This indescribable connection that made no sense yet made perfect sense at the same time.

Sitting down on a chair at the edge of the dance floor, legs spread out and arms crossed against my chest, I tried to pretend her defiance wasn't affecting me. She stood a metre or so away, swaying her hips to the hypnotic beat and kept her eyes locked with mine. Her confidence was such a fucking turn on. She never backed down from me and, for the first time in my life, I loved having a woman defy me.

She ran her hands up her body, brushing over her tits and under her hair, exposing her neck to me, before running them back down. Fuck this was torture. The sly smirk that played on her lips when she saw my jaw ticking and eyes roaming her body showed me she knew exactly what she was doing to me. She sauntered towards me in those provocative boots and leaned over, running her finger down my chest and torso. She smiled and bit her lip before she straddled my lap and started to grind on my pulsing dick to the music. My hands reached around to grab her ass cheeks as she rode me fully clothed, making me hiss. She quickly stood up and turned around, giving me a full view of her ass, wiggling it in my face before grabbing my thighs in her hands and dropping between my legs. Holy fuck. Slowly she rotated her hips until she stood up and sat on my lap, back to me. Sitting forward, my hands roamed her body as I kissed her neck from behind and she leaned back into me. I had forgotten we were even in public at this point, as the background faded away and all I could feel was her and the music. My very own incredible lap dance.

Abruptly, she grabbed my wrists and threw my hands away with surprising strength as she stood up and walked back on to the dance floor, making sure she gave me a little wink over her shoulder first. That was it. I had had my taste and I needed more. Following her, I reached forward and gripped her hips, slamming her back against my stomach as we started to move our bodies together, perfectly in sync. She lifted her arms around my neck and played with the back of my hair as we swayed and grinded to dance music. My hands ran all over her body and I honestly don't think I have ever been this turned on or hard in my entire life. What was she doing to me?

After a few more minutes, I had reached my fucking limit. Spinning her around, she looked up at me, her own intense want written all over her face as I picked her up by her ass. She wrapped her legs around my waist and I walked off the dance floor towards Finch and Angelo. My jaw clenched when I realised they would have been watching that entire scene. It was their job.

"Stiamo andando a casa. Assicurati che Elle torni a casa sana e salva... da sola," I ordered my men to stay with Elle and get her home safely alone and not with the boy she was hanging off at their table. That's how much I wanted Olivia right now. I didn't even care if some boy had his tongue down my sorella's throat. They nodded as I walked out of the bar, still carrying Liv as she wrapped herself around me like a koala.

"I love it when you talk in Italian," she breathed against my neck as she kissed my skin. I could not get back to the lodge quick enough.

"Ti farò urlare il mio nome tutta la notte bambola," I said fiercely, and she moaned, which made me chuckle, seeing that she had no idea what I said.

When we finally got back up to the lodge, all the lights were off, and I knew mamma and the kids would be fast asleep. I put her down so I could open the front door with my keys, but when I turned around, she was nowhere to be seen. "Olivia?"

"Come and find me," I heard her shout from around the side of the terrace. Smirking at her little game, I walked to the side balcony where the hot tub was and my feet nearly tripped over themselves. There was Olivia standing in her matching lacy underwear and bra, next to the hot tub. "Fancy a dip?"

She perched on the side of the bubbling water bath and I stalked towards her, every inch a predator ready to devour my prey.

"You will have to undress me," I commanded.

Her eyes flickered over my chest and she bit her lip. Unbuttoning my shirt slowly and pulling it off my arms, she ran her hands over my chest and abs, her seductive eyes following their trail. I stood as still as a statue, enjoying the feel of her delicate hands caressing my skin. She reached for my belt, unbuckling it and undoing my zip. I groaned as she brushed against my erection and her dazzling eyes flickered up to mine.

"Hurry up bambola, I am dying here."

She smirked as she hooked her fingers into my waistband and pulled them down. I sighed in relief as my dick sprang free and I grabbed her chin in my firm grip, smashing my lips against hers. She melted against me, her legs pulling me into her more. Reaching around, I unhooked her bra effortlessly and pushed my hand up underneath one of the cups, caressing her perfect tit and flicking my thumb over her nipple tenderly. She made that beautiful sound I love so much and I stepped back. "Take off your panties."

It was quickly becoming one of my favourite phrases. She stood up and wriggled out of them, completely naked on the decking before me. She turned and eased herself into the tepid water and I followed suit. The bubbles were burbling around us as we stared into each other's eyes. The tension grew, but it wasn't just sexual anymore. It was emotional. I wanted to tell her how I felt. I wanted to tell her who I was. But...I couldn't find the words. For the first time in my life, I was scared.

She glided towards me through the water and straddled my lap. Wrapping her arms around my neck, she leaned her head back in the bubbles and soaked her hair. I was mesmerised by her every move. The top of her tits on the surface of the water, the feel of her body on mine, the beauty of her face as she lifted her head once more and stared into my eyes. She was an angel. Sent down from heaven to tempt my mortal self. Sent to awaken my senses and emotions, a part of me that I had never let be. Her eyes were softly glowing in the outdoor light and her hair was slick down her back. If perfection had a face, a body, a voice – this girl would be it. Skimming my thumb across her cheek bone, she smiled down at me.

"What happens when we go back home tomorrow?" she asked quietly. Even though she had a confident expression, I could sense her nerves.

"Nothing has to change. We keep doing this."

She leaned into me, forehead resting on mine briefly before pulling back. "And what is this?"

Shit. She wanted to define us. I have never had a relationship before. I have never felt like that was something I wanted, yet I know it is all I want with Olivia. Just her. But things were not simple for us. I needed to sort shit out back home before I could bring her into any of this mess. It was too dangerous.

"Seeing each other. Being together like this," I replied. "But just until I get a few things sorted out, I think we should keep it confidential."

Her eyebrows pulled into the bridge of her nose and she seemed a little confused. "You mean a secret?"

"Not for long." I said quickly. "I just have some things I need to sort out and then we can be together."

"And by together you mean?"

I smiled and placed a tender kiss on her lips. "I mean you will be mine and I will be yours."

She seemed to ponder that for a short while and I hadn't realised I was holding my breath. "Okay."

"Okay?" I couldn't help the huge grin that spread across my face.

"Okay," she smiled back.

I kissed her. Softly at first, and then with graduated intensity she kissed me harder, deeper as I wrapped my arms around her back. She felt so small in my embrace. Our bodies meshed well together like they were always meant for this purpose. Her lips tasted like honey. The sweetest flavour and I couldn't get enough. When she knotted her fists in my hair, I groaned lowly, gathering her closer to me. We were tangled together as our tongues slipped into each other's mouths and my large hands ran up and down her dainty back.

I spun us around and lifted her onto the side of the hot tub, the cold air making her nipples little hard pebbles, so inviting. Pushing her legs apart, I knelt between them and took one of those nipples in my mouth, sucking and nibbling them with my teeth. She leaned back on her hands, giving me more access, and she dropped her head back as she moaned with pleasure. Her back arched, trying to push herself further into my mouth.

She was a sight to behold. Her incredible naked body perched on the side of the hot tub, steam from the water surrounding her with the ragged, snow-capped mountains and inky sky with twinkling stars as her backdrop. I ran my fingers from her face down her neck, breast, and traced the sexy little rose tattoo on her lower hip, enjoying the sight of her nipples hardening even more and her breath becoming shallow in anticipation.

"Anyone could see us Gio," she whispered, and I smirked. I glanced around at the lodge next door, which would be the only house with a front seat for our show, but all the lights were off. I wasn't worried. And I couldn't wait any longer.

"Only the stars are watching," I smirked as I placed light kisses and licked the drops of water off her stomach, travelling down to her sweet pussy. "Now lean back bambola and get lost in the stars." I nestled myself between her legs, holding her thighs apart and admiring her. Pink, wet and fucking delicious. I had only ever gone down on one woman before Olivia and after that time, I realised how intimate it was. I never wanted to do it again to the women I slept with because I never cared enough about their pleasure. But now, it is becoming my favourite thing to do. I inhaled deeply before lowering my head and flicking out my tongue for the first taste.

The contact caused a shiver to run through Olivia's body and she gasped. With my fingers, I spread her lower lips and ran my tongue from her entrance to her pulsing clit, causing her to moan loudly. I lived for that sound. I repeated the action slowly again but this time, darted my tongue inside her entrance and flicked my thumb over her clit.

"Oh god," she breathed. My head snapped up as I glanced up at her.

"God does not get to take any credit for my skills, bambola. You will cry out my name," My voice was dominant and demanding. But I knew she liked it like that. At least during sex. I delved back into her, lapping her gently, savouring every taste. Every couple of licks, I would swirl my tongue around her sensitive clit and suck it causing her to cry out my name.

Her fingers wove into my raven, wet hair, demanding more from me, and I was only too happy to oblige. Inserting two fingers and slowly massaging her, I sucked her little nub into my mouth and started my teasing flicking in a gentle rhythm. Her body trembled and her grip on my hair tightened as her orgasm built before my very eyes. Pumping my fingers in and out, faster and curling them up put pressure on that sweet spot and had her exploding in seconds as I continued to lick, flick and suck her clit.

"Gio! Ohhh," she cried out into the silence of the night, but I could feel she still had more to give. So, I pushed her over the edge and to beyond. I removed my mouth from her pussy but continued to pump my fingers in and out of her faster and harder, knowing what was about to happen. She screamed as she squirted into the hot tub and I had never felt so fucking satisfied. She looked flustered as shit and a little shocked as she panted heavily and came down from her intense high.

"What ha-happened?" she asked, slightly embarrassed.

"You squirted amore," I husked out, leaning up on my knees again and kissing her lips softly.

"W-what?"

I smirked. Good. That was her first time and it belonged to me.

"It's like a female ejaculation. Nothing to be shy about. It means you really *really* enjoyed it," I explained, with a cheeky smile. Her beautiful eyes widened, and that cute blush was back on her rosy cheeks. "But now it's my turn."

I gripped her hips and twirled her around. "Lean over bambola. Let me see that fine ass," I growled, and she did as she was told. Standing up in the water, I positioned myself behind her. She was kneeling on the seat, the water stopping at the top of her thighs giving me the perfect view of that pulsing pussy and rounded ass. Leaning her elbows on to the side of the hot tub, she waited for my next move. I could hear her breathing, wanting and needy. Running my hand down her back and down to her ass cheek, I gave it a squeeze and then a playful spank. She gasped at the sudden shock, and I smirked.

"You are the sexiest woman I have ever seen Liv," I groaned as I ran my other hand over her other ass cheek before giving it the same treatment. This time she moaned. Yes. My girl likes it a little rough.

Positioning my rock-hard cock at her centre, I brushed my tip up and down her slit, teasing her like she had been teasing me all night. She wiggled her hips, wanting to push herself back on it, but my firm hand on one hip kept her from getting what she wanted.

"Please," she begged, and I growled. Fuck, I loved it when she needed me.

"Please, what bambola?"

"Please...fuck me," she panted. I couldn't wait any longer. Without warning, I grabbed her hips and thrust inside her from behind. She was so tight and warm; it was my own little slice of paradise.

"Oh Gio...yes!" she screamed.

I drew back again, withdrawing my dick from her completely and she whimpered in frustration. Rubbing my tip against her clit again, I enjoyed watching her squirm. "Gio..." she begged once more.

"Si bambola?" I husked out.

"Stop teasing me or I will make you regret it," she groaned, a little anger in her voice and I couldn't help but chuckle.

"Are you threatening me?" I raised one eyebrow although she couldn't see my face as she hung her head down to her arms.

"Yes, I fucking am if you don't – "

I slammed back inside her mid-sentence, causing her to gasp loudly. I pulled back, entering her slowly this time, enjoying the feel of her walls clenching around my dick, sucking me in. After a few more torturous strokes inside her, I picked up my pace. Grabbing a fist of her hair tightly, my other hand on her hip pulling her back into me, I let go. I fucked her how I had always imagined from the first moment I saw her in that cute as fuck flower dress, messy hair and big, beautiful eyes. I used all my force, making her back arch and her screams to ring out into the night as each of my powerful thrusts became more fervent than the last. She was a moaning mess in minutes, and I had to fight the urge to come myself when she cried out my name and squeezed my dick with her inner walls. But I wanted more. I would always want more of her. Pulling her hair, causing her to stand up against my chest, I massaged and teased her breasts and nipples. She moaned as I pushed up into her from behind again, my hand around her throat and lips on her collarbone. She was so fucking perfect it was insane.

Pulling out of her swiftly, I sat down in the hot tub on one of the seats, staring up at her naked form. She turned, confused by the sudden withdrawal, and I reached out for her hand.

"Come and sit on my dick bambola. I want to watch you ride me."

Her eyes widened slightly but a seductive smile crept up on her lips. She lowered herself down in the water until her pussy was in line with my cock and she gripped my shoulders as she slowly slid down onto me. I placed my arms out on the back of the hot tub and leaned back, taking in the view.

"I want you to fuck me. I want to see you use my dick for your pleasure," I growled, and she bit her lip. She liked dirty talk. I could tell. I was handing all control over to her, which I had never done before with any woman. But I wanted her to make me come. I wanted to see how she rode my dick to give herself pleasure.

Keeping hold of my shoulders, she started to move her hips, rocking them back and forth and up and down slowly. I hissed at the intensity of filling her and having no control over how it was happening. It was a strange sensation, but I liked it. I closed my eyes briefly to focus on holding out longer than my body wanted to.

"Eyes on me Gio. You wanted to watch," she ordered, and my eyes snapped open. Oh fuck that was sexy. She started to ride me faster and deeper, throwing her head back as she stared at the stars. Groaning loudly, I fought the urge to grab her hips and start slamming into her, taking back control. No, as much as it went against my nature, I wanted to experience this. I wanted to watch her.

Her perky tits bounced with every movement and I couldn't take my eyes off them and her face. Her full lips parted and shaped into a perfect 0 when she hit that sweet spot every now and again. Her green and gold eyes stared deeply into mine. I gripped the hot tub tighter as I tried to hold on to my sanity. This woman was driving me crazy. I felt her nails clawing at my shoulders and neck as she fucked me harder and faster than before, causing a mix of pleasure and pain. This was once again one of the most intense sexual experiences of my life. In fact, she owns them all. Every time with her is insane.

She was close again, using my dick to get her where she needed to be. She leaned forward and sucked my lower lip into her mouth before tugging at it with her teeth, causing it to bleed. I was a goner. My hands went into her hair as I devoured her mouth until we were both gasping for breath.

"I'm going to come!" she cried, "come with me Gio!"

Again. Another order. And I couldn't stop myself. I grunted and growled out my orgasm, filling her completely as she screamed out her own. I swear I saw stars when I closed my eyes and came down from the height of bliss. She rested her forehead against mine as I wrapped my arms around her waist.

"That was..." she breathed.

"Stupefacente," I finished, and she smiled. I think she knew that meant amazing.

She climbed off me and I jumped out of the tub, my legs a little shaky and grabbed some towels. Once we were both out and walked into the house, the front door opened and in walked a drunk Elle with Finch and Angelo.

"Oh, have you guys been in the hot tub!! I want to get in!" she squealed and Olivia's face was a picture. I chuckled, pulling her in front of my body and wrapping my arms protectively around her, seeing as she was only wearing a towel. Even though they were my trusted men, they were still men.

"I really wouldn't if I was you..." I smirked and watched my sister's face screw up in disgust.

"Urgh! You guys are gross! Keep it in the bedroom," she shouted.

"I intend to," I answered back before lifting Olivia into my arms and taking long strides up the steps, her cute giggle echoing down the hall.

Vinny

Cecilia

"Don't worry, my love. It was just a heated argument and you both said things you didn't mean. Gio will come around," I ran my hand up and down Vinny's forearm as his hand gripped the gear stick.

"He is so stubborn. He knows I am right, yet he loves to test me. This deal that Sal wants with the Aianis is absurd. Why would we ever need an alliance with another family? It makes no sense to me to go into business with someone we cannot trust. Yet Sal has brainwashed Gio into believing we will gain power from this. We already have power. The Buccini name is feared across the country and we are the most successful Mala Del Brenta. Why join forces with rivals?" Vinny ranted, his hand gripping the steering wheel tightly. I reached up and ran my hand through his silvery hair and down the back of his head. He instantly relaxed.

"Because Sal wants more. This family. This power. It is all he has and he will always strive for more," I shrugged my shoulders. I understood my brother-in-law's strategy from a lawyer's point of view. Cementing an alliance between us and the Aianis would mean more deals, power and control over Northern Italy. But my Vinny thought with his heart. And his heart was loyal. He never went into deals with people he didn't like or trust. It was his main principle. "And as for Gio. You are too alike. That is why you clash. Gio is loyal to Sal, which is why he agrees with him. He loves you, but you are not boss darling."

Vinny rolled his beautiful brown eyes and pulled my hand to his mouth, kissing the back of it. "Thank the fucking lord for that. Enough about business. This is our night," he smiled. "You look worldly, my angel."

Batting my eyelashes at him, I felt the warmth of love rush through my body. Tonight was our 25th anniversary and he was treating us to a private opera performance and dinner. Suddenly, his eyes flickered up to the rear-view mirror of our Porsche and his jaw clenched. I knew my husband's body better than anything else in the world and from the way all his muscles tensed and his nostrils flared, something was wrong.

"What is it?" I asked.

"Security. We've lost them," his voice was hard. He was in underboss mode. I turned in my seat and looked out the back window and saw in the distance our men's SUV had come to a stop as two huge transits blocked their way. Suddenly, gunshots were fired.

"Fuck," Vinny gritted as I realised that whoever had blocked them had just opened fire on our men. Vinny slammed his foot on the accelerator and gunned us forward down the desolate road.

He dialled Sal's number on a loudspeaker.

"Vin," Sal's deep voice filled the car.

"I am being followed. They've taken security out. Unlicensed vehicles but I recognise one that looks like Leone's transit."

"Where are you?"

"East Verona. Back roads. I am going to try and lose them."

"I'm coming now." Sal hung up. The trees zoomed by in a blur and I gripped the handle of the car as my heart started drumming in my chest. It wasn't long until a transit was speeding behind us. It was clear by the way they were driving that this was a car chase. They were coming for us. Vinny kept his cool as he swerved skillfully around corners and took last-minute turns downside roads in an attempt to ditch them. When the first bullet hit the back window, I screamed. The sound of the metal on glass sent fear through my body. This was not my first car chase, but this was the first time I had been shot at.

"CeCe, take the wheel," Vinny ordered as he pulled his gun out of his trousers and clicked the safety off. My eyes widened as he leaned out the window and I grabbed the steering wheel, focusing on keeping it steady and straight. Vinny balanced, gripping the roof with one masculine hand and shooting at the car behind. I wanted to scream at him to get back inside for safety, but I reminded myself that he knew what he was doing.

I heard the shrill screech of tyres and a loud bang as I looked into the rear-view mirror and saw that Vinny had shot their tyres and the car had flown off the road and into a ditch. Vinny climbed back in, and I was about to let go of the steering wheel when I glanced down from the mirror and screamed. Another car had come out of nowhere and was speeding towards us head on.

Vinny took back control and swerved aggressively. Then we hit something hard, coming to a jolting stop. A tree.

"Are you alright?" Vinny asked in a rushed and frantic tone. I reached up and touched my forehead where a throbbing pain had started. My fingers were covered in blood as I pulled them away. I had hit my head pretty badly.

"Yeah," I managed to say.

"Stay in the car. Whatever you do. Stay in the car," he ordered. Before I could stop him, he had thrown open the door, climbed out, gun in hand and slammed the door shut. Tears brimmed in my eyes as complete fear overwhelmed me. Not fear for my life, but fear for his. Gunfire erupted outside and all I could do was slam my hands over my ears, sink down into the seat and whimper. He was just one man, taking on God knows how many...

Suddenly, the pummel of bullets at the car made me scream and the already fragile glass from our crash shattered on top of me. Before I could react, my passenger door was flung open and a dark figure with a black balaclava mask appeared. All I could see were his piercing green eyes behind the mask and I kicked his stomach before trying to scramble over the seats. I felt a grip on my ankle and insane strength as he pulled me back and wrapped an arm around my waist, hoisting me out of the car.

"Vinny!" I yelled blindly as I kicked and fought against the man who was carrying me towards a black parked SUV. All I could see was the blur of swiftly moving figures and the deafening sound of bullets being released through the air. But I couldn't see Vinny.

"Lasciala andare! (Let her go!)"

My kidnapper froze and the gunfire ceased. Everything fell eerily silent. All I could hear was my pounding heart in my ears. And then I saw him. Walking out from the shadows of the trees, tall and muscular and terrifying. My Vinny. His left arm was covered in blood and a sense of dread crept over me. He had been shot. Stepping over the litter of bodies on the tarmac, his dangerous eyes were on me and my kidnapper. His jaw tight and hand gripping his gun, pointing at the man behind me.

"Vinny," I cried when another masked man appeared at his side, pointing his gun at Vinny's head. I struggled to get free but the man's grip on me got tighter and I felt a knife against my throat, stilling me.

"Lasciala andare," Vinny's voice was almost unrecognisable as he glared at the man, not caring that he had a gun pressed into his temple.

"Abbassa la pistola," the man next to Vinny spoke deeply, commanding Vinny to lower his gun. No one moved. Time seemed to pause as the stand-off continued. I whimpered as I stared into Vinny's eyes, pleading with him to let them take me. We both knew he couldn't save us both. He slowly lowered his gun, his dark eyes glittering in the dim light.

The man holding a knife to my throat slowly started walking backwards with me in his arms towards the SUV where another man was hanging out the car door, gun poised at Vinny.

"Riccardo la vuole viva, (Riccardo wants her alive)," I heard him hiss to my kidnapper. A tear rolled down my cheek as I accepted my fate. They would take me. Maybe for ransom, more likely to torture me for information.

And then the world exploded in chaos. Three SUVs came skidding to a halt down the road and, using the distraction, Vinny grabbed the man's arm quickly, twisting it behind his back, pulling his body in front of his as a shield from the gunshots that the man hanging out the car suddenly sent his way. I saw Sal and our men crouching behind their cars as they opened fire on our attackers and Vinny pushed the dead man's body away and raced towards me.

"Noooo!" I screamed as the man holding me threw me to the ground and pulled out his own gun. I saw it in slow motion. The bullet left the man's pistol and hurtled through the air straight into Vinny's chest. He stumbled forward, clutching his wound, and his eyes found mine. Another shot was fired. Piercing his shoulder. He fell to his knees.

"NOOOO!" I scrambled to my feet as Vinny's body took another bullet to the chest. Sal raced in front of him and shot my attacker in the head with perfect aim as I scrambled towards Vinny on the floor. Pools of blood were seeping out under his body, and I threw myself on his chest. "No! Vinny!"

His eyes locked with mine and he raised his bloody hand to my face, cupping my cheek. "Ti amo con tutta l'anima. (I love you with all my heart)"

"No. No. Vinny!" I watched as life drained out of his eyes and his hand dropped down to the floor. "Ti amo! Ti amo Vinny!" I cried as the tears fell uncontrollably down my face, blurring my vision.

I felt a strong arm around my waist hoisting me off the floor and I clawed and struggled against it, trying to get back to Vinny's lifeless body.

"He is gone, CeCe! We have to go! More are coming. I have to get you to safety," Sal's *pained voice echoed in my ear, but I couldn't listen. I screamed and struggled against him as he pulled me away from my husband. My love.*

A vibrating noise jolted me awake and I touched my damp face as I tried to breathe through the insufferable pain. The heartbreak that would never leave me because that wasn't just a dream. That was reality. That was how I lost my Vinny and I have just lived through it all over again. I could feel the darkness inside me clawing to let it take hold.

Give up. He is gone. There is nothing but despair without him.

No. That is not true. There is family. My children.

The vibrating stopped and the screen on my phone flashed showing a missed call. I rubbed my face and wiped my tears away, taking a shaky breath. I checked the time and saw that it was 7am. The vibrating started again. Groaning, I leaned over to the bedside table and picked up my phone. I closed my eyes when I saw the caller ID. Sal.

"Ciao," I grunted into the phone.

"Cecilia," Sal's deep voice resounded into my ear, and I took in a sharp breath. It felt too raw to hear his voice right now after that flashback. "How did the deal go? Was it worthwhile?" He was straight to business as usual.

"Yes. It is done. Gio haggled a good deal, and they will use us for our connections with the Columbian channels. I am sure Gio can fill you in with the details when we are back." I said frankly, trying to make it clear that I did not want to speak to him right now.

"Bravo. I need Giovanni back tonight."

"Tonight?" My stomach dropped. I was dreading going home. I wanted to stay here in this little bubble of bliss a little longer.

"I will be visiting tomorrow."

"Okay."

There was a pause, and I was growing more restless by the minute. I could tell there was more he wanted to say.

"How are you?" His tone was laced with concern which made me prickle.

"Fine, you?" I faked my sweet sincerity.

"CeCe. Giovanni mentioned you were not doing so well at the moment. I wish you would let me take care of you," his tone softened slightly from its usual sharpness, and I felt my anger rising.

"I am fine. I do not need you to look after me, Salvatore. I appreciate your concern, but it is unnecessary."

He released a frustrated breath down the phone. "You know what I mean. If you would only open up to me, let me help you, CeCe."

"Like I said. I am fine. And don't call me that. Only one man ever called me that."

I knew that would piss him off, but I couldn't help it. He needed to know he could never replace Vinny.

"Have you taken your drugs Cecilia?" Gone was the kindness and warmth in his tone. It was now replaced with bitterness.

"Maybe you should be on them instead of me. It seems you have a split personality just as much as I do!" I snapped and hung up the phone. I was livid. Throwing back the covers and walking into the bathroom, I splashed my face with cold water. My hands were shaking as I opened the cabinet and took out my happy pills. I threw them back and stared at my empty reflection. Another day of numbness.

Countdown

Olivia

Packing my suitcase was bittersweet. I really didn't want to leave this place and this bubble that Gio and I were in. It's crazy how much a few days can change everything. I left Italy set on ignoring his advances and keeping my guard up, but he somehow had managed to break down every protective barrier I had around myself. He really had shown me a completely different side to him this weekend and I could no longer deny my feelings. I liked him. *Really* liked him. More than I have felt towards anyone before in my life. He just seems to get me. He understands me in a way that I don't even have to explain myself. It's refreshing after feeling so alone for so long.

I am really looking forward to getting back to Italy and filling Gigi in on my weekend. She is going to be beside herself when she finds out I really did fuck his brains out. Five times, to be exact. We had sex again last night and in the shower this morning. We can't get enough of each other. It was animalistic. I can't believe this is what I have been missing out on all these years. Although, I am pretty sure it is sex with Gio and not just sex that makes it fucking incredible.

I am not naïve to the fact that he will not be this version of himself all the time when we get back. But I am starting to wonder why that really was. The man I have spent time with this weekend is wonderful. Sweet, caring, funny, playful, cheeky and bloody sexy. Why can't he be like that all the time? Why is it that he must revert to being arrogant, intimidating and terrifying towards people? I didn't understand it. Was it a coping strategy for his stressful job? Was it to mask insecurities? I couldn't tell but I was going to find out.

There was a knock on my door, and I peered over my shoulder as the devil himself walked in with a mischievous grin. I knew that look.

"No! Unless you are here to help me pack, you can leave me alone!" He wrapped his arms around my body from behind and nuzzled my neck affectionately. I giggled as his stubble tickled my skin. "I mean it, Gio! We have to leave in half an hour, and I am nowhere near ready."

"We have to leave when I say we have to leave, so don't stress bambola," he husked against my ear. I turned in his arms and wrapped my arms around his neck.

"Well, that might be true, but your entire family will be downstairs waiting for me, and I am not about to have one of them, most likely Sani, come running into my room to find out what's taking so long and scar him for life!"

He chuckled lightly and leaned down, giving me a slow and sensual kiss. So unfair. When he pulled back, he smirked, knowing he had me in the palm of his hand. "Why do you always taste so delicious?"

"Lip balm," I quipped back, and he shook his head.

"No, it's you. You are delicious," He went in for another taste and I pressed my fingers to his lips, halting him.

"Are you going to help me pack?"

"No," he smirked.

I rolled my eyes and turned around, continuing to fold all of Gigi's outfits that I didn't need back into the suitcase. He let go of me and flopped down on my bed, playfully. I say my bed, but I haven't even slept in here since the first night.

"Maybe we can make use of the private jet's bedroom instead? Fancy joining the mile high club?" he flirted.

"You are outrageous! Your family will be in the next room! Definitely not!"

He groaned and propped himself up on one elbow as he watched me intensely.

"You're staring again!"

"Admiring," he corrected, and I smiled to myself. Such a charmer. "You are staying with me tonight."

I chuckled at his commanding tone. He likes to think he is in control, but we both know that it is only in the bedroom.

"Is that so?" I raised one eyebrow and he smirked.

"Yes."

"I need to go home. See Gigi. Give her back her clothes. Put a wash on. Do a food shop. Get some sleep," I gave him a knowing look. We hadn't had much sleep in the last two nights.

"All of that sounds extremely boring compared to what you would be doing if you were with me," he teased.

"Life is all about balance, Giovanni. The mundane tasks make us appreciate life's blessings," I couldn't help the smile that played on my lips as I pushed my toiletries into the front of the suitcase.

"That is possibly the nicest thing you have ever said to me," his face lit up and I stopped what I was doing to stare at him.

I looked at him blankly. "What did I say?"

"That I am a blessing. The greatest blessing of your life."

"I don't think that is what I said," I shook my head, trying to hide my amusement as he reached out for my hand, but I jumped back just in time. "You are a pleasant distraction at the most," I teased.

His eyes bore into mine with friskiness and I knew I was in trouble. The excitement bubbled inside me as his dark eyes narrowed.

"I am going to give you five seconds to run from me, Olivia. One."

"What?!"

"Two."

"And what exactly are you going- "

"Three."

My eyes widened as the look of pure desire mixed with dominance, made my heart flutter.

"Four."

I ran to the bathroom and felt him hot on my heels. I squealed as I tried to slam the door, but his huge hand gripped it just before it closed and I jumped back against the edge of the sink.

"Five," he growled as he grabbed the back of my neck and smashed his lips onto mine with ferocity. He devoured my lips and attacked my tongue with so much power and passion, I couldn't stop the moan as I gripped the side of the sink with my hands. His hands left my hair and went up under my top, groping my tits over my bra before he pulled it down and tugged on one of my nipples, causing me to gasp into his mouth.

I jumped up onto the sink and circled my legs around him as his hands left my breasts and travelled down to my thighs. Gathering up my skirt around my waist, he pulled my knickers to the side and pushed two fingers inside me quickly, causing my breathing to hitch.

"Always so wet for me bambola," he groaned against my lips. I hadn't even realised he had unzipped himself and released his boner when he replaced his fingers with his erection and slammed inside me with one powerful thrust. I gripped the sink tighter as he wrapped one muscular arm around my waist and started to fuck me mercilessly. Each thrust was faster and harder than the last, but he held me in place, filling me completely with his length. With his other hand, he teased my clit, and I couldn't stop myself from moaning into his mouth like a fucking porn star.

As I cried out my orgasm, a guttural, throaty growl from his chest filled the room as he released inside me and panted heavily.

"Now tell me again how I am not your greatest fucking blessing bambola," he husked, and I giggled into his chest. His peppery and masculine scent mixed with that smell that was just him, warmed me on the inside.

"Your dick is a blessing. I will give you that," I chuckled, and his eyes narrowed but a smile crept up his face.

"You better watch that mouth of yours, Olivia, or that blessing is going to end up in it!" he growled, and my core tightened. Oh, yes please!

"You think that would be a punishment?" I smirked and he threw his head back to the ceiling and groaned.

"Christ, how the fuck are you this perfect?"

I laughed, pushing his chest and causing him to slide out of me as I climbed down from the sink. "Great! Now I need a shower!"

"No time. We have to go," he winked, zipping up his flies and walking back into the bedroom. "Let my cum seeping out of you be a nice reminder of what a blessing I am!" I am going to strangle him.

**

As soon as we all climbed into the car and reached the lowest part of the mountain, Giovanni's phone came to life. My eyes widened as each beep sounded after the next, as what seemed like hundreds of messages came in. Wow. He really was a popular man.

I studied his handsome features as they scrunched up in irritation and then anger as he flicked through them. It was as if I was watching all the peace, happiness and relaxation from the weekend leave his body, replacing it with stress. I glanced at Cecilia, who was also noticing the change in his demeanour and she gave me a sad smile.

"He rarely gets any signal in the resort," she explained.

"No, I turned my phone off," he replied curtly, but didn't look up from his phone. "Cazzo" he growled angrily, and I glanced over to check Sani and Raya didn't hear. I knew what that word meant in Italian. Luckily, they were both iPad zombies and oblivious to their surroundings.

"Che c'è?" Cecilia asked and he ran his hand through his black hair before glancing up at me quickly. The look in his eyes made me feel uneasy. He turned to his mother and replied to her.

"Lo scoprirete presto quando torniamo a casa."

There was only one word I understood in that sentence. Casa means home. I wanted to ask what was wrong, but from the intensity on his face and then tension in the air, I thought it best to leave it alone. He could speak in English if he wanted me to know and he wasn't. That said volumes to me and I hated how much it hurt that he wasn't willing to share his problems with me.

Checking myself, I glanced out the window as we sped towards the airport. *Don't be so stupid, Olivia. You have spent three days with this man. He doesn't have to share everything about his life with you.* But I couldn't help the slow, looming dread that spread through me. The bubble had popped. Reality had hit us. And things weren't going to be the same. I had let myself get swept up in the idea of us together, but realistically, we didn't even know how it was going to work in the real world. He wanted to keep us a secret. Sneak about behind closed doors. Is that what the arrangement with that Mia girl was? Am I just another Mia? I knew in my heart that I meant more to him than that, but all the signs were there. Was I blind?

The short plane journey back to Italy was much the same. He no longer had a signal on his phone, but instead he had his laptop on his lap and was typing away. He hadn't said a word to anyone since we took off, only drank his whiskey and frowned deeply.

Suddenly, he slammed his laptop shut and exhaled a long-drawn out breath as he sank back in his chair. He looked exhausted already. Sensing me watching him, he turned his head to me and held out his hand, summoning me to him.

I stood up from my chair slowly and walked towards him. I could feel Cecilia and Elle's eyes on us and I stopped just in front of his parted legs. He grabbed my wrist and pulled me down forcefully onto his lap, lifting my legs over the side of the chair. He wrapped both his arms around me tightly and buried his head into my hair. I was shocked. I looked over at Cecilia and Elle, who had small smiles on their faces but quickly looked away pretending to be busy when they caught me. I could feel the tension in Gio's body as he held me tighter to him.

"Is everything alright?"

It was a stupid thing to say. I knew everything was not alright, but I wasn't sure what I could do if I had no idea what was going on. He breathed in my scent, and I felt his lips on my neck before he pulled back, resting his head on the chair. I swear I saw worry in his eyes. I pushed a strand of his black hair out of his face and he blinked up at me.

"Just a lot of shit has gone on in the last 24 hours and I had no idea. It's a mess and I am going to have to deal with it all immediately. I am sorry, Bambola, but it is probably best you go home tonight after all," he sighed.

Even though I had always planned to, I couldn't ignore the disappointment that settled in my stomach, but I wouldn't make him feel worse about it.

"It's fine. I was always going to anyway."

He gave me a knowing look and I smiled. He squeezed me tighter into him and I ran my fingers up and down his toned, tattooed forearm, admiring the ink work and hoping it did something to soothe him.

"Tomorrow. We need to talk. There are some things I want to tell you," he whispered. There was anxiety in his tone. It was unnerving to hear as he always spoke so confidently.

"Okay... about what?" I asked quietly, searching his eyes for the answers. He lifted his hand and traced his fingertips along my lips as he thought carefully.

"About me. About who I am. I want to be honest with you and tell you everything," he said deeply. "I just hope you don't hate me when I do."

I frowned; my eyebrows furrowed. "Why would I hate you?"

I could see the emotion in his eyes, but he hid them with a small smile. "Just remember who I am to you. Please. That's all I ask."

What?! He was speaking in riddles. Suddenly, the pilot announced we were landing and I reluctantly slid off his lap onto the seat next to him. He grabbed my hand, lifting it to his mouth as he kissed each of my fingers, and then looked out the window, still holding my hand in his lap.

I was so confused. What was he talking about? Who was he? And why would I hate him?

Are you home yet?

Olivia

As we stepped off the plane, I saw three cars parked on the runway. An incredible red Lamborghini and two black SUVs. How many cars does this man own?

Cecilia turned to me as we approached the SUV and I helped Raya into her seat. "Thank you for coming this weekend, Olivia."

"Thank you for inviting me. I don't feel like I really did much," I said guiltily, realising I hadn't really helped all that much with the children this weekend. I guess I had been a little preoccupied. She smiled warmly and touched my arm.

"You have done plenty." She climbed into the car, and I shut the door behind her, before it pulled away, leaving only myself, Gio and a few of his men behind.

"Angelo is going to drive you back. I am sorry I can't do it myself, but I really need to get back to the house," Gio said as he pulled my waist into his body and looked down into my eyes.

"It's okay. I can just get a taxi. I don't need Angelo to- "

"Don't fight me on this Liv," he grumbled, and I paused. He really wasn't in the mood, and I didn't want to make things worse, so I just nodded. His face softened slightly as he lifted my chin with his fingers and forced me to look up at him. "Don't worry, okay? I will sort out my shit and then we will talk tomorrow."

"Okay. I will see you tomorrow." I went to walk away but he pulled me straight back into him, slamming me against his chest.

"What? No kiss goodbye?" he smirked.

"I thought we were hiding this. Now we are back?" I argued, peering up at him through my lashes. His face twisted. As an answer to my question, he leaned down and grabbed my face fiercely in his hands and devoured my lips. I melted against him as his tongue slid into my mouth and then he teased my lips with his teeth. "I'm going to miss this," he husked.

"It's only for one night," I giggled, but his expression was hard to read. That worried look was etched on his features once more. Swiftly, he bent down and pecked my lips again before walking away with one of his men towards his Lamborghini. "I will text you later. Keep your phone on you or I will worry."

I saluted him, which caused him to smirk as he climbed into the driver's seat of his luxury car.

The drive back to Gigi's seemed to fly by as I was so consumed with thoughts of everything that happened over this weekend and how different everything was now. I smiled at the memories of the best weekend of my life, but I couldn't ignore the nervous flutter in my stomach. Something seemed off. What was he so worried about? What did he have to tell me? I had a feeling I would not sleep a wink tonight.

I thanked Angelo as I climbed out of the SUV. Climbing up the stairs awkwardly with my suitcase, I faffed about trying to find my keys for the front door.

"Ciao? Vivi qui?" A smooth voice from behind me made me jump and turned to see a man in his late twenties dressed in a very smart, tailored suit that probably cost more than my entire wardrobe in the stairwell. He was attractive with short brown hair and sparkling blue eyes, but he reminded me of some of Gio's men in the way he carried himself. Intimidating although the smile on his face was friendly.

"Sorry? I don't speak Italian," I mumbled as I found my keys and put them in the lock.

"Ah!" he held his hands up in apology. "Sorry miss. Do you live here? I am looking for a friend's flat but there are no numbers on the doors."

His English was very good and I smiled politely. It was such an old building they seemed to have forgotten to actually number the doors.

"What number is the flat?" I asked, looking the man up and down again. He didn't seem like the type who would have a friend living here, but then again, who am I to judge?

"Eight."

I frowned and tried to work out which floor that would be.

"Well, this is Flat three, so I expect it is a few floors up. Just count the doors," I smiled, and he nodded.

"Grazie. Ciao," he replied, and started climbing the stairs. I let myself into the flat and felt a rush of excitement to see Gigi and boast about how much amazing sex I had been having. I stopped dead at the sight before me. There in the kitchen was the huge, long-haired Viking. Completely naked. He turned when he heard me enter and smiled.

"G'day, how's it going?" his strong Australian accent boomed around the room. I looked away quickly, seeing that his privates were on full display, and felt my cheeks flush. Not that he seemed to be the least bit embarrassed about the situation.

"Hurry up big boy!" Gigi called before sauntering out of her room with only an oversized T-shirt on. It looks like I wasn't the only one having hot, wild sex all weekend. "Liv! Oh my god you are home!" She came flying at me, hugging me around my neck.

"And you have company," I smirked at her and she grinned. "I thought you never went back for seconds?" I whispered, surprised she was breaking her own rule.

"When the sex is this good, it's an all you can eat buffet," she winked, making me laugh.

"I got it!" Viking shouted, holding up the whipped cream. My eyes widened and Gigi bit her nails mischievously.

"I think I am going to go and do my food shop now," I said, grabbing some bags from the kitchen cupboard and throwing my handbag over my shoulder.

"You can always join us?" The Aussie winked and I gave Gigi a knowing look.

"You guys carry on," I sang as I walked out the flat, slamming the door shut behind me. I chuckled to myself as I walked back down the stairs and out onto the street. I guess we will both have a lot to catch up on later. My work phone vibrated in my bag and I paused on the pavement to pull it out.

Grinning like a fucking idiot when I saw it was a message from Giovanni.

You home? G x

I shook my head at how protective he was, but I have to admit, it was quite sweet when he wasn't being a crazy person.

Yes. Just heading out to do that mundane task of a food shop to give my flat mate some privacy! X

I started to walk towards the little mini mart at the end of the road and my phone vibrated again.

Alone? Be careful. Keep your phone on you. X

I scoffed at his message.

I am fully prepared for the dangers of the supermarket. I can protect myself with cucumbers if worse comes to worse. X

I saw him typing immediately, so I waited, biting my thumb nail.

Quite the comedian, aren't you? Text me when you are home. X

I clicked the phone off and placed it back in my bag with a secret smile. And that's when I clocked the black Range Rover. I only noticed it because, for a second, I thought it was Giovanni's. It looked identical with the tinted windows and huge alloys. I squinted my eyes to see if it was in fact his men. I wouldn't put it past him to have ordered his men to keep an eye on me. But then why was he texting if he was doing that? I started to walk down the street towards the supermarket, eyeing it suspiciously. I couldn't see who was inside. Feeling paranoid, I shook my head. I had been spending too much time with Giovanni, he was rubbing off on me.

After my uneventful shopping, I strolled out of the supermarket and walked straight into a wall of muscle. Dropping my two shopping bags all over the path, I cursed and dropped to my knees picking up my groceries. The man bent down and started to help me. I glanced up to say thank you as he handed me the potatoes and I froze. It was the same man from before. In the stairwell. He smiled at me but it didn't reach his eyes.

"Oh it's you," I said bluntly, standing up. "Sorry I wasn't looking where I was going."

"You should be more careful, Olivia," he replied.

I frowned deeply. Wait...How did he know my name? Suddenly, he grabbed my upper arm in a tight grip and pulled me into his chest. I gasped when I felt something hard poking into my stomach. Was that a gun? I glanced down and froze. It was a fucking gun!

"Don't be alarmed, gorgeous. We only want to have a chat. But fight me and I will pull the trigger." He glared down at me, and all his friendliness had disappeared. I gulped in fear, realising he was not bluffing. He pulled me towards the black range rover and the back door opened. Shoving me inside, I fell onto the expensive leather seats as he scooted in and slammed the doors. I raced to the other side and tried to open the door but, of course, it was locked.

The engine started and I saw two men in black suits in the front seats. Their side profiles were serious and fixed on the road. I turned quickly and looked over at the man who had kidnapped me and saw that he was rummaging through my bag.

"What are you doing? Who are you?" I shouted, my voice trembling a little at the end. Dread suddenly consumed me as I wondered if they were here for Henry. Were they taking me to him?

"Are you helping Henry?" I quivered.

"Whose Henry?" The man muttered as he clicked open my iPhone and read the texts from Giovanni with a small smile on his lips.

I frowned. If they weren't with Henry, what the fuck was this?

"Who are you?" I tried again, sitting a little straighter in the chair.

"My name is Lorenzo Leone," he replied calmly. I stared at him blankly as he looked up at me, his blue eyes locked with mine. "Underboss of the Leone family."

"Under what?" I asked. Am I supposed to know who he is? He gave me an amused look as he studied me curiously.

"You don't know, do you? Interesting."

"Don't know what? What is going on? Are you going to kill me?" I rambled. Surely, if they were, they would have done it already.

He chuckled deeply. "No. We are not. Like I said. We just want to have a little chat."

"We?"

The car came to a halt and the door closest to me opened. A man swiftly climbed in and sat next to me, sandwiching me between Lorenzo and himself. He was much older, probably double Lorenzo's age and had a few scars on his face giving him a menacing look, although the expensive, designer outfit he was wearing contradicted it. He turned to me, looking me up and down slowly and I felt a shiver run down my spine.

"Is this her?" he questioned.

"Si," Lorenzo answered and my head whipped back and forth between them both. "Although, she doesn't seem to know anything about…anything."

"Seriously, what the fuck is going on?" I snapped, getting irritated that no one was telling me a thing. Now I knew they weren't going to kill me; the fear was not in control of me anymore and I had found my voice.

"Language," the older man warned, and I narrowed my eyes on him. "Feisty one, isn't she?"

"Si," Lorenzo chuckled.

"Will you please stop talking about me as if I am not here and tell me what you want!"

The older man's grin was lazy but wicked, one-blunt-tipped finger smoothing over his lower lip, back and forth like a hypnotic pendulum.

"We need you to deliver a message. To your boyfriend," he said after a long silence.

"I don't have a boyfriend!" I replied, although I immediately knew who they were referring to.

"Really? So, you have sex with strangers in hot tubs all the time?" Lorenzo added.

My eyes widened in disbelief and my cheeks flamed. "What?"

"Don't be shy, little girl. You certainly weren't then."

"Stop teasing her, Lorenzo. My name is Riccardo Leone, and I am the Don of the Leone family," the older man held out his muscular tattooed hand to me and I looked down at it as if it was a snake about to strike. When I didn't take it, he narrowed his blue eyes and dropped his hand. Hang on. Did he just say don? As in the mafia?

"Don? Like a mafia boss?" I squeaked, my eyes wide. They both smirked and nodded.

"I see what you mean. How has Giovanni managed to keep you in the dark? It's impressive," Riccardo chuckled.

Giovanni? "How do you know Giovanni? What is going on?" I was losing my patience now and the panic in me was rising. I was wedged between two mafia men with guns who wanted something from me. I had only ever heard about the mafia from films and TV shows and, even then, I hadn't paid much attention. All I knew was that they were criminals and bad people.

"Giovanni Buccini, your so-called 'not- boyfriend', is the underboss of the Buccini family. The most powerful family in Northern Italy. And our enemy." Riccardo stated frankly and I swear my heart stopped beating, before it began thundering in my chest. What was he talking about? Giovanni wasn't part of the…

Something in me clicked. The wealth… the security… the guns… the fear

he evoked in people…
You aren't afraid of me, are you? Should I be? Most people are.
Are you dangerous? Yes.
You should know. I am a monster to many.
About who I am. I want to be honest with you and tell you everything. I just hope you don't hate me when I do.

Oh my god. It's true. I knew it in my bones. He was part of the mafia. Which means… His whole family is too! Cecilia, Elle, his uncle…

"His uncle," my voice choked with shock and Riccardo smirked.

"The asshole that is Salvatore Buccini? Yes, he is the Boss. Giovanni is next in line to take over."

I shook my head. How could I have been so stupid? This whole time they had all been lying to me. Having a good laugh behind my back? I had been in the company of criminals for weeks. I slept with… Oh my god. I dropped my head in my hands as the panic started to grow. *No. No. Don't have a panic attack now Liv. This is not the time.* I squeezed my eyes shut and started snapping my hair band against my wrist, trying to focus on breathing. *No! Hold my breath.*

"What is she doing?" I heard Lorenzo ask. I felt Riccardo shrug his shoulders next to me. When I couldn't hold it any longer, I exhaled loudly and opened my eyes. I was feeling slightly calmer. No longer on the brink of a panic attack at least.

"I get panic attacks," I managed to breathe, and I could feel their amused eyes watching me.

"You are in with the wrong crowd then, my love," Riccardo chuckled.

"What do you want from me?" I whispered as I regained my senses.

"Like I said. I need you to deliver a message to Giovanni. Tell him we want to meet him. Alone. He must not inform his uncle. He will know how to get in touch with us. And if he refuses, which of course, he will, give him these."

Lorenzo handed me a large brown envelope and my eyes snapped up at the terrifying man sitting to my right. He nodded for me to go ahead and open it. I pulled out blown up photographs of…me. And Giovanni. One of me on my bike, riding home from work one day. The next was of us climbing into his Ferrari the day we went to France outside my house. And last…oh shit! It was Gio nestled between my legs as I leaned back on the edge of the hot tub completely naked. My eyes were screwed shut in pleasure and my head tilted up to the night sky.

"That is my favourite," Lorenzo smirked, and I shoved them back in the envelope quickly, my whole body on fire with mortification.

"You've been following me?!" I shouted.

"Since the ice cream day, yes," Riccardo replied. "That's when we knew you were important. But we obviously needed to be more discreet after that, didn't we, Frankie?"

The man sitting in the front seat turned around and I gasped when I saw he was wearing an eye patch. He gave me a death glare as if I was the one that did that to him, or I was at least responsible for it. It made me cower back in my seat. "Frankie, here, was caught that day spying on you all and your boyfriend decided to make him pay. Show her Frankie."

The man lifted his eye patch, and I slammed my hand over my mouth at the grotesque sight of his mangled eye.

"An eye for a spy. Very creative of Giovanni," Riccardo stated and nodded for Frankie to lower the patch and turn around. I felt sick. Giovanni did that? He took someone's eye? Had he killed people? Of course, he had. He was the fucking mafia! Bile rose in my throat, and I knew I had to get out of here fast.

"She looks a little pasty, Father. Do we have a sick bucket?" Lorenzo chuckled next to me.

"Not cut out for this life, my dear?"

I slammed the photos into Lorenzo's chest. "Let me out of here now. Deliver those to him yourself. I don't want any part of this."

Riccardo's low, evil chuckle vibrated from deep in his throat as he ran his eyes over me.

"Too late for that little girl. You are in this whether you like it or not. Deliver the photos and relay our message. We will give him two weeks to meet with us or he knows what will happen."

"What will happen?" I choked out but I already knew the answer from the sadistic grin on this monster's face.

"You will be ours. To do whatever we like with…before we kill you," he smirked, and my eyes widened. I gulped down the terror that had emerged again. "But don't worry, sweet cheeks. He will agree. A man in love will agree to just about anything to save his woman."

"In love? He isn't in love? You have this all wrong! I am nothing to him but a nanny. I work for his family!" I hesitated when that cold smile grew.

"We will see. You are free to go."

The back door opened, and I practically scrambled out like a rat scurrying for food. My bags were thrown out of the door and onto the path after me. As soon as the door slammed shut, the SUV revved and zoomed off down the road. That bile that was still lodged in my throat threatened to projectile all over the street. I grabbed the edges of a rubbish bin and puked into it violently, earning a few disgusted glances from passers-by.

After a few minutes of being hunched over the bin, I felt like I had nothing left to give. My whole body was shaking as I picked up my bags of groceries and handbag. The phone vibrated inside it and with a trembling hand I pulled it out, already knowing exactly who it would be.

Are you home yet? X

I clicked the screen off as I felt my bottom lip tremble and tears brim in my eyes. My life was in danger once again and I was trapped. Because of another dangerous man. How could I have been so stupid?

Imposter

Giovanni

The moment I turned my phone on and gained a signal, the joy and relaxation of the last few days evaporated, and I was struck by stress, irritation and anger. Niccola had sent me the CCTV footage of Riccardo in our restaurant and, just as I thought, he was sending me a message. At one point, he looked directly into the camera and smirked. He knew I would see it. But why? What was he trying to achieve? Was he just attempting to rile me for what I did to his little spy? But then I noticed him writing something on a napkin in large letters before he got up and left. Zooming in on the footage, it read clear as day, PALARE which means talk. Talk about fucking what?

I then received another message from Mattio saying that Leone's men had been sighted in a few different locations in Verona in the last few days. He was trying to provoke me. But what was strange was that it was directed at me and not my uncle. He was targeting areas in my jurisdiction. My businesses and my territory. The fact my uncle hadn't called, made me believe that he wasn't aware. However, mamma informed me that Salvatore was coming to the house tomorrow, so maybe that was what he wanted to discuss.

Just before we boarded the flight, I saw I had five voicemails and several missed calls from Max. That put me on edge too. Max had been taking care of things while I was away and was staying at the mansion. For him to try to get hold of me that many times caused huge anxiety as to what could possibly be going on.

When I caught Liv watching me with concern on the plane, I felt ten times worse. I couldn't be the Gio she had just had an amazing few days with right now and she knew it. When I pulled her onto my lap, it was initially for her sake. To help ease her worry about me acting differently and trying to show her that it wasn't anything to do with her. But when I buried my head in her neck and inhaled her sweet-scented skin, feeling the warmth of her body on mine, I realised it was me that needed the reassurance. I was spiralling because I knew this couldn't last. I couldn't keep pretending to be someone I was not. If I really wanted to give us a fair chance, I had to be honest with her about who I was.

Climbing into the Lamborghini, I powered through my country roads that I knew like the back of my hand. My body felt tense and the darkness was starting to scratch at the surface, knowing that whatever shit I was about to deal with was keeping me away from my girl. The moment I left her at the airport, I felt uneasy. I hated being away from her. But I knew I was being overprotective and needy as fuck. Two things that she despises. So, I forced myself to give her some freedom tonight. It was for the best anyway, as I knew I would not be in a good mood for the rest of the evening.

Pulling up the long driveway of my estate, nothing seemed out of sorts. Everything was calm. It was only when I reached the front of the house and saw that mamma was standing outside the front door next to our soldiers with her arms folded that I knew something was wrong.

Climbing out of the car and striding towards her, I could see the fury in her eyes.

"What is it?" I growled.

"See for yourself," her tone matched mine as I looked over her shoulder into the lobby, but I couldn't see anything. As I marched past her, she grabbed my shoulder and pulled me back, looking hard into my eyes. "Keep control, Gio, and don't do anything rash. We will sort this out."

I frowned as I shrugged her off and marched into the house on a mission to find out what the fuck was going on.

"The lounge," I heard mamma's voice behind me.

As soon as I opened the heavy wooden doors to our private living room, I froze. Max's eyes widened slightly at my presence but he composed himself quickly as he stood up from the coffee table he was perched on. Directly in front of him, sitting on the sofa, was Camilla. She gulped in fear when she saw me, but slowly stood up too.

"What the fuck is she doing here?" I growled at Max.

"She lives here," he replied, getting right to the point. My eyebrows furrowed and my face screwed up tightly with confusion as I looked between them. Camilla immediately cast her eyes down to the floor.

"What the fuck are you talking about?" I snapped, my voice rising a few notches. Camilla's body visibly tensed.

"Boss and Francesco agreed she should move in with you to allow you both to get to know each other before the wedding. Camilla arrived yesterday. I tried to call and warn you." Max said carefully as he held my gaze. His eyes darted to Camilla to warn me to calm myself for her benefit, but I felt enraged.

"Without my consent? This is my fucking house! And she is not welcome here! There will be no wedding and she can get the fuck out!" I bellowed, pointing my finger at her as I took menacing steps towards them. Max stepped in front of her protectively and gave me a stern look which only made me more pissed off.

"Maybe we should talk in private, Gio. You need to calm down before you say something that will disrespect the boss."

"Fuck Salvatore! He may be the fucking boss, but that gives him no right to move a complete stranger into my house! And one from a rival fucking family!" My body was shaking uncontrollably.

Max glared at me, warning me to shut the fuck up. Anything I say, Camilla could tell her father and that would cause huge problems for everyone, but right now I don't give a fuck. He turned around and spoke softly to Camilla. "Can you leave us please? Go to your room and I will check on you later, okay?"

I shook my head with a chuckle of disbelief as she nodded and nearly sprinted out of the room. Why was he talking to her like that? As if he cared. And what fucking room? She doesn't live here!

"Seriously fratello, you need to calm the fuck down!" Max ordered as soon as she had left the room. I dove at him, grabbing him by the throat and choking him with all the rage I felt. His face was turning red as he clawed at my hand.

"I left you in fucking charge Max. I trusted you. How the hell did you let this happen?" I hissed. Letting him go with a violent push, he stumbled back, wheezing from my assault.

"What the fuck was I supposed to do, Gio? Sal and Francesco turned up together yesterday morning with her. Told me that I was to get her settled and familiar with the house before you returned. Then you and she will be able to get to know each other before you are married. Francesco even made a comment about you falling in love with her."

I scoffed loudly. "Sal has lost his fucking mind!" I pulled out my phone from my back pocket and started calling my zio's number.

"What are you doing? Don't. You are not thinking clearly!" Max dove at me, knocking the phone from my hands and I growled at him. "Gio! Just take a minute before you go all guns fucking blazing on Boss because we all know how that will turn out."

"I am not marrying her!" I shouted as I picked my phone up off the floor and pocketed it. Max was right. I needed to think clearly before speaking to Sal. I needed a plan.

"Just try to remember that this is not her fault. She is doing her duty as a boss' daughter. She is shit scared of you," Max spoke more calmly and I ran my hand through my hair for the millionth time.

"Good. She should be. Because I do not want her here. She can go back to her fucking father and I will deal with the consequences."

"Well, that is a fucking stupid plan and you know it!"

I fell back onto the cream sofa and groaned aggressively.

"The best thing to do right now is not react. If you are really serious about not going through with this alliance, then you need a bloody good way out of it and that is going to take time and strategy. Let her stay here. Keep up appearances and play along with their crazy shit while you and I figure this out."

"She can't stay here," I repeated. I knew Max was right. I knew that was the best and most sensible action to take but… Olivia. What the fuck was I going to tell Olivia? How was I going to explain who this woman was and why she was living here?

Suddenly, my eyes widened, and worry overwhelmed me. I pulled out my phone and typed a text asking if she was home. She replied quickly. We shared a few texts, and, for some reason, I instantly calmed down. She was safe and just talking to her had managed to help me regain control over my rage and think more rationally.

"What has happened? Who were you messaging?" Max asked curiously as he handed me the glass of whiskey he had made each of us.

"Olivia."

There was silence in the room as he studied my face and then shook his head, running his hand down it.

"What the fuck have you done, Gio?"

"I can't let her go," was all I responded.

"Didn't you think maybe it would be a good idea to sort all of this shit out first before you go and fuck the nanny and bring her into this mess!"

"Watch your mouth Max," I growled, giving him a menacing glare. His eyes widened.

"Oh fuck me! Do you have feelings for her? That is even worse! How did you think this was going to play out? You go to Boss and tell him, 'Sorry I cannot marry to cement an extremely important alliance that is crucial to our family's power and peace with the Aianis because I have fallen for the nanny?' Are you trying to start a war? Because that is what will happen between us and the Aianis. We already have Leones breathing down our necks, and you want to add another enemy?" he scoffed and took his glass to his lips, still shaking his head in disbelief.

I stood up abruptly and threw my glass across the room. The whiskey stained the cream carpet and the glass shattered as it smashed into the marble fireplace. "Don't fucking lecture me on my life and my fucking responsibilities Max. I know exactly what this means. But I am not letting her go. I can't."

"Then you had better come up with a better plan quickly."

"I will. Just keep her out of my sight. I want her out of the house tomorrow for the entire day, Max. I don't care what you do with her, just keep her away from Olivia."

I stormed past him and towards the door.

"Gio! Take it easy on Camilla," Max called behind me and I growled. I didn't give a shit about that woman. She was an imposter in my house.

Storming up the stairs towards my room, all I wanted to do was take an ice-cold shower and beat the shit out of someone. A punching bag in the gym was going to have to suffice as we had no enemies in the cellar right now.

I opened my bedroom door. My eyes widened and my jaw clenched. Her blue eyes showed so much alarm and fear as she stared up at me from the chair by the window. My chair. In my bedroom. By my window.

"What the fuck are you doing in here?" I bellowed, striding towards her. She cowered away from me.

"T- This is where your uncle told me to s-sleep. I- I didn't me- "

I didn't let her finish her sentence as I grabbed the top of her skinny arm and hauled up off the chair aggressively. I dragged her to the door, opened it and shoved her out.

"This is MY room. Stay the fuck out of it!" Her eyes filled with tears and her bottom lip trembled as she turned and raced down the landing towards the stairs. Slamming the door shut, I turned around and scanned my room, panting heavily. Now I knew she had been there; I could sense it. I could smell her perfume. I could see items had been moved. I snapped.

I ripped my bedding off my bed and threw it into the laundry, the smell of her perfume lingering on the bed sheets. I stormed into my walk-in dressing room and there hung up on hangers were all her fucking clothes. Ripping them down, I grabbed as many as I could and threw them out of my door onto the landing. I will deal with the rest later. I needed to release this fury inside me.

Taking two strides down the steps to the ground floor, I tore my T-shirt in half and kicked off my shoes. As I reached the gym doors, I pointed to one of my soldiers, Theo, who was standing nearby.

"Voi! Combattimi. Adesso. (You! Fight me. Now.)" I commanded and he nodded once and followed me inside.

Dangerous Dilemmas

Olivia

I didn't sleep a wink last night. Once I returned to the flat, Gigi took one look at my face and sent Viking on his way. I wasn't sure if I should confide in her about what had happened with the Leones or who Giovanni truly was, because I wasn't sure if she would be safe knowing it. I told her as little as I could without raising suspicion but also needing to talk to someone. I said some enemy of Giovanni's told me to give him a message to meet with them and I had no idea why. It was the best my scrambled brain could come up with. I then told her I didn't feel well and was going to bed. She seemed to buy it as she looked very concerned at how sickly I really did look from the shock.

Giovanni tried calling me when I hadn't texted him back, which I ignored. Realising that he wouldn't quit until I responded, I quickly typed out a message.

Home now. Not feeling well, so I'm going to bed. X

He texted back asking what was wrong with me and then tried calling again at 11pm but I couldn't answer. I couldn't speak to him. I didn't know how. Who was this man? That was the question I was trying to get my head around the entire night.

I couldn't stop replaying every conversation, every touch, every moment with him and it made me want to cry. Was it real? It felt real. But how could I be sure when I didn't even know who I was even sleeping with. He lied to me. I was so open and honest with him about what had happened in my past, which was a big fucking deal for me, and he still didn't tell me the truth about him. I trusted him, but he didn't trust me. Or he didn't care enough to want me to know. Once the shock had worn off, it was replaced with anger. Anger at them all. Cecilia for hiring me without being honest about what I was getting myself into. Elle. I thought she was my friend. She could have told me at any time who they were or at least dropped some hints, but she didn't. But mostly I felt deceived by Giovanni. After that weekend, I thought he was someone I could rely on. I thought he was someone I could trust. Was it all a lie just to get me into bed? Is it all a game to him?

But then my brain would take me back to those intimate and tender moments we shared over the last few days, and I knew in my heart it wasn't. No matter who he was, those moments were real. I think... And so, my mind continued to spiral with chaotic and conflicting feelings, flashbacks, and thoughts.

Once I heard Gigi going to bed, I tiptoed into the living room to grab her iPad. I spent hours researching and googling about the mafia. Obviously, most of it was fictional or from the history of Italian families and there didn't seem to be any information on current mafia groups or Giovanni. But why would there be? From what I have read, the families are so protected that hardly anything is ever leaked about them. When I read that most mafia families had successful businesses that they used as a front to launder money through, it all made sense. The hotels, restaurants, night clubs. It portrayed the image of a young, successful entrepreneur who had been given a legacy from his uncle's name. But the truth was so much darker. These weren't normal people. They didn't make their money in honest ways. They were criminals. Clever, powerful criminals. And Giovanni was next in line to run it all!

How didn't I see the signs? Now they were staring me in the face, it was so freakin' obvious! He had even warned me he was not a good person. That I should fear him. Yet, I didn't listen. I allowed my desire and sexual attraction for this man to override everything my gut was telling me. To run. And now look at the mess I am in.

As the first rays of a new day started to stream over the brown and beige rooftops of the city, I sat on my bed cross-legged, with the photographs from those Leone men in front of me. I knew I couldn't go to work today. I couldn't face any of them yet. Especially not Gio. I needed to get my head together before I could do anything. Pulling out my phone, I texted Cecilia.

Hi Cecilia. I am sorry, but I have a stomach bug and I won't be able to make it to work today. I will let you know how I feel later. Sorry again. Olivia.

That should buy me some time to get my head straight and come up with a plan. All night I had been going around in circles about what the hell I should do now. I came up with 3 different ideas.

1. Deliver the message to Giovanni, hand in my two weeks' notice and put an end to whatever this was with him. Pros- get myself out of this mess. Cons- no job, miss those kids, no Giovanni and potentially they might kill me for knowing who they are. Although I doubt they would if I had signed the confidentiality waiver and the thing that Giovanni wanted to tell me today was who he really was.

2. Run. Book a flight to another country and start over again. I had done it once; I could do it again. Pros- never have to see any of them again. Start over. I couldn't be used against Giovanni in whatever vendetta was going on between the two families. Cons- I would be on the run again. But not just from Henry. If the Leones were serious about coming after me and Giovanni didn't meet with them, which he might not, they could come for me too. But I am not sure I would be worth the fuss to them. If I was already gone, what

would it matter?

3. I go and speak to Giovanni and hear him out. I demand the truth about who he really is and what he does. All of it. Then I make a decision. Could I stay with him knowing what he was capable of? Would I want to? Pros- it might not be as bad as I think. He might still be the person I have just spent all weekend with. I might be able to get over the fact he is a criminal and be happy with him because he does…make me happy. Cons- I will still be used against him by those thugs. My life will always be in danger. Do I want to be part of their world? A world of violence and crime. The very things I have been trying to run from.

I fell back onto my pillows and covered my face with my hands. Whatever way I looked at this, it was a shit show. My work phone vibrated twice.

Two messages appeared.

Sorry to hear that, Olivia. Don't worry, I will have the kids today. Rest up and feel better soon. Cecilia.

Mamma just said you are feeling unwell? I'm coming over. Do you need anything? G x

I jolted up in bed when I read his message. Coming over? No! Shit. I quickly messaged him back.

No please don't. I am fine. Just a stomach bug and I really need to rest. I will speak to you later. X

I chewed on my thumb nail, staring at the screen as I saw him read it but not reply. A panicked feeling rippled through my chest. Fear. Was I scared of him now? Or just scared of seeing him and dealing with this? I couldn't work it out. Suddenly, his caller ID appeared and my heart leapt into my throat. Oh my god, he's ringing me. If I don't answer, I know he will come over.

I took a shaky breath and pressed the answer button with trembling hands.

"Hello?"

"Liv? Are you okay?" His deep, low voice was laced with concern and my stomach twisted into knots from the complicated feelings it provoked.

"Y-yeah. I just have a sickness bug. I am sure a bit of sleep and rest is all I need," I lied, hoping he couldn't hear the nervousness in my voice. Of course he did.

"You don't sound okay. Shall I call for a doctor?"

"No. No, really I will be fine."

There was an awkward pause.

"And you are sure you don't want me to come over and look after you?" My heart flipped at his words and tears brimmed in my eyes. How could this man be a violent criminal? I exhaled and shook my head as a tear slid down my cheek.

"Thank you, but no. I just need to sleep," my voice trembled slightly as I fought to keep control of my emotions.

"Okay." Another pause. "Will you text me later? Let me know how you are doing?"

"Yep."

"Okay good. If you need anything, just call me."

"Okay."

"Are you sure you are alright, bambola? You really don't sound yourself."

"Gio, I am fine. Stop worrying and let me sleep," I chuckled nervously, hoping that sounded more like myself. It seemed to work as he exhaled into the phone.

"I do worry about you. I'll speak to you later then?"

"Yes."

"Bambola... I miss you."

I dropped my head in my hands as my heart took on another level of pain.

"I – I have to go." I hung up the phone and grabbed my pillow, burying my face into it and screamed. Why did this hurt so much? Why did his lies and deceit make me feel like my heart was breaking in two? I shouldn't care this much. I'd only known him for a few weeks! Why can't I just cut him out of my life and be done with it? He was bad news. He will turn my world upside down and I may not survive it. So why can't I ignore this feeling manifesting inside of me? Why can't I let him go?

Because you love him.

Strategizing

Giovanni

"Bambola... I miss you," I sighed. I fucking did. It hadn't even been 24 hours since I had last seen her, but the thought of going a whole day without seeing her face or kissing her lips today had me feeling a frenzy of emotions.

"I – I have to go."

The line went dead. Fuck. I stared at my phone and squeezed it tightly in my hand, willing it to crumble. Maybe I shouldn't have said that. Was I coming on too strong? Was I scaring her off? *Stop overthinking everything, Gio!*

I have never been an over thinker. I was all about action. But with her, I find myself questioning everything. Something felt wrong. I know she wasn't feeling well but there was something else in her tone. Awkwardness. She spoke to me as if she didn't even know me just then. What was that about?

I dropped my phone onto my desk with a clatter and stretched my fingers out, allowing the sting of my red, raw knuckles to make me feel something physical. Fighting Theo last night helped me to relieve some of my anger, but he came off a lot worse than me. I had a few bruises on my body, whereas he ended up with a broken arm, cracked cheek bone and an impressive collection of cuts and bruises. He is still recovering in hospital now but face timed me earlier with a toothy grin. No hard feelings. He was my soldier and if I say, fight me, he will give as good as he's got. Clearly, it wasn't good enough.

A knock at my door caused me to lean back in my chair as mamma poked her head around. "Did you speak to her? How is she feeling?"

She strutted over and took a seat in the armchair opposite me. "Yes. She sounds like shit. But stubborn as ever, she doesn't want any help."

Mamma smiled and nodded. "Women are tough. If she says she wants to be alone, respect her choice."

I sighed deeply and played with my silver bands on my fingers, twisting them around in a rhythm.

"I am going to tell her. When she is feeling better, I am going to tell her who we are."

To my surprise, mamma nodded her head. "That is a good idea."

"What if she wants no part in this life? What if she leaves?" I asked calmly although my heart was pounding and my gut twisted at the thought.

"Then that is her choice. You cannot force her into something she does not want. Do you think you have done enough? Did you let her see the real you?"

I smiled as flashes of France entered my mind. "I think so. I hope so."

"Then it is up to her. Just be completely transparent with her. If she senses she cannot trust you at all, it will be game over. Even if she asks questions you don't want to answer, you must answer them honestly. And don't be surprised if she needs some space or time to think afterwards. Give it to her."

I listened carefully to my mamma's advice and nodded. It was sound. But I knew in reality, it would be a lot harder than that.

"And Camilla? What are you going to say about her?" Mamma's eyes narrowed as she studied me intensely. Mamma was nearly as pissed as I was at the situation. Camilla was now in one of the spare rooms on mamma's wing as I refused to have her on my floor. Max had already taken her off the premises for the day, so at least I didn't have to deal with seeing her around the house.

"I don't know. I fear it will be too much to tell her about that at the same time. But I want to be honest."

Mamma nodded and exhaled loudly. "What is your plan, Gio?"

I ran my hand through my hair and sighed. "I need time. Time to think of something that will appease Francesco and Sal more than a marriage alliance. But Max is right. If I refuse to even try to get to know her or have her in the house, then I will cause a rift and chaos without any plans to solve it. So, I have to go along with it for now. She has to stay here." Mamma tutted and folded her arms across her chest, anger on her features. "I don't like it any more than you do mamma."

"But you are not actually going to entertain it, are you? Get to know the girl? Because if you even think of playing Olivia along while bedding this other woman, then so help me God I wil- "

"Fuck mamma! I would never do that to Liv! The thought of even being with another woman makes my skin crawl. Liv is mine and I don't want anyone else," I shouted as I slammed my fist on my desk.

A slow smile spread across her face. "Good. I was just checking." She stood up and walked over to me, giving me a kiss on the top of my head like she used to when I was a boy. "I love you Gio. Your father would be a proud man."

A lump formed in my throat as she walked away and closed the door behind her. I hadn't realised how much I had needed to hear those words in the last two years. As much as I wanted my uncle's respect, it was my father's pride I craved. I gripped my jaw and ran my fingers over my stubble.

It's how you handle the darkness that is your secret power.

My father always used to say that. I don't think there was a day since I turned eighteen that I didn't hear him tell me that. And now I need those words more than ever. I was about to have a meeting with my uncle, and I needed to channel my father's control. I needed to make him believe that I was willing to try to form this alliance until I had a better alternative.

***

"So, you decided to leave me a present for my return from France?" I smirked at my uncle from across my desk.

"I am pleased to see it put a smile on your face," he chuckled. He leaned back in his chair and lifted one polished shoe over his knee, looking extremely relaxed.

"I would have preferred a little warning. I don't like surprises."

"Well, it was a good surprise, so what's the problem? Is she settling in well?" he raised one eyebrow as he grasped his hands together, weaving his thick fingers.

"Moderately. Though putting her in my room was a step too far. I like my privacy. She is in a guest room now," I said calmly. Fuck me, I should win an Oscar for this performance.

"Do what you want. As long as you treat her well outside of the bedroom, I don't give a shit. Once you are married, you can treat her however you like."

I smirked, pretending to enjoy the idea. "So, is there a reason for your visit today?"

"Do I need a reason to visit my favourite nephew?" I cocked my head to the side in disbelief and he chuckled. "There is a reason, yes. I have become aware of a potential alliance between Leone and Diego Barbieri. They are just in talks now, it seems, but if this comes to fruition we are in trouble."

I sat up straighter. This was serious. Diego Barbieri was the Don of the most powerful family in Southern Italy. "Agreed. So how do we stop it?"

"I think it is time." My eyes narrowed as I tried to comprehend if he truly meant what I think he did. "To get revenge for your father's death."

I exhaled loudly and dropped my head down, staring at my desk. I have been waiting for those words for two and half years. "You mean killing Riccardo Leone?"

"And his son. But we cannot be tied to this. If the commission finds out we are behind it, we are both dead."

I nodded in understanding. "This is why the alliance with Francesco is so important, Giovanni. The Aianis will have our backs. We can count on them for alibis and weaponry and resources that are not linked to us."

I froze as my body went cold. So that was what this was all about. An alliance to take out a common enemy. To take out the people who murdered my father. If I broke this alliance, we would be screwed. We would lose our chance at revenge. This was so much more complicated than I thought.

"I understand."

"Good. We will keep an eye on things for now and start strategizing discreetly. Bring Max and Leo in on this, but no one else for now."

I nodded, deep in thought.

"Your mamma is feeling better?" he asked, changing the subject suddenly. I blinked back at him as I tried to stop the spiralling panic in my head.

"Yes. Seems to be. Though she is not happy about the marriage arrangement," I answered truthfully.

"She will come around. She is emotional. She doesn't understand the sacrifices we must give up in order to be in positions of power."

I nodded again and he stood up. "I will be in touch, Giovanni. Start strategizing with Max and Leo. We will speak soon. Enjoy your present," he smirked wickedly as he walked out of the room with an air of arrogance and authority. I stayed glued to my chair as I tried to process what I had just heard.

Start strategizing… To avenge my father's death or get out of this marriage?

There had to be a way I could do both, surely?

The Boss

Cecilia

"Where's Liv?" Sani asked for the fourth time today.

"I told you darling. She is not feeling well. She needed a sick day. She will be back tomorrow, I expect."

He frowned but went back to building his Lego.

"Aren't you happy to spend time with your mamma instead?" I smiled and Raya nodded her head enthusiastically.

"Yeah, I guess you are okay," Sani said before bursting into giggles when I tickled him. He had Giovanni's dry sense of humour.

"My eyes are deceiving me! That cannot be Santino Buccini all grown up!" His voice immediately made my shoulders tense. Sometimes, I could have sworn he sounded just like Vinny when he lost his sharpness in his tone.

"Uncle Sal!" Sani jumped up from the floor and hurtled towards him. He stopped by his legs, not actually wanting to physically touch Sal. It was that intimidating aura he gave off. I watched as Sal ruffled his black curls and smiled down at Raya who had shuffled closer to me, unsure.

"Wow. Soraya, you are twice the size you were when I last saw you!" She hid her face behind her teddy, and I jumped to her defence.

"She is very shy."

His dark eyes moved from her to me, and he gave me a small smile and nod. "Cecilia."

"You are well?" I asked formally.

"Yes. You?"

"I could be better. Sani, come and finish your Lego. Children, I am just going to speak to your zio for a moment. I will be right back." I walked towards the playroom doorway, which Sal was blocking with his towering frame and he stepped aside for me to pass. I nodded to Marco to keep his eye on the kids as I took Sal into Sani's bedroom, away from the children's little ears.

"Cute bed," he said flatly, looking over at Sani's racing car.

I folded my arms across my chest and glared at him. "How dare you bring a stranger into my house to live without consulting me!"

He smirked and leaned back against the wall, folding his own muscular arms as he did. "Let's not get into this again Cecilia. I thought you would be happy that I am allowing Giovanni to get to know the girl he is going to marry beforehand."

"Oh! So, I should be thanking you? That you are trapping my eldest son into a business marriage that will only benefit you!"

"It will benefit us all."

"Bullshit! You only ever do anything for yourself! Whatever reason you have for pushing this on my son, is for your gain, so don't stand there and lie to me Salvatore!"

His dark eyes glimmered with controlled rage as they narrowed but an amused smirk formed on his lips.

"I am not forcing Giovanni into anything. He understands the importance of this alliance for the family, and he is doing what a good boss does. He is putting his family first."

"Enough with this *family first* crap! If you really cared about Giovanni, you would allow him to find happiness with a woman of his choosing and find a different arrangement with Aiani. You just don't want him to marry for love. That is the real reason you are doing this!"

His jaw tensed. He moved his lips into a pout and back as I saw his control slipping. I knew this was where I should back off. I was one more insult away from his hands on me, but I would be damned if I backed down from a bully.

"Why don't you marry her yourself, Sal? A pretty little thing with a tight ass. The arrangement is for her to be the next boss' wife. You are already the Boss. Marry her yourself if this alliance is so important." I snarled.

"I am old enough to be her father. How ruthless you are, Cecilia!"

"That has never stopped you sleeping with them before. Why not marry one?" I screamed in his face.

He lunged at me, grabbing my upper arms and spinning us so my back slammed against the bedroom wall. His death grip on my arms was so tight, I could feel my skin burning from the bruising that I was sure would appear.

"You know why I will never marry Cecilia. Don't act foolish," he growled.

Narrowing my eyes up at him, I spat back, "You are living in the past, Sal. Look at you. You are making yourself miserable and trying to bring everyone else down with you! And for what?"

"All I have ever done is try to look out for you and the kids. To care for you! When Vin died, who was there to pick up the pieces? Who held this family together? Who made sure you got the right care and help when you needed it?" he hissed in my face, his eyes glaring into mine with maddening desire and rage.

"Giovanni!" I shouted in his face.

"No!" he bellowed back; his voice boomed as it filled the room. "Who do you think Giovanni came to for help? Why won't you just let me care for you all?"

I knew it was coming but it still took me by surprise. He smashed his hard lips onto mine and gripped my head in his enormous hands as he kissed me forcefully.

I shoved him off me with all my strength and slapped him hard across the face just like I had on the night of the club. "Don't touch me! Ever!"

I stormed out of the room and locked myself in the bathroom as my breathing raged and my quivering body paced the floor, trying to get my adrenaline and fury under control. That man could get under my skin like no other. How dare he!

My phone vibrated in my pocket, snapping me out of the turbulent emotions rampaging through my body. Pulling it out, I paused when I saw it was another text from Olivia.

Cecilia. I need to speak to you alone. Please meet in town and do not tell Giovanni.

I frowned deeply at the message. Strange.

Of course. Where? Is everything alright Olivia?

I paced the bathroom floor as I waited for her response. This wasn't good. This didn't feel good. Why does she want to meet me alone and not tell Giovanni?

Near the Ponte Pietra Bridge on the river. 3pm. Thanks.

Too blunt. She didn't answer my question, which meant only one thing. Everything was not alright. Opening the bathroom door, I was pretty sure Sal would be long gone by now and walked over to Marco, who was standing rigid at the playroom door.

"Marco. I need to go into town. I will call Lucinda up to play with the children. If Giovanni asks where I am, please tell him I need some air and I am with Nic for protection. He nodded once in understanding. "I shouldn't be long."

Strutting down to the ground floor, I went into my office to grab my handbag and keys. A feeling of dread loomed over me. I had no idea what this could be about but I knew in my gut that Olivia had not come into work today for a different reason than a stomach bug.

Camilla Aiani

Camilla

Swinging my legs over the edge of the stone wall and looking out across the ocean, I inhaled the fresh sea air and closed my eyes. Calm. Tranquillity. Peace. Just for a moment, I could allow those feelings to wash away the suffocating torture that is my life. Just for a moment, I could forget who I was and what I had to do and just be present. A girl sitting on the edge of the world, listening to the sea.

A cough interrupted my quiet and I felt him take a seat next to me, dangling his muscular legs over the wall before handing me a takeaway cappuccino. Him. The man who I could never have yet wanted more than anything. The man who had quickly become the only thing I could think about and the only person I could trust in this hell hole.

"Grazie," I said as I took the cardboard cup from him, our fingers brushing and sending my stomach into a flutter of excitement. Pathetic. He gave me a small smile and looked out across the Mediterranean that calmly lapped against the wall below our feet.

We sat in a comfortable silence for a few minutes, and I took little opportunities to sneakily admire him. His masculine, rough hands were covered in colourful tattoos that held his coffee in his lap. The strong, furred forearms were decorated in the same ink that disappeared into his black T-shirt which hugged his biceps. His strong, square jaw line decorated with a full beard and brown hair pulled back into a bun. He was gorgeous. He was everything I always dreamed of in a man. The perfectly groomed and model good looks were not my thing. I liked ruggedness. I liked aggressively attractive. That was Maximus. But, of course, as my luck would go, he was not the Buccini mafioso I was being handed to in a business transaction. His cousin was. The man who terrified me more than my own father does. Even though Maximus looked every bit the scary thug, he wasn't at all. He was nothing like his cousin. He had shown me so much kindness and care since I was practically left on the doorstep of the Buccini mansion. I was under no false impression that Max was just as deadly as all the other men I had grown up around, but he was also different. I wasn't used to it. The only man who had ever been half as kind to me was my fratello but he was blood.

"You see that there?" His husky voice broke me out of my forbidden thoughts as he lifted his arm and pointed at the outline of a small island miles away. "That island is owned by my uncle. Do you want to hear a funny story?"

He turned his head to look at me and I nodded as my eyes connected with his sparkling green irises. I didn't care what he was saying as long as he was talking to me. I would listen to him talk all day if I could.

"A couple of years ago, there was a storm. A small boat was shipwrecked, and the survivors managed to reach the island. A young couple. They broke into zio's house and lived there for months before anyone realised they were there. They lived a life of complete luxury and took full advantage of Salvatore's assets until my uncle himself went there for a vacation and walked in on them fucking in his bed," Max chuckled.

I gasped, my hand covering my mouth as I stared out at the little, rocky island in the distance. The first thought that crossed my mind was I would give anything for that to happen to me. To become shipwrecked on an island and disappear. If I had Max for company, that would be even better.

"What happened to them?" I asked curiously.

Max quipped one eyebrow up suggestively and sipped his coffee. Oh. Of course. They were killed.

"That's not a funny story then," I commented back as I looked out at the island again.

"I guess not," he replied.

Silence fell upon us once again and I sighed deeply. "I don't think many stories end happily these days. Especially not in our world." I felt his gaze on me as I kept my eyes fixed forwards. Just knowing he was looking at me had my body heating up even more under the afternoon sun. "Why doesn't Giovanni want to marry me?"

He huffed loudly and ran his hand over his beard repeatedly, which drew my attention from the horizon to watch that hypnotic action. I wondered what it would feel like to play with it myself.

I knew he should lie to me. He should tell me that his cousin wanted to marry me to stop me from running to my Papi like I am sure they think I would. So, I was surprised when he told the truth.

"It's not for me to say and there is more than one reason. But it has nothing to do with you. You should never think that his actions or words are personal."

"But I don't understand it. He agreed to it two years ago. I was prepped for this role for two years! Being taught how to be an obedient wife. Knowing where my place would be and what would be expected of me. For two years, I have wondered who my husband was, and I was stupid enough to think he wanted me. But I knew from the moment he met me that I was a disappointment. I had one job to do and I failed immediately," I dropped my head and looked down at my hands as the last words choked out of me.

All my life, I have felt worthless. I was told from the moment I could understand it that my role was to look pretty. To seduce men and make Papi money. As soon as I grew boobs, my Papi shoved me in front of sleezy, old men and I had to bat my eyelashes and make them believe I was smitten with them until they signed the deals. I was relieved when Papi announced I was to be married two years ago, because at least I wouldn't be used as bait by him anymore. Instead, I would be one man's property and that was better than that.

Max turned his huge frame slightly and I gasped when he placed his hand on my chin and rotated my head to look at him. He kept his light grip on me as he stared into my eyes. "You did not fail at anything, Camilla. You can never be a disappointment. Gio is a fool if he doesn't want you."

My heart raced as my lips parted and his eyes flickered down to them, and I saw the desire as he glanced back up. *Please. Kiss me. Just one kiss.* I could resign myself to a life of misery if I could just feel those lips on me just once.

As if being electrocuted by his words, he quickly released my face and turned back to the sea, clearing his throat. I wanted to cry as I watched his jaw clench and he picked at the paper around his cup. I closed my eyes and inhaled a soothing breath.

"Do you want to marry him?" I swear his deep voice was laced with pain and it made my heart break. Did he feel it too? This thing between us or was it all in my head? Was I just latching onto the only man who had ever shown me an ounce of kindness?

"No," I said immediately. He looked across at me and I held his gaze. "But I must. If I don't, my Papi will kill me."

His handsome features took on a menacing look as anger took control. I have seen that look on many men, many times in my life. But somehow, this didn't scare me. His anger was not directed at me.

"Why would he kill you? You are his only daughter!"

"And his only chance of gaining favour with your uncle. This alliance means more to him than I do. I have known that for a long time. If I am the one who screws it up. There will be no mercy, daughter or not."

"Your Papi is an asshole."

"You are not wrong," I giggled sadly.

My father does not love me. Or my mamma. He never has. He has no respect for women. I have grown up being told I was not good enough from the moment I could walk. My hair is not blonde enough. My eyes are not blue enough. I am not skinny enough. My tits are not big enough. For my 16th birthday, when all my friends were given horses or jewellery, I was told I was having a boob job. Then came the hair extensions, the fake eyelashes, the Botox and lip fillers. And I can't remember the last time I was allowed to eat a cheeseburger. What I would do for a cheeseburger! If I ever tried to refuse any of his orders, I was quickly put in my place by my papi's back hand.

"Can I trust you, Cami? If I tell you something that I know I should not and would get myself killed if my cousin or uncle found out, can I trust that you will not tell your Papi or anyone?" His beautiful eyes bore into mine and I wanted to scream. Hand on my heart, I would never betray this man. In the short time I have known him, he has been the only decent man I have ever met. He means more to me as a friend than Francesco does to me as a father.

"Yes. You can trust me. I swear," I said quietly, not breaking our eye contact. He studied me for a few moments, clearly trying to decide if I was genuine or not. He nodded his head and looked out at the waves.

"Giovanni and I are going to get you both out of this marriage. We will find a way to keep the alliance that doesn't involve you having to marry each other."

My eyes grew wide and I felt panic rise inside me. No. They couldn't. My papi would kill me. I am as good as dead if I do not marry Giovanni. Seeing the panic on my face, he turned his body and grabbed my hand in his.

"Listen Camilla. I will not let anyone hurt you. Giovanni, my uncle or your father. No matter what happens, no one will touch you."

I shook my head as the tears started to brim in my eyes, the fear taking over. He could not protect me.

"No. Giovanni has to marry me. He must," I panicked as my voice cracked.

"Hey! Look at me. We will find a way out of this where you are both free and my uncle and your father still get what they want. You said your father just wanted an alliance with Sal, because who wouldn't want an alliance with the most powerful family in Mala Del Brenta? So, we just have to figure out a better deal for them both. But for the time being, you must play the part. Pretend everything is going well with Giovanni. Act like the loved-up fiancé to keep them off our backs."

"And if it works? What then? I am to be sent back to my family and sold to the next highest bidder!" I shouted; the tears were streaming down my face now. I couldn't help it. As much as the thought of marrying such a ruthless and cold man made my stomach knot, going back to the prison of my home was far worse.

He reached up and wiped the tears from my face with his thumb, my other hand still in his. "No. I will not let that happen. I said I would protect you and I will. We will figure this out."

"Why? Why are you being so nice to me?" I stared up into his eyes and saw the turmoil swirling in them. He lowered his hand and let go of mine.

"We should go. It's getting late," he said frostily, and jumped down from the wall, strolling over to his motorbike. I inhaled a shaky breath and wiped my cheeks as I took one last look at the rolling waves of the ocean.

But this time there was no calm. No peace. Just jealousy of their freedom.

The Truth

Olivia

As I sat on the bench by the river, I tried to tame the pesky hairs behind my ears that had fallen out of the messy bun of hair on top of my head. I looked like shit. I knew I did. My eyes were stinging from the tears and I was still pale from the shock. I needed answers. But I also needed to prepare myself for the truth. So, I decided to talk to the woman who could give it to me before I walked into the lion's den. I knew she was an honest person and we were very similar in many ways. That was how I knew that even if it was not what I wanted to hear, she would give it to me straight.

My eyes darted around the beautiful surroundings as the paranoia took hold. I had been followed for weeks. I was likely being watched now. It was a horrible feeling and one that made me want to lock myself away in Gigi's flat and never leave again. But I couldn't. I was never going to let another man control my life like that, even if they were threatening to kill me.

"Olivia?"

I turned and looked over my shoulder as I heard my name and the clicking of heels on the cobbled pavement. I stood up quickly and stared at her concerned face that looked me up and down carefully. One of Gio's men was standing guard behind her protectively and when she saw me looking at him, she waved her hand, shooing him away. He moved back a few paces to give us some privacy.

"Don't worry. Gio doesn't know I am meeting you."

I relaxed a little and nodded, sitting back down on the bench as she came to sit next to me, brushing the invisible dirt off it before she perched.

I looked out across the river at the buildings on the other side and tried to gather all my strength to not feel intimidated by this woman. Now I know who she is.

"Olivia. You are worrying me. What is wrong?"

"You are the mafia," I said coldly, still not looking at her. I felt her body tense next to me and the tension grew between us. "Are you going to deny it?" I turned and faced her.

To my surprise, a small, sad smile appeared, and she shook her head. "You are right. We are. Although we do not call ourselves that." My heart started pounding more violently at her confirming what I already knew. I held her gaze, willing her to continue. "We call ourselves Mala Del Brenta. We are the most powerful family controlling Northern Italy."

"And by controlling you mean what?" I asked bluntly. My tone was portraying my anger. I tried to keep calm, but this woman had invited me into her home to care for her children and fall for her son on an illusion.

She sighed and fidgeted with her gold bangle on her wrist. "I really think you should speak to Gio about all of this, Olivia."

"No. I am asking you Cecilia. Woman to woman. You knew I had no idea about who you really were and you gained my trust. You welcomed me into your family with open arms and fed me lies. You and your son. And now I want to know why. Why would you not tell me the truth? Are all your other employees in the dark as well?"

She took a deep breath. "No. They are aware. Everyone has a trial period when working for us and they must sign a confidentiality agreement. After two weeks, if they are a good fit, we tell them who we are."

I thought of Natalia. So, she knows they are criminals and she still told me to go for the job. But she obviously hadn't told anyone outside of work about who they really were because she signed their waiver. It was starting to make sense.

"And what if someone breaks confidentiality?" I asked, glaring into her brown eyes. She looked uncomfortable and shuffled in her seat.

"Olivia, I really think you need to hear all this from G- "

"You kill them? Or torture them? Threaten them?" I interrupted her, my voice raising slightly into a low yell.

"Olivia, I know how you are feeling right now. This is a lot to take in and- "

"You have no idea how I am feeling, Cecilia! You all deceived me! You kept your entire lives a secret from me! You gained my trust and…" I choked on my emotions at the end of my sentence. It was him I was really thinking of.

"I know how this feels better than anyone, Olivia. I was in your shoes thirty years ago! I was a normal girl from a sheltered background, who had just finished university and become a lawyer. I met Vinny and fell in love, having no idea who he really was. When I found out, I was feeling everything you are right now," she said with heartfelt emotion and I stared at her, narrowing my eyes. "Ask yourself this, Olivia. If I had told you who you were working for after the two-week probation would you have stayed? If you knew who we were, would you have given Giovanni a chance?"

"That is not the point, Cecilia, and you know it!"

"I know. But Gio had his reasons for wanting to protect you from this."

"Really? Because as far as I can see, he hasn't protected me from shit."

"He knew that you would never give him a chance without seeing the real him, Olivia. He let you in. He opened up to you and everything you shared in France was real. You are so important to him and you need to understand that he was only trying to allow you to see him for who he really was before revealing the truth."

"So, he was tricking me? Well, that is one way of getting into my knickers!" I snapped and she narrowed her eyes.

"He cares for you, Olivia. Don't downplay your connection like that," she replied sternly, and I scoffed.

"Cares for me? How can he care for me? He doesn't trust me. If he did, he would have told me who he was before he slept with me and got me so deep into this mess! This isn't fair, Cecilia. I didn't deserve that."

"You are right. You didn't. But it happened. I am just glad he has told you now and you can make your own decision about moving forward."

I frowned. She thinks Gio told me? "He didn't tell me! He has no idea that I know."

She looked taken aback as she sat up straighter and her face paled. "Then how did you find out?"

"Two lovely gentlemen who called themselves Leones," I said sarcastically, and her eyes widened in panic.

"What? When? Did they harm you?" She reached out for my arm, but I whipped it away.

"No. They didn't, but they did tell me the truth about Giovanni. They thought it was hilarious that I had no idea," I snarled, and her face took on that intimating and cold mask. She was pissed.

"Those men killed my husband, Olivia. They are dangerous people. You need to tell Giovanni right now what happened. You are in danger if they know what you mean to him," She growled.

"No shit!" I let my anger get the better of me as I folded my arms across my chest and stared out at the river. I heard her sighing deeply and looking around our surroundings, most likely checking to see if we were in danger right now. "Don't worry. They won't kill me for at least another two weeks apparently."

Her eyes rested on me and she rubbed her face with her hands. "Olivia," her voice was softer now as she seemed to get her own emotions under control. "Giovanni never lied to you. He may have omitted the truth, but he never lied. If you had asked him out right at any moment, he would have told you the truth. My son is many things, but he is not a liar."

"Oh, so it is my fault for not asking him directly if he is a mafia underboss?"

"Of course not. I am just trying to make you see that everything that has happened between you and everything he has ever said to you is the truth."

I sighed, closed my eyes and let my foot tap anxiously on the floor. That was what I was scared of. That all of this was real. That he was real because it would make it so much harder to walk away. I had to walk away. Didn't I?

"I am going to speak to him, Cecilia, but I need to know how bad this can get. I need to know it all."

She nodded in understanding. "He will tell you. You ask the questions, and he will answer them."

"And then what?" I glanced over at her and she gave me a sad smile.

"And then you have a decision to make."

"Like you did?" I said quietly and she nodded. "Did you ever regret it? Getting involved in all of this?"

"No. How could I regret true love?" She had tears in her eyes.

I looked away from her quickly as my own emotions threatened to overwhelm me. If I walked away from this, from him, I may never feel what I did for Gio, with any other man. He was like an addiction. So bad for me, yet he felt so good. But was it healthy? Was it toxic? Was there some twisted part of me that wanted him because of my past? How could I be with someone who could kill or torture someone as a job?

"No one is going to force you to stay, Olivia. If you can't do this; if you cannot see past the lifestyle to the man who adores you and will devote his life to you, then you must do what is best for you. For me, I couldn't think of a life without my Vinny in it. So, I stayed. I adapted. And you can too. It won't be easy, but I am here to help. So is Elle. But it must be what you want."

She took my hand in hers and squeezed it in support. I had never felt so conflicted in my life. It was as if nothing had changed between Gio and I if I didn't let it, yet, everything had changed. I know things now that put my life in danger. But then, my life was already in danger before I even met this man. I can't blame him for that.

"Okay. I will speak to him," I said more confidently than I felt. I stood up and walked past the bodyguard, who was obviously not just a bodyguard as she followed behind me. I still had no idea what I was going to do, and I realised that the only one who could help me decide was the man who could also break my heart.

Confessions

Giovanni

I couldn't concentrate. No matter how many times I tried to busy myself with work and phone calls, thoughts of her swarmed my mind. Something was off. I could sense it. I still hadn't heard from her and it was nearly 5pm. I wanted to call or text again, but I was trying to muster some patience and control. If she needed me, she would reach out. She said she needed time to rest and I was trying to listen to her wishes.

I groaned as I slammed my laptop shut on the desk. I had been trying to find solutions to my marriage alliance for the last two hours and I was getting nowhere. If this was just a straightforward business deal to make us all more wealthy and powerful, it would have been easier. But there was a deep-set vendetta behind the alliance. We both had hatred for the Leones, but ours was vicious. I had no idea Sal had been trying to come up with a way to get revenge for my father's death without the commission tracing it back to us, but of course he would never have let it go. They had been close. Opposite men in many ways, but my papi was his baby brother, only two years apart. Family first. That was their motto. If I went against this alliance, we would have no access to alibis, men who were not our own and the element of surprise. The Aianis could stab us in the back out of spite if we ever touched the Leones. I would effectively be losing my chance to avenge my papi's death, something that had lived in my blood like a parasite for two years. And for what?

Her face flashed in my mind and I dropped my head in my hands. For her. That's what. It was pathetic. This feeling. I had, without even realising it, turned into my father. I was contemplating putting a woman before my family. Before my duty. I was brought up to respect Boss and his decisions to strengthen this family above all else, yet I was contemplating going against everything I had built myself up to be for her. I never saw her coming. One day, I was the cutthroat underboss who cared for no one but his family and his name and the next, BAM, Olivia happened. It was unexpected. She was unexpected. I thought I was perfectly content with my life until she entered it with a feisty attitude, messy brown hair and big, bright eyes. She gives me hope that the world can be a good place. She gives me hope that I can be good. Not as good as she deserves, but I can try. I want to try. Fuck, listen to me. I am fucking whipped. And I don't even care.

But one thing remained. She still didn't even know who I was. I could tell her and she might run. Then that would solve all my problems. If she didn't want me. My stomach twisted into knots and I felt physically sick at the thought of her leaving me. Of her walking out of my life and never seeing her again. But if it was what she wanted, what could I do? As much as the thought calmed me somewhat, I couldn't exactly chain her up and keep her prisoner in the mansion just for my sake. She would hate me. I would have to let her go.

My phone vibrated on my desk and I grabbed it frantically. My heart soared when I saw her name.

Can you come over?

I stared at the words on the screen. No kisses. No affection. But she wanted me to come over all the same. At least that was something.

Leaving now. Do you need me to bring anything? Are you feeling better? X

I stood up and checked my appearance quickly in the mirror before dashing out of my office and down the stairs. Grabbing the first pair of keys I could find in the security room, I strolled out towards my Aston Martin and felt Angelo and Zane follow behind me without a word and climb into one of the SUVs. It was one of the most frustrating things about being an underboss. I had to have muscle with me wherever I went. I was more skilled and deadly than those two soldiers combined, but I couldn't always have eyes everywhere. Their job was to watch my back. To be on the constant look out for anything out of the ordinary so I could go about my day. My phone vibrated again as I climbed into the car.

No. I am fine. Thanks.

I frowned at her bluntness. She seemed…mad at me. Did she expect me to actually come and check on her today? Was this one of those situations where the woman says no but really, she means yes and gets pissed off when her man listens? I shook my head and slammed the door shut, starting up the engine. Women. Honestly.

Once I parked outside the shabby apartment block, I nodded to my men in the SUV to wait outside. I shoved the green door open that was barely hanging on its hinges. Someone should really get this fixed. It's not safe. Anyone can get in.

Climbing the stairs, two at a time, I stopped at her flat door and took a deep breath. I was excited to see her but also nervous. I knocked once and heard some shuffling from inside. The door whipped open and there she was. My immediate smile at seeing her soon faded when I saw the look in her eyes. Something was wrong.

I stepped forward and reached out my hand to touch her face.

"What's happened?" I frowned when she backed away from my touch and I dropped my hand.

"We need to talk."

My heart flipped. This can't be good. I had seen enough movies where those words meant a breakup or something along those lines. She walked away from me and sat down on the sofa, refusing to look at me. My nostrils flared as I tried to get my emotions under control. *Don't panic, Gio. Just hear her out. It is probably nothing.*

I took slow, deliberate steps towards the small sofa and sat down next to her, leaning my elbows on my knees and I turned my head to the side to look at her pretty face. She wasn't wearing any make-up and her eyes looked wild and... bloodshot. Had she been crying?

"Have you been crying? What's happened? Tell me," I didn't mean for my voice to sound so dominant and aggressive, but I was losing control at seeing her like this and not knowing why.

She looked up at me and glared. It had me frozen to the spot. Her anger was at me. "Tell me who you are."

"What?" My voice was barely audible as panic rose in me. Did she... know? How?

"I need to hear it from your mouth, Giovanni. Who are you?"

I swallowed as my eyes widened. Shit. This wasn't supposed to happen like this. I had it all planned. I was going to take her somewhere romantic and try to break it to her softly. Maybe she didn't mean what I thought she did.

"Liv. What do you mean? You know who I- "

She snapped. She stood up abruptly. "Don't you dare, Giovanni! Tell me the truth!"

Fuck. The look in her eyes told me everything. Hurt. Betrayal. Anger. It was all there. I reached for her hand but she pulled it away out of my grasp. I ran my hand through my hair as she waited for my answer. This was it. The moment I had been dreading.

"I am Giovanni Buccini. The underboss of the Buccini family in Mala Del Brenta."

I held her gaze as I spoke and saw her bottom lip tremble. She knew yet still a part of her didn't want to believe it.

"A mafia boss," she clarified, and I nodded.

"One day. Yes."

"And you didn't think to tell me? You enjoyed playing games with me, didn't you, Gio? The innocent, clueless nanny who you laughed at behind my back? How could I have been so stupid!" She shouted and I stood up, grabbing her arms and forcing her to look at me.

"You are not stupid, Liv. I am. I should have told you sooner. No one was laughing at you. I was trying to protect you. I knew I was no good for you Liv, but I couldn't stop. I couldn't stay away from you."

She shook her head in disbelief. "I confided in you Gio! I told you things about myself that were difficult for me. I trusted you! I let you in! Why couldn't you do the same?"

"Are you kidding me, Liv? I did let you in! I let you see a side of me that I have never shown anyone but my family. No. Not even them. When I am with you, I am the real me. I am not pretending. Who I am is who I have always been with you, bambola. If I didn't trust you, I would never have been able to show that side of myself. It fucking scares the shit out of me. It is so easy to be Giovanni the ruthless underboss. It is so easy to shut the world out and make everyone fear me and hate me. Letting down that front and being vulnerable is so much fucking harder. But I wanted you to know me. The real me."

"So, what are you saying? That the intimidating and ruthless Giovanni is an act? That is not who you are?" She folded her arms as she raised one eyebrow at me and I sighed. I could so easily say what she wanted to hear right now. Pretend that the darkness in me was an act, but I would be lying. It was as much a part of me as the side she knows.

"No. That is also real. I can't help who I am, Olivia. But what I am saying is that I am not that person when I am with you. I never will be," I said softly. I tried to step towards her again but she turned and walked into the kitchen, keeping a safe distance from me. I frowned. I wanted to hold her so badly. I hated that I was the reason she was in pain. If only she would let me, I could fix it. I could make it go away.

"I need to know," she spoke to the kitchen counter as her head hung down between her arms that were leaning on the surface. I stayed still, mentally preparing myself for what I knew was coming. The questions.

"I need to know it all."

Mamma's words echoed in my head. I had to answer every question honestly, no matter how bad it got. No matter how much I wanted to protect her from it all. She deserved the truth. Only then could she truly know what it would mean to stay with me. To choose me.

"Ask me anything," I muttered as my heart dropped. After this, she would either accept me or leave me. And there was nothing I could do about it.

She stood up straight and her enchanting eyes locked with mine. This time they were full of fear and my heart shattered into a million pieces.

"Are you a murderer?"

Confessions Part II

Olivia

"Are you a murderer?"

My heart was like a wild beast in a cage as I stared into his dark eyes. I could see the truth in them before he even opened his mouth.

"I have killed men. Yes." I held his gaze as I gulped. I had prepared myself for his answer but it still didn't make it easier to hear.

"How many?" My voice shook as the fear took over. But it was odd. I wasn't scared of him like I thought I would be when hearing those words. It was a fear of not being able to take it. Of not being able to handle his darkness. Hearing what he was capable of could break me and I had no control over it. I had no idea how I would feel once I knew all of this and it was terrifying. Walking away from him was terrifying, but so was choosing to stay.

"Too many to list," his jaw clenched, and his eyes filled with pain as he held my gaze. The silence stretched between us as I tried to hold my nerve.

"Why do you kill people? For fun?" I asked shakily. It was a stupid question, I know, but it was the first thing that came to mind. Henry killed Nate for fun. He did it because he could. There was no good reason behind it and, even though I didn't believe anyone had the right to take someone's life, I prayed Giovanni had a better reason for doing it than the thrill.

He frowned. His dark eyebrows pulled down into the bridge of his nose as he huffed loudly.

"No. It is not for fun. Although I would be lying if I said some of the men I killed deserved it and I took pleasure from ending their lives."

My eyes widened at his words. The words of a psychopath. A demented soul. Yet when I looked at him, he was still Gio. It was confusing.

"Why did they deserve it?"

"Part of our business is that we are hired to kill fucked up people. People who have done wrong to others. Murderers, rapists, paedophiles, sex traffickers. I enjoy killing them," his voice was hard, but every word had an edge to it. A hesitance. He was being brutally honest with me in order to gain my trust back, no matter what the cost. "But there are times when I have killed men for less. That is when I have to switch off my emotions and see it for what it is. Business."

"So, you always do it for money?" My curiosity was overriding my fear now as the questions came flying out of me with ease.

"Mostly. Yes." I narrowed my eyes, wanting him to elaborate. "Sometimes power. Sometimes revenge. We have rivals. Enemies. People who want to harm my family. We are the most powerful family in Northern Italy, which puts a target on our backs. Call it jealousy or a need to overthrow us, but our rivals will stop at nothing to tear us down." He took one step closer to me and I fought the urge to move back. He was testing me. To see if I feared him now. When I didn't move, the faintest smile played on his lips before his face returned to its intensity.

"So, you kill each other? Other mafia families?"

"We want to kill each other, yes. But there is a law. A commission made up of all the heads of families in Italy. We all signed a declaration of peace making the heads of families untouchable without consequences. If one head breaks the treaty, all hell can break loose."

"So instead, you torture each other? Take their eyes?" I dropped one hip with sass and crossed my arms as his face creased with confusion. Realisation hit him and his eyes widened.

"How do you know- "

"That you took a man's eye? I met him. Nice bloke," I replied sarcastically. His face changed completely. And now I truly was scared. Of him. It was the same expression he had the day we were in the piazza and the night I found him in the gym. Controlled rage and evil.

"What?" His voice was low and gritty, and my heart jumped into my throat. I took a step back and my body hit the fridge door. "Fucking talk to me Liv before I lose my shit. How did you meet him? Did he hurt you?"

"N-no. Last night. I went to the shops and when I came out a man..." I paused as my breathing became erratic from the look of rage on his face. "He kidnapped me. Put me in the car and they told me about you. About who you are."

He was so close to me now, but he wasn't seeing me. He was looking right through me in his fury. "Who? Who did that to you?"

"Lorenzo and Riccardo Leone."

He turned away from me abruptly, his hand on his jaw. His other hand was clenching and unclenching into a fist at his side. I could feel his extreme anger radiating from him.

"Did they touch you? Tell me the truth, Liv. Did they harm you in any way?"

I couldn't see his face, but from the way his shoulders were rising up and down in rapid breaths, I was glad I was spared the sight.

"No. I promise. They just talked to me."

That seemed to calm him a little as I heard him exhale deeply. I suddenly realised that he wasn't angry with me. He was scared. He thought they had done something to me. His fury was at them. I swallowed as I tiptoed towards him cautiously and placed my hand on his shoulder blade. He tensed at my touch. The atmosphere thickened around us.

"Look at me Gio," I whispered. He slowly turned and glanced down at my face. I held his haunted stare. "I am fine. They didn't do anything to me."

His face softened and he stepped forward carefully, wrapping his arms around my waist and leaning down to bury his head in my neck. I froze. I didn't know how to react. A part of me wanted to hug him back but a bigger part of me still needed time. I was still so unsure and didn't know what to think or how to feel about any of this.

"Just let me hold you, bambola. Just for one minute. I'm sorry I scared you."

My heart ached at his words and I fought the lump in my throat. I allowed him to hold me, the tension slowly ebbing away from his body and I closed my eyes to try to ignore his intoxicating smell or the warmth of his skin. I could feel myself caving. My resolve was wavering.

"Giovanni, please," I whispered, my voice coming out in a broken husk. He lifted his head and rested his forehead on mine, which only made it worse.

"Look at me, bambola. I am still right here. It's still me."

I couldn't. It was too soon. I pushed at his chest lightly and turned away as his arms dropped from my body.

"They wanted me to deliver a message to you." I walked over to the counter and picked up the brown envelope. I threw it down on the surface as it slid towards him. His face scrunched up as he picked it up and pulled out the photographs. That sinister look was back. Only this time I was more prepared for it. "They had been following me, us, for weeks. Since you took that man's eye. They threatened my life unless…" he glanced up at me and pure rage was swirling in those almost black eyes. "You meet with them alone. Without telling anyone. They said you had two weeks to decide."

He burst out laughing, taking me by complete surprise. But it wasn't his usual laugh. It was a calculating and dangerous laugh full of arrogance.

"That is fucking hilarious."

My mouth fell open and my eyes widened. Did he not care? That they were going to kill me?

"My life is on the line, and you find it amusing?" I growled.

"Bambola. Your life is not on the line. I will never let them get within one mile of you again. Their threats are void because I will never let it happen. I fucked up by letting you out of my sight yesterday, but they won't get that chance again."

"What do you mean? Why do they want to meet with you anyway?"

"To kill me. The first person you take down in the family is the underboss… Then the boss. Then the whole system falls apart. And I mean, you are staying with me now so pack a bag. You will never be out of my sight or you will always have protection around you. They won't be able to touch you."

My eyes bulged as I realised what he was saying. I was going to become his prisoner in his home like his mother. Never leaving the house. Always having to ask permission to do anything. To go anywhere. Is this what my life would be if I chose to stay with him? To give up my freedom and my life just to stay hidden away by his side? I didn't survive everything I had just to be controlled and scared again.

"No."

His head snapped up and his eyes narrowed, but I wouldn't let him intimidate me. Even after everything I now knew about him, I still believed he would never hurt me. He was a monster to many, but never to me. That I knew. I stood my ground as he put the pictures down carefully, never taking his eyes off mine in challenge. "No?"

"I will not end up like your mother, Giovanni. I am not going to be hidden away behind your mansion walls like a caged animal. I wasn't raised in your world and I do not have to accept it. I still have my freedom and I am willing to fight for it."

His nostrils flared as he fought to hold onto his control. I don't know why he was surprised. He should know me by now. The one thing I would never allow is for a man to control my life.

"This is not up for discussion, Olivia. Even if you don't want to be with me right now, even if you need some time to think about us, you are still coming back with me today and you will not be allowed out of my sight," his deep voice was demanding and hard.

I scoffed loudly, which made his nostrils flare. "You cannot control me Gio. I am not one of your men that follows your every command."

"I am not trying to control you. I am trying to protect you," he hissed, stepping closer to me. I wanted to step back but I knew it was a power move. I forced my feet to stay glued to the floor as he towered over me, glaring down into my eyes. They flickered down to my lips fleetingly and he licked his own, causing my stomach to flutter. *No Liv. Not now.* This man had just told you he was a cold-blooded killer and wanted to keep you locked away and you are thinking about kissing him? *Fuck I have issues.*

"Well, right now, I don't need your protection. They said I had two weeks. So that means I have two weeks to figure this shit out and make my decision."

He was so close to me now that I could feel his warm breath on my face. His beautiful yet fierce features were so smouldering and dark as he listened to my words and I saw the passion and desire in his eyes.

"And what shit do you have to figure out, bambola?" His voice was a low seductive caress and my centre ached with need. He knew what he was doing. He was trying to break me down using his most lethal weapon. Sex. And my body was falling for it.

Pushing my body against the kitchen counter, he trapped me there with his arms on either side of my hips. I gulped down my arousal and I tried to maintain my sanity and think clearly.

"It looks as though I have only two choices. Stay with you and live a life of confinement."

"But have the best sex and be worshipped every day," he smirked as he brushed his lips lightly against mine, causing my breath to hitch. "Or?"

"Or leave. Take the next plane out of here and disappear," I whispered, and he froze. His eyes burned into mine with a storm of emotions and his breathing became laboured.

"Is that what you want?" His tone was dangerously low and laced with hurt. We stared deeply into each other's eyes as we both heaved breathlessly. No, that wasn't what I wanted. Right now, all I wanted was him. His lips on mine. My lust was clouding my judgement once again.

In a flash, he had given in first. He grabbed my face in his huge hands and smashed his lips against mine possessively and with all the fire that burned within him. It was wanting, angry and raw as he forced his tongue into my mouth and claimed my soul. I moaned, my body melting against his as he lifted me onto the kitchen top so we were at an even height. My hands grabbed at his hair, pulling it and fisting it aggressively as his hands explored my back, groped my breast aggressively through my top and then wrapped around my neck, holding me to him. Every movement was a power struggle between us mixed with intense passion and feeling.

"Say you're mine Liv," he breathed against my open mouth and my senses snapped me back to reality. What was I doing? I pulled back from him and he stared at me with hooded eyes.

"I – I can't," I whispered, trying to push at his chest to give me some space. He held onto me tighter.

"Do you fear me, Liv? Do you believe I would ever let anything happen to you?" he growled, and I held his gaze.

"No. I don't, but that doesn't change anything."

"That changes everything, Olivia."

"It does not! You are still who you are! You will still do what you do and I just have to look the other way? I don't know if I can do that!" I shouted, matching his tone. I shoved him harder and jumped off the counter. This time he didn't try to stop me.

I paced the small kitchen floor as he sighed heavily. There was nothing he could say about that. It was true and he knew it. The silence stretched between us and every second that passed made me feel sadder than the last. This could never work.

"I can't let you go," his haunted voice whispered, breaking the silence. My heart flipped and tears sprang to my eyes. I can't do this right now. I needed time to process. Time to think. He was too confusing. His words, his actions, his beautiful face. He didn't seem like a ruthless killer to me, yet I knew he was.

"I need you to go," I choked, and he turned to stare at me. The look in his eyes nearly broke me.

"Bambola, please. Just come with me. You don't even need to see me. I will stay away from you, I just need to keep you safe," he pleaded. I nearly gave in. Those eyes nearly had me.

I shook my head. "I need space. I need time alone, Gio. Please."

His jaw flexed and his features tensed with irritation. He closed his eyes and exhaled before turning abruptly and storming out of the flat. I stared at the slammed door before I crumbled to the floor as a sudden wave of despair crashed over me. I couldn't be mad at anyone but myself. I told myself not to fall in love with him. If only I had listened.

Protector

Olivia

I was pacing the length of the small flat with my burner phone in hand and biting my nails for what felt like eternity. The conflict of emotions inside me was threatening to deplete me and I needed to talk to the one person who had always been there for me and would know what to say. Millie.

But if I called her, I was risking everything. I was putting her life in danger as well as my own. I had never felt more alone. But what if I destroy the burner later?

Allowing the sudden impulsivity and the need to speak to my best friend to take over, I dialled her number and let it ring three times before hanging up. That was the signal. Now I just had to wait. If she wanted to talk to me, she would find a pay phone and ring my burner.

It was nearly half an hour before the phone started vibrating. My heart was pounding my chest as I inhaled a shaky breath. A mix of excitement and nerves swirled in my belly.

I answered the call without speaking, just to be sure it was her.

"Liv?"

Her voice felt like home and the tears were already rolling down my cheeks as I released a loud sob of happiness. "Mills!"

"Oh my god Liv! Thank God you are alright. I miss you so much! You have no idea! Are you alright though? Where are you? Oh shit no don't tell me that. I am just so happy to hear your voice."

I laughed through my tears at her rambling as my heart swelled. "I'm alright. I miss you too. I just needed to speak to you. I'm sorry. I know I shouldn't have called." Panic started to fester in me as I realised the magnitude of this action.

"It is fine. I had to borrow a random colleague's phone to make an urgent phone call, saying my battery had died. You will still need to destroy your burner after." Her tone was serious and I smiled. She was always the bossy one between us. "I know you can't tell me much, but are you well? You aren't sleeping on the streets or anything?"

I chuckled. "No, I am good. I have a flat and a job. I am fine."

There was a pause. "Why do I sense that you are not then?"

I sighed deeply. Even after not seeing her for a few months, she still knew me better than anyone. "I've... met someone. A man."

My gut was telling me she was smiling through the phone. "That's great

Liv! You deserve to be happy."

"But… It's a really fucked up situation, Mills. I… I don't know if I can do it."

"What exactly?"

"Be with him." I groaned in frustration and not being able to tell her the whole truth. "He has an unusual job. He is a very dangerous man, Millie. He is… above the law." That was the best I could do. There was a long pause.

"Dangerous how?"

"I can't say. That's how dangerous it is."

She breathed deeply. "Shit. But he isn't hurting you? You are not in danger?"

I shook my head. I wasn't going to tell her that actually just being associated with him put me in danger. That wasn't what she meant. "No. No, he would never hurt me. I trust that."

"Okay. So let me get this straight. You meet a man who wants to be with you but you aren't sure if you can be with him because of his dangerous job."

I smiled. "Pretty much. There is more, but I won't get into it all. He is extremely protective and possessive, but it's not like Henry. It's because he cares. I still don't like it, but I know he is trying. He's trying to be better for me. I just don't know if it's enough."

I could almost hear her brain frantically trying to piece it all together. "Does he know? About Henry."

"Yes. He knows what happened. I told him."

"Liv, that is huge! You never tell anyone."

"I know," I sighed.

"Have you slept with him?" I smirked at the curiosity and excitement in her tone. She was the only person who knew how difficult sex has been for me the last five years apart from my therapist.

"Yes. Quite a few times now."

"Oh my god! You have? This is serious Liv! Do you love him?"

The question had me halting my incessant pacing as my heart pounded in my chest.

"I – I think so." I have never been in love before. I wasn't sure how it was meant to feel. But I knew that my feelings for him were unlike anything I had ever experienced.

"Fuckitty fuck!"

I laughed loudly. She was already making me feel better. "Then I say, your choice has already been made. As long as he is good to you and you trust him, I think you should go for it. And… you say he has a dangerous job. Can he protect you? From Henry?"

My eyes widened as I realised that there was no one better out there who could protect me from that monster. "Yes. He can."

"Win win. Maybe, in some fucked up way, you were meant to find him."

I sat down on the sofa as I processed her words. It was a nice way to look at it. That fate had brought us together when I needed him the most. Millie was right. I had never felt safer than when I was in his arms. But can I really accept the rest of it? The control? The possessiveness? The brutality of his world?

"Liv. I need to tell you something. I wasn't sure if I should say, but now I know you have someone who is looking out for you…"

"What is it?" Bile rose in my throat as I waited for her next words. I knew it would be about him.

"He broke into my family's house last week. Ransacked the place. Luckily, none of us were there and I don't think he found anything, but it was still scary. He is getting desperate, Liv," her voice was a low whisper and I could feel her fear through her tone. I gulped down my instant guilt.

"Mills, I am so sorry! It's all my fault… your family…" I choked.

"They are fine! Everyone is fine. The police have 24-hour surveillance on us now. He would be crazy to come back again."

I exhaled a shaky breath as my hands trembled. "He has stayed completely hidden this entire time. We cannot even be sure it was him but…"

"It was him." I said sternly. I knew it in my bones. "The police are no closer to finding him?"

"It doesn't seem so. I'm sorry Liv. What is your boyfriend's name?"

"He is not my boyfriend. It's complicated…" She sighed impatiently. "Gio."

"I like it! He sounds sexy! You need to tell Gio he is looking for you. If this man can protect you and you are going to stay in one place, then you will need him to know."

I dropped my head in my hands. I knew she was right. If I chose to stay; if I chose this life with him, I had to tell him why I was here.

"But Liv? If it doesn't work out for whatever reason, you need to run. Immediately. Get on a flight and go. Change your name again, do whatever it takes to hide. Henry will not give up on you, Liv. We both know that."

I wiped my eyes and exhaled. "Okay. I will. Mum… how is she?"

She hesitated. "Honestly? I don't know. She is under witness protection, and no one has seen her since you left. It is for the best. At least she is safe from Henry and Neil."

I nodded. That was good. That was what I wanted. Even though my relationship with her was strained and fractured after everything, I still wanted her to be safe.

"I have to go now. I am getting daggers from the colleague whose phone I have run away with!"

I chuckled. "Okay. I hate this. I don't know when I will speak to you again."

"I know. But you know I love you."

"I love you too."

"Laters baby."

I smiled as she hung up. And then all of the emotion I was keeping bottled up inside, erupted out of me as I fell down onto the cushion and bawled my eyes out. How was this my life?

***

I woke up early the next morning after another restless night and took a leisurely shower to try and wash away the pain of the day before. I felt emotionally drained. I barely had the energy to get dressed, but I forced myself into a pair of ripped denim shorts and a baggy top. I was going for the grunge look today to reflect my mood. Right now, I am leaning towards staying. Trying to give it a go with Giovanni and live in his terrifying world. Mills was right. I wasn't exactly safe staying with him, but I also wasn't safe without him. But it was my conscience that I was struggling with. He kills people. He does dodgy deals with dodgy people. He is a criminal. There will always be a risk with him. He could get caught. Thrown in jail. He could get killed like his father. I could as well. Was I willing to risk it all just to be with him? I will be going to hell for sure.

I strolled out into the living room and was surprised to see Gigi standing in the kitchen in yesterday's work clothes. She clearly didn't come home last night. She leaned against the kitchen top, taking a bite out of a bagel.

I raised my eyebrows suggestively and she smirked. "Good night?"

"Hmmm Hmmm."

"Which nationality did you sample last night?" I asked.

"There is only one I am sampling now. The man who likes to go down under," she winked.

"The Viking? Again?" I giggled as I caught on to her play of words.

"His name is Joel."

My eyebrows were halfway up my forehead now. She liked him.

"Good for you."

"So, I guess you two have made up?"

I frowned in confusion as she stared at me intently. "Huh?"

"Giovanni? Is he not giving you a lift to work?"

"I am not going to work today. I'm still not feeling well," I lied. Her eyes narrowed.

"Then why is he sitting outside the building?"

I jumped off the stool and raced to the window. There he was. My heart fluttered. He was lying on top of his Aston Martin bonnet, with his arms folded across his chest. A black SUV was parked behind him and I could see two bulky figures inside. What the hell is he doing? As I stared down at his enormous frame taking up the car, I realised he was wearing the same clothes as yesterday. I turned abruptly and darted out of the flat, down to the road.

As soon as I pulled open the creaky green door of my building, he sat up and looked my way. A cheeky smile tugged at the corners of his lips.

"Good morning, beautiful."

"What are you doing? Did you stay here all night?"

"Of course."

My eyes widened as he turned and slid off the car bonnet, leaning against it lazily. His eyes twinkled with mischief. "What?! Why? You are crazy!"

"You refused to come with me and I had to keep you safe."

I looked from him over to the SUV behind and saw Angelo and another man who I didn't know sitting in the front seats looking exhausted. Angelo nodded at me curtly. I stared back at Gio, who was now smirking at my reaction.

"So, you slept here all night? In your car?" I yelled in disbelief.

"I didn't sleep, no. But I did stay here all night, yes."

I was speechless. I didn't know what to say. It was possibly the most romantic and craziest thing anyone had ever done for me. Our eyes locked and at that moment, I knew I would stay. Without hesitating, I raced into his arms, taking him by surprise as I smashed my lips against his and wrapped my arms around his neck. He froze for a split second before kissing me back ferociously and holding me tight against his body. When we broke away, he peered down at me in wonder.

"Will you come with me now?" he panted, out of breath. His eyes pleaded and I brushed my nose against his and closed my eyes.

"Yes."

No More Tears

Giovanni

I couldn't stop the goofy grin plastered on my face the entire drive home with Olivia sitting next to me. I knew I had a long way to go in gaining her trust back and proving to her that she was making the right choice, but for right now, I just wanted to enjoy this little win.

I yawned loudly and felt her gaze on me before I turned and gave her a dazzling smile. She rolled her eyes, but happiness showed on her face too. I hadn't slept in over 24 hours. And with the two previous nights resulting in not much sleep either, I felt like a zombie. But it was worth it. There was no way I could have left her unprotected and alone in the flat after hearing what Leone did. They may say they weren't going to make a move for two weeks, but I wasn't about to test the validity of their words.

I will kill them before they get a chance to come near her again.

Now more than ever, I wanted to put a bullet in each of their skulls. Which just made shit more complicated. I needed to ensure this plan with Sal happened because she would never be safe as long as they were alive. As we pulled up to the gate of the mansion, I felt that crippling dread returning. I still had to tell her about Camilla. Luckily, Max would have taken her off the premises for the day, so I had time to do this right. I was going to be honest. Explain everything. About my father's death, my uncle's deal with the Aianis, the plan to kill the Leones and how I was going to get out of this alliance, but for right now, I had to play along. It was a huge risk. But I hope she will trust me when I say that I will never touch Camilla and I am not in the least bit interested in marrying her. It will only be a short time until Max and I come up with a better deal for the Boss's.

I glided the car into the glass garage and turned the engine off. She looked up at the mansion with a pensive expression.

"It feels…different now. Like I am seeing everything in a new light," her voice was soft and quiet. I couldn't imagine how she might be feeling about all of this. I was born into this life just like my siblings. We didn't know any different.

"Is it really that different from what you thought? I am still a businessman. I still love, care for and look after my family. The men here are all still here for their protection. I am still the same person I was in France, Liv."

She turned her head and stared into my eyes. The gold and green shimmering with a mix of emotions. "There is something I have to tell you."

"What is it?" My heart immediately raced. She looked so serious. Whatever it was… it was big.

"Not here. Let's go to your office. Somewhere private," she replied as she pulled the door handle open of the car and climbed out.

"Okay," I walked around the car and reached for her hand. We walked towards the front door as my nerves started to build. "There is something I need to tell you too."

Just at that moment, Max came jogging towards me with a pissed expression. I dropped Liv's hand. "Where the fuck have you been?" he growled. My phone had died in the middle of the night, so I hadn't contacted anyone.

"Out."

"Right well, while you have been out, shit has been kicking off!" His green eyes glared at me accusingly and I groaned. Turning to Liv, I asked her to go and wait for me in my office and I would be up soon. She nodded once, looking a little intimidated by Max's anger, and climbed the steps to my floor. I watched her go with a clenched jaw before returning my hard gaze to my cousin. "What is it?"

"Come and see for yourself…" he stalked away towards mamma's office and I followed. Once I was inside, I saw mamma sitting behind her desk with a face full of rage as she stared at her laptop screen. I walked around the other side and leaned over her shoulder as she sat back in her chair and pressed play on the CCTV footage of a hotel in Venice. I watched in confusion as I saw what looked like a small wedding ceremony happening on the grounds. The camera zoomed in on a black-haired woman walking down the aisle in an extravagant gown.

"Why am I supposed to care about a fucking wedding?" I growled in frustration.

"Wait. Look who the groom is," mamma's sharp tone made me narrow my eyes at the man standing at the end waiting for her. The camera followed her and when she reached the groom, mamma hit pause. My eyes widened. Lorenzo Leone. Underboss of the Leone family. He got married?

"Who has he married? Who is she?" My tone was aggressive. I looked up at Max, who exchanged a look with Mamma and then glanced back at me.

"Isabelle Barbieri."

All the colour drained from my face. The daughter of Diego Barbieri, Don of the largest Mafia family in Southern Italy. Fuck. They had an alliance. They were starting a war.

The silence spoke volumes. "Does Boss know?"

"Probably."

I stood up and ran my hand through my hair. This shit just keeps getting better and better. Fuck. I turned abruptly and punched a hole into mamma's wall.

"Giovanni! I just had that redecorated!" She scolded me.

"We need to work quickly if we are going to get you and Cami out of this marriage but still keep our alliance with Aiani. We are going to need him more than ever now," Max said calmly. How was he so calm? Wait. Why was he here and calling her that?

"Cami?" I spat. Why was he so familiar with her? Panic flickered across his eyes, but he kept his face neutral. "Where is Camilla?"

"Upstairs."

I froze when I heard Toni's voice and then a feminine voice in the lobby. I turned and looked at mamma and then Max as his eyes widened slightly. Toni was talking to Camilla. And they were heading upstairs. Probably to my office. Fuck, Olivia. I raced out towards the lobby and up the stairs. I could see them entering my office and my heart pounded in my chest.

"What are you doing here, nanny?" Toni's accusing, harsh tone made anger rise in me. I managed to get to the door and pushed past them both to see Liv standing behind my desk with a pale face and wide eyes. She was holding something in her hands. A file. My eyes flickered down at it and then back up to hers as they portrayed her pain. Her file. Fuck. No.

"You knew?" her voice was a broken whisper, and I froze.

"Who is this?" I heard Camilla's sickly soft voice behind me, but I couldn't move. Liv's eyes moved to Camilla and took her in, looking her up and down.

"Olivia. Who are you?"

"I'm Camilla."

"Giovanni's fiancé," Toni added. My blood ran cold. Olivia's tortured eyes darted at mine and something inside me broke at the hurt in them. She bent over slightly as all the air was knocked out of her lungs and she was struggling to breathe. I still didn't move. I was frozen in time.

"You're engaged?" She screamed breathlessly. I snapped out of my trance as she came hurtling towards the door, trying to escape. I grabbed her arm to pull her back.

"Liv! It is not what you think. Please. Hear me out."

"Get your hands off me!" she snarled. The look of pure rage and hatred in her eyes had me release her. She stormed past us.

"I don't understand…" Camilla whispered but Liv heard her. She turned on her heels and glared at my fake fiancé.

"Don't worry. He is all yours. I am just the nanny he fucked," she hissed with venom and raced out the room. Ignoring the smirk on Toni's face and the shock on Camilla's, I shoved past them after her.

"Liv! Olivia! Wait!"

I was intercepted by Max, who grabbed my shoulders firmly and stopped me reaching her as she catapulted out the front door.

"Let her go!" He hissed but I tried to push him off. "You go after her, you fuck everything up! Toni just saw all of that!" Mamma came running through the lobby and gave me a concerned look. "Go after her, Cecilia!" Max growled.

She nodded and ran out the door, her heels clicking against the stone floor.

"Breathe Gio. Get yourself under control and go back up there and make it seem like you don't care. That you were just fucking her. You must! For her safety and to not screw up this alliance!" Max growled and I closed my eyes, trying to get my erratic breathing under control. I had just got her back, only to lose her all over again.

***

Olivia

My body was trembling uncontrollably from the shock and pure rage. I had to get out of there. Away from him. How could I have been so foolish? To believe that he wanted anything more with me than to be his little sidepiece. His distraction.

I was just getting my head around who he was and what it meant for us. I accepted it to be with him. To take a chance and see where this could go. I was willing to give up my life as I knew it... for him. And all the while, he was engaged to another woman?! The most perfect model of a woman with blonde hair that hung halfway down her fake tits and a figure that would stop men in their tracks. She was as pretty as she was sexy and the kind of woman I had always imagined Giovanni to be with.

"Olivia! Stop!"

I could hear a voice behind me but the amount of ringing in my ears and the shards of pain in my gut were making it too hard to concentrate. I tripped over my feet as I tried to speed down the gravel driveway.

"He is not engaged! It is not what you think!"

The words caused me to freeze and try to catch my breath. I leaned my hands on the stone wall that curved down the driveway with the folder still in my hand. The folder. My entire life rolled into a bound file. Every important milestone and achievement. Personal information about me and my family. Even Millie was in there. And of course, the tragic event that haunts me even today. He had gone behind my back and found it all. But that isn't what hurt the most. It was the fact he lied. He pretended he didn't know. He let me believe that I was confiding in him when he knew all along. Thinking back to the moments when he suddenly changed around me. He stopped trying to sleep with me using his arrogant charms. It wasn't because he genuinely realised I meant more to him than just a hook-up, it was because he read about my past. He knew what he needed to do to get me in his bed.

He changed his tactics because he knew they wouldn't work. I have never felt so betrayed in all my life.

I felt a presence next to me as I stood up straight. "It doesn't matter," I growled at Cecilia. She knew all of this! "Why? Why did you allow me to be with him in France knowing he had a fiancé back home?"

"She is not his fiancé Olivia. It is a misunderstanding. It's a business arrangement between his uncle and her father. Gio had no say in it and is trying to find a way out of it. You must believe me," she pleaded, her big brown eyes looked terrified as I glared at her.

"Even if that is true and he doesn't want to marry her, that doesn't change the fact that he kept this from me. Another huge part of his life. What else is he hiding from me? He slept with me and made me believe it was me he wanted to be with when she was always there in the background. Why is she here, Cecilia?"

She sighed and looked around the lawns. "She lives here. But it is not permanent. She will be gone as soon as we can figure this out. It is more complicated than you can imagine Olivia and Gio wants you! Not her."

I scoffed, feeling the anger rising in me. "I just can't...I can't deal with this. My life is a fucking disaster as it is! I don't need this either." I started to storm away from her again, but she followed me, not backing down.

"So that's it? You are going to walk away from the man you love?" She yelled, her tone dominating.

"I didn't fall in love with that man! I fell in love with his words. Unfortunately, he was a good liar!"

"Olivia! Will you stop and think rationally for a moment? He should have told you, yes. He should have handled all of this better. I don't deny that. But he has never felt this way before, he is bound to fuck up when he is dealing with so much shit that is out of his control. Everything he has done has been to protect you. He never wanted to hurt you!"

I spun around in my converse high tops at her final words.

"Well, I know that is a lie! This!" I held up the folder and shook it in front of her. "This proves that he went behind my back, invaded my privacy, found out my weaknesses and insecurities and used them against me just so he could do whatever it is that he has been doing with me! At any point, he could have revealed what he knew about me but he didn't. He let me sit there and pour my heart out to him and he pretended he didn't know a thing! How can I ever trust a man like that?"

Her face paled and she stood motionless as she looked from the file to me. She didn't know. She had no idea he had done that. Ha. She doesn't know her son as well as she thinks she does. "You once said to me that as long as trust was there, then we could overcome anything!"

Her eyes held her sorrow as she realised I was done. Nothing she could say would make me want to go back to that house. "I'm sorry Cecilia. I can't work for you anymore. I hope you understand. If I must serve out my last two weeks' notice, I will, but only if Giovanni is not in the house."

She shook her head slowly. "If this is truly what you want, Olivia. You do not need to come back at all. I will get Elle to meet you with Sani and Raya to say goodbye tomorrow."

I nodded once as I swallowed the lump that was lodged in my throat. I was not going to cry in front of her. I was not going to shed one more tear over that man. I turned on my feet as the gate opened to the Buccini estate and I walked out of it for the last time. I stopped on the road and glanced back up at the long, winding driveway.

He was never mine in the first place but losing him still broke my heart into a million pieces.

Maze Of Secrets

Camilla

I had no idea what was going on.

Ten minutes ago, I had come out of my room and made my way down to the kitchen to grab something to eat and to hopefully bump into Max when that slimy right-hand man to Salvatore showed up. I hated the way he looked at me. The way his beady eyes raked my body and he licked his lips. I was just a piece of meat to him, and I was sure that if I didn't have the protection of being engaged to Giovanni, he would have tried something. Men like him always do.

"Buongiorno Camilla," his cold tone was masked with a fake smile, and I returned it without holding his gaze.

"Ciao."

"Is everything to your satisfaction?" His eyes sparkled with desire, and I gulped. "Living here, I mean?"

"Si. Everyone has been very welcoming," I lied. No one wanted me here. I wasn't a fool. Giovanni's mother hasn't said a word to me, leaves the room anytime I enter it and the staff look right through me as if I don't even exist. And Giovanni... Well, he is the worst.

"Bravo. Where is your fiancé? I need a word," he looked around the lobby with slow, calculated precision and my stomach dropped. If I was to play this part like Max said, I should act as if I actually know Giovanni in some form.

"He has been working. I expect he is in his office," I replied in what I hoped was a confident manner. The truth was, I had no idea where he was. I rarely saw him. His eyes fell on me again, lingering on my boobs before he gave me a small smile.

"Would you be so kind as to walk me up?" He asked. I nodded once and turned to climb the stairs again. He hovered behind me just so he could gawk at my ass. I knew men like him like the back of my hand. I also knew that this was possibly a test. He wanted to see Giovanni and I together and report back to his Boss.

When we reached the office door, I knocked once. There was no answer, but I could hear movement inside. Faking my boldness and familiarity, I decided to open the door anyway and prayed that Giovanni wouldn't bite my head off for it.

My face must have portrayed my surprise when I saw a beautiful girl, probably a similar age to me, standing behind his desk, flicking frantically through a file. I had never seen her around here before and my first thought was that she might be Elenora, the sister I have yet to meet.

"What are you doing here, nanny?" Toni spat. His tone was sharp and accusing and I immediately felt bad for the girl. When mafia men belittle women like that there is not a lot we can do. But to my surprise, she held his hard gaze and glared back at him with just as much menace. Nanny? She works here?

Suddenly, Giovanni's bulky and towering frame shoved me out of the way and I stumbled back slightly. It was as if time stood still the way that he looked at her and she looked at him. Both the colour had drained from their faces and, for the first time, I swear I saw a vulnerability in Giovanni.

"You knew?" she whispered to him. He didn't move, just kept staring. Sensing Toni's confusion as well, I realised I needed to seem involved in some way.

"Who are you?" I asked nervously.

Her green eyes, which were bright and unique with the gold speckles, looked me up and down carefully before she replied, "Olivia. Who are you?"

"I'm Camilla."

"Giovanni's fiancé," Toni added with a smirk. My eyes widened slightly when I saw the girl's face flash with hurt and then anger. She glared at the man before her who seemed to have lost his ability to move.

"You're engaged?" She screamed hysterically, the pure rage evident. In a flash, she was running to the door and Giovanni snapped into action. He tried to pull her back and nearly blew our cover when he told her it wasn't what it looked like, but she managed to get away from him. Was he in a relationship with this girl?

"I don't understand…" I whispered more to myself than anyone else, but Olivia heard me. She turned abruptly. The words she hissed in my face had me recoil. Poor girl. She thinks he used her. Giovanni raced out of the office after her and I stood motionless with Toni. Shit. How should I react? What would a fiancé do?

I sat down in one of the armchairs slowly, covering my mouth with my hand and feigned shock and hurt.

"So, he was fucking her after all?" Toni smirked. It was a rhetorical question. He was talking to himself. "And you didn't know?" I shook my head slowly and looked down at the floor. "Have you been fucking him too?"

My head snapped up with genuine shock this time. I opened my mouth to speak but I didn't know what to say. Just then, Max came into the room, and I breathed a sigh of relief. He looked down at me first and then his expression became hard when he glanced over at Toni. He didn't trust him either. I could tell.

"Want to fill me in on what the fuck that was all about Maximus?" Toni asked as he walked over to the liquor trolley and poured himself a drink.

"What? The nanny? Just an infatuated employee who believed she meant more to Gio than a quick fuck in the laundry room. No bother," he replied effortlessly. Was that true? He sounded convincing.

Toni turned around and stared at Max intensely, sizing him up. Max's handsome face kept its cool, neutral expression as he sat back in one of the armchairs. The atmosphere changed considerably as Giovanni bounded back in. He didn't look at any of us as he poured himself a whiskey and downed it in one before hissing. Strolling over to his desk, he sat down in his leather chair, his face cold and expressionless.

"What are you doing here Toni?" he snarled.

"How charming! We will talk about the real reason I am here after you tell me why that nanny was in your office alone and why you seemed to care so much about her finding out you are engaged." He strolled over to me and leaned his hand on the back of my chair, making me feel extremely uncomfortable. I noticed Max's eye's glance at where Toni's hand was, and his jaw clenched.

"She was snooping. She's been getting clingy since I started fucking her. That's all," Giovanni growled as he leaned back in his chair, still refusing to look at any of us.

"That still doesn't explain your reaction," Toni quipped, hiding his amusement behind his tumbler.

"She is a good fuck. And our nanny. If she quits, we are left in a shit situation."

"Hmm. Do you really think you should be fucking around with a nanny when you have this beautiful woman living with you?" He peered down at me and gave me a wink which made me want to gag.

For the first time Giovanni looked up and stared into my eyes. They were empty. I saw no sign of any humanity in them. He moved his gaze to Max briefly and then sighed. "I am not married yet. I was just having some fun before I have to walk down the aisle."

"May I be excused?" I asked bluntly. I didn't want to sit here and listen to any more of this. I didn't want to be in the same room as these men. They were all monsters. Except for Max.

Giovanni nodded and I stood up, brushing down my flowy dress. I could feel all of their gazes on me, but I kept my head down and walked out the door. I needed fresh air. I felt suffocated in this place.

Racing down the stairs, I didn't even bother putting any shoes on as I made my way out to the back gardens and headed for the hedged maze. I needed to get lost for a bit. To forget where I was and who I am in the company of.

I always loved mazes as a child. That feeling of never knowing which course will take you to your end destination. Just blindly following the curves and turns of the greenery and praying for the best. I used to panic as a little girl when I couldn't find my way out. But now I am an adult, and the excitement of such beautiful, innocent moments has been sucked out of me by responsibility and duty, it has taken on a different meaning. I no longer wanted to find my destination. I wanted to get lost. I wanted to be hidden and forgotten about.

I couldn't get Olivia's face out of my mind. That look of intense hurt and betrayal. She loved Giovanni; I was certain. And I am pretty sure he felt some way towards her as well. You would have to be blind to not see the panic and fear on his own face when he realised she was about to leave him. How could she love a man like him? I get that he is very easy on the eye, but he is a monster. He is heartless, cold and ruthless. But then maybe that is just what he shows me. That thing between them wasn't just about sex like he tried to convince us all. That was more. Is she the reason he wants out of this alliance?

"Cami?" I heard a deep voice call somewhere through the hedges and, by the way my stomach fluttered and skin tingled, I knew who it was.

"Max?" I shouted back.

"Where are you?"

I chuckled as I spun in a small circle and was completely surrounded by towering, evergreen bushes. "Hard to answer that. This is a maze if you hadn't noticed." I smiled as I heard him chuckle lowly.

"Are you alright? After that," his tone was serious, laced with genuine concern.

"Yeah. Why wouldn't I be?" I quizzed. It wasn't me that was hurt by that situation. I felt nothing towards Giovanni. He could fuck every employee in the house and I wouldn't bat an eyelid.

"You just took off quickly and looked upset."

I smiled and bit my bottom lip. He came after me because he was worried. That's so cute. "I was just playing my role. Like you said," I replied as I started walking forwards, hoping to try and find him.

"You're a convincing actress."

His voice felt more distant as I followed the curve of the hedge and I frowned.

"You were pretty convincing yourself," I shouted over my shoulder, knowing he was somewhere in that direction. I kept walking until I came to a fork in the maze. I waited to hear his voice before I decided which path to take.

"What do you mean?"

Left.

"They are not just fucking, are they? Are they in love?" I paused again at another crossroads.

"Maybe. I don't really know. Giovanni doesn't really open up about his emotions."

Left again.

The nerves started to build as I thought about taking this topic in a riskier direction. Would I be shot down? But if I don't try, I will never know. It is easier to talk to him now, knowing we can't see each other.

"What about you? Do you open up about your emotions?"

There was a pause as I slowed my steps.

"Who says I have emotions?"

I smirked. "I know you do. I've seen them."

Another pause. "What emotions have you seen?"

I stopped for a moment to really decide if I was going to do this. Was I really about to make it obvious that I liked him? I inhaled deeply. "You worry about me. You were angry when I told you how people have treated me. You seem happy when we are spending time together. And…I see passion and desire when I look into your eyes."

I covered my face with both my hands as soon as I finished. Oh my god, I had never done anything so bold in all my life. There was a long silence and I started to walk slowly forwards as my nerves were skyrocketing through my body.

"So, it appears I am human after all," his voice was a few tones deeper and it made my heart flutter. He sounded closer now. "But that doesn't make it right."

My heart was pounding. Was he admitting that he had feelings for me? "Why not?" I breathed so quietly; I was sure he wouldn't be able to hear me. I already knew the answer but that didn't stop the butterflies in my stomach fluttering wildly.

"Because you are not mine."

My feet stood rooted to the ground. He was right there. On the other side of that bush. I would just have to walk to the end and turn right and he would be there in front of me. His muscular, tattooed body ripped to shreds, his long brown hair tied back and those green eyes. A rugged, handsome Adonis.

"I wish I was." It came out before I could stop myself. Within seconds, he came striding around the corner and stopped a few feet in front of me. Holy shit. His chest was rising and falling steadily but with shallow breaths, lips parted and eyes burning into mine with intense need. It was a split second, but everything melted away and it was only us. I needed to kiss this man. I needed to know how it would feel to be kissed and held by someone who saw me for who I am and not just as an object. Someone who I wanted just as much.

I raced at him, barefoot in my flimsy sundress and he stepped forwards, arms open ready to grab me. The moment I felt those strong arms wrap around my body tightly and our mouths crashed into each other, my world was set on fire. His tongue teased its way into my mouth, and I moaned at the heavenly sensation of our breath mixing as one. The kiss was frantic, full of passion and desire as his hands roamed my body and mine grabbed at his dark green T-shirt, trying to feel every hard muscle of his torso and shoulders. When we were breathless with need, I pulled away and looked into his hooded eyes as we panted together. Fuck we should not have done that.

"At least I got to do that just once," I whispered as I pushed his strong chest to break free from his embrace.

He grabbed my wrist as I tried to turn away and pulled me straight back into him.

"Once was not enough," he growled before devouring my lips once more.

Goddammit

Giovanni

"Boss wants to push the wedding forward," Toni stated as he lounged back in the armchair in my office.

My mind was fucking spinning. All I could think about was Olivia. How badly I have fucked this up. Again. The string that my control and sanity were barely holding on to was about to snap. I couldn't speak because I couldn't trust what would come out of my mouth. So instead, I rubbed my hand along my jaw and waited for Toni to finish saying what he came here to say so he could get the fuck out.

"I expect you have heard about the marriage between Lorenzo and Isabelle, uniting our rivals with the most powerful head family in Southern Italy. You know what this means. We must take the Leone's out as soon as possible. Francesco will only support us once you put a ring on his daughter's finger."

I inhaled deeply and closed my eyes. Breathe. Control. Hold it together. Don't fucking shoot him. Where the fuck did Max fuck off to? I needed to be saved, before I did something I would regret.

A knock at the door caused me to open my eyes and I had never been happier to see my mamma's face. Although, she looked upset. Which could only mean one thing… Olivia had gone. My heart dropped and my anger rose.

"Sorry to interrupt, but how much longer will your meeting be? I need to speak to my son urgently."

"We are done," I said with finality, causing Toni to frown at me.

"I will take that as an agreement and we will get preparations underway," he growled as he stood up and nodded respectfully at mamma before leaving the room.

I leapt to my feet as soon as the door was shut and started my erratic question bombardment. "Where is she? What did she say? I need to go to her. Did you tell her it wasn't real? Is she in the house?"

Mamma raised her hand to still me. The look on her face was a mix of sympathy, sadness and anger. "She's gone."

I leaned over my desk with my fists in balls on the surface, my head dropping to my chest. I knew she would have. How could I blame her? The look on her face will haunt me forever. In one aggressive movement, I swiped everything off the surface of my desk onto the floor, glass shattered and my laptop smashed, but it wasn't enough.

"You did a background check on her? Did you know about her past before she opened up to you?" Mamma's voice was soft but I could detect the disappointment threaded through her tone. I squeezed my eyes shut and ground my teeth.

"Yes." I stood up straight and saw mamma shaking her head in disapproval. "It was before any of this became serious. As soon as I realised what she was dealing with, I put it away. I didn't read the whole file! I wanted to earn her trust and for her to tell me herself. How mad is she?"

"Mad isn't the word, Giovanni. She is hurt. She feels betrayed."

"I need to speak to her. I can fix this. Once I explain everything, she will understand." I stormed around my desk to head for the door but the pain of mamma's next words sliced through my heart and made me unable to move.

"She's quit Gio. She doesn't want to see you again. It is all too much for her."

My fists clenched at my sides and my breathing became laboured. No. I wouldn't accept it was over. She cannot just leave and walk away from this. I sprang into action, flinging my door open as it smashed against the wall and hurtling out of my office. I could feel mamma running after me.

"Gio! Giovanni! You go racing over there to see her now like this and you will make everything worse!"

"How could it possibly be any worse!" I bellowed over my shoulder.

"You are wound so tightly with anger and tension right now Giovanni, that if you go over there and force her into anything she will be terrified of you!" I stopped halfway down the staircase. "Give her some space to digest all of this. For her to get her own feelings under control. If you go storming round there right now, demanding she listen to you, it will not end well. You are both too stubborn."

I sighed deeply and sat down on the step to force my legs to stay still, dropping my head in my hands. Mamma was right. It would be like a fucking wildfire if we were in the same room right now and I would lose my shit if she tried to leave me. I felt mamma perch next to me on the steps. She didn't touch me, which I was thankful for. She knew better than to touch me when I was this wound up. The only person whose touch could calm me was the one person who didn't want to be anywhere near me.

"What do I do mamma? I can't lose her."

"Gio. You always knew there would be a chance this would happen. If she truly cannot be in this life, in this world with you, you will have to let her go." My head snapped up and I glared at her. She raised her hands up in front to calm me. "But... I think there is still hope. She loves you, Gio."

I froze. She what? "She loves me?" I whispered in disbelief.

Mamma smiled sadly and nodded. "I believe she does. And when you love someone, there is always hope. You just need to be very careful about your next moves, my boy. You need to show some patience and understanding."

I was still shocked by her words. Did Olivia admit that she loved me or was this just an observation?

"But you need to think carefully about this. It wouldn't be fair to pursue her if you do not feel the same way. This is an extremely dangerous game she is entering, especially with the new information we have. She would be safer if you let her go."

I shook my head. "The Leones know what she means to me. They have already threatened her life. She is not safe either way."

Mamma sighed and I felt her intense gaze on my side profile. "And what does she mean to you, Gio?"

I closed my eyes and allowed the terrifying and overwhelming emotions inside me some control to speak the truth. The thoughts and feelings that I had been trying hard to tame but now I knew they were pointless to try to ignore. They were too strong and I was in too deep.

"Everything. She means everything." I couldn't deny all I had felt since this intoxicating woman walked into my life. Desire, anger, lust, worry, and something even more dangerous- love.

When mamma didn't reply, I turned my head to the side hidden by my hands and saw her smiling.

"You love her?"

I nodded. "Si."

"Then you must fight for her, at all costs. But Gio, when I say fight...I don't mean to wave your gun around and force her to be with you," she smirked.

I scoffed. "Noted."

I stood up, feeling slightly calmer, and looked down at my mother, who had never failed me. She always had my back, no matter how idiotic I was. I bent down and kissed the top of her head. "Grazie mamma."

Walking down the steps, I called for Angelo, who was stationed at the front door on guard.

"Take one other soldier and guard Olivia's building. I will put you on shifts. Ring me if you see anything suspicious, no matter how small. Eyes on her at all times. If she leaves the flat, follow her at a safe distance and inform me. She won't be happy about it, but you are an extension of me and you will not let anything happen to her. Do you understand?" He nodded professionally. "Do this well, Angelo, and I will move you up the ranks quickly."

A small smile played at the corners of his lips before he forced his face to become expressionless again. He marched away to fulfil his order. Giving her some space from me was going to be the hardest thing I had ever done in my life, but I couldn't leave her unprotected. I'd give her a few hours to calm down, but I am not giving up on us. She thinks she doesn't need anyone, but she needs me. She just doesn't realise it yet. But I will make her see. One way or another, I will win her back. Because I fucking loved her. *Goddammit.*

Saying Goodbye

Olivia

"Gigi, please come away from there," I moaned as I flicked through the few TV channels we had on the small plasma. Gigi was peering out the curtain at the black SUV that had been parked outside the building since I returned home from the mansion yesterday. I recognised the beefy body and stern face of Angelo and knew Giovanni had sent them to keep an eye on me. A part of me was furious, but another part felt a little relieved knowing that someone was keeping me safe, seeing as the threat of Leones and Henry was still out there.

"I just don't understand it. Why do you have a bodyguard if you've quit?" She spoke, her eyes still squinting down at the car. I don't know what she was expecting to happen.

I didn't answer her and pretended to be engrossed in the Italian news that I couldn't understand a word of. I couldn't exactly tell her the truth. And now, being here, was going to put her in danger too. I had to leave. And soon.

"Oh! They are switching over!" she said excitedly. I groaned and flopped my head down on the cushion.

"Why are you so obsessed with this?"

"Because it is not every day, I have super hunky men standing guard over my flat! Maybe I should go outside and offer them a coffee? They must be thirsty," she smirked mischievously.

"No! You should definitely not. They are fine."

"It's Giovanni!"

I sat bolt upright and stared at her. She was pointing down the path and my heart started racing. He had sent me a text last night saying he wasn't marrying Camilla and he would give me some space, but he was not going anywhere and was ready to talk whenever I was. I wasn't ready to talk. It was too difficult. It was over and just seeing him again would cause too much pain. This thing that should have never started between us needed to end. I could never give him what he needed. I thought for a second that I could. That I could be that woman who could be in the chaos of his life, but I can't. Yesterday just proved to me that I couldn't trust him and I needed to move on before Henry came for me. Even as I tried to convince myself of those words, my heart tugged and I felt physically sick.

I stood up and raced towards the window. There he was. Standing in the road talking to Angelo. He looked unfairly gorgeous in grey suit trousers and a crisp white shirt; sleeves rolled up. Angelo nodded once at something he said and they swapped cars. Angelo climbed into Giovanni's Ferrari and Gio climbed into the SUV. My heart was pounding in my chest as Angelo sped off, leaving Giovanni and one other man sitting guard outside the building. I stepped backwards slowly, eyes wide.

What was he doing? Why would he come here? Doesn't he have more important things to do than sit outside my building all day? I threw myself back down on the sofa and grabbed the remote again.

"Aren't you going to go and speak to him?" Gigi asked, giving me a dubious look as she walked away from the window and into the kitchen.

"No," I replied.

"So, it was a pretty big argument then?" She questioned. She had been like this all morning, trying to get more information out of me as to why I quit my job and came home in a foul mood last night.

"No. No argument. He just wasn't the person I thought he was. We are complete opposites. It would never have worked, so it's better this way," I replied nonchalantly, avoiding her penetrating stare.

"Hmm. I'm not buying it. You were practically glowing when you first came back from France. What could have possibly gone so wrong in the last 48 hours?"

I sighed loudly, making it clear I did not want to continue this conversation. I picked up her iPad and started to look for flights. There was no point in hanging around here anymore. It was too dangerous. What was Giovanni expecting to do? Continue to monitor my life every day even though I no longer work for him? I felt suffocated. I needed to get away. Start fresh. Forget him.

Trying to ignore the knot in my stomach and the urge to cry at the thought of never seeing him again, I flicked through the list of flights out of Italy over the next few days. I had no plan. I had no idea where to go, but I knew I needed to keep moving. I had already stayed in one place for too long and knowing Henry was growing desperate just put me on edge now more than ever.

"What are you doing?" I jumped when Gigi's accusing tone interrupted my scrolling from over my shoulder.

I lowered the tablet and turned to look at her carefully. "I am going to leave soon Gigi. I was never meant to stay here as long as I did and it's time to go." Her eyes widened and she looked completely shocked and a little hurt. "Honestly, you are a friend I have made for life and I am so grateful for you letting me live here and being so amazing."

"Where will you go?" She whispered, tears welling in her eyes.

I smiled sadly at her. "Who knows? Maybe…" I looked down at the list of flights. "Iceland? I've had enough sunshine here and I have always wanted to see the northern lights!"

"I'm going to miss you! When will you go?"

"Soon. I need to book a flight and get all my finances together, but I am going to go as soon as I can."

She nodded slowly, letting it sink in. "Is this because of Giovanni? He did something to really hurt you, didn't he? I will kill him!"

I chuckled at the thought of her even attempting that and grabbed her hand on the back of the sofa. "No. No, it's not just about him. This was always the plan. You know I told you I left the UK to get away from my stepbrother? He might come after me soon and I need to keep moving."

She sighed deeply. "I understand. I just wish you didn't have to go."

"I know. Me too," I smiled sadly. But Millie was right. If it doesn't work out for whatever reason. Run. Immediately.

***

Bracing myself to step outside and walk past Giovanni in the car, I inhaled deeply and shook my head. I was going to go and meet Elle, Sani and Raya to say goodbye and I'd called a taxi.

I opened the green front door and waltzed out with my chin held high, avoiding looking in the direction of the SUV. I walked briskly over to the taxi that was parked on the curb and as I pulled open the car door, a strong hand slammed it shut again.

"Olivia. Please talk to me."

His voice sent waves of despair and need through me and I refused to look up at him. "Please move out of the way," I gritted.

"Not until you agree to listen to me. I need to explain."

"No. You don't. You need to move."

He sighed deeply and reached his hand up to my face to force me to look at him. I jumped back at his touch, anger rippling through my body. He can't do this to me. Can't he see how much this is hurting? How it was tearing my soul apart to even think of letting him go. The frustration on his face from my action formed a lump in my throat.

"I never read the whole file, Liv. I knew your stepbrother killed your boyfriend, but that is all, I promise. I stopped reading as soon as I realised that I cared about you and didn't just want to sleep with you! I wanted to hear it from you when you were ready to tell me, I swear." His brown eyes pleaded with me and I could see he was telling the truth, but I was still so mad.

"Yet you let me open up to you…cry on you! And you didn't say anything? You could have been honest, Giovanni. You could have told me you knew from a background check for the job!"

"I know. I'm sorry." He groaned, running his hand through his jet-black hair. A strand flicked back down over his eyes and I had to fight the urge not to touch it. He looked so fucking good. Why? Why was this so hard?

"It's too late. It doesn't matter now. I have to go," I tried the door handle again but he leaned his muscular body against the car. The driver tutted out the window and Gio shouted something at him in Italian in a rage. I glared at him for his outburst at an innocent man.

"It does fucking matter Liv. Are you telling me you are going to throw us away like last weekend meant nothing? Just because I didn't tell you I knew one little thing about your past?" he snapped, losing his patience. Fury erupted inside me at his words.

"It wasn't one little thing!" I yelled. "It was the worst fucking thing that has ever happened to me! Do you know what it feels like to have everyone gossiping about you behind your back? For your entire life to be splashed across every front-page newspaper for everyone's entertainment? I moved here to run away from it all. To feel safe. I told you about it because I trusted you and that was a big fucking deal! The fact you can stand here now and dismiss its importance just proves to me that you are not the man I thought you were!"

His jaw clenched and his eyes blazed with his own anger as I tried to shove open the door of the taxi and this time he stepped back, letting me climb in.

"And tell your men to stop following me! I don't need you or them to keep me safe. I can look after myself!" I shouted through the window. He stepped up to it, leaning down, his hand on the window frame to keep the driver from pulling away.

"I am not going anywhere, Liv. Until you are ready to talk to me, my men or I will be right here, protecting you from the Leones," he hissed and I scoffed.

"And I should be thankful? You are the reason I am in this mess with them! Just go back to your fiancé Giovanni!" I spat and his nostrils flared.

"Don't push me Liv, or I just might," he growled, and I wanted to slap him. So badly I wanted to slap him. And kiss him. How can one man cause such conflicting and intense emotions in me at the same time?

"Good! Go fuck her to forget about me! That's what you're good at!" I shouted and he stood up glaring. Thank God the driver slammed his foot on the accelerator, and we sped off because that look on his face was terrifying. I threw my shaking hands over my face as I fought back the tears that were threatening to spill. That was it. I knew I had pushed him away. It was what I needed to do, so why did it feel so wrong?

***

I smiled as I watched Raya and Sani chasing each other happily around the park. There were about five of Giovanni's men placed strategically around the children's playground and I would have laughed at how ridiculous they all looked standing guard over two children if I wasn't feeling so dead inside.

"I need to apologise to you Liv," Elle's soft voice came next to me as we stood awkwardly next to each other leaning against the metal fence. "I hope you don't hate me for not telling you who we are."

"I don't hate you, Elle. I was hurt, but I understand your position. I don't judge you for who you are or what family you come from. You are still my friend," I smiled at her sideways and she locked eyes with me.

"He is really sorry, you know? He knows he messed this up but he is really trying to fix it all Liv. Please just give him a chance," she pleaded in a broken voice. I sighed loudly and wrapped my arms around my body protectively. "You are the only one who can save him."

I narrowed my eyes at her in confusion. "What are you talking about? Save him from what?"

"From himself. You bring out a softer side to him. You make him lighter and a better person, Liv. Without you in his life, I worry about him. He will lose himself to his duty and I fear the kind of man he will become."

I turned my head away from her and watched the children playing happily. As much as that pained my heart to hear, I didn't believe it to be entirely true. Everyone seemed to think I had some kind of magical power over this man, but that was insane. I had only known him for a few weeks and we had only been together for a few days. He would have been the way he was in France with his family if I was there or not.

"I'm sorry. I know that it is unfair of me to put that on you. But it is true. You make him happy, Liv. And that is something he hasn't been for a very long time."

"He is engaged, Elle. I know it is an important alliance. I can't see how he will get out of it. Please, I don't want to talk about this anymore."

She folded her arms across her chest as she respected my wishes and stopped talking. After a few moments of silence, she asked, "What will you do now?"

I shrugged my shoulders. I couldn't tell her my plans to leave. She would tell Giovanni or Cecilia for sure and they would try and stop me. "I don't know yet."

"The bambinis are going to really miss you. We all are," she whispered. I sniffed, holding back the sudden emotions that surfaced. I was an emotional wreck at the moment. The truth was I was going to miss this family too. So much. I had grown so close to these kids and the thought of saying goodbye was breaking my heart.

"I suppose it is time to tell them," I sighed, pushing off the fence and walking over to them on the slide. I leaned on the metal frame as Sani climbed up the ropes to the top and Raya sat at the peak of the slide.

"Guys. I have to tell you something," I tried to keep my tone light and happy. They both stopped what they were doing and looked at me. "I have to go away for a bit. I have some new places to go and things to do and I am really excited, but I am also going to miss you both so much."

Sani's face scrunched up in confusion and irritation and for a split second he looked the image of Giovanni. "When will you be back?" Raya asked sweetly. I stroked her cheek and gave her a sad smile.

"I don't know. I might never come back," I replied honestly. I couldn't lie to them or give them false hope.

"Why? Did we do something wrong? Are we too naughty?" Sani asked bluntly and my heart broke in two. I shook my head quickly, reaching out for his hand.

"No. No, of course not. You two are the best kids in the world. You have been so amazing and I am so proud of you both. This has nothing to do with you, okay?"

"Then why are you leaving us?" He pulled his hand out of mine sharply and I saw the pain in his eyes.

"Sometimes things just happen and people need to make a change. I promise you, Sani, your mamma will find another wonderful nanny to look after you and teach you."

"I don't want anyone else! I want you!" He shouted, losing his temper.

"Sani," I tried to soothe him, but the tears of anger were welling up in his eyes.

"This is Gio's fault! I heard mamma say to Max this morning that he upset you!"

"No Sani. It's not your brother's fault. I just need to- "

"I hate him! And I hate you! I want to go home!" Sani pushed past Raya on the slide and whizzed down it before running to Elle. She looked up at me with worry and sadness and I fought back my own tears.

"I will miss you Liv," Raya whispered before sliding down and hugging my legs. She ran over to Elle as they all left the park and climbed into the black SUV. I sat down at the bottom of the slide and buried my face in my hands. That could have gone better.

"Signorina Jones?" I glanced up at Marco's enormous frame that was blocking the afternoon sun from my eyes. "I know it is not my place to say, but I have to thank you. For what you did for those children. They have never been so content." I couldn't stop the tears now. He shuffled awkwardly on his feet as he looked over at the SUV. "And I think you are making a mistake. This family needs you. And I think you might need them. I have worked for them for fifteen years and you have no idea the powerful impact you have made on every one of them in the last few weeks. I hope you know what you are giving up."

He nodded once out of respect and walked away towards the SUV, leaving me speechless. That was the most he has ever said to me since we met. I watched the convoy drive away leaving only one black tinted car parked on the side of the road. The one for me. I don't know how long I sat in that park for, but the sun had set and the cool evening breeze made me shiver before I picked myself up and made my way back to Gigi's. The black car crept along protectively behind me.

Rabbits

Giovanni

As soon as the taxi sped away, I saw red. I was wild with rage as I turned violently and slammed my fist into the green front door. Then my foot. Followed by my fist again. Yes, I was beating the crap out of a door. It broke off its delicate hinges and I threw it on the stone floor outside.

My breathing was ragged as the rage swept through me like a hurricane. I had lost my temper. Instead of remaining patient and calm with her like I intended, it ended in a heated argument. I said shit I didn't mean out of fear. She was trying to leave me and I snapped. What the fuck is wrong with me? And now I have ruined her fucking front door. I am on a bloody roll today.

A little old woman wobbled towards the entrance from inside of the building, her wrinkly face scrunched up in disdain as she looked at her smashed door on the floor. My anger died down as I tried to focus on not alarming her.

"Cosa è successo alla mia porta? (What did you do to my door?)" she looked at me with annoyance, as if I was a teenage pest vandalising her property. She wasn't far off.

"Scusa signora. Era già rotto, quindi l'ho rimosso per te. (Sorry miss. It was already broken so I removed it for you.)" I panted, with my hands on my hips. She eyed me suspiciously.

"Una porta rotta è meglio di nessuna porta, (a broken door is better than no door)" she accused, pointing her little finger at me as she stood in the doorway. Old, Italian women were feisty and you did not want to get on the wrong side of them. I gave her my best appeasing smile and saw her face soften.

"Farò in modo che tu ne abbia uno nuovo tra un'ora. Anche le migliori caratteristiche di sicurezza. (I will see to it that you have a new one in one hour. The best safety features too.)"

She rolled her grey eyes at me and tutted before waving her hand dismissively and hobbling back inside. I groaned and walked over to my soldier and ordered him to find someone to come and fit the best standard security door within one hour, no matter the cost. Climbing into the SUV, I called Marco, who I knew would be in the park waiting for Liv to arrive.

"Marco. Get one of the cars to stay behind and watch over Olivia. I am heading home."

"Si Boss."

He hung up and I turned the engine on and drove us back to the mansion. I needed something to occupy my mind today. I needed to focus on getting out of this arrangement but also planning an attack on the Leones. As soon as I arrived home, I inhaled deeply before making my way up to Camilla's room. As much as I hated it, I was going to need this woman's help to get information about what her father might want more than this marriage. I was about to knock on her bedroom door but froze when I heard heavy panting and moaning from inside. What the fuck?

I opened the door and there was my cousin on top of her on the bed, both naked and going at it like rabbits. My eyes widened at the scene. They hadn't heard me enter, so immersed in their passionate fucking.

"You've got to be kidding me?" I bellowed, causing Max to fall off Camilla and onto the bed. She scrambled with the sheets to cover herself, her eyes large. They both looked like deer in headlights, and I fought the urge to laugh hysterically. Max jumped up from the bed, scrambling to pull his jeans on, and I turned abruptly, marching to my office.

I could hear them whispering in panic behind me as I left them to freak out. This situation just gets better and better. Does Max not realise the fucking danger he has just put himself in? If anyone had walked into that room that wasn't me, he would be a dead man.

After a few minutes, they both entered my office, now fully clothed and looking sheepish. It was so hard not to laugh at my cousin's anxious expression, but I wanted to make him see how fucking stupid he was being.

"Testing out my fiancé to see if she was up to my standards Maximus?" I narrowed my eyes as his big green ones widened and he looked from me to Camilla and back. She was staring at the floor, avoiding my gaze, and I could see the slight tremble in her posture.

"Gio. Man, it's not what you think. I –"

"And what do I think?" I questioned, leaning forward on my desk.

"That- That I just fucked her for the fun of it." His gaze held mine and for a moment I was a little taken aback. That is exactly what I thought, but from the look in his eyes, there was more to this.

"I'll tell you what I think, Max. I think you are fucking idiot! What if it had been Boss or Aiani that had walked in there? You would both be dead."

"I know. It was stupid," he replied seriously. He looked over at Camilla who was still staring at the carpet and his expression softened. "But I don't regret it. I would do it again."

Is he fucking losing his mind? Does she have a hypnotic pussy or something? My cousin is not this person. He is logical. He thinks about every situation carefully.

"What are you saying?" I snarled. I really don't need to deal with any more crazy ass shit in my life at the moment.

"We've been spending a lot of time together and I – "He started but hesitated. He was beginning to look a bit flustered, losing his normal cool and laid-back aura. Shit, I recognised this immediately. This is how I felt when someone questioned me about Liv. He swallowed before fixing his gaze on me. "I love her."

Camilla's head snapped up in surprise as she stared wide-eyed at Maximus. I looked between them both as he turned and gave her a reassuring smile and she melted before his very eyes. I couldn't hold it in anymore. The insanity of it caused a bubble to rise in my chest. I burst into hysterics, causing both of them to stare at me like I had lost my mind. Maybe, I fucking had!

"This isn't an excuse, Gio! I mean it."

"You love her? The woman that Boss is forcing *me* to marry for an alliance. Wow! Max, you know how to pick them!"

"Says you! You fell in love with the fucking nanny!" He shouted back.

We both paused and stared at each other. Both our faces slowly creased into the widest grins and we were both hunched over holding our stomachs as we lost control of our senses. Camilla watched on in shock at the two of us laughing, not knowing what to say or do.

After a few moments, we both calmed down and I covered my face with my hands. Fuckkkkk! How did this happen? How have we allowed our lives to become so messy because of women? Something I vowed I would never let happen. I sighed as I sat down on my chair and gestured for them both to take a seat.

"So...what now? I am guessing this isn't a one-sided relationship?" I asked Camilla directly. She glanced over at Max, a pink flush on her cheeks before she looked back at me and shook her head.

"You can speak, you know? I will not bite your head off," I smirked. She was timid and terrified of me, but knowing how my cousin felt about her, made her family now. And I would chill the fuck out around her.

"Yes. I feel the same way," she replied quietly. I nodded and scratched my chin, deep in thought. Now what? "Do you have a plan yet? To get us out of this marriage?"

I glanced back at her, surprised that she knew. She smiled and looked at Max. He gave me an apologetic, small shrug of his shoulders. He had told her. Well, I guess that proves I can trust her.

"Not exactly. I was coming to ask you what it is your father really wants out of this alliance. Is it just the power of association?" I asked and she looked a little frustrated.

"Honestly, I don't know. My papi doesn't exactly include me in his ideas. He just gives the orders and I am expected to comply."

I chewed on my lower lip as I thought about this carefully. If I was Francesco, what is it I would want from Sal?

"Sal wants your papi's alliance as protection for us to take down our rivals. Your father will provide us with alibis and deals that are not directly linked to us and can go unnoticed by the commission. So, as long as Francesco is happy, Sal will still get what he wants. Do you think your father would be happy for you to marry a Capo?"

Her eyes widened and Max looked a little pale at my words. "No. The deal was that I was to become the next boss' wife," she replied sadly.

"What if I gave up my title? What if I stepped down from underboss and gave it to Max?"

Max sat forward instantly in his chair. "You can't! Gio, you have wanted to be boss your entire life! You can't give that up!"

"I can. And I will if that is what it takes."

"Salvatore will never allow it! You are his prodigy. He has been training you to take over since you could walk!"

"Then I guess we will see what is really important to him. As for Francesco, if Sal agreed, I can't imagine he would be happy with the change. We will need to find something to sweeten him up. Something that will make it less of a problem."

"I can try and find something out," Camilla said. "There are few people I trust back home who will do some snooping for me."

I nodded. "Be discreet. No one can know about this until we have everything figured out. Which means, if you two are going to keep fooling around, be fucking better at hiding it!"

Max sniggered and a small smile played on Camilla's lips. I was happy for my cousin. If we can pull this off, we may both get what we want. Suddenly, my heart dropped as I remembered that this wasn't the only thing stopping me from being happy. She needed to forgive me first, which somehow, I knew was going to be harder than dealing with my zio.

I dismissed them both and headed to my room to lie down. I felt drained. Drained of everything. I couldn't focus on anything but her. How much I fucking missed her. She had to forgive me. I had to find a way to show her how much she meant to me before it was too late. I could see it in her eyes. She was giving up on us. Simply sitting outside her building every night was not going to cut it. But I had never felt this way before or been in this situation. And I didn't have the first clue how to deal with it. I loved her but I didn't know how to show it. I didn't know how to tell her without her thinking I was lying or just trying to manipulate her, because right now she doesn't trust my intentions. And it fucking hurts. It hurts more than anything. But there was something else. I could feel it. Something in her eyes today when she drove away from me. Panic and fear. She was running from her feelings for me. That had to be it. Now I just had to work out how to make her want to stay.

Belle of the Ball
Olivia

"I can't believe you are leaving tonight," Gigi whined. She looped her arm in mine as we walked through the piazza of shops and restaurants. I was aware of two of Giovanni's men keeping a distance behind us but following us all the same. I tried to ignore them. This was my last day in this beautiful city and I wanted to try and make the most of it. There was nothing I could do about them and at least it made it feel safer for me and Gigi to be walking around absentmindedly. I stayed up all night last night, tossing and turning over Marco's words. They really got to me. And seeing the over-the-top arrangement of flowers outside my building with a note about the new security door from Gio had my heart rocketing to another dimension. But I couldn't stay. Things were just too complicated and I didn't have the time to hang around and try to solve my fractured relationships when Henry was coming for me. Everyone here was in danger until I left. Gigi, Elle, the kids, Giovanni. I can't risk bringing them into my mess. I would never forgive myself if anything happened to them.

"I still think you should come to the gala this evening. As your last night out with me. Come onnnnn, it will be fun! You could get a taxi from the event straight to the airport!" She beamed, excitedly. I smiled and shook my head.

"What are you going to do on your last night then? Your flight isn't until 2am, so are you just going to sit in the flat alone all evening? You have already packed. Come on! Come with me!"

I rolled my eyes as she swerved us into a very expensive shop with designer dresses. "I thought you were taking Viking as your date?"

"Joel…and I am. But he will be more than happy to have you tag along," she winked.

"Are you seriously thinking about a relationship with that man?" I questioned, trying to change the subject. She unlinked my arm and started rifling through the exquisite array of ball gowns.

"I don't know. He is quite sweet really. I know he likes to act the brute, but he buys me flowers, takes me to dinner, tells me I am beautiful. I've never really had that from a man before," she shrugged her shoulders and I smiled at her leaning against the glass cabinet full of sparkling jewellery.

"Well, you should expect that from a man! Nothing less. You've been selling yourself short for too long, Giulia. You deserve to be treated nicely," I argued.

"I think I am only entertaining it because he has a fucking huge cock," she said frankly and my eyes widened as the sophisticated shop worker glared at us disapprovingly. There she is. My horny flatmate. "Oh my! This one was made for your figure, Liv! Try it on."

She pulled a dark emerald, satin floor-length dress from the rack and held it against her body. It was gorgeous but I didn't need anything so glamorous.

"I don't think I will need that where I am going," I joked and she tilted her head at me.

"For tonight, silly! When you come to the gala with me and Joel."

I turned my back to her. "Gigi!"

"Olivia! It is your last night in this city and you need to go out with a bang! I am going to be coordinating the event with my boss so I need someone to keep an eye on Joel!"

"Oh, please sign me up," I replied with sarcasm. "Babysitting your boyfriend does not sound like fun to me."

"There will be a live band, free booze and food, auctions, a casino and, best of all, lots of incredibly good-looking people to ogle! There is always drama at these events! Oh, and did I mention it is for charity? Think of all the poor endangered wildlife that you will be letting down if you don't go!"

I sighed as I stared into her begging eyes. I took the dress from her and marched into the changing room to try it on. I would let the dress decide. If it fits me perfectly and I love it, I will go. If not, Netflix and chill...

Pulling the smooth material over my hips and putting my arms through the thick shoulder straps, I reached around and did up the buttons at the back that stopped halfway up my spine. The style had two side parts cut out, revealing my sun-kissed torso and a triangle neckline which flattered my breasts beautifully.

Shit. It was incredible. Looks like I am going to the ball.

***

I stared at my reflection in the mirror, and I almost didn't recognise myself. Gigi had one of her friends come over and do both our make-up. The girl was talented because you could no longer see those huge dark circles under my eyes from the lack of sleep I'd had this week. I styled my hair in large waves that fell down my bare back that was on show in this emerald dress. I felt expensive. I felt like it was prom night or something. I allowed myself a small smile before grabbing my clutch bag and heels to put on in the living room. I had been trying to think of a way to get to the airport without Giovanni's men following me and this was the perfect excuse. I would go to the ball dressed like this, but when I leave, I will be in trackies, a sweater and a baseball cap. They will not recognize me at all.

As I sauntered down the hallway, the Viking whistled, and I gave him a playful twirl as Gigi beamed at me.

"You look hot as hell girl!"

"So do you!" I held out my hands to her dress as she spun around on the spot. She was wearing a beautiful midnight blue floor-length dress with a sweetheart neckline.

"What about me? Share the love!" Joel faked his hurt at being left out of our compliments.

"You look rather dashing too."

"He scrubs up well for a beach bum surfer I guess," Gigi teased, and he grabbed her, pulling her into his chest and squeezing her ass. I looked away as that stabbing pain in my heart returned because it made me think of Giovanni. Gigi noticed and pulled away from him, giving him a knowing look as she nodded her head towards me.

"Guys. It's fine. Don't stop your PDA on my account."

"PDA?" Gigi asked.

"Public display of affection," Joel chimed in, giving me a wink. I have to admit, he did look good. Much more refined than he normally does, with his long sandy coloured hair pulled back into a bun and his beard trimmed to a point. He was wearing a black tux as well, which helped. Every man looks good in a tux.

"Are we ready to go?" I asked as I sat down to put on my black strappy heels. This whole outfit cost more than I cared to admit but I had been paid extremely well by the Buccinis and hadn't splashed out once, so I didn't feel too guilty.

"Si! Let's go party!" Gigi squealed as she pulled Joel out of the door by his suit jacket.

I grabbed my wheeled suitcase and took one last look around the small but beautiful flat I had called home for nearly two months. I swallowed my emotions and ignored the voice in my head telling me not to leave as I closed the door behind me.

***

Cecilia

I was squirting my perfume on when Elle waltzed into the room in her black, flowy ball gown and sighed heavily before dropping onto the bed.

"Elenora! Sit up! You will crease that dress!"

"Mamma, I can't stop thinking about this Liv and Gio situation. I feel terrible, as if I am going through a breakup myself. Do you think they will figure it out?" she huffed.

"Yes. I believe they will. Olivia just needs some time to get her head around all of this. It would have been a lot to just find out who we are but to find out that Gio was engaged and he had done a background check on her was too much," I replied sadly. I took out my diamond necklace that Vinny had bought me for a special birthday and gestured for Elle to come and clip it around my neck.

She dragged herself off the bed, her black hair curled over one shoulder and took it from me. "I hope you are right. She told me about her stepbrother. At least Gio knows he needs to protect her and is going out of his way to put his men on her watch."

I frowned. "What do you mean? He is protecting her from the Leones. Gio said her stepbrother was locked up in a hospital."

Elle clipped the back and let it drop. She shook her head, her beautifully waxed eyebrows furrowing. "No. She told me that he was dangerous and was looking for her. That's why she ran away from home. That's why she is here."

My eyes widened as I realised that Giovanni had no idea about this. Oh, Olivia is so much more stubborn and head strong than I thought! Why hasn't she told him?

"He doesn't know?" Elle cottoned on quickly.

"No. But he needs to." I slipped on my heels under my silver dress and made my way towards the door.

"Mamma. Wait. Don't you think Liv should be the one to tell him? You might make things worse between them if she finds out he knows this too."

I paused as I contemplated her words. She was right. But I also couldn't allow that girl to get herself killed out of stubbornness. She may not realise it, but she needed Gio just as much as he needed her.

"It's a risk I am willing to take if it means she will be safe."

I lifted the bottom of my dress and made my way up to his floor. Walking past his office towards his bedroom where I thought he would be getting ready, I paused when I heard shuffling inside. Pushing the door open, I walked straight up to his desk where he was leaning over paperwork, his shirt half undone, hair dishevelled and half a bottle of whiskey empty on his desk.

"What are you doing?" I said sharply with frustration.

"What does it look like I am doing, mamma," he replied tartly, causing my anger to flare.

"It looks like you are drinking yourself into oblivion while pretending to do work that can wait. Why aren't you ready? We have to leave in ten minutes."

He gave a dismissive grunt and I exhaled deeply. "This is an important charity event and you are required to show your face as the benefactor. It is the one good thing this family does every year and you are not missing it."

"I am not feeling in the most charitable mood," he mumbled as he circled some area on a map in front of him.

I sighed and walked over to his desk, taking the whiskey bottle away. He dropped his pen and leaned back in the chair, glaring at me.

"There is something you need to know but I am not sure I should tell you when you are in this state."

"I am not in any state. I have only had a few glasses. What is it?" he grumbled. Wow, he was in a terrible mood, but I guess I couldn't blame him.

"Do you know the reason why Olivia came to Italy?"

His face screwed up in confusion at my question. "We were all there when she told us at the dinner table."

"That wasn't the whole truth, Gio. Her stepbrother is after her. She is on the run."

His dark eyes widened with fury and his jaw clenched. "That is not possible. He is locked up."

"You didn't read all the files, remember? Perhaps he has been released?"

He stood up slowly and I had never seen such a frightening look on his face before. It was a red-hot solar flare of violent rage etched on his features. "Gio. Calm down. You have your men watching her. She is safe right now."

"How do you know this?" he gritted through his teeth.

"Olivia told Elle in France. Elle thought you knew."

"Do you know what that man did to her? He sexually assaulted her, emotionally abused her for two years and then stabbed her boyfriend in the back seven times while they were having sex." I gasped, my hand covering my mouth. That poor girl. I had no idea she had been through such an ordeal. "And you are telling me now that he is out there and looking for her?"

I could see in his eyes that he had entered a whole other level of darkness. I knew at that moment that no matter what happened between him and Olivia, he would not stop until he found her stepbrother and killed him. Most people would say I have screw loose to condone my son for being a ruthless murderer, but in our world, it was the norm and, in this situation, he had my blessing.

He pulled out his phone and dialled a number.

"Angelo. Dov'è Olivia?"

His eyes snapped up to mine as they grew wider. He listened intently to whatever Olivia's bodyguard was saying and a small, wicked grin played at the corners of his mouth. He hung up and I raised my eyebrows at him, willing for him to tell me what was going on.

"Looks like I am going to the gala after all." He stormed past me and raced towards his bedroom.

"What?" I shouted after him.

"She is there," he replied before he disappeared into his room.

I stood frozen on the landing. Well, this will be an interesting night, I am sure.

Run

Olivia

"I don't get it! Why? Why put olives in a drink? Vile little things!" Joel pulled out the stick of green olives from his drink and threw it on the table.

Gigi gave him a deep scowl as she picked it up and brushed the expensive silk tablecloth that now had olive juice and an alcohol stain. I chuckled behind my glass of champagne at the pair of them. They were total opposites, yet they worked so well together. Gigi liked the finest things in life but didn't have the means to back them up. She had that wholesome yet fierce attitude where she would always strive for the best but enjoy what she had while she had it. It was endearing. And Joel, well he just seemed to be all about having a good time. Happy to be here but I expect he was happy to be anywhere. He didn't take life too seriously and just lived in the moment. I envied them both. They were so free.

"Ah shit. Bitch face is summoning me." Gigi glanced over my shoulder at a stern-looking woman dressed very elegantly with a Bluetooth device in her ear. I knew Gigi hated her boss, but she put up with her because she knew pleasing her was the quickest way to the top of their company. "Can I trust that you will be on your best behaviour? Liv, please keep him in line!"

Joel feigned innocence and I giggled and nodded, waving her away. She dashed off, weaving through the elaborately decorated tables in the grand ballroom. This was by far the most extravagant event I had ever been to. It was stunning. I caught Joel watching Gigi saunter away with a look of admiration in his eyes and when his gaze flickered at me, a slow, knowing smirk spread across my face.

"What is that look for?" He arched one thick eyebrow up.

"What are your intentions with my friend Viking?" I hid my amusement and tried to keep a straight face but the way his eyes crinkled and his face lit up made it hard.

"Viking aye? That's sweet. Like my nickname. And as for your mate, lots of root," he winked.

I sat forward, amused. "Lots of what? Root?"

"Sex."

"Ah. So, you are the 'deny your feelings' type? Okay. That's cool," I shrugged. He narrowed his eyes and smirked at me.

"Ya reckon?"

"Yeah. It takes a true man to be able to admit his feelings for a woman. I don't hold it against you, there's not many of them left," I teased, lifting my champagne glass to my lips with a smile.

He nodded his head a few times. "Good on ya. Alright you got me. She's a good girl."

I smiled, knowing that was about as much of a confession as I would get out of this man. Suddenly, my mind swarmed of Giovanni. I never actually found out how he really felt about me. I guess I will never know. My mood sombered immediately as I stared around the room at all these sophisticated and wealthy people. I can imagine that this is the type of event the Buccinis come to all the time. I would never fit in with this world. I would always feel inferior, as if I didn't truly belong. Maybe sensing my sudden discomfort, Joel leaned forward on the table.

"A bit stuffy, isn't it? All this?" He whispered and I gave him a small smile and nod. "How about we have some fun? Liven it up a little? You game?"

I raised an eyebrow at him. "I am supposed to be supervising you to make sure that doesn't happen," I chuckled when he rolled his eyes and leaned his beefy body back in the chair. He still looked funny to me wearing a tux.

"Come on! I won't go crazy!" He peered over my shoulder and pointed behind me. "You see the auctions over there? Let's go and put crazy bids on them under fake names."

I burst out laughing as excitement danced in his eyes. That did sound quite fun. And it would be better than sitting here thinking about Giovanni all night. "Fine. You are a terrible influence."

We stood up and I linked my arm with his as we strolled over to the table of contents that was up for auction. As we approached it, I fought to keep a straight face as Joel put on a terrible British accent and said, "Oh darling! Look here, a two-week vacation to the Maldives. It has been two months since we last went. Shall I bid for us, my dear?"

"Oh no honey! Maldives is so overrated. I think I would prefer the superyacht."

"Good choice. The five we already have are not enough," he smirked as he leaned over the table and picked up the pen. I tried to peer over his muscular shoulder to see what he was writing.

$6,000,001 Mr Justin Sideher.

I slammed my hand over my mouth and had to turn my back to hide my laughter from the man who was working behind the auction table. My laughter immediately died. Our eyes met across the room. Suddenly, we were alone in the crowd. My heart hurtled into a frenzy as neither one of us moved. Those chocolate brown eyes blazed with so many unsaid words and emotions, and I felt as if I had fallen into an abyss, unable to find my way out. Giovanni. What was he doing here?

I felt a strong hand slide around my shoulder and Joel's fake British accent pulled me out of my trance. "Your turn sweetheart. What are you going to bid on?"

I almost jumped back from him as I looked up at his smiling face. I opened and closed my mouth as my brain tried to catch up with what was happening. I glanced back over at where I had seen Giovanni standing on the other side of the room to check I hadn't imagined it. But there he was. Mouth-wateringly handsome in a tailored and intrinsically detailed wine-coloured suit and black shirt open at the collar. I saw his dangerous eyes rake down my body and freeze on Joel's hand that was resting on my arm and his jaw clenched. He looked furious. No, he looked deadly. Now I knew who he was and what he was capable of, panic rose in me as I realised Joel was in danger just by being stood next to me. I turned quickly, my eyes wide and Joel's happy features changed to concern.

"You alright?"

"You need to go. No. I need to go," I muttered as I turned to walk away from him quickly. He grabbed my wrist to stop me.

"Liv? You look really scared. What's going on?"

I don't know how he had made it across the room so fast, but in the blink of an eye, Giovanni had grabbed Joel's arm that was holding my wrist and twisted it behind his back, pulling his body awkwardly into Giovanni's chest. My eyes widened as Giovanni wrapped his hand around Joel's throat and growled in his ear. "Don't you fucking touch her."

"Giovanni! Let him go! Now!" I screamed, causing lots of people in close proximity to turn around and stare at us. Gio's menacing eyes locked with mine and I gulped. He must have been able to see the fear on my face because he slowly released Joel and pushed him away. Joel's face was full of icy fury as he charged towards Giovanni and I jumped in between them both. Even though I was sure Joel was more than capable of winning a fight, he had no idea who he was taking on.

"Joel! No. Stop. This is a misunderstanding. Please." Joel stopped his rampage but kept his angry glare over my head fixed on Giovanni. I had to get one of them away and I knew if I walked off with Joel, it would only make everything ten times worse. Turning on the spot quickly, I stepped towards the man that was making my body burn with anger and arousal at the same time and pushed him away. His eyes were still locked in a death glare with Joel's, but as he felt my hands on his chest, pushing him back, he glanced down at me and his face softened slightly.

He wrapped his arm around my waist and turned away, pulling me towards the dancefloor.

"What are you doing?" I hissed up at him but he ignored me and continued to drag me along. Taking rapid steps in my heels to keep up with his pace, I looked around the room and spotted Cecilia, Elle, his cousin I had met at dinner that time, and... that woman. She was here. His fiancé? They were all watching us intensely with looks of worry on their faces.

When we reached the middle of the dance floor, he pulled me into his chest forcefully, wrapping one arm around my waist so tightly his fingers were digging into my skin and his other took my hand. I glared up at him, unable to comprehend what he was doing.

"Are you fucking kidding me? You want to dance?"

He looked down at me and I recoiled slightly at the terrifying look on his face. His chiselled features were rigid with pure rage and I could feel every muscle in his body was tense.

"Yes. Because I need to calm the fuck down before I commit a murder in front of all these people. And holding you is the only thing that will calm me," his voice was so deep and grisly that my core tightened in response. Why? Why did seeing him like this… at his worst…turn me on? Why wasn't I running for the hills? What the fuck is wrong with me?

I didn't say anything, just stared up at his strong jaw, perfect full lips and dark eyes. He had the face of an angel but the mind of a killer. I allowed myself to become mesmerised by his beauty one last time, tracing every curve to memory because after tonight, I will never see him again.

After one song had ended and another started to play, I felt his hard, muscular body relaxing slightly and his thumb started to caress my skin on the small of my back as we moved slowly to the music.

"Who was he?"

His voice was calmer now, but it still had an edge to it. I rolled my eyes and looked away from him, my nostrils flaring. "Don't roll your eyes at me bambola. Tell me who he is before I lose my shit again."

"He is a friend. Gigi's boyfriend. So yes, once again, you lost your fucking head over a man who did nothing wrong," I snapped at him. Now it was my turn to be angry. This is how it would be. Even if I could look past the crime, the violence, the betrayal, he would always be this man. He would always try to own me. See me as his property. I was no one's property and he needed to understand that.

"This is why we would never work, Giovanni. Forget your job, your family, the fact that you are engaged to that woman over there. You see me as something you own and I will never allow a man to control me like that."

"I am not trying to control you, Liv. I am trying to protect you. Everything I do is to protect you," he growled down at me.

"And Joel? What were you protecting me from then?"

"He was stopping you from walking away. He had his hands on you," he hissed, anger flashing in his eyes again.

"And in France? The gay man I was dancing with? How were you protecting me then? Don't you ever stop to see how I am feeling in those moments. That I am happy and not looking to be saved!" I argued. His jaw ticked as he realised I was seeing through his excuses. "Admit it, Giovanni.

You don't act that way just because you are being protective!"

He snapped. He pulled me up against him so tightly that I could barely breathe. My lungs felt like they were being crushed against his chest as he grabbed the back of my neck, so my face was inches from his.

"Fine. You want the truth. I hate it. I can't stand it. I can't see you with another man. I can't watch a man put his hands on you and not want to rip his fucking head off. I am trying to be a better man for you but there are some things I just can't fucking tolerate."

My lips parted as my heart drummed in my chest at being this close to him again, this intimate. His eyes bore into mine in challenge and I held his gaze.

"Then that is why this will never work. Let me go. I am leaving."

I pushed his chest as hard as I could and wriggled out of his embrace. Picking up the hem of my emerald dress, I weaved and dodged my way through the crowds of people and tables to make it to the door. I had to escape. I had to get out of here. I had to run.

A Final Farewell

Giovanni

She sped away from me in a flash of emerald and I raced after her. Her petite frame squeezed through the throngs of people easily, while I was getting more and more aggravated as people stepped in my way. Flying through the exit of the grand hall, I searched the lobby frantically for any sign of her. The sway of green satin caught my eye as it disappeared behind a door. Marching towards it, I yanked the door open and found myself in a cloakroom with an array of guests' coats and jackets hanging on the rails and a woman in a uniform standing behind the desk.

Her professional smile faded when she saw the look on my face. "Fuori. Adesso. (Out. Now.)"

She scurried from the room just as Olivia stormed around the corner of the racks, halting when she saw me. She looked so unbelievably gorgeous in that green dress that caressed every inch of her beautiful body and her bright eyes and wavy hair that cascaded down her back. She was too good for me, and I knew it. I didn't deserve her. I will never be as good as she deserves, but I can't let her go. I would be as good as I was capable of. That had to be enough.

My eyes travelled down to the handle in her hand and I froze. A suitcase? My eyes darted back up to hers as she visibly gulped and then made a dash for the door. I blocked her way and she stepped back, huffing angrily.

"Where are you going?" I growled, my voice harsh and demanding. I couldn't help it. She was trying to leave me.

"That is none of your business," she hissed, attempting to get past me again. I grabbed the suitcase out of her hands and she gasped when I threw it effortlessly across the room. It landed with a thud on a rack of coats and her eyes narrowed and nostrils flared in anger.

"What the fuck?"

"Why didn't you tell me?" I forced my voice to soften as I stepped towards her. She backed away and stared up into my eyes.

"Tell you what?"

"About Henry? That he is out there and is looking for you?" Her stunning eyes widened, and she looked away from me, the emotion causing her lip to tremble. "If he wants to get to you, he will have to go through me first."

"That is why I am leaving Giovanni! I cannot bring you into this or your family! It's not fair. I have to keep moving, I am already putting your life in danger with the Leones and Henry is coming. I can feel it. My demons are not yours to fix!" She shouted as she folded her arms across her chest protectively.

"You are wrong, Liv. I would ruin myself to protect you."

She peered up at me through her dark eyelashes, fresh tears brimming at the edges. "I would never ask you to do that."

"You don't have to. Don't you get it, Liv? If you were to simply whisper my name, I would fall at your feet. I am intoxicated by you. You are everywhere. In every thought, in every decision. Do you think I enjoy this? This infatuation? The constant need to know you are safe. You can hurt me like nobody else ever can." I grabbed her small face in my huge hands and forced her to look into my eyes to see that I was baring my soul. A tear slipped down her cheek.

"Then stop it! Stop caring about me. This will never end well for either of us. You are not meant to be with me, you are meant to be with her. This is too messy! Just let me go!" She cried, as she forced my hands off her face.

Something inside me snapped. Why couldn't she let me in? Why couldn't she see that I would never let anything come between us?

"I CAN'T! You are killing me Liv! The fact that you think I could possibly let you go just shows how oblivious you are about the power you have over me."

Her eyes flashed with anger. "I am killing you? You are engaged to another woman, Giovanni! And even if you don't want to marry her, that doesn't change the fact that you must! I know what it means! I know by choosing me over her you will start a war of families! I've done my research! I can't let you do that."

"I really don't give a shit. If you ever think I will be able to look into anyone's eyes the way I get lost in yours or that I will feel even a fraction of the way I feel about you for her, then you are a fucking fool!" I bellowed, losing my temper.

She scoffed, her eyes fierce. "So now you are insulting me?" She tried to walk away from me and head for her suitcase but I pulled her back by her arm and pushed her against the wall.

"Yes, because you are being a stubborn ass bambola! Don't run away. Stay with me," I demanded, my hard gaze burning into her eyes.

"Why should I?" she growled back, my body flushed against hers, pinning her to the wall. She's so mad at me right now but she looks so fucking hot that it is taking everything in me not to kiss her senseless.

"Because you love me," I husked against her lips. She pushed at my chest, forcing my lips away from hers.

"I- I can't do this. Don't make this harder than it already is, Giovanni." Her silent tears were running down her face now and my heart felt like it was about to explode. I stared down at her as if I could see into the depths of her very soul and she shook her head. "Please. Don't look at me like that."

"Like what bambola?" I breathed, my chest brewing up and down in a slow rhythm, hands on her hips, holding her in place.

"Like you fell in love with me," she whispered.

"Maybe I did."

"Stop it," she bit back through her tears as her fists punched my chest. I let her take her frustration out on my hard pecs for a few moments before I grabbed her wrists and held them above her head against the wall.

"I will never stop Olivia. You are pushing me away because you are scared. You and I are it. Stop running from the truth. I love you dammit. I FUCKING LOVE YOU!" I screamed in her face. Her eyes widened and her lips parted. I saw my words break her. She gave in to her weakness for me. Her ache for my lips, the longing for my body on hers. She couldn't resist it no matter how hard she tried. I knew it because I felt it too. She was my weakness.

The hunger as her lips smashed against mine caused an explosion of emotions between us as I released her wrists, and my hands roamed her body. She was tugging frantically at my clothes, ripping them off me with so much need, as I grabbed at the length of her dress and tore a slit up the side of it to allow me access to her pussy. My dick pulsed in my trousers. It ached to be inside her. To claim her again. She had me under a spell, making me feel incomplete without it. Our tongues were fighting with need as we devoured each other's mouths and I lifted her as she wrapped her legs around my ass, pulling my groin into hers. From this position, all I had to do was unzip my fly and I'd be inside her in a heartbeat. Using my free hand, I did just that. She gasped into my mouth as I filled her completely in one powerful thrust.

It was too much, yet not enough. I had never felt like this before. Such intense passion and desire to take every inch of her as my own out of fear. Fear of losing her. I moved my hips back slowly only to push up into her again as she cried out against my lips. Moving faster and harder, I pounded into her with all the intensity I felt. I groaned and moaned as she clenched around me and raked her nails along my back as I buried my head in her neck and kissed her skin. We both screamed out our orgasm so raw and full of emotion as I shuddered inside her and panted heavily.

Her body was shaking against me violently and when I pulled my head back from her neck to look at her, my heart shattered like glass in my chest. She was crying. She looked away from me as I slowly slid out of her and lowered her to the floor. I reached my hand up to wipe her tears but she moved away from me quickly.

I stood, confused and not able to comprehend what was happening as she grabbed her suitcase and raced to the door.

"Liv?" I pleaded, genuinely not caring how pathetic I sounded.

She turned and looked back at me with so much sorrow. "I love you too,

Giovanni. So much. But I will destroy everything you have. That is why I have to let you go. I'm sorry."

She ran out the door, suitcase in tow, and I stood frozen by her words. No. She thinks she will be the death of me. She thinks I would be better off without her. She couldn't be more wrong. Grabbing my shirt from the floor, I raced out after her as I threw it on and started to do up the buttons. My eyes darted around the lobby. I saw her walking out through the revolving doors and sprinted through the luxury hotel lobby to get to her.

The cool evening breeze hit me as I ran as fast as I could towards her. She rushed down the stone steps towards a taxi. "Olivia!" I shouted.

She turned as she reached the pavement and that's when my acute senses took over. Something wasn't right. Her teary eyes locked with mine and her face creased with confusion when she saw the genuine panic on my face. Everything that happened next was as if the world stopped spinning and time slowed right down. I glanced to her right and saw a homeless man who had been sitting on the floor, dropping his handmade, cardboard sign, hand delving into his layers of clothing and producing a gun. Her gaze followed mine as she turned and saw the man charging towards her, the gun rising up from his extended arm.

I sprinted down the stairs and dived through the air as I saw him take his aim. The trigger clicked, the fire shot. I grabbed Liv's body against mine as I turned my back to the hitman and shielded her with my frame. The sudden pain was excruciating as I felt the bullet pierce my skin and lodge inside my body. My eyes widened as I looked down at Liv who was beneath me on the floor. I saw her mouth open and I knew she was screaming, but I couldn't hear a thing, with the ear-splitting ringing in my ears. I raised my hand to her face and stroked her cheekbone with my thumb as the darkness crept upon me.

The last thing I saw were those terrified green eyes with gold speckles that I loved so much.

Bit Of An A-hole

Olivia

"Olivia!"

I turned to see Giovanni racing towards me but he paused momentarily as if he could sense danger. His gorgeous features frowned deeply with worry as his eyes moved from me to my right. I followed his gaze and saw a shabby looking homeless man dropping his sign and my eyes widened when I saw he was holding a long, silver gun. His determined expression was fixed on me and I knew I was his target. He stood up quickly, his arm extending as he pointed the barrel directly at me.

My body froze and my heart stopped when I saw his finger on the trigger. I screwed my eyes shut and braced myself for the impact of that metal bullet lodging itself in my flesh. But it never came. Instead, I gasped because the air was compressed from my lungs by the weight of a large, incredibly heavy man caging me to the stone floor. I opened my eyes and peered up into Giovanni's wide chocolate pupils that had dilated with pain. My heart felt like it had been torn out of my chest as I realised that he had been shot. I screamed as I watched his eyelids droop. He brushed my cheek with his thumb before his eyes closed fully and his head fell onto my chest. Other gunshots were fired, and people were screaming and running, but all I could do was cry out as the shock and despair rushed over me. I tried to roll him off me to the floor as I cradled his head in my hands. I looked up and saw another body on the floor. The homeless man. Angelo was racing towards us with his gun in his hand.

"Help him! Angelo! Help!" I screamed as my tears fell on Gio's lifeless face. Angelo rolled his body to the side to look at the gunshot wound in his back and his face creased with concern. He whipped off his suit jacket and pushed it against Gio's back as I stroked his face in my lap. Whimpering and pleading for him to wake up, I didn't even hear the police and ambulance sirens that came to the scene. As the paramedics came to his aid, I was pulled away to give them space by Angelo's muscular arms. I sobbed into his chest. He couldn't die. This is happening again. I looked up when I heard a deafening wail of intense pain. There, being held back by police officers was Cecilia and Elle, clawing to get to Gio's body, which was being lifted onto a stretcher, an oxygen mask over his face.

"Questo è mio figlio! Fammi passare!" Cecilia screamed again and again before the police finally let her pass as Gio was lifted into the back of an ambulance. She climbed in and they shut the door, before speeding away, the sirens blaring into the night.

"Olivia…Olivia what happened?" I glanced up and saw Maximus' concerned and angry face as his hands were on my shoulders. I looked down in a daze at my own hands and dress that was covered in Gio's blood and sunk to my knees on the stone floor.

I felt soft arms around my shoulders as Angelo spoke quickly in Italian to Maximus above me. I moved my head to the side and saw the stunning face of Giovanni's fiancé. Her blue eyes were looking into mine with worry as she spoke to me, but I couldn't hear anything she said.

Maximus kneeled next to her and I tried to focus on his lips that were moving. He was talking to me.

"Liv. I know you are in shock but the police are going to come and talk to you in a minute. I am going to ring our family lawyer. Don't say a word until he gets there, okay? Do you understand?"

"Giovanni…" I whimpered. "Is he…?" I couldn't bring myself to say the words.

"No. He's gone to the hospital. The doctors will do everything they can."

"The man…" I looked over at the body that was now covered on the floor and police were taping the crime scene off from the public.

"Angelo shot him. He's dead. When you speak to the police you tell them that Angelo is Giovanni's bodyguard. He has a licence for his gun."

"Scusate? Signorina? We will give you a ride to the hospital once you have been checked by a paramedic. We will need a statement from you."

Max and Camilla helped me to my feet as the police officer blinked at me with a kind expression. My body trembled as I nodded slowly. Maximus shrugged off his suit jacket and placed it over my shoulders before Angelo and I followed the officer and climbed into the police car.

***

Sitting at a table in the warm but depressing meeting room in the hospital, I shivered as I stared at my hands on the table. Even Max's jacket was doing nothing to provide warmth to my numb body. I recognised it as shock. It was how I felt five years ago, when I was dealing with the aftermath of Nate's death. Giovanni wasn't dead. I kept repeating it over and over in my head. I had no idea if it was true or not, but I couldn't allow myself to think the worst. I wouldn't survive it.

The door opened and an older, short and stout Italian man in a stripy navy suit walked into the room. His oval glasses perched on his bulbous nose and he gave me a small, reassuring smile.

"Miss Jones? My name is Alonzo and I am Buccini's lawyer. I am here to help you."

I blinked twice. "Am I in trouble? Am I being arrested?" I panicked. I knew that was absurd. I hadn't done anything wrong, but just being here like this makes you feel guilty.

"No, no. They just want a statement. But don't worry. I have requested a certain police officer to interview you. That is why it is taking them longer to arrive. He knows the Buccini family very well," he gave me a knowing look and I nodded my head. So, they were all corrupt. I had never been so relieved.

As Alonzo took a seat next to me, the door opened again and two police officers walked in. One woman and one man. They smiled at me like I was a small child as they sat on the opposite side of the table.

"Ciao. My name is Officer Haie and this is Officer Fabisona. Please state your name," the man said softly.

"Olivia Jones."

"And in your own words, can you please tell us what happened tonight, Olivia?"

I looked over at Alonzo, who nodded, giving me permission to speak.

"I was leaving the gala and I was about to get in a taxi when…" I paused as I fought back fresh tears. "When Giovanni called my name. He saw the man before I did. The homeless man. He…he had a gun and he was aiming it at me. He was going to shoot me."

The officers nodded and encouraged me to continue as I took a long, shaky breath. "I thought I was going to die. But Giovanni dove in front of me. He…he got shot. He saved me." The tears rolled down my cheek and I brushed them away quickly.

"And when you say Giovanni? You mean Giovanni Buccini? The well-known entrepreneur?"

I glanced over at Alonzo again, who nodded. "Yes."

"And what is your relationship with Mr Buccini?"

My eyes widened and my mouth opened but nothing came out. What was my relationship with him? "I- we – it's complicated."

"Is this relevant information for the crime?" Alonzo asked and the female policewoman glared at him.

"All information regarding a murder is important."

My heart sped up at her words.

"Murder? Is he dead? Is Giovanni dead?" I shouted, panic consuming me.

"No. No, he is being operated on as we speak. My colleague is talking about the murder of Nicholas Grisle. The man who tried to shoot you."

My eyes flared with anger. "That was not a murder. That was self-defence. Angelo works for Giovanni as a bodyguard, and it is his job to protect him. He was only doing his job."

"We are aware. But still one man has died and another is in a critical condition. We are just trying to fit all the pieces together. So please answer the question. What is your relationship with Mr Buccini?" the female officer, who was clearly not the corrupt one and taking her job very seriously, asked again.

I thought quickly. If I needed to make this seem believable without revealing the true reason as to why someone would want me dead, I had to think fast. I lifted my chin a little higher.

"I am his girlfriend."

The male policeman raised his eyebrows in surprise but kept quiet.

"And do you know of any reason as to why someone would want to harm you?"

I peered over at Alonzo, who looked a little worried. He was obviously hoping I would say the right thing.

"Giovanni is always receiving death threats because of his businesses. Jealousy over his wealth and power in the city. That is why he and his family have bodyguards. We tried to keep our relationship a secret for that reason. So, no one could use me to get to him. But it seems someone has found out."

The officers scribbled everything I said down.

"Do we know who he was, Nicholas Grisle?" Alonzo asked.

The male officer looked at us with understanding. He knew that Alonzo was asking if this was another mafia family.

"He was exactly what he seemed to be. A homeless man who has been living on the streets for many years. He was known to us for petty theft and small crimes. It seems odd that he would do something like this. We will look into the matter carefully."

I nodded and glanced down at my green dress. Gio's blood was now a dried stain on it. "Am I free to go? I would like to go and see him now."

The female officer went to speak but the male one beat her to it. "Yes, you are free to go. We will contact you if we need any more information."

"Thank you." I stood up unsteadily on my feet and Alonzo took my arm, helping me out of the room. As soon as we were outside, he turned to me with a beaming smile.

"You did well, Miss Jones. I think you will be very well suited to this life after all," he smirked as he guided me down the hospital corridors towards the waiting room. I scrunched my face up in confusion as I wondered how he could possibly know about me. Ah Maximus.

"I will take you to the family, but then I must get to the station to help Angelo."

Love Knows No Bounds

Cecilia

The moment I saw my first born hooked up to all those machines and wires, the sobs broke out of me once again. Knowing how close he came to losing his life had shaken me to the core. No mother should ever have to go through the pain of losing a child. It also brought back the gut-wrenching memories of losing Vinny the same way.

And all I felt was guilt. I did this. I pushed Olivia into his life. If he had never met her, this never would have happened. He would never have risked his life like that for anyone else. But he was his father's son and I would be a fool if I thought that he wouldn't do it again.

I held his unresponsive hand as I stroked his black hair away from his eyes and stared down at his beautiful face. He looked so peaceful.

"How long has it been going on, Cecilia and why wasn't I aware?" Sal gritted behind me after five minutes. I knew he was there, but thankfully he had given me a moment with my son before his interrogation started.

"A few weeks." I turned towards him as he glared at me with his muscular arms folded across his chest. "And don't you dare think about fucking this up for them, Sal! I meant it. I will never forgive you."

His jaw ticked as his dark eyes peered down at Giovanni's sleeping form. "This is why Cecilia. This is what I have tried to protect him from. He could have died! Just like Vin!"

I looked back down at my son as I nodded my head sadly. "Yes. He could have. But that was his choice. As much as you want to control everyone, Sal, people have the right to make their own choices."

"Like you made yours," his tone was low and laced with pain as my head whipped round to him. His face had softened, and he held my gaze. I don't know if it was the intense emotions that were still in control of me or the situation, but I suddenly felt sorry for this man. I had put him through a lot of pain over the years yet he still showed up when I needed him. He gave me a sad smile before he ran his hand through his silver hair and walked towards the window.

"If the Leones did this, they must pay."

"Will it be enough?" I asked.

He stared out the slats of the blinds with a vacant expression. If we could get proof that the Leones were behind this, then we could take the evidence to the commission and they could give us the green light to seek revenge. We wouldn't be allowed to kill them but we could still do something that would cause a chink in their armour.

"No. I want Riccardo dead, CeCe. And his bastard son. I want them wiped out for what they have done to this family."

"I know. I want the same thing."

Turning around, he fixed his gaze on mine.

"Then we need an alliance with the Aianis." My eyes must have popped out of my head at his words because he rolled his eyes.

"You can't be serious? When are you going to see what is right in front of you, Salvatore? Gio put Olivia's life before his own. He would never give her up. And you still want him to marry that girl?"

"Yes. That is the deal and when I give my word, I mean it."

"But it wasn't your word to give!" I screamed, losing my temper. How can we still be going around in these circles? If I didn't stop this, everything would end in disaster. Either Sal and Gio would be at loggerheads or Olivia would leave him. I stood up abruptly, not caring how desperate I seemed, and grabbed Sal's forearm over his suit jacket. "Please Sal. Don't make him do this. Don't put him in this position. You have the power to change the deal. You have the means to make a different deal that the Aianis could still be happy with. I know you do."

His molten eyes bore into mine as I pleaded with him, and he sighed deeply.

"You are right. I do." Hope rose in me on hearing his words, but it soon faded just as fast. "But I won't. It is the best and cheapest deal for such loyalty."

My nostrils flared as I narrowed my eyes at him. "There must be something you want, Sal. Please. Don't do this to my son."

His eyes met mine with a knowing look and I gulped. A small smile played at the corners of his lips. I stepped back immediately, releasing him from my grasp.

"Of course, there is Cecilia. But you already knew that." I shook my head slowly. "You."

Every muscle in my body tensed under his heated gaze. I had fallen straight into his trap. He was giving me a choice. Be his or put the burden of this alliance on my son. I felt numb inside. He stepped forward and ran his rough knuckles over my cheek.

"Your choice CeCe," he stated before leaving the room. I peered down at my son barely alive in the hospital bed and I knew I didn't have a choice. I would do it if it came to that. I would give up my life to allow him to live his. A mother's love knows no bounds.

Awakening A Monster

Olivia

"Hey," Elle's head poked around the heavily guarded door of Giovanni's hospital room. I lifted my head off the edge of his bed where I had been dozing in and out of sleep for the last few hours. "Your flat mate just dropped some clothes here for you. Are you sure you don't want to go home and shower? Get some proper rest?"

I shook my head with a smile as I stood up and took the bag of clothes from Elle. I had to get that blood-stained dress off me, but I refused to leave the hospital. I think Gio's family and the hospital staff were a little taken aback by just how stubborn I could be and they finally caved, giving me some hospital scrubs to change into, but I would be glad to be in my own clothes again.

She walked up to the side of the bed and glanced down at her sleeping brother with worry etched on her features.

"No change?"

I yawned loudly, covering my mouth as quickly as I could to avoid the lecture, but it was too late.

"No. No change."

She gave me a disapproving look. "Liv. You need to sleep. Or shower at least. The doctors said it could be twenty-four hours before he wakes up. It's only been twenty so just go and look after yourself."

"No. I am fine." I pulled out the leggings and long baggy top and felt relieved that I would at least feel comfortable in a moment. That was good enough. I didn't need to go home. I would only worry and want to be here again as soon as possible.

She huffed dramatically. "Just have a shower, Olivia. Use the ensuite there. I will sit here with him until you are back. Five minutes. Come on."

A shower did sound good, and I would only be in an adjoining room. I studied his handsome face for any signs that he might wake up, but he looked just as peaceful and deeply sedated as he had for hours.

"Ok. But will you knock on the door if he wakes?"

She nodded her head before shooing me away with her hands. I gave her a small smile, before I leaned over and kissed Gio's forehead. Briskly, I grabbed my clean clothes and locked myself in the bathroom, turning on the hot water.

***

Giovanni

A high pitched, constant beeping. Tightness on my chest. A low murmur of a feminine voice. Those were the first things I sensed as I regained consciousness. My eyelids felt so heavy when I forced them to flutter open, but I immediately shut them again when they were met by bright, fluorescent lights on the ceiling. Where was I? What's going on?

"Fidati di te per farti sparare solo per prenderti una pausa dalla vita. Per quanto ti meriti il resto, è meglio che ti svegli presto fratello. Tutti stanno cadendo a pezzi senza di te. Soprattutto mamma e Liv. (Trust you to get shot just so you can take a break from life. As much as you deserve the rest, you had better wake up soon Brother. Everyone is falling apart without you. Especially mamma and Liv.)"

Liv? As my sister's words caught up with my brain, my eyes flew open in panic. Olivia. The homeless man. I was shot. Was she okay?

I immediately attempted to sit up and cried out in agony as a sharp, stabbing pain rippled through my chest under the tight restriction of bandages.

"Gio! Oh my god! You're awake. Wait! Don't move. Let me call the nurse."

I was vaguely aware of Elenora faffing around my bed, pulling something off the wall as I attempted to sit up again, more slowly this time. I glanced down at my naked chest that was wrapped tightly in bandages and all the wires coming out of my arms. I pulled them out, wincing a little at the strange sensation.

"Giovanni! Stop! You have to stay in bed!"

"Where is she? What happened to her?" I husked out, my throat sore and dry. Suddenly, a swarm of bodies entered the room and began ordering me to lie back down and relax in Italian. I couldn't relax. Was she hurt? Did they shoot her still? Did they take her?

I was starting to lose my mind as I pushed the hands of nurses and doctors off me who were now becoming a little more persistent with their commands. I didn't give a shit if I was going to need restitching or if I was weak like they were telling me. I had to find her. I had to know she was safe.

"Liv! Liv!"

My head whipped around to my *sorella* as she banged violently on a door in the room. I froze.

Suddenly, the door opened and my heart skipped a beat when I saw Olivia standing there, hair damp, eyes puffy but completely unharmed. I could have cried. For the first time in my adult life, I felt like crying from the relief.

Our eyes locked and I got lost in the storm of green and gold that churned with emotion. She raced towards me, pushing past one of the doctors and flung her arms around my neck. I closed my eyes as I felt the warmth of her small frame against mine and her sweet scent of coconut and vanilla invading my senses. I held her tight with one arm that wasn't tied against my waist in a sling and buried my face in her damp hair.

I could feel her little body shaking as she cried quietly into my shoulder.

The doctors and nurses all took a step back, realising I wasn't going to try and leave anymore, and some of them departed. I don't know how long we stayed like that but when Olivia pulled back and rested her forehead on mine, both her small hands on either side of my face, I couldn't help but smile.

"I am so unbelievably mad at you Gio! You could have died!" She whimpered as my smile widened.

"It would take more than one bullet to bring me down, bambola."

She narrowed her eyes and shook her head in disbelief. Her beautiful face creased with pain and her eyes brimmed with new unshed tears. I reached up and cupped her face in my hand. "What is it?"

"I'm so sorry. It was my fault. I should have stayed. You were right. I was a coward."

I chuckled, a deep rumble from my chest that caused me pain, but it was worth it to see her face soften. "I can't believe my ears. Olivia Bennett, did you just admit you were wrong?"

Her eyes narrowed in that cute way they did when she was annoyed with me. I never thought I would be so happy to see that look again. I pulled her tighter into my body as I perched on the side of my bed. I was very aware that I was naked under the bed sheet and I was starting to get a little excited…

Moving my head to look at the man in the white coat who I expected was the lead doctor, I said, "Grazie per avermi salvato la vita dottore. Ma come vedi sto bene. Per favore, dacci un po' di privacy. (Thanks for saving my life doc. But as you can see, I am fine. Please give us some privacy.)"

He looked unsure but I kept my hard gaze on him. He knew who I was. "Devi fare un controllo completo, ma ti darò cinque minuti. (You need to be checked but I will give you five minutes.)" As he ushered everyone out of the room and Elle gave me a quick kiss on the cheek before she followed them out, I turned my face back to Olivia. She was still standing between my legs and had her arms around my neck as I held her against my body.

"Where were we? Oh yes. I was right and you were wrong."

She rolled her eyes but a smirk plastered on her face. "Even after a near death experience you are as arrogant as ever." Her smile fell as she looked into my eyes.

"Why did you do that? Why did you risk your life for mine?"

I brushed a strand of her hair behind her ear.

"Haven't you got it yet, bambola? This is who I am to you. I'd betray anyone for you. I'd kill for you. And I'll always dive in front of bullets for you." Her eyes widened with every word as she gulped nervously. "I love you, Olivia."

Her stunning eyes searched mine as I felt her heart racing in her chest that was pressed against me. "Ti amo Gio."

My face broke into the goofiest and widest grin as she told me she loved me in my own language.

"Did you just speak Ital-"

Her sweet, full lips were on mine in a flash and I closed my eyes and got lost in the magic of her. *She loved me.* She finally admitted it. This stubborn, gorgeous woman was mine. She was a rare gem. Strong, beautiful but precious. Delicate under the hard exterior. And now it was my job to protect and love her for the rest of my days. When a mafioso man finds his woman, nothing and no one will come between them. Nearly losing her has ignited something within me. My zio was wrong. He said love always makes us weaker. But with her in my arms, I felt stronger than ever. If they thought I was ruthless before, they have not met Giovanni Buccini in love. They have just awoken a monster. I will come for every single one of them who wants to cause her harm. They haven't seen anything yet.

Heaven

Olivia

"When is the doctor coming back? If he is not in here in the next five minutes, I am discharging myself," Gio whined as he pushed the plate of food away from him.

"You are not the only patient in this hospital! Stop complaining and eat something...please. The doctor said you need to get your strength up." I pushed the plate back towards him on the table over his bed and he groaned.

"It tastes like shit. Order me a pizza and I'll eat the lot," he smirked. I rolled my eyes and picked up his phone. If that was what it would take to get him to eat, then so be it. I knew this was the hardest thing for him. Just sitting here in this room, doing nothing. He wasn't used to it. He'd been here for three days now and he was itching to escape. He had taken many calls from his hospital bed all in Italian, so of course, I was kept in the dark about what exactly they were about, but from his tone and fierce demeanour when he was on them, I was glad I didn't know. I had agreed to stay. I was going to give this mafia life a go, but I was under no illusion that it would be easy. So as much as possible, I was going to ease myself into it. I didn't need to know everything Giovanni was doing in his business. As long as he was honest with me when I needed him to be, that was good enough for me.

"So...are we going to talk about the marriage alliance?" I asked, leaning back in my chair. His beautiful brown eyes flickered up to mine in panic at first, but when he saw I was chilled, he relaxed.

"I'm not marrying Camilla. No one is going to come in between us, Liv."

"I know. I just want to know what you and Max are planning. How exactly are you going to get out of this alliance and still keep everyone happy?"

He sighed deeply and rubbed his face with his hand. "I'm not. There is no possible outcome that will keep everyone happy. So, I am going to tell the truth. Salvatore already knows about us now and it will only piss him off more if he thinks I am trying to trick him."

I narrowed my eyes at his uncle's name. "He hates me."

Gio turned his head to look at my face as I lowered my eyes to my lap. If there was only one man that I thought could really come between Gio and I, it was him. And it made me nervous.

"He doesn't know you. Once he gets to know you, I actually think he will approve of you. He loves my mamma for her feisty nature, so I am sure he will love you too in time." He sounded confident in his words but his eyes showed his own insecurity.

"And if you are wrong? If he doesn't accept us together? If he still wants you to marry Camilla?"

"I will quit."

My eyes widened as I sat up straight. "Quit what?"

"All of it. Underboss. His legacy. I will give it all up."

I was momentarily speechless as I stared at his serious expression. He would give up everything he has ever known, everything he has ever worked for, to be with me. "Can you do that?"

He chuckled and shook his head. "I can do what I like, bambola. If this alliance is more important to him than me following in his footsteps, then that is his choice."

I leaned back in the chair, flabbergasted. As much as I wanted that to be true, my gut was telling me that it wouldn't be that simple.

"I can see you freaking out, Liv. Stop. I will take care of it."

"Do you know who was behind the shooting yet?" I asked carefully. I knew Gio would not let this go until he found out who was responsible, which was causing me huge anxiety. I knew I had to get used to this and quickly, but it didn't make it any easier, knowing he would go after them.

"No concrete evidence yet, but boss is working on it. Pretty sure we both know who was trying to kill you..."

I pouted my lips, deep in thought. It was the most obvious answer. The Leones. They said they would come for me if Gio hadn't met with them, but it hadn't been two weeks. Maybe I was trusting their words more than I should have. There was only one other person that I knew wanted me dead. Henry. But surely, he would want to do it himself?

I looked up at Gio as he fixed his intense gaze on me. It was as if he knew what I was thinking.

"Tell me about Henry."

I gulped and looked away quickly. "He escaped a few months ago. He killed a warden on night duty and managed to get out of the hospital. As soon as I heard that, I decided to run. I changed my last name, packed a bag of necessities and booked a flight to Italy."

When I glanced back at his stone face, I saw the hate he had for Henry raging behind his eyes. "And he is looking for you?"

"I don't know. I think so. Why else would he have escaped? I spoke to my best friend from home a few days ago, Millie, and she said he had broken into her family's house. He was obviously looking for something that would lead him to me." I released a shuddering breath as I rubbed my forehead. The stress was already increasing at just the idea of him getting closer to me.

"And that's why you were leaving? You were panicking?" His voice was soft, trying to understand my decision to run again, but his face was like stone.

"Yes. I should keep moving. Staying in one place too long is too risky. That was always my plan. Get a job, earn some money and then move onto the next place until Henry is found. But then I met you." I gave him a small smile and his expression changed. He pushed the table away from him as its wheels glided across the sterile floor. Holding out his tattooed hand to me, it swamped mine as I placed my dainty hand inside. He tugged hard and I nearly fell off my seat. I frowned when he chuckled, but he didn't give up. He tugged again, only this time, I moved with him, standing up and sitting on the side of his bed next to his hips.

"Closer," he demanded, and I saw the desire swirling behind those seductive, molten irises.

"What?"

"Closer bambola," He pulled my hand again, guiding me to climb onto the hospital bed and straddle his lap. He entwined his strong fingers with mine as he leaned his head back on the pillow and looked up at me. His other arm was still taped to his torso to keep him from ripping open his chest wound.

"You never have to be scared of him, Liv. He will never hurt you again."

I stared down into his determined eyes and, despite the conviction in his words, panic started to build within me.

"What are you going to do, Gio?" I whispered.

His gaze held mine as the silence stretched between us. His thumb circled the skin on the back of my hand.

"Do you really want to know?"

Did I? This wasn't just some business contract, this was personal. This was about me. I had to know. I nodded slowly.

"I am going to find him before he finds you. And I am going to kill him."

My heart pounded in my chest at his words. I had no doubt in my mind that he meant them. But they still made me feel sick. Not because he was going to kill Henry. If there was any man in the world I wanted dead, it was him, but because I was scared. Scared for Gio. Which was just ridiculous. But he had just been shot for goodness sake!

"Liv? What's going on in that pretty head of yours?" his voice was laced with concern.

"I- I don't want to lose you, Gio. I can't lose you. Henry will try and kill you. And the police…they are looking for him. Won't they be suspicious?"

The small smile that crept up his face caused me to pause my rambling. How was he smiling in a situation like this?

"You will not lose me, bambola. Not at his hands, I promise you. And you don't need to worry about the logistics. It will all be in hand."

My eyes widened slightly as I realised something.

"You are already doing this, aren't you?"

"I have my people out looking for him already, yes. Don't worry. He will never come near you and you won't have to see him ever again."

My lips parted as I tried to unscramble my brain to make sense of all of this. Was this really possible? I always thought I wanted Henry behind bars, but there would always be a chance he would be released in the future. What Gio was suggesting meant I would be free of him forever. I will never have to look over my shoulder again. Nate would have justice.

"Are you okay with this?" he asked carefully, his thumb still caressing my skin. It was a weighted question. It was him asking if I was okay with what he did and what he was planning to do. I was a terrible person because as I looked at this man who was so adapted to killing, all I saw was remarkably soft eyes that melted me to my core.

"Yes. I am okay with it," I leaned forward, placing my hand beside his head on the pillow as his face lit up at my acceptance. If this was the life I was choosing, I had better get onboard fast. "Kill the fucker."

Gio's eyes darkened immediately at my words as they filled with arousal. He licked his lower lip as his eyes flickered down to mine and I had never felt so empowered. So turned on. I was taking back my life. My control. This man was my saviour and I owed him it all.

"Fuck you are sexy when you are badass," he growled, gripping my hip with his free hand and pulling me up to rub against his rock-hard erection under the thin hospital sheet. I moaned as it worked its magic against my clit, only the sheet and my knickers as a barrier between us.

"This is deeply inappropriate! We are in a public place," I breathed, even though my hips were now rocking up and down his length on their own accord, causing pleasurable friction with every rub.

"That's never stopped us before," he husked.

He was right. And I didn't care. Leaning down, keeping my weight on my hands and avoiding his bandaged chest, I licked his lips before tugging at his bottom lip with my teeth. He groaned loudly and pushed his dick into my groin harder. The mere thought of him being inside me again made my body vibrate with need so strongly, I suspected I was more than ready to take him in one thrust. Our tongues were locked in a passionate entanglement as I continued to grind on his erection. I broke the kiss when I couldn't take it anymore. I could feel his cock pulsing under the thin fabric and as I sat back, I pulled the bed sheet away from him. I bite my lip at the sight of his perfect dick – long, heavy and strong. My pussy clenched for it. I felt empty and desperate without it. Grabbing the base of it with one hand, I positioned myself above it, and moved my knickers to the side with my other hand. Gio's eyes were on mine as I lowered myself onto him, taking him in as far as I could. Both our mouths dropped open as our breathing ragged at the blissful feeling of being one again. His hand was still on my hip, all he could do was guide me, but I was in full control here. And I knew he liked it.

Rocking my hips back and forth, he moaned as his eyes rolled before I leaned down and kissed him with ferocity once more. I started to lift my body up and down on top of him as I rode his dick as if it was my own personal fuck toy.

"Fuck Liv! Slow down baby, you feel too good."

I ignored him as my own pleasurable bubble was building in me. In fact, I increased my speed, practically twerking on his cock.

"Oh mio Dio. Sei così fottutamente stretto!" He roared and just hearing his sexy Italian words had me crying out my orgasm as he closed his eyes and growled out his own.

I was a panting mess as I regained my senses and peered down at his sated face under my eyelashes.

"I've fucking missed that," he exclaimed, and I giggled, nodding my head.

Suddenly, his phone vibrated on the side table, and I peered over to see the delivery man was outside.

"Pizza is here," I said, climbing off him and rearranging my knickers.

His gorgeous face broke into the biggest smile as I walked over to the hospital door to retrieve the pizza.

"Are you sure I didn't die and go to heaven?" I heard his deep chuckle behind me.

Maxilla

Maximus

"What do you mean the Leones were out of the country?" I snarled into the phone at Leo, our Capo of Venice. Venice was split into two territories. One half belonged to the Leones and one half to us. It was nearly unheard of nowadays for two rival mafia families to be sharing a city and it had been the cause of our feud for as long as I could remember.

"Lorenzo is on his honeymoon in Santorini and Riccardo took a private jet out of the country the day before the shooting," Leo replied calmly.

"Well, that doesn't make them innocent. In fact, that makes them even more suspicious. They were covering their backs. This could have been arranged prior to them leaving and they left the city to escape the fallout." I was just speaking every thought that entered my brain now. It was how I processed and unpicked information. I liked to present all the facts out loud to come to my own conclusions. I knew my zio was doing his own investigations into the shooting, but I like to look into things myself when it comes to Gio and I. We had always had each other's backs since we were kids.

"True," Leo agreed.

"But then, why would they attempt to kill Olivia when they had no reason to. They would have known it would start a war. So why run away? What would be their gain? It doesn't make any sense."

"Also true," Leo yawned. I was clearly boring him.

"Just keep tabs on the Leones' every move. Don't let a single bit of information slip through your fingers, no matter how insignificant it may seem. They are up to something and I don't like it. What about the Aianis?" Francesco was a snake and I didn't trust him as far as I could throw the fat fuck.

"Nothing alarming. They have no connection to the firearm used or the homeless man."

"But they have a motive... If they knew about Olivia and Gio."

"Si. How is Giovanni? Is he home yet?"

"Home today. And he is not going to be very fucking happy that we don't have this figured out yet. So, you better get cracking."

Leo groaned and hung up. Pocketing my phone, I threw my cigarette onto the gravel driveway and put it out with my combat boot. Today I was sporting ripped jeans, a loose tank top, with a flannel shirt tied around my waist. Every finger on my hands adorned thick silver bands and I had a long silver chain around my neck with a cross. I liked having all my tats on show as much as possible. Why get your body covered if you are going to hide them under a stuffy suit?

I knew I didn't look like your average mafioso. A biker thug was more the image I gave which zio thoroughly disapproved of, but just because I didn't wear designer suits and slick my hair back like my cousin and uncle, didn't make me any less of a fucking lunatic you shouldn't want to mess with.

I clumped up the stone steps into my cousin's mansion to look for her. I come here pretty much every day now. I knew I was playing with fucking fire but I couldn't help it. I couldn't stay away from her. She was my dream woman. Everything I had ever wanted. She looked like a fucking super model and gave off such a sweet, timid and feminine vibe. It drew me in immediately. She was my perfect type. But as I got to know her, I realised there was so much more to her than meets the eye. She was clever. Intuitive. She noticed things quickly and made her own intelligent judgements with hardly any information to go by. It was impressive. She didn't realise it but she had a quiet strength about her. I hated to imagine what she must have been through at the hands of her own papi. The man was a dickhead through and through. She has told me bits here and there, but I know there is more. For a woman to have gone through that all her life and still be such a sweet soul shows the strength of her character.

Luckily, because Sal had put me in charge of keeping her happy while Gio was away, no one had batted an eyelid at the amount of time we were spending together. We were falling in love in plain sight and it was fucking hilarious to know my zio unknowingly caused this.

I found her out by the pool, watching Raya and Sani playing in the water. She was relaxing on a sun lounger with just a skimpy bikini that showed off her insane figure and a pair of large sunglasses. My dick twinged in my jeans at the sight of her.

"Cami! Watch this! I can make a bomb!" Sani shouted from the diving board as he jumped in, causing a huge splash for such a small person. Cami squealed as the drops of water soaked her and she laughed so freely, I couldn't help the idiotic smile plastered on my face.

"Well, you might as well go in now!" I chuckled as I strolled out onto the decking. Raya ran towards me and hugged my legs before I scooped her up and gave her nose kisses. She burst into giggles as my beard tickled her face. She loved it when I did that. I put her down as Sani waved before diving under the water with his goggles on.

I turned and saw Cami watching me intensely, her head canted to the side and a pretty smile on her face.

"I was actually just about to go in!" she replied as she sat up and scooped her long, tanned legs off the sunbed to give me room to sit down.

"Who is watching the kids today?" I asked, looking around for Cecilia.

"Me," she said shyly, a small blush creeping up her cheeks. I smirked as I realised how much that would have meant to her. For Cecilia to trust her enough to watch the children. "It is only for an hour or so. She went to the hospital to help bring Giovanni back and there's loads of staff and Marco around, so it's not really just me but- "

I grabbed her hand in mine to calm her. She looked up at me with those big, blue eyes. "An hour or a day. It doesn't matter. She is beginning to trust you."

She nodded happily. I looked over at my two youngest cousins and groaned internally. That messed up my plans today. I was going to take Cami somewhere where we could be alone. Where I could be honest with her about everything.

I spoke to Gio last night on the phone. Together, we decided that we were going to come clean to Sal and Francesco. We had run out of time to find a better plan. I was going to marry Cami to keep the alliance and if they weren't happy with it being because I am a Capo and not in line to be Boss, Gio would offer to step down. I knew it was a long shot. Sal will never go for it. He has underestimated me my entire life. He sees me as the impulsive, cheeky younger nephew who makes a joke out of everything. But that couldn't be further from the truth. He had no idea that I studied hard in my spare time to learn about the ins and outs of business and constantly look into new deals or potential investments that would give the family more wealth and power. Gio had all that training from Sal and Toni himself. He was the chosen one. But I was cast aside like the no-good runt of the family. And I honestly didn't care. It was how I liked it. I had the freedom to do what I wanted within my territory and Sal stayed out of my way. Gio and I would have open discussions in front of Toni or Sal about ideas for upcoming deals. A few weeks later, Toni would be taking all the credit. Most people would feel disheartened by it but it just amused me. I liked that none of them except Gio knew how smart I was or how much potential I had. I was the dark horse of the family and I liked it that way.

But now things are about to change. I was about to be thrust under their radar and not in a good way. But sometimes life will fuck you sideways and you just have to change positions and enjoy it. When life gives you lemons and all that bollox. I glanced back at Cami as she watched the children with a smile and my heart leapt in my chest. I wanted to do this right. I didn't want her to think I was just doing this out of duty. Because I would marry her regardless. She deserved the fairy-tale and I know I look far from prince fucking charming but I was willing to try my best to give it to her.

"When Cecilia returns, meet me in the maze please. I'll be there waiting, however long it takes." I spoke quietly so the children didn't hear and her eyes sparkled with excitement.

"Okay."

I squeezed her hand before I stood up and left to get my plan in action. I would have given anything to just kiss her whenever I wanted but it would have to wait a little bit longer. Making my way down to the wine cellar, I pulled out a vintage champagne and grabbed two glasses. Hiding it in a duffel bag, I ransacked the fridge for strawberries and chocolates before I sneakily grabbed some throws from the private living room. Cecilia would have my balls if she knew I had taken them but seeing as she messed up my original plan of taking Cami to a private beach for the day, she owed me.

I made my way to the maze and after longer than I care to admit, I found my way to the middle. At least this place held some sentiment for us, so it wasn't a complete lost cause. I opened out the expensive, cashmere throws on the grass floor, before placing the Champagne in an ice bucket that I'd also sneaked out of the kitchen. Sitting down on the throws, I pulled the velvet box out of my pocket and leaned my elbows on my knees as I opened it in my hands. It was the perfect ring. A silver diamond band with a huge square solitaire. When I saw it, I instantly thought of her. I just hope she liked it. Snapping the box shut, I laid down on the ground and stared up at the clouds gliding across the bluest of skies that reminded me of her eyes. Now to wait.

***

Camilla

"Liv! Gio!" Sani bounded over to the couple who walked through the front door hand in hand. I smiled at Olivia, who returned it warmly. I hoped we could be friends. I've never really had any true friends, not ones that weren't interested in my family's money or influence anyway. My eyes flickered up at Giovanni, standing next to her. I almost had to do a double take. He looked so different. For one, he was smiling. A genuine smile. He ruffled Sani's hair as Sani started to ask him about what it was like to be shot and bombarding him with millions of questions. But it wasn't just the smile. He was wearing casual clothes and his hair wasn't styled back like normal, giving him that intimidating appearance. He looked youthful today. And happy.

His dark eyes locked with mine as he sensed me studying him and he gave me a small nod and smile. I grinned back, hoping that this might be a fresh start for us too. If this is the way he looked when Liv was around, then I really hoped she would move in.

"Were the children okay? They didn't give you any trouble?" Cecilia walked over to me and I shook my head.

"No, they were angels," I smiled. She raised one eyebrow in surprise before smiling. "Well, thank you Camilla."

"It was my pleasure. I don't want to intrude on family time. If you'll excuse me, I am going to take a walk in the gardens."

They all nodded as I turned to head out to the maze in the back garden.

"Cami! Wait a sec!" A voice behind me had me stop and turn. Olivia jogged up, her wavy brown hair flowing behind her. She was so effortlessly beautiful. "I just wanted to say, thank you." I scrunched my face up in confusion and she smiled. "How do I put this… thank you for not being a bitch and trying to steal my man."

I burst into a fit of giggles as she joined me. "You're welcome."

"I hope we can be friends. I think we are going to need each other with these men around," she added, and my cheeks hurt from how wide I was smiling.

"I would love that, Olivia."

"Please call me Liv," she gave me a quick hug and then pulled back. "I'll see you around the house I guess."

"You are moving in?" I asked excitedly.

"Yes. It looks that way." She waved as she took a few steps backwards before returning over to the Buccini family. I felt a weight lift off my shoulders as I made my way out onto the freshly cut back lawn. This family was so different from mine. I know they seemed ruthless and terrifying to begin with, but there was love between them all. So much love. It was the complete opposite to what my family was like. The only person I could vaguely tolerate was my nineteen-year-old brother, Enzo.

I really hoped I never had to go back to that place. That somehow all of this would work out for the best and I could stay. Suddenly, the realisation hit me. Olivia was moving in, which meant the alliance was off. After Giovanni's near-death experience, he wasn't fucking about anymore. He wasn't trying to hide his feelings for Olivia now. It was only a matter of time before I was sent back to my papi. I paused as I reached the entrance of the maze and leaned against the bush. I felt panic simmering to the surface and my heart was beating like crazy. I couldn't go back. If they didn't kill me, I would be beaten. Then I would be passed around to my papi's friends until he found another alliance that he would use me for. No. I would rather die.

I hunched over, grabbing my stomach as the pain of leaving all of this became real. Having to leave Max. I am going to run away. It was the only thing I could do. I couldn't saddle Max with the burden of trying to protect me from the inevitable. With my mind made up, I stood up straight and walked into the maze to find him. I will leave tomorrow. I knew he would help me. He could get me away from here, some cash, a new passport maybe. As I reached the middle of the maze, I froze at the scene before me. There was Max on one knee holding a box, his smile was so breath-taking I think it actually stole the air right out of my lungs.

"Wh-what are you doing?" I whispered as I looked around at all the roses on the floor, the blankets, champagne and food. My eyes flickered back to him on one knee and I slammed my hand across my mouth.

"Camilla Aiani. I know we haven't known each other for very long but from the moment I laid eyes on you, I knew. I knew you had become my whole life. I would go to the ends of the Earth for you without ever wanting anything in return. But I am going to ask for one thing… Just this once… And if your answer is yes…I will never ask for anything from you ever again because you will have given me everything I could ever want."

My eyes watered as his piercing green eyes bore into my soul, making me feel every word like a sonnet written just for me. "Cami, will you marry me?"

I opened and closed my mouth in shock. What? How? Was he insane? What about his uncle? My papi? They would kill him.

His smile wavered as I still stood frozen to the floor, unable to talk. I wanted to marry him more than anything in the world. But this was impossible…

"Cami? I know what you are thinking. That this is not going to work, that there are too many obstacles in our way. But do you trust me?" he spoke slowly, every word causing my raging heart to calm slightly. I nodded.

"Then trust this. Marry me. Please?"

As I stared down at his handsome face, I couldn't refuse him. I didn't want to. "Si. Lo sposerò te."

His face bloomed like a flower in spring as he jumped to his feet and scooped me up in his arms, before kissing my lips repeatedly, causing me to giggle against his beard. He opened the box as he stepped back and I saw the most perfect, elegant diamond ring. It was exactly to my taste. I gasped as he took it out of the box and held it up to me. "Do you like it?"

Tears were rolling down my face now, as I had never felt happiness like this. "It is stunning."

He took my hand and placed the ring on my wedding finger and I couldn't stop staring. "I can't believe it," I whispered through my tears of joy.

"No going back! You said yes now!" He chuckled, pulling me down onto his lap as he cracked open the bottle of champagne. I grabbed his face in both my hands and kissed him passionately as he put the bottle down and wrapped his strong arms around me.

"But how? The alliance…" I started, but he shook his head.

"This is all that matters right now. Me and you. We will tell them the truth. If they refuse to accept it, we will run. Go live on a desert island somewhere, drinking from coconuts and fucking like rabbits," he grinned.

"Can we do that anyway?" I giggled.

"We will do anything you want, princess."

I smiled down at him again as my heart nearly exploded in my chest. True love. I had always dreamed of it but never thought I would be lucky enough to experience it. My god, it was worth it all.

No More Secrets

Giovanni

I should get shot more often. The women in my life know how to look after me. But one woman in particular is doing a fucking ace job at it. Admiring my girl's beauty from my position on the king-sized bed, Liv propped up my pillow behind my head.

"So, this is the plan, Gio. You must take it easy. At least three hours of down time a day, the doctor said. Just because you are home, you can't go full speed ahead into underboss mode again. You still need to rest," she lectured me and I grinned like a Cheshire cat at how much she cared.

"Three hours a day in this bed with you? My pleasure."

She stood up, folding her arms across her chest with a disapproving smile. "No. Three hours alone. To sleep or just chill."

I frowned, shaking my head. "That just won't work. I will only come looking for you."

She rolled her eyes, but I held her gaze to show her even though I was in a playful mood, I was being deadly serious. I wanted her around me all the time. I'm not sure I will ever get any work done again.

"You are impossible." She wandered over to my dressing room and started pulling out all her clothes from the suitcase and folding them into neat piles on the floor. I watched her with a triumphant grin plastered on my face. She was here. With me. Moving her things into my room. Nothing had ever felt so right.

"Are you really sure about this? I can stay in one of the guest rooms," she glanced over to me from her knees on the carpeted walk-in and I frowned.

"Why the hell would you stay in a guest room?"

"Because it is so fast. Living together! We are literally going from a few days in France to breaking up to moving in in the space of ten days. What if we get sick of each other," she said seriously, but I could see the amusement behind her eyes. She knew that would never happen.

"When you know, you know," I smiled and she beamed back at me, shaking her head before she went back to organising her clothes.

"I will send some of my men to collect the rest of your things from Giulia's later."

She scanned the small piles of clothes, toiletries and make-up in front of her and shook her head. "No need. This is everything I own."

My eyebrows furrowed with confusion. She can't be serious. I pointed to her belongings that would barely take up one drawer in my wardrobe. "That...is all you own?"

"That is all I need," she shrugged back. "When you are on the run, it's best to pack light."

I dropped my arm back down. "Well, you are not on the run anymore." I reached for my phone and started typing a text to my personal shopper. I knew she was the same size as Elle. "What shoe size are you? Bra size?"

Liv's face did that cute little thing it does when she's confused and slightly annoyed. Her nose wrinkled, eyes narrowed and lips pouted. "Why do you need to know that? Gio, I don't need you to buy me anything! I have my own money."

"I am guessing a size 5 shoe and 34B?" I glanced down at her breasts admiring them in her little sundress and she scoffed loudly.

"Hidden talent?" she joked as she picked up her clothes and placed them in a drawer. I was right. One drawer and a few hangers were all she needed.

I smirked wickedly and finished the text message before she strolled out of the wardrobe and sat on the chair by the window. She smiled at me when she saw me watching her intently.

"What?"

"Nothing. I just like it. You being here. Making yourself at home."

She glanced out the window with a sweet smile as she looked across the well-kept lawns and swimming pool. "Who'd have thought...that one day I would be living in a bloody mansion! Definitely not me," she chuckled to herself. I turned on my side to watch her as she got lost in her thoughts.

"What was your childhood like? Growing up?" I asked, genuinely interested. I wanted to know every little detail about this woman. No matter how small or insignificant they may seem to everyone else. I wanted to know her inside out and for her to know me. For the first time in my life, I wanted to give myself completely to someone and I had no qualms about doing so. It was a warming feeling.

"It was okay. I can't complain. We had a roof over our heads, food on the table and I went to a good school and had nice friends. It was pretty normal really."

"Stop being vague bambola. I want to know everything. What is your first childhood memory? Did you have any hobbies growing up? What were you like at school? I bet you were a nerd," I smirked, and she whipped her head towards me with a cheeky grin.

"A-star student through and through," she beamed proudly.

"Of course, you were," I chuckled and patted the bed. She climbed off the chair and jogged over to me, jumping on to the bed like a little kid and lying next to me.

"Oh my goodness! Are these bed sheets actually made of silk? Who do you think you are? Hugh Heffner?"

Turning on my side slightly so she had my full attention, I smirked.

"Don't change the subject. I've noticed you do that. You change the topic when people ask you personal questions." Her face fell slightly as she stared up at me. I got lost in the vibrancy of her two-toned eyes as her expression became almost sad.

"I do that, don't I? I don't mean to. It's just after so many years of not wanting people to know what happened to me, I guess I have used it as a coping mechanism."

"I get it," I reached up with my one free arm to smooth her hair away from her face and she blinked back at me. She suddenly seemed so vulnerable. She was lowering her guard. Letting me in.

"My parents were hard workers. We never had a huge amount of money, but we managed. After my dad died, mum had to get a second job and we didn't have any other family close by, so I ended up in after-school clubs a lot or my friend Millie's family helped out with childcare. I think that is why I ended up feeling more comfortable in their house than my own. I remember wishing or pretending that they were my family when I was little. Then I would feel so guilty."

I led still and kept my gaze on her as she traced my tattoos on my hand that was resting on the bed between us. Again, I recognised it as a coping strategy. Keeping her hands busy or focusing on something else so she could freely talk without having to meet my gaze.

"I liked drawing and reading as a child. I also loved going down to the beach. Living in London, there weren't many beaches near us, but once a year, mum and I would pack the car up and drive down to Cornwall for a long weekend. We would stay in a caravan park and I would spend every minute I could by the sea. Even when it was far from sunny, which it isn't often in England," she smiled as her eyes flickered up to mine.

"I'd like to see your beaches in England."

She giggled and I wanted to kiss her, but I also did not want to distract her. She was opening up and I could slowly see she was feeling more comfortable about talking about herself. "I think you would be a little disappointed compared to the beaches you have here in Italy."

"Hmmm, I think it's your weather that would annoy the hell out of me! I hate the rain."

"Oh god, you would hate England then. It never stops raining! But I have always found the rain quite calming. I'm weird. I love thunderstorms too."

"You are weird," I smirked, and she pouted at me. Why was she so cute? "Ok so beaches, thunderstorms, reading and drawing, A-star student. Sounds like you were a dream child?"

She moved onto her back so she was staring up at the ceiling. "Far from it. I wasn't naughty. But I also didn't let people push me around and I NEVER did anything I didn't want to." She chuckled as she recalled some memories.

"Now that sounds more like the Liv I know."

"Mills and I used to sneak out of our houses at night just to meet up in a huge oak tree between our roads and drink her dad's stolen vodka. I don't know why we did it. We thought we were cool. But now I can't stand the taste of it! That was before everything changed."

Her body tensed next to me, and I knew instantly what she was referring to. Or who she was referring to. I didn't know whether pushing her to talk about this now would be a step too far, but to my surprise, she continued.

"Mum met Neil on a dating app. Ironically, it was me who suggested she sign up. She had never had a relationship since dad and I felt bad for her. She always worked so hard and when she wasn't working, she was with me or sorting the house. I just wanted her to find a man to bring a little joy into her life." Her tone was laced with sadness and regret, and it made my heart ache. "Everything was great to start with. Neil was nice to mum. Wined and dined her. Took her on weekends away. He had a good job and was also widowed with one child, so they had things in common. It was only after him and Henry moved in that things started to change. Neil became lazy. He expected mum to do everything for him. Cook his dinner, keep on top of the housework constantly even though she still had two jobs. He used to pick fights over the smallest things. If there was a plate left in the sink for more than an hour or if something in the house broke. It would be her fault. They argued like cats and dogs but he would always apologise quickly and make it up to her with a fancy dinner reservation or be overly affectionate. I told her to leave him, but she refused. I think a part of her just thought having him around was better than the loneliness of having no one. Soon the fire in her burned out and she became indifferent to the way he treated her. She just put up with it. She stopped fighting back."

I reached for her hand and gave it a supportive squeeze as I started to rub circles on her skin to soothe her. It was for my benefit as well as hers. This was hard for me to listen to. I didn't like the idea of anything bad happening to her but I knew I was about to hear it all. And I needed to. I wanted to know. So that when I found that fucker, he would pay duly.

"So, Henry was like his dad?" I asked, trying to understand if their behaviours were the same but she shook her head.

"No. Neil was an arse. But he wasn't violent, and he wasn't possessive or controlling. He just expected things from my mum that he had no right to and made her feel like shit when she didn't deliver. Henry was different. The whole situation was different."

I waited for her to continue and saw her inhale deeply before she released a shuddering breath.

"After the night he came into my room and tried to…have sex with me. He became so fervently angry. It was as if a switch flicked on in him and all he could feel was rage. Every second of every day. At first, I thought he was just mad that I rejected him, and he would cool off eventually, but when he started doing things to torment me, I knew there was something wrong. He would use any opportunity we were alone to try and intimidate me. Scare me. He would corner me in rooms. Purposefully, throw or bang things next to my head to make me jump. I would wake up and find him sitting in my room in the dark in the middle of the night. That's when I fitted a lock on my door. That pissed him off more. He would cut up my clothes if he thought they were too revealing. He started to follow me everywhere. I would be out with my friends in a café or park and he would walk past glaring at me. He would sit outside my friend Millie's house in his car when I was round there for dinner and knock on the door offering me a lift home. He was suffocating me. But the worst was his words. The things he would say. In one breath he would tell me I was worthless or a whore and the next he would be calling me beautiful and that I was his. He spread rumours about me throughout the village so no boys would want to come near me. He threatened any men who looked my way. He used to start fights with men who spoke about me to him and then would come home and tell me it was my fault that he had beaten them to a pulp."

My breathing was becoming laboured as I tried to control the lava of fury that was spreading through my veins. For two years, this had been her life before he even murdered her boyfriend. Fuck I don't think I have ever wanted to kill someone more in my entire life.

She turned back to me on my side. "I know what you are thinking. Why didn't I tell anyone? Why didn't I get help?"

I shook my head. "No. I wasn't thinking that at all."

"I tried. I spoke to my mum. But she was dealing with her own despair. Even though Henry was making my life hell, he had never been physically violent towards me. It got progressively worse when I turned eighteen and started dating Nate but I knew I would be gone soon. I knew I would be at university, miles away and the distance would make him forget about me. That he'd lose interest. And then that night happened. The night he murdered Nate."

"Come here," I whispered as I pulled her into my body and wrapped my arm around her small frame. She rested her head on my shoulder and I exhaled loudly. "I know that was hard for you to talk about. But I want you to know that even though I am possessive and protective of you, I will never be him, Liv. I will never cause you any harm or make you feel like you're not the most amazing person in the world to me."

She raised her head to look into my eyes and smiled. "I know. You are nothing like him. You are the only thing in my life that makes me feel safe. I love you so much Gio."

I leaned down and kissed her forehead. "I love you bambola."

"Shall we make a deal?" she said with a secret smile.

"I'm listening."

"I will stay with you for three hours every day while you rest and we will use that time to talk. To learn everything there is to know about each other. No more secrets."

The rage that I had felt just minutes ago, had simmered down as I gazed into her eyes.

"Deal."

She leaned down and kissed me. A slow, sensual and fucking delicious kiss. I would never get enough of her lips. When she pulled back, I frowned, wanting more.

"But maybe a little of that time could be spent helping me to relax in other ways?" I smirked, raising one eyebrow suggestively.

The desire swarmed in her eyes as she bit her lip seductively.

"You mean… something like this?"

She moved her way down my body, kissing my abs below my bandaged chest as she went, and I moaned as she unzipped my trousers. I lifted my head to watch her pull out my cock and hold the base of it with her little hand as she held my gaze.

"Hmmm," I hummed as she licked from the bottom to my tip and flicked her tongue over the top. I was growing instantly hard just at that action. When she took me into her talented mouth, I dropped my head back and groaned in appreciation.

"Fuck. Yes, exactly like that."

Stand By Your Man

Olivia

Waking up for the first time in the Buccini mansion felt oddly normal. Like I was always meant to be here. Feeling the weight of Gio's muscular arm draped over my waist and his scent swarming my senses was the nicest way I had ever woken up in my life. Turning around carefully so as not to wake him, I gazed up at his sleeping face and smiled.

No wonder this man could get away with murder with a face and body as gorgeous as his. There I go again. Thinking about him being a murderer. I sighed deeply as I took in his distinguished features. I was starting to train my brain to see his way of life differently. He was born into this role, and he had never known anything different. He told me that he did what he had to do to survive and to protect his family. That was always what drove him. When I think about it like that, I can understand it. Would I kill to survive? Yes. Would I kill to protect those I loved? Without a doubt. So how did that make me any worse than him?

Not many people can say that they have witnessed a murder in their lifetime. Yet I can. I watched the life drain out of Nate's eyes. I saw the pain, horror and fear in them. And I watched it almost happen to Gio too. So even though I couldn't pretend to understand what Gio did for a living, I had experienced it first-hand. It was a dog-eat-dog world he lived in and it seemed to be them or us. I was just going to have to accept that death and revenge were always going to be a part of my life now. Perhaps it was always meant to be. Perhaps it was my destiny. Because no matter how I felt about Gio's darkness, my love for him and his family was far greater.

I ran my hand over his bandage lightly and pulled at the corner to check his stitches. It healed quickly. Good. He was going to have physio for a few weeks, which he wasn't very pleased about, but I would force him. After yesterday, I realised I had a way to get him to do just about anything I wanted. I grinned mischievously as I thought back to how I turned him into putty in my mouth as I gave him what he described as the best head of his life.

"What are you smirking at bambola?" He mumbled with his eyes still closed. My mouth gaped open. How did he know?

"I can feel you watching me sleep, you weirdo."

I giggled and moved his arm off my waist, before climbing out of his bed. No, our bed. Oh, that feels strange. That all of this is now technically my home.

"Where are you going?" he groaned as he opened his eyes and reached his arm out for me that was not bandaged to his chest. I walked naked towards his bathroom- our bathroom and gave him a seductive glance over my shoulder.

"To shower. I have work to do," I replied.

"What work?" he called out.

I poked my head around the door frame. "I am your sibling's nanny, if you haven't forgotten?"

"Last I remembered, you quit!"

I smirked as he pulled himself upright in the bed and flung the covers off him. "Hmm, that was when I thought the man I loved who happened to be my boss was using me, marrying another woman and had gone behind my back and betrayed my trust."

I heard his heavy footsteps padding towards the bathroom as I turned the shower on. When I spun around, he was leaning against the door frame, stark naked. His tousled hair, tanned skin, rippling muscles and that perfect dick that was sporting its morning glory made my mouth instantly water. I don't think I will ever not be turned on by the sight of this man. He was something else.

"Ouch! Still too raw bambola. Don't remind me," he said with a twinkle in his eye. I stepped towards him and slowly started to undo the bandages on his chest. The doctor said I would need to rebandage them today.

"Well, I would like my job back if Cecilia hasn't found anyone else?" I asked as I started to unravel his chest tenderly.

"You don't need to work for us anymore. You can just spend time with the kids whenever you want. As part of this family," he replied, watching my face intensely.

"I like being their nanny and I like teaching them. It gives me purpose and I am earning my own money. I do not want to sit around this house all day doing nothing and living off you."

He smiled as I pulled the last of the bandage off and then he rolled his shoulder slowly, giving a blissful expression at being able to move his other arm again. "Does it feel okay?"

"Yes. It feels fine. Better. I don't even think I need the physio."

"Ahh ahh! You are seeing the physio whether you like it or not."

"Is that an order bambola?"

"Yes, it is. Each time you go, and you are not an ass to the physio who is only trying to do their job, you will be rewarded!"

His dark eyes narrowed with amusement as he wrapped both his arms around my waist. "What will be my reward?"

"You will have to wait and see," I smirked, walking us towards the huge three-headed waterfall shower. I carefully removed the padding around his bullet wound on his back and, to my delight, it looked amazing. He would have a scar for sure, but it was healing so well. Then I checked the stitching on his chest where they had operated on his lung.

As the water hit our bodies, I traced his chest with my fingertips and he closed his eyes. "You are going to have scars but they look better."

"Add to the collection," he smirked. I rolled my eyes as I washed him carefully. "What did I ever do to deserve you, bambola?"

I smiled as I leaned forward and kissed his toned chest. "I think I should be asking you the same thing. You are the one who saved my life."

He opened his eyes and peered down at me with so much love and devotion that my insides melted right there in that shower cubicle. "And I'd do it again in a heartbeat. You can have your job back, but you might have to fight Marco and Camilla off for the role now."

I chuckled as he turned and picked up the loafer and started to wash my body, caressing every part of me but paying particular attention to my boobs. He was definitely a booby man.

"I like Cami. I think we will be good friends and Max and her are well suited."

Gio looked down at me with an intrigued expression. "What?"

"Most girls would feel some kind of jealousy towards the woman that is living in her boyfriend's house with the intent on marrying him."

"Why? Should I be jealous?" I lifted one eyebrow with a smirk.

"Of course not."

"Well, there you go then. And I am not like most girls, Gio."

"No," he grinned. "You most certainly are not."

***

As I made my way down to the children's wing, I couldn't remember a time that I felt happier than I did right now. I knew we still had a lot of shit to deal with but I felt a sense of security and understanding between Gio and I, now that we were open to communicating and on the same page about everything. It was hard to imagine anything coming between us again.

"Signorina Jones, nice to see you back," Marco nodded at me as I approached the playroom.

"It's good to be back. And Marco? Thank you. For what you said. You were right. I do need this family," I smiled up at him from his towering height and a genuine smile crept onto his face. I knew I would do it one day. He is such a big teddy bear at heart. I now understood why Cecilia had chosen him as the children's main bodyguard.

Pushing open the door to the playroom, I could already hear their laughter. Sitting on the floor on cushions were Sani, Raya and Cami playing a game of fishing with wooden alphabet letters. It was a game I had invented before France and it made me so happy to see them still wanting to play it.

"Liv! Look! We are playing catch the letter game!" Sani shouted as he tossed his wooden fishing rod into the makeshift pond (bowl of water).

"I can see! Well done!" I strolled over and kneeled beside Raya. "Is there a spare rod for me?"

"You can share mine," Raya smiled up at me and I nodded.

"Thank you."

"It's okay. Here, take mine. I'll leave you guys to it," Cami held hers towards me as she attempted to stand up. I frowned. She always seemed to feel like she had to leave around all of us. Except the children. They seemed to make her feel comfortable.

"No. Please stay if you would like. I hear you have been spending time with these rugrats. Thank you."

She gave me a shy smile and sat back down on the cushion. "Yes. We have been having lots of fun."

"So, do we have two nannies now? You and Cami?" Sani asked as he pulled off the letter m from the end of his magnetic rod. I smiled over at Cami and nodded for her to answer.

"No Sani. I am just a friend who likes playing with you both. I am not a teacher like Liv."

"Are you Max's friend? Like Liv is Gio's?" Sani asked, looking between us both. I chuckled at his boldness. I loved that about him. He always spoke exactly what was on his mind.

"Yes, I suppose I am," she replied. And that is when I looked down at her hand and caught sight of the stunning engagement ring on her finger. I froze. My immediate thought was had Giovanni given her that to keep up appearances, but then I knew he would never. Which only meant one thing...

"Hey guys! It's a lovely day. Why don't we go for a walk around the grounds? We could go on a bug hunt."

"Yeah!" They both cried and jumped up excitedly.

"Urgh! I hate bugs!" Cami scrunched her nose and giggled.

"They are more scared of you than you are of them. That's what Liv says. You are a giant and they are only tiny," Sani held out his hand to her in support and my heart burst with pride. She took it with a smile.

"Ah well, I suppose I need to be brave then."

The four of us made our way outside and once the children had run off to look for bugs, I decided to broach the subject as Cami and I walked alongside one another. "Congratulations," I leaned in and whispered in her ear. She glanced over at me in shock and then looked down at her hand as my eyes moved to the ring.

"Oh." Her pink blush settled on her cheeks as she smiled like a giddy teenager. "Thank you. Max proposed yesterday. I still can't believe it."

My heart soared for her and Max. I hadn't spent much time with either of them but it was clear that they were deeply in love. They had fallen hard and fast. Just like Gio and I.

"You two are perfect together, Cami. I really wish you all the happiness."

Her smile faded and she suddenly seemed stressed as her shoulders tensed and she swallowed down her emotions.

"What's wrong?"

"I really love him, Liv. But what if love isn't enough? Salvatore and my papi control our lives. If they do not accept us together, we don't have many options," she sighed.

I shook my head as anger bubbled in my chest. How was that fair? In this day and age, people should be able to choose who they want to marry. "I don't understand that. This mafia culture you all live by. It's so oppressive."

She smiled sadly and nodded. "It is. But it has always been this way. The boss of the families has all the control. Everyone below them must follow their commands and stay in line or they will face severe consequences. It's been installed in us since birth. To respect the boss above all else."

"Do you really think your father will not allow you to marry Max? When he sees how much love you share?" I asked curiously. She scoffed and shook her head.

"My papi does not care about my happiness, Liv. He will see me marrying Max as a waste. He wants influence and sway over other mafia families. The only way he will get that is if I am married to a boss or soon-to-be boss. Marrying a capo would be lessening my rank as it is. I am the daughter of a boss."

My heart ached at her words. She sounded so defeated. "Don't give up Cami. Gio and Max are not going to. They will fight for us."

She stopped walking and turned to me, reaching for both my hands. As her blue eyes bore into mine, I saw her worry. "That is the problem, Liv. They are going to get themselves killed."

"What?"

"If Sal and Francesco band together and see this for what it is; a betrayal and defiance against them. There will be nothing to stop them from killing Max and perhaps Gio. Men have been killed for far less in these families."

My gut twisted as I realised just how dangerous this whole thing was. Not only was the threat outside of this family, but it was within its very walls as well.

"What do we do?" I whispered as she let go of my hands.

"We are doing the only thing we can do." She looked out over the grass as we saw Max and Gio smoking cigars on the back porch of the mansion, watching us. "We are standing by our men. No matter what the cost."

Reward

Giovanni

Stretching back in my chair and doing a few more of those exercises the physiotherapist taught me a few hours ago helped to ease the tightness in my chest and back. I had come to my office to try and get on top of matters that I had ended up giving to Max to take responsibility for in my absence. He had kept everything running smoothly, but I didn't like not having a handle on things.

I pulled up the CCTV footage we had installed outside the front of the Leone mansion and watched for any developments over the last 24 hours. Everyone was certain it was them who hired the hit on Liv but the more I thought about it, the less likely it seemed. They had backed off from her completely after they gave her the message to tell me to meet them. They hadn't been sighted in Verona and my men who had been watching over Olivia hadn't seen anything suspicious. So why that night? Why pay a homeless man to shoot her? It didn't make any sense. They had their own skilled hit men who could do the job far better. And after Max informed me that neither of them were in the country when it happened, it seemed even less likely.

But then, if it wasn't them, who else would it be? Henry? Possibly. But I had a feeling he was at a point where he had nothing to lose. He would come after her himself, not pay someone else to do it for him. I was growing more and more frustrated that my private investigator had not found him yet. I hated the idea of him being out there on the loose.

Also, Cami had managed to hear some rumours circulating around the Aiani household that one of Francesco's most trusted soldiers was missing. I knew it couldn't have been the homeless shooter as the police have identified him as a man who had been living on the streets for years but it still seemed like a coincidence to have one of his men missing around the same time.

One thing remained though. The Leone's were starting a war. They have formed an alliance with the most ruthless and powerful family in the Cosa Nostra. The only family that could truly take us in numbers and power. And they were still responsible for my father's death. They thought they could use Olivia to get to me. That I would fall into their trap and meet with them alone? What do they take me for? A fucking mug?

But I can't lie and say I wasn't curious as to what they possibly wanted to say to me. I was eighty percent sure it was a trap, to either take me hostage for influence over Sal or to kill me. But there was still that small part of me that wondered if there was some other reason.

All of this was just adding to my fucking headache and body tension as I realised that nothing was falling into place. It's like I had the outer edge of a jigsaw but was missing the centre pieces.

A knock on the door startled me from my thoughts and when Olivia's head popped around it, I beamed.

"Are you busy?"

"I am never too busy for you bambola. Come in," I leaned back in my leather chair and curled my finger, demanding she come inside. She gave me a flirtatious look before she opened the door wider and revealed her body. She stepped into my office and closed the door, locking it from the inside. My eyes travelled down her body and my eyebrows furrowed at what she was wearing.

"Why are you wearing my robe?" I also noticed she was wearing heels.

She turned and leaned back against the door and the look in her eyes made me instantly hard.

"I heard you were a good boy today for the Physio."

My lips curled up into a sly smirk as I clasped my hands together. "I was."

"Well, I guess you deserve your reward then." I knew my heated eyes would be giving away my excitement as she slowly started to undo the knot in the belt. "Your personal shopper came by today. Gave me far too many things that I do not need Giovanni." Her voice was a seductive purr, and I couldn't take my eyes off her as she opened the robe and let it fall to her feet.

Holy shit.

"But I decided there was no harm in keeping a few items. What do you think?"

I gulped as my eyes roamed every inch of her mouth-watering curves in the sexiest lingerie I had ever seen. It was all black lace but had extra thin straps over her hips and breasts, giving a bondage vibe as well as a suspender belt and sheer stockings. She looked fucking incredible. She prowled towards me like a lioness as I sat motionless, enjoying the view.

"Cat got your tongue?" she smirked.

"Bambola, you look insane," I growled, my voice a deep rumble and I licked my lips.

She put her hands on the arms of my chair and pushed me back so she could give herself enough room to perch on my desk in front. I leaned forward and ran my hands up her thighs, but she pushed them off, wagging her finger at me. I frowned as I sat back in my chair again.

"Ah, that is not your reward. I seem to remember a time when you enjoyed watching me… touch myself."

Her eyes held my gaze, and I bit my bottom lip. Fuck me. Please tell me she is going to give me a show.

"Hmmm, but I never got to see you come. I felt robbed."

She smiled with sass and my raging boner was now becoming really fucking uncomfortable in my trousers.

"Well how about we put that right?"

She leaned her hands back on my desk and lifted each of her heels onto the arms of my chair, spreading her long, slender legs wide in front of me, giving me the perfect view. I grabbed her ankles in my hands to stop me from diving at her. Lifting one hand, she first caressed one of her tits in her lace bra, playing with her nipples through fabric, and I licked my lips again. My mouth was watering. Her lips parted and she moaned softly, causing my dick to pulse against the restriction of my trousers. I dropped my head back against my headrest as my hooded eyes watched her hand travel further south where she started to rub herself over her knickers. I groaned as I watched her breathing increase, and her fingers working in circular motions. She was so fucking sexy, it was insane.

"Let me see you bambola," I husked, and she met my command by pulling her black lace knickers to the side and showing me her sweet, pink pussy. She started to pleasure herself and when she pushed two fingers inside her vagina, I practically growled. My breathing was hard and my jaw tight as I watched her bringing herself closer. When my eyes flickered up to hers, I groaned as I realised she was watching me intensely. Just like she did that day behind the door.

"You are so fucking gorgeous Liv. Look how hard you make me," I breathed as I unzipped my trousers and pulled out my erection. I was rock hard as I slowly started to move my hand up and down my length, pleasuring myself as I watched her. Her eyes watched me hungrily and she started to become breathless as she circled her clit again. Her legs began to shake on the arms of my chair and I kept my eyes glued on her face so I could watch her climax. She dropped her head back, her tits rising and falling with frantic breaths as she cried out her orgasm. I had to stop pumping myself or I would have fucking cum just watching her.

I dove at her. I had enjoyed the show but my whole body was craving to touch her myself. To fuck her until she was screaming my name. Grabbing the back of her neck, I crashed my lips against hers as she was still coming down from her pleasure and pulled her lace material down from her breasts so I could play with her beaded nipples. She moaned loudly against my lips as she wrapped her legs around my waist, pulling me into her. I was still fully clothed with just my dick out as I pushed her down to lie flat on the surface of my desk. I placed feathery kisses down her body, giving each nipple some attention from my tongue and teeth until I reached her soaking centre. Hooking her legs over my shoulders, I knelt and devoured her pussy, moaning against her wetness as she shook on the table. Keeping her in place with my firm hand over her stomach, I enjoyed every lick, flick and suck of her clit, before I plunged into her centre and fucked her with my tongue. She was a moaning mess by the time I had had my fill and I stood up, staring down at her spread wide for me on my desk. She looked up at me through her dark eyelashes, panting heavily as I wrapped my hand around her neck and positioned myself at her entrance.

"I am going to be fast and rough, bambola. Tell me to stop if it's too much," I ordered, and she gave me a seductive smile.

"Be as rough as you like, Gio. I love it," she breathed and I roared as I slammed inside her hard and deep, pulling her body down onto my dick by her throat. I didn't stop there as I pounded her tight pussy relentlessly as she screamed my name and ordered me to fuck her faster. Without warning, I pulled out of her and grabbed her around the waist, flipping her so her stomach was against my desk. I groaned at the sight of her delicious ass bending over my desk and pushed her legs out wider so I could settle between them.

Rubbing my dick up and down her dripping slit, she whimpered and begged for more. I eased into her slowly this time as I felt myself fill her to the base and she cried out at the intensity. Once I was fully inside her, I spanked her ass cheek and she screamed in pleasure and pain, which made me smirk. She tried to move against me but I leaned over her body, my weight holding her still and whispered, "Shall I make you cum on my cock, bambola?"

"Yes," she panted, and I nibbled her ear lobe.

"What are the magic words?"

"Fuck me now!" She growled, impatient and feisty as always. I chuckled.

"Good girl." Grabbing her arms behind her back, I held on tightly to them as I did what she asked of me. I fucked her hard, fast and deep. Seeing her bent over my desk like this in this sexy lingerie and heels while I was still fully dressed was the most erotic fuck of my life and I doubted I would ever get any work done on this desk again. Watching the pleasure on her side profile, cheek to my desk as I claimed her again and again, had me close to coming. When I was sure she could handle more, I went deeper, rougher, pulling her body back by her arms. Her tits bounced against the surface of my desk as she screamed my name.

I felt her walls clench around me as she came on my dick and she wasn't quiet about it. I couldn't hold back.

"Fuck Liv!" I growled as I plunged into her one last time, lost in her. I released her arms and rested my hands on the desk at the sides of her slumped body as I tried to calm my breathing. I pulled out of her slowly and she gasped as I sat back on my chair, utterly spent.

She stood up and turned around. I grabbed her hand and pulled her down onto my lap as I kissed her lips.

"That was quite a reward."

"I seemed to get something out of it too," she smirked and I chuckled, burying my head into her neck and kissing her skin.

"How am I supposed to ever get anything done in this room again? Every day I will have the memory of you spread over my desk in this insanely hot underwear."

"Life is all about balance, Gio. Work hard to play hard," she winked at me and I kissed her lips. Shit, I was getting hard again. Suddenly, my office phone rang, breaking our kiss, and I groaned.

"Aren't you going to get that?" She asked.

"No, let it go to voicemail." I leaned back towards her, sliding my tongue across her lips again as I heard the beep. My zio's deep voice was an instant mood killer.

"Giovanni. Francesco, Enzo, Toni and I will be coming to the house tomorrow at 10am to discuss wedding plans. I expect Maximus and Camilla to also attend. Don't fuck this up. Ciao."

Dropping my head back against the leather chair and closing my eyes, I inhaled deeply.

"If the stick up his arse was any bigger, he'd be a frickin' tree."

I laughed loudly at her insult and she gave me a dazzling smile. "I have to agree. I guess there is no time like the present. Are you ready bambola? Tomorrow is going to be intense."

"You want me to be there?" she asked, surprised.

I have thought about this a lot. All the different possible ways to tell Sal and Francesco that the wedding was not going ahead. I knew she would be in danger the moment it left my lips from the Aianis, so I wanted her with me where I could protect her.

"Yes, I want you by my side. Always."

The smile she gave me melted my cold heart.

The Alliance

Olivia

"So, what is your plan exactly?" Cecilia asked as she paced the cream carpet of the private living room in her black silk pantsuit. She looked nervous. She looked how I felt. But I was trying to hide my anxiety for Gio's sake. He didn't need to be worrying about me when he had so much stress to deal with already.

"We will tell him the truth. I will make it clear that I am with Liv and Max will marry Camilla to maintain the alliance. If Francesco is not happy with that, I would suggest Max becomes underboss."

"And if they don't go for any of it? You know how ugly this could get, Giovanni. Do you really think it is best to have Liv and Camilla here?" Her brown eyes flickered at me and I sat up straighter.

"I want to be here, Cecilia. We have a right to be. This is about us after all," I glanced at Camilla who was sitting next to Max on the opposite sofa and she gave me a smile of unity.

Cecilia breathed in deeply as Giovanni leaned back on the sofa we were both perching on and threw his muscular arm around the back of me. "Mamma, try not to stress. You never know, this could all work out for the best and we may get what we all want."

She scoffed loudly and shook her head. The door of the living room opened and we all tensed until we saw Elle strolling through, looking as beautiful and trendy as ever. She was wearing a mini leather skirt with a baggy black T-shirt tucked in and killer studded ankle boots.

"What are you doing here?" Cecilia asked as Elle walked past Max and Cami, giving them both kisses on the cheek before she came and sat next to me.

"Showing my support for my favourite couples, of course. You didn't think I was going to be left out of the drama, did you?" she teased, and Cecilia looked at Giovanni for help.

He raised his hands up in surrender. "Not my idea. These three women come as a package deal now."

I grinned at him over my shoulder as I turned back to Elle and gave her a wink.

"Sal is not going to be happy with this."

"Cecilia, come and sit down. Relax. No one has died yet," Max smirked as she paused her pacing to give him a death glare. She was so on edge and I can't say it wasn't making my insides curl at the sight of her out of character behaviour. Gio placed his huge hand on my knee and I looked down and realised my leg had been bouncing with nerves. His firm but soothing grip calmed me as he caressed my skin with his fingers.

"What's all this?" The unmistakable and intimidating voice of Salvatore Buccini caused my heart to race. We all looked over at the doorway as he strode in with an air of authority and arrogance, his black eyes scanning each of our faces but resting on me. I gulped as I saw the pissed-off expression at me being here. "I didn't call for a fucking family reunion Giovanni. This is a business meeting. All of you out," he commanded.

No one moved, which caused his square jaw to tick with irritation.

"This business meeting affects everyone in this room so they will all stay. This is my house and theirs. If you wanted a private meeting, you could have hosted it at yours," Gio kept his voice polite and calm but it also had an edge of authority. Challenge. I could now feel my heart thundering against my rib cage as the two most powerful men in the room glared at each other.

"Sal. Gio is right. This does affect us all. Please let them stay," Cecilia stepped up to his uncle and placed her hand on his pin-striped suit jacket. His face softened ever so slightly as he looked at her.

"I don't see how this affects anyone but Giovanni and Camilla."

"Please. Take a seat and we will explain everything. Before Toni brings Francesco in. Please Sal. Hear them out."

I couldn't stop staring at Cecilia. I was in awe of this woman. Just moments ago, she was a nervous wreck and now she had that calm and stern mask on and was commanding the most control and power of this terrifying man. He huffed angrily but listened to her as he undid his suit button and took a seat in an armchair.

I finally felt like I could breathe again, but I knew we were only just getting started. Gio gave me a reassuring smile before he pulled himself up off the sofa and walked over to the mini bar in the room. We all sat in silence as he poured his uncle a dark coloured drink and strolled over to him confidently to hand it over.

After Sal took his first swig, Giovanni spoke.

"I understand the importance of this alliance with the Aianis and I know that it is vital we have their support going forward. However, I believe there is a way of keeping that alliance and still allowing us all to get what we want."

"What are you saying Giovanni," Sal hissed. "If you are choosing that nanny over your loyalty to this family, so help me God. You will regret it."

I swallowed my fear as his molten black irises blazed with rage when he looked my way. I noticed Gio's body tense, his back muscles rippling in that tight black shirt, but he kept his cool.

"Her name is Olivia. This is bigger than just me and my feelings, Boss. Yes, I am with Olivia and trust me when I say no one will come between us.

But this is not just about me. Camilla is also in love with someone else."

Sal's eyes widened as his head snapped to Camilla.

"I don't see why I should care about that. This is a marriage alliance to benefit both families, not some fucking match-making mission."

"But that is what I am trying to say. We can still keep the alliance and she can marry the person she chooses," Gio stated calmly.

"Who?" Sal's curiosity snapped.

"Me," Max said, standing up from the sofa, crossing his hands in front of his body. His eyes held his uncles in challenge, and we all held our breath.

A slow, disbelieving chuckle started from Sal's chest and soon turned into a raucous, vindictive laugh. "You? She is in love with you?"

No one spoke and I could feel my own anger building at his harsh dismissal and lack of respect for Max.

"Maximus and Camilla will marry instead and keep the alliance," Gio raised his voice slightly over Sal's laughter and I could hear the irritation in his tone. He was protective of his cousin too. The only person who didn't seem surprised or upset by Sal's reaction was Max himself. He held his gaze on his uncle, his face expressionless, and waited patiently.

"You are all fools if you think Francesco will go for this."

"He will have no choice if you order it. We all know you have the upper hand in this deal. If you change the conditions, what can he do? He will not back out of such an association, that will bring his family phenomenal power and wealth," Max spoke confidently, as if he had rehearsed this. He probably had.

Sal's laughter stopped as he raised his hand and rubbed his bristly, grey stubbled jaw.

"And why would I do that? That just sounds like far too much trouble than it's worth. I gave Francesco my word that his daughter would be married to a future boss and I do not go back on my word."

Gio walked away from Sal, back towards me. Our eyes locked and he gave me a small smile before turning back to his uncle.

"I understand and respect that your word is loyal Boss. Which is why I am willing to give up my title to Maximus. I will happily allow him to step up to underboss and I will become Capo. He is more than capable of such a role and if this alliance and your word is as important as you say, it is a sacrifice I am willing to make."

Everyone watched as the colour drained out of Sal's face and he turned a shade of grey. His eyes narrowed and his nostrils flared. He looked lethal.

"It is, of course, your choice, Boss. Whatever is best for the family," Gio added before returning to his position on the sofa and leaning back, placing his arm behind me on the back of the chair. I gave him a sideways glance as he continued to watch his uncle like a hawk. Fuck, I loved this man. I wasn't sure what I was expecting, but it wasn't that. He held his own with so much grace and discipline of his emotions and I couldn't be prouder.

Suddenly, the door opened again and Sal's lap dog, that bastard, Toni, waltzed in with a shit-eating grin followed by a short and overweight man who looked exactly how all those mafia bosses in the films looked. He had an arrogant and aggressive aura with an unpleasant face and I immediately hated him. How could someone as beautiful as Cami come from a man like that? Her mother must be gorgeous.

"I see the whole Buccini family are as excited about this wedding as we are. How lovely that you all wanted to be involved," he smirked as he took a seat on the sofa closest to Cami and Max. His beady eyes fell onto her and he looked her up and down slowly.

"Daughter. You look well. I trust your fiancé has been taking good care of you?" His tone was almost sarcastic. He didn't really care.

"Si papi," Cami's voice was a timid whisper and I watched her body shrivel just in his presence. It made my blood boil.

"This is my son, Enzo. Underboss of the Aiani family."

I quickly noticed a young, skinny man with dark blonde hair and blue eyes sitting next to his father. He was wearing a grey suit that looked too big for him and he nodded his head once to all of us in greeting. He couldn't be more than nineteen years old. How was he an underboss already?

"Cecilia, you are looking ravishing as always," Francesco's eyes roamed her body suggestively as he didn't try to hide his desire for her and I felt Gio's body tense next to me, but it was Sal who quickly changed the subject.

"There has been a change of plans."

My eyes widened in disbelief as the words left his hard lips. Everyone else seemed just as shocked as they stared at the Boss in anticipation.

"What change?" Francesco's tone was dangerously low as he narrowed his eyes at Sal. The air felt like it was sucked out of the atmosphere from the tension that surrounded us all.

"Camilla is not going to marry Giovanni. She is going to marry Maximus. Our Capo of Trieste."

Gio sat forwards instantly as he looked across at Max. Camila was beaming from ear to ear as Max looked down at her with a smile, but her smile soon fell at her father's outburst.

"Him? This thug? A CAPO? That was not the arrangement we made, Salvatore. You promised my daughter would be the Boss' wife! She is worth more than some worthless Capo of Trieste!"

"Watch who you are raising your voice at Francesco," Sal snarled from his position leaning back in the armchair. Both bosses were in a stand-off, and everyone waited with bated breath. "When Giovanni becomes Boss, Maximus will be underboss, so there is no difference in positions for the future. The alliance still stands."

What? I couldn't believe my ears. Was Salvatore siding with Giovanni?

Was he actually allowing this to happen? Max to marry Camilla and Gio to keep his title?

"This is barbaric even for you, Salvatore. We had a fucking deal," Francesco hissed. "My daughter is not marrying a fucking capo!"

Abruptly, Francesco stood up and stormed towards Cami, grabbing her violently by the wrist.

"Get up you whore. We are leaving!"

The next few moments happened at such rapid speed that my eyes and brain had a hard time keeping up. Maximus had pulled his gun out of his ripped jeans and had forced it into Francesco's temple. Enzo, the son, had his gun pointed at Max from over his father's shoulder and Gio had jumped up and was aiming his gun at Enzo.

The only man who hadn't moved in the room was Sal as he lounged back in the armchair with an amused expression at the scene before him.

"Get your fucking hands off her, you piece of shit!" Max growled at Francesco. My heart was pounding in my chest as I looked at Cami's terrified face.

"Who do you think you are speaking to, boy? I AM A FUCKING BOSS AND YOU ARE A DEAD MAN."

"Funny that... yet it is you who is one trigger away from your brains being plastered all over the fucking wall, *Boss.*"

"Enzo will see to it that yours is next!" he hissed as he released Cami's arm with a shove, dropping her back to the sofa.

"And it would be fucking worth it," Max snarled with a grin.

"Drop the gun," Gio ordered Cami's brother, whose eyes darted from Max to Gio and back again. No one moved.

An amused, low chuckle erupted from Sal's chest as he raised his tumbler to his mouth and took a slow sip of brandy. His sinister eyes looked at each of the men carefully.

"Enough. Lower your weapons. No one is dying today."

Gio was the first to slowly lower his gun and Enzo followed. Max pushed the barrel into Francesco's head once before dropping it back down and sitting next to Cami on the sofa. He put a protective arm around her and pulled her to his side as Francesco clenched his jaw and turned back to Sal.

"Now. I can see you are not happy with the new arrangement, Aiani. So, I am willing to make an amendment. You can add one more thing to our contract that will only benefit your family and not ours. Then we can call it even and move the fuck on with killing the fucking Leones," Sal's tone had returned to its serious, intimidating manner. I caught Cecilia's eye as she hovered behind Sal's chair and that nervous look had returned. My stomach clenched with anticipation. Shit, this was all so intense. I mean I knew it would be. These were the fucking mafia! But it had only been ten minutes and already we'd had guns flying.

Francesco brushed down his suit before sitting back down on the sofa. He seemed to have regained some control, but the fury still blazed behind his eyes.

"So, what will it be? 50% of all Columbian channel deals? Unlimited access to our best soldiers?" Sal spoke in a bored tone as he rotated his tumbler in his hand, his shiny watch, catching the rays of sunshine through the window.

It was fascinating. Watching these men in action. I was starting to realise that everything Sal did was calculated and precise. Toni hovered in the background watching everyone and everything like a secret assassin. A spy in the shadows.

Francesco sighed as he lifted one leg over the other, his polished shoe bouncing up and down as he scanned the room. His eyes fell on my beautiful friend sitting next to me and he cocked his head with a sly smile that made my skin crawl. Elenora. No.

"You have a niece? The stunning Elenora Buccini, isn't it?" His voice had the venom of a poisonous snake. I felt both Gio and Elle's bodies tense either side of me. I grabbed her hand in her lap protectively as I peered up at her expressionless face as she visibly gulped.

"My daughter is not part of this arrangement," Cecilia stepped forwards, hissing.

"No, she wasn't. But I think it is rather fitting now, don't you? You have my daughter for your... capo. I will take yours for my son."

"No fucking way," Giovanni growled as my mouth dropped open.

"You can't! Sal!" Cecilia pleaded as she turned to her brother-in-law in desperation. He lightly drummed his thick fingers against the arm of the chair as he seemed deep in thought.

"It seems like a fair exchange."

Giovanni jumped up from the sofa and I grabbed his hand to stop him from doing something he would regret. Elle seemed frozen in a state of shock next to me.

"He is a fucking kid! My sister is not going to marry him or become part of your fucked up family!" Gio bellowed.

"Salvatore! Please do something," Cecilia cried as she fell to her knees at the side of his chair, grabbing his arm.

"There is nothing I can do. If this is the price to pay for your son's freedom, then this is what must be done." He said sternly without looking her way, and a lazy, wicked smirk grew on Francesco's face. No. She couldn't go and live with that vile monster. The man- no boy beside him- looked just as shocked and terrified at the prospect of suddenly being given a wife.

"Over my dead body!" Giovanni shouted in rage.

"Then marry my daughter!" Francesco bellowed back.

"Stop!"

We all froze as we turned to look at Elle who was hiding her face beneath her hair as she looked down at her lap. Her hands were shaking as she glanced up slowly at Giovanni and then me. I could see the emotion in her eyes.

"I'll do it. I will go with them."

A Shocking Turn of Events
Cecilia

No. I can't let this happen. Not Elle. Not that family. As I looked wide-eyed and pale-faced at my eldest daughter and the pure terror in her eyes, I knew what I had to do. I was willing to do it for Gio if it came to that and I was willing to do it for Elle. I knew what would happen once she was handed over to that vulture. She would be treated like an object, used for Francesco's entertainment, and that wannabe Boss next to him wouldn't be able to do a thing about it. He was just a boy himself.

"Then we have a deal," Francesco smirked, licking his lips as his eyes roamed Elenora's body and she gulped.

"My sister is going nowhere with you," Giovanni growled, glaring at Francesco.

From my position kneeling on the floor next to Sal, I looked up at his expressionless face. He could stop this. He was the only one who could stop this from happening without bloodshed. He had all the power and he knew it. Yet, he was doing nothing. Because he gained nothing.

My heart plummeted in my chest and my lips trembled with the intense emotions of guilt and betrayal towards Vinny at what I was about to do.

"No. Stop." I shouted, causing everyone to pause. My eyes were locked on Sal's face as he turned his distinguished features towards me. Holding his gaze, his eyes sparkled with curiosity and hope as he realised what I was thinking; what I was about to say.

Leaning up to his ear, I whispered, "Smettila e io sarò tuo. (Stop this and I will be yours.)"

My voice wobbled on the last word and as I moved back from his ear, the look in his eyes was a mix of disbelief and joy. I nodded slowly as a small smile curled at the corners of his mouth and he reached for my hand, giving it a squeeze.

"Non c'è ritorno da questo. Sei sicuro? (There is no going back from this. Are you sure?)" He grumbled under his breath but everyone in the room heard him and were watching us both intensely, unaware of what had just been promised.

"Si," I said with conviction. I had made up my mind. My happiness was a small price to pay for my children.

The widest grin spread across Sal's face and for a moment, I was transported back to the night I first met him. A handsome young man who had the world at his feet.

Abruptly, he stood up and ran his hand through his silvery hair. He walked over to the mini bar and poured two glasses of brandy. No one spoke or moved, they just watched him intensely. The atmosphere in the room was so thick you could cut it with a knife. Strolling back over to the group of us, he stopped in front of Francesco and offered him one of the glasses.

Francesco gave Giovanni an evil, triumphant smirk as he took the glass from Sal and both men raised their tumblers in the air.

"To our alliance," Francesco stated before bringing the glass to his thin lips.

"No." Sal said calmly but with clear venom laced through his tone. Francesco paused, his bushy eyebrows tightening in confusion. "To your death."

In a flash, Sal had whipped out his gun from under his suit jacket and shot Francesco between the eyes.

I fell from my knees to the floor in shock as the girls screamed and Max and Gio jumped up pointing their guns at Enzo who had turned as white as a sheet and cowered away from his dead papi's body slumped next to him on the sofa.

Silence took hold of the room once more as every one's eyes bulged at Sal, who lowered his gun and placed it back in his gun harness under his suit jacket. He rubbed his jaw as he turned his attention to the young, shaken boy next to him.

"Congratulations are in order. Enzo Aiani. New Boss," Sal smirked, and the boys' blue eyes widened as he looked from Sal to Gio and Max who still had their guns aimed at his head. "That is if you are willing to still hold onto your end of our original deal?"

Enzo visibly gulped as he realised he was being given two options. Form an alliance with Sal or end up like his father.

Turning his head, he peered over at Cami, who was pale from the shock of watching her father murdered in front of her very eyes, but to my surprise she didn't seem upset. She nodded slowly at her brother.

"Si. Formerò un'alleanza con te. (Yes. I will form an alliance with you.)"

"Clever boy. And I am assuming you will take care of this sticky situation with the commission for me? As your first task of Boss," Sal nodded towards the bloody head of Francesco and took a sip from his Brandy.

Enzo nodded slowly. "He died in a drug cartel gone wrong."

Sal beamed as he turned to look at Giovanni over his shoulder.

"I am impressed already. Guns down." He nodded towards Toni, who pulled out some paperwork from his briefcase.

"Let's end this drama and sign the contracts. You are now a very rich and powerful young man, my boy. But don't you ever forget who gave it to you and who can just as easily take it all away," Sal snarled, his intimidating and hostile tone was back.

Enzo gulped down his fear but stood up slowly and reached his hand out to Sal, who shook it with force.

Everyone else sat in silence and possibly unable to actually make a move as their brains tried to piece together what exactly had just happened. Gio and Elle kept giving me glances of concern which I refused to acknowledge. They would have questions. They want to know what it is that I said to Sal to make him do what he just did.

I forced myself to stand up from the carpet and walk over to where the men were setting up the contracts on the coffee table. This was my role. I had to witness every signature for contracts between our family and business deals.

I watched Enzo's hand shaking as he signed his name on the line his papi was supposed to. The original deal was still in place except I had to change the marriage clause from Giovanni to Maximus. Once everything was signed. Everyone started to filter out of the room and our men were called in to dispose of Francesco's body discreetly.

I stormed out of the living room alone, feeling an overwhelming sense of panic creeping up on me when a firm hand grabbed my wrist.

"We need to talk," Sal whispered slowly as I turned my head around.

"Yes. I think we all need to talk." Giovanni hissed at both of us before storming away. "My office. Now."

Liv raced after him as they climbed the stairs and I turned back to Sal's grinning face. My stomach dropped. "It's time he knew the truth, CeCe."

He let go of my wrist and started up the stairs after my son as I stood frozen in the lobby. My worst nightmare was coming true, and I could do nothing to stop it.

***

Giovanni

What the fuck just happened?

I stormed into my office, feeling extremely on edge after that shit show. I mean there was a part of me that was elated. We got what we wanted. I am keeping my position and no longer have to marry Camilla. Max and Cami are going to be married and we keep the original alliance that we need in order to take out the Leone's. I should be shouting from the rooftops how happy I am but I couldn't. Something was going on between Sal and mamma and it left me feeling cold.

Liv entered my office after me, pausing to watch me pacing the room, hand on hip.

"I- I don't know what to say," she spoke quietly.

"That shouldn't have happened. Not that it is a bad thing. It's fucking great for us but… Boss would never have done that to save the alliance. Murdering a fucking boss is downright risky even if it is meticulously planned and he just did that on impulse! Why? Why would he do that?" I spoke loudly, trying to get all my thoughts out quickly before Sal and mamma came up.

"I don't know. Whatever your mamma said to him must have worked," Liv said carefully as she stepped towards me and put her hands on my arms to stop my frantic movements. I pulled her into my chest, hugging her tightly to try and calm the uneasy feeling inside me.

"But what could she have possibly said for him to do that? For him to risk everything?"

Just at that moment, my uncle waltzed into my room with a gleeful look on his face which faltered slightly when he saw me hugging Liv. She tried to pull out of my embrace but I held her to me tighter. I needed her right now.

"What was that Boss?" I asked him directly as his dark eyes flickered from Liv back to me.

"I suppose it is out of the question to expect her to leave? This is a family matter after all."

"She is family now. And I expect you to treat her as such. She stays."

His eyes narrowed at my tone but his smile returned as mamma walked into the room looking extremely nervous and pale.

"Fine. Shall we all sit down?" My zio walked over to an armchair and pointed at it for mamma to take a seat. Her terrified eyes scanned his face and then mine before she silently sat down next to him. My jaw ticked as I looked between them. Something was definitely wrong here.

Releasing Liv, I perched on the edge of my desk with my arms folded as Liv did the same next to me.

"Don't look at me like that, Giovanni. I am still your Boss," Sal growled when I could no longer hide the anger and irritation on my face when no one spoke.

"I am just trying to understand what exactly made you think it would be a good idea to shoot the Aiani Boss in my house?"

"What is the problem? You got what you wanted?" He shrugged.

"What if Enzo goes straight to the commission about this? What is stopping him?"

"He won't. Because we have his sister and I have made it very clear that if he betrays us, I will send her head back to him in a box before the commission can get to me."

Liv gasped next to me, her hand slamming over her mouth and Sal chuckled.

"You better toughen up girly, if you want to be in this world."

"But why kill him? Why not just try to negotiate a better deal?" I asked. I already knew the answer but I wanted to hear him say it.

"You know why, Giovanni. He would never have given up on Elenora. And I would have been backed into a corner seeing as you fucked up the first deal so royally. So, I had no choice."

"But you were happy to hand her over," I growled, the anger returning at the thought of my little sister going to live with that family. With those men. "What changed?" I glanced over at mamma accusingly, knowing she had something to do with his sudden change of mindset.

The look my uncle gave mamma made my blood run cold. "Cecilia, do you want to tell him or shall I?"

Mamma's eyes widened as she fiddled with her fingers on her lap. She looked so small and vulnerable suddenly and I stood up straight. "Mamma? What is going on?"

"I- Sal and I are going to be together now."

I froze. What did she just say? My eyes roamed her face to my zio's who looked like the cat that got the fucking cream. "What?"

"You heard her, Giovanni. Your mamma and I are in love and we will be getting married."

Even mamma's head snapped up in surprise at his words. I couldn't believe this. This had to be some kind of sick joke.

"We will all be a proper family now. Like we always should have been," Sal said as he smiled at mamma, who looked like she wanted to cry or run away.

I snapped. "This is a joke, right? You are fucking with me? You can't be serious?"

Sal stood up quickly, his eyes darkening with fury. "I am deadly serious Giovanni, so calm the fuck down."

"You are my uncle! She was married to your brother! What the fuck is going on?" I bellowed as mamma flinched in her chair and Liv gripped my bicep in an attempt to calm me, but I was too far gone.

No one spoke for a few moments, and I held my uncle's stern gaze in challenge. "That is not entirely true, Giovanni."

"Sal... no! Please don't," mamma whimpered as the tears started rolling down her face.

"He deserves to know the truth, CeCe."

"Know what?!"

"Non sono tuo zio. Sono tuo papi. (I am not your uncle. I am your father.)"

The ground crumbled from beneath my feet.

Past Mistakes
Cecilia

"Gio!" I cried as the look of complete shock and betrayal engraved into every one of his handsome features.

"Is it true?" he hissed, stepping towards me.

"I- I don't know. It might be. Gio, I am so sorry! Please let me expl-"

"You have had 29 years to explain!!" He erupted, his nostrils flaring and eyes burning with so much hurt as he glared down at me. He fled from the room and Liv gave me a sympathetic look before she ran out after him.

Turning my attention to the man that had just ruined my life, I glared at him with every ounce of hatred my body possessed.

"How dare you! How dare you do that to him! To me!" I screamed, standing up from the chair to run from him. I couldn't be anywhere near this man right now.

He slammed his hand on the door before I could get to it and blocked me in. "It is time he knew, Cecilia. Now we are going to be together, he had a right to know."

"No! I don't even know if you are his father, Salvatore! How could you do that?"

"He is my son! I have known it from the moment I laid eyes on him. I am sorry it had to come out the way it did, but you could have changed all of this a long time ago! I am sick and tired of waiting, Cecilia. You are mine now and Giovanni is my heir. I will give you some space to calm down, but then I will send for you. You will be moving in with me and we will be married by the end of the week."

He opened the door swiftly and made his way down the stairs where Toni was waiting for him in the lobby. I raced to my bedroom and locked the door before falling to my knees in despair. I don't know how long I stayed there, curled in a ball on the floor, sobbing. But when the tears had dried up and emptiness took hold, I pulled myself up and walked into the bathroom. Holding up my fragile body by placing my hands either side of the sink, I stared at the reflection of a broken and defeated woman. I had no strength left in my bones; no tears left to cry.

This was all my doing. This was all my fault.

30 years ago…

"*Congratulazioni CeCe!*" my friend Nadia raised her champagne flute in the air and clinked her glass with mine as I beamed back at her. I had just secured my very job at a new law firm and I have to admit, I had never been prouder of myself!

"*Grazie!*" I took a sip of my champagne as my eyes scanned the packed club that Nadia had dragged me to celebrate. The fluorescent beams were showering the bodies that were grinding and jumping about on the dance floor and I felt suddenly over dressed in my work suit while all these other twenty-something girls strutted around in their skimpy dresses.

"You should have let me go home and change first!" I shouted over the music to my friend who was also dressed in suitable clubwear.

"No! You look great! Sexy and sophisticated! I wish I could wear suits at work," she whined.

I chuckled and shook my head. Nadia worked in a little corner coffee shop and had done since we finished university. She was a bit of a wanderer and still didn't know which direction to take her life. Unlike me, who had always had a carefully mapped out plan since I was five.

I placed my hand over the top of my glass as Nadia attempted to top it up. I was in a good mood today. No, I was feeling incredible! And when I feel this way, I tend to go a little crazy after a few drinks. It's like a button on me is pressed and I think to hell with everything and just go for it. Which is a lot of fun but can also get me in a lot of trouble which I really do not need now. I was trying to be taken seriously as a newly qualified lawyer.

"Come on! At least finish the bottle with me," she pleaded and I tilted my head.

"Urgh. Fine."

She whooped with glee as she poured more champagne into my glass. That was the moment my night changed. Over her shoulder, I could see a swarm of people suddenly acting quite bizarrely, as if a celebrity had just walked in or something. When they all parted, I saw what all the fuss was about. A group of very attractive and sexy men all dressed in black with bulky bodies were pushing through the crowd with serious expressions. They were clearly protecting someone important. As they came closer to our table, my eyes fixed on a striking man with jet black hair, high cheekbones and dark eyes between them all. He looked dangerous. He looked like the ultimate bad boy. Just my type. No. I was trying to change. After all the terrible failed relationships of my past, I had promised myself to stay away from the bad boys. But I have to admit, this one was pretty tempting.

He was wearing a very well fitted, tailored suit and rings on every finger. As he walked past our table, his eyes locked with mine and my stomach flipped. Yes. Sexy as hell. He never took his eyes off me as he walked past with an arrogant swagger, until he disappeared with all those men behind a black curtain at the corner of the room. I turned my attention back to Nadia, who was watching me with an amused expression, wriggling her eyebrows.

"What?" I feigned innocence as I took off my suit jacket and threw it over the back of the chair.

"I saw the eye fucking that was just going on. Don't even try to deny it!"

I rolled my eyes and downed my champagne.

"Let's dance!" I shouted, pulling her off her chair by her arm to change the subject. We spent the next hour or so dancing to upbeat music and drinking. I could feel myself getting looser and I was past the point of trying to be my best version of myself. I was having a good time and so I should! I had earned it. Wearing my grey, tight pencil skirt, cream silk shirt and heels, I stood out like a saw thumb in this crowd, but I didn't care. I had freed my long blonde hair from its bun and undid some of my buttons on my shirt to give a little glimpse of cleavage in my lacy white bra. That would have to do.

"Signorina, per favore, vieni con me, (Miss, please, come with me)" A deep voice from behind me on the dance floor caused me to turn around. There was one of those huge, muscular men all dressed in black with a stern expression.

"Come mai? Chi sei? (Why? Who are you?)" I snapped back, looking him up and down while I carried on dancing to the music.

"Il mio capo vorrebbe parlare con te." He told me his boss wanted to speak to me and I quickly made the connection that the sexy stranger I had been ogling was who he was referring to. Excitement bubbled inside me mixed with the alcohol and I knew my new good girl act had gone out the window.

"Bene. Portami da lui. (Okay. Take me to him.)"

Waving Nadia goodbye, which she barely noticed, with her arms wrapped around some guy, I followed the beefcake towards the black curtain I'd seen them disappear behind earlier. As he pushed it aside, I found myself in a private room with casino tables, a bar, dancers on poles and lots of little booths with sofas and tables. There weren't many people there. Maybe around twenty, all men apart from the dancers.

As I walked towards the end booth with my guide, I felt a lot of provocative eyes on me but I held my chin up higher. Stopping in front of a table, there were two men leaning back on the sofa in the booth, smoking cigars. One I didn't recognise and the other was Mr dark and dangerous. His brown eyes raked down my body hungrily until they came back to my face. He didn't smile or show any emotion as he continued to stare, taking deep drags from his cigar.

I became impatient. He was the one who called me here after all. "Your friend here said you wanted to talk to me. So, are you going to speak or shall I go back to enjoying my night?" I snapped, folding my arms across my chest.

Amusement danced across his molten eyes as he studied me for a little longer. I huffed loudly, about to walk away when he boomed, "Tutti fuori! (Everyone out!)"

I stood still as I watched every single person in the private boudoir leave immediately. Wow. This guy had some power or at least authority over these men.

"Me included?" I asked, curving my eyebrow up at him once we were alone.

He placed his cigar down in the ashtray and stood up swiftly, taking a few menacing steps towards me, so he was towering over me. He wasn't extremely tall but was at least half a head above me. I stood my ground, showing he didn't intimidate me even though he kind of did. A small smile played on his lips when I didn't move or break his penetrating gaze.

"Donna grintosa (feisty woman)," he smirked as he picked up a strand of my blonde hair in his fingers and flicked it over my shoulder. "What is your name?"

"CeCe. What is yours?"

He licked his lips slowly as he made me wait with anticipation. "Salvatore, but you can call me Sal."

"How kind of you," I teased, and his smile grew.

He lifted his rough hand and grabbed my jaw in a firm grip, brushing his thumb over my bottom lip, smudging my red lipstick. I stood frozen. I would never let a man touch me like this normally, but there was something about him that made me want more. He was the scariest yet most attractive man I had ever met and just that action had my core tightening and body aching with arousal.

"I have been waiting for a woman like you for a long time," his deep voice and the proximity of his face to mine, had my mind spinning, but I wouldn't give in to him so easily. I guessed he was a man who liked a bit of cat and mouse.

"And what makes you think the wait is over?" I bantered back and he chuckled deeply.

"Because you will be in my bed within the next hour."

I scoffed loudly, pulling my jaw from out of his grasp.

"You are pretty sure of yourself, Sal. What if I am not interested?"

I was. I can't deny that my mind was racing with thoughts of how good he might be in bed.

"We both know that is a lie." He ran his ringed finger from my lips down my throat and chest, until he reached the swell of my breasts. My breathing became laboured as he moved my silk blouse to the side to reveal my lacy bra. "From the moment I saw you tonight, I knew you would be mine."

I narrowed my eyes at his words. "I belong to no one."

His eyes darted up from my breast to my face and I gulped at the intensity of his heated glare. "You are mine if I say you are mine. Just give me one night to prove it to you."

He ripped open my blouse, the buttons popping off and I gasped as he cupped one of my boobs and flicked his thumb over my nipple that was concealed under the lace material. He leaned down and tugged my lower lip with his teeth and I moaned. I couldn't help it. I knew sex with this dangerous stranger would be the thrill of a lifetime. And didn't I deserve a reward for my success at work today?

"One night?" I breathed against his lips.

"We'll see," he mumbled back before weaving his fingers into my hair and claiming my lips. And I gave in to him. For one night only. I was Salvatore's.

After my one-night stand with Sal, I snuck out of the hotel room without leaving any contact information. It had been an amazing night filled with raw and passionate sex but that was all I wanted from this man. He was bad news, and I could tell he was extremely dangerous. Someone that I didn't need in my life or to ever see again.

A few days later, I walked into the small interview room in the police station, where my new client was being detained. I paused when I saw his muscular frame, bulging muscles and thick black hair from the back. My heart flipped in my chest as for a moment I thought it might have been Sal. But I knew it wasn't. This man was bigger, taller, more muscular and a strange tingle of anticipation danced across my skin just on seeing his back profile. Squaring my shoulders and lifting my chin, I strutted into the cold, unwelcoming interrogation room to face my first ever client. I worked for the local law firm and, as it was his right, he was allowed a civil court representative as well as his personal lawyer. Looking around the room though, his lawyer had not arrived yet, as only one police officer stood on guard by the door.

The click of my heels echoing against the walls, caused him to turn his face towards me for the first time and, honest to God, my heart skipped a beat before it came alive with instant excitement. His swarthy features flickered with surprise as he took in my body, dressed in a formal pantsuit and blonde hair tied up in a high ponytail. He had the darkest olive-black eyes, tanned skin, a slightly dimpled square chin and roughly carved cheekbones. He was the most devilishly handsome creature I had ever laid eyes on.

I buried my instant attraction to this man deep down in the pits of my soul. I would not turn into some love-sick puppy on my first real case. I was a professional and I wasn't going to let some sex-God bad boy derail me.

I pulled out the metal chair on the other side of the table and took a seat, placing my leather briefcase on the table. I could feel his intense stare as I clicked it open and pulled out my files.

"Good afternoon, Mr Buccini. My name is Ms Tessaro and I have been assigned by the court to represent you."

"I already have a lawyer. Though now I am starting to think I may have the wrong one," he flirted, causing a flutter of butterflies in my stomach.

"Well, now you have two. Which I think you are going to need all the help you can get with these charges."

A slow, deliberate smile made him look even more dashing and I had to glance away from his face quickly, so he didn't catch the blush that was spreading up my chest and onto my cheeks. What on earth was wrong with me? I do not let men affect me like that!

"Do you know why you are here?" I began in the most professional tone I could muster.

"Hmmm. I think there was a mention of murder or something," he replied coolly, his voice a deep husk. He said it as if the idea was amusing to him. Murder…Cecilia…did you not hear that?

"Si, Mr Buccini. You have been arrested on suspicion of first-degree murder. This is a very serious charge." I added when I saw he was still smiling as I spoke. Irritation brewed inside me as I realised he wasn't taking any of this seriously in the slightest.

He sat back on his chair, spreading his thick legs out lazily and rested his bound hands on the steel surface of the table between us. My eyes flickered down to his masculine and powerful hands as he started to drum his fingers on the table in a hypnotic motion. It drew my attention so much that for a moment I forgot what I was about to say.

"You don't seem the lawyer type to me," he said with a smirk, his dark eyes twinkling.

I narrowed mine to him. "What do you mean by that?"

"Just that you take me as someone who likes to live dangerously perhaps… Life is boring you, isn't it, Ms Tessaro? You are looking for some excitement, that's why you are here representing me," he teased arrogantly.

I glared at him. "No Mr Buccini. I do not like to live dangerously. That is why I am sitting on this side of the table, on the right side of the law, unlike you."

"Yet you are happy to be representing a man who is accused of being on the wrong side of it? You should know nothing's ever what it seems. Sometimes it is fun to be naughty," he smirked.

"So, you are— "

"Innocent until proven guilty," he interrupted, his heated gaze flickered down to my cleavage in my shirt and then up to my lips. Just that obvious seduction made my body temperature rise.

"Are you saying you are innocent of these charges?" I asked, trying to get back on track and steer the conversation away from me.

He sighed impatiently as he tapped his knuckles on the table. "I did not kill the drug lord."

"But I am guessing you know who did?" I raised an eyebrow at him as he leaned forward on the table. Suddenly, I had a waft of an earthy and musky scent that made my mouth water. His cologne.

"What is your name?"

I blinked back at his dismissal of my question and inappropriateness of his. "I have already told you my name. It's Ms Tessaro."

"Your first name."

"Why is that important?" I asked with irritation. Urgh, this man was infuriating.

"I'd just like to know the name of my future wife so I can inform my family when I get home," he grinned, flashing his pearly white teeth. My eyes widened and I looked away from him.

"Mr Buccini. Please can we get back to— "

"Vincenzo."

"Excuse me?"

"My name is Vincenzo. Vinny or Vin for short. But you can call me whatever you like…"

"Well, I will call you Mr Buccini then," I snarked, and he chuckled deeply from his chest. I squeezed my legs together at the erotic sound.

"As you wish. But I will call you angel until you tell me your name."

He was enjoying this. Teasing me. I huffed loudly in annoyance and picked up the papers from the table, trying to find the information I needed him to sign.

Suddenly, the door opened and a chubby man in a tailored suit strolled in looking a little dishevelled and rushed.

"Scuse! I was stuck in traffic!" Two more police officers filed in behind him and my eyebrows furrowed in confusion. "Why is he cuffed? Free him at once," the stout man ordered, pushing his glasses up the bridge of his nose.

The police officers walked over to Vincenzo and took the cuffs off his wrists as he smirked at me from across the table.

"Wait. What's going on? Who are you?" I asked, frantically.

"I'm Alonzo. Mr Buccini's lawyer. He is free to go."

Vincenzo stood up slowly, his huge frame suddenly feeling rather intimidating from where I was sitting, so I stood up to match his position.

"I don't understand." I said quickly. This was my first case. He was accused of murder. How could he go free?

"I presume you are a civil court lawyer? There has been a misunderstanding and the charges have been dropped. Mr Buccini had nothing to do with this murder. You will no longer be needed," Alonzo said to me dismissively with a nod of the head and turned to walk from the room. I couldn't believe it. My first case and it wasn't even a case! It was a complete waste of my time.

I watched as the insanely hot but frustrating client in front of me gave me a cheeky wink and strolled out of the room as a free man. I huffed loudly and grabbed my notes, shoving them in my briefcase and stomping out in a rage. I was so looking forward to having this assigned to me and now I looked like a fool.

Once I walked out of the station through the entrance doors, I stood on the pavement and closed my eyes, inhaling a deep breath.

"You seem upset, angel? Anyone would think you wanted me locked up," that deep rumble of vocal perfection made me spin on my heels and lose my balance. I stumbled forwards but before I fell to the ground, I felt strong arms wrapping around my body and pulling me into a rock-hard chest. That intoxicating scent invaded my nose and I glanced up in shock at the face of Vincenzo Buccini.

"Are you making fun of me?" I snapped, trying to wriggle out of his grasp, but he held me to him tighter, causing my heart to race.

"Oh angel, I would never dare." He smirked down at me. Suddenly, his face turned serious as his ink-spilled eyes bore into mine.

"I am no angel, Vinny." I looked up at him through my thick eyelashes. I couldn't ignore the euphoric feeling of saying his name out loud. I guess he was no longer my client and a free man. I might as well flirt back. He licked his lips and held his bottom lip between his teeth, which made me so turned on in the middle of a police car park, that it should have been illegal.

"I didn't think you were. But I am no angel either," he lifted his hand and grabbed my ponytail in his fist, pulling it down and forcing my face up to his. I gasped as my lips parted and breathing hitched from the look of desire in his eyes.

"You don't scare me," I whispered, keeping my eyes locked with his.

"Then why can I feel your heart beating so fast?" he husked, lowering his face and brushing his lips lightly against mine. My eyes fluttered shut and then opened again when he pulled back. I wanted more.

"Because I want you to kiss me."

His chest heaved up and down in laboured breaths at my words and his expression was so serious and brooding, it made me want to moan.

"If I kiss you angel, no one else will ever kiss those lips again."

I stared up at him as I realised what meaning his words held. He would claim me. Never allow me to be with another man. And for some reason, I knew they weren't just *words. He meant them. I did the only thing I had ever been so sure of in my life. I kissed him.*

Staring back at my reflection in the mirror thirty years on, I couldn't bear to look at myself. I did this. I slept with both Vinny and Sal within the same week and by the time I found out I was pregnant I was head over heels in love with Vinny and I freaked out. The baby could have been either of theirs but as I had only had sex with Sal one night, I hedged my bets on Gio being Vinny's. Sal of course has never dropped it. He has convinced himself from the moment he heard I was pregnant that the baby was his.

I refused to acknowledge it as a possibility. For the first year or two of Vinny and my relationship, Sal made my life hell. He would pester me and constantly try to get me alone. Tell me he loved me at any chance he got. That he would give it all up, this life, if I would run away with him. But I refused every single time. I loved Vinny. Vinny was the one I chose. I was always surprised that Sal hid what happened between us from Vinny. I think he liked that he and I had a secret together. I wanted to tell Vinny, but I knew it would rip the family apart. Vinny hated to think of me being with another man and it would have killed him if he had known I had slept with Sal even if it was before I had met him. So, I waited. Eventually, Sal stopped trying. When their father died and he became Boss, he threw himself into work and kept his distance from me. It was a huge relief. I knew the reason he paid special attention to Gio growing up and gave him special treatment compared to his other nieces and nephews was because a part of him believed he may have been his son, but we never spoke about it. He never brought it up. Not until today. Not until right now.

And now my dirty secret was out there. Sal had everything he wanted. Me. His son. The family. And what did I have left?

I opened the bathroom cabinet and stared at the pill bottles that contained my sanity. Grabbing them on impulse, I flicked the lids off and poured the pills down the toilet before flushing them away.

If Sal wanted me, he could have me. But I wasn't going to make it easy for him. He should be careful what he wishes for.

Deep Dive

Olivia

It's been nearly two days since Sal dropped that bomb on Gio and I am starting to become really concerned about him. He has gone into a dark place in his mind and closed himself off completely to everyone, including me. He's still there in body but there is a vacant and cold look in his eyes every time I speak to him. He is refusing to speak to Cecilia and find out what the hell all this means and how it could possibly be true. He is burying his head in the sand and refusing to deal with it. Instead, he has thrown himself back into work, his physio (which at least that is a good thing) and swimming. He barely slept last night and when I woke up at 5am he wasn't in bed.

Sighing heavily as I gazed out of Sani's bedroom window at him doing lengths in the pool which I am sure was against his doctor's orders, I felt helpless. He was hurting and I had tried to be soft, patient and understanding. I have tried waiting for him to want to talk about this but how long was he going to push everyone away for?

"Olivia?" A nervous, vulnerable voice from the door caused me to spin on my feet to see Cecilia wearing a black floor length dress. She looked just as awful as her son did. The bags under her eyes showed her lack of sleep and the dullness of her usually vibrant skin was concerning. But again, it was her eyes that spoke volumes. They were only full of sorrow. I was starting to realise that all the Buccinis had that gift. They spoke with their big, brown eyes.

"Cecilia, hi. How are you doing?" I spoke softly as I walked towards her. I hadn't seen her since that day in Gio's office. She had locked herself away in her wing and said the only person she would speak to was Gio but of course he never went to see her.

She stared at me as if I had asked the most ridiculous question in the world.

"Sorry," I sighed, "Of course you are probably feeling as shit as Gio is."

Her dull eyes suddenly sparked with anger.

"I do not need you or anyone else telling me how shit I have made my son feel, thank you very much!" She snapped at me and I cowered back from the shock of her outburst. She had never raised her voice at me before. She had been stern and intimidating, sure. But never like this.

I didn't move and continued to watch her carefully as she sighed loudly and ran one hand through her blonde hair, pulling at it slightly by her scalp.

She was not acting herself at all but after everything, I suppose that wasn't a surprise.

"Sorry," she muttered under her breath.

"No, I'm sorry Cecilia. I didn't mean it to sound the way it did. I wasn't blaming you, I- "

"You should blame me. This is all my fault," The anger had dissolved and her bottom lip trembled with emotion. She was all over the place.

"Cecilia. Shall we sit down? The children are in the playroom with Marco and Cami and I was just tidying their bedrooms so I have time to talk if you want to?"

She looked around her youngest son's room as if she suddenly realised where she was. She walked over to his bed and picked up his very loved teddy that he slept with every night and breathed it in before slumping down on his racing car bed. I strolled over to her and took a seat.

"I met Sal first. A night out. It was a stupid one-night stand," she started, her voice muffled by the teddy she was clinging to. She lifted her head up and inhaled deeply. "I never expected to see him again. A few days later, I met Vinny and it was love at first sight. I know that sounds cliché but it was. The instant connection and chemistry I had with him just made me want to throw away everything I had ever known to be with him. We slept together the same day we met. I know what that sounds like. Sleeping with two men without really knowing either of them but I wasn't always like that. They both had this power of me. Over my body and my emotions."

I nodded slowly, knowing exactly what she meant. I am not even sure how I managed to hold off from sleeping with Giovanni for so long!

"By the time I found out who Vinny really was and made the choice to stay, I was madly in love. I was then introduced to his family and was shocked to walk into a room with Sal sitting on the sofa smoking a cigar and drinking a brandy. I always remember the look on his face when he saw me again. He thought I had found him. He'd been obsessed with looking for the girl who left him in a hotel room apparently. He jumped up with a beaming smile which soon fell when Vinny put his arm around me and introduced me as his girlfriend. Sal and I never told Vinny we had slept together but it didn't stop Sal from wanting more. By the time I realised I was pregnant, I was in too deep with Vinny. I was head over heels in love with him and I was scared I would lose him if I told him the truth. I prayed the doctor would say I was early on in the pregnancy but when I found out I was already two months, I could have cried. The dates matched the same time I met the brothers. I had no idea who the father was. But I lied. I told Sal Gio was Vinny's for certain. I stuck to that story for 29 years. But clearly Sal never believed it."

I reached for her hand and looked at her beautiful side profile as she stared at the floor. Her lip trembled as she spoke about what had caused all of this. I really felt for her. She did what she thought was best in a difficult situation. Knowing how these mafia men are about their women, I knew she did it to protect her relationship and the family. If she had told him the truth, it would have torn the brothers apart. But unfortunately, it was Gio who was now suffering the consequences of her decision.

"I am sorry Cecilia. That you have had to carry the weight of that secret for so long."

"I haven't. I have convinced myself that Vinny is Gio's father. Even if it isn't by blood, Vinny was still his father. He raised him. He loved him. He was the best role model Gio ever had," tears fell from her face and she quickly wiped them away. She suddenly pulled herself together and sat up straight. "I know he doesn't want to speak to me. So, I came to tell you that I am leaving. I am moving in with Sal."

My eyes widened at hearing this. After the shock confession that Sal could possibly be Gio's dad, I had completely forgotten that Cecilia and Sal had announced they were together. Is this really what she wanted?

"Cecilia, I hope you don't think I am stepping out of line here but I have to ask. Do you love him? Salvatore?"

She chuckled sadly and shook her head. "I will never love another man after Vinny."

"Then why are you agreeing to this? Why are you going to be with him?"

"Oh you poor, naïve girl," she stood up suddenly and I frowned. Her mood had changed again and she now seemed cold and angry. "Life is all about sacrifices Olivia. Sal will be here to get me in two hours. Look after my children for me."

My mouth dropped open at her words as she strutted towards the door. "What? Wait! You are leaving Sani and Raya here?"

She turned quickly to look back at me and once again her face showed sudden sadness and intense emotion. "Yes. They will be better off here with you all. Where I am going… I will not be able to care for them."

She stormed out the room, leaving me standing speechless. How? How can she leave her young children to go and live with that man? What did she mean, she wouldn't be able to care for them?

I rubbed my forehead as I felt a headache coming on. This family was something else. There was never just one calm day in this house. Making up my mind, that enough was enough and Gio needed to speak to his mother before she left at least, I made my way downstairs and out to the swimming pool.

He was floating on the water, head over the edge of the pool with his eyes shut when I stomped out onto the decking. He squinted open one eye against the sun to see who was rampaging towards him and shut it again when he saw me. Charming.

"Giovanni. Enough. You need to speak to your mother before it's too late."

"I don't need to do anything," he said in a bored tone. I folded my arms across my chest. He was stubborn but I was too and I don't give up.

"Cecilia is leaving in two hours. Sal is forcing her to move in with him."

He didn't move or speak, just continued to lie in the pool with his eyes closed.

"She told me what happened thirty years ago. If you go and speak to her, she will tell you too."

"I don't want to know. How can I believe anything she says to me? She has lied to me my whole life."

I scoffed loudly which caused his eyes to flicker open and jaw clench. "Gio! I get that you are feeling betrayed and angry and you have every right to feel that way. This is so unfair on you but don't you want to know the truth? Can't you at least hear her out before she leaves?"

"No."

"Fine then you will listen to me. Your mum met Sal on a night out. They had a drunken one-night stand and she didn't even know who he was." Gio abruptly jumped out of the pool, pulling his body up onto the side and grabbed a towel. He tried to storm away from me but I continued. "It was before she met your dad! Before she fell in love with him."

"Which dad?" He snapped back at me over his shoulder. I grabbed his bicep to try and stop him from hurtling away from me again. He shrugged me off aggressively and I lost my footing. My arms were flapping as I stumbled at the edge of the pool but it was too late. I was falling. Fully clothed, in my little dress, straight back into the water.

"Liv!" I heard Gio shout before I went under. I sunk down to the bottom and started to kick up but felt a strong arm around my waist hoisting me through the water to the surface at speed. When we broke through, I inhaled the air sharply and wiped my eyes.

"Are you okay?" His voice was full of panic as I blinked back at him, while we treaded the water to keep us afloat. His arm was still around my waist holding me to his naked torso. I burst out laughing at the serious expression on his face. Did he think I couldn't swim?

His face softened slightly when he saw I wasn't harmed, and a smile stretched across it for the first time in days.

"I can swim, you know! You didn't need to dive in and save me," I giggled as he pulled us over to the shallow end where we could touch the floor.

"How was I supposed to know that? I'm sorry. I didn't mean to push you," he said with pain in his eyes.

I wrapped my arms around his neck and kissed his lips. He froze momentarily but as I sensually licked his lips with my tongue seeking access to his mouth he relaxed and gave into the kiss. It was slow and sweet. Everything it needed to be to get him to drop this concrete wall he had built up around himself. When I felt like he had truly let go, I broke away and gazed into his eyes.

"Come back to me Gio," I whispered against his lips. He closed his eyes and rested his damp forehead against mine. "I love you and I want to help you but you have to let me in."

I wrapped my legs around his waist as his hands roamed my back under the water and he sighed.

"I know. I've been a dick. I just… It is a lot."

I pulled my head away from his and stroked his dripping black hair out of his eyes. "It is. But we can deal with it together."

"Okay." He huffed. "Tell me."

I told him everything Cecilia had said to me and I also mentioned that she didn't seem herself; that her emotions were all over the place. He listened intently and his dark eyebrows tensed with concern. I knew deep down he loved his mother more than life and he worried about her. "She is hurting too, Gio. Just don't let her leave here thinking you hate her."

He nodded slowly. "I won't."

"So, what are you going to do? You know that what Sal is saying might not be true. And even if it is, Vinny is still the father that raised and loved you. Nothing will ever change that."

He leaned his head back and stared up at the sky. "I know. It's just I always wondered… I always felt torn between those two powerful men in my life. A part of me has always connected to Sal, the darker part. What if I am more like him than I thought? What if he is really my father?"

"You are still you, Gio. This doesn't change who you are. You don't even need to find out if you don't want to. Vinny raised you as his own whether you were his biological son or not."

"I need to know," he whispered. "But I am afraid of what it will do to mamma if I get a paternity test."

"It is your choice Gio. She will respect it because she loves you."

He stared into my eyes and I felt my heart ache for him. For what he was going through. "Thank you bambola. You keep me sane."

"And you drive me crazy! But I wouldn't have it any other way," I smirked as he kissed me again.

Sugar And Salt

Giovanni

Wrapping a towel around my waist and then a huge one around Olivia's body, I noticed her dress sticking to her tempting curves, making me horny as hell. I have been in a bad place the last few days, so we haven't even been physical. I switched my emotions off. I couldn't deal with the betrayal and pain of my mamma's deceit but also the soul-crushing thought that my papi was not in fact mine.

I have always looked up to Sal for the way he conducts business. He is a force to be reckoned with and is a shrewd and ruthless Boss which in turn, has made this family the most successful Mala Del Brenta, but I have never seen him as a father figure. He has taught me how to kill a man without allowing them to scream. He has taught me how to close the most savage of deals to ensure our family always comes out on top. He has taught me how to provoke fear and respect from men. But he did not teach me how to ride my bike. He did not teach me how to respect and love the women in my life. He did not teach me how to own my mistakes and learn from them. My papi did that.

Liv was right. Even if I was not Vinny's son by blood, I was still his son. I still loved him as my papi. Nothing would change that. But I wanted to know. I had to know if Sal was my father. He was convinced he was. And I didn't like that he could use that to his advantage. I wanted to be in the know. I wasn't sure what I would even do with the information if he was my father. I would most likely keep it to myself, but at least I would know.

There was one thing that was bothering me more than anything about all of this though. I could understand that Sal and mamma may have had a past. But how can they consider a future together? It wasn't right. It was an extreme betrayal to his brother and mamma's love for Vinny. I witnessed their love. Their marriage. It was true and pure. It has only been two years since papi's death and she is considering moving in with Sal? His brother? It didn't make sense. Mamma would never do this unless she had good reason. I did need to put my own feelings aside for the moment and get to the bottom of this. Mamma would never leave Raya and Sani like that.

Once Liv and I reached our bedroom, we dried and dressed quickly so I could catch mamma before Sal arrived. Liv sat on the end of the four-poster bed in a pair of shorts and cami as she towel dried her hair. I was pulling on a clean black shirt when I noticed her biting her lower lip with a pensive expression on her face.

"What are you thinking about?" I shouted from the dressing room.

Her eyes darted up to my face with a flash of panic and she shook her head. Oh hell no. I had to know now. Strolling towards her as I did up my buttons, I lifted her chin to look up at me.

"Liv?"

She sighed deeply, worry and turmoil were evident on her pretty face.

"There are things I want to say but I am not sure if I should… everything considered."

My eyebrows pulled into the bridge of my nose as I frowned. "No secrets, remember? There is nothing you can't say to me."

"You have to promise you won't do anything rash… don't fly off the handle Gio," she warned. Well, that was like poking a bear with an iron rod. I was instantly on high alert and my heart rate increased. "Forget it," she muttered when she saw the look on my face. She tried to stand up and walk away but I pulled her back to me.

"Olivia. You know I will not let this go now. So, save us both the hassle and just tell me."

"Okay…" she huffed back down on the edge of the bed. I folded my arms across my chest and stared at her expectantly. "I hate Salvatore."

I couldn't help it. I burst out laughing. Was that it? Not many people liked him, so it wasn't exactly a shock. "Well, I already knew you weren't his biggest fan," I joked, but her face stayed rigid.

"I don't trust him and I like to think I am a good judge of character. I know he is your… family and I hate to speak badly of people you love, but he is not a good man Gio, and I think you should be wary of his intentions."

I smiled as I reached out and stroked her cheek. "Okay bambola. I am under no illusion Sal is a good man. He doesn't try to be. He is what he is but he does care for this family in his own way. But you don't have to like him."

Anger burned red hot in her eyes and my smile faded. She pushed my hand away from her face.

"Don't patronise me, Giovanni! You are not listening to what I am saying. I can see the signs… I can feel it… it is not right."

I frowned as I saw how stressed she was getting over this.

"What isn't right?"

"Sal. The way he is with Cecilia, for example. He is… he acts… like Henry did with me."

I froze. "What?" My voice came out as a low growl. What was she talking about? I had seen Sal around mamma all my life and he had never seemed hostile or manipulative in any way. Yes, he was protective of her and they argued now and again, but mamma argued with everyone.

"He has a hold over her, Gio. Not a healthy one. I asked her if she loved him and she said she would never love another man after Vinny. So why is she doing this? Why is she going with him? It can't be out of choice. He must be forcing her in some way. He is manipulating her and controlling her. The way I have seen him look at her… it's unnerving. I think he is borderline obsessed with her. And then there was the night of the club…"

She paused and looked up at me with so much worry. My mind was already spinning, trying to unpick and think carefully about everything she was saying, but I couldn't see it. I had only ever seen how much he cared about her in all the times I have seen them together.

"What about the night at the club?" I gritted through my teeth. I knew from the look in her eyes I wasn't going to like what she was about to say.

"I didn't tell you because Cecilia swore me not to. She is dealing with Sal by herself, Gio. Just like I thought I could deal with Henry alone. And she knew if I told you, it would cause a huge amount of trouble and that is why I really need you to breathe and listen. Do not react."

"Liv…" I growled impatiently.

"I walked in on Sal pinning your mamma to a table by her throat when they were arguing."

Rage coursed through my veins, like a flood of darkness as my chest rose and fell in angry breaths. He laid a hand on my mother. He dared touch her with force. Suddenly, I felt fury like no other that my papi would have felt if he was still here to protect her. If he was still here, this wouldn't be happening full stop.

"Gio…" I heard Liv's worried voice behind me as I stormed out of our room towards mamma's wing. Throwing open her bedroom door, her frightened eyes widened from her position on the edge of her bed. She was surrounded by suitcases and looked so small in comparison to the mountain of possessions she had packed.

"Gio?" she whispered.

"Is it true? Has Sal dared to lay his hands on you?" I bellowed. Mamma's big brown eyes looked behind me at Liv, who I knew had just come sprinting into the room.

"You told him?" Mamma shouted in anger.

"I'm sorry Cecilia. I had to. You shouldn't be with Sal."

"This has nothing to do with either of you. Just leave me be," she snapped.

"Is it true?" I shouted in rage, losing the last of my control over my temper.

She hid her face behind her hands and her lips trembled. When she pulled them away, she looked me square in the eyes. "Yes. But it is not black and white Giovanni. I hurt him too. I slapped him before Liv walked in and saw us."

I growled out my frustration as I paced the room, my fists clenching and unclenching at my sides. I would go fucking ballistic if I was in a room with him again. Family or not. No one touches the women I love.

"Why? Why are you going with him mamma?" I yelled and all the colour drained out of her face. "And do not stand here and feed me more bullshit. I have had enough of the fucking lies in this family. Be honest."

"He is in love with me. He always has been. He agreed to stop the alliance if I accepted him."

I froze as I stared at her. "He blackmailed you to be with him? To leave your children and move in with him? What else is he doing, mamma? Has he forced himself on you?" My voice trembled with red-hot fury and she shook her head quickly.

"No. No. He wanted Raya and Sani to come with me but I didn't want them to. They are happier here. I will come and visit them. It will all be okay. Just let it go, Gio."

"Let it go? Listen to yourself mamma! You are being forced to be with a man you hate! Why? To protect me and Elle from a forced marriage?"

"Yes. That is exactly why Gio. I have had my big love story. I have experienced the wonder of true love. I will not allow Sal or the Aianis to take that away from you or Elle. You do not need to worry about me, darling boy. Sal will look after me. I know he is no gentleman but he loves me and he will care for me even if I do not reciprocate his feelings. There is no way out of this. Sal will kill anyone who stands in his way and I will not allow that to happen." She stepped forward and raised her hand to my cheek. "I am a big girl. I will be fine. You will see. It is a small price to pay for my children's happiness."

"Mamma, I will not let you do this. I cannot let you leave with him."

"You can. And you will. Because you must protect your family. You must do what is right for everyone, not just one person. That is what it is to be a good Boss and you will be the best Boss there has ever been in this family, because you will be nothing like him."

I shook my head as a tear rolled down her cheek. "I am so sorry Gio. About everything. But I promise you, I am making it up to you now. Let me do this for my children. This is my choice and I am okay with it. Do NOT confront Sal over this. You know how it will end."

"I will get you out of this, mamma. I promise."

She smiled sadly at me. "I do not need saving, my love. I am fine."

A knock on the door made us all spin around to see Mattio. "His men are here to escort you, Signora Buccini. Shall I send them up for your belongings?"

"Si. Grazie, Mattio."

She leaned up to kiss my cheek before she walked from the room with that cold mask pulled over her face, never showing the flurry of emotions she was hiding.

I closed my eyes and ran both my hands through my hair. Two small arms were wrapped around my waist and I felt Liv's head resting against my back. "We must help her, Gio. We can't let this happen."

"Maybe she is right, Liv. Maybe she doesn't need saving. She said he loves her and will care for her."

"Sugar and salt look the same, Gio. It doesn't mean they are." I turned to face her as I held her against my chest. "Just because he says he loves her doesn't mean his intentions are good."

"I know." I replied, leaning down and kissing the top of her head. One thing was for certain. I no longer trusted Salvatore Buccini. Whether he was my father or not, he had lost my respect and my loyalty.

More Than You Know

Maximus

I flicked off the engine to my Harley outside the Buccini mansion and pulled off my bike helmet. My smile widened when I saw my fiancé sitting on the stone steps waiting for me. My fiancé. It felt so right just saying those words. Cami jumped up and raced towards me, throwing her hands around my neck and kissing me while I balanced my chunky bike between my thighs.

"Someone is happy to see me," I smirked, and she pouted while she sorted out the mess of my long brown hair my helmet had caused.

"I hate being away from you."

"Not long now and you will be with me all the time," I smiled.

As soon as the alliance was finalised with her brother which was a fucking epic turn of events, I wanted Cami to move in with me in Trieste but with all the shit going on here and Liv needing the extra help with Raya and Sani, Cami decided she wanted to stay and help until it all settled down. Even though I wanted her all to myself, I admired and loved how much Cami had thrown herself into this family and wanted to help them.

"Can't you just move in here too?" she pleaded, giving me those big, blue doey eyes that made this rough man melt into a puddle.

"You know I am here as much as I can be. I will stay tonight, yeah?"

She nodded and I pulled her back into me by her top and kissed her again.

"About fucking time fratello! Put her down and get your ass inside." Giovanni called from the entrance of the mansion. I broke the kiss and looked over at my grinning cousin, rolling my eyes.

"Fuck off. You have your woman in your bed every night so give me five fucking minutes," I shouted back and he smirked.

"I'll give you two." He walked back inside and I glanced back at Cami. She took my helmet from my hands as I climbed off my bike and threw my arms around her waist, pulling her into me properly. I squeezed her ass in her little denim shorts and moaned.

"Two minutes is definitely not enough time for all things I want to do to you," I growled as her girly giggle caused my dick to stir.

"Then you will have to show some patience, Maximus. I will make it worth the wait tonight," she winked at me, wriggling out of my arms and grabbing my hand. She pulled me along to the mansion as I let my heavy boots scuff the gravel and groaned in frustration which made her laugh some more.

Once we made our way out to the back gardens of the mansion, I spotted Gio and Liv sitting at the marble outdoor table while Raya and Sani were busy playing on the lawn. After greeting Liv, I pulled out a chair and grabbed Cami's hips before she could sit down herself, so she was on my lap. Giovanni rolled his eyes with a smirk.

"Thanks for coming Max. You two are the only people we trust right now and we could really do with a sounding board," Liv said as she stood up and grabbed me a beer from the ice bucket on the table. She hunted around for the beer opener, but I dismissed her, taking the beer with a grazie and biting the cap off with my teeth.

"Yeah, things are pretty fucked up in this family right now," I agreed. After Boss murdered Aiani and claimed Cecilia as his before telling Gio that he was potentially his real father, I think all our heads were a fucking mess. I knew my uncle was a determined man but I had no idea just how far he would go to get what he wanted. As soon as the truth was out, I saw through it all. I don't think he ever intended to keep Aiani alive. I think he knew forcing Giovanni into a loveless marriage was the quickest way to manipulate Cecilia. It wasn't a secret that the woman would do just about anything for her children and he knew it.

He had lost my trust and Gio's. But the problem was... apart from murdering his ass, there wasn't a lot we could do. I have never liked the man but I have respected him as a Boss, but I knew Gio had a complicated relationship with him. Now more than ever. Not only could he be Gio's father but he was also the Boss of Mala Del Brenta. As much as we were all pissed at him right now, he still had extreme loyal followers in our family. All the other capos, the soldiers and Toni were loyal to him. He was untouchable.

The commission were the only ones who could overthrow his position but that would mean ratting him out to them about Aiani which was out of the question. We were not fucking snakes.

"So, what are you thinking?" I asked Giovanni directly. He leaned back in the chair, rubbing his stubbled jaw as he watched his siblings playing.

"Firstly, I want a paternity test without Sal's knowledge. Secondly, I am going to go to meet with the Leones."

I sat up straight in shock, nearly knocking Cami off my lap. "You can't be serious? It could be a fucking trap Gio!"

"I know," he said sternly as he reached for Liv's hand. She was watching his face intensely and I could see the worry in her eyes. They had already talked about this clearly but when Gio makes up his mind about something, he is going to go through with it.

I huffed loudly, running my fingers through my free-flowing hair. I had wondered myself why the Leone's wanted to meet with Gio but the risk was too high. The fact they would only meet with him alone and with no security was suicidal. He'd be walking into the palm of their hands and praying for the best. They were our biggest rivals and had just formed an alliance with Barbieri. It was a terrible idea to meet with them.

"I have a strong feeling that they have something on Sal. Obviously, I don't fucking trust the assholes and they could be trying to cause shit between our family but right now, I don't trust Boss either and I need to know what they want to tell me."

"You really believe that is all they want? To talk?"

"I don't have a fucking clue. But Liv can't stay behind these mansion walls for the rest of her life, which is the only way to keep her safe if I don't meet them."

I scoffed loudly. "So, this is about Liv?"

He narrowed his eyes at me. "No. This is about all of it."

I leaned back, my mind swirling with all the possibilities that could come from this. Most likely they will kill him or torture him. Or keep him hostage for something they want from Sal. Or the least likely option, they really did have something to tell him and would let him walk away unharmed after. He was going to do this no matter what I said so I had to find a way of making sure he had some protection walking in there. My eyes lit up as the idea came to me.

"The commission. I will go and meet with them and tell them where you are and what is happening."

He held my gaze and nodded slowly. "That way if they do harm me in any way, Boss will have the evidence to warrant retaliation…"

"I don't like this. Can't you at least take some of your men with you?" Liv panicked. It was clear Gio hadn't gone into a huge amount of detail as to how dangerous this situation really was.

"No. The message was clear. Meet them alone without informing Boss. If I don't want to risk him finding out I am meeting them, I have to go alone."

"Then I want to come with you!" She grabbed his arm that was holding her hand and he chuckled.

"No fucking way, bambola."

"He is right, Liv. You will put him in more danger if you go as well. They could use you against him at any point," Cami replied softly, and Liv huffed back in her chair.

"Then I want to go with Max to the commission. I have to do something."

I shrugged my shoulders at Gio. It wasn't a bad idea. She would at least be safe with me and the commission.

"Fine. But you do not leave Max's side," he sighed, and she gave me a cheeky grin. This little firecracker was the most perfect woman for Giovanni. In fact, she was the only woman for him. That much was obvious.

"When?"

"Tomorrow. I already sent a message to the Leones."

"How?"

"Angelo. He is my most trusted soldier and proved his loyalty to me time and time again. He delivered the message this morning and they accepted it. I am to meet them in neutral territory in an underground club."

"Well that sounds promising," I scoffed.

"I need you to hang about here today. I have invited Boss over and I'd like you to be present as I am sure he will be bringing Toni."

Now this did surprise me and from the look on Liv's face, she wasn't too pleased about it. "Okay. What are we discussing?"

"I am going to clear the air with him. Make him believe I am okay with him and mamma to keep him off my back and not suspect my distrust."

I nodded. It was a good idea. If we were to meet with the Leone's discreetly, we had to make it seem like Gio had accepted everything and the debris of the monstrous storm Sal had caused had settled.

***

The four of us sat in Gio's office staring across from each other as the tension grew. My hostile glare was directed at Toni. I have always hated this man. He was a brown nose who couldn't get his head any higher up my zio's ass. And the way he looked at Cami made my blood boil.

"I am guessing you have calmed down enough to want to discuss a few things now son," Sal stated boldly. I noticed Gio's body tense as Sal called him son, but he kept his cool.

"Clearly there is a lot to discuss."

Sal nodded. "I know it must have been a shock. I apologise."

"Why do you believe I am your son?"

He chuckled gruffly and his eyes held a knowing look as if the answer was obvious. "Well apart from the obvious physical resemblance, you share my ambition and ruthlessness Giovanni. I knew what potential you had from the beginning. You were born to spill blood, boy."

I rolled my eyes and rested my ankle over my leg as Gio held his gaze. That didn't mean shit. Vinny was just as ruthless as Sal when he wanted to be. The difference was, he had integrity. Gio was far more like Vinny in every way than Sal but I wasn't about to point that out.

"So, you have believed me to be your son since I was born? And you never said anything? Why?"

Suddenly, Sal looked uncomfortable. It was a strange sight to see. The unshaken Boss shuffled in his seat and pushed his hand through his full head of silvery hair.

"Your mamma. She chose Vinny. It took me a while to accept it, but I did eventually. I loved her and wanted to see her happy. And she made Vinny happy. When my papi passed away and the family title fell to me, I had something else to live for. So, I let it go. I watched from afar but loved you all the same. I only ever wanted what was best for you Giovanni."

I narrowed my eyes on Zio. He seemed genuine but it was hard to accept that as the truth when I had never heard him speak so vulnerably in all my life. Gio seemed to be thinking the same thing as he sat back in his chair and clasped his hands together, deep in thought.

"Why now then? How did you and mamma decide now was the right time? Don't you feel any guilt towards your brother?" I sensed the slight anger in Gio's tone and saw his nostrils flare. He needed to keep calm if we were going to pull this off.

"Vincenzo has been dead for two years. It is not like he is stepping on anyone's toes," Toni cut in and I glared at him with hatred.

"We are well aware how long Vinny has been dead for," I snapped.

"All I want to do is look after your mamma, son. I have never stopped loving her and after Vin was murdered by those fucking scumbags, we have grown closer because I have made sure she has been cared for. I am not trying to replace Vinny. I know I never will, but she deserves to have a chance at happiness again."

Again, his words seemed heartfelt, but I didn't buy it. He just lied and we knew it. He said Cecilia and him had grown closer after Vin's death. Cecilia has outright told Gio that she hates him.

Gio sighed deeply before he spoke. His face remained cool and expressionless but the whites of his knuckles as he clenched his fists below the table told me otherwise. "Then we are on the same page. As long as mamma is happy then so am I."

Sal's face broke into a genuine smile. "I am glad to hear it and she will be too. This is how it always should have been Giovanni. You are my heir and the future of this family. I will be thinking of retiring once Cecilia and I are married and this will all be yours. my boy."

My combat boot stopped bouncing on my knee as I froze from his words. What?

Gio sat up straight and his jaw clenched. "Married?"

"Of course. Why wait? We will be married by the end of the week. Then Toni will get everything together and I will sign the business over to you."

"And mamma has agreed to this?"

"Of course," Sal's smile fell as he narrowed his eyes on Giovanni. Shit. Gio was about to blow and Sal would know that he was not really onboard.

I jumped up from my chair and reached my hand out to my Zio with a beaming smile.

"Congratulations Boss. That is wonderful news."

It was enough to distract him as he stood up, did up the button of his blue suit jacket and shook my hand firmly.

"Grazie Maximus. Of course, you will be benefiting from this as well. Once Giovanni is Boss, you will be Underboss."

I smiled and nodded with respect as I felt Gio standing up behind me. I stepped back and gave him a knowing look. He had seemed to have regained his control and held his hand out.

"Sorry, that was just a bit of a shock. Congratulations. I am happy for you both."

Sal looked down at his hand before he pulled Gio into a hug, shocking every one of us in the room. Boss does not hug. Ever.

"Grazie figlio. Ciò significa più di quanto tu sappia. (Thank you, son. That means more than you know.)"

Gio lifted his hand and held the back of Sal's head firmly which looked like a moment of genuine affection. He locked eyes with me over Sal's shoulder as he tugged a hair follicle quickly, distracting Sal by saying, "I hope I am going to be the best man?"

Sal chuckled. "Of course you are."

I peered over at Toni who couldn't hide his jealousy quick enough, and I gave him a wink before slapping him on the shoulder. If I ever became Boss in the future, this fucker would be first to go and he knew it.

Sweet Love

Olivia

"Come on munchkins, time for bed!" I shouted for the zillionth time as Sani and Raya ran circles around me in their pyjamas, their hair still damp from the bath and in no way seeming the least bit ready to wind down. They had been playing up a little more than usual since Cecilia left to live with Sal which was understandable. They were confused and strangely excited. Cecilia came by earlier today and spent some time with them and told them about the wedding. She made it seem like it was going to be a small party with cake and music which I guess was true. Even though her voice was upbeat, and she had a smile plastered on her face, her eyes were void of any emotion.

"I am counting to five and if your bottoms are not in your beds, there will be no story tonight!" I used my teaching voice which caused them to halt in their screaming and to stare out at each other, contemplating my words. It lasted a whole three seconds before they squealed and started jumping on Sani's bed.

"Right! Time to call in reinforcements... you made me do this!" I warned as I strolled towards the door. They paused their jumping and watched with anticipation in their eyes as I gave them a knowing look and opened the door.

Marco was stationed outside, ever the obedient protector and I nodded at him to enter. A small smile played on his lips which he transformed into a stern expression as soon as he entered the room.

"Ahhhh!! It's monster Marco!" Sani screamed, pushing Raya out the way as he leapt off his bed to run.

"Monster Marco is feeling hungry! And naughty children who aren't in their beds are my favourite snack!" He boomed as I folded my arms across my chest and watched with a smile as he stomped like a giant towards the frantically running bodies around the room.

"Quick! Get in your bed Sani so he can't get us!" Raya shouted excitedly as she raced through the adjoining door to her room.

Sani did some weird action man roll across the floor and through Marco's legs before hitting his bum and laughing as he sprinted to his bed and climbed under the covers.

"Owww! No! They escaped again! Looks like I will have to try again tomorrow night," Marco spoke loudly as he straightened up and walked back towards me. We gave each other a sly fist bump before he left the room and I walked over to Sani's bed to tuck him in.

"Good night you crazy kid," I smiled as I kissed his forehead.

"Liv... is zio Sal not going to be my zio anymore? When he marries mamma will he be my new papi?"

Anger rose in me as I thought about how messed up this all was and how confused these two little people must be feeling. "No Sani. No one can replace you papi. From what I have heard, your papi was a very special man and he loved you very much."

"I don't really remember him that much," he said sadly and I swallowed the lump in my throat.

"That's okay because he is always with you. Even if you can't see him, he is right here." I poked his chest, indicating his heart. "The people we love never really leave us."

"Do you have a papi, Liv?"

I smiled sadly at him as I stroked his black curls away from his face. "I do. Just like you, he's right here." I rested my hand over my heart and he nodded in understanding.

"Good night sweet boy," I tucked him in as he grabbed his teddy and turned on his side.

After I tucked Raya in and closed her door, I had to take a moment to compose myself. These little people who meant so much to me were the ones who were going to suffer through this family's mess. They needed their mamma. We had to stop this wedding from happening but how?

Making my way towards the stairs to the top floor, I paused when I heard giggling and laughing from behind Cami's door. I smiled knowing at least one good thing had come out of all this mess. When I entered our bedroom, I found Giovanni dozing on the bed, shirtless in a pair of grey joggers with the TV on in the background. I tiptoed towards him, so I didn't wake him up. As I reached his side, his eyes flew open and as quick as lightning, he grabbed my hips and flung me onto the bed, caging me beneath his enormous frame as I squealed.

"I thought you were asleep!" I chuckled as he ran his nose up my throat.

"I was but my body knows when you are near," he mumbled as I ran my fingers through his hair. "Did they go down okay?"

I scoffed. "In the end. Sani asked if Sal was going to be his new papi."

Gio groaned and rolled off me, holding his hand over his eyes.

"Are you going to let Cecilia go through with this?" I asked, pulling myself up on my elbow.

"I don't know how I can stop it, Liv. I have tried my best to persuade her not to go through with this, but she is adamant it has to happen. She has stopped answering my calls now because she knows what I am going to say. I know you feel his feelings towards her are toxic Liv but with no proof that he is or has done anything wrong, my hands are fucking tied."

I sighed because I knew he was right.

"Can you explain the commission to me? I feel like I should know a little more than I do before I walk in there tomorrow."

"They are made up of previous and existing members of all the mafia families in Italy. Over fifty years ago, all the Boss' of every family signed a treaty to try to bring some peace amongst us all as there was so much hate and bloodshed. It was bad for business and hard to keep us out of the press and justice system when people were constantly having shoot ups in public places. Because of this treaty, we are unable to kill anyone from another mafia family unjustly. The commission works as a jury. If we believe a member has broken the treaty, we take our evidence to the commission, and they decide if it is enough for retaliation."

I rolled onto my side as I ran my fingertips across his hard chest.

"So, by going to them tomorrow and telling them where you are and why, the Leone's will not be able to harm you?"

He looked down into my eyes and gave me a small smile.

"That's the idea."

"But they still could?" I hated this. I hated the idea of him meeting them alone and just hoping for the best.

"Yes. But if they did, they would be breaking the treaty and then we would be given the green light to attack them."

"But then it would be too late! They would have already killed you!" Bile rose to my throat and my gut twisted at the thought of the amount of danger he was about to put himself in.

"I am taking Angelo with me if that helps," he ran his knuckles over my cheek, and I frowned. No, that did not help ease my worry at all. "And they also will not have any of their men. The arrangement is to meet alone from both sides."

"But it could be a trap?"

"Yes."

I huffed loudly and he chuckled. How was he feeling so calm about this? How was he not freaking out like I was?

"Bambola, I know it's hard but try not to worry about me, okay? I will have my alarm watch on so if anything goes wrong, I will send an alert to Max immediately and he will be able to inform the commission. That's when Max will need to tell Sal."

I rubbed my hands down my face as I fought back the intense emotions I was feeling. I wanted to scream or cry or just shout at how unfair this was, but I knew that was immature and wouldn't help in any way. I had signed up for this. This danger came with being with him. I had to grit my teeth and stay strong.

"Okay," I whispered. He pulled me back to lie down in the safety of his arms and I stared up at his gorgeous face. I had fallen so madly in love with this man, but I was starting to realise that every day in his world, I risked losing him. It was a hard pill to swallow but it reminded me that life is precious, and it could be taken away at any moment.

"I love you Gio. Please don't die," I was being deadly serious, but he laughed loudly before kissing the tip of my nose.

"I won't. I have far too much to live for Bambola."

The air sizzled with emotional and sexual tension as I held his gaze as we stared at each other with intensity. Just a few months ago, I had no idea this man existed and now he was my whole world. I could see the depth of his own emotions in those mountain brown eyes, and I slowly inched my face closer to his so I could brush my lips against his. My hands threaded through his hair as our noses caressed and his lips parted slightly encouraging me to continue. I licked his lips sensually before he gripped my body tightly and deepened the kiss with passion. Within seconds, our clothes were discarded on the floor, and he rolled on top of me, entering me in one slow, delicious stroke. We clung to each other's bodies as he gazed down at me, his black hair hanging over his forehead. He covered my body so perfectly with his as we moulded together, him filling me completely and pausing. His dark eyes burned with love and desire before he leant down and kissed me so tenderly it made my insides melt and burn at the same time. I needed him to move, I felt so full, yet he wasn't moving and my need to feel him taking me, claiming me like he does, was too much. My back arched off the bed as I racked my nails along his back, my body pleading with his to end this pleasurable torture.

Just as I was about to cry out and beg for him to move, he did. Pulling out of me so slowly only to push back in hard causing me to gasp into his mouth. My eyes shot open as he repeated it again and again. Out slowly, powerful thrust in. I felt like I was going to explode. Every slow, deliberate massage inside me was met by a groan from him as he plunged back inside and a whimper from me as he glided back out so slowly. It was an unbearable pleasure like I had never felt before. The intense feelings building inside me were enough to make me want to cry. His fingers tightened around my back as he tried to hold onto his control to keep this torturously slow pace. Each thrust back in was harder and deeper than the last as he growled in appreciation and I dug my nails into his back, needing more.

"You. Are. Mine," he breathed with affection with every thrust and for the first time ever, those words didn't scare me. They were true. I was completely and utterly his, mind, body and soul. And he was mine.

"I'm yours," I moaned back and I felt all his back muscles ripple under the palms of my hands as those words caused him to lose control. He claimed my lips with so much passion and need as he started to really move inside me, hitting that perfect spot over and over until I was crying out his name against his lips and he gasped out his own orgasm inside me.

With our foreheads stuck together with sweat and both of us breathless, we held each other tightly as we tried to regain our senses. That was the most intimate and loving sex we have ever had. A tear rolled down my cheek as I felt overcome with how much I loved this man.

He rolled onto his side, still holding me to him and stroked my hair without saying a word. We stayed entangled like ivy as my eyelids started to feel heavy. The last thing I heard as I drifted off to sleep was his sweet words in my ear.

"I would walk through fire for you. Ti amo bambola."

Without a doubt, so would I.

Bound To Revenge

Giovanni

I stared down at my nonna's stunning engagement ring in the black velvet box. Mamma had left it on my desk for me to find before she went to Sal's with no message or explanation. I didn't need one. I always knew why my nonna had left this ring to me, much to my mamma's annoyance and confusion.

When I visited her on her last days on this Earth, she had placed it in my hands and said this belongs to the next consorte della mafia (mafia wife) and I would know when I found 'the one'. At the time, I had no interest in finding 'the one' and I did not want to marry for love so I gave it to mamma, knowing how much she loved it. I snapped it shut and placed it in the safe in my office. If I survived today, that ring would be on Olivia's finger.

Strolling down the steps towards the entrance of the mansion, I smiled when I saw Liv, Max and Camilla all chatting by the front door.

"You all set?" Max gave me a stern look as I pulled Liv into my arms and tried to hold onto the memory of how her body felt against mine one more time. I knew what I was potentially getting myself into. I was armed with a knife and gun with Angelo as extra muscle but if it was a trick and they were not alone, I would be fighting my way out of there with a slim chance of making it out alive.

"Of course," I replied, keeping my voice calm and steady. I wasn't afraid of dying. Far from it. I had grown up knowing death was natural and an everyday risk in my world. It was what I would be leaving behind that scared me more. My family. Liv. I was their protector and without me, who knows what would become of them.

"Do you have the address and details of the meeting point to inform the commission? And the photos?" I asked and Max nodded, tapping his rucksack that was hanging over his arm.

I squeezed Liv tighter into my body before pulling her head back from my chest and kissing her lips swiftly.

"I'll see you tonight, bambola. Don't get into any trouble while I'm gone," I warned with a grin. I was trying to keep the mood light but the intense worry in her eyes was evident.

"Please come back," she whispered and I kissed the tip of her cute little nose.

"Always," I said seriously, holding her gaze as her eyes watered. I needed to leave before those eyes made me change my mind about what I was about to do. Pulling her arms away from my body gently, I walked away leaving her standing with Camilla as I strolled out the mansion with Max and Angelo. The Lamborghini was already parked out front, ready for us. I was going to take my fastest and most garish car to make a point. People would see it. People would recognise it.

Max grabbed my shoulder and gave it a firm squeeze as I nodded to him in understanding. We didn't need words. Just as I was about to climb into the passenger's side, I paused.

"Max?" He turned slowly and held my gaze. "If I don't make it back…"

"I know. I will protect this family with my life. Olivia included. You have my word."

I nodded once and climbed in before Angelo ignited the engine, roaring it to life.

***

As we pulled up outside the desolate nightclub, I scanned the outside of the rundown building and assessed my surroundings. It was broad daylight, so there was hardly anyone around this side of town that was normally hustling and bustling as soon as the sun set. Graffiti along the walls outside and the metal shutters signalling the club was closed gave off a hostile vibe.

Angelo and I both sat in silence, our eyes, ears and bodies on high alert, searching for any possible danger. Nothing. We waited a few more minutes before a side door opened down the alleyway to the right of the building and a large, muscular man stepped out the heavy door, nodding our way.

"You know the plan? We go into together but if it's a trap, you get yourself out and back to Max immediately. I have the alarm watch on so he will know you are on your way. That is an order, Angelo. No trying to be the hero, got it?" I narrowed my eyes at my most loyal soldier and he nodded professionally. We climbed out of the car and made our way towards the Leone soldier who put his hand out to pause us as soon as we came near.

"Niente armi. (No weapons,)" he spoke firmly.

I gave him my most menacing glare. "Non sono uno sciocco. Non entrerò senza la mia pistola. (I am not a fool. I will not be entering without my gun.)"

The man and I stood in a standoff as I waited for him to realise I was not going to back down. Slowly he moved away from the entrance, allowing us to pass through into the gloomy corridor. It stank of sweat and stale alcohol as Angelo and I were guided down some stairs to an underground level. When we reached the end door, the soldier knocked once before opening it wide and gesturing for us to enter.

"Giovanni Buccini, the one and only. How wonderful it is to finally meet you," a deep, swarve voice came from the darkness of the room. There was only one dim light swinging from the ceiling, causing a tiny spotlight over a metal table in the centre of the room. I narrowed my eyes, keeping my senses on high alert as I tried to make out how many men were in here. Two.

"What is with the dramatics? Do we not live in the 21st century," I stated as I lifted my hand and flicked on the light switch next to me, flooding the room with artificial light.

There on the other side of the table were the two men I had despised all my life. The Boss, Riccardo Leone and his son, underboss, Lorenzo. They were both leaning back lazily in their designer suits staring back at me. Riccardo had a wicked smirk plastered on his face but Lorenzo was showing me just as much hate and hostility that I am sure I had written all over my features.

"Apologies, my son likes to create a mood," Riccardo laughed lazily as Lorenzo's eyes narrowed on me.

"I am more of a 'get the fuck on with it' type," I replied, walking up to the table and pulling out a chair opposite them.

"I can respect that," Riccardo replied, opening his suit jacket and delving his hand inside. I tensed, my hand moving to my gun as I kept my eyes fixed on his movements. When he pulled out two cigars, I relaxed ever so slightly. I still couldn't trust that this wasn't an ambush until I was back out that door, driving away unharmed. "Would you care for one?"

I nodded, leaning forward and taking the freshly cut cigar from him. A soldier walked over to me and held out his Zippo, lighting the end as I puffed at it.

"As lovely as this is. I don't think you asked me here to share a cigar and a whiskey Leone."

"I am pleased to see you are a man of your word. Only one soldier in attendance and I can assume your Boss is in the dark about this little meeting?" He raised one eyebrow as he puffed on his own brown stick.

"Currently, yes. Although the commission is aware of my whereabouts in case you were thinking of not keeping your word."

His eyes danced with amusement as he nodded. "You are a sensible man, Giovanni. Just like your father."

My jaw tensed and for a moment I wondered if he could possibly know.

"I always liked Vincenzo. He would have made a fine boss and he was a fair man. Did he ever tell you that we had a drink once?"

Anger spiked to the surface of my skin as I listened to the man who murdered him speak as if they were f*cking friends. When I didn't respond but continued to glare at him, trying to hold onto my control not to put a bullet in this f*ckers head right here and now, he spoke again.

"We happened to be in the same club one night in Venice. Obviously, that should have ended in bloodshed but your father sent a bottle of whiskey my way and asked for a night of peace so he could enjoy his evening with your mother. I was blown away by the gesture from such a notorious rival and he gained my respect that night."

"So much respect that you put out a hit on him and tried to kidnap my mother," I hissed, my voice so deep and laced with aggression I noticed Lorenzo slightly shuffling in his seat.

Riccardo's eyes became serious as he held my gaze, never backing down from my aggressive stance. "That is what you have been made to believe. That is why you are here. So, we can set the record straight."

I scoffed loudly and stubbed out the cigar in the ashtray on the table. "So, you are here to plead your innocence? Let me guess, you have heard rumours that my uncle is seeking revenge and you are shitting your Armani pants?"

"I would love for Salvatore to attempt anything towards my family. I am sure you are aware our family has grown recently," Lorenzo interrupted with a sly smirk. I smacked my lips together as I moved my burning gaze to him.

"I hear congratulations are in order. Although, please send your wife my deepest sympathy," I snapped back causing his smile to fall.

"That is not why you are here, Giovanni. Yes, we are aware that Salvatore is taking measures to target us, hence our alliance with Barbieri. I am sure you can understand we are only protecting our backs in case it ever comes to a war. Just like your alliance with the Aianis. But I am hoping it will not come to that," Riccardo leaned forward, his scarred face shining under the artificial lights.

I ran my tongue along my teeth as I folded my arms over my chest and glared at these men. "Go on then, let's hear you pin my father's death on someone else... Who is it to be? Francesco? A lower rank family member? A drug lord?"

A heavy silence fell between us as the room thickened with sudden tension and I grew more and more impatient by the second.

"Firstly, we are not pinning your father's murder on anyone. We are here to tell you the truth and the facts. What you choose to do with it is up to you," Riccardo spoke seriously as Lorenzo pulled out a large file and iPad from his briefcase. He placed it on the table and slid it towards me. I narrowed my eyes as I stared at it and back at them.

"What's this?"

"This is all the information we have gathered from our investigations over the last two years on the death of your father. This is all the evidence that points to the people who were responsible for that night."

I didn't move as I tried to understand what this meant. If they were telling the truth, they knew they were being framed for Vinny's death and had been doing their own investigations to clear their name. But why were they giving it to me? Their rival?

"If this is everything you say it is...why have you not taken it to the commission? Why give it to me?" I questioned suspiciously.

Lorenzo spoke first. "Because if someone killed my father, I would want to know first so I could be the one to bring justice, not the commission."

My heart started thundering in my chest as I saw no malice or distrust behind his eyes. He was telling the truth. Whatever was in this file was the truth. I was feeling more and more certain. Leaning forward, I moved the iPad off the top of the file and opened the binder. No one spoke but I could feel their gaze on me as I skim read the first page of a CCTV report. It was in Leone's garage and the date on the still video shots was the day before my papi's shooting. The white vans with the Leone number plates were lined up in their garage. The same vans that stopped my father's security and killed them. I flipped to the next page and saw footage of two men with black balaclavas breaking into the garage.

"Two of our vans were stolen from our out of city garage a day before the shooting. We believe those vans were used in the attack on your father," Riccardo stated the obvious. This proved nothing. The Leone's could have easily set this up themselves to make it look like a robbery. I flicked to the next page where there was evidence that the vans were reported stolen the next day by Riccardo himself. They were found, burnt and abandoned a week later by police.

"This does not prove your innocence. My mother heard one of your men say your name from their lips that night. That you wanted her alive."

"Keep reading," Riccardo stated calmly. I flicked through more pages of CCTV footage of the city and froze when I saw the vans pulling out of an abandoned car park the night of the ambush. The licence plates had been changed but they were the exact same model of the stolen vehicles. Except they weren't leaving Leone's territory. They were leaving the Aianis. My head snapped up and widened as I glanced across at Riccardo. He nodded.

"Play the first video on the iPad."

My hands were starting to tremble with rage as I picked it up and pressed play. The CCTV footage had zoomed in on the driver of one of the vehicles. A brown-haired man with green eyes. I didn't recognise him as anyone I had ever met.

"We did a background check on that man. His name was Quintin Vallis. He was one of Francesco's head soldiers. He was leading the ambush and the man who attempted to kidnap your mamma. I believe Salvatore shot him during the attack, although his death is said to have been a drug deal gone wrong in our findings."

The Aianis. Were they behind this all along? They killed my papi? But why? Sal was trying to make a deal with them at the time of the shooting. I remember vividly that was what I was arguing with my father about. He didn't want to form an alliance with them, but Sal and I thought it was best to gain more power. Is that why they killed him? Just because he was against it?

Fury blazed through my veins like red-hot lava as I realised that Francesco was already dead. I would never get to torture him or kill him at my own hands for what he did. But I couldn't tell the Leone's that or I would be corrupting my uncle.

"So, Francesco did this because my father was standing in the way of an alliance?" I gritted through my teeth.

"That is what we thought but we wanted to be sure. We sent an undercover spy into their family posing as a soldier," Lorenzo stated, and my eyes widened. Cami said that one of her father's soldiers had suddenly gone missing. He must have been their spy and come back to the Leones now. That was fucking risky but brilliant.

"And?"

The two men looked at each other carefully before Riccardo sat up straight and clasped his hands on the table, staring deeply into my eyes. "Our man climbed up the ranks quickly. He became one of Francesco's most trusted men. He managed to gain important entail and record conversations in meetings as well as phone calls. This is not going to be easy to listen to Giovanni, but you deserve the truth."

My blood ran cold as I realised this was it. This was the moment everything would change. I would find out exactly who killed my papi and why.

I swiped to the next video on the iPad, which was an audio recording, and pressed play as my heartbeat pounded in my ears.

"We had a fucking deal. We got rid of Vincenzo for him, and you would make sure Camilla married Giovanni. Why the fuck has it been a week since Camilla met him and we have heard nothing?" The familiar, sleazy voice of Francesco echoed through the device. I froze on hearing my name. But what came next had all the colour draining from my face.

"We still have a deal. But the family needs time. Salvatore needs to ensure it is the right time to approach Giovanni with this." Toni's voice came through firmly and clearly. I would recognise it anywhere. The voice of a fucking traitor.

"You tell Salvatore that I did not risk everything to sit and fucking wait for my daughter to become a boss' wife. I want your end of this fucking deal to be finalised as soon as possible or..."

"Or what, Francesco? Do not threaten Salvatore Buccini. We can quite easily throw you to wolves if you do not play nicely."

"This was his idea! He came to me with this arrangement! To kill his brother and frame the Leones! I can just as easily go to the commission myself!" Francesco raised his voice down the phone.

"And who do you think they will believe? A grieving brother or a rival boss?" Toni chuckled.

There was a long silence and I stared blankly at the iPad.

"Fine. Tell Salvatore he has two weeks. I have already waited two years to make this marriage happen and I am losing my patience. You back out of this and you will have enemies surrounding you in every territory."

The phone call ended and I sat motionless. All I could focus on was my breathing. The heavy breaths in and out, my chest rising and falling, nostrils flaring as I tried to take in as much oxygen as my body needed to not pass out. I couldn't... believe it. Yet, I had just heard it with my own ears.

Salvatore, with the help of Toni, plotted his own little brother's death. Why? Why?

"As I said before, you can choose to do what you want with this information. If you want us to take it to the commission for them to deal with the injustice themselves, then we will, but we thought you-"

"No."

Riccardo paused at my interruption. I glanced up at them for the first time since the audio played and by the looks on their startled faces, I knew I looked like a monster.

"I will deal with this myself."

I stood up abruptly, taking the file and iPad with me. I nodded at Angelo, whose own face looked pale and sickly from shock, to follow me out.

"Giovanni!" Riccardo called from his chair. I turned slightly, not really seeing him through the rage that had now manifested through every fibre of my body. "You owe us for this. But don't think we are allies now. Only a monster can take out another monster. You will do well to remember that." He said in warning, reminding me that even though they were not responsible for any of this, we were still rivals. I halted in my steps towards the door and spun on my feet to glare back at them both.

"Olivia. The shooting. Was it you?" I growled, but I already knew the answer.

"No. She's far too pretty to kill."

My jaw ticked and I grabbed the door, slamming it open violently as it hit the wall, the noise echoing around the room. I could barely see or hear through my shock and anger as I stumbled out of the building into the daylight again. I squinted my eyes against the blinding sun as I heard the beep of the Lamborghini unlock. Climbing in, I gripped my hair in my hands as Angelo started up the engine silently and sped us out of the city back towards Verona. As we reached the open roads that snaked around the rocky landscape of the coast, I couldn't take it anymore. I couldn't bear to be in this small space. I needed air. I needed to breathe.

"Ferma l'auto. Adesso! (Stop the car! Now!)" I ordered.

Angelo swerved to the edge of the cliff and turned off the engine as I climbed frantically out of the car. I hunched over, hands on my knees as my head spun and the bile rose in my throat. Taking deep breaths in through my nose and out of my mouth for a few minutes, I started to regain control over my body and slumped to the dirty cliff edge.

I had no idea how long I sat there for, staring out over the horizon, but I felt every emotion possible in that time. Disbelief, shock, denial, confusion, betrayal, despair, disgust and anger. That last one was the one that stuck. How could he do this? How could he murder his own brother?

So, he was in love with mamma… he believed me to be his son… was it all out of jealousy? That Vinny had everything he wanted. There had to be more to it than that? I was willing there to be more to it. Something unforgivable that papi had done but no matter how hard I racked my brains I knew there was nothing. Nothing except… me. Vinny was next in line to be Boss because Sal had no children. But he believed he did. He believed it was me that should take over. That I was his rightful heir. And he wanted mamma for himself. The only person in the way of getting everything he wanted was my papi. The cold, hard truth was right there staring me in the face. And now I knew he was capable of killing his own blood, I knew in my heart it was either him or Toni that must have put the hit on Olivia. They just weren't expecting me to jump in front of the fucking gun.

An hour or so must have passed as I sat with my volatile thoughts before I heard Angelo's boots on the road behind me.

"You will not speak a word of this to anyone, Angelo," I spoke firmly, and I knew he was nodding behind me.

"What are you going to do?"

I gazed out at the horizon as the sun started to set. This was the moment that would change everything. My entire life was about to implode but I knew what I had to do.

"I am going to kill Salvatore Buccini on what he thinks is the best day of his life," I gritted through my teeth as my brain swirled with a vengeful plan.

"From this moment, I pledge my loyalty and allegiance to you as Boss," Angelo bowed his head as I stood up and took his hand. He knew what this meant.

I kill Sal. I become Boss. And I was ready to rip the fucking crown right off his head.

The Commission

Olivia

"Try not to piss anyone off today, Liv. Best you leave all the talking to me," Max winked as he climbed out of the SUV. I opened my door before he could get to it to help me out and stepped onto the quiet driveway of what looked like a large vineyard.

"I might be feisty, but I am not stupid Max. I know when to bite my tongue." He gave me a knowing look with a cheeky smile which I returned. "Where are we? Is this a vineyard?"

"Yes. The commission are geniuses setting up their workplace where they have an endless flow of wine."

We walked up to the entrance with two Buccini soldiers following closely behind. Once we were inside the beautiful, old stone building, Max walked over to the welcome desk and spoke in a hushed voice to the man in a fine suit. He nodded before disappearing behind a door and Max turned to me, leaning his elbow on the desk.

"Now what?" I whispered.

"Now we wait to be seen. Want a glass of wine?"

I looked over my shoulder to where Max was nodding to and saw an elegant bar full of unsuspecting visitors here for a day of wine tasting and grape picking. Max walked up to me and held out his tattooed arm. "We could both use a drink right now."

I placed my hand in his elbow as we walked up to the bar and both perched on wooden bar stools. After the barmaid had poured us each a smooth, full bodied red wine and I took a sip allowing the warmth to travel through me, I sighed.

"Have you heard anything yet? From Gio?" My mind will not allow me to relax. No matter how much wine I drank in this place, I knew I would still be on edge. Just knowing he was in such a dangerous situation right now was making me sweat and my gut twist.

"Liv, he only left an hour ago. He has an alarm watch on him which will alert me directly if he is in any real danger. Try not worry," he lifted his wrist with the sleek black watch adorning it.

"How can I not worry? The Leone's are your biggest enemies! Do you really believe they are going to let him go without harming him when they have such a perfect opportunity?"

Max held my gaze as he took a sip of his wine and put it down on the bar slowly. "Yes. I think they know something. Something big. Something that is going to fuck our lives up completely."

I frowned in confusion. "Like what?"

Max sighed, rubbing his jaw. "I don't know but I am starting to think it could have something to do with Sal. Since all this shit has come out about him and Cecilia, my suspicions have been growing."

I leaned forward urgently, still just as confused. "Max spit it out please. Remember I am new to all of this and I need all the information."

His green eyes locked with mine and I could see his mind spinning. He wasn't sure whether he should tell me without Gio's approval but I needed the distraction more than anything.

"I think Sal might have killed Vinny or at least played a part in the attack."

My eyes widened in shock and my mouth hung open.

"What? But Vinny was his brother? Why would he-" and then it hit me. Cecilia. Gio. Sal believed they belonged to him. He had been obsessed with Cecilia for years and watched her choose his own brother over him and raise a child that could be his.

"But why then? Why 27 years later?"

Max huffed and grabbed his wine, downing it in one. "I've been wondering the same thing. Around the time of Vinny's death, we were all growing concerned about the Leones. They were growing rapidly in numbers and some of our biggest clients were starting to work with them as they were offering their services at competitive rates. It was pissing Sal off. He wanted to knock them back but without the commission's approval there was nothing he could do."

"So you think he framed them for Vinny's murder? In the hope that the commission would let him retaliate?" I was starting to catch on to Max's trail of thought quickly and he nodded.

"But it didn't work. There wasn't enough evidence. I always wondered why we could never get enough from the scene. I mean we should have at least been able to identify one of the bodies of the soldiers who killed Vinny, but Sal always said when they went back to the scene after making sure Cecilia was safe, the bodies were gone. What if that was a lie? What if Sal was the one who got rid of them himself?"

"But surely he wouldn't have been alone in this? Buccini members would never agree to a hit on their underboss?" I asked, my heart now speeding in my chest.

"I don't think he used our men."

I shook my head in disbelief. It was hard to imagine that Sal would go to such lengths to get what he wanted. To have his brother murdered so he could kill the Leones and get to Cecilia and Gio. Could it be true? In my heart, I knew it could be. Sal reminded me a lot of Henry except he was a lot smarter. When he wanted something or believed something was his, he would do anything to have it. I saw that with my own eyes when he shot Francesco.

"Does Gio know? Are we going to tell the commission?"

Max shook his head. "No. I have only just come to this conclusion today as I have been trying to understand why the Leones would want to meet Gio. And no. We cannot say a word to the commission, not without evidence. That is very important Liv." He gave me a stern look and I nodded. I suddenly felt very out of my depth here. What was I doing? I was about to meet members representing every mafia family in Italy in one room and who the fuck was I?

"Mi scusi. Sono pronti per te," a polite and formal voice said behind me. Max nodded and jumped off his stool, holding his arm out to me again.

"Ready?"

"No," I whispered in a shaky voice, and he smiled widely.

"Come on. Let's go and say hello to my papi."

"What?" I whisper-yelled in his ear as I took his arm and we followed the escort down a narrow stone corridor to the back of the building.

"My papi is the Buccini representative. He was a soldier who worked his way up the ranks for years, then ended up marrying my mamma, who is Sal's sister, and then was elected a member of the commission."

"Wow. That's… impressive."

Max chuckled deeply and I could see the pride in his smile. "Yes. He is my inspiration."

After climbing an ancient staircase where the walls were decorated with enormous antique and renaissance paintings, we approached double doors with gold-framed detail and I squeezed Max's arm with nerves. He gave me a reassuring smile just as the doors were opened by two beefy men in black and we walked into an exquisite room full of paintings, statues and art. There in the middle of the room was a long, mahogany table with around twenty or so men all wearing expensive, designer suits.

Max walked us to the head of the table and bowed his head at them all in respect. I quickly copied him and as I looked up, I saw that all their curious and very intimidating eyes were on me and not Max.

"Who is this? It is not every day we have a beautiful woman visit us." One middle-aged man asked. I was relieved that they were talking in English. Before Max could answer, I let go of his arm and stood up a little taller.

"My name is Olivia Jones and I am Giovanni Buccini's girlfriend. I am here in his place."

Silence fell around the room. Some of the men seemed surprised or shocked by my confident introduction, while others narrowed their eyes and looked me up and down with suspicion.

"And why has Giovanni sent his woman and Capo instead of seeing us himself?" Another asked. As my eyes darted around the room, I tried to work out who Max's dad was and representing the Buccini family. No one stood out.

"He is currently meeting with Riccardo and Lorenzo Leone alone," Max said calmly.

"What?" One man stood up abruptly and Max smiled. "Alone? That is suicidal!" This man had the same green eyes as Max and I guessed it was his father from the obvious concern he had for Gio.

"No it is not. Our family signed the treaty just like yours. Riccardo would be a fool to kill Giovanni." Another man shouted. Clearly a member of the Leones.

"That is why we are here. To inform you of what is happening, so if, for whatever reason, Giovanni does not make it out of this meeting, you all know who is responsible." Max opened his bag and threw the pictures of me and Gio onto the table as well as an image of some Italian writing on a napkin and a map with the location they are currently meeting at.

"Two weeks ago, the Leones cornered Olivia and threatened her life unless she delivered Giovanni a message to meet with them alone without informing Salvatore. Riccardo had been sighted in Verona multiple times, sending discreet messages to Giovanni like this one here." Max lifted up the photo of the napkin as all the men studied it.

"Why?" Another man asked.

"We don't know. That is why Giovanni had decided to meet them. To hear what they have to say."

"We want to be kept informed of this development, Maximus. Whatever the outcome of this meeting," Max's father said firmly, and he nodded. "You call me the moment you hear from Giovanni."

After a few more questions from the commission about the meeting, we were sent on our way. As soon as we climbed back into the SUV with the two soldiers who had been waiting for us in the bar, I checked my phone for anything from Gio. My heart plummeted when I saw I had nothing. Glancing over at Max, I saw he was doing the same. When he felt my gaze on him, he turned his head and gave me a reassuring smile.

"I am sure he is fine. No news is good news, right?"

I nodded slowly as I watched the beautiful landscape zoom past my window, repeating those words over and over in my head.

A Close Encounter

Camilla

"Cami! I'm hungry," Sani moaned from the floor where he was playing with his train set. I glanced down at my watch and saw it was gone one pm and it was probably time for their lunch. I had never really been the maternal type. I didn't have a lot of experience around children so Sani and Raya being left in my care today was daunting to say the least. But I was going with the approach of giving them what they want to make them happy and keep the peace.

"Ok. What would you like? I will go and make you something."

He paused his play, eyes rolling up to the ceiling and finger tapping his chin. "Finger sandwiches like Liv makes them. And chocolate. And apple juice. And some melon."

I repeated the list back to him and he nodded. Ok. I could do that. I had never made finger sandwiches before, but I am sure it is not rocket science. Standing up from their playroom carpet, I brushed down my light blue sundress.

"What about you Raya?"

"The same please," she smiled sweetly. She was such an angel. I grinned back before making my way to the door. After asking Marco to go inside and play with them while I made their lunch, I found myself hunting around in the spacious, modern kitchen that I swear was barely used by any of the family members. It took me forever before I even found any plates, but I was determined to be of some use today. Max and Liv had left to visit the commission hours ago and Gio was meeting the Leones. I felt slightly useless in this whole mess but if I could at least do a good job of taking care of these kids, then I was at least doing something.

Bending down to rummage in a cupboard for some chocolate, I didn't notice anyone enter the room but as soon as that intimidating, sly voice startled me, I jumped up from my position and gasped.

"Quello è un bel culo con cui mi stai prendendo in giro (That is one fine ass you are teasing me with.)"

My blue eyes widened, and my skin itched with disgust as I saw Toni leaning against the kitchen door. His hazel eyes roamed my body as he slowly licked his lips before biting his lower lip aggressively and letting out an appreciative growl. He was wearing more casual clothes than I had seen him in before, ditching the tailored suit for a white shirt and blue jeans. The shirt clung to his body, showing that he was indeed still a man built like an ox despite his age.

I gulped down my instant fear and lowered my gaze to the kitchen island, busying myself with preparing the lunches. I was going to ignore his sleazy comment. It didn't deserve a response.

"Sto parlando con te troia. (I am speaking to you slut.)" He hissed when I didn't acknowledge his presence. I slowly lowered the butter knife to the table but kept it firmly gripped in my hand as I glanced up at him.

"Is there a reason you are here Toni?" I asked politely, trying to keep the nerves at being alone with this man out of my voice.

"Where is Giovanni? I need to discuss details about Boss' wedding tomorrow."

Shit. We hadn't counted on Toni or Sal coming by the house today. Thinking quickly on my feet, I used my knowledge of Giovanni's businesses to pull the wool over his eyes.

"He is out. In town, taking care of some business at the restaurant."

Toni huffed in irritation and folded his muscular arms across his chest. "Maximus then?"

Panic started to rise in me as I realised, I couldn't avoid letting him know that I was here alone.

"He just popped out but will be back any minute I am sure," I lied, hoping that will be enough to keep him from trying anything. I knew from the moment I met this man, he wanted me. He had made it extremely obvious in every interaction we had ever had.

"Well, I suppose I will just have to wait then," he turned and shut the kitchen door behind him before he waltzed over to a kitchen bar stool and sat down keeping his leering gaze on me the entire time. My heart started pounding in my chest as I kept my eyes cast down and spread the butter of the bread. I did not think he would come and wait in here with me.

"Why don't I go and call Mattio? He could make you comfortable in the living room with a brandy while you wait?" I said sweetly.

"No. I am good here. I prefer this view," he smirked as he picked up a strawberry and bit into it roughly.

I remained silent as I tried to speed up my sandwich making so I could get away from this leech as fast as possible. Grabbing the butter and ham off the counter, I turned to place them back in the fridge and as soon as I shut the door Toni was standing behind it, making me jump. A sadistic grin spread across his chest as my hand rested on my speeding heart drawing his perverted gaze down to my breasts in my blue sundress.

"Such a shame about your papi. He was a useless bag of shit at the best of times but still to be shot in front of his own children like that was brutal. Not that you cared," he hissed as he took a step towards me, forcing me to step back.

"W-what do you mean? Of course, I cared," I stuttered as I glanced down at the bread knife I had left on the counter and was now inching further away from. I didn't care in the slightest that my father was dead. I hoped he rotted in hell.

A low chuckle left his chest as he kept taking menacing steps towards me, forcing me back into a corner in the kitchen.

"You don't fool me, Camilla. You are just some little whore, who spreads her legs for men to make them love you, aren't you? Your papi told me what you were good for."

My breathing was becoming erratic, and my ears were pulsing with my heartbeat as panic took over.

"First you fucked Giovanni and then Maximus. I am feeling left out," he pouted, evil lurking behind his eyes.

"I have never slept with Giovanni. I am marrying Maximus because we are in love. He will be back any minute," I choked out as my lower back hit the kitchen counter by the sink.

"Oh, you delusional slut, how could he love you? He loves to fuck you, I am sure. You are a very tempting woman," he sneered, pressing his huge frame up against my front, caging me in. I could smell cigars and brandy on his breath, and it made me want to gag.

Using all my force, I tried to push him back while finding my voice. "Max will be back any minute and he will kill you if you even lay a finger on me."

He laughed loudly as he grabbed my jaw in his large hand firmly, forcing me to stare up at his face.

"You think I fear Maximus? I am two ranks higher than him in this family and you no longer have the protection of being Giovanni's fiancé or Francesco's daughter. You sealed your own fate, and I am finally going to enjoy seeing for myself what a little whore you really are."

He slammed his hard, dry lips onto mine using his hand to pull me into him and his greying moustache scratched my skin. My eyes bulged wide as I tried to fight him off, but it was like punching a steel door. I battered his chest with the bottoms of my fists as he groped my ass, pulling my dress up to my waist. My body was in full fight mode as I knew I possibly had seconds to try and get away from this man or at least scream for help from one of the soldiers, but would they even help me? This was their consigliere. They were loyal to him and would more than likely look the other way. I could only help myself. Grabbing his throat with one hand I tugged him away from his lips to give me just enough room to quickly jab him in the Adam's apple, followed by a swift stamp on his foot. His grip on my body loosened and I darted away from him making a run for the door.

A burning sensation from my scalp and aggressive yank backwards, caused my body to smash straight back into his as he grabbed a handful of my hair to pull me back. My eyes watered from the pain of his fist tugging at my hair.

"You fucking bitch. I am going to show you just who you are dealing with," he growled in my ear as he released my hair only to backhand me so hard across the face that I fell to the floor. Before I had a moment to regain my senses from such a powerful blow, he had a fistful of hair again, yanking me up to my feet and slamming me over the kitchen island. I screamed loudly as my head pounded, cheek stung, and he grabbed my arms behind my back forcing my chest to the cold surface. Tears were streaming down my face as his huge frame leaned over my body and he hissed in my ear, "Mine now."

I could see the bread knife on the counter just inches away from me but with my hands tightly restricted behind my back I had no way of reaching for it. A sob escaped my mouth when I felt him pull my knickers to the side and insert his fingers roughly, causing me to cry out.

"Hmm, what's wrong, beautiful? Do I not make you wet like Maximus?" He chuckled as the pain from him forcefully pushing another finger in made me whimper. My mind went numb, and I closed my eyes when I heard him unbuckling his belt. Once again, I was reminded of what I was put on this Earth for. To be used for men's pleasure. How could I believe I would ever escape it?

***

Maximus

As the SUV pulled up in front of the mansion, I couldn't help the wide grin that spread across my face, knowing I was about to get a kiss from Cami. This woman had turned me into a soppy bastard from the moment I met her. Even being away from her for a few hours was torture.

Liv and I climbed out the car and made our way upstairs to find Cami and the kids. When we reached the playroom, Marco was being dressed up as a princess by a giggling Sani and Raya but there was no sign of Cami. Immediately, my senses were on high alert.

"Oh wow! You make quite the damsel in distress Marco!" Liv chuckled as she walked into the room.

I scanned it carefully and looked at the open bathroom door. "Where is Cami?"

"She is downstairs making the children's lunch," Marco replied in a professional tone that just seemed ridiculous as he was wearing a tiara, fake earrings and pink lipstick. I nodded with a smile and made my way down to the kitchen and that's when I noticed something didn't seem right. Apart from the men stationed at the front door, there were no soldiers around the lobby.

Picking up my speed, I rushed towards the kitchen, needing to see Cami. A strange, unsettling feeling was prickling across my skin when I saw the kitchen door was shut. It was never closed. Flinging it open, it took a second for my brain to register what I was seeing. There was Cami bent over the kitchen island, her dress up to her waist, arms being held behind her back, her eyes screwed shut in fear and pain. Standing behind her was Toni. I watched as he pulled his fingers out from her and started to unbuckle his belt.

RAGE.

I had never felt anything like it before in my life. I lunged at Toni, growling loudly as I tackled him to the floor in one violent attack. His huge frame smashed into the porcelain ground beneath me and I saw first shock and then anger in his eyes. But I didn't give him a chance to react as my fist went flying into his face. Straddling his body, I pummelled his cheek, nose and mouth, blood squirting out in many directions. He managed to swing his own fist, connecting with my cheek but in my blind fury, I didn't even feel its impact. He was built like a tank and I knew he would be able to dominate me if I didn't get him into a delirious state quickly. Never stopping my vicious beatings, I thought he was starting to lose consciousness but he suddenly took me by surprise when he leaned up and reached behind my back pulling my gun out of my trousers. I reacted fast, grabbing his arm as he tried to bring the gun around to aim at my head. I slammed his arm down on the floor multiple times until the gun flew out of his hand and slid across the kitchen floor away from us.

I could hear Camilla crying behind me and the sound distracted me enough to give Toni the upper hand. He tossed me off him onto the floor, climbing on top of me and strangling my throat. His bone crushing hands were in a fierce grip as I tried with all my strength to pry his hands off me. I could feel my face turning red from the lack of oxygen as I stared up at his mangled, bloody face.

"Stop! You're killing him!" I heard Cami scream and suddenly she had jumped onto his back, stabbing a knife into his shoulder. He released one hand from my throat, grabbing her hair over his shoulder and slamming her head into the marble kitchen island. She fell to the floor, knocked out and I growled, fighting back with the little strength I had left to kill this mother fucker. But he was too strong. I could feel my vision blurring as white dots danced across my eyes from the restriction on my throat. Panic started to set in.

"Get off him!" I vaguely heard a shout from behind Toni's back but I couldn't make out who it was. Then Toni's eyes bulged. His hands loosened their grip as I coughed and wheezed for air. Blood seeped through his white top and I realised he'd been shot. Shoving him off me as he spluttered and choked on his own blood, his eyes wide, I wanted to make sure he died a painful death. Grabbing his face in my hands, I pushed my thumbs into his eye sockets until they popped and blood trickled down his face. His screams were silent as he choked on his blood and took his final breath.

I fell back on the floor and looked up for the first time at the person who had just saved my life. The gun fell from her trembling hands as she dropped to her knees.

"Is he dead?" She whispered.

I crawled over to Cami who was still unconscious, blood trickling down from a small cut on her forehead. I frantically checked for her pulse, bile rising in my throat. She was alive. She would be okay.

I looked back over at the shaken woman who had just killed a man for the first time.

"Yes Olivia, Toni's dead and you just saved my life."

Innocent Murder

Olivia

I – I just killed someone.

I just shot a man in the back twice.

My whole body shook with adrenaline and shock as I fell to my knees, eyes glued on the body of the man I just murdered. Murdered. I am a murderer. Blood started pooling from beneath him, staining the porcelain kitchen floor.

"Yes Olivia, Toni's dead and you just saved my life."

I heard the words, but I struggled to process them. Toni? As in Sal's right hand man? I am dead. I am more than dead when Sal finds out. But he was trying to kill Max. He would have killed him if I didn't stop him. I had no choice.

I dragged my gaze away from Toni's body and saw Max cradling Cami in his arms, her eyes closed and a trail of blood snaking down the side of her head. When I came down here to help Cami make the kids lunch and heard loud grunting and a woman crying, I immediately sensed danger. I ran into the kitchen and saw the huge man toss Cami off his back like a rag doll and she fell to the floor. That's when I caught sight of Max's face, scarlet red as the life was slowly being drained out of him. He was fighting against the man but he was losing. In a blind panic, I saw the gun near my feet and picked it up shouting to the man to get off him. But when he didn't and I saw Max's eyes roll into the back of his head, I pulled the trigger. The second time was an accident. I was expecting a loud noise but the gun was silent so I thought it hadn't worked. It was only when the blood started seeping through the man's top that the magnitude of what I had just done hit me.

"Olivia! Liv!"

I blinked rapidly as my brain caught up with Max's voice. "I need you to go and get Marco. Only Marco, okay? No one else can know about this. Got it?"

At that moment, Cami stirred in his arms and relief flooded through me. She opened her eyes, gritting her teeth as her hand went straight to her wound on her head.

"Cami, take it easy," Max soothed as I watched him move slightly into her view and brush her hair from her face. Her beautiful blue eyes widened as she looked up at him and remembered what had happened. She burst into tears and turned into his chest, hugging him tightly as he stroked her hair and muttered something in Italian over and over. When she calmed down a little, she looked over at Toni's body and then up at me. Her bottom lip quivered again.

"Liv! Thank you," she cried.

I shook my head, still not understanding what was happening.

"Olivia. Listen to me. I have to get Toni's body out of here. I need Marco. Can you go and get him for me?"

I nodded slowly as I stood to my feet. I walked towards the door and opened it.

"Liv! Lock the door after you, okay?" Max shouted from the floor. I did as he asked and made my way up to the playroom in a state of shock. I had no idea how I had just managed to manoeuvre my body through the house and as I pushed open the playroom door, Marco jumped up immediately with concern on his face.

"Signorina Jones? Are you okay?" He asked, walking towards me. I glanced up at him.

"Max needs you. In the kitchen." My voice didn't sound like my own as I heard it fill the room. Was that me talking?

He nodded once and raced out the room, clearly sensing something was not okay.

"Liv, we are watching the Gruffalo! Come and sit with us," Sani ordered from his bean bag in front of the Plasma. I seemed to manage to find my way over to them and perch between these two innocent children that had no idea what I had just done minutes ago. I stared blankly at the screen as the little mouse character said, "Don't call me good! I'm the scariest creature in this wood."

A small bubble of laughter formed in my throat and then before I knew it, I was laughing hysterically from the shock. I had no idea why I was laughing but I think it was a coping mechanism to avoid having to deal with the other emotions that were festering in my body. Sani and Raya looked at me with amusement but not really understanding what I was finding so hilarious. As I took some deep breaths and calmed down, I realised I was also crying, tears were streaming down my face and I quickly wiped them away.

"If you think this is funny, wait until the Gruffalo runs away from the mouse," Sani announced.

I had no idea how long I sat there but the show was over and a superhero cartoon was now playing when Marco and Max finally entered the room. I turned my head on their arrival and saw the concern on their faces.

"Where's Gio?" I asked. I suddenly felt so fragile. I wanted to feel safe again. And I only ever felt safe in his arms. But he wasn't here. Where was he? Suddenly, remembering that he had gone to meet the Leones and still wasn't home, I jumped up from the floor.

"He is on his way back. I just received a call. He is fine, Liv. He's coming back," Max said carefully as he rested his hands on my shoulders. Tears welled up in my eyes as the relief rushed over me and my knees went weak. Max quickly pulled me into his chest and hugged me tightly which was exactly what I needed to hide my emotions from the children.

"Everything is going to be okay Liv. Why don't you go upstairs and lie down for a bit? Marco will watch the children," he whispered.

I nodded slowly, grateful to have a moment to myself.

"What happened to…his…"

"Don't worry. It's been taken care of."

I pulled out of his embrace and stared into his green eyes. He had a swollen eye and lots of cuts and bruises on his face as well as hand marks around his neck but you wouldn't think it hurt, the way he seemed more concerned about my mental state.

"Where's Cami? Is she okay?" I asked quickly.

"Yes. She is downstairs being checked over by our on-call doctor and nurse."

"Okay," I muttered. I had so many more questions suddenly brewing in my mind but I knew now was not the time to ask them in front of the children.

"Do you want me to help you upstairs? Run a bath for you?" Max asked kindly but I shook my head.

"No thank you. I can do it myself."

He nodded and let go of my shoulders as I walked past him and made my way to our bedroom. As if on autopilot, I strolled into the bathroom and turned on the taps to fill the enormous bath, pouring in some bubble bath as I sat on the side. I stared at the water flowing from the taps numbly until the level was close to the top and turned it off. Shredding my clothes, I stepped into the balmy water and let it sooth my body and relieve the tension every muscle held.

As soon as I closed my eyes the scene flashed in my mind again. The sight of Cami passed out. Max's face as he was being strangled to death. The weight of the gun in my hand. The feeling of pulling the trigger. The blood. I splashed my face with the water, rubbing my eyes knowing my mascara would be running below them but not caring in the slightest. I killed a man. And not just any man. The consigliere of the most powerful mafia families in Northern Italy. What was Toni doing? Why was he trying to kill Max? What had happened? What did they do with his body? What will Gio think? Will Sal find out? Will I go to prison? Will he kill me?

Closing my eyes, I sank down below the water level, submerging my entire body. Holding my breath under the water was the only thing I could do to stop the panic attack that was rising within me. That and Gio. Where was he?

***

Giovanni

I pulled out my phone as Angelo sped down the country roads towards the mansion. In my complete dismay and fury, I hadn't contacted anyone that I was alright and I suddenly felt so guilty, knowing they would all be worrying about me, especially Liv. I rang her mobile but it rang out with no answer. I frowned. She knew she always had to keep her phone on her or I worried. What the hell.

I rang Max next, my heart pounding in my chest. From the moment, I heard his out of breath voice on the phone, I knew something had gone down.

"Gio? You're alright?" he panted.

"I'm alive. What's going on? Why can't I get through to Liv? Why are you panting?" I spoke frantically.

"Toni's dead."

My eyes widened and I glanced over at Angelo who furrowed his eyebrows, hearing Max's voice through the phone.

"What?" Some shuffling noise could be heard and then a slam that sounded like a car door. "Max? What the fuck is going on?" I was losing my patience as he huffed breathlessly down the phone.

"Give me a fucking second to catch my breath. That bastard is heavy fuck," he growled and I don't think my eyes could get any wider.

"Wait! You killed him?"

"No. I tried. I walked in on him about to rape Cami and beat the fucking shit out of him but the guy was a bulldozer and got the upper hand. He knocked Cami out and was strangling me to death."

Rage boiled through my veins at the thought of Toni doing that to Cami and Max. But knowing what I know now, I wasn't fucking surprised.

"So, who killed him?"

There was a slight pause before the name I least expected to leave his lips entered my ear.

"Olivia."

Panic, worry and anger mixed together made a lethal blend as I realised she must have witnessed this. That she was in danger herself. That she was the one who had to kill Toni.

"What? How? Is she okay? Where is she?"

"She shot him. Thank God she came in when she did or I wouldn't be here speaking to you right now, man. She's okay but she is shaken up badly. You need to get back here as soon as possible."

I glanced at Angelo, who slammed his foot on the accelerator in response.

"Fuck!" I shouted down the phone as I ran my hand through my hair. This fucking day. I should have been there. I should have protected her from this. Sensing my thoughts, Max sighed deeply.

"You can't protect her from everything Gio. Sooner or later, she is going to have to defend herself or those she loves if she is going to be in our world. I am just pleased she deemed me worthy enough to defend," he chuckled but I couldn't bring myself to see the funny side. Liv just killed someone for the first time and knowing what she has witnessed in her life, I knew she would be so hard on herself. And I am not even there to comfort her.

"Just check on her Max. Look after her until I get back. I should be home in half an hour."

"Okay."

"Did anyone witness it? Why the fuck weren't my men around?" I snarled down the phone.

"I am guessing Toni sent them all off on a break. He obviously knew Cami was alone, the fucking scumbag," Max's tone was laced with pure hatred and he took in a deep breath to calm down before he continued. "No one saw. Only Marco knows. He just helped me shove the body in the boot of a car. I will get rid of it later tonight."

I ran my hand down my face as the stress built. What the f*ck were we going to tell Sal? He would definitely work out Toni was missing by morning. I couldn't have him suspecting any of us to ensure my plan would work. But right now, I was more concerned about Liv. I knew she would be a mess but I couldn't deny that I am not secretly impressed and proud that she did that to save Max. This woman just keeps on surprising me and I fucking love it.

As soon as we pulled up outside the mansion, my door was open, and I was already out of the car before the engine had stopped. Darting into the house, I ran into the living room where I could hear muffled voices and saw Cami led on the sofa, Max sitting next to her and Dr Halsorino and a nurse attending to them both.

"Where is she?" I demanded as the nurse let go of Max's battered face so he could answer me.

"Upstairs. In your room."

My heart was palpitating in my chest as I raced up the stairs to the top floor and sprinted into the bedroom. When I found it completely empty, panic rose in me. "Liv?" I called out but there was no answer.

I ran over to the closed bathroom door and tried to open it but when I realised it was locked, I knocked softly. "Liv? It's me. Open up."

There was no response. My breathing became erratic as the panic started to consume me. A flashback of a very similar scene entered my mind from two years ago; knocking on mamma's bathroom door with no answer. The steam coming out from the bottom of the door. I broke the door down and found Mamma trying to drown herself in the bath with a slit wrist. It was one of the worst days of my life so far.

"LIV?" I boomed, now desperate to know she was okay. When there was still no answer, I stepped back from the door and kicked it with so much force the lock shattered into pieces on the floor. I dove into the steamy room just as her body shot out from under the water at the intrusion. Without removing any of my clothes, I leapt into the bath and pulled her up into my arms, holding her against my chest. Only then did I realise my whole body was trembling with fear. Fear that I had lost her.

"Gio?" She whispered in surprise as I pulled her head back from my chest. Even though her make-up had run down her face and her hair was soaking wet, she still looked as beautiful as ever.

"What were you doing?" I growled, unable to keep the hurt out of my voice that she might have been trying to end it all. That she might not be able to handle this life.

"I-I was- holding my breath," she stuttered. Her eyes filled with tears and her bottom lip trembled. My eyes scanned her stunning green irises with those ember sparks.

"Why?" I asked more softly.

"I was t-trying to stop the panic attack," she whispered, and I exhaled loudly. Our eyes locked and I felt overwhelmed with love and admiration for this woman. She was my entire universe, and I could never let anything happen to her. I would not survive losing her ever. I now knew just a fraction of hurt mamma must be living with every day.

I leaned forward to capture her lips with mine, melting the world and all our anxiety away as she wrapped her arms around my neck and threaded her fingers through my hair, deepening the kiss. Within seconds, she was clawing at my soaked shirt, and I was frantically undoing my trousers and standing up in the bath to remove them before diving back down and pulling her onto my lap. She gasped into my mouth as I entered her quickly, needing her to wash away the horrors of the day. She needed me too. That much was clear. In this moment, all we would feel was each other. Our love. Our connection. Our pleasure. It was what we both needed more than the air we breathed. Wrapping my arms around her tightly, I moved in and out at a pleasurable pace as the tears rolled down her cheeks and I kissed her hard, trying to take all her pain away.

A Wedding or a Funeral?

Olivia

I dug my nails into his toned back as the euphoric feeling heightened to the precipice of pleasure. This was my safe place. Being in his arms. Feeling him inside me. Every touch, every kiss, every breath mixed with mine was calming me and the world was fading away. It was just him and I.

I gripped my hands in his hair as the water splashed around us when he quickened his thrusts to push us both over the edge of heaven. We both cried out at the same time, gasping and panting our orgasms into the room.

I lowered my forehead against his and closed my eyes, trying to hold onto this moment in time. I didn't want to face reality. I didn't want to come back down to Earth and face what I had done.

"Bambola?" His silky, soft voice beckoned me back. "Are you okay?"

I slowly shook my head against his, never opening my eyes. I was scared of what I would see. I had killed a member of his family. What if he never forgave me? What if this changed everything?

"Liv, look at me. I am right here," he whispered. Reluctantly, I opened my eyes and was met by his beautiful pools of brown that shimmered with so much love. It made me immediately want to cry again.

"I- I killed him. I killed Toni. I'm so sorry!" I whimpered as I let it all flow out of me, shaking in his arms. He gripped me tighter to him, before cupping my face in his hands forcing me to hold his gaze.

"You have nothing to be sorry about Olivia. You saved Max's life. Toni was trying to rape Cami. That asshole deserved everything he got. You rid the world of a monster."

I released a shaky breath as I let his words sink in. Is that really what happened? He was trying to rape Cami? It suddenly all made sense. The guilt dissolved and was replaced with so much anger. How dare he do that to her? And then try to kill Max!

Seeing my change in mood, a small smile played on Gio's lips as he leaned forward and kissed me briefly.

"My little badass bambola," he smiled.

I wasn't ready for jokes yet. This was all still too serious. Even if he was a monster, he was Sal's consigliere and there would be extreme consequences for killing him, I was sure. Sal didn't strike me as the type of man who would forgive something like this easily. "What about Sal? He will find out and he will- "

"He will do nothing. A dead man can do nothing."

I froze hearing his harsh words and the seriousness of his tone. I pulled my head away from his to search his face for meaning.

"What do you mean?"

His nostrils flared and he closed his eyes momentarily, clearly trying to get some control over his sudden fury. When he opened them again, I saw his darkness. It should have scared me, it would anyone else, but I knew it was not directed at me. It would never be directed at me.

"Sal killed Vinny. He orchestrated the entire thing. Him and Toni worked with Francesco to frame the Leones for killing my father."

My mouth dropped open, and I gasped. Max was right. It was all Salvatore. Everything this family had been through was because of him.

"I am going to kill him, Liv."

My stomach flipped as the fear of Giovanni taking on Salvatore caused dread to infect every inch of my body. I had seen first-hand how ruthless his uncle was and clearly the lengths he would go to get what he wanted. "I am so sorry Gio. But he is Boss! How are you going to do it without him knowing you are coming for him? Please tell me you have a plan Gio and you aren't just going to pull your gun out and shoot him in the head? What about all his loyal soldiers? What about the commission?"

My mind was working a thousand miles a minute as the panic started to flood through me. He brushed my hair away from my face with a small smile. "Shh, I have a plan. Don't worry. It's going to take some organising, but it will work. I know it will. The water is getting cold, let's get out of here and find Max and Cami and then I will explain everything." I nodded slowly, my mind still whirling with everything that had happened today. As I stared up at my gorgeous man all I could feel was grateful. He was alive and back in my arms. That was all I cared about right now.

"Turn around and let me wash your hair," he commanded. I did as he asked, his large hands massaging my scalp and then tenderly rinsing it off with the shower head. I closed my eyes as I let him take care of me, knowing he needed it as much as I did.

***

"I fucking knew it!" Max shouted as he paced the private living room floor, hand on his hip and other hand running through his long hair. His face was looking better after just a few hours. He had a few butterfly stitches on his right cheek and lip and bruising around his eye. The marks on his neck were no longer flaming red but it was still obvious he had been in a pretty fierce fight.

Cami was sitting next to me on the sofa, a small bandage on her forehead. She seemed surprisingly okay for someone who had just been sexually assaulted and nearly raped. She seemed more concerned for Max than herself.

"I just said to Liv this morning that I had a feeling that was what the Leones wanted to say. And there is evidence?" Max asked, looking over at Gio who was slouched in an armchair with a whiskey in hand.

"Loads of it. I have it all. The Leones did a thorough job of getting every incriminating detail so there was no way Sal could worm his way out of this one. There are voice recordings of their meetings, phone calls, and emails. The lot. Toni was the one it was mainly going through. The middleman so to speak. But Sal agreed to it all. It was all for his benefit. Get rid of the Leones. Get rid of Vinny so he could get to mamma and me." Gio rubbed his jaw as he said the last sentence, emotion flicking through his eyes. I knew there was a part of him that felt guilty. That he somehow felt like Vinny's death was his fault. That it was because of Sal's obsession with him and Cecilia that Vinny was killed. Elle, Sani and Raya lost their papi because of it.

"Cecilia! We have to tell her," I said quickly, realising that she was living with her husband's murder.

Giovanni sighed deeply, the world suddenly seeming too heavy for his shoulders.

"I will but not until it is safe to. This will kill her. She will blame herself."

We all sat in silence for a few moments as the truth of those words sunk in. He was right. This will tear her apart, but she had a right to know. She deserved to know who was responsible.

"So, what is the plan? I can't wait to kill the second of Satan's spawn," Max grinned with malice. "Liv already put one down so let's get on with the second."

"I am going to take all the evidence to the commission first thing in the morning. They will obviously accept that Salvatore is guilty of murdering his own underboss and trying to frame another mafia family for it. I will ask for permission to allow the Leones retaliation rights. I cannot be seen as the one who will kill Salvatore as it will cause problems within our family. I need soldiers and capos to believe that the Leones killed him and then the truth can come out about what he did to Vinny through the commission, keeping my hands clean in the whole thing."

Max nodded. "That is a good plan. You will have everyone's respect and loyalty as Boss immediately and when it comes out that Sal killed Vinny, no one will see the need to retaliate against the Leones. Vinny was loved by everyone. But don't you want to be the one to kill Sal? Instead of handing him over to the Leones?"

A slow, dark smile stretched across Gio's face as he looked up at Max. "I will be. I have already sorted it with the Leones. On the way to the wedding, we will be ambushed by Leone men. They will take both Sal and I hostage. Max, you will then inform mamma what has happened and bring her to the Leones. Tell her everything. She will want to watch him die. At that very last minute, I will be released in front of Sal and the depth of my betrayal will become clear. I will kill him myself."

Max whistled and chuckled loudly. "Savage! Killed by his own son on his enemy's territory. There is no bigger fuck you then that!"

"I am not his son," Gio growled. Max raised his hands up in apology and I sighed. I really hope now more than ever that the paternity test came back negative. That Sal really was not his father because I could see in Gio's eyes that he was going to kill Sal no matter what that envelope said. But I would hate for him to have to live with the fact he killed his own father.

"What about Toni?" Cami asked quietly next to me. My heart tugged at his name and the reminder of what I had done but it was far less crippling now.

Gio and Max spared a glance at each other as they thought deeply. I knew I had added to this mess. It was just another thing they had to try and manage without Sal becoming suspicious.

"We act oblivious. Toni is missing. We know nothing. I will ring Sal tonight and tell him Max just had a scrap in a club with a Leone soldier. That should cover us for a short time," Gio replied.

"Problem is… Toni was last seen here. By the men he sent on break. It will get back to Sal that he was here today. What if we made Sal believe the Leone's had him? Had captured him on his way back?"

"It could work but it is a risk. He could call off the wedding to try and find Toni," Cami added.

Gio shook his head. "He won't. He has waited thirty years to marry mamma. He won't let anything stop him. Even though the Leones are supporting this, I still don't trust them. They could play Sal and I off against each other if I give them too much information about Toni. I would rather play dumb. He is missing. We know nothing."

We all nodded in agreement. Once we went through some more of the fine details of the wedding day, I felt completely exhausted. Cecilia would come here to get ready with us girls while Gio and Max would go to Sal's house to get ready with his uncle. We would tell her everything and that the wedding would not be going ahead. We would wait for Max so we knew that the plan had worked and Gio and Sal were at Leone's territory and then Cecilia and Max would go along if she wanted to confront Sal before Gio killed him. It was a confident plan but there were still so many risky factors at play. We were trusting the Leones once again to keep their word. We were hoping Sal still went ahead with the wedding without Toni. And we were praying that Cecilia would be onboard. My heart broke for her as I thought about the pain she was about to endure.

***

Cecilia

I stared blankly at the floor to ceiling mirror as two women made last minute adjustments to the silk fabric of my ivory suit for my wedding day. *My wedding day.* It was almost laughable. I refused to wear a dress.

The sharp sting of a needle caught my thigh as one of the young designers pushed through the fabric and I hissed at her. Her eyes widened and she started to apologise profusely but I had already lost my patience.

"I've had enough. Get me out of this. Now," I snarled and they stood up from their positions and carefully took the suit jacket off my body. It's been three days since I stopped taking my medication, and I was starting to feel the effects. My patience was at an all-time low and I felt my moods shifting like the breeze.

After changing back into my designer tracksuit, I returned to my position on the sofa of the theatre room in Sal's house and pressed play to the mind-numbing movie. This is where I had hidden myself away for the last two days. Watching films, eating crap and drinking wine. What else was there to do? I couldn't bring myself to see my children. To have to force the happiness on my face to avoid them worrying. I didn't have the energy for it. I didn't have the energy for anything.

It must have been evening by the time Sal walked into the room with a pissed expression seeing the state of me and the contents of bottles of wine and empty food packets. The staff had informed me dinner was ready and Sal was waiting for me in the dining room, but I ignored them. Just like I was ignoring his judgmental glare now.

"Cecilia. Enough. Look at the state of you. Get up and come and eat dinner now."

"I'm not hungry," I replied coldly, causing his jaw to tick and fists to clench at the sides of his tailored trousers.

"I have been patient. I have given you space to get used to this change but my patience is wearing thin now woman. All I asked is that you have dinner with me every night. One thing."

"And I said, I am… NOT… HUNGRY," I shouted, my anger taking control. Why can't he leave me alone? I watched as his own control snapped and his eyes darkened with fury. He leaned forward, grabbing my upper arm with force and yanking me up from the sofa. "Get off me you bastard!"

He ignored my thrashing and screaming as he threw me over his shoulder and marched out of the cinema room, through the extravagant lobby towards the dining room. He threw me down aggressively into a chair where a meal had been placed on expensive crystal plates and laid out like a bloody fine dining experience. I glared up at him and folded my arms across my chest in defiance as he pulled out his chair next to me and sat down. Without saying a word, he picked up his knife and fork and started to eat.

After a few minutes of not touching my food, he looked up with a menacing glare.

"Eat."

"You may be forcing me to be here, but you cannot force me to eat!" I smirked.

"I am not forcing you to be here. You agreed to be with me. You chose this. Deep down there is a part of you that has always wanted this and the sooner you get onboard the better it will be for everyone."

I burst out laughing which caused him to grind his teeth.

"You are delusional! What choice did I have? It was either my children's happiness or mine! You knew full well I would do anything for my children, and you used that against me. I will never want this! I will never want you!" I screamed and, in a flash, he leapt from his seat and grabbed me around the throat, pulling me up to my feet. His dark eyes glared down at me as he tightened his grip, restricting my airways enough to hold me in place but not enough that I was gasping for air.

"You wanted me once before. You will want me again. You cannot deny that I was the best sex of your life," he growled. His face was inches from mine, his lips brushing against mine seductively.

I narrowed my eyes as I prepared myself for the aftermath of my words. "No. Vinny was."

To my surprise, he laughed. Loudly and sadistically.

"Liar!" He smashed his lips against mine, forcing his strong tongue into my mouth and pulling me into his body. My fingers stretched down to the table as I gripped a knife and held it against his throat, breaking the kiss. Panting heavily, we stared at each other as I pushed the blade against his skin.

"Do it. Go on Cecilia. Slit my throat and be rid of me if that is what you really want," he released my neck and stood there, holding my gaze as my hand started to shake. A slow, triumphant smile slowly tugged at the corners of his mouth when he knew I couldn't do it.

"You see. Somewhere inside you, you still have feelings for me. And once I make you my wife tomorrow, I will expect you to give into those feelings." He took the knife from my trembling hand and placed it back down on the table, before returning to his seat. Anger and frustration reached their peak as he arrogantly took a bite of chicken from his fork, smirking at me.

Seeing red, I grabbed my own crystal plate piled with food and threw it against the wall, food and glass smashing everywhere.

"I HATE YOU!" I screamed hysterically before storming from the room.

"And I love you, wife," he shouted with an infuriating cackle, his booming voice following me down the hall like the plague that I would never be rid of.

Hidden in plain sight

Olivia

"So, when do we tell her?" Cami whispered as I poured out four glasses of champagne in the private living room of the Buccini mansion. I glanced over my shoulder at Elle and Cecilia. Cecilia was dressed in her elegant ivory wedding suit and Elle was curling her hair. There was a vacant look in her eyes as she stared at her reflection in the mirror in front. Elle was doing a great job at talking her ear off about anything and everything under the sun but Cecilia hadn't uttered a word all morning.

"Soon. Gio told me to wait until he messages me, but just look at her Cami. She is miserable. This feels like we are torturing her for no good reason. The sooner we tell her this wedding isn't happening the better."

Cami nodded in agreement as we both picked up the flutes and made our way over to them.

"You look gorgeous, Cecilia," Cami said as she handed her the champagne flute which Cecilia took without saying a word. She knocked back the champagne in one go and the three of us shared a concerned look. I couldn't keep up the façade. It wasn't right.

"Cecilia. We have something to tell you," I said carefully as Elle's head snapped up at mine. Her eyes gave me a 'what the fuck are you doing?' look. I shrugged and pointed to Cecilia and Elle sighed deeply as she looked back at her mamma.

Squatting down in front of her mother, Elle took the empty champagne glass from her hands before holding her beautifully manicured hands in hers. "Mamma?"

Cecilia looked down at Elle for the first time and gave her a small smile. "Oh Elenora. You look lovely, my dear."

Elle smiled but it didn't reach her eyes as the magnitude of what she was about to say to her mum, caused her voice to catch and she cleared her throat. Elle had taken the news of who had killed her papi badly but she knew she had to be strong for her mother right now.

"Mamma, the wedding is off."

Cecilia shook her head slowly and held her hand up to Elle's face. "How many times must I say it my love, I must do this for you. Let me do this for my children."

"No mamma. You don't have to. You won't have to. Salvatore will not be at the altar to marry you."

Cecilia's perfectly groomed eyebrows furrowed as she looked from Elle up to me. I moved around so I perched on the coffee table next to Elle for support. "What do you mean? Why not?"

"Mamma, Sal...Sal killed..." Elle's voice broke as she choked on her words and tears sprang to her eyes. Cecilia's concerned eyes darted from her daughter to me in question.

"Cecilia. This is going to be very difficult to hear but we want you to know we are all here to support you and we love you. Giovanni is dealing with it and it's over. You will never have to see Sal again."

Cecilia suddenly stood up, impatience and unease evident on her confused features. "What are you talking about? What happened?"

I took a deep breath as Cami handed Elle a tissue to wipe her eyes. "Cecilia, Gio met with the Leones. They had gathered evidence over the last two years to find out who was trying to frame them for Vinny's murder. They gave it all to Gio."

Cecilia froze and, regardless of the blush that had been applied to her cheeks just minutes ago, she looked deathly pale.

"What? It was the Leones. They killed my Vinny."

I shook my head carefully, maintaining eye contact with her. She visibly gulped.

"No mamma. It wasn't them. It was Salvatore. Sal and Toni worked with the Aianis to kill papi and frame the Leones for it," Elle managed to whimper.

Cecilia stumbled back on her heels, shaking her head until her legs hit the sofa and she fell with a gasp.

"No," she whispered, her eyes wide but looking right through us. "No. That's not possible."

I raced to her, falling to my knees in front of her as I took her hands in mine, forcing her to see me.

"It is true. Sal killed Vinny. That is what the alliance was about. He had promised Gio would marry Camilla in return for their men attacking Vinny. Sal planned the whole thing."

Tears sprang to her eyes as she continued to shake her head. "No. NO! Why? Why would he do that? Why would he kill my Vinny? He loved him. He was his brother!" Cecilia jumped up from the sofa as she paced the room hysterically, her whole-body trembling.

None of us spoke as we let her come to the realisation herself. I couldn't break her heart more than it already was. I couldn't force the words out of my mouth. She suddenly screamed. A noise that was full of so much pain and heartbreak as she fell to her knees and Elle rushed to her side, cradling her in her arms as Cecilia broke down in tears and unbearable cries.

Tears left my own eyes as I watched the strongest woman I know fall apart in front of me. This was so unfair. She didn't deserve this. None of them deserved this. All because of one man's selfishness. All because of one man's obsession. Salvatore Buccini was just like Henry. Of that I was certain.

It felt like the longest time before Cecilia's wails simmered down to sobs and Elle helped her up off the floor, back to the sofa. I poured her a glass of water and placed it on the table in front of her as her red-rimmed eyes stared at it without blinking.

"It was me, wasn't it?" Her voice was barely audible. "He killed him because of me."

No one confirmed it. We didn't need to. We all knew what Sal's reasons were. She released a shuddering breath as she glanced up at me for the first time since she heard the words that changed everything.

"What is Gio going to do?"

"He has informed the commission. They have agreed to let the Leones retaliate. They will stage an ambush on Gio and Sal and take them to the Leone estate. That is when Gio and the Leones will confront Sal and he will kill him," I said as calmly and clearly as I could.

She nodded slowly. I wasn't sure if she really understood or registered my words as that vacant expression returned to her face. My phone started vibrating on the table and I stood up and walked out of the room to take it when I saw it was Giovanni.

"Hey, you can tell mamma now. We are at Leones place. They have Sal in an interrogation room. Everything is going to plan," his voice was a low whisper, and I bit my lip.

"We've already told her. I'm sorry, but I couldn't hold it in anymore, seeing what this was doing to her."

He sighed, "How did she take it?"

"Not great as expected. I think she has gone into shock now. I will give her some time and then ask if she wants to see Sal before...you know."

"Ok. No rush. The Leones will be torturing Sal before they let me at him anyway," he replied nonchalantly. My gut twisted at those words. Torturing. I knew Sal deserved everything he was about to get and more, but I still hated the images that came into my mind.

"Are you okay?" I asked softly. Gio was strong and he was angry, but this still couldn't be easy for him. Sal was still his family.

"I'm good. I will be once he is out of our lives and can no longer manipulate or fuck with my family," he growled. "I have the paternity test." My eyes widened. I didn't know it had come. "It arrived this morning. I haven't opened it. I don't know if I can."

My heart broke for him and I wished I could hug him. "Remember whatever is in that envelope changes nothing. Vinny was your papi. No matter what."

"I love you bambola. I have to go."

"I love you too. Be safe."

He hung up and I stared at the phone, chewing my lip. I couldn't wait for this day to be over.

"Liv! She's gone!" Elle came running out into the lobby with panic.

"What? Who?"

"Mamma! She said she wanted to use the bathroom. I just went in and she climbed out the freaking window!" She screamed as she bolted to the front door. Cami and I raced out after her.

"She took the wedding car! It's gone!" Elle gripped her hair in her hands as she looked down the driveway. Angelo came running out towards us.

"Olivia. Is there a problem?" Angelo asked.

"Cecilia. She has gone."

He turned his back to us, pulling out his mobile and speaking aggressively in Italian. When he got off, he turned back to me.

"She is with Nik and has taken the wedding car. She has asked to go to the Leone mansion."

Shit. I pulled out my phone and started to frantically type out a text to Gio, warning him his mother was on her way.

"What do we do now?" Elle asked.

"You need to stay here with the kids and in case she comes back. I will go with Angelo and see if we can catch up with her car. Cami, Max is on his way here, so you might as well wait and come up with him." I felt like I had to take some control of this situation as the two women stared at me wide-eyed and nodded.

There was still one wedding car parked on the driveway with a driver ready to go inside. We had needed to make the whole wedding look authentic to the rest of the mafia family. Only Nik, Marco and Angelo were aware of the true plan to kill Salvatore today, as they were the only men Gio truly trusted and were more loyal to him than his uncle.

Angelo nodded at me as we skipped down the steps. I grabbed the hem of my blush pink bridesmaid dress and slid into the backseat of the car as Angelo climbed in next to me.

"Leone estate," Angelo ordered the driver as I frantically typed away on my phone to Gio to let him know the new plan. The car pulled aggressively from the gravel and made its way out of the grounds and onto the roads of Verona. Gio hadn't replied to my messages, but I hadn't expected him to. He would be busy killing his uncle/father most likely. My battery warning symbol flashed on my phone, and I cursed as the screen went black.

I had no idea what would be going on in Cecilia's head right now. Was she going to try and stop Gio? Was she going to confront Sal or kill him herself? My heart was pounding with the adrenaline at this situation. Leaning forward to look between the two front seats, I peered out the front window ahead to try and spot any sign of Cecilia's wedding car up the road. And that is when my heart stopped. I glanced up into the rear-view mirror and was met with the pair of bright blue eyes that haunted my nightmares under a black driver's cap, staring straight at me.

My whole body turned to ice and I was paralyzed with fear. Henry.

Veil of Betrayal

Giovanni

I never knew I could possess so much control.

Sitting across from the man who killed my papi and the man I was convinced put a hit on Olivia, I grinned as he put in his cufflinks and pulled on his Tom Ford tailored cream jacket. The only thing that was keeping me calm and collected was the knowledge that by the end of today, he would no longer be breathing.

Staring up at his smug face as he checked himself out in the mirror made me want to laugh. He had no idea. No idea that he was about to face his death at my hands. He thought he had won. Everything he has ever done, was for this moment in time. He had mamma. He was marrying her. He was Boss. He had his heir. The Aianis were our allies not by choice but still. He was one step closer to destroying the Leones. Yet all of this was an illusion. He had achieved none of it.

"Still no word from Toni?" Max asked as he leaned against Sal's bar in his gentleman's room where we were all getting ready.

A deep frown set on Sal's face. "No. He wouldn't miss this. Something is not right."

I took a slow sip of my whiskey before answering, "Do you still want to go ahead with the wedding? Or shall we try and track him down?"

Sal coughed gruffly and cleared his throat as he smoothed down his jacket. "No. We will go ahead. If he still hasn't shown up by the end of the day, then we will start the search party."

I smirked into my glass. Selfish. I didn't expect any less from him. Toni had been his best mate since they were kids and his right-hand man for twenty-seven years. Yet, he has no concern for his whereabouts on his wedding day. Just more proof that Salvatore Buccini was only ever out for himself.

"I wonder what Vinny would think about all of this," I couldn't help but prod the beast. Sal's dark eyes narrowed at me through his reflection in the mirror at my mention of papi.

"What do you think he would think?" Sal spun the question back on me. Clever. He was checking my loyalty.

"I think anything that makes mamma happy he would be okay with. And she is happy right?" I asked.

A fake smile plastered on his face as he turned to me. "Of course. She has never been happier. Though I am not sure her meds are entirely accurate. She has seemed more…emotional as of late. I shall investigate it after the wedding."

Irritation brewed within me. I was sure my mother's moods towards him had nothing to do with her medication and more to do with the hate she possessed for her brother-in-law. I shuffled in my seat and sat up taller. Now to test the waters on the topic of Olivia.

"Weddings all around in the Buccini family," I smiled as I raised my tumbler to Max. He returned my celebration by raising his and Sal turned to pick his own glass up. "First you and mamma, then Max and Camilla. Makes me think I should pop the question too."

For a split second, Sal's hand froze on its way up to bring his drink to his mouth. It was the smallest reaction, but I caught it.

"Though I am not sure Olivia is perhaps the right woman to be married to a Boss," I added.

Max's eyes widened slightly until he caught my eye and realised what I was doing. Sal turned to me, suddenly fully invested in our conversation. "I thought she was the love of your life?"

I shrugged, "I may have been letting how good her pussy tastes affect my judgement. I don't think she is cut out for this world after all, but we will see."

I had never seen a wider grin on Boss' face. "I could have told you that Giovanni. But I guess the truth always comes out eventually."

I pursed my lips together to avoid the laugh I was suppressing at his words. There was no doubt in my mind that he wanted Olivia out of my life, and he would go to any lengths to achieve it. Even more reason to end him.

"I couldn't agree more," Max said with a grin as he looked over at me.

"Very wise words indeed, papi," I said calmly even though it physically hurt me to call him that, but it had the desired effect. His face broke out into a genuine smile when heard that word from my lips. "Shall we go? We must not keep your bride waiting?"

***

The wedding car was speeding down the cliff roads and I glanced up ahead when I saw the junction that I had agreed with the Leones would be the ambush point. I had managed to persuade Salvatore to be unarmed in his wedding suit, promising that I had my gun and his soldiers had theirs. He agreed easily to my surprise, his genuine happiness helping to distract him.

"You know when I first saw your mamma, I knew I would marry her one day," he suddenly interrupted the silence in the car and I turned to look at him. He was staring out of the window, deep in thought. "I saw her first. She was always meant to be mine. But life doesn't always work out the way we want it. Sometimes, we must fight for what we want because life doesn't hand you everything on a plate, son."

I stilled at his words. It was almost a confession. He didn't know that I would be able to read between the lines. That I would understand the true meaning of his words.

Suddenly, the breaks of the car slammed on as Sal's soldier noticed the convoy blocking the road ahead. Sal's eyes glazed over when he saw Riccardo and Lorenzo standing in front of several cars with their arms folded and sinister smiles.

"Fucking Leones," Sal hissed as I pulled out my gun from the back of my trousers. "Pass me your gun," he demanded his driver who hesitated slightly before passing it back to Sal. Shit. I wanted him unarmed for this.

"Plan Boss?" I asked frantically as I looked out the back window at two other SUVs that had suddenly blocked us in from behind. Sal growled when he saw it too.

"Take as many of them out as we can. If they get too close, we jump."

My eyes widened as I realised what he meant. "Off the fucking cliff?"

"Si. If they capture us, it's game over Giovanni. At least if we jump, we have a chance of surviving." He flung open the car door and opened fire on the Leone men. I did the same, ensuring I missed every time. This was not going to fucking plan. I ducked behind the shelter of the bullet proof door as bullets plummeted our way.

Fuck. I couldn't let Sal get shot here. I couldn't let him jump either. It was a huge risk but I had to knock him out. Keeping low, I snuck around the back of the car hoping the Leone soldiers behind us didn't open fire on my ass or I was dead. Sal was too distracted shooting forwards to notice me approaching behind. Using the handle of my gun, I hit him hard on the back of the head and he fell to the dirt floor, unconscious. Glancing at the Buccini driver, I saw blood all over the window of the car and realised he had already been taken out.

"Tieni il fuoco! Salvatore è fuori! (Hold fire! Salvatore is out!)" I shouted. This was the moment it could have all gone wrong. Had I put too much trust in my enemy? They could easily kill me themselves right here and take down the whole Buccini family. The only security I had is that the commission had only given approval for Sal's death and not mine.

The gun shots stopped. I slowly stood up, with my hands in the air as two Leone soldiers came running towards our car. They tied Sal's hands behind his back and threw a hooded bag over his head before dragging him over to a SUV. I walked up to Riccardo and Lorenzo.

"Thought you said he wouldn't be armed?" Lorenzo narrowed his eyes on me.

"He wasn't. He took his soldier's gun."

"Well, that was fast thinking to knock him out or we might have killed him on this fucking dirt road and where is the fun in that?" Riccardo grinned.

I climbed into their car with them and we all drove back to the Leone's mansion. As soon as we arrived, I walked away from the men to ring Olivia. There were always two soldiers on my guard, watching me suspiciously as I spoke in a hushed voice down the phone. As soon as I was done, I pocketed it and walked into their estate. The soldiers led me down to the cellars below the house which is where their interrogation and torture rooms were. I was put in the room next to where they were holding Sal.

After a few minutes, Lorenzo came in. We did not like each other. That much was clear. Where Riccardo seemed to enjoy at least trying to be civil towards me, Lorenzo never hid his feelings. And they were fucking mutual.

"He has just woken up. Father is going to start the torture now and I had the idea of making it seem legit that you were being tortured too," he smirked. I chuckled as I folded my arms.

"And let me guess? You offered to be the one to do it?"

"Of course. We want him to truly believe you are dying right?"

I huffed loudly. "Nothing to my face. It's my best feature," I smirked.

He walked over to a cabinet that was full of torture devices and held out two options. A leather whip with metal spikes attached or a steel poker. We had one of those ourselves. You scorch it until it glows and scar the skin. Hurts like a mother fucker but it would leave less scaring than the whip.

"Poker," I shrugged as I sat down on the metal chair and rolled up my trouser leg. I wasn't about to let him scold just any part of my body. Lorenzo's eyebrows raised at my choice but a sadistic smile spread across his face as he used a blow torch to heat the poker until the end glowed a vibrant orange.

He strolled over to me when it was ready and I mentally prepared myself for the insufferable pain of burning flesh.

"Remember, the louder you are the better," Lorenzo chuckled before he slammed the poker up against my calf muscle. I roared louder than I normally would at such pain and hissed as my skin sizzled against the steel.

Lorenzo removed it and I took some deep breaths. "Again," I muttered.

He pushed it against the same wound which felt like I was being burnt alive as I screamed in agony and groaned until he pulled it away. If this was a true torture, I wouldn't be making a sound. Biting down on my tongue rather than give them the satisfaction of hearing a peep out of me but that wasn't the purpose. I wanted Sal to believe I was being tortured so it would make my deceit so much sweeter when I walked in there to kill him.

***

Salvatore

The back of my head was fucking throbbing as I came around to darkness. Suddenly, the fabric over my head was whipped off me and I was confronted with bright lights and the face of my nemesis. Riccardo Leone.

I didn't have time to say a word, before his fist connected with my cheek and I spat blood out onto the cement floor of my interrogation cell.

"Nice to see you too, Amico," I smirked, blood lining my teeth before he hit me again.

"If you are that pissed off I didn't send you an invite to my wedding, you could have just called," I chuckled as his smile grew.

"Oh, you still believe you are getting married today. That's precious."

Anger rose in me that I was in fact here and not at my fucking wedding. The one I had waited thirty fucking years for.

Riccardo whistled and laughed, shaking his head as he walked over to a cabinet and leaned against it.

"Cecilia Buccini. I don't blame you. She is one fine piece of ass. If I wasn't happily married already, I would probably have taken her for myself."

I hissed at him through clenched teeth. My jaw tense as my eyes burned with hate. She was mine. No other man will ever have her.

"Tell me Sal. Did you really believe that she would jump straight into your arms as soon as you killed her husband or were you playing the long game?"

I clicked my tongue and glared at him. As if I would ever admit that I killed Vin to him. If I did make it out of this alive, I wouldn't ever risk CeCe or Giovanni knowing the truth.

Yes, I planned the murder of my only brother. He didn't deserve everything he had. He was born the lucky one. He had charm and charisma. Everyone who met him loved him. My papi even preferred him to me. I was the first born so I was the heir. I had to live up to every one of my father's high expectations whereas he could do whatever the fuck he wanted. He was mamma's favourite too, the crazy old bat. She made him soft. She made him lovable. And then he stole the only person I had ever wanted love from. Cecilia. I found her first. She was mine before she was his. Yet, he wormed his way in and stole her from me. He turned her against me. And when he started to do the same to Giovanni, I knew it was time to get my revenge. I waited patiently for years. Watched him have it all. The loving family. The perfect woman. The respect of our men. But I would not allow him to take Giovanni from me. He was my son. He was my heir.

That little gold-digging slut was trying to take him too. But that should all be solved by the end of the day. The fact Giovanni was even doubting his relationship with her was a fucking bonus. Hopefully he won't even go looking for her when he finds out she's missing. That psychotic little prick better stick to his word and take her far away from here. Hopefully, he kills her. He has it in him. You can see it in his eyes.

"No longer in the mood for talking Salvatore?" Riccardo sneered, as he fastened metal spiked knuckle rings to his hand. "You see… I know what you did. I know you plotted to kill Vincenzo with Francesco and tried to frame us for it. What a convenience that Francesco is no longer with us to back up the story."

I refused to open my mouth. I had no doubt he was probably knew the truth and was not bluffing. He would have been looking into Vin's murder the moment he heard I was pinning it on him. Which is why I needed them gone. Him and his son.

After a few rounds of beatings, the metal spikes piercing my jaw and stomach from his blows, I panted loudly.

"What do you want, Riccardo?" It was time to negotiate my release. I would find something this fucker wanted more than my head. Everyone had their price.

Suddenly, a loud roar and painful scream echoed through the walls. My eyes widened and my nostrils flared as I knew it was Giovanni.

"Name your price Leone. Anything you want as long as you release me and my son."

His eyebrows shot up in surprise at my words and a sadistic grin stretched over his scarred face, making him look ten times more monstrous.

"Son? Well, that does explain a lot doesn't it, Salvatore?" I growled in his face when I heard Giovanni screaming from whatever torture they were giving him. "The truth. That is all I want."

I narrowed my eyes at him with distrust. The truth?

"About what?" I groaned through the blood that was pooling in my mouth.

"About everything," His blue eyes sparkled with excitement.

"You want me to admit I killed my brother? You want me to clear your name with the commission? I would never kill my brother. But I know it wasn't you who did. I know it was Francesco. That is why I put a bullet in his skull myself."

Riccardo folded his arms across his chest as he chuckled, shaking his head. "Oh Sal. That is almost believable. But I have the proof you see." He walked over to a laptop and pressed play. Toni's voice filled the room as well as Francesco's as I listened to the two fucking idiots speaking so openly about Vin's murder and our alliance. My jaw ticked.

"You have Toni?" I hissed, realising it was my consigliere that has betrayed me.

"I wish I could say I did. I would love to torture that prick but unfortunately not."

Suddenly, the door swung open and my eyes widened when I saw Giovanni strolling in. I would have been happy to see he was well if it wasn't for the dark, evil look in his eyes that was directed at me.

"Giovanni. Whatever they have told you is a lie. I did not kill Vinny. I would never, he was my brother," I said calmly, trying to tug at the cable wires around my wrists.

Giovanni cocked his head to the side as he leaned over and pressed a button on the laptop. My voice filled the room. It was a private conversation I had with Toni at Aiani's residence. I felt the colour drain from my face as I said the words, "Don't even bother putting Vin in a coffin. Just bury him in the dirt."

Within seconds, Giovanni had kicked me in the chest, causing the chair I was sitting on to fall backwards and he was on top of me, pounding my face with his fists. I was barely still conscious, my eyes barely open and head spinning when he finally climbed off me and pulled my chair upright.

"You think you are so clever, Boss. You think you pulled the wool over all our eyes? I have known for days. I know what you did. Toni took a trip to the meat grinder. And you will be joining him very soon."

My heart sped up as the realisation hit me. This was all planned. Giovanni betrayed me. He worked with the Leones.

My blood boiled at the disrespect and deceit of my own son.

"I am your father! How dare you!"

I could just make out his face as he bent down to my level. "Let's find out, shall we?" I squinted my swollen eyes as I saw him pull out an envelope from his suit jacket, "I got a paternity test."

Ripping it open, I could barely focus as he stood up straight and scanned the page.

"Looks like you were wrong."

I shook my head as my heart plummeted in my chest.

"No. You are my son," I muttered, spitting blood onto the floor.

"According to this DNA test, I am not." He bent down again and stared straight into my eyes. "Even if it said you were, you would never be my father. Vinny was a far better man and father than you would ever be and I would kill you to avenge him regardless."

I dropped my head to my chest as I let his words sink in. Just at that moment, the door flew open and a vision in white stormed into the room. I squinted my eyes as I saw the most beautiful woman in the world to me, her eyes bloodshot and only hatred behind them.

"CeCe?" I whispered.

Her hand slammed across my face in one powerful slap, causing my head to whip to the side.

"You bastard!" She screamed.

The Devil's Deceit

Olivia

I was frozen in my seat as our eyes locked. No. How could it be? How did he find me?

Time stood still as he kept his eyes on me in the rear-view mirror. He knew I knew it was him. My heart was pounding in my chest and all I could hear was ringing in my ears as panic consumed me. As soon as I moved my eyes from him, I knew everything would change. He would do something...

I slid my hand discreetly towards Angelo's leg next to me and nudged him, keeping my eyes on Henry the entire time. I felt Angelo move his head towards me and I knew he would see the terror on my face. Within seconds, Angelo swiftly reached into his suit jacket to retrieve his gun, but Henry was fast. He turned and shot my bodyguard in the head, blood sprayed all over me and the car windows as Angelo's body slumped down on the seat. I screamed, bringing my knees up to my chest and cowering in the corner of the chair. I tried frantically to open the door to throw myself out of the car. I didn't care how fast Henry was zooming down this road, I would rather take my chance than stay in here with him. But, of course, it was locked.

"Livvy! Baby. Calm down," his voice was soft and smooth, as if he hadn't just killed a man seconds ago.

My breathing was erratic as my chest moved up and down in panted breaths as I stared at Angelo's lifeless body. His eyes were still open, with a gunshot wound in his forehead. Tears sprang to my eyes as sobs escaped my lips.

"I have missed you so much, Livvy. You look good. I like your hair," Henry smiled at me through the mirror, and I stared at him, wide-eyed as fear crippled me.

"W-where are y-you taking me Henry?" I choked out as I tried to recognise my bearings or a place we might be near. But only trees surrounded us. I had no idea where we were.

"Somewhere we can be together. You enjoyed the chase didn't you, Livvy? You loved making it hard for me. But I found you in the end, just like you wanted me to. I will always find you."

He removed the black driver's hat that had covered his face and ran his hand through his shaggy blonde hair. He had a stubbled jaw and tired skin. But his eyes still shone brightly like diamonds. Cold pools of ice.

My brain was frantic as I tried to think of a way to get away from him. I looked over at Angelo's body and saw his hand still under his suit jacket. A gun. Angelo would have a gun on him. But I was too far away. Henry would see me reach for it and could shoot me before I could even get to it. Then I glanced down and saw on his other arm that was resting on the chair between us the black alarm watch on his wrist.

My heart flipped in my chest. I could send an alert. It was bound to go to Giovanni or Max. But I needed to distract Henry.

I sat up slightly in my seat, his eyes darting at my movement in the mirror.

"How did you find me Henry?"

A sadistic smile made me gulp as I slowly inched my hand towards Angelo's watch.

"I knew you weren't in the UK after I ransacked your bitch of a best friend's house. I found your scrapbook you made with her when you were kids. All the places you wanted to visit. But the fucking pigs were on my back so I couldn't exactly hop on a plane discreetly."

I tugged at the band of the watch slightly as he spoke, pulling Angelo's arm towards me. "So, I couldn't believe my luck when some mafia bloke cornered me in an underground bar one night. Told me you were in Italy and his boss would pay for me to fly out by private jet to come and get you." I froze at his words.

"Who?"

"Your boyfriend's father. Salvatore something."

Oh my god.

"I've been here for a week, Livvy. Growing impatient to see you. But Toni said I had to wait until today. That today was the day."

I hit the screen of the watch and saw the red dot that would send an alert. I pressed it quickly and looked back up at Henry. His eyes had narrowed and he suddenly looked pissed. That look I was all too familiar with.

"What are you doing, Livvy?"

It was now or never. He slammed the brakes of the car as I dived at Angelo's body for his gun. The sudden jolt of the car caused me to fall into the footwell before I could pull the gun from the harness. Henry had climbed into the back and was now on top of me as I scrambled to reach up for the gun in Angelo's jacket.

"Don't be a fucking idiot Liv!" Henry growled as he grabbed my arm and pulled it above my head. He pulled Angelo's gun out of his jacket and smirked at me before throwing it into the front of the car. Without missing a beat, I headbutted him hard in his nose twice until he groaned and shifted on top of me, sitting back. I booted him in the privates as I scrambled over to the front seat and opened the passenger door, grabbing the gun as I went.

Racing through the trees, my heart was thundering in my chest and my eyes scanned my surroundings frantically for any sign of human life. Every so often, I would look over my shoulder to see if Henry was after me but all

I could see were trees. Losing my balance, I tripped over a large tree root and fell face first. Quickly, I shuffled to my feet and hid behind a large tree trunk, the gun in my hands. My chest was rising and falling in shallow breaths as I tried to focus on keeping my fear and panic at bay.

"Livvy, you just love to tease me, don't you, you little slut? I am sick of these games you keep playing. Don't make me lose my patience!" His angry voice sent a shiver down my spine, and I held my breath. I had only ever shot a gun once and I managed to hit my target easily, but this was different. Toni wasn't moving and I had a clear aim.

I heard twigs snap close to the tree I was hiding behind and bile rose in my throat. Knowing I only had this one chance made my hands shake as I held the gun, poised ready to shoot. When I heard another branch snap even closer, I jumped out from behind the tree and shot at where I thought Henry was standing. But he wasn't there. Suddenly, I felt a hand around my mouth and my body was slammed back into his chest. I struggled against him, but he ripped the gun from my hand, another shot fired into the air as he tossed it away.

He lifted me with a strong arm around my waist and his other hand still over my mouth, muffling my screams, but I was not going to give up. I fought against him, trashing my arms and legs. Without warning, we both fell backwards towards the forest floor and a sharp pain struck my head before everything faded to black.

***

Giovanni

"You bastard!" The sound of mamma's violent slap echoed around the room and I could feel her fury and hurt radiating from her body.

"CeCe," Sal's voice was soft, almost pleading.

"Don't! Don't you dare! You are the most vile, despicable man who has ever lived. Vinny loved you! You were his older brother. You were supposed to protect him!" Her voice broke with emotion as her body trembled. I stepped forward to pull her back from him but she shrugged me off, never taking her accusing glare off his bloody face.

"He took everything from me!" Sal snapped, his body lunging forward in his chair, which was hopeless as he was tied so tightly to it, there was no chance he could get free.

"He took nothing from you! I never belonged to you. I was never yours in the first place. You were a drunken mistake that I have regretted every day for the rest of my life," she spat and he roared at her aggressively, spitting blood on the floor again.

"How could you ever think I could love you, Sal? You are not capable of love. You are not deserving of it. You will die knowing that no one loved you. I don't love you and never have. Gio doesn't love you. Everything you set out to do has failed. It was all for nothing!" She screamed in his face.

The evilest sound vibrated from his chest as he started to laugh. Soon, he was roaring like a mad man as mamma stepped back, shaking her head. I glared at him as I watched whatever he found so amusing possessing him like a demon.

"You are wrong CeCe." He looked up at us through his half-closed eyes that had swollen from my beating. "I achieved one thing."

My heart started thundering in my chest when his eyes locked with mine and I saw the malice lurking within them.

"How is Olivia?"

My eyebrows furrowed in confusion but my body was on high alert as soon as her name left his lips.

"What have you done, Sal?" Mamma whispered as she raised her hand to her lips.

"Love makes us weak, boy. You will thank me one day," he chuckled, and I lunged at him. My blood boiling with a mix of fury and panic.

"WHAT HAVE YOU DONE TO HER?" I screamed in his face as he continued to laugh.

"Not what…who…" he gave me a bloody, toothy grin and I froze.

"Henry…" I breathed as his words hit me like a ton of bricks.

"I am sure they will be very happy together. He seems like a nice man. Fucking demented, but who isn't? Toni messed up the homeless man hit so royally that I realised I would have to get rid of her myself. Luckily, Toni knew all about her past and tracking her stepbrother down was pretty easy."

All the colour drained from my face and my gut twisted so much I thought I was going to throw up. It all made sense. I couldn't find Henry because Sal already had him. He had been under his protection.

Suddenly, my watch vibrated on my wrist as a red alert came in from Angelo's watch. I glanced up at mamma with pure panic written all over my face.

"Go! Now," she shouted. Without a second thought, I raced from the room just as Max and Cami arrived.

"Stay with mamma! Make sure that fucker dies!" I shouted as I sprinted past.

"Where are you going? Gio?" Max shouted, but I didn't stick around to explain. As soon as I got outside, I saw two of my SUVs on the driveway with my men waiting that had come with Max.

"Keys!" I shouted at Nik who was hovering by the open door of the driver's seat. He threw them to me quickly before climbing into the passenger's side as I started up the engine. I pulled off the watch and threw it in Nik's lap as I drove like a maniac out of the Leone estate.

"Get the GPS off Angelo's watch and put it in the satnav," I ordered.

My hands gripped the steering wheel so hard; the whites of my knuckles were on show as I tried to take deep breaths. The satnav was taking me to the middle of nowhere. To a road that runs through the woods at the bottom of a rocky mountain. The darkness within was rising to the surface as my mind ran wild with all the sick possibilities of what could happen if I didn't get there in time. I can't let anything happen to her. I promised I would protect her, and I would not fail her now. I slammed my foot on the accelerator as the car revved down the empty roads towards the location. It was taking too long.

As the satnav informed me we were nearly there, my heart was in my throat when I saw nothing but a desolate road and trees that stretched for miles. I slowed down as I scanned the woodland for any sign of them.

"There!" Nik shouted, pointing half a mile down the road. As we came closer, anger took over my senses when I saw a huge body on the side of the road. Pulling over, we leapt out of the car and I gripped my hair when I saw Angelo's dead body. The watch was still flashing on his wrist. I growled and punched the door of the SUV when I realised that I had no way of tracking Liv anymore.

"Boss! Look here. There are tyre marks on the road where he had taken off at speed."

I jumped back in the car, winding down my window as I hung out of it to track the tyre marks on the dirt road. After a few miles, they veered off into the woodland. Following them as far as I could until we came to one of our own black cars we were using for the wedding today, abandoned in the thick forest. I turned the engine off and climbed out. There was no one insight and we would have to walk the rest of the way, but the adrenaline coursing through my veins was keeping me focused.

Would I find her?

Without question.

Would I save her?

Always.

Would I kill him?

Abso-fucking-lutely.

Unhinged

Henry

She was even more beautiful than I remembered. Every night I had pictured her face before I fell asleep but she had changed. She is a woman now. Striking. Perfect.

I stroked the soft skin of her sun-kissed arm with my knuckles as my eyes raked over her body. Her tits had grown. And she had wider hips. I could tell from the figure-hugging dress she was wearing. I knew seeing her again would make it all worth it. She knew I would find her. She knows I can do anything.

The pin dropped the night I killed that boy. She wanted this. She wanted me to prove my love to her before she would give herself to me fully. For two years, I thought she was just stubborn. That she was just a fucking tease. And it made me livid. But then I realised. The night she went to that party, she left me hints. A condom on the floor of her bedroom. That barbie skank I fucked to get extra information about her told me Livvy was planning on sleeping at her house that night. My girl wanted me to stop her. Everything she has done is to try and make me prove myself to her. That I am good enough. That I will do whatever it takes to be with her.

When they put me in that mental asylum full of nutters, I knew it was just another test Livvy wanted me to pass. They try to stop me, but they can't. Nothing will stop me. Those therapists said I have an 'antisocial personality disorder.' That I am a sociopath. That is what I allowed them to believe. I noticed in that place that most people have a weakness. A conscience. They feel empathy towards others, especially people they believe to be depressed or troubled. I let them believe I was one of those people. That they could help me. But I didn't need help. I am happy with who I am. That is why Livvy chose me. She knew I could take care of her without feeling remorse for the things I had to do to keep her safe.

She stirred in my arms on the cot bed of the warehouse I had been staying in this past week. We had to stay here one more night and then that Sal bloke would fly us out of here for good tomorrow.

Her stunning eyes blinked rapidly as she reached up to where she hit her head. The blood had dried now and she would be fine. I made her better. Just by letting her sleep in my arms.

"Shhh, just a little bump. You always were a fucking clumsy bitch," I chuckled as her green and gold eyes widened and she stared up at me. Her eyes were always my favourite thing about her.

She jumped off the bed and away from me, putting her hands out as she scanned the room. I frowned as I sat up on the bed and sighed. Looks like she wasn't done testing me yet.

"Where are we, Henry? Why are you doing this? Why can't you just leave me alone," she shouted as she ran to the door and started banging on it. There was no use. I had already locked it.

"Don't make me angry now, Livvy. I didn't come all this way to argue with you. Come and sit down," I tried to remain calm, but the more she banged on that bloody door, the more aggravated I was becoming.

"Olivia," I warned.

Jumping to my feet, I grabbed her around the waist and threw her down on the bed, straddling her hips as she hit me over and over with her tiny fists. This was just foreplay to her. She knew what pleased me. She knew I liked this. I grabbed her arms and tied them to the metal frame of the bed with some rope I had found in the warehouse a few days ago. I thought it might come in handy.

"P-please! Please Henry, don't do this! You don't have to do this. You can let me go. I won't tell anyone. Just let me go," she whimpered. The fake crocodile tears running down her face. I grabbed her jaw in my hand, forcing her to look at me.

"Isn't it enough yet, Livvy? When will it be enough?" I shouted.

"W-what? I d-don't understand."

I sighed deeply as I released her jaw and ran my hand over her hair, pushing it out of her face.

"I knew I fell in love with you from the first day I saw you. I also knew that was what you wanted too. You needed my love to ensure I didn't crawl away from you. You spun me into your web Livvy. You left me hanging. Watching. Tormenting me. You knew that I wouldn't want to leave you, even though it was hurting me. You were hurting me and you were enjoying it."

I leaned down and lifted a strand of her hair to my nose and breathed in that intoxicating scent. "I can smell it on you now. The scent of seduction, lust and control. Every day you tested me. Every day you knew what you were doing to me. It was all foreplay for you. For us. A twisted game you created to make me prove my love for you. Have I not proven myself, Livvy?"

She shook her head as her bottom lip trembled with emotion. "You had everyone fooled. But I was not as stupid as them. I knew what you wanted. What you need. That's why you are with him, right? He is me. You thought I was gone. That they had won. So, you found someone to replace me. But I'm here now. We can be together now."

"No! Henry, you are not well. Please."

Anger rose in me that she was still playing these games. "How can you still do this to me Olivia? How can you force me to be this person? He didn't get it. He didn't know you like I did."

"Who?" she feigned confusion.

I scoffed. "Nate. I had to kill him for you. That was the first test, wasn't it? You are so lucky. Lucky that I can crush those that stand in our way. But you know that, don't you? That's why you continue to test me."

"Henry... no. I never- "

"I knew. From the first time I saw you. I was in love with you. And you knew. But they didn't know, did they? That's why they had to die. I get it now. That's what you needed from me, to show them that it's just us."

A loud bang sounded from somewhere in the warehouse and my head snapped towards the door.

"OLIVIA!" A loud male voice boomed.

"Gio!" Livvy shouted back and I slammed my hand over her mouth, putting my finger to my lips. I peered down into her wide, beautiful eyes and I saw the answer. This was my final test. Once I killed him, we could be together. She would be mine.

***

Olivia

He is fucking unhinged! He has truly lost the plot. He is so much more dangerous now than he ever was before. This isn't just about his ego or possessiveness. I can see the craziness in his eyes. He believes his own lies. He believes I want this. That I want him. There is no way out.

I whimpered as he continued to stroke my hair and stare into my eyes as he spouted his insanity. He was either going to kill me or keep my hostage forever. I know which one was worse.

"OLIVIA!"

My heart flipped and relief flooded through every cell in my body when I heard his voice. He'd found me.

"Gio!" I managed to shout just before Henry slammed his cold hand over my mouth. He raised his finger to his lips as my muffled cries fell against his hand.

"Olivia!" Gio shouted again, his voice was deep and aggressive as he grew closer to our hiding place. Henry grabbed a T-shirt and wrapped it around my head to stuff my mouth as he stood up and started rummaging in a duffel bag. I watched in horror as he pulled out a large knife and smiled at me with excitement.

I tried to scream but the fabric in my mouth restricted any noise from flooding the room as Henry stalked over to the door and stood against the wall. I watched with wide eyes as Henry winked at me and got in a fighting stance. Gunshots were suddenly fired at the lock on the door and, in one powerful bang, Gio had kicked the door in. He saw me first lying on the bed, my hands tied above my head and my mouth gagged as I tried to scream at him to watch out. As soon as he stepped into the room towards me, Henry pounced forwards, knife in the air ready to attack, but Gio sensed him coming and dodged out of the way at the last minute.

All I could do was watch on in horror, my heart in my throat as Henry turned and sized Gio up. The look on Giovanni's face was one I had never seen before. He looked lethal. Henry jumped forward, attempting to stab Gio once again, but Gio grabbed Henry's outstretched arm and dislocated his shoulder so forcefully, Henry fell to his knees crying out in pain. I heard the pop that sent a shiver through my body as Gio let go and Henry held his shoulder with his other hand, the knife clattering to the floor. Gio smirked as he grabbed a handful of Henry's hair and punched him so powerfully in the face that Henry fell back on the floor. But Gio didn't stop there. He kicked him in the stomach numerous times and then once in the face, causing Henry's body to twist on the filthy floor and blood to pour from his nose and mouth.

"You are no match for me, you sick fuck," Gio spat as he pulled out his gun and shot Henry in one of his thighs. "So, you can't run away."

Nik came waltzing into the room and yanked Henry up as he screamed in pain, dragging him out as Gio ran over to me, pulling the top from out my mouth as the tears were flooding down my face. He got to work untying my hands as I whimpered and sobbed. As soon as my hands were free, I sat up and flung myself into his arms. He held me so tightly against his chest.

"Did he hurt you? It's okay bambola. I'm here. He will never hurt you again. It's over."

"No. No, I thought I was going to- I thought I would never- "

"I know. I know. You're safe now. I promise." He lifted me up swiftly, cradling me in his arms as he carried me out of the abandoned warehouse and to a car. I hid my face in his chest when I heard Henry shouting my name from the car he had driven me here in.

"Stai zitto quel cazzo di bocca!" Gio shouted over to Nik. Suddenly, Henry's shouts were muffled and Gio placed me down in the front seat of a car.

"I will be right back," he said softly when I gripped his arm tightly as he tried to walk away. I nodded slowly as he stepped back and closed the door. I watched as he walked over to the wedding car and opened the boot. Both Gio and Nik dragged Henry out and threw him into the boot before slamming it shut. Gio said something to Nik before he walked back over to the car and climbed into the driver's seat. He reached for my hand and squeezed it.

"What is going to happen to him? Where are you taking him?" I asked as he pulled out of the woodland and back onto the main road.

"My yacht. I will deal with him later. First, I need you to be okay."

I looked down at his hand on my lap and realised it was shaking. His whole body was shaking. My heart ached as I realised how traumatic that was for me but also how it must have been for him. He needs me just as much as I need him. This is how we worked. We were each other's lifeline.

"Pull the car over," I ordered, wiping the dried tears away from my face.

"What?" He looked at me with utter confusion.

"Pull the car over. Now," I said more sternly, and he swerved to the side of the road. I opened the door and climbed out, walking to his side of the car as he slid out the driver's side.

"Liv- what are you- "

I jumped up into his arms, wrapping my own around his neck and my legs around his waist as I held onto him like my life depended on it. His beautiful brown eyes widened as he held me tightly and I lowered my head until our lips met. The passion, love and relief exploded inside me as our lips parted against each other and I felt his tense body melt with mine. He pushed me up against the car door as our kiss became frantic with emotion and his hands explored my body as mine weaved through his hair. It was a kiss that could have lasted a lifetime and I would have died happy. When we finally broke away out of breath, he rested his forehead against mine and a single tear slid down his cheek.

"I was so scared, Liv. I thought I had lost you," he whispered, and my heart felt like it was being squeezed inside my chest.

"I know. But you didn't. You saved me. Again," I said, looking into his eyes. "You always save me."

"But you saved me first," his voice choked as it filled with genuine emotion and I held his gaze. "You saved me the day you walked into that interview."

My smile grew as my eyes filled with fresh tears. "I love you so much."

"Ti amo bambola."

Broken People Fix Each Other

Cecilia

As I stared into this monster's eyes, I realised I never really knew Salvatore Buccini at all. I knew he was ambitious. I knew he was dangerous. I knew he was possessive. But I also believed he was loyal to his family. I believed that deep down, buried underneath the years of darkness that had hardened him, there was the potential to be a good man. Never a great man like Vinny but a man who put his love for his family above all else. Family first. That was his and Vinny's motto they created together. But it was a lie. A beautiful, deadly lie.

This man didn't know love. He didn't understand the meaning of it. If he did, he would never have killed the only person who loved him. Tears threatened to form in my eyes as I thought of the love of my life. The innocent man who had his life snatched away from him by the man he respected the most in this world.

"Leave us," I commanded in a fierce tone as Maximus turned to regard me with concern.

"But Cecil- "

"Leave us! Everyone out," I ordered again as a slow smile spread across Sal's face.

After a moment's hesitation, Max nodded to Riccardo and the men left the room, closing the door behind them. I walked over to a chair placed at the corner of the room and dragged it until I would be sitting down facing Salvatore, only a metre away.

"Why?" I gritted through my teeth.

"Because I love you, Cecilia. You were-"

I didn't need to hear any more about why he killed Vinny. My heart couldn't handle it.

"No. Why get rid of Olivia? You say you love me and you want to marry me. You said that you would have chosen me thirty years ago. Then why not allow Giovanni the same?"

He pouted his lips to run his tongue over his bloody teeth, his swollen eyelids blinking back at me.

"Because he is my heir. Love will make him a pathetic boss. He will have a weakness. A target for our enemies as long as she is alive."

I shook my head as the fury grew within me. I felt like I was hanging off the edge of the world, clinging onto the cliff with my fingernails before I surrendered to the fiery depths of hell fire beneath me.

"So, if I had chosen you over Vinny, you would have been a pathetic boss?" I snarled.

He chuckled deeply, wheezing through the pain it caused him to do so. "No. Because I am made of different stuff. If you had let me raise Giovanni as my own, then so would he. Perhaps then he could keep his little slut."

It was my turn to burst into laughter. "You are insane. Did you forget the results? You are not his father! It is over Sal. You have lost everything. And Gio will find Olivia and save her. He will marry her and love her the way a man is supposed to love a woman. He will be the greatest boss this family has ever had. He will have everything you never did! And do you know why? Because he has Vinny's blood running through his veins!"

The pure evil and unfiltered rage that took over his features made me delighted. I knew that would hit a nerve. Not break his heart because he doesn't have a heart to break but at least cause him pain.

"So, what's the plan Cecilia? You are going to kill me?" He leaned back in his chair, his evil eyes twinkling with amusement. "You don't have it in you, my love."

I narrowed my eyes as I thought of what would hurt him the most in this world. Because death was too easy for him. He needs to feel the pain he has caused me. That he has caused my children. Sani and Raya will grow up never knowing the wonderful father they should have had. Elle will never have Vinny to walk her down the aisle on her wedding day. Giovanni's children will never feel their nonno's love. I will never grow old with my soul mate. Because of this man. Because he took it all away from us. The overwhelming despair and fury invaded my mind and body like the black plague. Sweeping through me, killing any form of happiness or hope I had left in this world.

"No. I am not going to kill you."

His grin grew as his eyes searched mine. But when he saw something unsettling behind them, his smile fell. "Cecilia…"

"You say you love me. That I am the only person you have ever loved. Everything you have done up to this point has been for me, right?"

His lips parted as his breathing grew short and rapid.

"But you overlooked one major detail."

His eyes narrowed as I reached for Riccardo's gun on the table.

"That I would rather die than live in a world where I was loved by you."

"Cecilia!" Panic gripped his tone as I lifted the gun and held it to my temple with a shaky hand.

"Don't you get it yet Salvatore?" I choked as I hovered my finger over the trigger, his frantic eyes darting from my finger to my face and back. My face was wet from my silent tears. "Everything you did; everything you are, will kill the very person you say you did it all for. I would rather cease to exist than be loved by you."

Suddenly, his eyes glazed over with a steel mist and his jaw clenched.

"Then kill yourself, Cecilia. I will be sure to follow you and torment you in the next life too. I will never let you have peace. I will never let you go even in death. You will never be rid of me!"

Letting the depth of despair and rage take control, I felt my hand turn the gun on Salvatore's head and my fingers squeezed the trigger. The sound of the gunshot rang in my ears as I screamed. Suddenly, there were bodies in the room as I fell to my knees and sobbed. The walls around me were caving in and my body was shrinking. Blood was everywhere. Bright like the roses in my garden. It was rushing towards me like a tide, coming for me. Drowning me. I could hear my name being called in the distance and my body was moving with the current. I wasn't in control. I could fight to survive or I could let it take me.

"It's okay Cecilia. You're okay," the deep voice soothed from the sky.

"Vinny?" I whispered, blinking my eyes but all I could see were the rolling ruby waves overhead before they engulfed me completely.

***

Olivia

Gio walked out of Cecilia's bedroom looking forlorn and exhausted. I stopped my pacing and stepped towards him, touching his arm.

"How is she?"

"Still staring at a blank wall and refusing to talk. I found her empty pill bottles in her desk drawer. She must have been off them for days. The doctors are on their way, but I don't know what to do. I don't want them to take her without her consent, but I am worried she is suicidal again," he huffed, his eyes full of pain and worry.

"I am not sure what went down before she shot Sal but when I raced in, she was in a bad way. She was calling me Vinny as I carried her out," Max shook his head and puffed out his cheeks.

"What do you expect? She killed Salvatore after finding out that he killed papi to be with her. That is enough to break anyone. And she hasn't been on her meds! How didn't we see it?" Elle grunted as she leaned against the wall in the corridor.

"There has been a lot going on, Elle. And we haven't been around her for days. How were we supposed to know?" Gio's tone was defensive, and I started biting my nails. That wasn't entirely true. There had been signs that she was struggling but Gio was right. With everything else going on, we had failed to see it as more than her hate for Sal.

"Can I try?" I asked quietly as I looked between the siblings. Elle shrugged and folded her arms across her chest while Gio glanced down at me, unsure.

"I don't think it will be of any use, Liv. She needs professional help right now," he groaned.

"Then there is no harm in trying," I stroked his arm before standing on my tiptoes to kiss his cheek.

The curtains were drawn, and the only light was coming from a bedside lamp on Cecilia's table. The frail outline of her body was curled up in a foetal position under the satin bed cover. As I approached the side of the bed she was facing out from, my heart ached when I saw the face of a broken woman. Pale and expressionless. Her brown eyes were staring straight ahead at the cream bedroom wall, unblinking.

I sat down in the plush armchair next to her side and looked down at my hands in my lap. I didn't speak. I knew just having company after such a traumatic event was sometimes all you needed.

After what felt like eternity, my head snapped up when I heard her quiet voice.

"I would have done it."

My eyebrows furrowed as I stared at her. She continued to fix her gaze on the wall ahead.

"Done what Cecilia?" I asked softly.

"Shot myself. If I believed he truly loved me in those final moments, I would have done it."

I swallowed my shock and instant concern at her words. She was going to kill herself in front of Salvatore.

"But he didn't love me. Because you would die for those you love not let them take their own life. Vinny died trying to save me. Sal told me to kill myself."

I leaned back in the chair as tears sprang to my eyes.

"Why were you going to do it Cecilia?"

"Because I thought it would hurt him. If everything he did was for me, then losing me would be the worst thing to happen. But even that wasn't enough. Vinny died because of me. My children don't have their papi. You were nearly taken by your stepbrother. All because of me."

A large tear rolled down her cheek to the tip of her nose and dropped to the bed.

"No. You are wrong." I sighed deeply as my inner demons came to the surface. "I used to think it was my fault. That Henry tormented me. That Nate died. That my mum couldn't even look me in the eye after it happened. That Henry killed an innocent warden and God knows who else to find me. I always thought it was because of something I had done. That I was the reason all of this was happening. But I know now, it wasn't me. It was him. Everything he did; every decision he made was because of his own unhealthy obsession. It was nothing to do with me really. If it wasn't me, it would have been somebody else. I believe that now. I can see that now. And it is the same for you Cecilia. Salvatore made you believe everything he did was for you but how can it be when you didn't ask for any of it? When not once did you give him the impression you wanted him? You are a victim, Cecilia. You are not the cause."

Her bottom lip trembled and more tears fell from her eyes. "But how can I go on? How can I live with the knowledge that Vinny's death was because of Salvatore's obsession with me? How can I live knowing I nearly married the man who took him away from me? I don't deserve to."

I jumped up from the chair and lay behind her in the bed, throwing my arms around her as she started to sob uncontrollably.

"You will live because he doesn't get to win. You will live because you are strong and you are loved. Salvatore is gone and you are still here. That happened for a reason. Vinny was always protecting you. You can still feel him, right?"

She nodded her head as I stroked her hair away from her face.

"Listen to him. What is he saying?"

Her lips pursed together as she closed her eyes. "Angel be strong. Fight."

I smiled as the tears ran down my face too. "That's right. You have so much to live for. You have so much to take Vinny along for. He wants to see it all with you Cecilia. You must live for the both of you."

She turned in my arms to face me.

"I need help Olivia. Please help me get better."

"Always. Broken people fix each other. One day at a time."

She nodded slowly. "One day at a time."

Him and I

Giovanni

"È a bordo. Lo yacht è pronto per partire (He is onboard. The yacht is ready to go)," Nik informed me as I watched the car drive away with mamma and Elle inside. I released a calming breath knowing she was going to get help. She had agreed to go back to the rehab clinic after her chat with Olivia. Once again, this woman was saving my life. How she got mamma to even speak is beyond me.

Today has been a fucking day. But it wasn't over yet. There was one last loose end to tie up. I nodded to Nik in appreciation as Liv looked up at me from under my arm.

"What did he say?"

Turning towards her, wrapping my arms around her waist, I held her gaze carefully.

"I have to go and deal with Henry now," I tried to keep the aggression out of my tone at even saying that bastard's name.

She swallowed her sudden nerves and fear as her green and gold eyes danced with emotion. She nodded slowly.

"I want to come with you."

I inhaled sharply. I wasn't sure that was such a good idea. No, I knew that was a terrible idea. Because what I had in mind to do to that asshole, I didn't want her to see that side of me. She thought she knew what I was capable of, but really, she had no idea. Not when it came to people who hurt her.

"I don't want to watch," she quickly added when she saw my uncertainty. "I just need closure. And I need to be in the same place as you. I need to be with you," she whispered, a slight blush forming on her cheeks in her unexpected shyness.

My heart fluttered in my chest. She was so fucking adorable. Knowing how much this woman hated to rely on and need others, those words meant a lot. She was admitting for the first time that she needed me. Not just to protect her, but to be there for her.

"Okay bambola. You don't get seasick?" I raised an eyebrow and a small smile pulled at her lips as she shook her head. "Then let's go."

I turned to Nik, who nodded and climbed into the driver's seat of my Rolls Royce as I held the door open for Liv to climb in. We drove to the harbour in silence, holding hands the whole way. I didn't know what would be running through Olivia's head right now, but from the calm and serene look on her face, I knew she was okay. It was nearly over. Henry was about to pay for everything he did to her and she would be free of him, once and for all. And I would make sure they never found his body.

Normally, when I know I am about to torture and kill a man, I have to shut off my mind and my emotions and retreat to a dark place. Block out the reasoning and moral compass within me. But this time, I didn't have to do that. I wanted to feel everything. I wanted him to look me in the eyes and see me. Not Giovanni, the ruthless mafioso, and not Gio, the protective family man. But me. I was both. I was who she chose. I was who she wanted and I was the one who would love her for the rest of my life. I wanted him to know who I was to her and who he will never be.

As we walked onboard the luxury superyacht with immaculate and high-tech designs and interior, I squeezed Liv's hand in support. She held her chin up higher with a determined expression which made my heart soar. I was in awe of her strength, facing her abuser and tormentor for the last time.

I led her down to the lowest level of the yacht where I knew my men would have detained Henry and stopped outside the door to the room.

"You are sure?" I asked quietly. Her stunning eyes flickered up to mine and she nodded with conviction.

"Yes."

I opened the door and we stepped inside the lavishly decorated room. In the middle, tied to a chair, was Henry. His head hung to his chest, dirty blonde hair hanging down covering his face. Wearing ripped black jeans and a black T-shirt, I could see that he was in shape but nowhere near the size of me. He lifted his head when he heard us arrive and his eyes locked with Liv's, which made rage erupt through me like an electric current. I hated the way he looked at her. Full of desire and possession.

"Livvy," he breathed. I couldn't contain the fury in me as I stepped forward and punched him in the nose, breaking it as he groaned.

"Say her name again and I will keep breaking more parts of your body," I hissed, grabbing his jaw in my hand. I felt a small hand on my shoulder as Liv stepped forwards and I dropped his bloody face and looked down at her by my side. She was staring at him with a clenched jaw and fire in her eyes.

"I feel sorry for you, Henry. That you will never understand. I am not going to stand here and tell you all the ways you hurt me or try to make you understand all the pain you caused because you will never admit guilt. You will never show remorse. And I don't need that from you. Look at me," she said, stepping closer to him.

I instinctively wanted to pull her back, to shield her with my body from his sleazy, sadistic gaze, but I fought it with every fibre of my being. She needed to do this her way.

"You didn't break me. I didn't just survive you Henry, I fucking flourished. I found love. I found family. I found happiness. So, I have to thank you. Because if it wasn't for you, I wouldn't be where I am today."

A guttural growl escaped his throat as his icy blue eyes shimmered with hate and anger and I smirked behind my strong girl.

"Once I walk out that door, I will take a deep breath, never think of you again and start a new chapter in my life. And you…will be left in the hands of the man I love. The man I chose in every lifetime and the next. Goodbye Henry."

She turned on her heels, grabbed me by the back of the neck and smashed her lips against mine. I wrapped my arms around her back as I lifted her from the floor and kissed her back.

"You fucking slut! You're a pathetic whore who no one loves! He will grow sick of your shit one day, Livvy! Only I know what you need!"

My body tensed at his words as I slowly lowered her to the ground. She held my face between her hands as she smiled up at me, ignoring his words completely, before she walked out of the room without looking back.

"Liv! Olivia!" He screamed in rage after her as I fixed my deadly gaze on him and welcomed my darkness.

"You believe you are what she needs?" I said calmly as I walked over to the polished oak dining table that showcased an array of my torture devices, guns and knives.

"I know I am, and she does too! This is all a sick game to her and you are just another fool she has taken along for the ride," he spat.

I chuckled deeply as I picked up a black dagger that my men had found in his belongings. "Oh and what a ride it is!"

His eyes blazed with jealousy as he glared at me from his position. Twisting the sharp point against my fingertip, I looked up at Nik, who was standing behind Henry.

"Pop his shoulder back in and cut him loose," I demanded. Henry's brows tightened in confusion when Nik bent down and roughly sorted his dislocated shoulder before cutting the cable ties around his wrists and ankles, freeing him from the chair. He jumped up, stumbling on his wounded leg, rubbing his shoulder as he looked frantically between me and Nik.

"Nice dagger," I held it up in front of my face as his eyes narrowed. "Just like the one you used to stab Nate in the back, right?"

A vindictive smirk stretched across his face, pulling his lips away from his teeth. "Nearly identical."

I nodded as I stabbed the knife powerfully into the oak table and let go, the blade warping and swaying until it stilled.

"I'll make a deal with you, Henry."

His eyes flickered between Nik and I suspiciously as his jaw ticked.

"If you want to truly prove to Liv that you are the man she needs, then you need to stop being a fucking coward," I smirked as I started to undo the buttons of my black shirt.

"Coward? Do you know how many people I have killed for her?" He snapped and I raised my eyebrows.

"But how many of those people did you give a fair chance to defend themselves? You see Henry. Liv wants a real man. One who fights for her. So, my proposal is this...fight me. Face to face."

He ran his tongue over his teeth as he contemplated my words. I smirked when I saw a flicker of uncertainty.

"What's wrong? Can you only kill a man when they are unprepared? Anyone can stab someone in the back, Henry. But to look a man in the eyes as life drains out of them...that is what real men are made of."

I couldn't contain my delight as my provoking words had the desired effect. He stood up taller and ran his hand through his long blonde hair as he glared at me with so much hate.

"I will even allow you to have your precious dagger, seeing as you have a wounded leg," I pulled it out of the table and threw it on the carpet between us.

"There are two of you. How is that fair?" He growled, looking over at Nik who was standing like a wall of muscle in the corner of the room.

"Nik will not move. This is between you and I."

"And if I kill you? He will kill me!" Henry shouted and I shook my head.

"If you kill me... You will walk out of here a free man," I held his gaze. He had the widest smile on his face as he swiftly bent down and grabbed the dagger in his hand. Seems he still wasn't brave enough to actually take me on in a fair fight, but it didn't faze me. I would still beat his ass to an inch of his life.

I pulled off my shirt. It was Prada and one of my favourites. I didn't want his blood ruining it. I stepped towards him menacingly and he moved quickly, side stepping away from me. I smirked as I stood still, raising my fists and beckoning him forwards with my fingers.

His nostrils flared and he dived at me, attempting to stab me in the stomach with the knife, but I dodged out the way easily. We circled each other once again.

I pretended to dive forward, causing him to flinch and I laughed loudly. His eyes blazed with anger at my trick and I saw something in him change. He wanted me dead. He was going to go for it now and I couldn't fucking wait. The adrenaline ramped up as our eyes locked and gone were the jokes. Now it was time to stop messing about. Now it was time to show this fucker exactly who he was dealing with.

When he came at me again, I grabbed his arm holding the dagger up in the air, and landed a powerful punch to his stomach, causing him to bend over before kneeing him in the face and pushing him away. He fell back on the floor but quickly scrambled to his feet again as he glared at me, puffing his cheeks with rapid breaths.

"Come on Henry. I expected so much more from you," I sneered as he roared, flying towards me and jabbing the dagger towards my chest. I knocked his arm away, but he swiftly punched me in the face with his other fist and I was surprised that it caused my lip to bleed. Not bad.

I turned and punched him square in the jaw, causing his body to turn to the side. Before I could move out of the way, he flung his arm back and the blade sliced through the skin on my hip. I hissed as I slammed my hand over it and stumbled back to quickly assess the wound. It was only a surface cut, but it was enough to allow my rage to take control. Flying towards him, I knocked him to the floor and grabbed his wrist that held the knife. With all my strength fighting against his, I took the blade to his throat as he gritted through his teeth, his body shaking to battle my strength as the blade pressed against his skin. A trickle of blood started to run down his neck, but I didn't want it to be over yet. He hadn't suffered anywhere near enough. I pulled the blade away and was pummelling his face with one fist while slamming his arm down on the floor with the other. The blade fell from his hand, and I slid it away from us. He punched me in the stomach and then the jaw in my moment of distraction and I fell to the side of him. Just as he was about to climb on top of me, I booted him hard in the stomach with my foot, causing him to fly back into the wall. Leaping to my feet, I beat every inch of his body, blow after blow, until he fell to his knees on the floor, blood covering us both.

"GET UP!" I bellowed aggressively, but his eyelids drooped, and his head rolled. I grabbed his hair and pulled him up to his feet just to send him back to the floor with my fist.

He groaned and spluttered through the blood pooling in his mouth, and I knew he couldn't fight any more. I stepped back and nodded to Nik as I wiped the blood from my mouth with the back of my hand. Nik threw Henry back onto the chair as I walked over to the table and grabbed a sharp knife. Nik dragged the chair over to the table with Henry on it and placed his arm on the surface. His chin was resting on his chest, barely conscious. This should wake him up.

I cut off his finger. His head fell back as he screamed in agony, but it did nothing to appease the beast within. I was only just getting started. I then cut two more off.

"Now you are awake, let's talk. How many times would you roughly say you have called Olivia a slut? Whore? Bitch?"

He mumbled something incoherent, and I sighed. Using the knife in my hand, I grabbed the collar of his T-shirt and cut it off his chest. I slowly sliced his skin with the knife repeatedly. Small cuts for every demeaning word he had ever said to her until his body was a mass of slits and blood. I stepped back to admire my work as he squirmed against Nik's tight grip in the chair, screaming and crying for mercy. I grabbed his tongue and cut half of it off.

"How many times did you stab that boy in the back, Henry?" I asked coldly as I placed the smaller knife down and picked up a sharp, thin blade. When he didn't answer me, I grabbed his hair on top of his head and forced him to look at me. "How many times? Use your hands."

"S-se," he mumbled, unable to talk through the blood and half a tongue in his mouth as I dropped his head back. I held up his hands and counted the remaining seven fingers I had purposefully left. I stabbed the blade into his shoulder and his harrowing scream echoed around the room. I repeated my action six more times in different areas of his body, being sure to miss any vital organs to keep him alive a little longer.

Tears were rolling down his face and his skin had paled from the loss of blood, but he was just about hanging onto his reality.

Next, I picked up the baseball bat. Feeling nothing as I stared at the blubbering mess of a man, I savagely beat his arms, breaking every bone in them and then shattered his knee caps. He lost consciousness through the pain and I threw the bat to the floor. Glancing up at Nik, who stood up from restricting Henry's thrashing as he was no longer needed, I said, "It's time."

He nodded and lifted Henry's battered, bloody body over his shoulder and we walked up to the back deck of the yacht. The moon was hanging low in the sky, illuminating the inky, black surface of the water that stretched as far as the eye could see. My driver had brought us out to the middle of the Mediterranean Sea so there would be no witnesses or chance of anyone finding his body before the fish had their fill.

Two of my soldiers had already prepared the cement blocks on the floor as Nik threw Henry's body down on a deck chair and the men pulled his shoes off. They strapped his feet to the top of the blocks and a cement weight was tied around his neck tightly as Henry groaned, waking from his little nap.

His eyes flickered open and closed as he tried to comprehend what was happening.

"I will be sure to make Olivia very happy for the rest of my life. Thank you for sending her to me Henry." I smiled as I stepped back and nodded to my men, who dragged him to the edge of the deck.

"No!" He panicked as he realised what was about to happen. I stared into his eyes and saw the fear of death in them as I nodded once more and they threw him overboard.

I closed my eyes as the adrenaline and satisfaction reached its peak. Turning on my feet, I walked briskly inside and headed to the bathroom to wash off all of Henry's blood before Olivia saw me for the monster I am.

Olivia

I heard the splash. Scrambling up off the lounge sofa and running to the balcony, I looked over and saw three of Gio's men hovering at the end of the yacht, looking down into the black water and I knew. Henry was gone. Forever.

Relief and an overwhelming feeling of freedom washed over me as my hands started to shake and I blinked back the tears. I was finally free.

A movement below the balcony caught my attention and I just managed to catch a glimpse of Gio's black hair and shirtless, bloody body walking back inside. I turned and raced through the lounge and out into the extravagant lobby to the staircase. Was he hurt? Was he okay?

I frantically flew down the stairs to the ground floor and searched for him in every room. When I flung open the door to a small bathroom, I froze.

There was Giovanni, shirtless and leaning over a sink. His beautiful face, his toned chest, his muscular arms and his deadly hands; all covered in blood. My heart pounded in my chest as my first thought was that it was his. That he was hurt. But as his head turned and I locked eyes with his gorgeous mountain brown irises, I knew he was fine. It wasn't his blood.

It should have scared me. It should have made me feel physically sick. But as we held each other's gaze, his chest rising and falling with shallow breaths, all I felt was overwhelming need, desire and love. This was the true Giovanni in all his fucked-up glory, and I was here for it. For him.

"Liv…" his deep voice was laced with worry at me finding him like this and I knew I had to make him see. I accepted him in every form. I ran at him, jumping into his arms. Our lips connected and everything in me came alive with electricity. He was my addiction. He was everything. His callous hands clawed at my dress, ripping it off over my head as I wrapped my legs around his waist, and he slammed my back against the bathroom door. Our tongues were frantically fighting for more as our kiss became crazed and my hands gripped his hair aggressively. I felt him rip my knickers in half and skilfully undo his flies without breaking the passionate kiss. As soon as he pushed himself into me, I gasped into his mouth, digging my nails into his shoulders as he started to move in and out, massaging every inch of me with his length. His dark eyes burned into mine as our foreheads touched and his thrusts became more possessive and demanding as he squeezed my ass in his hands.

I was crying out his name within minutes as he growled out his orgasm. Without saying a word or putting me down, he walked us over to the shower, his dick still inside me and turned on the scalding water. As he submerged us under the downfall, all the blood washing away from our bodies as it ran down the drain, he kissed me again. Slow and sweet. Loving.

"It's over bambola. And now they will all know."

I stared down into his eyes as he looked up at me with admiration and love.

"Know what?" I whispered.

"That Giovanni Buccini in love is as deadly as they come."

I claimed his lips once again as we got lost in each other for the second time. But this time, it was a promise. A promise to a new beginning. A promise of a life as one. Just him and I.

So Much Better

Olivia

Two months later

"I can't believe that you have never tried a Maraschino! You live in Italy Liv, it's criminal!" Gigi laughed at me as I took a sip of her cherry-flavoured cocktail and winced at the sweetness.

"Hmm too sweet for me. I think I'll stick to the Godfather," I smirked, stirring my own cocktail with the straw.

"I bet you will," she winked and giggled. After some serious discussions, Giovanni allowed me to tell Giulia and Millie who he really was. They had to sign an oath and I had to ensure they really knew how serious it was that they didn't gossip around town, but I trusted them both entirely. It felt so nice to have friends that I could speak to about my life now. I had Cami and Elle of course but they were born into this life, and I was still adjusting and learning the ropes.

"How is Cecilia doing?" Gigi asked as I leaned back in my chair, basking in the last of the afternoon sunlight from the quaint courtyard bar in the Piazza.

"Better. She is home now and taking everything a day at a time. She is spending all her time with Sani and Raya around the house which is so nice to see."

"Glad to hear it. That woman deserves some peace," she sighed and I nodded my head.

"So how is Viking?" I wriggled my eyebrows and she huffed loudly.

"Back in Oz. But we have arranged for me to fly out for a trip in a couple of weeks' time, so we'll see. Talking of trips." She sat up straight in her chair and peered over my shoulder. "I think there is someone here who has come to visit," she grinned.

I turned in my chair and my eyes widened when I saw the bouncing brown hair and beaming face of my beautiful best friend jogging towards us.

"Millie!" I screamed in disbelief as I flung myself out of the chair and charged towards her. We crashed into each other and laughed when we banged heads. She squeezed me so tightly as the tears of happiness flowed down my cheeks. We had spoken nearly every day since Henry's death and after Gio agreed to let me tell her what had happened and who he was, she had been saying she would come and visit as soon as she could get time off work. But this was still a surprise.

"Oh my god! What are you doing here? Is this real? How are you here?" I mumbled through my shock and giddiness. She chuckled as she pulled out of my embrace and looked at me.

"Well, your boyfriend is a pretty demanding man and when he sends you a private jet with the order to get on it for an all-expenses paid trip to Italy to come and see your best friend, how can you say no?"

My eyes bulged and my heart fluttered. "Gio did this?"

She nodded. "He is pretty special, Liv."

I smiled as I wiped my tears away and suddenly realised I had not introduced Gigi. Grabbing Millie's hand, I pulled her over to our table as Gigi stood up and grabbed Millie into a bear hug.

"Thank you for looking out for my bestie Giulia," Millie smiled as Gigi released her.

"Oh, it's been super easy! No drama at all," Gigi replied sarcastically causing the three of us to all burst into laughter.

After a few more cocktails, Gigi excused herself to give Millie and I time alone. We chatted and laughed for hours as if no time had passed until the sun had set and the cool evening breeze made us chilly.

Millie reached for my hand suddenly, a loving but serious expression on her pretty face. "I am so happy for you Liv. And proud of you. You are just glowing."

I smiled back, my eyes flicking down to our entwined hands on the table. "I have never been so happy Mills. I just wish you were here all the time. Then my life would be complete," I chuckled.

"Well, who knows! You may convince me to stay!"

"Really? Why didn't you say? I can show you all the best places and make you fall in love with Verona!"

"Great! Let's start now. Take me to your favourite place in the city," her eyes sparkled with excitement, and I felt a bubble of happiness fizzle inside me.

"Ok but you must promise you won't laugh. It holds a special place in my heart now and even though it may be a tourist attraction, I love it."

"You had me at 'don't laugh'," she beamed, and I rolled my eyes.

We left the bar with two of Giovanni's men following us behind protectively. Millie kept looking back at them, a little unsure but I just squeezed her hand.

"Just ignore them. You soon forget they're there."

As we approached Casa di Giulietta, I started to tell Millie all about the day I first came here with Gio and how I thought he was the sexiest, most infuriating man I had ever met. I was mid-sentence when we reached the arched alleyway and the sight before me stopped me in my tracks. The path was decorated with candles all the way through it and rose petals covered the cobbled floor.

"What the- " I paused and pulled Millie back. "Someone is obviously in there Mills. We better not go in."

Millie ignored me and stepped into the empty archway and shrugged. "There's no one there. Oh Liv, come and see how beautiful this is. No wonder you love this place," she said as she continued to walk through. I quickly caught up with her, my eyes wide at the sheer beauty and romantic ambience that had been created by all the candlelight and flowers against the graffiti of lovers' names on the walls. When we reached the empty courtyard, there was a stone stand in the middle with a bottle of champagne and a rolled-up piece of paper.

"Millie, I really think we should go. Someone has obviously hired this out for a romantic evening."

Once again Millie ignored me and walked over to the letter that was tied up with a silk ribbon. She glanced up at me with a smile as she lifted it. "This has your name on it."

My eyebrows furrowed as I briskly walked over and took it from her.

Olivia

It was handwritten on the side of the scroll. "What?"

"Open it," she said with a devilish grin and I suddenly realised that she knew something I didn't. With a trembling hand, I unravelled the paper to reveal a handwritten letter.

Dear Juliet,

I am writing to you to tell you about a girl. A girl who has changed my life.

Before her, there was an emptiness in my heart. It consumed me and at times, the entire world was overcast with subtle shades of grey and black. A never-ending winter. But then she fell (quite literally) into my life bringing vibrant colours, sunflowers and warmth. And my heart was renewed. I suddenly had hope and light in my life because of her smile. Because of her eyes. Because of her laughter. I live for them. I am in awe of her. Of the quiet strength she possesses. Of the gentle care she has for others. Of the way she knows her own mind with such certainty.

I never saw it coming. I don't know how, or when it happened but I fell madly in love with her. A love so unexpected yet so simple. There is no longer her and I. There is only us.

But I have a confession. I once saw love as a weakness that could only ever end in one's demise. I told her that love always ends in tragedy. I was wrong (Don't tell her- I will never hear the end of it).

When defending you, she once asked me, 'What is the point of living if you aren't really living at all?' I understand it now. Life is not worth living without love. Love for your family. Love for your friends. Love for the world we are each apart of. She taught me that. And in return, I promise to love her for the rest of my life, if she will have me.

So, Juliet, you may never have had your happy ever after, but I know that I will. All because I met a girl. A girl who changed my life and stole my heart.

Forever grateful,
Giovanni Buccini

I glanced up as the tears fell from my eyes and my hand slammed over my mouth when I saw Giovanni walking towards me looking extremely handsome in his casual jeans and T-shirt that clung to his muscles. This was my favourite version of him and he knew it.

My mind was whirling and the intense love I felt as he stopped to give Millie a hug before walking over to me made me swoon. But then he did something I was completely unprepared for. He took my left hand and got down on one knee. He held out a black velvet box and opened it to reveal the most exquisite diamond ring I had ever seen.

I gasped and Millie squealed behind him.

"Bambola, will you marry me and let me love you for the rest of our lives?"

A huge sob escaped my lips as I had never felt happiness like it. I dived into his arms, wrapping mine around his neck as I sobbed with so much joy.

"Is that a yes?" he chuckled, as he tried to pull me back to look at me. I laughed loudly as I wiped my eyes and peered into his.

"Si, si, si!"

He laughed, his dimple in his cheek making my stomach flip and Millie screamed behind us. I couldn't stop giggling as he placed the stunning ring on my finger.

"I knew you were a soppy romantic at heart," I chuckled, remembering how he had teased me months ago about loving this place.

"Only for you," he smiled before he held my face in his hand and kissed me.

Our love story may have not be a fairy-tale romance but what we found was so much better. We found ourselves in each other.

Coming soon...

Tempting My Mafia Princess

If you loved Tempting My Mafia Boss, come and join Elenora Buccini as she embarks on a journey of self-discovery, dangerous liaisons and most importantly her own mission to find true love.

@aurawrites31
Face.book.com/AuthorAurawrites

About The Author

Aura Rose grew up in England and started writing fiction during the covid pandemic in 2020. She lives with her husband and daughter and is a true romantic at heart. She has written a trilogy of supernatural e-books on dreame app. Her first book, The Last Alpha, just came 3rd place in Stary III Writing competition and its sequel, Dark Love placed in the top five books on the app as voted for by readers in the ACE competition. Tempting My Mafia Boss is her first published book on Amazon. It is also available as an e-book on Kindle Unlimited.

If you enjoyed her work and would like to stay up to date with new content and projects, you can find her on social media.

@aurawrites31
Facebook.com/AuthorAurawritesReadersPage

Printed in Great Britain
by Amazon